MW00930284

THE
PALACE OF
DREAMS

ALSO BY JODI LYNN ANDERSON

The Thirteen Witches series
The Memory Thief
The Sea of Always

My Diary from the Edge of the World

The May Bird trilogy
The Ever After
Among the Stars
Warrior Princess

Thirteen Witches

BOOK 3

THE PALACE OF DREAMS

JODI LYNN ANDERSON

ALADDIN

NEW YORK   LONDON   TORONTO   SYDNEY   NEW DELHI

ALADDIN

An imprint of Simon & Schuster Children's Publishing Division

1230 Avenue of the Americas, New York, New York 10020

First Aladdin hardcover edition March 2023

Text copyright © 2023 by Jodi Lynn Anderson

Jacket illustration copyright © 2023 by Khadijah Khatib

All rights reserved, including the right of reproduction in whole or in part in any form.

ALADDIN and related logo are registered trademarks of Simon & Schuster, Inc.

For information about special discounts for bulk purchases, please contact Simon & Schuster Special Sales at 1-866-506-1949 or business@simonandschuster.com.

The Simon & Schuster Speakers Bureau can bring authors to your live event. For more information or to book an event contact the Simon & Schuster Speakers Bureau at 1-866-248-3049 or visit our website at www.simonspeakers.com.

Designed by Heather Palisi

The text of this book was set in Adobe Caslon Pro.

Manufactured in the United States of America 0223 FFG

2 4 6 8 10 9 7 5 3

CIP data for this book is available from the Library of Congress.

ISBN 9781534416499 (hc)

ISBN 9781534416512 (ebook)

For Gwen

PROLOGUE

I n the woods a girl is walking, her long dark hair in a ponytail, a quiver of painted arrows slung over her shoulder. Behind her lies the house in which her family sleeps.

It takes several minutes for her to reach the ladder. She tries the bottom rung, and it holds her weight. The girl—only human and, till now, earthbound—climbs into the sky, toward the moon.

While she's away, the animals talk, in their way; the trees whisper through their roots; the undergrowth points branches at the beauty of the dark; the night flowers bloom so that they, too, can gaze up at the sky. Nocturnal creatures hunt and are hunted; they speak quietly of scents and directions to burrows, telling each other "stay away" or "come closer" or "I am here."

When—later that night—the girl returns, she walks home softly and full of secrets. Annabelle Oaks lies down envisioning the danger her future holds: she pictures arrows piercing wicked hearts. She envisions a time when witches are ended and her loved ones are safe. She hears soft breathing in the night, her sister in the bed across the room. Outside, an owl hoots softly. Years from now, another owl will determine her fate.

The forest, alive and watchful as it always has been, settles down to wait for morning. Light-years away, on a distant planet, a dining room table inside a rickety hotel gets its second coat of furniture oil. In the dark, Annabelle listens to the house around her as it rests. She breathes in the dark, and she dreams.

PART 1

CHAPTER 1

"We're getting there," says a woman's voice in the dark.

I'm not sure who the voice belongs to. I reach out to see if I can touch someone—my mom, my brother . . . but my hands touch nothing. I wonder if I even have hands at this point, because when I try to reach them up and touch my face, I feel nothing.

Besides the voice, only one thing seems to exist: a pinpoint of light I see in the dark ahead of me. It might be a tiny dot close by or an immense glow a million miles away.

All I know is that moments ago, I somehow stepped into a hole in a magazine. And now I am hurtling—across space, underneath space, or maybe through no space at all.

"Soon the universe will suck us back out into existence again, like being sucked through a straw," the voice says. "Just let yourself relax. You don't have to do a thing. It'll feel squishy, but not painful." The voice has just the slightest hint of a Spanish accent. Silence passes for a moment. Then, "I'm Wanda, by the way. Wanda Luna. Sorry we have to make our introductions as disembodied consciousnesses, but a mal tiempo, buena cara."

"Disembodied whats?" another voice chimes in. I think it's Germ.

"Oh! Here we go," Wanda interjects. "It's coming up. Try to squeeze yourselves together . . ."

"Squeeze?"

"Just, you know, tuck it all in. Like you're trying to make yourself as small as possible. Better if you're not all dangly."

I'm panicking now. I don't know how to tuck myself in so that I'm not all dangly. I slurp in a deep breath as the pinprick of light grows from a dot to a softball to a sphere the size of a house, bright and blinding and beautiful.

My toes get sucked toward it first. The pull gets more and more intense as it climbs up my feet, my ankles, my legs. And then the sound becomes deafening—there's a whooshing as the light engulfs me. Up is down and down is up, and just when I think I'm hurtling up at a spinning starry sky, I find myself hurtling down toward all-too-solid land.

I scream and a moment later hit the dirt, hard. There are several thuds around me as others make impact. Almost immediately Ebb is kneeling beside me, watching me with concern. He hasn't hit the ground at all, since he's a ghost.

"Rosie," Germ breathes, sitting up on the other side of me, shivering and catching her breath. It's chilly, the air crisp and cool.

"I feel like something's gonna happen," says Aria, who's landed on her stomach, "but . . . no idea what." And then she lurches forward and vomits. She wipes her mouth and says, "Okay. It happened."

A few others wretch, and then, on shaky legs, we stand, gaping at each other.

"Everyone all right?" the woman named Wanda asks, brushing dust out of her dyed brick-red hair. We all nod, dazed.

"It's fine. I broke my fall with my face," says Clara dryly, adjusting her hair back into its perfect bun. We are a gathering of dazed travelers. My best friend, Germ; and Ebb, who's dead. My mom, Annabelle; my twin brother,

Wolf. Aria and her big sister, Clara; and Wanda—the last two I only met a few minutes ago in the stomach of the time whale who was helping us to flee a burgeoning black hole. We are standing on a barren, white, dusty expanse that disappears into a black horizon. I don't know where we are, but it's not anywhere on Earth.

"What's that smell?" Aria asks.

"Burning stars, most likely," Wanda answers, nodding skyward. Above, thousands of stars encircle us—burning so bright that a person could read by their glow. "If I've got things right, we're on a dwarf planet called Glimmer 5 about a hundred and ten light-years from home. Still in the Milky Way, so that's something." Wanda brushes off her skirts, stamping dust off her wooden leg and tossing her flamboyant hair briskly. "It's lucky you had the magazine," she says to Germ. "There couldn't be a better place to route ourselves, really."

I know she's talking about Germ's well-worn copy of *Pet Psychic: The Outer Space Issue*, which we have apparently just stepped through. I know it, but it's hard to *believe* it. And then, so much more comes back to me—all lost in the haze and confusion.

"We left Chompy," I whisper. Our whale, alone and scared at the bottom of the Sea of Always. Instinctively I reach for the shoulder straps of my backpack to retrieve my *Lumos* flashlight, only to remember that the flashlight's gone—and my bluebird, Little One, with it—destroyed by witches.

"We left *the world*," Aria adds, her voice cracking, leaning closer to her sister.

I hear a groan, and it takes a minute to realize it's come from me, rising out of my own chest and through my mouth.

The war against the witches on the beach.

The blanket made of nothing left behind.

The black hole opening above the earth.

We gaze at each other, in shock. Is it all gone? The sea? Our town? Countries? The world?

The more I get my bearings, the more I want to crumple up and dissolve.

Beside me Germ is ashen, her reddish freckles vanished as they only do when she turns pale. I jar her gently, but she doesn't speak. My mom, too, is silent, and next to her my brother shivers.

"The others who came with you . . . ," Aria ventures, turning to Wanda, confused. And now that comes back to me too, a white-bearded man and two teenage boys who appeared on the whale but aren't here now. Wanda tries to wipe the dust off her flushed cheeks but only manages to spread it into larger swaths.

"They could be dead, or lost in space if something went awry as they came through the hole," she says. "It's a hazard of this kind of travel. But hopefully they diverted somewhere safely." She's quiet for a moment, thinking. "We'll have to assume we're the only witch hunters left."

"But *how* are we left?" Aria says. "How are we even here?"

Wanda only presses her lips together tightly, and then starts to walk purposefully in the direction of the empty horizon.

"I'll catch you up on all of that," she says. "But right now, we need to see what's what. A mal tiempo, buena cara," she says, repeating what she said when we were falling through the air. "In bad weather, a good face," Wanda translates as she settles into a purposeful gait, her wooden leg thumping in a steady rhythm on the ground. I don't know where she could be heading. I see nothing but empty gray land in every direction. And then a noise . . . like a whimper . . . comes from behind me. I turn to see my brother, thin and shivering, backing away from us.

I reach out to touch his shoulder. "It's okay, Wolf," I say, trying to sound more hopeful than I feel. But as I step closer, he jerks away. Then he turns, and—shoulders hunched, seeming in the moment more animal than boy—

he walks and keeps walking. He doesn't look back over his shoulder as he slinks away toward the horizon. My mom is turned toward him like she's watching a sinking sun.

"He'll come back," Wanda says as we watch him go. "It's a tiny planet, from what I've read. You could circle it in an hour." My mom's eyes stay glued to my brother as his figure gets smaller. I look at Wanda uncertainly. She only turns and keeps walking.

The gray landscape slopes ever so slightly beneath us. I soon understand that Wanda wasn't kidding about circling it in an hour. The planet is small enough that I feel the curve of it under my feet. The only signs of life are a few straggly, parched trees with crooked trunks and pointy limbs, and some snow-white shapes in the distance, winged and waddling.

"Space geese," Wanda explains. "They eat the moss that grows along the rocky hills. It only rains once in a blue moon here, and not much light for anything else to grow. It's always dim, always looks like the cusp of evening. Always chilly." She looks back at Ebb, who's floating along beside me. "There's no such thing as night and day. You won't fade away, no matter how long you stay."

This is good news. Back home, ghosts fade if they're

away from their graves too long. But Ebb only frowns, lost in his own thoughts. And I know he's thinking about his parents, how close he was to haunting them in 1934, to seeing their lives in the past unfold. I want to hug him tight, but he's too ephemeral for me to do it.

"You talk like you've been here before," Aria says. And Wanda, glancing back at us, vigorously shakes her head.

"No, but I've known about Glimmer 5 most of my life. And, luckily, I had the means to get us here." She holds out her hand, closing her fist to better display a ring on her finger. It's a small silver circle, with the top poking up like a wing or a fin. I hadn't noticed it when we were on Chompy, but then again, we were in a whale at the end of the world, watching a woman draw a hole in the fabric of space and time. I was a bit distracted.

Now she squints. "We landed too hard—I've broken it." She wiggles the delicate metal fin with her hand, and it lists to one side crookedly. "Traveling across this much distance is not something I've ever attempted. And I wouldn't have, if the world . . ."

She clears her throat, all business.

"Just to be clear on what you've told me: the world's witches wove a blanket of *nothing* that turned out to be a black hole. You killed them, but the blanket remained."

THE PALACE OF DREAMS

She looks around to verify this, and we vaguely nod. But to be honest, we're still trying to grasp it ourselves.

"The Nothing King's been imprisoned in his *own* black hole," Wanda continues, "locked up there by the Moon Goddess for millennia, but now these twin black holes have been connected across the universe like a tunnel, so the Nothing King could come through it and drag Earth in . . . and obliterate it. If that hasn't happened yet, I imagine it soon will."

Wanda says all of this matter-of-factly, as if she's talking about taxes, or dusting. Meanwhile I feel Germ sway a little beside me, clearly distraught. I've never known her to be quiet for so many seconds in her life.

"Unfortunately," Wanda goes on pragmatically, "a black hole is a gaping suck of darkness that nothing can resist. Once you're close enough, there's no turning back from it. A speck of *dust* can't survive it. Light can't; even time can't. Certainly *Earth* couldn't. Only the Nothing King could ever survive it, since it's what he's made of."

Wanda looks around at each of our faces gravely, and then brushes her hands together brusquely, as if her entire way of being is facing bad weather with a good face.

"So . . . what do we do?" Aria asks.

Wanda shrugs. "For now," she says, looking beyond us

at something in the distance, "we get our bearings." We all turn and follow her gaze to see a small rocky hill made of gray stone, about fifty yards away.

"What are we looking for, Wan?" Clara asks.

"A view," Wanda answers decisively.

With Wanda and Clara in the lead, we set off in the direction of the rocks, and crest the hill, where from the top we see nothing but empty space in every direction, stark and beautiful and gut-wrenchingly, vastly empty. Suddenly I think of the Moon Goddess. Does the moon still exist? Does *she*? The thought takes my breath away.

"Should we see Earth from here?" I whisper. "Is it . . . gone?"

Wanda taps her wooden leg nervously. "It's not Earth we're looking for. It's Rufus Glimmer, the man who built the League of Witch Hunters." And then, having seen enough to know where she's going, she walks back down the hill, leading the way across the emptiness. We have no choice but to follow.

"A witch hunter . . . lives *here*?" I ask, gazing around at the emptiness. Wanda shakes her head.

"Not a witch hunter himself," she answers. "Actually, he's a bit of a coward. But if anyone in the galaxy can help us, it's him."

CHAPTER 2

"Don't trip on that defense shield," Wanda says, pointing offhandedly at a small, strangely shaped yellow rock as she skirts around it ahead of us. "I'd bet that the more of them we see, the closer we're getting, so that's good. Looks like we bypassed his alert system by coming in the way we did."

Beside me Germ, usually so sure-footed, stumbles over a rock, dazed. I try to steady her, but I'm feeling even clumsier than usual. I'm still getting used to my own longer legs, which grew like weeds when the Time Witch stole a year of my life from me in London. I keep glancing at Aria and Clara with a weird flutter of jealousy, their arms linked together, clinging to each other, reunited after years apart. I scan the horizon for Wolf, but there's no sign of him.

"Rufus," Wanda says, "is a genius. And also a thief. Fairly selfish . . . and not bad on the ukulele, so I've heard. He's a legend, really."

Aria and I cast each other a confused glance.

"From what I know, he was born with the sight, but—unlike you and me, who turned that sight to hunting witches—he chose to use it to invent things. He hoped inventions would make him rich.

"I guess he turned himself into a scholar of moonlight, trying to harness the invisible energy of it to come up with all sorts of things he could sell on TV—toasters that can crisp a bagel at the speed of light, goggles for seeing ghosts. Problem was, none of his inventions would *behave* in front of people who didn't have the sight—which, of course, is most people. Moonlight can be stubborn that way.

"Still, in studying the forces of moonlight and magic, he happened to learn more about witches than anyone else on Earth. And I'll say this for him: he shared what he learned.

"He wrote a kind of newsletter, sent to and passed

around among all the witch hunters he could track down—detailing all that he discovered about witch weapons and magic. Those letters are really what made the scattered witch hunters all over the world into a *league*, the newsletters getting passed from hand to hand until they were wrinkled and worn and barely legible. They connected us.

"He gave me the idea for my weapon." She holds up her fist to indicate her ring. "It's a seam ripper, for cutting holes out of the invisible fabric. The blade is here, underneath. I've mostly used it to cross distances, but I did rip a hole through Hypocriffa's hat once."

"But how did Rufus end up here?" Aria presses, never one to beat around the bush. "On a random rock across the galaxy?"

Wanda shrugs. "He came here to hide. As I'm sure you all know, all too well, witches won't tolerate a threat once they learn of it. And eventually they learned about *him*." She raises her hands and drops them, skirting around another defense shield. "Luckily for Rufus, his inventions were better than anybody knew. Good enough to get him off planet Earth. He'd figured out enough about moonlight and motion, he'd stolen enough equipment from international space agencies, to travel at astronomical speed. Next time we got a letter, it was from space." She offers a tiny faltering smile. "Filling us in on the progress of his projects here on Glimmer 5. Though"—she looks around uneasily—"it seems those updates might have been a little exaggerated."

Following her line of sight, I see very little that might merit an update, except for more and more clusters of defense shields, growing sharply in number as we walk.

"Rufus is, first and foremost, a survivor. He values his own skin," Wanda says. She leads the way up a slight rise, and pauses briefly at the top. "Ah. Here we are."

At first, what's before me is so impossible, it seems like a mirage.

A rambling structure stretches across a vast dusty plain below us. Crookedly built, it sprawls in all directions, as if someone started making additions to it and forgot to stop.

Most of its doors and windows are hanging off the hinges, the screens in its windows torn. The yard around it is strewn with debris: hubcaps, old signs, metal lumps that might be broken-down cars. A sign along the building's roof pulses and blinks in rainbow colors, though several of its letters have fizzled out. TH H TEL T THE DGE OF THE GAL XY, it reads.

"The Hotel at the Edge of the Galaxy?" Aria asks.

"Like I said, it's the only place I could think of to come

to," Wanda says, "but luckily for us, it's also the *best* place. Rufus will know what to do."

Dazed, we limp into the Hotel at the Edge of the Galaxy, Wanda holding open two rickety wooden doors.

Inside, we find ourselves in a threadbare lobby, comfortingly warm after the chill air outside, thanks to a fireplace blazing in one corner. Hallways branch off in three crooked directions as if they were tacked on in a hurry, and to our right stands a reception desk with a silver bell covered in cobwebs. A bank of wooden mail slots line the wall behind it, empty. Wanda leans forward and rings the bell. We wait. I look to my mom for reassurance, but she's looking out the window for any sign of Wolf.

Wanda taps her wooden leg and is lifting her finger to ring the bell again, when suddenly we hear a *tut, tut, tut* down one of the halls. It takes another moment, but eventually a shining ghost materializes through the wall behind the desk and comes to float his elbows just beside the bell. He has a goatee and round eyeglasses, over which he gazes at us in distaste. He busies his hands with his wrinkled bow tie.

"Welcome to Glimmer 5," he says stiffly, "your relaxing home away from home. May I help you?"

We stand there wordlessly. Considering how deserted the planet is, it seems he could be a little more surprised by our arrival.

"We've just come from Earth," Wanda explains, "which is in danger of being sucked into a black hole, if it hasn't been already. The Nothing King has returned. This was the only place where we knew we could be safe."

The man stares at her for a minute, sniffs, and then picks up a pen. "And how many of you will be staying with us tonight?"

For a moment, none of us can speak—even Wanda seems taken aback. She gazes around at us, and counts under her breath.

"Eight," she says.

The man with the goatee—Fabian, his name tag says—nods.

"Dinner is at six in the parlor. If there's anything we can do to make your stay more pleasurable, please let us know. Zia will lead you to your rooms." He rings the bell again, several times, until a second ghost appears, a girl, maybe fifteen. She's wearing a sequined corset dress, and sparkling barrettes in her hair. At least *this ghost* does a double take when she sees us.

"Zia, please show these guests to their rooms," Fabian says.

He looks like he's trying to remember something he's supposed to recite as he turns back to us and tilts his head. "We hope you find our service out of this world."

Wanda opens and closes her mouth, at a loss for words. The ghost girl, Zia, not very subtly rolls her eyes.

"Thank you," Wanda finally says.

And then Zia turns and leads us into the crooked left-side hall.

CHAPTER 3

"I'm so glad you're here," Zia says as she walks us through several connected hallways—some painted, others half-wallpapered as if done with scraps of whatever was available. "We haven't had a guest since a few ghosts found their way here fifteen years ago. I sometimes think I'd die from boredom if I weren't dead. Though I heard that happened to a ghost in Delhi once, actually just completely vanished from boredom."

She tugs at her translucent black wavy ponytail and raises an eyebrow at us, the bronze glow of her luminous cheeks echoing the amused twinkle in her hazel eyes.

"I like her style," Aria says to me. I wonder if she means Zia's sparkly clothes or her attitude or both. Somehow I step on my own feet three times as I contemplate this. I can tell straight off that Zia's the kind of person—like Germ—who's never met a stranger (in other words, the opposite of me).

It gets more and more obvious as we walk that the Hotel at the Edge of the Galaxy was built without a plan. We pass stairways tucked awkwardly into corners, comfy parlors tucked around the corners of seeming dead ends, guest rooms that—from their narrow doorways—appear at first to be closets. There are so many nooks and rooms and hallways that it's hard to imagine you could ever explore them all. And all of it is worn and faded: peeling paint, overstuffed couches, and sagging beds. Still, despite the gaping ache in my heart, seeing the dim chilly night beyond the windows soothes me and assures me that we are at least safe, at least for the moment.

"We keep the fireplaces blazing," Zia says, "even when no one's here. We don't have to worry about running out of logs because the fires run on moonlight; also no ashes or smoke that way, which makes it easier for me. Rufus has drilled it into us to be always at the ready, always remember our scripts. Customer service and all that." She gives us a deadpan look, and for a moment her eyes linger on Fred, Ebb's spider, who's perched on Ebb's shoulder and is as dead and translucent as Ebb himself.

"You all look terrible, by the way," she adds, glancing around at all of us and giving Ebb a sideways smile. "You look like my aunt Nahla that time she had to have her kidney out."

"Um, thanks?" Ebb says uncertainly.

"But how could he do all of this?" Aria asks. "Build a hotel *here*?"

"Eh." Zia taps her chin. "Thievery, physics . . . magic. I guess back on Earth, Rufus was kind of a magpie, collecting every scrap of metal or knickknack or unguarded heirloom he could get his hands on. From junkyards, aviation museums, people's houses, whatever. He brought it all with him, loaded into a stasis compartment on the back of his ship. He also brought me and Fabian. We had nothing going on back home, so we volunteered."

"Rufus thought the League of Witch Hunters would defeat the witches," Wanda adds, the *tap, tap* of her wooden leg punctuating her words. "And that once the witches were dead, people would get back their sight. And that once people had the sight"—she shrugs—"they'd get really into space travel. He was gonna get in on the trend early with his hotel."

We blink at her.

"You can't be serious," Aria says flatly.

"I said Rufus was a genius." Wanda shrugs again. "I never said he was realistic."

At that moment, Zia turns and says, "Your rooms."

We're in a back corner of the second floor. Zia directs me and Germ into one room and Aria and Clara into the next.

"These rooms smell old, but they also have the best views," she says. "Not that the views are great or anything. It's just flat land out there, really. There are robes in the closet, but they're scratchy."

"You should really be in charge of the marketing here," Aria quips.

Zia grins and then steers Ebb to a room at the other end of the hall, before giving Wanda one across a small parlor.

"My son and I will sleep in the same room," my mom says. I shoot a glance her way, feeling a little left out. But she doesn't notice my look. "Maybe somewhere quieter?"

"No problem." Zia turns and leads her away up a small flight of stairs, which gives us a few minutes to put down what few belongings we've carried with us from the belly of the whale.

Germ and I—in room 8, according to the placard on the door—share a set of bunk beds, a desk, and a narrow window that allows a view of the stars. I lay my backpack full of books on the desk as Germ climbs into the bottom bunk without a word and burrows in, until her pale freckled forehead and a swath of reddish-blond hair poke out just above the covers. It isn't like her at all, but I know without her saying it that she's thinking of her family—all the Bartleys left behind on Earth—and I don't know what to say. Next door, in room 9, Clara and Aria are murmuring to each other. I long for someone to murmur with too.

Then Wanda returns, appearing in the doorway. She stands at the threshold for a moment, thoughtfully intense.

"This is the main thing I've been thinking since we left your whale," she says as if thinking out loud, twirling her ring on her finger. "I can understand that the witches made a black hole and that the Nothing King traveled through it from his own. What I can't understand is *how* the Nothing King got out of the one he was *in*. Everyone *knows* that the Moon Goddess locked him into that hole eons ago, with her very own key."

I am about to point out that most people do not know that the Moon Goddess exists. But she presses on.

"It doesn't make sense. She wouldn't have let anyone

get hold of that key. And *that's* really where Rufus comes in. If we could find that key, we could at least have a fighting chance of somehow locking the Nothing King back in. Without a key to lock him up, we might as well not even hope to stop him. And if anyone knows enough about witches and magic to help us find that key, it's Rufus."

Just then, Zia reappears.

"Can you give us directions to Rufus's quarters?" Wanda asks. "We need to see him right away."

Zia blinks for a moment, surprised. "He has the owner's suite up on the fourth floor, two lefts, up the stairs, and then a right." Wanda pivots on her heel to start immediately, but catching her up short, Zia adds, "But he's not here."

Wanda goes still, swiveling back to Zia. "Not . . . in the hotel?"

Zia bites her lip, sensing she's just punched us in the gut. "Not on Glimmer 5. I went to clean his room this morning, and his bed was unmade and his closet empty." She frowns. "He left a note."

"Did it say when he'll be back?" Wanda asks.

Zia watches us sympathetically. She's wary now, as if she doesn't want to say. "You'd better come see for yourself."

CHAPTER 4

ufus's room is perched crookedly at the highest, farthest corner of the hotel. Stars glint beyond the huge window across the room, which holds an unmade four-poster bed, scattered books, and more souvenirs than I've ever seen in one place: painted Dutch clogs, an engraved wooden fan, a Russian nesting doll, a pencil sharpener shaped like the Eiffel tower, a pair of socks embroidered with the words "I ♥ NY."

There's a fireplace opposite the bed, and now Zia points to a piece of paper lying on its mantel. Wanda crosses the room, dodging the mess, and picks the paper up to read aloud.

Dear Zia and Fabian,

I'm sorry to say I've decided to abandon this venture.

Wanda swallows and looks up at me with a heavy dread in her eyes, then continues.

On reflection, I'm unsure Glimmer 5 will ever be the premier destination for space visitors I dreamt of. The echoes of my failure will repeat in my heart for a long time to come with shining clarity. I plan to go somewhere quiet, to read, think, and try to replicate my experiences by copying them in my journals, which I will one day publish. I'm sorry.

Humbly,
Rufus Glimmer

Wanda studies the letter for another moment. It's the first time since I've met her that I've seen her shaken—and that includes when we told her the world was probably ending. After returning the letter to the mantel, she crosses the room and opens the empty closet, then gets on her knees and looks under the bed. She stands and runs her hands along the souvenirs, lifting them one by one as if to feel their weight. Finally she turns to me and Zia with one of the I ♥ NY socks in her hand.

"He's lying," she says.

She gazes at the sock she's holding ever so carefully.

"Rufus wouldn't say things like 'on reflection' and 'humbly.' He always signed his newsletters, um, well"—she clears her throat—"'Ingeniously Yours.'" Zia and I exchange a glance. "And it's no coincidence," Wanda goes on, "that he chose now of all times to vanish, right when the Nothing King has escaped. Something made him flee. Something bad."

She turns her attention more directly to the sock again.

"I don't think he's actually *left* Glimmer 5 at all. I think . . . he's here."

She hands me the sock. A long silence follows.

"Here?" I finally ask. "In a sock?"

Wanda nods. "These other things"—she gestures

around the room full of knickknacks—"are just camou-flage. This sock is the one that matters. It's the weight that gives it away, like it's heavy and light at the same time. It's a time bauble, all right. He must have gotten it off the Time Witch somehow, probably planned to sell it for a fortune in the gift shop or something." She rubs her hands together as if brushing dust off her palms. "But now . . . now he's hiding *in* it instead."

Another long silence comes and goes.

"Rufus," I finally say, "is hiding in this . . . *I love New York* sock?" I cast a confused glance at Zia, who looks, frankly, as if she's excited to have something interesting happen at last.

"Welcome to *seeing*, Rosie," Wanda says matter-of-factly. "Size and space and time and place don't mean what you used to think. And neither do the boundaries between them." She looks me up and down, while I wonder if I'll always feel like I'm just beginning with the sight. "You're going to need a new weapon," she says. "And we'll need to talk to Clara and Aria."

"Why?" I ask.

"Because we need to go in after him."

Before I can react, Wanda, her leg tapping out a vigor-ous rhythm, has already hurried out of the room.

✦ ✦ ✦

After winding through the hallway, we find the sisters' room empty—though, I can already tell which bed's Aria's from the way she's draped scavenged fabrics over her lamp in a sophisticated kind of way so that it looks more like a French boudoir. Opposite, Clara's bed is as smooth and tight as a soldier's.

One of the few things I know about Clara is that *she* knows time baubles, since she was trapped in one—a snow globe—with Wanda for years. A time bauble holds a slice of time stolen by the Time Witch, like a memento of her favorite moments, kind of like a postcard. But I still don't really understand how a person ends up in one. Or how *I*, specifically, will end up in one.

We find Clara and Aria out in front of the hotel, kneeling over a strange metal object half stuck in the dusty ground. Walking up to them, I think how you could never mistake them for anything but sisters. They've both got the same ballerina buns in their black hair, similar constellations of freckles along their brown cheeks. But that's where the similarities end. Clara holds herself like the general of a small army—alert and intent and straight-postured—while Aria is sort of effortlessly graceful. And Clara has a pencil tucked behind her ear, like at any moment she will need to jot something down. I'd like to know the ways Wolf and I are alike and different too, but he hasn't returned.

"It's definitely supposed to fly," Clara says, seeing us approach.

"It's a messenger." Wanda crouches beside them and gently tugs the thing out of the ground. It looks like a rusted coffee can with gears attached to a pair of flaps that appear to be wings. "That's how Rufus used to send his letters. Much faster than the speed of light."

I'm about to ask how that could be possible—especially with what looks like a piece of junk you might find at a dump, but Clara stands and announces, "There's something else." She takes the messenger out of Wanda's hands as she leads us around the corner of the hotel to a rusted-out shell of an enormous building—plain and square but big enough to hold a fleet of buses. She throws us a *Hold on to your hats* kind of glance before she yanks open a pair of enormous rusted doors.

We stand peering into the twilit shadows.

"There's a light switch," Clara says, laying down the messenger and feeling around along the wall. At the same moment, Aria reaches into her pocket, pulls out her slingshot, and shoots a pebble into the air as she hums a melody that sounds somehow like light. The pebble lands on the other side of the room, casting a glow all around us long enough for Clara to find the switch.

I catch my breath at both the sudden brightness and what it illuminates.

We're in a workshop, but not like any I've seen. Everywhere there are hulking, jagged shapes: a sleek biplane dangling from a set of chains in the ceiling far above, a deflated hot-air balloon draped on a partition, a torn kite with a silver motor attached to its tail, angled gliders shaped like arrows, a parachute slumping over a rack. All along the rusted walls are enormous drawings, clusters of calculations, diagrams of planets, sketches of moonbeams lined with equations, crisscrossing renderings of what I think must be the invisible fabric of space and time.

Space suits (at least, I think they're space suits) dangle from hooks along one wall, half-sleek and half stitched together with scraps, with tiny jets at the back. I run my hands along the sleeve of one, and as I touch it, the suit lights up and begins to breathe on its own—rising and falling—before blinking out again. The whole place feels old and new at the same time.

"All these broken, miraculous things," Wanda breathes.

"I guess he abandoned them over the years, as the dream of a world with the sight kept getting further away."

Clara is standing with her back to us at a far corner of the room now, dwarfed by the shadow of some kind of aircraft. It's silver-plated and streamlined, several plates missing or singed or bent, and it's half made of glass covering it from the middle up to the roof like windows. It has one left-leaning, singed silver door, emblazoned in bright yellow zigzagged letters: ASTRAL ACCELERATOR. Clara tugs on one of the panels, and it comes off in her hand.

"That's the ship he came in," Wanda says. "He mentioned the name in his letters."

I lean my face against the glass and see frayed and decaying seats and some kind of cockpit.

"I found some blueprints, for a lot of the things in here," Clara offers, moving beside me. "Most of his inventions ran on moonlight instead of gas." She points out the back door of the hangar to a small pond full of glowing silver light.

"Delivered by the Brightweaver," Wanda says. "He wrote about her. They were friends."

My heart flutters. *Were.* When I last caught sight of the Brightweaver's clouds and cloud shepherds, they were being sucked across the sky toward the black hole.

"Well, its flying days are over now," Clara says, laying gently on the ground the metal plate she's pulled off. "In addition to falling apart, it's missing the piece that keeps it from overheating and exploding." She points to a small spiral-shaped notch beside a flap in the back.

"Do you think you could fix the messenger, Clara?" Wanda presses. "Enough so it can fly to Earth and see if Earth is still there?"

"Clara's witch weapon is a tool kit," Aria explains to me with pride, nodding to a satchel over Clara's right shoulder. I try to picture Clara screwdriving a witch to death. "She can fix just about anything."

Clara wiggles the flapping wings of the messenger, which lift for a moment of their own accord before giving off a puff of thick black smoke and falling limp.

"I can fix cars, Peanut, not spacecraft."

Aria casts me an embarrassed glance.

I bite back a smile. *Peanut?* Aria, who listens to sophisticated bands and can captain a whale and basically saved our lives?

"I'd have to make this thing strong and smart enough to survive a trip across the galaxy," Clara goes on, "then find proof of life, then get back here without being spotted by the Nothing King or his crows. It's a big ask." Nevertheless, she pulls her pencil from her ear, then a pad of paper from her back pocket, and starts writing down calculations.

"Speaking of big asks," Wanda interrupts. "We came out here to ask you something else, actually. We're going into a time bauble. Well, we *are* if my ring has at least enough juice left to get us in. We need you to make sure we can get out again."

Even Clara, who must be used to Wanda's brusque manner by now, looks taken aback. I shudder a bit.

"We might not get out again?" I ask.

Wanda looks at me, then examines the reinforced toe stitching of the sock. "Well, I doubt it's a witch trap like Clara and I wandered into. But even on their own, slices of time can be dangerous. You can't tell by looking from the outside what cluster of moments a bauble contains. Never know what you'll stumble in on," she says. "They can be beautiful moments or horrid ones. We'll need you both"— she nods to Clara and Aria—"on the outside to haul us out if we get into trouble."

"Why Rosie?" Aria asks protectively.

Wanda eyes me. "I think Rufus would like her," she says simply. "They're both dreamers." Then she brushes her hands along her waist, unruffled as always. "Now let's go eat. I'm starving."

CHAPTER 5

We make an incomplete dinner group as we gather in the dining room that evening at a long oak table lined with candles, a fire crackling in a fireplace in the corner.

Germ stays in bed, and Wolf is still somewhere on the planet running wild. I sit beside my mom, but she's distracted, looking for him through the window. She seems completely unfazed by Wanda's news that I'm going into a sock.

Given that the world is hanging in the balance, it's

strange to think of eating *anything*, let alone a candlelit dinner, let alone on a planet twenty-two thousand light-years from home. Still, I *am* starving, and Fabian and Zia serve a miraculous feast: hot bread rolls and five kinds of cheese and a roast and cake and jam and fruit.

"When a fridge runs on moonlight, it keeps things fresh forever," Zia explains, holding a tray loaded with sweet buns and laying them down on the table with a friendly smile.

It's Ebb who notices that something's off as he gazes at Fabian, who's primly laying silverware beside Clara's and Aria's plates. "How are you doing that?" he asks. "Carrying stuff? Like, real stuff?" Ghosts back home can't do much of anything except drift around and be kind of useless, given that they're wispy and barely exist. Fabian only sniffs and murmurs something about teaching not being in the job description.

"Rufus figured it out," Zia says, looking around the table to include the rest of us. "He'd brought me and Fabian here and he needed our help to get this place off the ground, so he did some calculations and some experiments, and now . . ." She uses her filmy translucent hand to push a candlestick an inch along the table, to demonstrate. "Voila. It has to do with electromagnetism. Ghosts can sort of . . . channel electromagnetic waves. Sometimes accidentally, when they're mad or upset." (I think of the Murderer, getting so angry with me that he knocked an axe off a wall.) "But also when they just *really* concentrate."

"I haven't even been able to move a feather," Ebb says, clearing his throat, "since I died."

Zia holds her hand out toward the candle she moved and runs her hand through the flame, making it flicker. "It takes five minutes to learn. And then it's like whistling; once you learn the trick of it, it's easy. I'll teach you." She puts the hand that passed through the flame on Ebb's arm encouragingly. I feel a strange, small pain as she does. If I tried to do that, my living hand would slip right through him. "And when Fabian and I do it together, we can lift bigger things, so it'll be nice to have a third."

Shaking off my discomfort, I stand from my chair to reach for the butter, but somehow my feet get tangled in the legs of the chair and I fall against the dining room table.

Fabian snickers behind his hand and pretends it's a sneeze before vanishing into the kitchen. I'm too embarrassed to breathe.

"It's because you've grown so much since your time got stolen by the Time Witch, Rosie," my mom offers, putting her hand over mine as I sit back. "You don't know exactly where your body is yet."

"I *know* where my body is!" I say in a mortified half whisper, and cast a self-conscious glance at Ebb, who's frowning at me thoughtfully. I look back at my mom, but her gaze has already gone back to the window. Though the clock on the sideboard says it should be night, the dim, dusky light outside has not changed, just as Wanda said.

"There's a vending machine on the third floor, near the library, Rosie," Zia offers, settling into the seat on the other side of Ebb. "After dinner you should go check it out. I'm sure there's something in there you can use as a new weapon."

Vending machine? I try to picture making a new Little One out of a bag of Doritos, or a can Coke. Not to mention, how could there ever be another Little One? She was irreplaceable.

"Thanks, Zia," I say, giving her a shy smile.

"Man, I miss eating," she sighs, gazing around the table as we stuff our faces. "I could eat a house if only I had a living stomach."

"I sneezed spaghetti out of my nose once when I was alive," Ebb says. "Now I'd give anything to have spaghetti coming out of my nose if that meant I was eating spaghetti."

Zia barks a laugh, and Ebb's frown fades a little. And then Fabian reenters the room. For a moment, there's an awkward silence.

"And now we'd like to share with you all a very special welcome video," Fabian announces stiffly as Zia meets our eyes apologetically. Fabian clicks a remote he pulls from a shelf, and a large hologram appears above one of the sideboards. Zia and Fabian move to stand on either side of the image, smiling widely as they've clearly been instructed to do.

The hologram shows a man, old and thin, mustachioed and black-haired with streaks of gray at his temples, in a plaid suit, an orange bow tie, and a fedora with a matching orange feather. Across the table, Aria and I exchange a look. His outfit and his giant smile remind me of this guy on a commercial back home who says his cars are priced so low, he's "practically giving them away."

"Hi there. I'm Rufus Glimmer," the man in the hologram says with a grand arm gesture. "Welcome to Glimmer 5. My dream was to create a space travel destination for all of humankind to enjoy, and I thank you for joining us! While you're here, my staff and I hope you'll take advantage of all the planet has to offer."

Three-dimensional images of the Hotel at the Edge of

the Galaxy flash above the sideboard. Only, in this version, it is tens of stories high, with gleaming windows and polished chrome. There are people relaxing around the lush green grounds, playing games, reading, boarding shuttles into space.

"Levitating shuffleboard," Rufus narrates cheerfully, "an extensive library, space excursions and globular cluster tours, space-goose hunting, the death-defying astral-drop." An image appears of a smiling person in a pressure suit parasailing behind a spacecraft. "And for our ghostly patrons, we have one-way trips to Limbo on our crown jewel, the Astral Accelerator shuttle."

Onscreen is the broken old shuttle we saw in the hangar—but here, it shines as a high-tech space cruiser, gliding gamely toward a bright glowing puff of cloud on which ghosts are standing, smiling, chatting, and playing golf.

"The Astral Accelerator uses the most cutting-edge physics and magic technology in the galaxy. Fueled by moonlight, using its fine-tip instruments to weave between both the space-time fabric *and* the invisible fabric, it can glide through the warp and weft of existence without friction, travel many times faster than the speed of light, and three times faster than even *our* fastest messenger, getting you to Limbo quick while also putting on quite a show."

The hologram version of the ship shoots off a stream

of fireworks, with its passengers oohing and aahing behind the windows inside.

"The craft is equipped with seats for twelve passengers and has state-of-the-art luxuries like panoramic windows and reclining leather seats, and its finest technology is also its tiniest." Between his thumb and forefinger, Rufus holds up a small spiral tube pulsing with light. Across the table, Aria nudges Clara, raising her eyebrows. The object he's holding is exactly the size and shape of the piece that was missing from the ship. "The Glaciation Matrix, which will keep you cool and comfortable no matter what speed you're traveling at, or what unstable atmospheres you pass through along the way. So relax and enjoy."

Meanwhile, above the sideboard, the 3D Astral Accelerator blasts up toward the ceiling gracefully, full of ghosts smiling and waving out the window. I notice that the ghosts are just repeats of Fabian and Zia.

Rufus appears one last time, his smile wider than ever. "Please contact our helpful hosts for more information about all the wonderful amenities we have in store for you! We hope your stay is out of this world!"

The hologram disappears, and Fabian leaves the room while Zia sighs and returns to her seat. Aria and I exchange meaningful glances. Rufus comes across as . . . a bit slippery.

"What's Limbo?" Clara asks, adjusting the pencil in her hair as she looks around at the rest of us. Several of us shrug. Even Wanda doesn't seem to know the answer.

"I've always heard about it," Ebb offers, looking at Zia uncertainly for her guidance. "It's kind of a *non-place* for ghosts. If you're a ghost and you're tired of drifting around Earth getting ignored by the living, haunting houses that get constantly renovated or whatever, you can go to Limbo instead."

Zia nods. "It's only a few thousand light-years from here. Rufus adapted his shuttle so it could make the trip, but"—she shrugs—"he never got the customers. I doubt they would have wanted to go anyway," she adds.

"Why not?" Aria asks.

"Well, once a ghost enters Limbo, they can never leave. Which means never moving Beyond."

I look at Ebb, who's frowning. Moving Beyond is something mysterious, even to ghosts. It's what happens to most spirits when they die and float up into a sparkling pink kind of halo that circles Earth. If a ghost doesn't move Beyond, it's because they have unfinished business even though they don't know what it is.

I know, without Ebb saying it, that he's thinking of his parents. In our small gaggle, as young as we are, we all

love people who have gone Beyond: Ebb's parents; Clara
and Aria's parents; my dad, who I've never met but have
missed all my life. I can't imagine giving up the chance to
see them. But where *is* the Beyond now? Where is anything that was once in the sky above the world?

As I'm ruminating on this, the swinging door of the dining room comes flying open with a *wham!* and we all jerk.

Wolf stands on the threshold, shirt off, hair wild, blood
on his cheeks, and a dead space goose dangling from
between his teeth. He's holding something sharp and
shiny in his hands that looks like a piece of broken mirror.
My heart flutters and pounds.

Mom shoves back her chair and hurries over to him.
She hesitates for a moment and then gently pulls the space
goose from his teeth.

"Good job, Wolf," she says shakily. "You caught us
something for dinner tomorrow. I'll see what I can do
about cleaning it."

The rest of us sit, gaping in shocked silence.

"He's found the Glasslands," Fabian sniffs, having
drifted in again. "Everything there is razor-sharp. Hope
he doesn't hurt anyone."

"The area got hit by a shower of molten glass millions
of years ago, that froze and splintered as it hit our atmo-

sphere," Zia elaborates. "It's the one place on the planet we don't like to go."

"Sorry about that," I say, trying to offer an excuse for him and quell my pounding heart at the same time. "He was kind of . . . raised by a witch?"

"Oh." Zia nods for a moment, clearly concerned, and then tries to brighten the mood. "Oh well," she offers. "We've all got our *stuff*."

I tremble a grateful smile at her. But inside, I feel panicked. I thought that finding Wolf would be like twins reuniting in the movies, that we'd understand and love each other instantly and be able to finish each other's sentences. I'd pictured us back home and safe. I'd pictured him speaking actual words, sharing thoughts and jokes with me. I'd pictured him at least liking me. But instead, Wolf hasn't said a word, much less a sentence, and it turns out he hunts space geese with his bare hands.

One thing is certain, and it's dawning on me so fast that it makes me dizzy. Whoever I was picturing when I crossed the world and all of history to save my brother—that person doesn't exist, and maybe never did.

After dinner, I climb the stairs to the third floor, getting lost several times and jamming my elbow against a wall while going around a corner. (I guess I *don't* know where my body is after all.)

I find the vending machine Zia described, in a vestibule across a comfy little library with a roaring fireplace. There are two machines side by side, one full of glass soda bottles that look straight out of the old days, and another with a black curtain hanging behind its glass, obscuring what's inside. The first machine is marked REFRESHMENTS at the top. The second has a tiny flashing neon sign that reads EVERYTHING. I blink at it, confused.

"It's just what it looks like, an Everything Vending Machine."

I startle and turn. Zia is standing there with a broom. She casts me a friendly smile and steps up beside me.

"How much money do you have?" she asks. "It takes all currencies."

I fish in my pockets. I find one old penny at the bottom of a hole in my pocket.

Zia shrugs. "That'll get you something, just nothing glamorous. Push the green button and it'll show you your options." She nods to a panel to the right of the mysterious curtained window.

When I do, the curtain opens.

Several rows of prizes turn in circles before my eyes,

dotted with flashing lights like a casino. Everything is in miniature: bags of Doritos the size of my thumbnail, but also cars, thimbles, what looks to be a Jacuzzi, a tiny roller coaster, a castle . . .

"They're just models of what you get. The upper shelves are getting into the really high-budget stuff," Zia explains. "A castle will cost you about fifteen million dollars."

"You mean," I sputter, "if I put that much money in, I'd get a castle out?"

"Well," Zia says, shrugging, "in theory. The idea is that you're supposed to be able to input a location and the machine would deposit the actual castle there. But the only things you can really get are, like, the Doritos and stuff that just come out in the slot. *You* can only afford the row down there anyway."

I lower my eyes to the one-penny items sitting forlornly along the bottom row. There's a mini box of cereal that looks like its expiration date was probably 1985, a plastic spider ring . . . On the third rotation, I notice a miniature pocket flashlight. It's definitely not as nice as my *Lumos* one. But it *is* in the same ballpark at least. Beneath it are numbers: A1005.

Zia, seeing my interest, jabs her finger at the glass. "You just key in the number."

I put my penny into a slot to my right and tap in A1005, and the curtain closes. There's a little thud in the slot at the bottom of the machine. I retrieve the flashlight and study it a moment in wonder before turning it on. A tiny anemic stream of light shines through Zia and onto the wall behind her. We both look at it, underwhelmed.

"I guess that would light up . . . a very small corner of a . . . small room," says Zia, trying to be encouraging. I can almost hear my heart making a *womp, womp* sound of disappointment.

Not knowing what to say, I turn to cross the library. But just when I'm at the threshold, Zia calls after me.

"I'm happy you're all here," she says. "It's nice to have another ghost around too," she adds, looking thoughtful. "Fabian's kind of a stick in the mud, so it's lonely." She pauses for a moment. "How did he die?"

I blink for a moment before I realize who she means. "Ebb?" I ask, and she nods. "Um. He drowned."

Zia takes this in, her eyes darting away from mine. "He looks good"—she clears her throat—"for someone drowned."

Something about the way she says it pricks my ears a bit. I've never really thought about whether Ebb looks good or not, but I suppose he does.

"Usually the drowned ones are all bloated and purple and blue," Zia clarifies, turning her broom in her hands. "I myself fell off a hotel balcony on a visit to my relatives in Morocco."

"Um, I'm sorry," I say, for lack of something better.

"Don't be," she says. "I broke my neck, so it was quick. Well, let me know if you need anything in the night. I'm always up. Though, of course you'd know that about ghosts, since you know Ebb."

In our room, Germ is still burrowed in her blankets. But leaning over her, I see she's awake, staring at the ceiling, just her eyes and pale freckled forehead showing.

I tuck my flashlight into my pocket and sit on the edge of the mattress, laying a hand on her shoulder. My fingers feel bigger there than they used to. I still can't fathom that I'm older than her now.

Still, she's my best friend, and seeing her so broken feels like seeing a lion with its mane shaved, like Aslan in the Chronicles of Narnia. Germ is the person whose courage always makes me strong. I feel a sudden surging hatred for the Nothing King, for making my dazzling, indomitable best friend feel this way.

"Did I ever tell you about the pizza poem D'quan wrote

me?" Germ says to the ceiling in a soft voice, tugging her blanket to below her chin.

I play dumb. D'quan is Germ's boyfriend back home, and he's everything Germ usually isn't—soft-spoken and ruminative, and always writing poems. She *has* told me about the pizza poem, about a million times, but I shake my head anyway. "It compared my eyes to pepperoni slices from Luigi's downtown," Germ says, "but still, it was a really nice poem." She clears her throat. "Now I don't know if he's alive. Or if Bibi is alive. Or if my fam . . . my family . . ." She breaks off and gathers her breath. "If the world."

The covers have slipped down a little from her face, and a tear trickles its way down each cheek. "Back when we were traveling through the Sea of Always, I felt like every day we spent on Chompy meant us being one day closer to getting home. I could practically taste it, that real normal life like we used to have, waiting for me to come back. But now there's no point counting. Because there may be nothing and no one to get back to."

I nod. Germ loves home—she's a star around which people orbit—but she left all that behind to come with me on a journey that's gotten stranger and scarier each time we've gotten close to finishing it. I've always leaned on her for help being brave, and now I want her to be able to lean on me. But I don't even completely know who my new thirteen-year-old self *is*. All I know is that I trip on chairs and feel a pinch when Zia touches Ebb's arm.

Just then I hear footfalls in the hall, and I turn as the door opens.

"Hey," Aria says, looming in the doorway. "Clara says things are all set for the morning sock expedition. Did you get your weapon?"

I hold up my paltry pocket light sheepishly. Aria winces.

"Well, it looks . . . like . . . it's easy to carry?" she says, and we'd laugh if things weren't so unfunny otherwise. Instead Aria's eyes go to Germ and she frowns. She comes and sits beside me on the bed, and wraps her arm around my waist to join our huddle. Germ is now full-on crying, tears coming fast and furious. Luckily, unlike me, Aria seems to know just what to say.

"Germ, you helped me find my way back to Clara. And I'm gonna help you find your way back to your family if it's the last thing I do. I know you feel hopeless, but that's fine because I can be hopeful enough for both of us."

I squeeze her arm. When we met, Aria wasn't hopeful at all. But I suppose finding out your sister was trapped in a snow globe on your dresser for several years can make you think *anything* is possible.

Aria opens her mouth to sing. The song is wordless. It curls out in blue and red tendrils around Germ's bed, wrapping the three of us up in its light like a hug, like a reminder that all is not lost.

It is so beautiful that later—after a long walk—when I'm sitting in my bunk trying to write, by Glimmer 5's strange twilight, a story to wrap around my flashlight, I try to write a story that feels like Aria's song, one with the feel of things not being so bad as they seem.

When I finish, I wrap the piece of hotel stationery I've written on around my flashlight. I've gathered a cup of moonlight from Rufus's pond, and I submerge the flashlight into it. The moonlight feels strange on my fingers as I do, a dryness that looks like it should be wet: a cross between both water and air, impossible as that seems. I put the cup on the side table by the window, hoping the stars will help. And then I go to sleep, waiting for Little One to come back. The words I've written scroll across the dark behind my eyelids:

Once when we thought we'd won, we'd actually lost. Once, something that meant everything—food, water, trees, land— was gone.

But also once there was a bird who could fly through any-thing. This bird did not need food, or water; it didn't need trees or a place to land. All the things other birds might depend on, this bird could do without.

I don't know what the bird looked like; it couldn't quite be seen. But I do know it was tired, and beaten up by all of its battles, and weary from trying to reach the safety of the sky yet never quite arriving. This bird was trying to be something but it hadn't found out what.

And still, anytime it lost itself, it simply lifted its wings and moved. And because it moved, it lived. It found that it could survive even the emptiest of emptinesses. It found that emptiness had something behind it, too.

CHAPTER 6

wake to the same dusky glow that was outside my window when I fell asleep, but my body tells me it's morning.

It takes a moment to realize that I'm being watched. Standing on the foot of the bed, blinking at me with her head tilted to one side (either groggily or dizzily, I can't tell) is . . . a bird. Glowing, translucent, magical.

I shudder.

"You're not Little One," I whisper, trying not to wake Germ. Did I leave my flashlight on? I could have sworn it was off. Also, should a person's witch weapon be wandering around when she is sleeping?

Carefully I slide my legs over the edge of the bunk and climb down the ladder, then tiptoe to where my flashlight sits in the cup of moonlight on the windowsill. I waggle its switch and shine its dim light onto the floor. The bird flutters to the end of the beam.

We look at each other. She's definitely not like Little One at all. Little One was a bluebird, for one, and this bird is more like a hawk. But also, she's shabbier and smaller than any hawk I've ever seen, like she was the runt of the litter (or nest). Her feathers are a mottled gray and white (Little One's were a brilliant blue), and several of them appear to be missing. She looks hungry and what my mom would call *rangy*.

She chirps at me in a friendly way before walking in a circle like she's confused about where she is. She seems loosely tied to my flashlight beam but also able to stray away from it. Then she tries to bite my toe.

"Wow, that bird's awko taco." Germ, awake, is sitting up in bed, rubbing her eyes. "Awko taco" means "awkward" in Germ speak.

"She's like," I breathe, "a fake Little One." It comes out more like a sigh. Little One was light and zippy, childlike and bright. This . . . *creature* is molting, apparently. And moody. And still pecking at my toe.

"Maybe that's what you should call her," Germ suggests. "'FLO' for short."

I nod, watching the shabby hawk as she flutters crookedly up from the ground and perches on my hand, then appears to try to shove her head into my arm. "Flo" doesn't seem quite right.

"Or maybe 'Flit,'" I reply.

Germ leans back, then curls back under her blankets. And then—my eyes going to the clock—I remember that I have somewhere to be. With the new bird hopping along ahead of me, I hurry into the hall and up the stairs, toward Rufus Glimmer's room.

Parted for years, reunited for less than twenty-four hours, Clara and Aria are bickering.

"A whole planet to ourselves, and you stepped on my foot," Clara says.

"Your feet are too big to miss," retorts Aria dryly.

Wanda is standing with her arm draped along Rufus's mantel, studying the sock from yesterday as if it contains the secrets of the universe.

"At least I don't have giant thumbs," Clara says.

"My thumbs are amazing."

I enviously watch the sisters—who seem way too familiar to have been apart for years. (I'm pretty sure neither of them enjoys long walks amongst shards of glass and catching living geese with their teeth.) Wanda casts them a disapproving glance, which she then turns to Flit.

"This," she says, watching Flit peck at my pinky toe, "is the weapon that helped to destroy eleven witches, you say?"

"Um. She—she wasn't like this before," I stammer.

"Well," Wanda says uncertainly. "Between your bird and my barely functional ring that won't even get me to the Glasslands—I tried last night—this should be interesting. Still, I've been doing some experimenting, and I think the ring should get us inside the sock, at least. Though, I have to say, getting *in* is the easy part. It's making sure we get out alive that manners."

I take this in with a nervous lump in my throat.

"Aria and Clara are here so that if we're in for more than an hour, they can break us out again."

"And how do we do that, exactly?" Aria asks, clearing her throat.

"Whatever you did the last time," Wanda says. "With the singing."

Aria glances at me, uncertainty in her eyes. When she broke Clara and the others out of the snow globe, it was kind of by accident. But, maybe because she wants to prove herself to her older sister, she just adjusts her hair bun and nods. "Sure, no problem."

Wanda lays the sock down on the ground.

"Make sure not to step on us," she says breezily, which only makes me feel more nervous.

Wanda puts both hands on my shoulders as if she's testing out whether I'm sturdy enough to survive what's about to happen. Then we crouch beside the sock, and with her ringed finger she traces a small hole in its fabric. The tiny hole glimmers slightly, indicating that it's not just actual fabric she's sliced but something else as well, some layer where space and time and magic meet.

"That'll be big enough," she says, then tilts her head, leaning closer to the sock. "Do you hear something?"

I do. From the tiny hole comes a faint noise, like the distant rumble of a train.

My mind shoots back to other times when I've heard sounds and seen movement coming from places they shouldn't be: voices drifting out from a mouse hole in India, strange movements in a shop window in Russia.

"Maybe this slice of time is from a train station," she

says. "Watch that you don't step on the tracks. We have to keep our wits about us and orient ourselves quickly. Now." She clears her throat. "You have to nudge the tip of your shoe in, just the tiniest bit."

Slowly I move the tip of my shoe against the hole. The stretching and straining begins *there*, at the front of my foot. Soon I feel a pressure all around me, squeezing me from all sides. The next moment, my organs feel like they're being smushed and I have the strange sensation of my skeleton being turned inside out. Then suddenly the pressure releases and I feel my feet on the ground.

And then I'm knocked against a wall.

A crashing, ripping sound surrounds me. Something flies across my vision and strikes my chest, and I scream, crumpling to the ground, trying to grasp what's happening. Wanda appears a moment later, and she too is knocked off her feet and onto her back. We're being battered—by *wind*, I realize. So strong that it pins us where we lie.

A room surrounds us—or what used to be a room. It's being pulled apart. A window shatters, its glass flies everywhere, and I hide my face with my hands. A mirror crashes to the ground.

Wanda, across the room, is trying to get to me, but keeps getting buffeted back. Stuffed animals whip across the floor; a wrought-iron bed slams into a wall, hard enough to break through it. The noise is deafening, and beyond the shattered window I see wood splinters flying. A stinging in my skin tells me I've been cut.

And then, suddenly, silence.

Wanda and I are curled on the ground, panting, gaping at each other. The buffeting has stopped. Wanda peels herself off the floor and hurries toward a window; I follow.

Beyond the decimated wall of this room, a pillar of dust is spinning away, thin at the bottom, expanding upward in wild gray curls. Around it fly splinters of wood, shards of split furniture, uprooted bushes.

And then it spins into a wall of trees and out of sight.

"Tornado," Wanda breathes, still trying to catch her breath. "So sorry, Rosie."

She stands to study me, brushing debris off my body. Rapidly she examines the cuts on my arms, then grabs a handkerchief from her pocket and dabs at them. "We're lucky we got here at the tail end of it. If we'd come a little bit earlier . . ." She looks at the mirror shattered on the floor. "Not that we're out of the woods yet. It'll reset soon."

I want to ask what she means by "reset," but there's so much to take in. There's no rhyme or reason to what has been destroyed around us. A wall, a dresser, and a bed are shattered. A dollhouse, a lamp, and a rabbit stuffie in the corner remain in place and intact. Dust motes and pillow feathers dance through the air. There seems to be the faintest smell of smoke in the air, though I can't tell where it's coming from or if I'm imagining it.

"We're in a kid's room," Wanda says gravely. "The moment a child's world is destroyed. How horrible that she would keep a slice of time like this. Not that it's surprising."

I wish I didn't get what she means, but I do. *Despair is a witch's greatest thrill; it is like the air she breathes*, I remember reading in *The Witch Hunter's Guide.*

Thinking of the witches makes me think of my witch weapon. I flick Flit on. She flutters across the room and perches on the ear of the stuffie bunny, then hops toward the roof of the dollhouse but doesn't quite make it and bumps her breast against the chimney.

Around us, the room blinks.

"Ah! There we go," Wanda says. And now, without asking, I see what "reset" means. With a shimmer in the air like heat rising over hot tar, our surroundings have blinked back to what they must have been before we came— everything in its place, like a computer glitch righting itself. The moment has reset to before the storm's arrival.

Wanda gazes out the window and upward, at a sky that is not a real sky but more like the wrinkled gray fabric of a sock.

"We probably have about ten minutes till the tornado arrives again."

"Again?"

"A time slice just repeats itself over and over forever. But it usually only spans minutes, maybe fifteen or twenty at the most. We should hurry." She glances at her finger, touches the fin of her ring doubtfully.

I swallow hard; weathering the tornado again is the last thing I want to do.

"Rufus?" Wanda calls into the room. "Are you here? It's Wanda Luna from the League of Witch Hunters. We're here to help." She runs her hands behind the newly intact curtains, feeling along behind them. "We need to look for anything that might be out of place in *this* time and place," she explains to me.

Lifting my flashlight, I shine Flit around the room, but she immediately starts pecking at a dangling piece of curtain. As we search the room top to bottom, I try to be more patient with her foolery by remembering I'm not perfect either. We look through the drawers of a dresser, under bundles of blankets, in the closet.

Wanda is a genius for searches, apparently. She peels up the rug to see if there's a trapdoor underneath, feels along a bookshelf for a secret latch, taps the ceiling with a broom for hollow spots. There's a door leading into what I think must be the hall, but when I open it, all I see is another shimmering wall.

"It goes nowhere," Wanda explains. "I learned that the hard way when we were stuck in the snow globe." She swipes at a pile of pillows, looking in every place where a hidden thing the size of a human could be. "Though, that was a much safer time slice than *this* one. We were inside an attic in Switzerland during a snowfall, a stillness and loneliness that the Time Witch wanted to keep, I suppose. Instead of tornadoes, we were surrounded by old plates and dusty porcelain dolls. So we were lucky. Though, we all know porcelain dolls can be pretty scary in their own way."

She gives me a faint smile, and goes on talking as she hunts about the room doggedly.

"It was my own fault, really, that we got trapped. Raj and the boys and I had found a set of the Time Witch's tracks that led straight to the snow globe. I thought I was being clever, guessing that she'd gone inside." Wanda stops for a moment to listen to the air, seems to hear nothing, and then resumes knocking along the floor for hollow hiding places underneath. "I knew about time baubles by then. I should have known it was a trap."

She looks around, gauging what corner of the room to try next. "Don't know how many years went by before I managed to set up a signal, a light I could turn on and off in the attic to tell the outside world we were there. Of course, poor Clara's the one who noticed it and ended up getting trapped too. And now poor Raj and the boys are dead or lost, God knows where."

She steps to the window to check the progress of the storm. Moving behind her, I scan the horizon. Is the wind picking up in the faraway trees, or am I imagining it?

"I know what it's like not to know," I say, trying to commiserate. "When I first found out about the invisible fabric, I thought my dad might still be a ghost haunting the world and that I might run into him. I had this big excited hope about it." I bite my lip self-consciously. I never got to know my dad like Wanda knew her friends, but I've missed him so badly, every day of my life. "Then a cloud shepherd told me he's gone Beyond."

Wanda turns to look at me for a moment, sympathetically. "Cloud shepherds don't always get things right," she says. "They have a lot to keep track of." I'm about to ask her what she means, when she goes very still, putting her hand on my arm. Beside me, Flit lets out a nervous trill.

"The storm's returning," Wanda says. As if on cue, I hear a distant rumble of thunder.

Wanda starts knocking things over impatiently now, shoving the dollhouse and several toys out of the way to feel along more sections of wall, her hands trembling. I stand watching helplessly, having run out of places to look. The sound of the approaching storm grows louder; Flit begins to half screech, half chirp. A breeze drifts in through the open window. The hairs on the back of my neck stand up.

On the flat horizon outside, I see it, a growing swirl of dust, zigzagging across the plains toward us. It intersects with a house in the distance and swallows its roof—then spits out the pieces. Wanda notices it too.

"Time to go," Wanda says.

She tugs me toward the door and opens it, then ushers me into the shimmering haze. Just as she does, I hear a loud creak of splintering wood behind me. But then we're past the threshold, and it feels like my bones are being stretched like taffy.

The whole thing goes easier than shrinking, like my body's rubber-banding back to its normal shape. In no time, Wanda and I are life-size, looking at Aria and

Clara, who are sitting on the bed playing poker. Clara is explaining the rules of Texas Hold'em to Aria, even though I know she already knows how to play.

They glance up as if they've forgotten we were gone, but in a moment they're up, anxiously studying our faces for what we've discovered.

There is a long silence.

"He's not there," Wanda says flatly, looking out at the spinning sky beyond Rufus's window, the vast emptiness of the landscape, and then at Flit pecking at nothing on the floor.

She glances down at her cracked ring, then slides it off her finger and lays it on the mantel.

"I think we're alone out here."

And then, like a sleepwalker, she walks out of the room.

CHAPTER 7

The days begin to pass on Glimmer 5, light-years away from home or any other signs of life. If we had time to save Earth, we're running out of it.

With Rufus Glimmer—our plan A—being unfindable and maybe gone for good, we enact a plan B: Aria and Clara set to work on getting Rufus's messenger to fly.

It isn't much of a plan. Even if they repair the machine and send it toward home, we can't be sure it'll find anything at all. And even if it does, we can't do anything about it anyway. But still, it's the only plan we've got.

Wolf makes a habit of disappearing at daybreak to roam the planet, and Germ stays in bed—so I spend most of those early days perched on a rock in the yard, watching Clara and Aria work on the messenger. Clara's got everything in her tool kit—pliers, drills, a rock hammer, a chisel, a saw, duct tape, paper clips, a pack of gum—and she figures out a way to use every tool she's got. She works on the little tin can as it gives off foreboding little zaps, dipping wires into moonlight before she reinstalls them.

Wanda, meanwhile, gathers up some of the blueprints Clara found and sets up a sewing room in the back of the hotel. She starts tackling the pressurized space suits, unearthing all sorts of sewing implements from the shelves in Rufus's hangar and using her seam ripper to try to whip the suits into shape. She enlists Aria to help with the helmets, tiny speakers, and sewn-in microphones, which can connect to each other by a kind of intercom. When she needs a break from the messenger, Clara helps Wanda tune up the jets that propel the suits. My mom cleans the hotel from top to bottom, because she's too anxious about Wolf to sit still. She beats the dust out of pillows, launders our measly pile of laundry (we only escaped the world in what we were wearing), wrestles the cobwebs out of corners, scrubs the insides of fireplaces. When she's not cleaning, she's watching Wolf out the windows, or trying to track him down so he can eat and get bathed. But he usually only comes in to steal things. Shards of glass aren't the only shiny things he collects; spoons, tools, and door-knobs are also on the list.

Mom's so preoccupied with my brother's strange hab-its that sometimes I think she forgets I'm around. But just when I start to feel that way, she'll do something to show that I'm on her mind too. Like when I pass her cleaning a window or a mirror, she'll swipe a message onto the glass with her finger, then blow warm air on it to make it show up. *Love you, Rosie,* it'll say. Or *You're a star.*

Even Ebb is busy. Every morning, he wanders off with Zia to practice electromagnetic energy on pebbles, branches, and tumbleweeds—getting excited as more and more things move beneath his hands. He and Zia drift around the grounds stretching their hands at things like sorcerers, and soon they're even *building* something: a greenhouse.

It's Ebb's idea. He shows Zia how to listen to the few scrubby plants that grow on Glimmer 5, how to read the slight bends of branches and listen to the slurp of roots, as a way of repaying her for the "electro" lessons. I know I shouldn't feel left out, watching them, but I do. It's just that nobody—my mom, Wolf, Germ, Ebb—is *with* me in quite the way I planned.

To pass the time when I get tired of watching Aria and Clara, I take the winding stairs to cross the library to Rufus's room, and read his letter again and again, trying to decipher the mystery of it.

> . . . unsure Glimmer 5 will ever be the premier destination for space visitors I dreamt of. The echoes of my failure will repeat in my heart for a long time to come . . .

One night, as I'm walking back to my room, going over these words in my head, I hear voices coming from Clara and Aria's room. I wander to the threshold and peer in. Clara is lecturing Aria on the importance of double-checking your circuits before sealing a piece of machinery.

"Rosie," Aria says with relief when she sees me, and gestures me to her side of the room, which is looking more like a Parisian boudoir by the day, with piles of frayed, colorful pillows and string lights that Aria's somehow finagled.

"Pass me that screw, Peanut," Clara says, holding her

hand out toward Aria without looking at either one of us. She's got the messenger on her lap, and a screwdriver in her other hand.

Aria passes the screw, blushing—the "Peanut" thing is really getting to her—and Clara twirls the screwdriver to tighten something, a small puff of rainbow light swirling around the screwdriver as she works.

"I didn't know a tool kit could be a witch weapon," I say, puzzled.

"Well, they come in handy for things like this," Clara says, still focused on the wing. "But in a pinch I could probably hold my own against a witch by using them as projectiles." She lifts the messenger, with its newly tightened join, out to Aria, who takes it, cradles it in her lap, and sings to it. As she does, a thread of music winds from her lips down around the part, soldering it tighter together.

"I never saw myself as much of a smelter," Aria says to me dryly, "but here I am."

"Pay attention, Peanut. You get distracted too easily."

"You do know I survived for years on a frozen island and sailed a whale across the sea of time?" Aria retorts, casting me a side-eye glance as I stifle a grin. But Clara doesn't seem to register it, and I can tell it hurts Aria's feelings that Clara treats her like such a kid. The funny thing is, Aria is the least distractible, most resourceful person I know. But once a little sister, always a little sister, I guess.

Restless, I flick Flit on and watch her wander under the bed, getting her head tangled in a dust bunny and sneezing. I frown.

"She'll come into her own," Aria says, comforting me. "Remember when my slingshot was all wonky and blew things up?" I smile softly. "You and Flit probably just have to grow into each other, trust each other, like me and my voice when I was so angry."

"But I'm not angry," I say.

"Hey, Rosie," Clara interrupts, "your brother took off with my silver pliers earlier. Would you mind getting them from him? I'm worried he might bite me or something if I try."

Aria casts her a *Could you be more subtle?* glance.

"Of course," I say, and stand, my face burning with embarrassment.

Outside, I find my brother by the pond; as I get closer, I see lumps strewn along the edge of the bank beside him and realize they are books. *The Witch Hunter's Guide to the Universe* is lying facedown on the dirt, one corner touching the pond's surface. Annoyed, one by one I start to gather the books that *used* to be in my backpack, but Wolf doesn't seem to notice me. He's got a glowing silver needle—no doubt scavenged from Wanda's sewing area—and a pile of sparkling, broken glass and shiny silverware beside him. Somehow he's sewing and knotting it all together with moonlight-dipped thread. It looks like he's making a medieval torture device.

"You've been to the Glasslands again," I say. And then I realize with a sinking stomach, what he's making is actually a horrible kind of blanket. And I think of another kind of blanket made by the Time Witch. *How long can you live with a witch before you become part witch yourself?* I think, before I can push the thought away.

He jerked at the sound of my voice, and now—careful not to cut himself—he tucks his creation into my backpack, which is lying open beside him.

"Wolf," I say firmly. He looks up, startled, and I point to my backpack. "That's mine."

Wolf glances down at the backpack, then at me. I lean over to take it from him, but he lays his hand over it.

"You can't take people's things," I say, spotting Clara's silver pliers lying in the dirt. I scoop them up and tuck them into my pocket.

Wolf's expression doesn't change, and he doesn't move his hand. I glance around helplessly, frustrated, then snatch up *The Witch Hunter's Guide* where it lies beside him in the dirt. Finally, at a loss, I plop myself down on the ground, flipping it open and thumbing through it just to have something to do with my hands. I skim past the pages full of all the witches we've killed and open it to the one we haven't.

The Nothing King: The most powerful of all witches.
Specialty: Nothing.
Skills: Nothing.
Curse/familiars: Crows.
Victims: Everyone and everything.

After a moment, I sense Wolf scooching to my side. I don't know whether he's trying to see the book or just wanting to be close.

"What do you think he looks like?" I ask, more to myself than to him. "Did the Time Witch ever say anything about him?"

Wolf doesn't answer. And then, out of nowhere, he rests his head on my shoulder. I sit very still.

"Can you talk to me?" I say, feeling a quiver of hope. "Can you talk at all?"

Wolf doesn't answer.

"Have you dreamt of being part of a family like I have?" I whisper. "And of laughing with me?" I place my hand on top of his, but he flinches, and stands up quickly.

And then he slinks away, taking my backpack with him.

That night, in the warmth of the second-floor parlor, most of us—the lonely residents of Glimmer 5—huddle against the emptiness of the world and talk about home.

Wanda tells us about her life as a seamstress growing up in Argentina with her grandmother—the one who taught her to tackle everything with a brave face—before witch hunting all over the world, learning to speak four languages in the process and eventually setting up a dress shop in London. She tells us how she first stumbled on to the companions we lost after Chompy—"Raj and the boys," she always calls them—while trailing the witch called Miss Rage, whom Aria, Germ, and I remember all too well.

Clara and Aria talk about their childhood and what Clara remembers of their parents, who died hunting witches when Aria was too small to remember it. Every time Aria offers up some detail about their past that she *does* remember, Clara corrects her. Even when Aria brags about how Clara hot-wired a time whale to whisk them to safety on a frozen, deserted island.

Zia shares how she died balancing on the rail of a balcony, on a dare. "I'm fairly good on a tightrope," Zia offers. "My dad was an acrobat. But this time . . ." She makes a falling motion with her hand while letting out a sharp whistle.

Of course Zia has a bold and flamboyant death story, I think. She seems kind of perfect.

"At least you didn't fall asleep in a sea cave at high tide," Ebb offers. "That's the most absurd death you can have."

"Nah," Zia replies. "My great-aunt Elora choked on a biscuit."

This elicits one of Ebb's rare smiles. Which elicits one of the tiny pinches in my heart that I don't like.

My mom shares stories too, but hers are more clouded. Her memories have returned since I defeated the Memory Thief, but there are holes—perhaps left by memories that will never come back. Some things she half remembers, if at all, and her recollections are full of lost months, lost people, lost moments. She says she and my dad went to watch *Mary Poppins* at a retro theater for their first actual date, but she doesn't remember where. She talks about her mom and her twin sister, Jade, who I didn't even know existed before the summer my mom got her memories back. I breathe in the stories of these family members like air, thrilled to have a grandmother or an aunt to hear stories of.

"My mother could turn a turnip into a feast," Mom says. "That was her weapon, as weird as it may sound—cooking. Though you'd have to be a pretty slow witch to get cooked." She smiles. "Your aunt Jade had the sight too, but she never wanted to be a witch hunter like me, even though she had the gift for it. She loved to make intricate and miniature things: tiny houses out of toothpicks, sculptures out of soda cans, jewelry boxes with interlocking parts, puzzles out of cardboard with a thousand tiny pieces. She used to replicate clouds outside with whipped cream at the dinner table; she could remember them perfectly even after they'd passed and re-create them. We adored each other."

She smiles sadly, growing wistful. I know she hasn't seen Aunt Jade in years, that my aunt went off to Switzerland and joined a convent.

My mom falls silent, no doubt wondering the same thing we all wonder *all* the time: Are the people we love okay? Do the Alps and the Great Wall of China and New

York City still exist? Are there still buses, and meadows, and schools?

Through the window, we catch a glimpse of Wolf far off across the front field. Germ has appeared beside him; she slipped outside without us hearing her, and is sitting with him by the pond.

He's squatting on his haunches at the pond's edge, his shoulders hunched, his posture miserable. Beside him, Germ sits cross-legged. For a moment, I see something similar in their postures of grief and wildness, two restless people slumped by sadness.

"I'll go see if Germ needs me," I say, moving to stand up. But Wanda gently stays me with one hand.

"Sometimes only people who are grieving can understand each other," she says. "Might be best to let them be."

Is that what my brother is doing? Is that why he can't speak? What is he grieving for when *we're right here*?

I'm his twin and the one who should be able to understand him, but I can see that Germ might be the only one who actually does. Wolf scoots a little closer to her, settling back into staring at the water. And together, the two seem to relax, both laying their hands open at their sides as if surrendering or catching starlight in their hands.

CHAPTER 8

I wake to screaming; the clock says it's long before morning.

Stumbling, half-dazed, into the hall, I realize it's coming from my mom's room and hurry in that direction. I burst through the door to find my mom standing over Wolf in his bed, thrashing and writhing and shrieking. Mom grabs him up and pulls him against her, hugging him tight.

I turn to see everyone—Ebb and Zia, Clara and Aria, Wanda, Germ, even Fabian—hurrying to the door, wide awake and addled, and I wave them away for privacy. And then I step fully into my mom's room and close the door softly behind me.

I sit on the edge of Wolf's bed in the dark as my mom gently comforts him.

"He had a nightmare," she says.

I reach a hand toward Wolf's shoulder to try to comfort him, but that feels too familiar, like I really know him, so I let my hand drop.

As my mom slowly murmurs him back to sleep, her long dark hair a messy shadow around her face, my eyes adjust to the curtained room around us, and I notice that she and Wolf have been painting.

My mom's paintings are familiar to me, characteristic swirls of light and nature. But Wolf's are different: packed from edge to edge with screaming ghosts, witch shapes looming large, beasts with open mouths full of sharp teeth. Wolf is a gifted painter like my mom. But the world inside his head is as misshapen as a witch's heart.

I watch my mom watch him sleep.

"I have something for you," she whispers, surprising me, and stands. "C'mere, Rosie." She walks to her bed and sits on it, patting the space beside her before turning to open the curtain. I sit on the bed, which is now bathed in dusky light, as she leans over and pulls something from inside her pillowcase.

"When you were gone on the whale, and I was going over my memories to pass the time, I remembered this." She removes her hand from the pillow and opens her palm, revealing a glistening pebble dangling from a thin silver chain. "I had tucked it away under the floorboards for safekeeping, right near where I'd hidden *The Witch Hunter's Guide*."

The pebble has a dim glow, and I realize after a moment that the glow is not coming from the dusk outside but from the stone itself.

"I'm glad you didn't discover it when you found the *Guide*. Because I want to be the one to give it to you. It's from the Moon Goddess." My mom squints as if trying to recall something fuzzy. "I met her once, just like you did, when I was young and just about to head off across the world to hunt witches. It feels like a dream, but I know it happened. I walked through the woods while the rest of my family slept, and I climbed the ladder to the moon."

I take in this piece of her forgotten history, of her past that—for so long—has been as hidden to her as it's been to me.

"It's moonlight in its purest form," she goes on,

"concentrated into a piece of moonstone crafted by the goddess herself. Like moonlight times a thousand." She leans forward and clasps the necklace around my neck. "I think she wanted me to have a little piece of light, as I faced the fear ahead of me. And now I want that for you."

I let my hand wander to where the stone lies against my collarbone. I feel lit-up inside, but I think it's more my mom's attention than the stone itself; for the moment, she is focused on *me*. But it makes me wonder if I'm greedy. Because even now, I want more. I want Wolf to be the brother I thought he would be, I want my dad to be alive, I want my mom to be more of a mom than a witch hunter. Even if we had Earth back, I'd want those things so badly.

"The Memory Thief stole years of your childhood from me, and then the Time Witch stole *more*." I know what she means. Since the Time Witch stole a year from me, I don't know who I'm supposed to be—like, I'm not quite a kid now.

"I can't get any of that time back, Rosie. But never forget, you are my shining light. I hope this reminds you of that."

We sit there not talking for a while, watching the stars out the window. A question burns in my mind, but I'm scared to ask it. Finally I whisper, "Do you think Dad would have liked me?"

My mom pulls in her breath, and then lets it out. "Your dad loved you, even before you came. And he would have found you to be even more wonderful than he expected." She looks over at Wolf, then lifts her shoulders helplessly. "I'm sorry you can't meet him, Rosie. Sometimes you get the thing you want—but in a different way than you pictured—like a happy ending nestled into a sad one. We're not the family you pictured, but we'll be okay in the end."

I nod, but I'm not sure I agree. I know it's pointless to long for a family that includes a living, loving dad. But knowing that doesn't make me want it less.

She gives me a gentle squeeze, and then tugs my sleeve. "Now off to bed," she says. "Don't worry."

As I wander into the hall, still twirling my moonstone between my thumb and forefinger, I wonder, What would my dad say about Wolf? Would he say not to worry that Wolf paints monstrous things, and kills wild animals with his bare teeth, and screams in his sleep?

Wolf may be my missing half, but what kind of a half is he?

Too wired and full of these questions to sleep, I stand in the hall. It doesn't help that since I suddenly became thirteen, I feel restless to the tips of my fingers.

I wander into the library and choose a book, one with a faded cover, called *Fairy and Folk Tales of Ireland*. I head to the parlor, but instead of reading, I just sit on the couch and stare into the roaring fire, flicking Flit on and off. And then I notice Fred the spider, up in one of the corners of the room, finishing up a poem in his web:

> *From time to time*
> *The clouds give rest*
> *To the moon beholders.*

"Oh, Fred, I love you," I murmur.

Fred gets all his poems from me, and I learned that one in fourth grade. It's by a man named Matsuo Bashō, and in a few words, it captures the world.

"He loves you too."

I startle. Ebb is standing in the doorway. I don't know how long he's been there. He floats in and sits beside me on the couch weightlessly, putting his feet up and leaning back, then lolling his head to the side to look at me, and particularly at my necklace. Ebb notices things, always.

"Can't sleep, huh?" he asks.

I shake my head.

"What's the matter?"

"Oh, you know," I say. "The end of the world. My twin brother teetering on the edge of evil, possibly."

Ebb smiles softly and crookedly. "That's nothing. I've got to worry about moving tumbleweeds with my hands." I bark a dry laugh. Then Ebb holds out his hand palm up on the couch, nodding to me to put my fingers in his, which of course I can't.

"Go on," he says.

Suddenly, feeling awkward, I lay my fingers down on top of his, even though they flop right through. Ebb turns to face me and starts making the strange motion of kneading my fingers like dough, even though of course I can't feel it.

"My mom used to do this for me when I couldn't sleep, back when we were alive. She called it the dizzle dazzle, but it's basically just a hand massage. It always made me drowsy."

I side-eye him. "You know you're transparent and unable to actually give hand massages, don't you?"

Ebb ignores me. "It's the thought that counts," he says, continuing to move his ethereal hands around my fingers. "It's the placebo effect."

"Placebo effects don't work if you say they're placebo effects," I say.

Ebb shrugs carelessly. And something about his shrug kind of tugs at me in a painful way. I like the way he shrugs, is the thing. And I don't know why, since it's a normal shrug, as shrugs go.

"I'm sorry, Ebb. You were so close to seeing your parents . . ."

"It wouldn't have been real anyway," he says softly. "I would have only been haunting them."

He looks up at me from under his eyebrows, sadness furrowing his forehead. I have a weird urge to smooth out the wrinkles with my fingers.

"What are you two up to?"

We look up to see Germ standing in the doorway, and Ebb stands quickly, like he's embarrassed.

"I was worried about you." Germ looks back and forth between us, a twinkle of curiosity in her eyes. "Is Wolf okay?"

I nod. "Ebb was trying to help me sleep," I say, feeling guilty for some reason.

I stand and follow Germ into the hall and down the stairs, waving over my shoulder to Ebb without a backward glance. Placebo effect or not, I feel a warmth all along my fingers.

CHAPTER 9

The next morning when I wake up, I find Germ standing on the ladder at the end of my bed, studying me intently over its ledge.

"What's happened?" I ask, groggy and blinking.

"*You* tell *me*," she says.

"What?" I sit up, rubbing my eyes, thinking back to the night before, with Ebb.

She's squinting at me, as if she's sizing me up, when suddenly our door bursts open and slams against the wall, zinging on its old rusty hinges, surprising us. Aria is standing there, dark bags under her eyes but a huge smile on her face.

"Come see," she says.

By the time Germ and I pull on our hotel robes and don our sneakers, we find that the hotel has been deserted. We soon see that everyone is gathered in a knot in the yard out front.

It's not until we make our way into the group that I get a glimpse of what everyone is staring at. A crooked, rusted, but also whirring and alert, mechanical owl. Aria and Clara watch us for our reactions, Aria bursting with pride. We are—appropriately—stunned.

"We disguised it as an owl," Clara explains, "because crows are scared of owls, so maybe the Nothing King's crows will steer clear of it."

"And we thought of you, Rosie," Aria adds. "With that owl from Harry Potter and everything."

"Can we call him Zippy?" Germ asks.

I suppose, even depressed, she can't resist her love of naming pets. Clara nods, clearly not caring about something so trivial either way.

"He's agile," Clara explains, "with extremely good eyesight, and he's smart. He's got a homing beacon powered by—what else?—moonlight, which means it's not a *typical* homing beacon."

As Clara continues, Germ holds a finger out to the owl and rubs gently along its metal ear tuft as it tilts its head appreciatively.

"We can send him right to your neighborhood in Maine and instruct him to bring something back as proof that Earth is still there. We'd want something from one of your houses. That way we'd know it's not a trick from the Nothing King. And there's nothing left of the hut where we lived on the island." Aria looks at Clara sheepishly. "Since I knocked it down."

"Could the Nothing King do that? Trick us that way?" I ask.

"We know so little about him," Aria says, "so we thought we'd better guard against it." She points to a tightly woven mesh bag dangling from Zippy's claws, that opens to the size of a basketball. "He's got a little stasis compartment here. It protects whatever's inside completely and time-lessly. It can hold a flower from a favorite plant, or a loved one's mitten, and even after a million years it wouldn't decay or die."

"How long will it take him to travel to Earth?" I ask.

"Well," Clara says, "it's about twenty thousand light-years from here to Earth, which means if he traveled at the speed of light, it would take twenty thousand years." I feel my heart drop to my feet. "But since he runs on moon-light, according to Rufus's notes, the messenger—" She clears her throat. "Um, Zippy will take about four days. Roundtrip."

Everyone stays silent. This is so shocking, it is almost impossible to believe. Then again, we came here through a hole in a magazine.

"Can he bring a message home?" Germ asks. "Telling people, if he finds them, that we're alive and where we are?"

Wanda shakes her head. "As tempting as it is, we have to be careful. Zippy has to stay secret. You saw how the Time Witch's spies were everywhere; I bet the Nothing King's crows are swarming the planet right now. If there's one thing we have over the Nothing King, it's that he doesn't know we're out here."

While we are standing there listening, I feel the prick-ling weight of someone watching me, and glance up to see Wolf standing at the edge of the circle. He's looking intently at my collarbone. His eyes widen as they meet mine. He's longing, I'm sure, for the shiniest thing he's seen since he arrived. I shake my head slowly, and ner-vously tuck my necklace under my shirt collar.

"Rosie, Germ," Clara says firmly, "you live close to one another, right?" We nod, our houses just a bike ride across the woods from each other. "Take some time with Zippy this morning to tell him the distinguishing features of your houses, and a little bit about your lives there so he can bring back something that you recognize . . . an item of clothing, a favorite plant, a box of cereal that you know will be in the cupboard. Once I get some logistical information from you, I'll program the geographical coordinates so you don't need to give him directions or anything." I try to think of what directions I would possibly give from Glimmer 5 to Seaport, Maine. Take a left at the sun?

"Bring him back when you're done," Aria instructs us, "and we'll launch him just before dinner."

For the next couple of hours, we do as we're told. We tell Zippy about our favorite pillows (we nicknamed them Sponge Boy and Pancake when Germ was sleeping over once), clothes that might still be in our closets, old boxes of Pop-Tarts at the back of a cupboard gathering dust. True to form, Germ goes off on a tangent about her pet iguana, Eliot Falkor, that threatens to sidetrack the whole endeavor.

"Sorry," she mutters when I nudge her. "My therapist just yawned whenever I talked about Eliot Falkor's feelings," she says, "but Zippy seems really interested." I keep my mouth shut, both because Zippy is a robot and because I, too, have sometimes yawned listening to Germ talk about Eliot Falkor.

Finally, when all is ready, we return Zippy to Aria and Clara in the hangar. And then, just before dinner, we all—Fabian and Zia included (though Fabian stays several feet away from us as if he doesn't want to be seen with us)—walk to the hill we visited the first night we arrived.

Wanda makes a speech about how Clara and Aria have brilliantly repaired the messenger, which I can barely hear because the sisters are bickering about whether Aria's old enough to drive if we ever make it back to Earth. (Clara thinks driving's too dangerous.)

After Wanda finishes, we stand in silence, staring out at the star-filled sky. Then Clara holds the owl perched on her arm like a hawk, calm and confident as she gazes out at the vastness of space that surrounds us.

"Don't let us down, Zippy," she says. She gives her arm a strong jerk upward, and Zippy lifts off her arm in a crooked kind of flap.

As the messenger rises, a tiny thread of smoke emits from one of his ear tufts and then evaporates. He nose-dives, but lifts at the last moment to avoid crashing into the ground at the bottom of the hill. My spirits nose-dive too. Watching, I can't imagine Zippy making it off Glimmer 5, much less all the way to Earth and back. Finally he flutters higher, furiously agitating his metal wings and listing to one side.

After a minute more he seems to straighten out. He weaves into the darkness, occasionally plunging before righting himself again, getting farther and farther away until he is only a speck in the distance.

"Time for the thrusters," Clara says.

And then the speck suddenly streaks like a shooting star into the dark, disappearing. For a moment, my spirits rise, then fall again. Even the streak looks lopsided.

We stand watching in silence, not meeting each other's eyes. Wanda turns to all of us with a wooden smile. "Well," she says through her teeth, "this ought to go well."

"We'll know in a few days if he's coming back at all," Clara says.

We all nod vigorously, trying to look hopeful. But long after everyone else has walked inside and Aria and Clara have gone off to have a well-earned sleep, I stand watching the empty sky as if I could see if Zippy makes it. Nothing reveals itself except the vast and empty dark.

I don't know that by the time he returns, everything will have changed.

CHAPTER 10

For nights after Zippy leaves, I'm up late, restless, wandering the halls. On the fourth night it begins to snow, and I stand in the parlor watching it fall in wonder. The night seems full of promise, the way the arrival of snow always makes things feel. And so, feeling like I could be lucky, I make my way to Rufus's room, take his note from the mantel, and read it for the thousandth time.

On reflection, I'm unsure Glimmer 5 will ever be the premier destination for space

visitors I dreamt of. The echoes of my
failure will repeat in my heart for a long
time to come with shining clarity. I plan
to go somewhere quiet, to read, think, and
try to replicate my experiences by copying
them in my journals, which I will one day
publish. I'm sorry.

Humbly,
Rufus Glimmer

Why would a man write a letter that doesn't sound like him at all?

And then a small and subtle idea occurs to me that I haven't thought of before. Is it because he wants attention on the words themselves?

I reread the letter, but this time, I look at each word as its own separate thing—as if each word carries weight. And soon, my pulse picking up a bit, I notice a pattern.

Reflection. Echoes. Repeat. Replicate. Copy.

All of these words mean some version of doubling.

It can't be a coincidence.

I glance over at the sock, still on the floor where we left it. I know the smart thing would be to wait for morning, wait for Wanda to come with me. But I'm a shy, inward kind of person. I think best alone and when no one is expecting anything from me.

It's not hard to find the hole in the sock, since I've been through it once before.

Once I've flicked her on, Flit looks more agitated than usual . . . like she, too, is nervous. I lean close to the sock and listen. This time, I know it's not a train I hear but a storm that could rip me apart. I have to time things just right.

I wait for the roar of the storm to come and go.

And then I nudge the tip of my toe into the hole in the sock, and—for better or worse—I shrink.

In the bedroom, time has already reset itself. Stuffed animals, the bed, the curtains, the walls, are all in their places. Beyond the unbroken window, the view is peaceful and unprepared for the coming storm.

With Rufus's letter trembling in my hands, I look around the room. *Reflection. Echoes. Repeat. Replicate. Copy,* I think. *Reflection. Echoes. Repeat. Replicate. Copy.* Do these words even connect to this time slice at all?

I look around for anything that's double—double doors, double curtains, double drawers. I rummage in the closet and rummage in the dresser drawers. *Doublemint gum?* I think absurdly. *Double-sided tape?*

Minutes pass quickly as I look under the bed. I pull off the bedspread. I pull all the clothes out of the closet. Flit begins to trill a panicked note, and starts pecking at the letter.

In the distance, I hear a rumble. I walk to the window and see the swirl of dust far away.

My hands are shaking harder now. Snatching my letter out of Flit's beak, I read it again. And this time, I notice something new.

"Shining clarity."

I scan the room frantically with a sudden idea. My eyes alight on the mirror that was shattered the last time we were here. My heart stops. At the same time, I can feel a slight vibration in the ground of the storm coming closer.

Reflection. Echoes. Repeat. Replicate. Copy. Every single one of these words describes a mirror.

I cross the room, feel along the mirror's edges before looking behind it, but there's nothing hidden there, no secret latch into a hidden room, no loose board hiding a passageway to Rufus Glimmer. Outside, the tornado is approaching. I have to go, *now.*

I glance back at the mirror, panicked. And then, feeling foolish, I try a last resort: puffing warm air onto the glass like my mom when she leaves me her little messages.

To my shock, my breath reveals something . . . a letter *y*, smudged onto the glass by someone's finger. My pulse begins to pound.

Puffing again and again, until my head begins to ache, I reveal more letters: *y oor pen.* Soon, an entire sentence has revealed itself.

My door is open.

Underneath the sentence is an arrow, pointing diagonally down and to the right. Looking in that direction, I see the dollhouse that I know from last time survives the storm intact. A chill runs down my neck.

Its door is open. And there appears to be a tiny hole in the empty space within it—another hole like the one Wanda made has been cut into the air itself, leaving a pinprick of strange light.

I walk closer and kneel to peer between the curtains in the windows, but they're all closed. I can just see, through a slit of an opening, the edges of a living room.

The storm is coming now in earnest, rattling the room. If I'm leaving, I should go now. If I'm staying, I need to act.

How much can you shrink before you disintegrate? I'm already the size of a ball of lint inside a sock. Flit stands nervously beside me, clearly resisting her urge to flee. I weakly offer her a panicked smile. You can say a lot of negative things about Flit, but it looks like she doesn't bail out when the chips are down.

Taking a breath for courage, I wiggle a pinky into the hole, and the now-familiar sucking feeling overtakes me. And in a moment, I'm inside.

I'm in a foyer, standing next to an umbrella stand. And, of all the things I think I might find here, I am still, somehow, surprised.

A fire crackles in the doll-size fireplace, in a living room with a floral couch and a frilly armchair and an ornate lamp. There are clothes draped over the armchair and the chandelier, notebooks lying open here and there with labels like *A Compendium of Magical Vehicle Parts*, *The Complete Moonlit Engine*, and *Starting Your Own Exo-Solar Business*. An old TV sits in a corner of the room and shows several live-cam views of the starry skies surrounding Glimmer 5.

In the one tidy easy chair sits a thin man with gray-streaked black hair, wearing a plaid suit. His fingers are paused on the strings of his ukulele as he looks at me in surprise.

"That was quicker than I expected," he says with a smile that doesn't reach his eyes.

CHAPTER 11

I've found him, I think over and over and over again. *I've found him, I've found him, I've found him.*

"You can have a seat if you'd like," he says. "The storm outside won't hurt us. We're in a time slice within a time slice." He smiles again, a toothpaste-commercial smile. "The planet's defense sensors didn't tell me anyone had come. Must have used a seam ripper, eh? That would be the only way to get in without me knowing it. Not that I'm trying to keep visitors out—only witches."

I nod. "My friend's ring is a seam ripper," I say. "It

brought us here." Rufus taps his foot a couple of times, like a twitch. He looks like a nervous man trying to look relaxed. "We came to Glimmer 5 looking for you," I say, and falter, as Flit waddles back and forth along my thigh uncertainly. "I'm Rosie Oaks, with the League of Witch Hunters. We thought you were in danger."

Though his eyebrows rise a little as I say my name, Rufus looks pleasantly perplexed, tilting his head. "The league." He nods. "I remember them." He shrugs. "I just needed some down time," he explains. "It's exhausting, running a planet, even without the guests. Even a small one like Glimmer 5. You *know* you're burned out when you have to retreat to a dollhouse stuck inside an endlessly repeating tornado to get some R&R." He smiles tightly at his own joke. "How are things on the outside? How are Zia and Fabian?"

"They're . . . confused," I say. "And wondering where you are." Rufus taps his foot again, then lays a hand on his knee as if to stop himself. "As for things on the outside, I'm sorry to tell you, but they're bad. The Nothing King came to Earth through a black hole the witches created, and Earth might have been swallowed by it. We might be the only witch hunters left."

Rufus rocks back and forth in the chair, turning his

gaze to the ground. "That's terrible. I had no idea. I'm very surprised."

I feel a prickle along my skin, feeling certain that Rufus is not surprised at all. But why would he lie? I look around the room, wondering if this is some sort of trap.

"My friend Wanda Luna thought you could help us. She thinks there's a part of the story of the Nothing King's appearance that we don't know. He was locked into his black hole, and only the Moon Goddess had the key. Wanda thinks someone stole the Moon Goddess's key to get the Nothing King out . . . and that it couldn't have been a witch who did it. She thinks you might have an idea of who it might have been, or how to find out."

Rufus nods, his face softening into something slightly more genuine.

"Well," he says, "I do agree that it couldn't have been a witch who stole the key. A witch couldn't have gotten anywhere near the Moon Goddess. Moonlight burns them." He scratches his mustache thoughtfully. "It had to have been a human. But anyone who might have those answers for you—everyone on Earth—is, by your account, out of reach. Possibly forever."

"We sent a messenger. To find out."

Rufus takes this in, straightening up a little with pride. "Oh? Which model did you use? The Meteorite-7? The Comet?"

I shrug. "We call it 'Zippy.'"

Rufus leans back. "Fastest things in existence that I know of, my inventions. The ships are even faster than the messengers. Though, they've fallen into disrepair, I'm afraid. And if you want to work on the Astral Accelerator, you'll need to reattach the Glaciation Matrix," he says off-handedly. "It's in the freezer."

Rufus clears his throat and shifts in his chair.

"Right now I'm working on a new moonlight-powered laser gun." He nods to a goofy-looking plastic water gun lying in pieces on the floor. "I hope at least you're enjoying the hotel? You know everything in it is for sale, more or less? Everything here as well." He glances around the frilly but messy dollhouse room. "Would you be interested in purchasing a miniature gumball machine? Or a miniature piano? Some doilies?"

I shake my head, and his face falls in disappointment.

"I'm not saying the Hotel at the Edge of the Galaxy is what I pictured, mind you. I had bigger dreams for it— an entire fleet of space vehicles, adventures all over the universe, a towering main building with views. There are other life-forms out there, you know . . . majestic planets, star births just waiting to be witnessed, endless possibilities. It would have been lovely to share it with the world. And I wouldn't have minded making a little money in the process. Of course, things haven't worked out quite the way I pictured. The witches . . . they persist."

"Well, *one* witch does," I say. "We killed the rest."

He looks up at me sharply. I sniff self-consciously as Rufus glances over at Flit, who appears to be trying to peck off one of her own claws.

"*You* killed witches," Rufus asks, "with *that* weapon?"

"Um. She—she was different before," I stammer.

Rufus stares at me for a long time, his smiley persona gone. And then he glances over at the fire, which has sputtered and gone out.

"Oops!" He stands and bustles to the fireplace, shifts the splintered fragments of wood it contains this way and that to get it going again. And I realize suddenly why I smelled the faint scent of smoke the first time I visited the tornado-ravaged room: it must have been drifting out of the chimney of this dollhouse. "I forgot to bring matches when I came," he says, "so it's a process. As for your weapon, it—*she*—has changed, and you're not willing to embrace that yet. You'll never be truly strong unless you do."

He pauses for a second and smiles at my surprise; this time the smile is genuine.

"I've learned a lot about all things magical in my time, Rosie. And a little bit about people, too."

I don't answer, because how can I say that—despite his words—with his fake smile, and his exaggerations, Rufus seems like a bit of a fraud?

"Look at this wood." He nods at the fireplace. "There's a reason why fires are hard to light. It's because there's nothing harder for something like wood than changing into something else. It doesn't want to let go. I read that somewhere once, and I'd say it's the same with you and your weapon. When a witch hunter truly trusts her gift and where it can lead her, she has to let go. When she does, miracles can happen."

"Like what?"

Rufus shrugs. "Dunno. I saw it almost happen once in Dunkirk, to a witch hunter named Clotilda. But she spontaneously combusted."

"That's not encouraging," I say.

Rufus finally gets a flicker of flame going, and then blows on it till the fire is crackling again. He stares into it for a few long moments, then settles back into his chair, his sales-y demeanor now gone completely.

"I have a hungry mind," he says. "I read fast. I ask questions. And moonlight has helped. At times, I've been able to use it to figure out pieces of the past. And so, I know a little of the Nothing King. I know," he goes on, "that he is impossible in battle. That his crows gobble everything in their path, taking bites out of the world around them just as the Memory Thief's moths once took memories. As for their master, he's made of *nothing*, so he can be *anything*. He's a shadow, a shape-shifter. He's all the witches, trolls, goblins, terrible accidents, and horrible news stories you've ever heard of wrapped into one. He is the fear and the emptiness. Ultimately, the Nothing King is the void at the root of *all* the witches—and you can't beat a void, Rosie, because it's not there."

Rufus takes a long, uneasy breath. "Rest assured, once Earth is gone, he's coming for *us*. He's coming for the rest of the universe, now that he's free."

Rufus clasps his hands on his lap and studies them, his shoulders hunched, then raises his eyes to meet mine. And for now, his eyes are truthful.

"This is the sum of what I've learned, as the oldest witch scholar alive, Rosie. Even dead, even with twelve of them destroyed, the *witches win*. And I don't want to be involved when they do. I'm safe here, at least for now. I like being alive. I like my things. A witch hunter has to be willing to change—to die—like the wood in my fireplace. I'm not brave enough to do that."

He nods, as if trying to agree with himself. But even with these words, Rufus seems uncertain. And then, with a flutter of recognition in my chest, I see something familiar, in the last place I would expect it to be, perched on his mantel: a small square cross stitch, threaded with a pink-and-blue house.

You are the cloud-builder; you are the grower of wings, it reads. *You are the one whom Earth entrusts its stories to; you are the singer of songs. . . .*

"I've seen that before," I say, pointing to it breathlessly.

Rufus's eyes shoot up to mine in surprise. I stand and cross the room.

"This is from the Brightweaver's cottage," I say. "It hung on her wall." I turn to look at him. "How did you get this?"

I run my fingers along the beautiful stitches, remembering the Brightweaver, who sews moonlight into people's hearts to bring them hope. I think of the funny and strange things she liked to say, like, *There's only one thing and we're all it.*

Rufus waves a hand vaguely and looks for words to answer, while Flit flutters up to my hand. She nuzzles into my palm as if to bask in the warmth that even just *thinking* of the Brightweaver brings to my spirits. Rufus watches her, alert, while *I* watch Rufus.

"How did you get this?" I repeat, watching his eyes. The silence in the room hangs so thickly that I can almost touch it. Rufus breathes in deeply. I feel like, if I move, I will frighten away a butterfly.

"I lied to you, Rosie," he finally says. "And I have something to show you."

He stands as if the effort to do it weighs heavily on him. And then, gesturing with his hand, he leads me out of the room and up a flight of stairs, then down a hall past three frilly bedrooms. He continues up another set of stairs to the dollhouse attic—but does not turn on the light. Flit glows weakly in the thick black dark ahead of me.

"Here we are," Rufus whispers, as if someone might be listening. He approaches a dollhouse-style woodstove, cast in the very faint glow of Flit, and looks around as if to make sure we're alone. Then he opens the stove door and pulls something out of it.

He sinks to sit, cross-legged, on the floor, and I sit facing him in the dark. In his arms, Rufus holds a basket—a sewing basket, to be specific. I've seen it before, but it takes a moment to place where.

Rufus hesitates, as if he's not certain he's doing the right thing. In the quiet and hush, he cradles the basket carefully in his hands.

"What's in it?" I ask when it seems he'll never speak.

Rufus gazes at me, all his fakeness and restful easiness gone. "If the world is indeed destroyed, Rosie," he says, "this is all we have left of it."

CHAPTER 12

"The night I went into hiding in this dollhouse, it wasn't because I needed a vacation, like I said in my letter. It was because I'd had a visitor."

He cups the sewing basket in his hands, running his fingers along the lid almost lovingly.

"I was out on the hill, watching some strange disturbances in the eastern sky. *Now* I know what those disturbances were: the flight of the Nothing King through his wormhole, rippling the cosmos along the way. But at the time, I couldn't comprehend what it meant. And then, scanning the sky, I saw her coming. She streaked here like a comet, silver in a blur of wings. You've heard of angels, visitations. It was like that."

"Who?" I ask.

Rufus looks at me as if it's obvious. "The Brightweaver, of course." He gives me a moment to take this in.

"We'd met each other years before. Someone I'd borrowed money from to fund my inventions was eager to collect . . . if you catch my drift. I was cornered, and wished myself up to the clouds, and there she was. She's been instrumental in all of my endeavors since, particularly with her gifts of moonlight that power my inventions."

"I've seen the pond," I say.

Rufus nods. "Yes, you would have. In any case, the Brightweaver herself had never come here until that moment when I saw her streaking across the sky." He pauses. "She was terribly rushed, and terribly scared, so I knew that whatever we were dealing with was catastrophic. She told me the same things you did, about the Nothing King's escape. Except, being in the clouds, she'd seen more. For one thing, she'd seen the moon get sucked into the black hole, the Moon Goddess along with it." He pauses to let me take this in. My chest begins to ache.

He shifts where he sits. "She only stayed here a few

minutes. She said I was the only person she'd thought to come to, and she insisted that we talk in complete secret. Once we were alone, she gave me this."

He looks down at the basket again.

"I suppose," Rufus goes on, "she had sized me up pretty well over the years. She said that if there was anyone in the universe capable of keeping a thing of value ferreted away, it was me. She said she was entrusting me with something more precious than anything I could imagine. And that I had to keep it safe and secret, even if that meant giving my life to protect it. But then," he goes on, tilting his head, his eyes hooded as he remembers, "she said something almost the opposite of that. She said that if the moment ever came when I felt, in my gut, that I needed to give it away, I should trust it."

I glance down at the sewing basket, trying to understand.

He looks at me. "As you can imagine, I was confused. I pressed her for more information. All she could tell me was that someone might need this object desperately before all was said and done. I tried to ask more, but she was in a terrible rush. She said she couldn't leave her shepherds, that she needed to try to save them. And then she promised that if she made it through, she'd come back in a day or two for the basket. But day after day after day has passed . . ."

His face grows solemn and pale. "And she never did. And now here I am. I came across the galaxy to escape witches, and now I'm hiding something that makes me a target."

I wipe my eyes, which are filling with tears, for the Moon Goddess and the Brightweaver and all her misty, breathtaking shepherds who kept their eyes on the world.

"You'll think I'm silly, Rosie, hiding here on Glimmer 5 all these years, and now tucked away in a dollhouse in a slice of a moment that never ends. But I'm not ashamed of abandoning Earth and its witches and witch hunters, of not wanting to die. Still, I care about the League of Witch Hunters. And I won't betray an entire planet." We both look down at the basket. "My gut is telling me this basket is for you."

I swallow, hard. "What's in it?" I ask. "Did she tell you?"

He nods and opens the lid. A glow comes from within, illuminating our faces as we peer into its depths. Within the hollow of the basket, mist swirls, sparkling and flashing, like lightning in a cloud.

I look up at Rufus, squinting in confusion.

"It's the Museum of Imagined Things," he says, as if I should recognize it. "It's a palace filled with all of the world's dreams."

I stare into the sewing basket.

"What?" I whisper. "How?" I remember the Museum

of Imagined Things from that one and only time I visited the Brightweaver, a towering building made of clouds that reached so far into the sky, I couldn't see the top of it. The Brightweaver said no one even knew if it *had* a top. It can't be in a basket.

Rufus understands my confusion. "She said she'd had just enough time to ravel it up and tuck it somewhere to take with her," he explains. "She said, in a pinch, the basket was the first thing she thought of."

"But how is that possible?" I ask, though I should know by now that the invisible fabric makes possible many things that seem impossible.

"It's made of nothing but mist and light," Rufus says. "So it takes up barely any real space."

I blink down into the churning mist in the basket, remembering how the Brightweaver once described the museum: *Every note of music ever played, every picture ever created, every dream ever dreamt, every word that ever left a person's mouth—even the dreams of trees, and animals.* All collected by the cloud shepherds, an archive of the world's imagined things.

"If there's any chance for the world, it lies here," Rufus says. "The Nothing King wants to snuff out all that this basket holds—the *maybe*s and the *possible*s. Those are worth everything, I think. Imagination is the opposite of witches, and the Nothing King knows it. If Earth survives, it's only because he plans to use it as a lure—to draw out whoever is keeping this palace hidden. I'd wager he'll keep the void at arm's length till then, and that his crows are scouring the galaxy for this right now."

I swallow, and now I understand why even here in this dollhouse attic, when we are probably the size of specks of dust, Rufus is scared that someone is watching . . . listening . . .

"But, I still don't understand how it can help me find the key," I say.

Rufus tents his fingers over the basket thoughtfully. "You need to solve a mystery, one that happened on a planet that's beyond your reach." He runs his hand over the rim of the basket. "The only echoes of what happened, the only fragments and whispers of it, would be here. Within this museum, I'd bet, is the memory, the dream, the story of the key—who stole it, what happened to it, and where it is now. This"—he tilts the basket gently—"is the only place left to look." He scratches his nose awkwardly and smiles his toothpaste-commercial smile, looking like he doesn't want to give me bad news. "Granted, you'll be sifting through things that have been dreamt up since the beginning of life on Earth. It'll be . . . a lot."

I gaze down into the swirling mist. "Do I just shrink again to go in?"

Rufus fiddles with his mustache. "I wish it were that simple. But the museum isn't like a sock or a dollhouse or a toy oven. The Museum of Imagined Things is, by nature, dreamlike, *unreal*. To enter it, I think—and this is just a theory—you have to become dreamlike yourself. And if you can manage that, the place's wildness—the unfettered nature of what it holds—could make it easy for you to get lost or stolen, or to disappear forever. Not all imagined things are good, Rosie."

I blink at him, feeling a tremor in my chest. "You said that's your theory. Does that mean you don't *know* how to get in?"

Rufus scratches his nose again. "I have no idea."

My heart sinks to my feet. Rufus knows more about magic than anyone else alive. With each new thing he says, the task feels more impossible. And though I've felt that way before, it now seems like nothing compared to this.

"Then again, Rosie, I'm no witch hunter. You'll have figured out by now that in cases of instinct, hunters' weapons often guide them. And I'd bet the museum is an instinctive place. Maybe your weapon can help."

We both gaze at Flit, who is gagging on a feather

she's somehow gotten lodged in her throat. My hands are trembling.

How do you search a building that doesn't end? One that might never let you *in* in the first place? Of all the undoable things I've needed to do since the night I burned my stories and woke to a world of ghosts and witches, this seems the most undoable. Because even if I can find out who got the key and where it is, we'd still have to retrieve it somehow, then beat the apparently unbeatable Nothing King into a black hole, and then manage to lock him in.

Rufus seems to follow my thoughts. "It's a sliver of a chance, I understand that. But the Nothing King won't stop until there is . . . well . . . nothing, period. He wants there to be no such thing as anything at all. Wanting that is the reason he exists."

Rufus pauses gravely.

"There's one more thing, Rosie, and it's important. Whoever stole the key was a traitor. Traitors can be anywhere—even in your midst right now."

I shiver. My mind goes to Wolf before I can stop it, to his life with the Time Witch, to all the things that have made him strange and unnerving.

"If I give you this basket, it's in return for a promise,

that you'll tell no one it exists, or that you found me. I fear that if I'm discovered here, our secret will be discovered too. Rest assured that if anything malevolent arrives on Glimmer 5, I'll know about it. But I'll only emerge from here if I have no choice."

"Can I tell my mom at least?" I ask.

He tilts his chin to meet my eyes. "No one. And I need for you to make me a second promise, the same one I made to the Brightweaver. That if this . . . this small bundle of ether in here is threatened, you'll die to protect it. Do you promise?"

I swallow. I feel suddenly as if the museum, and the care of it, will somehow be the end of me.

"I promise," I say, and shiver. Flit has hopped up onto my shoulder, and she shivers too.

Rufus slides the basket into my hands. I gently close the lid.

He smiles softly. "I have a good feeling about you." And then he glances at Flit. "I'm not so sure about your friend, though," he adds, and I can't tell if he's trying to make a joke or not.

Rufus places his hands over mine on the basket. "All that's left are the unseen things that we let ourselves believe are the least important. Take care of them, Rosie; they're all we've got."

CHAPTER 13

For all the trouble it took to get in, it takes only a few minutes to make my way out of our hiding place. Rufus escorts me out of the dollhouse, through the tornado-ravaged room (this time everything around us is shattered—the tornado has come and gone) to the exit. Without lingering, he turns to hurry back toward the dollhouse, casting a quick nervous wave over his shoulder just as I step onto the threshold. A moment later I am standing full height in Rufus's hotel room again.

I breathe a sigh of relief, clutching the basket to my

stomach. I listen at the door for anyone passing by, then tiptoe toward my room—sure that any moment, I'll be seen. But the hall, and even my room, appears to be deserted, Germ's bed empty and unmade.

I find a spot in the closet to hide the basket, deep under a pile of sheets. Once I'm sure it's safely tucked away, I walk into the hall again. The entire floor is silent. I peek into the nearby bedrooms, all empty.

"Hey, anybody?" I call. My voice echoes. No reply.

Worried now, I head to the common room, then up to the library. No one. I search the parlor near the Everything Vending Machine, the lobby, the dining room downstairs. Finally, through the window by the table, I catch a glimpse of them. They're all together, standing across the front field, clustered in an agitated circle. Something's happened.

At first only Ebb turns to see me approach. And then, for a moment, Wolf turns too, and I watch him watching my necklace like he wants to pull it from my throat.

"What's happened?" I ask, bracing myself. Aria reaches for my hand and tugs me close as she casts a glance at Germ, who I see now is trembling. My heart drops under my ribs. And then, pulled within the circle at last, I catch a glimpse of what everyone is staring at.

Zippy is lying on the ground.

The mechanical messenger looks like he's been through a war. He's slumped on his side at a strange angle, missing an eye and a wing, three of his talons ripped off.

And then I spot, lying beside him, something else—which he's kept safe in his stasis compartment despite whatever's destroyed him. Our messenger has returned with something so shocking, I can barely fathom it.

And it means—I realize—two things.

That the thing he's brought back is for Germ.

And that Earth still exists.

Eliot Falkor, Germ's pet iguana, sits on the sand beside Zippy, looking dazed. (Though, admittedly, that is his usual expression.)

Germ kneels beside him. Against all odds, he's been carried across the galaxy to us, looking well fed and bored. Germ cups him in her hands and lifts him to her face, weeping tears of joy onto his scales.

"Do you have a headache?" she whispers hoarsely.

A splutter startles us, and for a moment our eyes move to Zippy again. Sparks fly from the owl's neck joints. It shudders as if it's taking a breath. And then, the intrepid messenger who's brought hope back to us all collapses in a puff of smoke, and falls over, lifeless.

PART 2

Earth spins gently, and above, the black hole waits.

The world's people look at the sky because they can barely look anywhere else. They sit outside around campfires, or on the roofs of apartment buildings, watching the ink spot in the sky. In towns, they crane their necks upward as they walk. By day, the sun rises and sets as it always has. But the world has gone wild without the gravity of its moon.

It's been twenty-five days since the moon disappeared. In the moon's absence, night animals roam daylit highways, winds rage through streets once untouched by storms, *tornadoes rip up ancient woods. In waterfront towns and cities, the ocean is eating the shores, and people retreat inward. At first, they don't see the invisible creatures that travel alongside them, iridescent hummingbirds and chameleons and peacocks . . . the familiars of eleven dead witches, returning gifts that once were stolen.*

A woman in Egypt gets her memory back; a man in Ireland loses his rage. This is multiplied by thousands. And everywhere, everywhere, carried in the mouths of glowing hyenas, the sight, too, is being returned.

People who began their day believing that souls weren't real find, by sunset, that their homes are full of ghosts they never noticed. People see shining crows, more of them every day, perched on stop signs and along temple roofs, market stalls, traffic lights, and grocery stores. In other words, thanks to seeing, people see the danger coming. They begin to believe in witches—especially because, all over the news, there are three people who claim to have hunted them. These witch hunters say they've come from the belly of a whale with tidings of space and moonlight. They announce themselves to the world like a jazz band: Raj and the Boys.

In Seaport, Maine, in the house on Waterside Road, gathering ghosts talk of these changes—the black hole, the hunters, and how people who never noticed drifting spirits before now

jump at the sight of them . . . ask if they would mind leaving
the bathroom . . . stop them for directions.

Still, the gossip isn't what's brought so many more ghosts
here than usual. After floating in from the woods, from the
sailors' cemetery, from all over the town of Seaport, they con-
gregate in the halls and along the stairs, to hover by the night-
stand next to Annabelle Oaks's bed. On it are three framed
photos: a man smiling at the prow of a fishing boat; twin sis-
ters hugging long ago; and a girl, maybe ten, short for her age
and shy. Beside the photos is a book about lost children, lying
open. Hansel and Gretel.

It's this book the ghosts have come for. Around it they gather,
more coming all the time. The pages lay open to a drawing of a
shadowy forest, a dangerous cottage, a trail under trees; a story
of danger as old as words. The ghosts gaze down at the page,
and then they simply . . . climb into it. All night, they pour into
the room, and then they're gone. And no one can say exactly
how they've done it. Or where they end up.

CHAPTER 14

Being carried away from Earth by a robotic owl, then across the galaxy to a foreign planet, really takes it out of you, apparently. Eliot Falkor sleeps for days. But Germ won't put him down for anything, not for dinner (he sits on her napkin), not when she goes to the bathroom.

"Aren't his eyelashes beautiful?" she asks, her pale cheeks glowing. "Aren't his claw nails sweet?" "Does he look stressed to you?" But Eliot looks the same as usual: kind of blinky. And I'm not sure he has eyelashes.

"If only we knew what he saw in the world before he left," Germ says. "Ebb, what do you think he's thinking?"

Ebb, our resident animal expert because he pays so much attention to nature, shakes his head. "I can tell if an iguana's thirsty, not decipher an eyewitness account of what he saw before he left Earth," he says, throwing a crooked smile my way, which warms me inside. He leans down so that he's eye to eye with Eliot. Eliot darts his tongue out, and Ebb sticks out his tongue in return. This makes me snort a laugh, which clearly pleases Ebb.

"He doesn't appreciate it when you do that," Germ says flatly, and Ebb sits back, casting me another playful look.

"There are more useful things I can think of that Zippy could have retrieved," Wanda says, listening in on the conversation as she walks by. "But it's wonderful to see you two together."

We all nod. Of all the ways that Eliot's arrival has transformed us, Germ has been transformed the most. Her restlessness and bounciness are back. She stalks the hotel grounds like she's ready to leap into the sky and fly to Earth on willpower alone, talking about all the things she wants to get back to: tacos, strip malls, elevators, Frappuccinos, movies. (Strangely, I find I don't miss these things like she does.) She even starts going for runs, circling the planet and returning quickly because she doesn't want to be away from Eliot too long. She's back to being the restless, fearless best friend I've always known. And of course, I know why: there's just too much news to draw from Eliot's arrival.

One is that it's obvious someone's been taking care of him. He's been eating, and his ears have been oiled just the way Germ likes them to be. This can only mean that Germ's family is alive, because no one else would carefully oil the ears of a random reptile like that. Two is that, if Germ's family is alive, it means there's a very good chance that most people—the people of the world—are alive.

Finally, it means that Earth is not in a black hole yet. Which means that the Nothing King is waiting. Which means he's waiting for something that is most likely lying in my closet under my pile of sheets.

And all of this means that things are more urgent than they've ever been, because it means we need a plan.

I've learned that it's both wonderful and terrible to hope. But that's what I do, every morning while Germ is out walking with Eliot. I sit huddled in our closet and hope, trying to talk and wish the museum into letting me in.

I try everything I can think of, shoving in both my feet, pulling the mist out with my hands. I try sending Flit into the basket first, but she keeps coming out coughing. I try bargaining. ("Please let me in. I'll polish your wicker if you do.") Nothing. I borrow Wanda's ring and try to shrink my way in. *Nothing times two.*

Inevitably, terrified that this miraculous chance to save the world could slip away, Wanda calls a meeting about what to do next. We discuss the possibility of Aria and Clara trying to repair the Astral Accelerator.

"Impossible," Clara says. "Without the Glaciation Matrix we'll catch fire *pretty much* the minute we take off. And making a Glaciation Matrix is *pretty much* beyond my skill level."

"Oh," I say, coughing, taken off guard and remembering what Rufus said. "Um, I think I saw that in one of the freezers."

This sets the whole group on a mad search to find out which freezer, and soon enough Aria shows up pinching the tiny spiral between thumb and forefinger, a spiral that might just be our ticket to reaching Earth if the rest of the ship can be fixed. The next thing we know, the attempted refurbishment of the Astral Accelerator has begun.

"I'm sixty percent . . . sixty-two percent sure we can get her up and running," Clara says the following afternoon while we are taking a five-minute breather from salvaging parts from Rufus's other machines. "But it'll take time, and she still won't be able do anything spectacular. The ship's tiny; it has no weapons. It's not . . . like an X-wing from Star Wars; it can't fight. It'll go *fast*. From what Rufus said in his video, it could get to Earth in a matter of hours. But to actually face off against the Nothing King, we'll have to leave the ship, head out into open space in our pressure suits, and use our witch weapons."

"We just need to *get* there," Aria insists. She's sitting on the floor cross-legged, trying to bring Zippy back to life. "You get us there, Clara. We'll do the rest."

Clara looks at her for a moment, like maybe—just for a tenth of a second—she's caught a glimpse of the Aria that Germ and I know. The one who's unafraid, and not a kid anymore, and a leader. (Wanda seems to be our ringleader these days, but if I were going to pick between Aria and Wanda for president, I'd put my money on Aria.) Then Clara shakes her shoulders as if shaking it off. "Don't know why you're wasting your time on that messenger, Peanut," she says "It's already done its job."

Aria shrugs. Her shoulders hunch a little, but she keeps on tinkering.

"How long to fix the ship?" Wanda says, walking over to join the conversation.

Clara stands looking at the Accelerator, a hand on her hip. "Maybe three weeks, possibly longer."

I think we're all silently wondering if that's too long.

"If that's what we can do, it's what we can do," Wanda says, and nods. "We have to use that time to track down the key, if we can."

A long silence stretches around us, and my heart pounds with the power of my secret.

"I may have a way to find the key," I blurt out abruptly. Everyone looks at me.

"Where?" Aria asks.

I clear my throat. "Um. I can't tell you."

This draws an even deeper, more confused silence from the group. It's Wanda who breaks the tension.

"You really think you have a chance at finding it, Rosie?" she asks.

I swallow. "I *might*," I say. I expect her to push back on this, to grill me. She's a seasoned witch hunter after all, and I'm a kid—or at least I *was* one up until recently.

"Well," she says, giving me a hard pat on the shoulder. "You focus on finding the key through the incredibly secret source you can't tell us about, Aria and Clara will get the Accelerator running and install this Glaciation thing that was in the freezer, and the rest of us will start strategizing how to fight Nothing back into a black hole so that he can be *locked in* in the first place." She clears her throat. And then she seems to rethink her tone. "But . . . no pressure."

She looks over to Germ, sitting against a wall of the hangar snuggling Eliot Falkor. "Germ," she snaps, though not unkindly. Germ looks up, startled out of her snuggle reverie. "Figure out what your weapon will be. You'll need it."

After Wanda leaves, Germ, Aria, and I look at each other, overwhelmed. But Clara gets back to work, pencil tucked behind her ear, unruffled as usual.

"And I thought *Aria* was as cool as a cucumber," Germ mutters to me as we walk back to the hotel, leaving the sisters behind to fix the only spaceship that can save the world.

I throw one last glance back over our shoulders at Clara and Aria, both busy at their work again. "I guess everything's relative," I say.

"Well, I did it," Germ announces later that night, appearing in our bedroom doorway with Eliot Falkor perched on her shoulder and a smile stretching from ear to ear. I've been in bed, flipping through *The Witch Hunter's Guide* uselessly, waiting for her to go to bed so that I can try my luck with the sewing basket again.

"Did what?" I ask, laying the book down on my lap.

Germ pulls something from behind her back with a flourish. It's a little pink teddy bear holding a silk heart with the words "Home Is Where the Heart Is" embroidered on it. I stare at it for a moment.

"Picked out my weapon. From the Everything Vending Machine."

"That's not a weapon. That's a stuffie."

Germ looks at the teddy bear, then at me.

Germ deflates a little. "I figure we can hug it before we go into battle, and he'll give us courage," she says. She sits down on the edge of her bed, pulling Eliot off her shoulder and onto her lap. "Also, I'm pretty sure he'll shoot lasers out of his eyes."

"Wolf said he'd watch Eliot tomorrow morning during my run," she goes on, changing the subject. "Well, he didn't *say*. I asked him and he nodded."

I don't mention it, but I worry Wolf will end up roasting Eliot over a campfire and eating him.

"Be careful with Wolf, Germ," I offer gently.

Germ waits for me to elaborate.

"Don't you think . . ." I falter. "Doesn't it seem like maybe him living with a witch all those years has turned him, possibly . . . bad?"

Germ takes this in as if it's never even occurred to her. But Germ thinks everyone is wonderful.

"Eliot would sense if he was bad," she offers.

"How would he tell you?" I ask.

She shrugs, trying to summon an idea. "With his facial expressions."

Eliot's face is of course permanently expressionless, and I try to keep my face that way now. But I'm worried for Germ, for all of us. I'm so tempted to tell her about the Museum of Imagined Things, just to underline how careful we have to be about anyone who might betray us. But, knowing my promise to Rufus, I swallow the words.

Germ goes off to dunk her new teddy bear into a bucket of moonlight by the hangar and leave him out in the front yard all night so that he will turn into some kind of fluffy stuffed weapon. While she's gone, I try the sewing basket again, but as usual, nothing happens. I give the basket an impatient kick, then regret it. Have I just knocked down a shelf full of dreams or something? I wonder.

I hide the basket and climb up into bed, boiling with frustration.

"You okay?" Germ asks, walking back into the room.

I let out a small grunt.

"You know what always helps me when I'm annoyed?" she offers. "Going for a run."

I blink at her because I don't run.

"Or . . . a walk?" she offers.

I let out a frustrated sigh, but still, I take her advice. Fabian is in the lobby polishing the already-polished desk, and his sniffing accompanies me out the door.

Under the stars, I feel myself grow calmer. I take my flashlight out of my pocket and flick on Flit, and she darts and flutters ahead of me, clumsily tripping along but also a little bit beautiful in the dusk and starlight. I look around for Ebb, but he's nowhere in sight. There is only Wolf by the pond, his jagged blanket of glass twinkling in his lap, reflecting the glittering starlight above. I approach him reluctantly.

"Hey, Wolf. Have you seen Ebb?"

My brother looks up at me, expressionless, then holds the blanket out to me. I don't know what he wants.

"That's, uh . . ." I clear my throat. "Nice," I say. I reach toward it, meaning to make a gesture without actually touching it, but—intentionally or not—Wolf's hand jerks slightly, and I end up slicing my finger on a jagged edge.

"Ouch!" I drop my flashlight. As quick as lightning, Wolf leans sideways to scoop it up. He looks at it for a moment, then directs its beam (and Flit) at my moonstone necklace.

It happens in a flash. Flit collides with the moonstone, light into light, and a brightness flashes in a silver streak from my chest to a nearby tree and sets it on fire.

"Wolf!" I yell.

I yank off my hotel robe and fling it over the flames to smother them, singeing my hand in the process. When the flames have sputtered out, I glare back at Wolf and snatch my flashlight from his hands. He hangs his head, looking at his feet.

"Is everything okay?" I hear a voice ask.

Startled, I glance up. Zia is standing on the rise looking concerned, but she's not the one who asked. Ebb is standing beside her. Holding her hand.

For a moment, I stare at them in surprise. And then my chest feels like it has caught fire too.

"I um . . . we . . ." I look at the ground, then at Wolf, and my face feels like it's more ablaze than the tree was. A strange, new kind of hurt courses through me, devouring my ribs. "It was just—Flit just . . . ," I stutter. Even Ebb looks uncomfortable. He drops Zia's hand gently.

And then, of all the humiliating things that could happen, Flit lets out a long, pained trill, like she's wounded.

"Um, bye," I say loudly, and turn on my heel, holding my flashlight against my stomach.

And then . . .

I don't walk. I don't slip away subtly.

I run. I run in the most embarrassing way possible back toward the hotel, Flit fluttering along at my feet and sounding like a wounded hyena.

Turning her off, I slam the lobby door behind me and take the hallway stairs two at a time up to my room, where I scramble up onto my bed as if I'm being chased, then mush my face against my pillow. Germ, sleeping like a brick, doesn't rouse. It hurts to breathe.

I think about how Ebb once said that he'll always be thirteen, and I'll outgrow him. But I never knew exactly what he meant until now. He meant we will lose each other.

"I like him," I whisper out loud, then shudder, and look to make sure I didn't wake up Germ. I *like* Ebb. And I've never wanted to like anyone, much less someone dead. Realizing it is like being poked in my lungs with a sword.

Under normal circumstances I would wake Germ up and tell her everything. But this time, I just can't bring myself to do it. Never have I been able to keep a secret from Germ for more than twenty-four hours, and now I'm keeping two.

I feel like, if I'm the kind of person who likes Ebb, I am not the person I used to be. Just like with the night I burned my stories, things have changed, and I don't want to be older. But I *am* older despite myself.

I only find I'm crying when I touch my hands to my cheeks. I sit up, swiping the tears with my palms, and hold my fingers open. In the strange Glimmer 5 dusk, they glisten like light.

When I fall asleep, I dream that Flit is me and I am Flit. In the dream I want to go back to being a person and not a bird, but I can't even turn my head to look back at who I used to be. I flutter to the sewing basket and open the lid with my beak. And this time, there's a tunnel inside it leading down.

When I wake, with a jerk, Flit is perched on the foot of my bed, watching me. Even though I'm sure I turned her off. We stare at each other, and Flit's eyes look knowing and powerful, or maybe I'm just imagining it. And then she vanishes, as if she's been caught out doing something she isn't supposed to.

Then I hear a whisper.

"Come away."

At first I think it's from the hallway; maybe Wanda

and my mom are looking for me, or even Ebb, to see if I'm okay. But something crosses my vision: a tendril of white mist like a tiny cloud drifting past my face.

I sit up and look around as more puffs of fog float toward me. Looking downward, I gasp. The floor is obscured by a thick layer of mist roiling out from under my closet door.

I turn on Flit, who stares at me cluelessly, even though I'm giving her a look that says, *Did you do this? In my dream?* And now I can hear the whispers more clearly, and they're not coming from any voice I know.

"Come away, o human child. Come away, come away."

I recognize the words, from *Fairy and Folk Tales of Ireland* that I got out of the hotel library. It's from a poem called "The Stolen Child" that, of course, I was drawn to because of Wolf, about a child following a fairy away from the world because the world is just too sad, sometimes.

Below me, Germ begins to snore. I scooch to the bunk ladder and climb down, my pulse pounding in my ears. Quietly I open my closet door. More mist whirls around my feet and billows across the floor, and Flit flutters in and out of the clouds. I can barely see the sewing basket at all, but there's a bright hole in the middle of the mist where it should be, clouds puffing out of it like out of the stack of a locomotive.

I step up to the side of the hole, looking down, unable to see into it. I look back at Germ in her bed. And then I gently close the closet door.

The fog envelops me. From deep within the hole I hear distant echoes—cries and calls of wild animals, far-off laughter, a scream. The chill I've felt since we arrived on Glimmer 5 gives way to a warm, thick humidity.

I sit down on the edge of the hole, my feet dangling into thin air beneath me. Flit hops up beside me gamely. After a moment, I see that there's no way down but to just let go.

"Come away," the whisper says. "Come away."

Heart pounding, I slide off the edge of the hole, and in.

CHAPTER 15

I land on something that bounces under me. The ground feels almost pillowy, and as the mist evaporates and trails away, I look down at my feet to find I'm standing on a surface that's as thin and gossamer as a spider's web.

The more shocking thing is my feet themselves. My entire body, in fact. It shimmers, translucent, ethereal. I hold up my palm, and I can see right through it. I sweep my arms out and around, watching them glow.

To enter, Rufus guessed, *you have to become dreamlike yourself.* And he was right.

"I'm almost a ghost," I breathe to Flit, who chirps softly, not nearly as shocked as I am. Maybe it's not such a big deal to her, since she's already made of invisible fabric. And other than being transparent now, I guess I *do* generally feel like the same confused, nervous person I was a minute ago.

Gazing around, I see I'm in a long tunnel stretching away in both directions, its walls curving softly overhead, ridged and wrinkled. Flit flutters into a wall and bounces backward, but the wall bounces too. Reaching out to touch it, I watch the wall give slightly under my finger. I may be like a ghost, but this whole place is ghostlike.

"Which way?" I ask Flit doubtfully. "Rufus said my weapon might guide me."

If a bird can shrug, that's what Flit does. So instead I listen for the voice—the one I heard from my room—and catch it still whispering in the distance, though much fainter than before. "Come away, come away." And then a faraway animal shriek shakes the soft, squishy floor beneath me like it's Jell-O.

Flit and I look at each other. *Not everything imagined is good,* Rufus *also* said.

I swallow and will myself to walk forward, my feet rebounding gently like I'm walking on a trampoline. Tunneled halls curve off to my right and left, though some also curve down or up. I peer into one after another, breathing in the warm, thick air.

I must not be looking where I'm going, because when Flit lets out a sharp trill, I stop short at a jagged, open gap, staring down into an abyss.

"Thanks," I whisper. Carefully I skirt my way around it. A few feet farther down, the hall pinches in on itself so that I have to scoot sideways to get through. This is a treacherous place, a treacherous place that's also been rolled and stuffed into a basket.

The whispering voice has gone quieter; I can just barely hear it ahead of me. It leads me to the foot of a narrow set of stairs that goes upward and then disappears altogether. Whatever's above sounds like a rain forest—squawks, growls, echoing screeches, but also laughter, angry voices, rushing water. There's also light flooding down the stairs, so bright that, coming from the dimness of Glimmer 5, I blink.

Flit blunders up the stairwell, and I follow her into the light and space above. And catch my breath.

A palace of dreams.

I'm standing at the edge of an immense space. Arched, misty, multi-tiered ceilings—made of clouds and infused with sunlight—soar high above. Light blazes from beyond the walls through holes in the mist, illuminating puffs of clouds floating back and forth overhead, some so close that I can reach out my hand and touch them, my fingers making dents in the mist. There isn't an angle or corner anywhere in sight—webbed walls curve in the shapes of leaves, hallways peel off like roots branching off a tree. What's more, the whole place feels *wrinkled*, like a shirt that's been balled up and shaken out again.

It's not the shape of the room, though, that has shocked me. It's the life. A flock of purple birds flutters and squawks above, then dives and disappears into a hallway, knocking a bronze statue over as they go. A giant—at least three times as tall as the tallest person I've ever seen—sleeps at the foot of a spiral staircase that leads into a jagged hole in one of the ceilings. A goat nibbles at the bark of a tree full of golden apples. A stream meanders through the very center of the floor, and a figure made of gray smoke drinks at the water's edge and then, seeing me, ducks out sight. Flit flutters to my shoulder and hides under my hair, and I can't tell if she's scared or delighted.

Even with all its strangeness, this is a place gone awry.

That much is clear from the start. The Museum of Imagined Things is a mess.

Across the vast floor, I spot a bank of misty wooden desks shaped like flower petals. Signs hover in the air above each one, changing again and again into different languages until they eventually spell out words I recognize: *Ask about our audio tour!*

But at the desks, there is no one to ask. My mind immediately goes to the cloud shepherds. If anyone would have worked at the info desks, it's them. They were the ones who brought all the world's dreams into the museum and would have kept it organized. But now, stuffed into a basket, with no one looking after it, it's gone a bit wild.

I swallow, wondering where to begin, keeping my eyes on the sleeping giant. And then someone brushes past me. He looks back at me as he rushes on, an arrow protruding from his chest—*a ghost*, eyeing me briskly. "A dragon's broken out of Nightmares again," he says, then hurries off toward a cloudy column that rises into unseen heights above. He pushes a small bright button there and waits by a set of silver double doors I didn't notice, tapping his foot impatiently as he casts glances toward the stairwell behind me. And then I realize why. A sound—the animal screech we heard before—echoes from its depths, startling me. The ghost gives me an apologetic wave as the silver doors open and he steps inside, disappearing.

Glancing behind me, I hurry in the same direction. I jam my finger against the button and peer toward the stairwell again.

"Must be an elevator," I say to Flit, who, no surprise, is not turning out to be the guide I hoped she would be. "Hope it comes back fast," I breathe, nervous. Then, glancing at the wall beside the double doors, I see—etched in silver silken thread—some kind of directory. Now that I'm really noticing, I realize that it goes all around the room. Every inch of wall I can see is embroidered with the same faint silver thread, divided into columns, and blinking until it lands on the only language I can read.

On the left-hand side of each column are numbers in no particular order. On the right side are what I can only guess are all the Imagined Things, arranged loosely by topic.

Dreams about Wild Horses
Dreams Dreamt by Wild Horses
Dreams Dreamt by Trees
Tragic Love Stories

Happy Love Stories
Love Stories We're Not Sure
Whether We Should Be Happy or
Sad About
Beloved Stories of Upper
Cambodia
Songs about Days of the Week
Songs about Caterpillars
Maps of Imaginary Places
Mind Maps
Maps of Dreams of Real Places
That Have Been Changed Slightly
in the Dreaming (for example,
your house but with a pool full of
gumballs)
Conversations Held between
Carnivorous Plants
Conversations Held by
Invertebrates
Movies about Samurais
Movies Set on Trains
Musicals
Movies Only Movie Buffs
Would Love

The list goes on and on. As I scan it, it fills me with wonder. *How could all these things exist? What does a tree dream or a collected conversation even look like?* But also . . . it crushes me. The things the museum holds are truly endless, and it's all arranged by a logic that is completely illogical.

My heart sinks. Even if I knew exactly who stole the key, I wouldn't know how to find out where it is now. This is more than finding a needle in a haystack. It's finding a needle in a *football field* full of haystacks.

Beside me, the elevator doors open. But I just stand there, dazed, until Flit bites my ear.

"Ow!" I say as she flutters into the elevator ahead of me. She perches on the floor, tilting her head and watching me. I blink at her for a second, wondering about her. Is she trying to lead me after all? After a moment, more because of the escaped dragon than anything else, I follow her inside and the doors close behind me.

On the curved, gossamer wall is a cluster of numbered silver buttons. I stare at them blankly, supposing they work the way the ones on the Everything Vending Machine do, by punching in the combination of numbers you want. Of course, I don't know what I want, but I tell myself miserably that choosing *anything* is better than choosing nothing at all. And so, using my newly glowing fingers, I press four random buttons: 1809.

The elevator jiggles to a start and begins to lift, and we sway buoyantly upward like a balloon—moving straight, then at diagonals, sometimes dipping down and up again. My stomach dips with every turn; I close my eyes and hope that of all the things gone wild in the Museum of Imagined Things, the elevator isn't one of them.

Somewhere in this vast place is the answer to who stole the Moon Goddess's key. And up into the museum, with no idea of how to find it, I go.

CHAPTER 16

Floor 1809, when we come to it, is cozy, nothing at all like the vastness of the lobby below. The foyer on this floor is cramped and earthy like the inside of a burrow, and halls extend in all directions like hollow roots of a tree. There are signs at the crooks that mark each new hallway, indicating that I'm in a cluster of dreams: NIGHTMARES OF FORGETTING TO WEAR CLOTHES TO SCHOOL, DREAMS OF ACTORS COMING TO YOUR HOUSE.

Somewhere far below I hear the distant roar of the

dragon. Hesitating, I wonder if it's worth even looking in Dreams, since what I want is more of a memory. But I suppose whoever stole the key could have *dreamt* about it afterward.

I pick a branching hallway—Dreams of Old Friends—and walk forward, finding that it dips down so steeply, I eventually have to slide my way to the next corridor, this one lined with holes in the walls just big enough for a person to climb through. Leaning my face toward one of the holes to peer in, I find I'm looking into a café where two people at a table are holding hands, talking as if I'm not there. For a moment, I could almost laugh. I'm seeing someone's dream!

I continue walking, peering into every hole I pass at people's most beautiful and terrifying dreams: valleys full of snakes, beasts hiding in closets, clay houses with wings, a bus shaped like a monkey, and so on. Down the next hall, and the next, and the next, as Flit hops clumsily ahead, I watch for any dreams that might resemble *That Time I Betrayed the World by Stealing the Moon Goddess's Key*. But I don't find anything that fits.

And then the hall just ends and the floor comes to a stop, like it's been torn. I inch up to the edge of it, and leaning forward to peer down at the atrium, I see—with a nauseous wobble—over a thousand stories below. My heart flutters.

"We'll be lucky to make it out of this place alive," I say to Flit. She squawks and ruffles her feathers, as if trying to shake off the danger.

I turn in the other direction. The halls begin to open into more cavernous spaces, though there are also more huge precipices and drop-offs I have to steer clear of. Soon, the doors start to change. They're no longer holes but wide and tall doorways with red velvet curtains. Voices echo from inside.

"I don't think we're in Dreams anymore," I say. "Seems more like Movies." I suppose everything that was ever made into a movie (or a painting or a book, for that matter) was imagined first. I suppose real and imagined things overlap that way.

But Flit isn't paying attention; she's bobbing up and down, listening to a soft thread of music in the distance that I hadn't, till a moment ago, noticed. She starts chirping along with the tune, tilting her head from side to side, but I can't make out the tune.

Peeling one pair of nearby velvet curtains apart, I see two people singing a beautiful song I have never heard, in a language I don't know, holding out their hands to each other in the rain. I reach my hand out into the storm, and pull it back, dry.

"Make that Musicals," I say.

Flit hops down the hall in the direction of the distant song she first noticed, bobbing and flicking her feathers like she's dancing.

"Flit, we've got to keep moving," I say. "There won't be anything about the key this way."

Flit ignores me, but then, seeming to catch wind of something, she stops and tilts her head, then begins purposefully hopping down the hall in another direction. This time, I follow.

Up ahead, the halls grow cooler, mustier, more *ancient-feeling*. Round wooden doors line the walls, and I open them one by one, revealing scenes of women galloping on horses, families arguing, tricky spiders, mysterious strangers, unsavory transactions on trains. It's not until I see a snow-covered clearing with a wrought-iron lamp post and a faun-like man waiting beside it that I realize where we are.

"We've found Stories," I say to Flit, a grin stretching across my face.

My breath comes faster now. Somewhere in this place are Hogwarts and Hogsmeade, Cittàgazze and El

Dorado . . . if only I knew how to find them. But even if I never do, I feel how, even so far from home, this place is *my* place. And how strange and special it is that humans build all sorts of worlds aside from the one they're born in.

We walk onward, Flit still hopping along like a bird on a mission, and for a moment I have the fantastical hope that she's taking me straight to Platform Nine and Three Quarters. But then she does a sudden about-face. Trilling shrilly, she flaps to a round wooden door to my left and perches on its knob.

"What is it?" I ask. Flit rubs her beak along the knob as if she's trying either to turn it or to wipe something off her face. I approach, hesitate, and then grasp the handle and pull the door open.

What I see beyond it is a forest full of shadows. A trail under thick overgrowth leads deep into the woods, with little white specks of *something* dotting its path. The hairs stand up on the back of my neck.

"I know this story," I say.

Up in the sky, through the gaps in the trees, I can make out just the vaguest shape of words made of clouds, as if written in the white trails of planes:

Next to a great forest there lived a poor woodcutter with his wife and two children.

"Did you bring us here on purpose?" I ask Flit, turning to her. Or is it a coincidence? The story is one that my mom kept in our house, close by her bed, about two lost children in the dim wild woods. The specks on the path are bread crumbs. Without warning, Flit flies through the doorway and starts pecking at them.

We're looking into *Hansel and Gretel.*

"Flit," I hiss, stepping in after her. As I do, I remember the danger of the place. There's a witch here, one who puts children into ovens. I don't know what an imaginary witch can do to a figment of a girl, but I don't want to find out. A cold wind rustles through the trees, like a fear as old as time.

I'm corralling Flit back toward the door when I see something . . . just the slightest movement of someone behind a tree, watching us.

Flit stops eating, alert. I take two steps back and am about to stumble through the doorway, just as a ghost emerges into the clearing. He's missing one arm, and the other is covered in tattoos of giant squids, mermaids, anchors, dragons. He floats toward me, then stops short as if he can't believe his eyes.

I know how he feels.

Of all the stories, in all the world, in a museum in a

sewing basket on a planet light-years from Earth, somehow I am standing in front of Homer Honeycutt.

"Rosie Oaks, as I live and breathe," he says.

And you'd think that that would be the most shocking
thing possible. But then Homer does something no ghost
has ever done before. He lunges forward, and hugs me.

CHAPTER 17

"Yer not dead, are ye, Rosie?" Homer says, pulling back and studying me as if for flesh wounds. "Tell me yer not a ghost!"

I shake my head. "I'm not dead," I gasp. "But how can you touch me?"

Homer squints at me thoughtfully, and then seems to have a glimmer of recognition. "Yer a figment, aren't ye?" he says, sizing me up. "A figment's really just a smidge away from a ghost. So yes I can touch ye." He pokes my shoulder with one finger, grinning. "And I'm thrilled to see ye, long as it doesn't mean yer dead. Come in, come in. These doors let in a draft."

He tugs my sleeve, then quietly closes the open door behind me.

"What are you doing," I sputter, "in *Hansel and Gretel*?" I haven't seen Homer since I left Maine on Chompy the whale. Back at the sailors' cemetery in Seaport, he was the town gossip. But like all the ghosts I've come across, he still hasn't learned what unfinished business keeps him from moving to the Beyond.

Homer waves away my question. "I'll tell ye all that in due time. But what of Ebb, and yer mother?" he asks urgently. "And yer twin ye went lookin' fer? And yer loud redheaded friend?"

"Everyone's okay," I breathe. "Well, except Little One." I look at Flit, who's run out of crumbs to eat. "Little One didn't make it. This is Flit."

Homer glances at her with the same bemused expression everyone does when they meet her.

"Well, she's brought ye to the right place at least," he says kindly.

"But . . . how did *you* get here?"

"You first, Rosie," Homer presses curiously. "What brings you to the museum?"

"I'm here looking for something," I admit, not sure if I should say more. Homer narrows his eyes, waiting to hear more, and so I tell him the short version of everything that's happened since we last saw each other: the hunt for all the witches on Earth, rescuing Wolf from the Time Witch, the arrival of the Nothing King. I tell him about Glimmer 5 and the sewing basket. (I figure I don't need to keep a secret from someone who's actually *inside* the secret.) Finally I tell him how finding the person who stole the black hole key is the only way I can hope to discover where the key might be now.

Homer nods all the while, his eyes sharp and thoughtful.

"Some of these rumors have followed you and your friends," he admits, "though, when the black hole appeared, I figured you must be dead or drowned. It's not just ghosts who know about you now, Rosie. The world's changed since you killed the witches and freed up the gifts they stole. People see the invisible things now. Ye've been brave, child. Ye've come a long way from the girl I met in the sailors' cemetery who knew nothing about ghosts."

I'm not sure I like the idea of people knowing about me. I don't even like it when my classmates notice me back home.

"I haven't come far *enough*," I say. "I'm in an infinite

museum trying to find clues to a key that may be lost on Earth, for all I know."

Homer studies me. "Well, I may be able to help ye there, Rosie. With all the ghosts in these parts gossiping about the end of the world, ye hear a thing or two of how it all might have come about." He grins. "Come along," he says, and turns to float along the path into the shadowy, forbidding woods. After casting one nervous backward glance at the door through which we came, I follow.

"It's a strange overlapping kind of place, the museum. Course, now that you mention we're stuffed inside a basket, it makes sense that it all seems to be unraveling a bit: imaginary creatures on the loose, baddies from nightmares running about in the halls. Floor 6976 is swallowing folks whole, I hear . . . just sucking them into oblivion as soon as the elevator doors open."

The forest around us is lively with the sounds of birds and squirrels scurrying through the trees, but there are other sounds. Up ahead, I see that Flit is approaching a small cottage that makes my skin crawl just by being near it. Inside, I see a shape creeping beyond the windows.

"Don't ye worry, Rosie," Homer says. "The witch in there won't see us when she comes out to lure the children; the story's on a loop and we're not in it. Still, I hate to be around for it; gives me the chills. By the way," he says over his shoulder, glancing at Flit, who's plucked two of her own feathers out as we've walked, "I hate to break it to ye, but it seems yer friend might have mange."

"She might be molting," I say unsurely. "Where are we going?"

"To see a woman," he says, "who told me something you might find interesting. But better for ye to hear it secondhand than third. Lord knows I've heard so much news of the world since I got here, I don't want to jumble any of it. In the meantime, I can answer yer question of how I got here." He slows, and hovers for a moment beside a pine tree, glancing back at me. "Ye talked about shrinking into things like baskets, but have ye ever seen something move inside a *picture*, Rosie? Or words shimmer in a book?"

Caught by surprise, I nod. A memory flashes of standing in a house while hunting the Griever and seeing a waterfall move inside a painting. As strange as voices coming from a mousehole.

"Well," Homer says, and shrugs, "what ye're seeing when that happens is a doorway, a thin place in the invisible fabric where real and unreal meet. By stepping into a certain painting, or a certain story, ye can reach the place its maker imagined." He pauses. "Well, that is, if yer a ghost. Given what ghosts are made of, we're the only ones that can. Of course, all those places are stored here, in this museum."

Homer scratches his whiskers and begins walking again.

"I only first heard of the whole thing a few years back. It doesn't happen with *every* book or painting, mind you, but books and paintings are the place it's most likely to happen. I heard that one ghost even got here through a chalk drawing on a sidewalk, though I heard that from Pammy Mesnick, and she's usually full of stuffing. Honestly, for a long time I didn't really give it much thought. Besides, according to the rumors, the doors only went one way, which was off-putting, to say the least."

He shakes his head gravely. Up ahead, I hear voices and laughter, getting closer with each step. "But then came the black hole. Desperate to flee, me and some friends hurried to yer house to see if we could find one of these doorways we'd heard so much about. I tried all yer mom's paintings first, and some books left lying open in your room, but nothing. Then we found *Hansel and Gretel* on your mother's nightstand, open to a painting of the witch's cottage. And it had that kind of shimmer we'd heard of. So old Ewen Ironsides offered to be the guinea pig. He went through easily enough, so I spread word among the ghosts of Seaport to get out while they could, and then I came through. I've been here ever since. And that's how I met the lady I'm about to introduce you to. Ah, here we are."

We come around a bend in the path, into a clearing that looks like a medieval village square surrounded by timber-framed houses. And in the square is . . . well . . . a party.

Ghosts loll on stone walls and cluster on the porches of houses and shops, talking loudly. They swagger through the square, some in rags riddled with bullet holes, others dressed up in modern suits or Bermuda shorts, drinking out of frosty mugs, arms around each other, singing.

Also, they eat. I see ghosts gobbling giant turkey legs, slurping bowls of soup, devouring platefuls of candies and cakes. As we stand there watching, two ghosts climb out of a well at the center of the square, looking dazed.

"That old well is where the book spits them out," Homer explains. "Or *in*, I s'pose. Once they realize what this place is," he goes on, "they'll start livin' it up so fast, it'll make yer head spin. Ghosts can eat here, Rosie, and drink, and buy things, and move things. Even *I* went a bit wild when I arrived, to be honest with ye. I mean, imagine being dead for who knows how many years, never getting your favorite meal or venturing off the property where ye died, and then BAM."

I'm momentarily distracted from what he's saying by a dead train conductor riding by on a unicorn—neither of which seem to belong in *Hansel and Gretel* at all. Peals of laughter issue from a nearby pub. Homer points in the direction of the laughter.

"That's where we're headed."

We cross the square, and he leads me up an old set of steps and indoors, where—across the crowded room, up on a small balcony—I see a woman in a red suit with a red rose on the lapel, who stands surveying the room as if she owns it. Her eyes light on us, and she smiles.

Homer grins back at her, even blushes a little. The woman comes down a set of stairs in the corner.

"Homer!" she says, hugging him and squeezing his hand. She waves for us to follow her, and leads us down a hall behind the stairs to a quieter, sumptuous back parlor where we are alone, then gestures for us to sit on one of the plush couches.

Homer clears his throat. "Fen, this is my friend Rosie Oaks." Fen raises one eyebrow at me, smiling. "She needs to talk to you. She's a witch hunter and—"

"I've heard about her already," Fen says, sizing me and

Flit up. "She entered the museum about"—she looks at her watch—"four and a half hours ago. Can I get you anything, Rosie? Cotton candy perhaps? A bike?"

I shake my head and murmur, "No, thanks," confused.

"Fen's a woman who knows how to get things, Rosie," Homer explains. "You need something, she'll figure out how to find it for you. Directions, treasures, all sorts of things she's scoured from nearby imaginings—pets, cars, games, food . . . lots of food . . ."

"Unicorns?" I ask, remembering the ghost we passed in the square.

Homer nods, tapping his nose. "Fen makes sure ghosts who come here get whatever in their wildest dreams they ever hoped they'd have. Been doing it fer years. And in return all she wants is—"

"Gossip," Fen interjects, her eyes twinkling. "Do you have anything for me, Homer?"

Homer blushes again and stammers a bit, and now I suddenly realize why. Fen loves gossip as much as he does. She's basically his soul mate.

"*Hansel and Gretel* is probably the most popular story to hang out in anywhere in the museum," Homer boasts, "thanks to her. Even *if* our days are numbered here like everywhere else's."

"Why are your days num—"

"I know everybody here," Fen adds proudly, interrupting the question I'm about to ask. "Every ghost on this entire floor, and plenty of others. You can't lose a sock anywhere in the entire Nightmares section without me hearing about it."

"That's . . . impressive," I say. She studies me, satisfied, and Homer clears his throat.

"It's your extensive knowledge that actually made me bring Rosie here, Fen. I want te ask about something ye told me shortly after I arrived. A dangerous piece of gossip ye'd gathered . . . and one I think my friend Rosie might want te hear."

Fen studies me, her arms crossed, intrigued, her hawkish eyes sparkling. "What have you got for me in return, Homer?" she asks.

Homer grins. "There's a ghost down on sub-basement twenty, says they've been to Limbo and back. I'll get 'em to fill ye in on what they saw."

"I'll find out myself, soon enough," she says with a smile. "But all right, then." She gleefully looks around as if to make sure we're not overheard, the way Bibi West back home sometimes does when she's about to spill someone else's secrets. Then Fen turns to me.

"I have a nephew who died as a teenager when his ship sank off the coast of Jakarta, where he's from. He's a mischievous, handsome sort; name's Bo. Several years ago I caught wind that he was in the museum, in Conversations Held by Omnivores about the Weather, and I went to greet him. He'd come through a doorway in Paintings of Nature a few days before and was looking for a place to hide, the most obscure place he could hide anywhere in the museum, he said."

I blink, confused. "But the museum was always on a cloud above the world. Isn't that hidden?"

"Not enough, I guess," Fen replies. "You see, Bo saw something he wasn't supposed to see." She widens her eyes, savoring the weight of her own words. "A meeting . . . between a woman and a witch."

She pauses. I don't realize I'm holding my breath until Homer gives me a gentle nudge for me to let it out as Fen goes on.

"His story went something like this: Up till a few nights before, he'd been roaming the little stretch of boardwalk near the seaside where his ship sank. One night near twilight, he saw some kids had dug a pit in the sand, and he'd floated down into it, peeking his head out every now and then to startle the seagulls. Typical Bo."

"Well, he was so preoccupied that he didn't notice all the ghosts hurrying away from the area. When he finally looked around and saw they were all gone, he couldn't figure out why until he saw her. She'd just sat down on a bench at the edge of the boardwalk a few feet away and was looking out at the water." She pauses, lets the silence linger for a moment. "The Time Witch."

Homer nudges me. I'm holding my breath again.

"Of course, she was the reason the ghosts had scattered. We always do at the sight of a witch. But the strange thing, the thing that was really eerie, was that there was someone *living* with her. A woman, twirling something small in her hands." She pauses, seeming genuinely nervous for a moment. "Bo couldn't move. He knew he wasn't supposed to be seeing whatever was happening. So he stayed where he was, and that's how he overheard the conversation between them."

"What did they say?" I ask breathlessly.

She looks at me, then relaxes her shoulders, defeated. "Bo wouldn't tell me."

I feel myself deflate.

"He said it would put me in danger too, if I ever knew. Nothing could convince him to talk. And if *I* couldn't convince him"—Fen gives a knowing look from under her eyebrows—"I don't think anybody could. But from the way he spoke, I'd bet anything that it had to do with what that woman was twirling in her hands."

"Doesn't that sound, Rosie," Homer interjects, "like it could have been the key?"

I nod. I feel almost certain that it was.

"What did the woman look like?" I ask.

Fen tilts her head, thinking. "It was interesting. He was very specific about the fact that she looked sorrowful. And something else: he said she had tiny hands. 'The Frowning Woman,' he called her."

"And you don't know where Bo went after you saw him?" I ask.

Fen shakes her head. "Like I said, he was looking for someplace where he could really disappear. But even if you found him, I don't know how you'd get him to tell you what you need to know. He's willful, Bo. We've got that in common."

"We'd still like to try," I murmur.

Her eyes go back and forth between me and Homer thoughtfully. "Well, you would know him by the flat, dangly life jacket he wears—one that didn't do him any good when he drowned because he forgot to inflate it." Then she reaches to her lapel and pulls the rose from where it's pinned. "If you find him, give him this. It'll let him know I sent you. And I'll keep my ears open in the meantime."

I put the rose into the pocket of my pullover.

"Thank ye, Fen," Homer says. "I guess we'd better take our leave. This one's in a rush trying te save the world and so on."

Fen nods, with a wry smile at Homer's sense of humor. "When are you going to the boats, Homer?" she asks.

He frowns. "Don't know if I will."

"We won't have a choice in the end," she says, her smile fading.

I look at Homer quizzically as we turn to leave, but he avoids my eyes. We trail through the village square, and this time I feel ghosts watching us, even as they stuff their faces with cotton candy and turkey legs and sing their songs.

"Word's spread that you're Rosie Oaks," Homer explains in a low voice. "They're taking your measure, so stand up tall."

"Measure of what?" I ask.

Even as we cross into the shadows of the trees, I can feel their eyes watching my back.

"Of whether you killed eleven witches like they've heard. And whether you can kill the Nothing King, too."

CHAPTER 18

"I'm familiar with the place by now, mind ye," Homer says, "but I still get a little turned around now and then."

We're winding through the labyrinthine halls of the museum, but we keep having to turn around at dead ends, or stop halfway up stairwells that lead nowhere. Now Flit hops along crookedly beside us as Homer turns and leads us down a peculiarly noisy—*noisy* but somehow not loud—hall. The deeper in we get, the more the echoing space sounds like the inside of a big domed train station, as if a crowd is milling around and murmuring. And then I begin to see, up ahead, lines of colorful shapes—*letters*, I realize with a gasp—floating through the corridor in front of us.

"Are those . . . ?" I ask, coming to a stop.

"Words. Sentences. Paragraphs. All of the above," Homer answers, sidestepping into the hall to our right and reaching out a finger to poke a sentence snaking past through the air. "All the words ever spoken are in this part of the building."

The sentence—in a language I don't know—wiggles, then rights itself and slithers away. All down the hall, lines of words snake this way and that. In shock, I watch a rogue *n* break off the end of *I'll be there at ten* and sneak into a crack in the wall. Homer nudges a coiled-up paragraph out of our way with his foot.

"So, every conversation anyone ever had is here?" Homer nods, and I promise myself I'll come back. What better place to look for a chat between a woman and a witch?

And yet, as we wind our way deeper, the hallways of words grow only more and more numerous, bigger and bigger halls stuffed to the ceiling with exclamations and questions and paragraphs bumping into each other, crashing into walls, soaring, rolling on the ground.

"We're only just at the periphery of it," Homer points out. "There are multitudes of rooms the size of stadiums in here."

My hope flags. Talking with Fen was a stroke of luck, but how will I ever find *one* conversation? Or a ghost named Bo who doesn't want to be found?

I gaze at Flit ahead of me as she tries to peck the center out of the word "lethargy," getting all tangled up in the process. *Was* it a stroke of luck, us finding Homer and Fen? Or did Flit lead me to *Hansel and Gretel* on purpose?

I think about the dream I had of her getting us into the museum. As awkward and molting as she is, I wonder if there's more to her than I think.

"What did Fen mean, Homer, about you going to a boat? And not having a choice?"

Homer looks at me sheepishly. "Well, I was reluctant te say, Rosie. On account that it means this might be the last time we see each other."

"Why?" I choke, startled.

The way Homer looks at me makes me remember his age, that he's been around an incredibly long time. He is careworn and tired as he gazes into my eyes.

"Would ye like to see, Rosie?" he asks gently. "It'll be a bit of a detour."

I nod.

After stepping into the elevator a few minutes later, Homer pushes a button that looks like a minus symbol, then 786.

"It's on a negative floor," he explains, "way, waaaay down."

We lurch and bob and float downward for so long and travel so far, it feels like we might just drop out of the bottom of the museum. When the doors open, it's onto a dim hallway, misty and foggy and smelling of damp stone. A crowd of ghosts is moving past, all headed in the same direction, and Homer tugs me into the throng.

The hall gets mustier, colder, and darker as we go, until we emerge into an enormous sloped space the size of a football field, like a great cavern. The gray floor stretches about halfway across from left to right, then ends in empty, misty space. Along its edge, foggy ether laps like water at a shore. And floating on the ether is a line of boats like long canoes, in a single-file line. One by one, the boats pull up to let ghosts climb in, then float away on the fog down a long tunnel into darkness, and out of sight.

"We came te the museum te hide, Rosie," Homer says,

"but we're not safe here anymore. We're leavin'." He nods to the crowd around us. "The gossip is that the Nothing King is hunting for this place. And if that's true, he will find it. He'll find the sewing basket you harbor, an he'll find us all eventually. And so, we only have one choice, to go."

"But go where?" I ask, swallowing the lump in my throat.

"Limbo."

I take in a breath. "That's where the boats are taking them?"

Homer nods. "Over the years, as more and more ghosts came to the museum through the doorways, we became something of a nuisance. The cloud shepherds didn't like having things thrown into disarray. You saw how it was in *Hansel and Gretel*. Said it messed with their record keeping, among other things. Ghosts were taking things from the places where they belonged, making a mess, getting things confused about who was Beyond or in the museum or haunting Earth or what. Course, now the cloud shepherds are gone, ghosts are having their way with the place completely."

"Anyway, to make the shepherds happy, the Bright-weaver made this kind of back exit. A ferry that would take any ghosts who were willing off to Limbo. Most ghosts resisted till now. But with the Nothing King coming . . ."

I watch the ghosts, so sad and mournful as they climb into the boats.

"On Glimmer 5," I say, "we have this shuttle that's supposed to go to Limbo. It's broken down, though."

Homer takes this in. "It's not where most of us wish to go, Rosie. But whatever our unfinished business is that, once resolved, would let us go Beyond, we haven't figured it out in time. I'll be leavin' soon meself. But I'm so glad you got here before I did. I'm glad I didn't miss ye."

I stare at him, my heart aching. Just when I've found him, Homer Honeycutt is leaving. And then I have a hopeful thought.

"Aria and Clara are trying to fix our shuttle. Maybe we could come get you and the other ghosts in Limbo on our way to fight the Nothing King. You could fight with us. Maybe *that's* your unfinished business."

Homer shakes his head gently. "Oh, Rosie, ye know all too well, ghosts are helpless creatures. Ye know we can't change anything, can't move anything. Not to mention we're notoriously rather cowardly."

"Ebb's learning to use electromagnetic energy to build

a greenhouse," I press helplessly. "Maybe it could be used to fight the Nothing King."

Homer doesn't reply. He only gazes back at the departing ghosts, and then raises and drops his hands. "C'mon, my friend. I'll take ye back up."

In the bright atrium, the giant is gone from his sleeping spot, and the dragon is still nowhere to be seen, but a massive boulder has landed in the stream. Homer crosses the space beside me.

"Ye know yer way from here?" he asks at the top of the stairway from which I originally came.

"I think so. As long as there's not a dragon in my way."

Homer pats my cheek gently with his hand. "The last time we parted," he says, "all ye had to worry about was killing a witch. Now look at you." He smiles sadly. "I don't know if I'll see ye again, Rosie, in this life or the next." We gaze at each other. He seems to be weighing something in his mind.

"Tell Ebb, if you and yer crew find yourselves in the neighborhood of Limbo on yer way to fight the Nothing King, I'd fight alongside ye, though I don't really know how. And I'd round up a few ghosts to come along if I could."

JODI LYNN ANDERSON

My heart leaps, and I lean into Homer and give him a hug.

"Good luck, Rosie," he says. "If I never see ye again, good luck."

Then he turns, floats back across the atrium into the elevator, and is gone.

CHAPTER 19

or the next ten nights, just after Germ falls asleep, mist seeps out from under our closet door, enshrouding the floor of our bedroom. For the next ten nights, the museum—fickle and flighty, familiar and strange, terrifying and wondrous—invites me in.

I search any place I can think of where a ghost might want to hide. I wander into paintings, tromp along painted hills and under smudged trees. I circle through dreams of lush forest villages, in the shadows of mountains filled with giants. I wind my way through stories of castles, and beasts, and best friends.

Leaving on my first night, I learned that getting out requires bouncing on the soft floor of the hallway until I'm high enough to grab the rim of the hole and clamber out—not easy for a clumsy girl like me. But soon I get the hang of it. And every time, the basket closes itself behind me.

In the Halls of Words, I search for the sentences Fen's nephew Bo overheard. But while I encounter plenty of conversations about garage sales and spy missions, bitter arguments, recited recipes, and whispered secrets, I find nothing spoken between a woman and a witch about a key that could set the Nothing King loose to end the world.

On these nights, Flit wakes first, appearing before I reach for my flashlight, which continues to be unsettling. We meander through the tangled halls of the museum, sometimes unintentionally circling through places we've already been, Flit chirping and bobbing whenever we come near the Hall of Musicals and trying fruitlessly to lead me in. But mostly she's more helpful than not, charting our course more and more confidently, bumping into walls less often. She's even growing some adult-looking under-feathers. ("I guess she's really molting after all," Germ says one night at dinner.)

Each morning just before what dawn should be (on a sunless planet, it's not really anything), I sneak into bed and claw out a couple of hours of sleep. It's not enough, but then again, I'm not the only one who's sleep-deprived.

"I don't know if this is really preparing us," Germ mutters to me one afternoon when my mom has gathered us to practice our weapons. Germ's trying to get her teddy bear to do something "weapon-y" (her word, not mine). She throws him, rolls him, flings him from Aria's slingshot. And while he does occasionally shoot a very weak bit of light out of each eye, I wouldn't necessarily call them laser beams.

We attack targets that my mom hurls into the air—mostly plates and cups from the hotel. Flit, like Little One, transforms into the shapes I imagine—a leaping badger, a dart, a falcon—but it's like her heart isn't in it. She doesn't attack the targets fiercely, as Little One might have done. While Germ messes around with her stuffie, Aria and Clara can barely keep their eyes open. And Wanda—though she does manage to take nice slices out of some flying cutlery—is not the witch hunter she was before her ring got broken.

And I can't fight the sinking feeling that nothing we're doing is going to help us. If the *Time Witch* took our weapons—our breakable, drop-able arrows and slingshots and flashlights—how much easier will it be for the Nothing King? Beside me, Aria yawns.

"It's the Accelerator," she says, out of breath after shattering a target with a high note and a gray pebble from her slingshot. Beside her, Clara is busy with her toolbox, using her tools to double as projectiles; miraculously, they boomerang back to her. "We were at it forever last night, welding parts, wiring control panels. I've managed to bring Zippy back from the dead, but the Accelerator . . . I don't think we'll get a real night's sleep until it's done." Aria turns her weary eyes on me curiously. "Any closer to finding out about the key?"

"I'm not sure," I say. "Maybe a little."

She nods and tries to hide her disappointment, but Aria has no poker face. Still, we've come a long way from all the eye rolls she gave me when we met. She lays a hand gently on my arm. "Try to step it up, Rosie. We don't want to be found first."

"I know." I nod. In the distance beyond, I see Ebb and Zia putting up the windowpanes of the greenhouse, invisible energy buzzing in front of their hands, and I feel a dull throb in my stomach.

In the hours when I sleep, I have strange and wild dreams. I dream that I'm changing, that I'm becoming the mist that drifts out of the museum, the air that people breathe. In the dreams, I'm not afraid but happy.

I dream too about Flit. That I'm growing her wings and tail feathers and I have a bird's heart. I feel so calm about it, so safe and peaceful, I don't want to wake up. But one morning, something pulls me out of the dream. Someone breathing.

I come awake, blinking in the dark, startled to see a light coming from my chest. Looking down, I see Flit, not nestled on top of my rib cage but *in* it. Flit, glowing inside me, asleep. And then I realize that I'm being watched.

It's not Flit whose breathing has woken me, but Wolf's. He's halfway up the ladder of my bed, watching me. Correction—watching my necklace.

I jerk up to sit, and he stumbles back down the ladder, startled. My hand flies over my collarbone. "Get out!" I yell, angry now.

Wolf turns on his heel and runs out of the room. In half a second Germ is climbing up beside me, wrapping an arm around me, and I drop my face into my hands.

"I thought it would be different," I say. "I wanted us to be a family."

"He loves you, Rosie. He's just . . . figuring things out."

I bite my lip. "He's figuring out how to strangle me

with a glass blanket and set trees on fire and steal my necklace."

Germ is thoughtful for a moment, rubbing her eyes and becoming more alert. "I read this story in *Pet Psychic* once, about a family who had this pet dog that was way too wild for them. They thought the dog didn't care about them either way, so they gave him to someone in Canada. But two days after they gave him away, he escaped and started making his way back to them. They kept getting calls from people who'd seen the number on his collar. And every call was closer and closer to their house."

She goes silent. I blink at her. She gives me a look like, *WHAT?*

"What happened to the dog, Germ?"

"Oh, he became a mascot of some small-town police department he came across in Ohio. Now he solves crimes. That's how he ended up in *Pet Psychic*."

I blink at her some more. "He never came back to them?"

She shakes her head.

"Um," I venture, "so the moral of the story is, the dog didn't love them that much after all?"

"Well, I mean, he gets to solve crimes, so what dog in his right mind would pass that up?"

I pull my knees up under my chin and pluck the blanket. It feels like we are getting slightly off topic.

"You're still his sister, is what I'm saying," Germ tells me. "He loves you even if you don't think he does. Show him you care. Do something nice for him."

"Like," I reply dryly, "something nicer than traveling through time and hunting eleven witches to rescue him?" But Germ doesn't hear my sarcasm. She only nods earnestly.

"I know you don't like . . . um . . . putting yourself out there. Being so shy and everything. But maybe that's something you could change. For him."

I shrug noncommittally. But getting rejected in general, and possibly having my heart broken by my brother, seems scarier than fighting witches, I think. And being Germ's friend has always been the only way I "put myself out there." I've always leaned on Germ to do it for me.

By the time I lie back down, I've almost forgotten that Flit was inside my chest. But now, in the dark, I wonder about it.

The nuzzling into my neck, the climbing into my chest. Appearing in my dreams. It's like she wants to *become* me.

But if I let that happen, who will I be then?

CHAPTER 20

t's on the eleventh night searching the museum that I find my next clue. Weirdly, it's when I'm hoping not to find it.

It's deep in the night. I'm hungry and half falling asleep and about to give up. But just as I'm weaving in what I think is the direction of the elevator, Flit flutters up to my shoulder and pecks on my shirt, urging me down a hallway.

"Flit, I can't," I say through a yawn. "We've got to go to bed."

She tugs at my ear, then pecks at my collar, protesting. Relenting, I follow her around a turn, then another. Eventually I find myself in a wing we've never come to before, staring at a sign arched above a doorway in golden letters: MIND MAPS. I remember, vaguely, seeing it listed in the directory down in the lobby.

Inside, instead of being loud and busy or colorful like the rest of the museum, the place is deserted and hushed. It looks like a library, with austere shelves rising up in row after row on either side of a large space, stretching on and on and out of sight. Each shelf is crowded to the brim with paper scrolls rolled up and tied with string.

I run my hand along a few of the scrolls, and then gently remove one and flatten it out to view it. The paper is traced with countless branching trails, almost like the veins of a leaf—with tiny little pictures drawn along the branches, so small that I can barely make them out.

"The cloud shepherds must have compiled these," I say to Flit, who tilts her head, listening. "I bet they mapped everything they gathered. Like, connecting all the different things people imagined and dreamt back to the people they came from." It's kind of breathtaking to think about: maps of each person's dreams, memories, words, all in one place.

I wander farther down the line of dusty shelves, where scrolls are clustered alphabetically, and I sift through them as I walk. I wonder if I spoke another language if the library would arrange itself differently, the way the signs in the lobby changed until I could read them, and I bet it probably would. Eventually I find myself in the *N*s. On a whim, I turn toward the *O*s, then down aisle after aisle, searching for the name "Oaks."

It takes almost an hour of searching, but eventually I find my mom's scroll—marked with her name and the symbol of an arrow underneath. My hands are trembling now. I push my own mind map aside, and then my grandmother's. Something's been nagging me since Homer and I spoke with Fen, the way she described the Frowning Woman her nephew had seen—the sorrowful features and tiny hands. It reminds me of the way my mom described her sister's creations: tiny, miniature, intricate—the kinds of small things made by small fingers.

Jade Oaks, the scroll I retrieve reads, in a gold loopy scrawl.

"There are a lot of people with small hands in the world," I say to Flit, looking for reassurance. She seems too nervous to reassure me (in addition to not being able to talk). I also know it's far-fetched to think that, of all the people in all the world, my mom's sister would have any-thing to do with stealing the Moon Goddess's key. And yet, Aunt Jade did have the sight, which puts her closer to all things witch-related than most. The worry is there inside me, and I want to prove it wrong.

I unroll the map.

My aunt's mind branches across the page in pictures, zigzagging into tiny veins that meander through draw-ings of food, houses and buildings, musical notes, views of mountains. Most of it is too clustered, tangled, and minuscule to make out. But I do see that one particular place is dim and gray, with an etching of two little girls. The branching paths around them are scribbled out, as if something there is better left forgotten. Near one of the scribbles is a drawing of a crow.

I stand back, letting the map roll up in my hands, troubled. I tie it with its string, replace it on the shelf, and swallow a lump in my throat. I was hoping that the map might put my mind to rest. Instead I feel more worried than before. But since I have no idea how to decipher the map, it's probably time to call it quits for now.

Back in my room, I stand by the window for a while, thoughtful, watching Ebb in the yard outside, where he's sitting alone watching the stars. I think maybe I will go out and see him, but then I don't. Maybe I'm not so brave at all.

I climb into bed at around three a.m., full of wishes, and with a warning in my heart.

CHAPTER 21

"How long have you been keeping this from me?"

I wake, confused. Germ is sitting cross-legged at the foot of my bed; the clock says it's 10:03 a.m. I never sleep this late.

Germ is waiting for an answer, but I'm still half-asleep and trying to make sense of what her question is. My eyes zip to the closet, which is closed, then back to her.

"What are you talking about?" I croak.

She sighs and levels her eyes at me. "You're going to have to tell him, you know."

I blink at her. "Tell . . . who . . . what?"

Germ rolls her eyes, waiting for me to fess up. When I don't, she says decisively, "Ebb."

For a moment, relief courses through me. She's not talking about the museum at all. But then I realize, this is almost as bad.

"I woke up last night," she says, "and you were standing at the window watching him like this." She arranges her face so that it looks ridiculously wistful and mushy, blinks her eyelids a lot, then returns to her regular expression.

"And you've been acting weird around him. Like, really weird. And also he tried to give you a hand massage." She lays these facts out with the brash confidence of a detective solving a case.

My mind scrambles for words to deny it. But . . . well . . . *of course* Germ knows. She's Germ; she has a radar for romance that no doubt stretches across time and space. She was *born* thinking about love. Not to mention, she knows me better than I know myself. If there's one thing that can pull Germ out of worrying about the imminent end of the world, it's people having crushes on people. Frankly, it's a small miracle that she didn't figure it out before I did.

"It's horrible," I finally admit with a sigh, looking away from her.

I expect some stern words from her, she looks so serious. But then her mouth widens into a huge grin that she can't seem to stop.

"Why are you smiling?" I croak.

"Because this is great," she whispers back gleefully. "You said you love him."

"No. Nope. That's not what I said."

Germ brushes this aside as an irrelevant detail. "Rosie, you have to tell him," she repeats. "I mean, leave it to you to like a ghost. You're never gonna be into normal stuff, no offense."

I shake my head, pulling my knees up to my chest as if I could shield myself from her enthusiasm. "Germ, I can't get my mouth to say basic words to people even at the best of times, much less about something like *this*, to him. Also, he has a girlfriend, who's dead. Because he's also dead. They fit, and I don't. There's a million reasons not to say anything to him."

Germ shrugs. "D'quan and I have differences too. He likes Dungeons and Dragons, and different kinds of dice annoy me so—"

"That's not the same as him being dead," I interject.

"Mm," she says skeptically. "Sometimes when he made me play it with him, I felt dead with boredom."

I want to laugh, but I'm too distracted by also wanting to barf.

"Rosie," Germ presses, "you fought eleven witches to the death. You can tell someone you like them."

I answer by giving her my stubborn look, which visibly deflates her. I'm not bragging when I say that my stubbornness is legendary. She turns to begging.

"You know I can't keep this secret. You know that about me."

"We've got bigger things to think about," I say.

But there's a triumphant shift in Germ's posture as I say the words. "Exactly. The world might be ending. And if you can't tell someone you love them when the world is ending, when can you say it?"

"I didn't say I love him," I say.

Germ waves a hand like she's swatting away a fly. "He's known you your whole life. He *just* met Zia."

"But she's pretty great."

Germ contemplates this, softening a little. "That's true. She is great."

I kick her slightly with my foot.

"But, Rosie," she adds, "you've got to do it soon. We're going to leave this planet, fight the Nothing King, and possibly die. Even if we make it out alive, Ebb will go Beyond—since surely there's no bigger unfinished business than saving the universe. You probably won't have another chance. This is it."

I take in what she's saying, even though I don't want to. It's almost like I'm split into two Rosies. One who's quiet and wants to hide, and the other, newer one who wants to take the first Rosie by the shoulders and say, *Make room for yourself in this world.* Deep down, I know Germ is right. I know that if I don't ever tell Ebb how I feel, I'll regret it.

"Easy for you to say," I counter weakly, though I'm already giving up. "You say everything you think to everyone."

"I know. It's awesome," she says, and beams.

"Extroverts," I murmur.

"We're the best," she says.

"Okay." I relent, though it makes me sick to say it. "Okay, you're right, I have to tell him."

"Great," Germ says.

"Great," I say.

She blinks at me. "Like, this morning?"

Panicked, I feel like my heart is trying to escape my chest. "Later."

Her shoulders sink. "I'll give you till tomorrow night bedtime, Rosie. If you don't tell him by then, I'll tell him myself."

I put my hand over my queasy stomach. If anything could be more awkward than telling Ebb how I feel, it would be Germ doing it. Her communication style could basically be described as "bulldozer meets wrecking ball."

"I promise," I say.

But after she's gone off to breakfast, I can't even picture it.

Over the next few hours, as I sit next to Ebb at breakfast, and then outside, where he's watering new plants, I can't bring myself to say anything. I decide to ask him if I can talk to him about something later. Then at least I'd be committed, but even that's too scary. And then Aria starts talking about how it should only be a couple more days till she has Zippy running, and distracts everyone enough to let me off the hook.

What I *do* manage to do is act bizarre around him for the rest of the morning, and then avoid him for the rest of the afternoon. At dinner, he and Zia stay away, practicing Ebb's new skills by pushing around some geese out by the Glasslands. And so by bedtime, I'm no closer to confessing anything and my nerves are twanging in all directions.

Deep in the night I enter the museum as usual, my feet taking me back to Mind Maps. I don't know how to read Jade's map, but I know it's vitally important. I pore over it for at least two hours, tracing with my fingers the tiny drawings, the scribbles that block things out. But it's like being locked out of a riddle; the map hints at answers I can't see.

"This is useless," I say to Flit, who's perched on the back of the chair across from me, looking as flummoxed as I am. "This map shows enough to worry me but also tells me pretty much nothing."

"Shhh!"

Flit and I both go still, alert. I listen for a moment to the silence around me. I could have sworn someone shushed us. And then, out of the corner of my eye, I see a shape moving, and I turn toward it.

I'm so shocked, I could fall out of my chair.

A cloud shepherd is peering around at me from behind a shelf about fifteen feet away, holding his misty finger to his misty lips. He's an elderly-looking blob of white fluff, pointed at the top like a dollop of whipped cream. He floats out from behind the shelf and comes toward us, carrying an armful of scrolls tucked under his elbows. He shelves them one by one as he approaches us.

"We must whisper in the library," he says in a voice that sounds like several soft voices woven together. I gape at him.

"Sorry," I whisper back.

The cloud shepherd nods, then sprouts a misty goatee and a wild head of hair, turning suddenly younger. I remember this: the voice that sounds like many voices, the constant shape-changing of the first cloud shepherd I ever met, deep in the woods near my house back home.

"I thought you all were gone," I whisper, "lost to the black hole."

The cloud shepherd transforms again, this time into a woman with long braided hair. She's frowning. She holds her misty hands out in front of her, and within them a tiny mist scene unfolds: figures of shepherds being swept away in a wind. One shepherd, not as quick to hurry out of the museum as the others, left behind. *Luckily*, as it turns out. She closes her hands together and the scene disappears.

"We were left behind," they whisper sadly. And it comes back to me that the cloud shepherd I once met also spoke as "we." This time too, I feel like I'm in the presence of someone—or many shapes of a someone—serene and wise. A *they*.

"Can I help you with something?" the shepherd whispers.

I'm about to shake my head when I realize there's something I'd *very much* like help with.

"I'm trying to figure out what this map means," I say quietly. "I'm trying to decipher it."

"Ah." They nod, brightening, and growing a long beard instantly. "You need to take it to the viewing room." They point to a velvet curtain in a distant corner. "Through there."

I glance at the curtain and swell with hope. "Thank you," I whisper back.

"Please place the map in the bin when you're finished, to be reshelved."

I nod furiously.

The cloud shepherd smiles gently and then floats toward the stacks, reshelving more of the scrolls calmly as if they could do this day in and day out for all eternity and be perfectly content. I watch them drift around a corner and out of sight, and wonder if they're the only cloud shepherd left in existence and if I'll ever see them again.

After tucking Jade's map under my arm, I head for the viewing room and step inside, Flit hopping along beside me. It's so dark, I can't see anything around me except a small box lit by a red light to my right. The light illuminates the words "Insert Map Here," and a long narrow slot below it.

I hesitate and then unroll the map and gently feed it into the slot.

As soon as I do, colored lights come from above, illuminating an exact replica of the map the size of the entire floor. A path winds all through the map, branching off into the darkness in all directions, almost like a trail on a game board. A sign appears in red overhead: WELCOME TO THE MIND MAP OF JADE OAKS. PLEASE STAY ON THE DESIGNATED PATHS.

And then, just as I'm about to step onto the path, a little girl appears in front of me. She's three-dimensional but also transparent like me. She's standing with her back to me, but, seeming to suddenly notice my presence, she turns to look over her shoulder. There's a question in her eyes, which are shaped like my mother's, deep set and wide. Her hair, like my mom's, is dark.

"Are you Jade?" I ask, my voice shaking.

She smiles but does not speak.

"Can you show me what I'm looking for?" She just looks at me, waiting. "Can you show me the scribbled-out parts in your mind?"

The little girl's smile falters, subtly but unmistakably. She reaches for my hand, and though we're both figments, she holds it and then leads me forward.

We walk ahead into darkness.

CHAPTER 22

Aglow grows ahead of us, and when we reach it, I see it's not just a glow but a scene. A woman is rocking twin babies, trying to get them to sleep, while something delicious-smelling simmers on a stove nearby. The woman looks a bit like my mom, but she's got a mouth shaped like mine. She also has wings.

Since these are memories from my aunt Jade, I think the woman must be my grandmother. All around me I hear humming and feel warmth. I feel the beat of a heart pounding under my feet—like we are witnessing some-

THE PALACE OF DREAMS

thing more mysterious than memories, half-imagined and half-real.

"Is this the way you see the world?" I ask the Jade who guides me. She only watches me with mournful eyes, then holds out her hand for me to take again, and leads me on.

Our next stop is a glowing scene off the trail to my left, the same twins grown to maybe five years old. One is waving for the other to follow, saying there's nothing to be afraid of. They're walking into school. By how nervous they are, I think it's their first day of kindergarten. The walls and the ceilings of the room are plated with gems. Jade treasures this place, I think. Her sister—my mother—is wearing a cape and holding a shield, leading the way into the classroom full of kids.

"She's your hero," I say to the guide Jade, who nods.

The five-year-old Jade we're watching slides into a desk seat and begins to tie knots in a piece of yarn. In her nervous hands, the yarn becomes a lattice of elaborate crisscrossed stitches. I realize she is copying a spiderweb that hangs in the corner of her classroom, her fingers working out her first-day nerves by making art. The glow of the scene fades.

My guide and I continue down the path, which now

winds through a shadowed forest, and Flit, twitching, draws my eyes to a shape moving on a tree branch. It's a crow staring down at us with gimlet eyes—it's not real, just a piece of Jade's memory like everything else, but still I shiver. Jade shakes her head as if to warn me not to go near it. When it takes flight, swirling toward the sky, it leaves a shadowy trail in the air behind it like—I notice, with a chill—scribbles.

The deeper we go, the more convinced I become. The mind map is a place to see Jade's life *as she remembers it*. With wings and capes and shields and light, it shows the way she sees herself and others. Most scenes involve my mom: a birthday party where she eats cake with her hands, a recital where she sings confidently (even if kind of badly) from the stage while Jade stands behind her, trembling and shy.

And I feel a pinch of something familiar, watching them. I'm more like my aunt Jade than I am like my mom. I would hide behind Germ forever if I could.

The next scene shows Jade ten years old or so, sitting at her bedroom window, weaving creations out of wire and beads: forests, landscapes, tiny houses full of wire furniture so true to life that it's eerie. She copies a tree beyond her window by sight, and it seems that she can render each of its branches perfectly, an exact replica in miniature.

My mom appears in the doorway, a halo above her head and a dinner plate full of food for Jade in her hands. Beyond the house a breeze stirs up, and I see the silhouettes of crows out in the yard. My guide squeezes my hand and moves on.

The path gets dimmer up ahead, where Jade and my mom and a third friend play. My mom and the friend traipse off into the woods, so enthusiastic in their talk that they forget Jade is behind them. Three crows flap around in the sky overhead, leaving tangled trails of scribbled shadows in their wake.

Next comes a school art fair, where people gather at my mom's display, a collection of her bold, bright paintings. Far back—impossibly far, on the other side of an immense space—I see Jade, her tiny wire creations laid out on the table in front of her, too small and subtle to be noticed. A crow is trapped in the building, fluttering a visible, frantic path up near the ceiling. Then another scene: Annabelle and Jade, teenagers now, sitting at dinner. Annabelle is showing everyone the bow she's crafted for witch hunting. Her mother is praising her for it, and Jade is shrinking under the table. Two crows, perched on the windowsill, observe them. My heart starts to sink.

"You always got forgotten," I whisper to the little girl holding my hand. And the crows circling and scribbling through these scenes are Jade's way of trying to forget, too. She doesn't answer, but I understand too well what being the quiet and forgotten one is like. She gazes down the path but hesitates to go any farther. A cold wind blows toward us from ahead, and a scatter of crows comes with it. Flit is up on my shoulder now, shivering against my neck.

But now it seems Jade is determined to lead me on.

Dry leaves whirl across our way. The night gets colder, and I wrap my arms around myself and shiver. Little Jade bows her head down against the wind, and it's strange, because we are approaching a night in summer.

I feel a deep foreboding, coming to this scene. There is something in the air—heavy, electrical, painful.

The two girls, Jade and Annabelle, are asleep in their beds in the dead of night. Scores of crows roost in the trees beyond their window. With a start, Annabelle wakes and looks at the moon, then slides out of bed, gathers her arrows onto her back, and sets out into the night and the woods to reach it.

Jade, awake but still, waits until she's gone. Then she, too, slides out of bed and follows.

I hold my breath.

"You were there, the night my mother climbed to the moon."

Little Jade tilts her chin, just the slightest hint of a nod. She stares at me, as if she's *willing* me to guess her secrets.

"You snuck up one night by yourself. Did you pretend to be her?"

The girl doesn't answer. But a heartbeat sound surrounds us, and a coldness.

"Were you trying to find out what it was like to be brave?"

My guide does not respond.

There's one more scene to see. A teenage Jade is in her bed; it's morning. She wakes and sees a note lying on her dresser. Her sister has gone. I understand this scene because I know the past. It's the moment my mom leaves home to hunt witches. She has left her family without saying goodbye.

The crows, beyond the bedroom window, now cover the lawn.

"She broke your heart," I whisper to Jade.

Ahead of us, the path is blocked by crows completely. I can't see farther.

The girl looks up at me and I look down at her.

"What did you do?" I ask.

And she vanishes.

CHAPTER 23

It's been a long journey into the past, and yet I only have to walk a few feet to remove the map from the viewer. The room goes dark, and I stumble my way out through the curtains into the library. Flit flutters onto a table and runs her beak along one of her new adult feathers.

"Aunt Jade is the Frowning Woman," I say to her. "She has to be." Flit tilts her head and turns her dark eyes to mine. "She had gifted hands, so she'd be good at stealing, and she knew how to be seen without really being noticed, and she looked just like my mom. *And* she was angry," I add. "Most of all, that." Somehow, I think, some night, disguised as a witch hunter whom the Moon Goddess trusted, Jade managed to steal the goddess's key.

My mind spinning over and over on this, we wind our way out of the museum to catch what little sleep we can. But when I try to drift off, it's my guide Jade's mournful eyes that float in front of me, full of sadness, and anger, and loss. I can't decide if they also hold regret.

Where is the key now? It haunts me all the following day as I sit at meals and help Aria and Clara collect spare parts, as I go through weapons drills. *If it really was Jade who had it, did she give it to the Time Witch? Has it been destroyed?* I have so many questions, but the only ghost who might have answers doesn't want to be found.

"Not hungry, Rosie?" my mom asks at dinner while I stare down at my food.

"I'm just tired," I mutter. I can't look her in the eyes. Even if the museum weren't a secret, I wouldn't tell her what I suspect. Not before I know for sure and not before it can help. If I'm going to break her heart, I have to have a good reason.

That evening, I put off going straight to my room and

into the museum, while also still avoiding Germ. I walk softly through the halls of the hotel. I wander into the parlor and stand looking out the window, watching the stars. I know I should get a move on back to the museum for clues, but I linger, feeling endless inside. And then I hear someone clearing their throat, and Ebb comes floating into the room.

"Hey," he says, pleased and uncomfortable all at once. And suddenly I remember with a lurch of my stomach that I'm supposed to tell him I like him . . . by "bedtime," which is basically now. All day, I've let the thought slip.

He gives me a questioning look. "You okay?" he asks.

"No. I mean. Yeah. Um." I feel my cheeks flaming up. I lean a hand on the nearest piece of furniture to try to look at ease, but I slightly miss it and awkwardly fall to the side a little. "What are you up to?" I croak.

Ebb studies me uncertainly. "I was taking Fred for a walk. Got the idea from Germ and Eliot Falkor. Fred doesn't cover a lot of ground on his own, and I thought he might like sightseeing."

I look down at my feet, then out the window, pretending not to be interested. But it's so cute that Ebb is walking his spider, I almost can't stand it.

Suddenly my lips feel like they're sweating. We're alone, and my time's up, and this might be the only private moment we'll get. But the more I try to work myself up to begin, the more my heart threatens to fling itself out through my ribs and run screaming out the window.

Ebb floats up beside me and looks outside.

"Sometimes I just want to be one of those stars," I finally say, to cover the silence. "Then I could just watch the universe do its thing and not have to do anything scary myself."

Ebb smiles. "You wouldn't have any eyes. Or a brain. So you couldn't really watch anything, technically."

I shrug. "Maybe that's what it's like to go Beyond—you get to see everything even if you don't have eyes."

"Speaking as a bystander, I'm pretty sure life is bigger than that for you now, Rosie. You couldn't stand on the sidelines anymore."

I flick Flit along the floor like it's a nervous tic. I sometimes forget that Ebb has known me forever. *Say it,* I think.

"Well," I offer, abruptly faking a yawn and stretching my arms, "I was just about to go to bed."

Ebb gives me a furtive glance. He's slightly disappointed, which gives me a flutter of hope.

"Night," I say, wanting to melt into the floor, or at least spontaneously combust like Clotilda the witch hunter. But just as I'm turning toward the hall, the worst of all possible things happens.

Germ walks into the room.

She looks startled. "Hey," she says, her eyes darting from me to Ebb and back to me. I blink at her and give a nervous laugh.

She looks at Ebb again, and a grin spreads across her face. She checks her watch, glances back at me, and then unsubtly shoves me back into the room I was just about to leave.

"Rosie wants to tell you something, Ebb," she says flatly. And then she takes off.

I turn to face Ebb. He looks confused.

We stand there for a moment while I mentally catalogue the different ways I can break off my friendship with Germ. I clear my throat.

"You okay, Rosie?" he asks.

"Yeah, I wanted to, um, talk to you about something," I say, with a feeling like I'm floating above my own head. Can you have an out-of-body experience from just trying to tell someone how you feel about them?

"Okay." Ebb puts Fred up into his corner web so he can give me his full attention.

I stand there for several long seconds. I glance at Flit to try to put my eyes somewhere that isn't Ebb's face.

"It's Flit," I finally cough out. "There's something weird with Flit."

Ebb looks concerned. "What's happening with Flit?"

"Well," I say, "the other night I dreamt I was becoming her, and then I woke up and she was in my chest. Like, not *on* my chest but in it. It's like . . . we merged, a little. Or something. I thought you might have some ideas."

Ebb looks thoughtful, the way he usually does when I share important questions with him. I breathe a sigh of momentary relief.

"Maybe it's a good thing," he says. "Some ghosts say that when ghosts move Beyond, our separations from each other vanish."

I think on this. I'm not sure that, if I wanted my separations from someone to vanish, I would want it to be with a goofball like Flit.

"But we're not dead," I say. "I mean *you* are. You and Zia are, which is good." I pause. "I mean, not good, but good . . . for your *relationship*?" *What am I saying?* "I only mean that you couldn't like somebody who's not dead." I bite my lip and then clear my throat, but words continue to tumble out. "Ghosts belong with ghosts, is what I'm saying, not with people like me."

Ebb tilts his head, confused.

At this moment, of course, Flit flutters up to my shoulder and starts chirping madly, then bites my ear a few times, then flutters around my head, agitated. Ebb, squinting, seems to be catching on that somehow I'm not saying what I really mean to be saying. But just as he opens his mouth to press me further, my own words jar me.

"Ghosts belong with ghosts," I repeat, a chill running down my neck.

Ebb gazes at me, then at Flit, as if he's putting something together. But even that suddenly falls away from my mind.

"What are you trying to tell me, Rosie?"

I stare at him, relief and disappointment rushing in at the same time. Because I've just thought of something big, and I need to leave immediately.

"I gotta go."

And then I turn on my heel and hurry away.

Back in my room, Germ has—in her miraculous way, given that she only pushed me into the lion's den of confessing my feelings a few minutes ago—fallen peacefully asleep. (Even when she's full of suspense, Germ borders on being a narcoleptic.)

I open the closet. It only takes a moment before the

mist starts pouring out of the sewing basket, and I'm about to climb in when I hear a voice behind me.

"Rosie."

I swivel. Ebb has floated in through the bedroom wall and is looking at me, hurt and confused. Frantically I hold my finger to my lips.

"What were you . . . ," he whispers, glancing up at Germ. "What did you mean when you said . . ." And then he stops. He's spotted the mist pouring out of my closet. He hovers there for a moment in shocked silence. "What *is* this, Rosie?"

And in that moment, I give up. Because, well, if I can't trust Ebb, I can't trust anything in this world.

I sigh. "You might as well come with me," I say.

And I turn to lead the way.

CHAPTER 24

Naturally, the first place Flit tries to take us is the Musicals.

"She always does that," I say to Ebb. "She likes to dance." He has barely said anything as we've wound our way up to the high floors of the museum, understandably speechless as I've led us farther into its depths. I set a path toward where the Halls of Stories begin.

"You look . . . dead, Rosie," he says.

"I know. Homer thought I *was* dead. But I'm just a figment."

"Homer? He's here?"

As we walk, I tell him everything, about the night the sewing basket first opened and how I ended up in *Hansel and Gretel*, about Homer and Fen and Bo and the Frowning Woman with the delicate fingers. About the boats to Limbo, and the mind map and Aunt Jade, her love for my mom and how my mom hurt her without even knowing it.

Ahead I hear the echoes of a tune. Then another.

"What's that?" Ebb asks.

I think for a moment. It doesn't sound like the kind of tune that I've heard drifting out from Musicals.

The hall we're following, after several feet, opens wide, into a space like an enormous domed theater, and music begins to drift all around us, its sound making shapes we can see: trees, streams, wind.

"It's like a sound forest," I breathe.

As we walk, sonatas form blue puddles at our feet, pop songs leap in bubbles past our shoulders, arias make neon arches above our heads.

I smile at Ebb, who grins too before his eyes dart away. "This is the coolest," he says.

Finally, after making our way reluctantly away from the caves of music, we find our way to the edge of Stories.

Once we're there, it takes a while for me to find what I'm looking for.

It does not look inviting. The long narrow hallway ahead is dark, light bulbs flickering along the ceiling as if they're about to go out. Cobwebs hang across our path and need to be batted away as we walk. Behind wooden creaky doors, we hear screams. Mournful ghosts drift up and down the corridor, staring at us.

"When I was talking about how ghosts belong with ghosts," I say, in a low voice because this feels like the kind of place to whisper, "it made me think . . . if a ghost really wanted to blend in, to be completely camouflaged, he'd come here."

Ghost Stories.

"I think it's called 'hiding in plain sight.'"

I stop a ghost who happens to be floating past us. "Excuse me, have you seen a young guy in a deflated life preserver? Probably looks really stressed out?"

The ghost shakes her head.

I ask more and more ghosts as we go, winding from one cobwebbed creepy hall to the next. We ask a ghost who looks like—and might in fact be—Henry the Eighth. We ask someone who looks like they might have died of plague. For ghosts who love to gossip, they really don't seem to have any information on Bo at all.

Finally one ghost says he did see someone matching the description down in Ghost Stories about Dark Stormy Nights, in a tale featuring a creepy house. So then we start asking about that story in particular. It's not too long before we find someone who knows where it is.

"I can take you there if you'd like."

The ghost turns around and shuffles along the dark hallway, and we follow. Eventually he leads us to a tucked-away corner with a shabby, faded doorway. He nods toward it. "I'm off to Limbo," he says. "Good luck to you." Then he turns and floats away.

We open the door slowly, and with lightning flashing and illuminating our faces, we walk in.

We're in a barren field at dusk. A cold wind is whipping clouds across the sky, and there's a gloomy dampness in the air. It's about to rain. The occasional lightning illuminates, in the distance, a rickety old house at the edge of the field, its shutters flapping in the breeze. An owl hoots nearby. Beside me, Ebb shivers, and I give him an ironic look.

"I've haunted your house for a long time, Rosie," he says, defending himself, "but that's what I'd call a haunted house."

We walk closer, nearing a jagged, leafless tree. Beneath it, a ghost in a cowboy hat stands looking in our direction.

"We're looking for a ghost named Bo," I say to him. "A teenager. Wearing a deflated life preserver?"

The ghost just stands there, staring off into the distance, and says nothing, as if we're not even there. And then I realize, he's part of the story; he doesn't see us.

We turn toward the house and climb the front stairs warily, Ebb drifting closer to me. The door creaks as we open it, and the interior is dark except for the flashes from the lightning. A woman in rags crosses in front of us and vanishes through a wall. Someone below the floor is wailing.

We climb more stairs to a hallway. Finally, in a creepy mildew-streaked bathroom, we find him.

Fully dressed and wearing his life preserver, he's lying in the bathtub with his eyes closed. I give Ebb a look, my heart in my throat.

"Um, excuse me?" I whisper hoarsely. "Um, Bo?"

The ghost doesn't move anything but his eyes, opening them and looking at us sideways.

"I'm"—I clear my throat—"Rosie Oaks. And this is my friend Ebb, and . . ." Suddenly remembering, I reach into my pocket and pull out Fen's rose.

But Bo does not take the flower I hold out for him.

"We're trying to save the world, and, um"—I swallow nervously—"you might be our only hope."

Bo stays silent, watching us. And then I think of something else.

"I know you're afraid. But the Time Witch is dead. And the woman you saw with her, she's in Switzerland, I think."

Bo's eyes glint in the next flash of lightning. "Why do you think that?" he asks suspiciously.

I hesitate. "She's my aunt," I admit.

A long hiss escapes Bo's lips. He sits up slowly, plucks the flower from my fingers. He stands, dripping wet—though, clearly he is always dripping wet. He has now got a twinkle in his eye that doesn't seem quite right on a ghost who's been hiding in terror for his life.

"Then you've got bigger problems than I do," he says, and slowly smiles. "I thought *my* aunt was a lot." His eyes drift to Flit. After a moment, he holds out his left hand and Flit jumps onto it. She bats her little bird eyelids at him.

"The ghosts have been talking about you, Rosie Oaks. You're fighting an impossible fight, and you need to know what *I* know if you hope to win it."

He brushes his bangs out of his eyes so charmingly,

he might as well be on a beach with a piña colada in his hand.

"Lucky for you, I'm a fan of impossible fights."

Bo smiles, rather handsomely, I must say. "I'll tell you my secret, Rosie Oaks. I suppose it'll be the life or the death of all of us."

CHAPTER 25

For some reason, this feels anticlimactic. I stare at Bo, confused.

"I thought . . . I thought it would be harder to convince you," I explain. "Your aunt said—"

Bo tucks his hands into his pockets, stepping out of the tub. "I may have played it up a little with Fen, if I'm being honest. I *am* in hiding, but really it's more from *her* than a witch."

"But why?" I ask, befuddled.

"Well, you met Fen. She likes to be in everybody's

business. If you were a sixteen-year-old ghost, free in a museum full of endless possibilities, and had to have Fen hearing about your every move and having opinions about them, wouldn't *you* go into hiding?"

We blink at him; I try to fight back a smile.

"Not that I'm *not* scared of having seen and heard what I saw. I am. But." Bo shrugs. "Keeping off Aunt Fen's radar is the main thing. Anyway." He looks at both of us and then leans against a wall casually. "You wanna hear this thing, right?"

We nod eagerly. Bo nods too, and leads us to an empty room none of the ghosts seem to like. And then, sitting on the couch in the creepy house, he tells his story.

"It was a normal evening haunting the seaside near where I'd died," Bo begins, petting Flit, who's perched beside him on the arm of the moldy chair. "There was a small stretch of boardwalk I liked to float along in the evenings, watching the living eat ice cream and buy souvenirs and so on. I was passing the time by trying to startle the seagulls."

"I heard," I say.

"Well, you get bored, you know?" He winks. "And seagulls are funny. By the way, did you see that video where that seagull keeps walking into a store and stealing packs of potato chips?"

Ebb merely blinks while I say, "*Of course* I have."

"It was *her* I saw first," he goes on, the smile fading from his face, "the woman on the bench—her sadness was just that striking. Took me another second to notice the Time Witch taking a seat next to her, relaxed as you please, her watches dangling around her neck." I shiver at his description of the Time Witch, which I know all too well. "By the time I realized she was there, all the other ghosts had taken off and I was too late. I couldn't leave my little pit in the sand without drawing her attention. Naturally"—he shakes his head—"none of the living walking down the boardwalk saw the witch at all. I suppose they thought your aunt was talking to herself when she spoke.

"It was clear they'd made a plan to meet and talk," he goes on. "And because I couldn't move from my spot without being noticed, I stayed, just a few feet away, far too close for comfort. And heard everything they said." He scratches his chin thoughtfully. "Your aunt seemed afraid, but also, I got the feeling she was determined. She said she had something the Time Witch wanted. She reached into her pocket and pulled it out with shaky hands."

"Was it a key?" I press breathlessly.

Bo looks at me. "Not like any key I'd ever seen," he says, then pauses. "But yes, I believe it was a key. It was circular, and intricate, silver and bright, with little shining twists and turns in the middle. Even in the dim night, it glowed. Made of moonstone, I think." He leans back, scratching Flit's head gently, his eyes going to my moonstone necklace. "Like that. I could tell the witch wanted to jump out of her skin when she saw it, but of course she didn't want to let on.

"'I'm in a good mood, so I'll take it off your hands,' she said, 'rather than lay a curse on you for calling me here.'

"It was so obviously a lie. She wanted the key badly, but for some reason she didn't just stop time and take it. I guess maybe she was curious about your aunt, or maybe she was playing with her. For whatever reason, the witch told your aunt she could ask for something in return."

Some instinct makes me want to stop Bo right there. I think that, whatever my aunt Jade asked for, it's going to be something I don't want to hear.

"I'll never forget what she said after that. She said she wanted the Time Witch to take away the very next person her sister had come to love after her. The Time Witch said she already knew who that would be. She said she knew of a sailor. She said she'd make it look like a sinking so that no one would ever suspect the truth—or their bargain."

I feel my breath shudder in my chest. Beside me, Ebb watches my face in concern.

"And with that, they had a deal," Bo concludes.

"And she gave the Time Witch the key?" I whisper, though my body trembles as I ask.

Bo nods gravely.

"So when you last saw it," Ebb clarifies, "the key was with the Time Witch." Bo nods again, decisively. "Then it went with her into the sea where she drowned," Ebb says flatly. I suck in a breath, swaying slightly.

Bo thinks for a moment, then shakes his head. "Your aunt asked her about that. The Time Witch said she would destroy it, once she'd used it."

"That's worse," Ebb says, wincing.

"I think your aunt wanted to make sure no one would ever know what she'd done."

I can't even speak. I don't know why I ever hoped for anything else. The chance was always tiny that, even if we found out who took the key, we'd be able to get it back.

"And then," Bo goes on, "the witch was gone. Just there one minute . . . and then not. I suppose she stopped time for a few moments as she left."

He lets out a long breath, folding his hands in his lap and rubbing his fingers against each other. "I waited until your aunt had walked away before I floated out of my hole. She was far down the beach by then." In his lap, his hands go still, his face grave. "But as I stood there watching her retreat, she turned, very deliberately, and her eyes glared into mine, even from that distance. She'd seen me, Rosie. A woman with the sight and witches on her side. And she was letting me know it." He shrugs. "That night, I came here through a doorway—a painting of a landscape I knew about in a boardwalk shop—and never looked back."

"But you said you're not afraid of her."

"Well," Bo thinks out loud, "there was something else in that look on her face, besides a threat." He squints, remembering. "Shame. The more I've thought of it over the years, the more I feel sure she was really too ashamed to come after me."

We sit in silence for several moments, and everything seems to tumble down around me.

"So that's it," I choke, my voice like sandpaper. "This whole search was over before it even started. My aunt stole the key and gave it up, end of story." Flit leaps from the armchair into my lap and lays her head gently against my stomach, wanting to be held, but I can't move. All this time, we never had a chance at all. "The Time Witch destroyed the key long before we ever looked for it."

"Well, yes and no," Bo says in a small, steady voice. We both look at him, startled.

"What do you mean?" I ask.

He shrugs. "There's still the matter of the other one."

"Other one?" Ebb and I say at the same time.

Bo looks at my face, then at Ebb's, intently. "She had it tucked under her shirt, but she drew it out once the witch was gone, like she couldn't help but check on it. It was identical, knotted, intricate, bright, made of moonstone just like the first."

I look at him, utterly confused. "What are you talking about?"

My skin keeps switching from hot to cold. Flit flutters around Bo's head, moving the way my heart does, in painful, hopeful beats.

By the time Bo says it, I know what I hope he'll say. But as always, it's scary to hope. And then his mouth spreads into a triumphant smile, and now I see what Fen means, about her nephew being something of a troublemaker.

"I'm talking about the copy," Bo replies. "I'm saying that your aunt had two of the same key."

CHAPTER 26

O ut in the hall, my legs grow too weak for me to walk. I
sit down on the floor and lean my back against a wall.

"Rosie." Ebb tries to comfort me, crouching
beside me. "This is good news. *Jade has a key.* And if Zippy
found Eliot Falkor, he can find *Jade*, too."

I nod furiously, knowing he's right. For anyone else,
recreating the moon key would be impossible. But for Jade,
who could copy every bend in the branch of a tree or every
curve of a cloud from memory . . . it makes perfect sense.
I realize, thinking it through, that it's possible she never

even *stole* the original key in the first place . . . but copied *it* too from memory. Maybe she only ever needed to climb to the moon in my mom's stead and get a glimpse of it.

Still, my skin won't stop swimming in chills, because slicing through all of these thoughts is something far more painful: the favor Jade asked in return for her gift. The sinking the Time Witch promised her.

The sailor.

My dad.

"I thought the sinking was an accident," I say, paying no mind to all the ghosts skirting around us in the hall, "but it was the Time Witch who took him. He would have lived," I whisper. "He would have read books to me. He would have been here to help."

I try to stand, but my knees wobble.

"Rosie," Ebb says, his eyebrows knitting in concern. "Let's go somewhere. Till you feel better."

He straightens up and looks around. He doesn't know the museum like I do, but he decides on a direction and begins to lead me, down one story hall after another. I don't know how he manages it, but—with Flit helping (they're in cahoots, apparently)—after scouring a cluster of fantasies and fairy tales, he comes to a stop at whatever door he seems to have been looking for.

"C'mon," he urges, nudging me.

We both look at each other, startled. Being a ghost, Ebb has never *nudged* me in my life. We both laugh for a moment, then fall silent awkwardly.

Ebb opens the door and tugs me forward. Right onto the lawn of a story that, I realize with a gasp, is all too familiar.

Because I wrote it.

We are standing on a mountain looking down at a valley, and the valley is full of birds—parrots, robins, lorikeets, blue jays, crows, hawks, herons—circling overheard, squawking in the trees in flocks.

I gawp at Ebb, then back down at the lively and beautiful world below.

"This is the story I wrote when I was trying to make Little One," I say in wonder. The sky seems so close that it feels like we took a handful of stars and threw them just above our heads. I can hear the sounds of birds hunting in the night, and also distress calls, and greetings, and songs. A few feet down the hill below us, a snake swallows a nestful of eggs.

It's a beautiful world. But it's also a dangerous one, just like I imagined.

I scan the view for some glimpse of Little One herself.

But instead, in the distance, I see the moonlit shimmer of the ocean, and it makes me realize how—in all my stories—water is always there somewhere in my mind. Calm, peaceful, safe.

"I've used my stories to try to save a lot of things," I say to Ebb softly, "but one thing I've been trying to save without even knowing it is my dad."

Ebb just stands very close to me, his face full of sadness.

"I know that doesn't make sense."

"It doesn't have to," he says. "I get it."

We stand for several minutes, quietly, looking down on a world that only truly exists in my brain. In the sky, in thin cloud shapes silhouetted against the dark sky, I see words, just as I did in *Hansel and Gretel*—dim, almost faded completely, but there.

. . . it was a world where sometimes baby birds got taken by snakes . . . and sometimes mean vultures won in the end. But . . . there were also birds who made nests out of beautiful shells, and birds who fought badgers and rattlers and raccoons for their babies . . . birds who sang even when they were in cages.

Ebb is watching my face. I look at him and blink away the tears forming in my eyes.

"Thanks for bringing me," I say. "It's like a reminder, sort of. To keep going."

"Don't thank *me*. You're the one who came up with this goofy place."

I smile, and we stand for several minutes gazing at the vast sky, the vast sea that came from one small human mind, full of fears and hopes and things I can only reach for but never really reach.

"I wonder where Little One is in this place," I say.

"Off fighting baddies, like her maker." Ebb nudges his shoulder against mine again. "So weird I can do that," he says.

"Yeah, weird," I agree.

He holds out his hand and raises his eyebrows in a question. "Dizzle dazzle?" he says, and crookedly smiles. "It's the answer to everything."

Heart in my throat, I lay my hand in his, and he rubs my fingers—this time for real. I think maybe I could tell him. Maybe I could be that brave.

He's watching my face uncertainly. And now my heart is pounding through my chest again.

"Why did you write this story?" he asks.

I swallow. "I wrote it so bad things don't happen to good birds anymore."

Ebb nods thoughtfully, gently letting go of my hand. "Before, in the library, when you were talking . . ."

"I was just talking," I say.

"You never just talk."

I stand there for a minute saying nothing, which only proves his point.

"I thought . . . ," he goes on, "you might mean you and me." He glances up at me nervously. "When you said that thing about how I couldn't like somebody who's not dead."

By the feel of it, a flame seems to be devouring my face. "I was just saying Zia's a ghost, and you're a ghost," I offer, though I know this is nonsensical.

"I'm not with Zia anymore," he says.

"Oh," I say. "I'm sorry."

Ebb shakes his head. "Don't be. My heart wasn't in it." He hesitates, and looks at me again, nervous. "The problem is . . . well, this kind of thing . . ." He gestures to the valley below us. "Your brain is so weird, and wild, and beautiful." He clears his throat. "I can't like someone else. Because there's nobody like you, Rosie Oaks."

I am as still as a deer in headlights. The only things I can move are my lungs.

"I mean, I'm dead, and you're alive, so you'll outgrow me soon, which is not ideal. But, if there's a chance . . ."

"I like you too," I say. It's just four words, but some words tower over others.

I take Ebb's hand back into mine. Soon things will be different between us. But for now, he and I are made of the same ethereal air and we're the same age. For now, he lets go of my hand, and brushes a piece of hair out of my face like he's being brave. And I don't turn away, because I'm being brave too.

And when we kiss—since we're made of the same magical stuff that's brought us this far in the first place—I feel it.

CHAPTER 27

My mom sits in her room, painting a tree. Unnoticed, I stand in the doorway watching her work and wonder if it's a tree from when she was a kid. It looks like the tree in her yard that Jade copied with her hands.

It's taken me a while to get here. Since morning I've been hiding in my bed from what I have to do. Even Germ's excitement, informing me the Astral Accelerator has started up at last, hasn't been enough to raise me. Neither has the thought of getting to see Ebb (who held hands with me the whole trek home through the museum last night). But finally I am here. I can't put it off forever.

My mom has hunted or been hunted by witches almost all her life. And here she is, still strong and fighting, and I'm going to break her heart with a few little words. Every second that I hold them back, I hold back the breaking.

"Mom?" I finally say.

She looks up from her canvas, startled. We read each other's faces, and I can tell she realizes—even in that instant—that I'm going to say something bad.

"I can't tell you how I know this," I begin, the museum still my secret, but I tell her everything else, all I know about Aunt Jade, and the Time Witch, and the key, and my dad.

When I finish, I lift my eyes from my hands to study her face. To my surprise, she does not look shocked. Sad, heavy, resigned, yes. But shocked, no.

"I see," she says. As if that's all she can say.

I blink at her for a few moments. "Did you . . . already suspect?" I ask.

Mom sits quietly for a long time.

"I didn't want to," she says, "but in some part of my heart, yes. It makes the puzzle pieces fit."

I wait for her to elaborate.

"She was certainly capable of copying the key." She smiles faintly. "She once built my father a *watch* because the original was too expensive." My mom shakes her head in wonder. "So why not a magical key?" She pauses. "It was a gift she had, but so subtle and small that most people didn't appreciate it. Meanwhile I was fierce and loud and thoughtless, sometimes. I knew she was pulling away from me. I knew I'd hurt her, but I never quite knew how." My mom twirls her paintbrush slowly in her hands.

"I think some part of me always knew there was something pained and dangerous brewing in Jade." She lays down the brush, and I try not to think that some part of me thinks I know that about Wolf, too. We sit in silence for a long time, and I feel so sad. Because I think that even if there weren't witches in the world, there would always be hurt people hurting other people.

"What do we do?" I ask. "Can we send Zippy to steal the key from her? You know where she is, right? In that convent?"

My mom glances out the window, where Wolf is doing his usual thing: sewing his blanket of glass.

My mom nods. "I know where she is." Then she stands, and sighs. "I'll write to her." She brushes her hands together as if she could easily brush away how hurt she is.

"I'll tell her I'm sorry. And I'll ask her to send us the key."
She moves to her desk and sits down, pulls some hotel
stationery out of the drawer. "We'll send the letter with
Zippy. Aria says the owl is functioning again."

"But . . . ," I say, and trail off. There are too many buts
to name. *But she's the person who betrayed the entire world.*
But she'll betray us too. But my dad.

My mother turns and lays a hand on her desk, smiling
sadly. "I'm not a fool, Rosie. I know there are lots of reasons not to trust my sister. But the way I see it, we have no
choice. Jade will have that key well hidden—too well for a
rusty owl from the edge of the galaxy to find." She shakes
her head, seeming to falter only for a moment. "And I
can't think she truly grasped the magnitude of what her
anger was making her do. I'll tell her we're a part of each
other, despite everything. And just hope that influences
the choices she makes."

"But . . ."

"It's settled, Rosie," my mom says with finality.

Sometimes I forget that this is supposed to be my
mom's job, to make decisions so that I don't have to. It's
what I've wanted all my life, for her to take care of things
instead of me. But now, I worry she's making the wrong
choice.

"I'll ask her to send the key back with Zippy," Mom says. "And then we'll go after the Nothing King with it. And that will be the end."

The look on her face tells me the discussion is over. And that it's time for me to go.

The hotel, rambling as it is, feels tight and stuffy as I wander its halls. Fabian is stoking a fire in one of the sitting rooms, but fades out of the room as I pass. Eventually I admit to myself that I'm looking for Ebb, and retreat outside to see if I can find him.

Walking toward the lake, I see Zia, who nods at me in a friendly enough way but doesn't approach me to talk. I wave awkwardly, and she waves back, combing her other hand through her ponytail and looking happy enough. I have a feeling nothing gets Zia down for long.

Up ahead, Wolf is squatting in front of the same spindly tree he set on fire, sewing. I stop, and then adjust my course in his direction. I sit down beside him while he looks over at me furtively, then at my necklace, then away.

I gaze out at the still water, thinking of my mom and her act of foolish hope. Like it or not, her fate is entwined with Jade's; they are two halves of a whole. And it's the same for me and Wolf.

I shift, and Wolf looks over at me. I reach behind my neck, unclasp my necklace, and hold it out as I move closer to him.

"I love you," I say, "whether you're the brother I expected or not. Whether you love me back or not."

He stares at the necklace glowing in my hand. He wants to take it, but he's not sure.

"Go on," I say. "I want you to have it. You like shiny things more than I do."

My twin looks at me another long second, then takes the necklace from my hand and drapes it around his own neck. I help him clasp it.

He sits for another long second. Then out of nowhere, he hugs me.

"Thanks," he says. I shudder.

His voice sounds thick and cracked, like it's been let out of a jar that's been buried under an Egyptian pyramid. Wolf simply turns back to staring at the necklace as if he didn't say anything at all.

Someone—Wanda—clears her throat behind us.

"Your mom has called a meeting," she says.

Ebb is the first one to notice me when we get to the hill. He turns and gives me a quick wave before glancing away. Fabian and Zia soon trail up. Once we're all gathered, my mom—with slightly trembling lips but otherwise unflappable—prompts me to tell the group what I've learned about Aunt Jade and the key. There are muffled gasps, but afterward, the silence seems to last forever.

Aria is the first to speak up. "How do you know all this, Rosie?" she asks, but I shake my head. My eyes meet Ebb's, and he gives me a flash of a smile like sun passing through clouds. My heart flutters annoyingly.

"I can't say. I'm sorry."

"We don't need to know Rosie's source," my mom says. "All we need to know is that Jade gave the black-hole key to the Time Witch, and she kept a copy for herself. And now we have to get that copy back."

While they listen grimly, she tells them the plan she laid out for me this morning.

"So what you're saying," Clara replies, tilting her head and looking troubled, "is that we have to rely on the person who betrayed us in the first place to now NOT betray us by sending back the key. Then Zippy Part Two has to make it back under the Nothing King's radar. Then if that works out, we need to climb aboard the shuttle we've only just barely got running . . . to cross the galaxy and surprise-attack the Nothing King into a black hole . . .

and then use the key to somehow lock the door."

There's a long silence.

"That's basically what I'm saying," my mom answers after a moment.

"Oh," Clara says, her mouth twitching sideways as she looks around at all of us. "I thought you were gonna say we had to do something hard." Then she grins sardonically.

Aria and Germ snort. Even Wanda seems slightly amused. I suppose laughing makes us feel brave. And so in the end, what's left of the League of Witch Hunters— the courageous, amazing, exhausted, hopeful, lopsided group of people that I love—take it pretty well. With the exception of Wolf. I don't know how he takes it because he doesn't say anything at all.

"Can the Astral Accelerator be voyage-worthy by the time Zippy's due back?" Wanda asks. "Five days from now?"

Aria glances at Clara and they reply simultaneously:

"No," from Clara.

"Yes," from Aria.

They furrow their brows at each other.

"Yes," Clara corrects herself, watching Aria's face and softening a little. "Aria's right." Aria secretly widens her eyes at me, shrugging and pleased.

"Good," Wanda says. "The pressure suits will be ready to go too, and I'll load them in before launch day." We all look at each other. The pressure suits look like a cross between aluminum foil and scrap quilts, and Wanda knows it. "I know, I know. They're not fancy. But they'll keep us alive and breathing and mobile when we're off the ship. Anyway," she adds, "the hardest part won't be surprising the Nothing King. It'll be luring him."

Now we all turn quiet again.

"I've thought and thought and thought about this," she continues, "day and night. Our weapons can help beat the Nothing King back. But our best chance of getting him *into* the black hole will be to lure him to it, to tempt him to cross its event horizon with something he can't resist, and let gravity suck them both in."

Everyone looks at each other, stumped.

"There's nothing that would make him get that close by choice," Clara says.

Except . . . *Except*. I have the sinking feeling I know of something that would work. And using it means breaking a promise.

"I have something," I say.

CHAPTER 28

That night, we send Zippy to Earth for a second time, this time to find the person who betrayed us and ask for her help.

What my mother has written to Aunt Jade is between two sisters—personal and private. None of us ask to see it before she stands at the top of the hill and tucks the envelope into Zippy's beak.

"I'd like to sing a blessing," Aria says, stepping forward. "For long shots."

She thinks for a moment, gathering her tune in her

head. And then she sings in the way only Aria can, and shoots her slingshot up into the sky where we plan to launch Zippy. A shower of pink light blooms in the sky before it disintegrates, raining down over our heads, but evaporating before it touches us.

My mom lifts her arm and lets the owl go.

Later, when everyone is asleep, I take my last trip through the museum. Ebb comes with me. My heart beats a weird rhythm to have his fingers touching mine as we spread the word to every ghost we see: for those who haven't already left, the time to head for the boats to Limbo is now.

The trip is not a secret. Everyone on Glimmer 5—with the exception of Rufus, who I still haven't given away—knows about it. I've broken my promise and told the truth, because the museum is the only lure we've got to use, the only thing we could fling toward a black hole that the Nothing King would go after. I don't know if I'm making the right choice, but to win the world, it seems, we have to risk its dreams. I hope that it's enough.

When we hurry into *Hansel and Gretel* to find Homer and warn him that it's time to go, we're disappointed but not surprised to find that we're too late. We're also relieved.

The village square, the buildings and pubs that were so full of liveliness and laughter, are empty. Homer—and all the ghosts who were here in the village that first day I entered—has already gone.

Far from Glimmer 5 across a lonely galaxy, three witch hunters—who've survived entrapment in a snow globe and an escape from the belly of whale— are meeting with top space agencies to discuss how to rescue seven people plus a ghost from outer space, so that they can help to save the world.

It is not going well.

The people in charge are just getting used to the idea of witches in the first place. It's hard for them to get their minds around witch hunters, too, and how those witch hunters could *help fight a black hole. Not to mention, the technology to cross the galaxy is far beyond their grasp; no one can duplicate Rufus Glimmer's machines. Finally, there are budget concerns.*

In the end, the world's leaders grant Raj and the boys three rickety old shuttles that can only make it to where the moon once was. Raj and the boys have to make the best of it, which is not much. And so, on a wing and a prayer, Raj writes a letter to the editor and sends it to as many papers as he can. He writes about the world's witches and the kids—Rosie, Aria, and Germ—who destroyed almost all of them with a flashlight, and a slingshot, and whale friendship. And then he waits for the world to respond. He wants his letter to make the League of Witch Hunters grow, even if that League is running out of time.

In cemeteries, living people chat with their dead relatives for the first, and possibly last, time. Far beneath the Sea of Always, ghosts in every moment of the past hear rumors of the future and wait on the fate of the world. In Seaport Middle School, kids and ghosts make friends and share rumors. The most stunning is that students Gemma (Germ) Bartley and her quiet friend Rosie Oaks have been secret warriors all along, and are off fighting the world's most fearsome things.

On the morning when the fate of the world is decided, the kids don't notice the trees outside the school pointing branches at the sky. Then again, very few people notice this anywhere—the birches in Siberia, the fir trees in Sweden, the old oak in the Bartleys' yard—all the trees telling people to look. The kids don't see how, miles above, an owl is crossing the sky.

On a mountainside in the Alps, a woman with small hands and tiny gifts stands on a stone terrace and watches the night close in. She's haunted, staring at the view of everything she's done. Preoccupied as she is with what's above her, it's not unusual that she should see the owl long before anyone else would notice it.

It lands on the rail of the terrace where she stands, and hoots at her in a mechanical way.

She walks to it and reaches out her hand.

CHAPTER 29

ack in Seaport, when I was little, I used to crawl into tiny spaces to hide. I'd climb into the hollow of a tree, or curl up with my knees to my chin under the dining room table, and watch the world from my cozy spot—hidden, secretive, a small spy gazing at the big world.

I feel like all of Glimmer 5 is this hidden space as we wait for the news Zippy will bring. Knowing what waits for us if he's successful—a journey, a battle, an awful witch no one's ever even seen—makes the stillness and silence of this planet suddenly feel so safe. I savor it while it lasts.

It's four nights since we sent the owl. We're taking shifts to watch for him through the long, dim dusk. Above, the stars circle wildly and I watch the gorgeous bright universe, feeling happily small. I'm nestled against a nook in the hill, cross-legged, while Wolf runs across the horizon with my moonstone glowing from his neck. He's restless tonight, even more than usual, circling the lake like he can't sit still. I wonder if he's afraid.

"Want some company?"

I look up to see Ebb, who waits for me to nod, then drifts down onto the ground beside me. Flit leaps to his shoulder and starts to peck his ear.

"She likes you even more than she likes bread crumbs," I say. And then I add, with a smirk and a little courage, "So do I."

"You like me more than bread crumbs? I'm honored." Ebb's mouth tilts up at one side in a smile, and he tries to put his hand on top of mine. But of course, we're not in the museum anymore; I'm not a figment, and his fingers pass right through mine. Ebb's smile fades. Only in the basket we're about to throw away could we ever even touch.

There is a cluster of feathers close to where we're sitting—shed by some passing space goose. Ebb scoops them up, sort of *pushing* them forward with the energy from one hand, then blows on them. They drift above his palms, their fine feathery tufts quivering. He pushes them up into the air, and they fall around me like snow.

I smile. "You're getting good at that."

"When I'm able to direct it, it's like wind blowing into a sail. With more ghosts, we could do more—like, make a bigger push. We could help. With the fight."

This is why I can't help but like—like *like*—Ebb. He's been trying to help me since the moment I met him. Since even before that.

"She's not upset, by the way." He clears his throat. "Zia. She says it doesn't have to be weird. She says she probably only liked me because I was the only other ghost around anyway. Well, besides Fabian."

I nod, glad, smirking, and then shaking my head. "I'm still not a ghost, though," I say.

"You *are* inconveniently alive," Ebb jokes, but wistfully. He puts his hand beside mine, and it's enough. For now, at least, we're here. One day we'll have to say goodbye, but not tonight.

I think about my mom and dad, and something Wanda said about moonlight one of the nights we all stayed up talking. She says moonlight is magic because it's a promise even in the dark. She says she thinks something like moonlight lies on the other side of every ending. I wonder if it lies past the end of me and Ebb.

I open my mouth to say this, knowing as I do that I might tangle the words into a pretzel. But Ebb is looking away from me, squinting at some distant point across the sky. His body has gone upright and alert, and then he stands.

I do the same. Following his gaze, I see nothing. But Ebb has got better eyes than me.

"What is it?" I whisper.

He tilts forward as if he can close the gap by leaning.

"Something," he says. "Something's there."

I strain to see, and finally I spot a shape in the darkness far away. I gasp.

It's Zippy! Flapping madly for home.

I've never wanted to hug Ebb more. I am dizzy with relief.

Ebb, though, is still tensed as if to leap. Straining again, I soon see why. Our messenger is not alone. There's a shape behind, following. And then I see that there's more than one; there are a lot of shapes. The closer Zippy gets, the more of them come into view . . . more and more and more . . . an impossible number . . . thousands.

And soon they're close enough for us to make out what they are.

Crows.

"The Nothing King," Ebb says. "He's found us."

We stand, and run for the hotel.

The ground is doing strange things as we run. For a split second, I fear it's opening to swallow us.

"Rufus's shields," Ebb says. "They're rising."

Dodging them, but only barely, I watch the yellow rocks rotate themselves until they're underground, rusty silver cannons rising in their place. I leap away a moment before one shoots a burst of moonlight at the sky. Behind us, a swath of crows plummets down, destroyed.

The door of the hotel is thrown open as we approach. Aria stands in the doorway, half-asleep and gaping at the sky. To our right, Wolf, too, is loping in the same direction we are, looking over his shoulder in terror. Aria waves frantically as if it could make us faster. A moment later we barrel into her and into the lobby. My mom and Wanda are just arriving from the hall.

"What is it?" my mom gasps as Fabian and Zia appear through a nearby wall, and then she steps past us to look outside. "What has Jade done?" she whispers.

Wolf is the last one in. Aria slams the door behind him and turns the lock. For a moment we stand in silence, paralyzed, looking at each other.

And then it begins.

Thud.

Thud. Thud. Thud.

The crows hit the hotel like missiles.

Beside me, there's a *crack*. I see a black beak poking in through the wall by my head. Fabian, standing right near it, hurries through the same wall he came out of, disappearing.

"Weapons!" Aria yells.

We race to our rooms, where Clara and Germ are just stumbling into the hall, Clara with her tool kit and Germ clutching her stuffie. Flicking Flit on, I race ahead of them to the parlor window, then turn my back to the wall beside it for shelter. A crow barrels through the glass with a crash and skitters across the floor, where Flit becomes a cat and devours it. I peer outside. The defense lasers are shooting at the crows, but the crows are also dive-bombing the lasers—landing on them in hordes and ripping them out of the ground, and eating them.

They are, in fact, eating everything. They land on trees and gobble up the branches. They land on patches of dusty earth and gobble up the rocks. Perched on rusted machinery in the yard, they devour that, too.

More and more birds dive-bomb the window as Clara and I pick them off. Flit's now a bear, shredding them into mouthfuls, while Clara swings a hammer in one hand and a wrench in the other. Below, there are crashes and yells as the others join the fight.

A few more crows crash into the room, where we quickly destroy them. And then all goes quiet. It's so sudden that we can only look at each other in shock as we hear the others running up the stairs. Clara and I step back to the window as Aria races in behind us.

Looking out, we see that the crows have landed. The ground, the yard, the hangar are covered with them, roosting, ruffling feathers, nipping each other, letting out the occasional *caw*. As far as the eye can see, every inch of Glimmer 5 is a shivering, breathing, shifting blue-black. For now, they've stopped eating.

It's Aria who notices the sky first.

"Why can't I see the stars anymore?" she says. At first I don't get what she means, but then she draws my attention to a corner of the sky that's gone strangely blank. A cloud has moved in—though what it's made of, we can't tell. A moment later, the stars come into view again, but as we stand there confused, a flock of space geese rises on the horizon like they've been startled. And then—before our eyes—they fall from the sky, dead.

Whatever blankness is out there, it's coming closer. It moves from sky to land as dust clouds rise up and disperse, getting closer and closer. The moonlight in the pond lifts in a kind of whirlpool, then falls down again to settle. The tree Wolf set fire to creaks and falls over. Then a junked-out car at the edge of the yard opens and closes its doors.

"It's him," Clara says. "It has to be." I realize in horror what she means.

"He's almost here," Germ adds, holding her stuffie in front of her like a shield, her hands shaking.

We stare and stare, but we can only mark his progress by the things that rise and fall. *Shape-shifter*, Rufus said, made of *nothing*, so he can be *anything*. *He is the fear and the emptiness.*

And then, out in the yard just below our window, a human shape rises up from the dust, the silhouette of a man in a crow-feather cape that looks like it contains pure emptiness, a feather hood over a shadow where a face should be.

He stands still for a moment, his blank face steady as it's turned up toward us. And then he disintegrates into the ground and vanishes again. The window, what's left of it, swings slowly open on its hinges, then goes still. There is a long silence.

"He's inside," Clara breathes. As we stand there looking at each other, I feel a tickle on my arm, and turn, leaping as I see the sleeve of my pullover unraveling—the thread being pulled by some unseen force into the air and disappearing inch by inch. Clara takes her hammer and swings it at the air, and I get just a glimpse of him—a tendril of dust like a vine recoils, shivering and withdrawing through the window. We have only a moment to stare at each other in alarm as another dusty tendril comes snaking into the room, this time from the hallway. A parrot-shaped Flit attacks it fiercely, flying at it and retreating again and again, trying to get a bite, until it once again recoils.

For a moment the house goes still. "He's playing with us," Aria whispers.

From the corner of my eye I catch a shape in the shadows, beyond the threshold of the door. I turn to see the crow-hooded man watching us.

We turn to loose our weapons against him, but he collapses into the floorboards, and as he does, the floor beneath us shakes. Aria screams. Books fly from shelves, and a cupboard in the corner topples toward Germ just as

Wanda brandishes her ring and slices it in half. The glass shards on the floor lift and spin, slicing at our arms as Aria, screaming a high note, hurls a stone into the fray.

And then something goes wrong with Flit.

Bird-shaped, she flies to me and clings to my chest, claws digging in to the fabric of my shirt. She scratches at my rib cage as if she wants to get inside and hide. I thrust my flashlight forward, imagining her into a shield, but she only clings there, panicked and retreating when I need her most. "Flit," I gasp. "Stop . . ."

Outside, the crows have kicked up again into the air, and now they're eating and bombing everything in sight. Thousands go after the hangar walls, and the next moment the roof collapses with the deafening sound of metal being smashed inside. Aria moans. *Our ship.*

Still shaking Flit off, I jerk at the sound of a wall collapsing nearby, and turn to see that a hole has appeared beside the door.

But it's not the Nothing King who has put it there.

Rufus Glimmer is standing in the crumbled opening, his plastic laser gun in his arms. He takes aim into the swirling shards of glass and fires. Hit, the swirl of glass flies backward—through the window and clear across the field outside.

We stare in shock and all rush to the window, crowding together.

"I don't see him moving," Clara says, holding an arm against Aria protectively. Rufus comes closer to me, laser poised and ready, but all we see is crows, no indicator of where the witch might be. And then, turning to scan the room, I realize something I've been too scared, till now, to notice.

"Where's Wolf?" I say.

CHAPTER 30

We barrel down the corridor, slamming into each other as we stumble to my room.

The first thing I see is that the roof is gone. Peeled off like the top of a can. The second is that my brother's already here.

He stands next to my bed, trembling and looking at me, my backpack on his shoulder, with his blanket of glass dangling out of the top. A hand rests on his arm—the Nothing King is behind him, like a friend. Wolf shakes his head as if to warn me back. I shudder when I see my sewing basket in his arms.

Too shocked to move, I feel Rufus lift his laser beside me. The Nothing King's arm shoots like a vine toward him, and hits Rufus's skull with bone-cracking force. Rufus falls with a sickening thud to the floor.

The witch then wraps an arm around my brother and hoists him onto his back, where Wolf clings with his free hand.

I lurch for the basket, but it's too late. I'm only in time to meet Wolf's eyes as the two joined figures lift, soaring up and out of the roofless room.

For a moment, in the sky above, they're a picture that makes sense: a boy raised by witches, and a witch come to take him home. And then, blurring into the night, they're obscured, either covered by a dark cloud or becoming one.

The crows take off behind them, flapping in a cacophony of iridescent light. They rise into the air, in a wave of thousands of shapes, and are gone.

Behind me, my mom lets out a shattering wail. Wanda sinks to the floor next to Rufus, to see if he's breathing.

And only then do we know, for sure, all the things we've lost.

PART 3

CHAPTER 31

A twilit, lonely planet at the edge of the galaxy is no place to bury a man who fought for the world, whether he was a witch hunter or not.

And yet that's what we do.

Wanda leads the ceremony, which is short, and quiet, and of course small. She doesn't say much. I think we all feel too empty for it, like everything has fallen down around our ears, as we stand in a broken circle at Rufus's grave.

The hotel is wrecked in the distance behind us, its roof

gone, half its walls crumbled, its rubble still clouded by dust in the air. The hangar's no better. So many things destroyed. All that genius flattened in an instant. Part of me is glad that Rufus is not here to see it.

The dining room is our camp now. It's one of the only rooms with four walls and a roof. We'll sleep there tonight, having gathered blankets and pillows onto the floor.

But no one's ready to sleep. So in the yard, Wanda builds a firepit to warm us, piling up chairs, chopped-up doors, pieces of old cupboards. Germ holds Eliot Falkor to her chest as we huddle together, thankful to have found him under her bed, alive.

We sit in silence as the night grows long, keyless, Rufus-less, basket-less, and brother-less. Our ship has been smashed and the museum is gone. We're stranded, maybe forever, unless the Nothing King returns to finish us.

My mom surveys the scene with circles around her eyes.

"Wolf didn't mean it," she whispers. "He made a mistake." I raise my eyes to Ebb, who's sitting across from me, hunched over with his arms crossed. He gives me a meaningful look like I am the thing he worries about most.

"It's hard to let go of what you know," he offers. "Witches are what he knows."

My mom takes a breath, then walks off into the distance, looking up at the sky as if Wolf might fall back out of it. About twenty yards past her, Aria kneels beside a flattened Zippy, poking and prodding. The owl is so obliterated this time, there'll be no building him back up, but she lingers a long time, studying him. Nearby, in the ruins of the hangar, Clara's been inspecting the Astral Accelerator. Tucked beneath the angled wing of a glider when the hangar roof fell, it's singed along one side and its lights are smashed, but it still looks something like a spacecraft.

"Do you think it's working?" I ask as she wanders back to the group.

"It depends what you define as 'working,'" she says. "The welded bits held, so mostly it's sound. The Glaciation Matrix is a mess, though, half-shattered. I could get the ship to travel; I just don't know if I could get it to travel without incinerating us. And we wouldn't know until we tried it. Anyway, what's the point? He's long gone."

"Even if you could go after him, you wouldn't have the key," Zia agrees. She's not trying to be cruel; she's just speaking the truth. She's been picking up unbroken plates and piling them up while Fabian floats around, looking more put out than usual.

But as we've talked, Aria has approached the edge of

our circle. It takes us a while to notice the look on her face, but one by one, we do, gazing up at her from the fire. Her expression is too striking to miss: tense, and serious, and on the verge of saying something. I cross my arms over my chest. I don't think I can take one more piece of bad news.

Aria tries to start a few times, and then stops, each time clearing her throat. She moves her hands against each other, and I realize they are cupping something.

"Zippy is done for," she says, and we nod, unsurprised. She continues to stand there; it's obvious she wants to say more. "But he brought something back."

I could swear every single hair on the back of my neck stands up. Sometimes you sense something life-changing before it comes.

Aria holds out her hand.

In her palm is a small, glowing silver circle with a twisting knot in the middle, delicate, almost impossibly intricate. It glows like the moon.

We all know what it is without asking, of course. And at the same time, we know we were wrong about Jade. And that when the Nothing King tracked Zippy, it wasn't because she told him to.

How could it have been? When she's sent us the key, after all?

CHAPTER 32

After eight weeks and four days since we landed here, we are leaving Glimmer 5. Overnight we've gone from stillness to urgency, from a forlorn quiet to a loud buzz of plans. The Accelerator might not catch the Nothing King, but then again, it might. Rufus once said, in his welcome video, the ship was three times faster than his fastest messenger. And many times faster than the speed of light.

Inside the ship, Wanda has installed the pressure suits she's been stitching and repairing since we got here. Clara worked on the Accelerator all night, getting it as ready as it's possible to be. Only the Glaciation Matrix remains half-broken, blinking like a warning where it sits in its slot. But, according to Clara, even if we stayed for *weeks*, she couldn't fix it. We have to take our chances. We have to go now.

Wanda and my mom have been packing up supplies: food, water, blankets. Germ's made a special bed in one of the ship's onboard compartments for Eliot Falkor, which puts Ebb's arrangements for Fred the spider (who will just ride in his pocket) to shame.

I stand by our launch spot practicing new moves with Flit, trying to solve whatever went faulty with her when we fought in the hotel. My heart's skittering so fast in my chest that I can barely hear myself think. I twist Flit into a whorl of light, and for a moment the light snakes up my arm as if I, too, am part of it. I shake it off, and Flit lands on the ground and shakes her feathers in annoyance.

We're leaving this place, I think. We're going home, if there's still a home to go to. And I find I am both so ready and not ready at all.

"I'll keep an eye on the heat," Clara says, hunched over the back of the ship as I walk up to her and Aria. They're both staring at the Glaciation Matrix. "If this doesn't hold up, we'll know it. The ship will start to heat up and melt before incinerating us."

"So before we're exploding toast, we'll know we're about to be exploding toast," Aria interprets helpfully, giving me a side-eye. "At least our fiery death won't be unexpected."

Our new plan, admittedly, is not much of a plan. We no longer have the sewing basket to use as a lure. We don't have the element of surprise—at least, not surprise that we exist. Not to mention that our weapons appear to be almost useless against the Nothing King.

"Almost useless is not the same as completely useless," Germ offers when I say this out loud, standing by the ship as the last tweaks are made.

"We just have to get there, is the plan," Wanda says. "Get there before it's too late, and then fight." She puts a hand on her hip as we all gather, the last of our preparations done. My mom stands beside her. "I keep telling myself he's the worst witch in creation, but . . . he's also—"

"The only witch," my mom finishes for her, and Wanda nods. "He's the last one. Even now, I don't know all there is about witches," Wanda continues, looking around at us, a quiet misfit group that's all that's left of the League of Witch Hunters. "But we've come this far."

Aria, beside me, leans over and hangs the black-hole key around my neck. I move to shake my head, to refuse to be the one to carry it.

"You started this hunt, Rosie," she says. "It feels like you should be the one to end it. If you can."

I look around at the group. Everyone, even my mom, seems to agree with this. Aria looks down at Flit, who's nudging me, nagging me.

I've got something I need to say to everyone, and even Aria probably won't like it. But Flit won't stop with her insistent pecking till I do. Finally I say it.

"I know we're in a rush to get to Earth. Like, the greatest rush of all time. But there's a stop we need to make along the way."

They all look at me, and wait for me to explain.

As we gather for launch and survey our ship one last time, the Astral Accelerator doesn't look like much.

Its silver main doors squeak more than hiss as they open. Inside, the seats have been patched back together, and the control room, though functional enough, looks like it could be out of a movie from the eighties, with lights and controls blinking steadily. Not to mention, it smells a little bit like old cheese.

Outside, Zia and Fabian stand off to the side of the boarding ramp, waiting to say goodbye (though, Fabian clearly sees this a formality).

"It's going to be so boring without you all," Zia says as I approach her.

"Will you be okay here with everything like it is?" I ask. We've invited them to come with us, but they've both chosen to stay. Given the choices, I don't blame them.

"We'll fix it up," Zia replies. "We're ghosts, so we don't need much." Zia scans the landscape, the broken hotel, the debris-littered plain. "There's no hard feelings, Rosie. Rufus was a dreamer . . . and you're a dreamer too. I like that; I think this is the kind of place that a dreamer could make something grand of. Come back sometime if all goes well. We'd love to see you again."

"I hope your stay was out of this world," Fabian says stiffly to each of us as we filter toward the ship. We all take last long looks around the landscape; it might be the last time we set foot on solid ground. Even Glimmer 5's emptiness seems a bit cozy now that we're leaving it.

One by one we turn and climb aboard our ship, which domes over our heads like a snug bubble, its freshly polished windows wide and clear. I fight the nervous habit of checking for my backpack—it's gone. And I think of *The*

Witch Hunter's Guide to the Universe, left on the desk in my room. (I know it by heart, and if we don't make it, at least it will survive.) Aria and Clara settle into the cockpit, and the rest of us filter into seats in the back as their voices come over the intercom.

"I'm driving, Peanut," Clara says, not knowing the ship's mic is on. There's the sound of shuffling as they switch navigator and captain seats. "You're crowding me," Clara adds as she settles into her spot.

"You know this is a ship built for ghosts, right?" Aria retorts. "I can't be, like, nonexistent size."

Settling in beside me and buckling in, Germ looks at me and smirks, and we see Aria glancing back from the door of the control room at us with a deadpan look.

"Please stand clear of the closing doors," a smooth robotic voice announces a moment before the doors squeak shut. "If you are one of our human passengers, please note that gum is prohibited. Ghosts who are heading to their final and eternal place of residence, any gum you died chewing is ephemeral, so feel free to chew away. The trip to Limbo takes approximately two hours, depending on the flow of cosmic dust. Please enjoy your flight. We hope your journey is out of this world."

Our group settles into the ship, crowded but not

cramped. The ship is made to watch and wonder from. So, as small as it is, the big sweeping views out the window distract us. The backs of all the seats are printed with a kind of tourism logo: *Limbo. Not the Best Outcome, but Also Not the Worst.*

"Their marketing could use some work," Germ says, tucking Eliot Falkor into his compartment, then propping her teddy bear behind her head. My mom and Wanda are in front of us, while Ebb is on my other side. Which means Germ keeps waggling her eyebrows at me. And even though we're headed on a mission that might involve being incinerated, I'm a little bit excited to have the seat next to the boy who I like, and who likes me.

"Initiating power," Clara announces through the mic, and beneath us the Accelerator rattles to life, sounding like Germ's brother David's Camaro after the muffler fell off. Clara's voice trembles just slightly, which is not reassuring. We can hear her flicking several more switches. Aria glances back at us apologetically.

"Initiating lift," Clara says.

Now the ship really begins to shake and jerk as it thrusts upward unsteadily. It tilts one way and then the other like Zippy did—but now all of us tilt with it—and then it lifts and drops so fast that I think I might be sick.

Finally it lifts again, veering so wildly as we pass over the hill, I think we'll crash into it.

"Hold on," Clara booms, pulling at the levers up front but keeping her cool. Finally things smooth out, and the shuttle makes progress. Through the huge windows, we watch Glimmer 5—and Zia and Fabian—fall away below us. I can just see the tiny shape of Rufus's makeshift gravestone across the plain.

Then comes a deafening whoosh as we start moving forward.

"Usually there's noise cancellation," Aria yells back to us. "That's kinda broken. Things should quiet down once we turn off the thrusters." She grimaces a smile back at us, trying to be encouraging.

"We're gonna die, aren't we?" Germ asks. Then she glances at Ebb, and swallows. "Sorry, Ebb. Not that being dead is so bad."

"No offense taken," Ebb says.

"I don't guess we'll ever see this place again," I say to both of them.

"No, I don't think so," Germ replies. And the feeling is thrilling, and scary, and a little bit sad. She sits for a minute. "Can you even picture it?" she asks. "Actually going home? Actually winning? Then growing up and living in the suburbs or something? It makes me worry, the fact that I can't even picture it. Like, if I can't picture it, it can't happen."

I hesitate. To be honest, I can't picture it either . . . and imagining is supposed to be my gift.

Soon we're rising beyond the haze of Glimmer 5's atmosphere, and then even the rubble of the hotel becomes too tiny and distant to see. We lurch to full speed and head into the darkness as the reality settles in that this rusty, rickety, singed piece of metal is the only thing protecting us from the vast airless space around us.

Germ hands me her teddy bear.

I stare down at it, then up at her as she nods encouragingly. After a moment, to please Germ, I give it a hug. When I do, it begins to glow. And the glow wraps all around me, making me go warm and soft. And I feel, suddenly, okay.

"That's amazing," I say, feeling calmer already.

Germ takes the teddy back matter-of-factly. "Love is my superpower," she says casually, as if it were obvious. And I know she's right, and it always has been.

We fly, though not on a direct course, in the direction of home. Whether it's still there or not is anybody's guess. Before we get there, Aria and Clara plan to navigate us to the one stop we have to make on the way.

We set a course for Limbo.

CHAPTER 33

"Is it warm in here, or is it just me?" Germ asks.

"I don't get warm, I'm dead," Ebb replies unhelpfully.

"It's warm," my mom says from the seat in front of us, fanning herself with her hands and glancing around the ship, looking anxious. It's been heating up for the last hour.

Personally, I've been wanting to think it was all in my head. But Aria keeps throwing worried glances at us from the cockpit, and I know we're all wondering if we'll even make it to Limbo at all before the Accelerator melts. I flick Flit nervously along the aisle, both of us restless.

"I've been thinking," Ebb offers, "if Homer and a few ghosts do come with us, we could push our energy together to sort of . . . propel ourselves toward the Nothing King and then *push* him toward the black hole. Like a strong wind." My mom and Wanda turn to kneel in their chairs and rest their arms on their seat backs, listening. "I just need a few minutes with the ghosts to teach them how to do it," Ebb goes on, "the same way Zia showed me."

Wanda, my mom, and I look at each other. It's a good plan, as far as I can tell. I just feel nervous that if it doesn't work, I'll have taken us out of our way and wasted valuable time.

"It'll only be a few of you," my mom says, "so it may not be this huge blow to him. But it might be enough to get the upper hand so the league can do the rest with our weapons. You and Homer and whoever he gathers up, you'll be the forward charge."

Her words make me anxious; the forward charge is the first to rush into danger. But Ebb nods eagerly, glowing brighter than I've ever seen. And because I know him, I understand why. After countless years of being on the sidelines, the ghosts are going to fight.

"Mind you don't get past the event horizon," Wanda warns. "Once you've crossed the threshold, there's no escaping the pull of the hole. Even for ghosts."

"You blow him in the right direction, Ebb," my mom says. "And then we"—she looks around at me and Germ and up toward the cockpit—"will give him everything we've got at exactly the same time. We get him into the hole." She turns her gaze to me. "And Rosie will lock it up."

"Yeah, about that," I say. "How will I find the keyhole?" I worry that to get close enough to lock up the black hole, I'll have to cross the threshold, too.

"I think when you see it," Wanda says, "you'll know."

"And if that means getting too close and risking getting sucked in," my mom says, "Wanda and I will take over. If it comes to that, Rosie, give the key to me."

I look at her. I know this is hard for her to say to me. But it's even harder to hear.

"And what about Wolf?" Germ interjects. "What do we do about Wolf?"

The circle grows silent.

"We avoid hurting him if we can," Wanda finally says. "But ultimately we do what we have to do. It's Earth that's at stake."

My mom turns and sinks down in her seat, silent. Feeling suddenly claustrophobic, I unbuckle, get up, and walk to the front of the ship. I crouch beside Aria, who reaches out and holds my hand.

"At least when we stop," she says, "we'll cool down. Shouldn't be much longer."

We're silent for the last stretch of our journey, as we approach the outskirts of Limbo. We know we're close because Aria's navigation equipment tells us so, but also because the air around the ship gets denser and foggier as we go.

"How many ghosts do you think Homer rounded up?" Aria asks.

"Maybe a dozen?" I answer uncertainly.

Aria nods, thinking her own thoughts. "Well, we used to be only three people in a whale," she says, "and we did okay." We exchange shaky smiles.

We strain our eyes into the haze, hoping for our first sight of Limbo. I wonder if it will be anything like Rufus showed in his video, bright and beautiful. Secretly I harbor the wish—the one I can never stop making—that my dad will be there waiting for me, now that I know cloud shepherds don't always get things right.

Up ahead, a shape is looming out of the fog, round like a planet but dim. Clara glances over at Aria and me quizzically.

"Is that it?" she asks. Nobody answers. Because what we are looking at is really no place at all. It's just a huge ball of gas and mist, and nothing more. "This can't be right, Peanut. You must've navigated us wrong."

"The locator says this is the place," Aria replies.

"This is not a place, it's a soup." Nevertheless, Clara steers us into thicker and thicker fog.

"We just have to reach the pinging," Aria says, pointing to the radar screen on the console, "about five hundred yards in. Looks solid."

"I'll pull us in," Clara says doubtfully, "but the visibility's nil." She bites her lip as she weaves us into a mist so thick, I fear we'll never find our way out again.

This is a place to get lost in forever, I think. A moment later, as if reading my mind, the ship's navigation instruments hum to sleep.

"We're somewhere not on any maps now," Aria murmurs. The whole ship seems to have gone silent.

"I'll try to head toward the point where we saw the last ping," Clara says.

We drift along for another few minutes, and it's as if we're all holding our breath. And then—just as I start to picture what being lost in a fog forever might actually entail and how quickly we'd run out of food—a dark space opens around us, like a cave of clear air inside the mist. Up ahead we see, with relief and dismay, where the ping came from. It's nothing but a small wooden dock.

"The boats from the museum," I say, "they must arrive here." I've told them about the underground river of mist. But I didn't picture the destination like this, forlorn and in the middle of nowhere. We pull up to the dock, and the ship gives a guttural clunk as Clara powers it down.

All but for Ebb, we don our space suits. One by one, we climb out of the ship onto the dock, Ebb making sure to stay back from the mist's edge, since one misstep into Limbo's mists could lose him his chance of ever moving Beyond.

Somewhere buried deep in the fog, we hear moaning. *Ghosts.* Taking a few steps toward the sound, I find my left foot suddenly touching nothing, and Aria has to grab me back before I fall through the mist into thin air.

Clara studies the dock beneath us. "It only stretches about ten feet, and then it ends. On all sides, only fog."

"It's probably only for ghosts to enter," Wanda says. "Nothing solid here at all."

"But how can we reach Homer if we can't go in?" I press, on the edge of panic. We've spent all this extra time to come here, and now there's no way to even reach the ghosts we've come to retrieve.

"Homer?" Ebb calls into the mist. The moaning continues, many voices joined together but none of them responding to us.

"Homer?" I yell louder. Germ winces and points at her ears because when I yell through the speakers of my helmet, I also yell through the intercom into everyone's eardrums. "Sorry," I mouth.

Ebb stares up at the wall of fog. "I'll need to go in and find them," he says. "That's really our only chance."

His eyes settle on mine. And then after a moment, I realize that *everyone* is looking at me. I'm the one who talked with Homer and chose to come here. I'm the one they want to make the decision.

I shake my head. "I don't know," I whisper, glancing up at Ebb. I flick on Flit. She glows at my feet, and as I watch her, she watches me. And I know what she's trying to communicate without even moving a muscle. My heart believes in Homer, is the thing. My heart believes that his unfinished business is with us.

Ebb, still watching my eyes, steps forward decisively.

"If I'm not back within an hour, it means I can't leave. You'll have to go without me."

My breath flutters in my lungs. Germ and Aria clasp their arms together. Ebb walks to the edge of the dock, and turns his back on the fog for a moment to say goodbye to us.

He looks at each person—me last, holding my gaze a moment before he backs off into the fog, and vanishes.

As we wait on the dock, Germ and Aria sitting beside me with our heads huddled together, the moaning in the fog continues. Around us, the ship creaks, and occasionally there's a foreboding *zap* from the Glaciation Matrix.

I try not to think of how Ebb might already be lost to us forever. But then, as we sit, something begins to change—the fog itself. Little by little, the gap in the mist is shrinking. The haze is closing in on us.

"I think it's trying to squeeze us out," Wanda says. "I think the living aren't supposed to be here too long."

Misty tendrils stretch across the Accelerator's windows as the minutes tick past.

"What happens if the gap closes completely?" I ask.

"I have a feeling we never find our way out," says Wanda. She casts a look at me. "We can't wait much longer, I'm afraid, Rosie."

"Rosie," Clara says hoarsely, "it's almost been an hour. I don't think he's coming back."

I shake my head. "We can't leave," I say.

But Clara climbs aboard and begins to power things up, the spacecraft humming to life.

And then something looms up at the front of the ship, throwing its arms out as if at the glass, and we all startle in surprise. It's Ebb.

He turns to float toward us, and for a moment I think he's grimacing in terror, his eyes are so wide. But then I see he's smiling—beaming, in fact. We get to our feet.

"Anybody with you?" my mom asks urgently. "We've got to head out."

"They're coming," Ebb says, still oddly beaming, just as I see another shape emerge from the fog. Homer! And now I see that there are other shapes emerging behind him too.

"I've brought some friends, Rosie," Homer says.

He winks at me, then takes a deep breath to concentrate. He raises his hands and, using the technique he's clearly just learned from Ebb, uses them to push the mist back . . . and back . . . and back.

As the clouds curl away from the dock, I see that Limbo's not a lonely place at all, and my heart soars. Thousands of ghosts are gathered before us, hovering in a crowd and waiting. Homer turns to grin at me.

"Turns out, Limbo's as boring as Hades," he says. "These here are the ghosts who'd rather take their chances with

you lot." My eyes meet Ebb's in shock as Homer turns serious. "And anyway," he adds more solemnly, "they're ready
to fight for the world they knew, even though they'll never
live there again. Ebb told me the plan, and I've spread it
to the rest of 'em. In the meantime, I hear we're on a tight
schedule."

"How will they all fit on the ship?" Clara asks, tense.

"We don't need to fit in," Homer replies simply. "We'll
just hold on te the back. Don't mind us a bit."

And then he gives us a thumbs-up and leads the crowd
toward the stern of the ship.

This is how, so many light-years from home, the ghosts
of Limbo—a motley group of thousands who have never
solved their unfinished business and who have lost their
chance to go Beyond—join the League of Witch Hunters
to fight for the world.

"Initiating power," Clara announces as the ship shudders once again to life. We hurry into our seats while
the automatic voice talks about the closing doors. Once
settled, I look a question at Ebb. How will he handle
knowing that he'll never go Beyond?

But he thinks my eyes mean something different, and
he answers a question I don't ask.

"Your dad wasn't there, Rosie," he says.

Departing Limbo, I'm pretty sure we create a spectacle the galaxy has never seen: the ghosts hold on to each other in a chain, with Homer at the very front grasping the back of our ship.

As we pull away and thrust slowly forward, our fellow fighters stream behind us like the tail of a kite. When we are free of the mist, I see that they stretch for miles across the darkness of space. I watch them through the back window, the glow of them almost bright enough to blind a giant . . . or maybe even a witch. And I feel, for the first time since the night the black hole chased us to the bottom of the sea, like we can actually beat the Nothing King after all.

CHAPTER 34

It's the only time I'll ever fly across the galaxy, so I wish I could see it, planets drifting past us, a glimpse of the rings of Saturn or the icy blue glow of Neptune. But since we're moving faster than the speed of light, it's not that kind of ride.

I think about how Rufus must have felt when he crossed it all in the other direction, setting off from Earth, fleeing witches in search of a place to call home. I wonder if he felt excited or only just scared to reach the unknown. I think about how brave he was to make a life across the galaxy and build a dream out of nothing but a gray rock floating in space. *A space travel destination for all of human-kind to enjoy*, run on the magic of moonlight. I can see the appeal for a dreamer like Rufus, a place where the only limits of what you could build for people to see would be what you could imagine. Like the best theme park ever made.

On board, the ship feels static and still, while outside, the galaxy blurs past so fast, it looks like endless beams of light. It also feels *hot*. The temperature inside the ship has crept up another degree, according to Aria, and we're all overheated and anxious and quiet. From the back, I can see Aria hunched over her console with tense shoulders, her hands clutching the panel as if she could keep the heat at bay by will alone.

Sitting next to my mom now, while Ebb keeps moving in and out through the back of the ship to make plans with Homer, I lay my head on her shoulder.

"We've got strength in numbers now," she tells me. "He won't expect that." Hands folded together, she studies her fingers, which are trembling.

"Eighty-six degrees," Aria announces to the rest of us in back.

I keep my head on my mom's shoulder, and her arm stays around me. I never got to do this as a kid, and it's too late to make up for all our lost time. But I enjoy it while it lasts. I'm trying to picture what waits for us ahead, or what becomes of my family when we face Wolf, but I can't.

Though my flashlight is in my pocket, Flit has flicked herself on and is sitting on my lap. She cuddles against my stomach, looking like there's nowhere else she'd rather be, like just being with me makes things okay. And—maybe just a little—I feel that way about her too, as strange and flighty as she is. For whatever reason, I feel safe enough that I fall asleep.

When I wake, it's to utter silence.

The ship's engines are quiet. The temperature has miraculously dropped. We are standing still.

For a moment I panic, wondering if we've lost power. And then I see that everyone else is already at the front of the ship, staring out the window.

"What—" I say, and Ebb and Germ look back at me while Aria waves me forward. I walk up behind them to see what they're staring at, and catch my breath.

The black hole lies off our starboard side, distant but enormous, like an open mouth surrounded by a ring of light. A streak of light hangs out of it like a long noodle of spaghetti.

"It's eating something," Aria says.

"Stars," Clara replies gravely. And I wonder, my stomach churning, if this is how the black hole ate the moon and its goddess, sucking them in and spitting out the light like chewed-up food. Even from here you can see how the hole is a place there's no coming back from.

"This is as close as I feel comfortable getting," Aria says. "I'm staying well away from its pull."

And then we see something else, a planet ahead of us, luminous against the emptiness around it, as blue as a bluebird and full of life.

Germ grabs my hand and clutches my fingers, because everything we love outside of the people on this ship is there on Earth. And snaking around it is a shadow.

The shadow is mottled and crisscrossed, like a web, and it shimmers and moves and surrounds the world. I try to understand what I'm seeing. The strangest thing is how Earth, too, is moving. Sideways, as if it's being tugged.

"Are those . . . ?" I ask.

"Crows," my mom answers.

How many crows would it take to cover the earth? A million? A billion? Whatever that number is, that is what we're looking at.

The crows are dragging Earth in their claws like they

would drag a snake, across the horizon and in the direction of the vast void of the hole. I think back to a night by a fire at the beginning of the world, Dread and the Time Witch talking about the web the witches laid around the world and the Nothing King's return. *He has only to grab hold of the world and drag it back in.*

I couldn't really imagine it till now.

"But where's the Nothing King?" Germ asks. "Did we beat him here?"

Clara moves her fingers on the console, and before us floats a hologram, a closer image of the shifting restless shimmer of the crows. There's a strange coordination to the way they move, like they can read each other's minds. As we watch, they stretch one way, then the other, like stretching a pair of arms.

"We need to wait for them to get closer to the black hole," Wanda says, "before we attack."

We swallow, because that means waiting till Earth is closer too. And at the rate the crows are moving, that means soon.

"How do you fight a cloud of crows bigger than a planet?" Germ whispers, hugging her teddy tight. But nobody answers . . . because nobody knows.

"Tell the ghosts to get ready," Wanda says to Ebb, her

face drawn and tense. "When the crows are within range of the hole, we'll send you in. For the rest of us, it's time to disembark."

We gather our weapons and hurry back into our space suits (Germ tucking Eliot Falkor against her heart in a special pocket Wanda made). I'm suddenly terrified and weary, like I've been awake for a thousand years. My body trembles, thinking of my brother. *Where is he?*

I turn the dial at my wrist, and oxygen begins to hiss into my mask.

"Opening doors," Clara says. One by one, we use buttons along our wrists to direct ourselves outside the ship and into the weightless expanse of space. We come to float in a kind of line, staying close together, dwarfed by what's in front of us. And then we see them, the ghosts moving in a wave from the back of the ship to surround us. They stretch around and flank us, ghosts as far as the eye can see—with Ebb and Homer in the lead. My heart lifts.

In the distance, the crows around the world move in a new way, as if startled. They spill into a shape: arms, legs, a cloak, a hood, an empty place where a face should be. For a moment, the whole shimmering mass goes still.

"They've seen us," says Wanda.

"They're one and the same," my mom breathes in wonder. "The Nothing King and his crows. He's all of them at once."

We try to grasp it, that the Nothing King is a million creatures ready to devour us.

Then, like exploding drops of ink, the crows fly off Earth and scatter, then regather in a giant horde that moves toward us at incredible speed.

"If that's true, he's moving fast," Wanda says.

Ebb, standing at the head of his army, looks to us for a signal, and Wanda nods. He meets my eyes for a moment, and then yells something to the ghosts that I can't quite hear. Crackling with electromagnetic energy, the ghosts surge forward, hurtling toward the crows with greater and greater speed as the crows hurtle toward *us*.

I can almost see the wind grow before our luminous companions; the crackling energy from all their hands outstretched forms a kind of light shield around them—like the one made by Flit once but a thousand times larger—sparking like a moving lightning storm.

The ghosts leave a sound like thunder behind as they soar toward the massive body of crows, the ghosts and the billion birds heading toward each other on a collision course. As the two meet, the crows waver like they're being blown backward. And then they spread out, the mass of black wings like arms reaching for an embrace.

As they surround the ghosts, the crows dive in from all sides, pecking, devouring, smothering. And soon the ghosts are lost and buried in the sheer number of the birds, and we can't see them or their crackling light at all.

"They're eating them up," Aria cries. A few ghosts race back toward us—Ebb among them, but not Homer.

And then the crows disperse, scattering in all directions like a supernova.

There is nothing left behind.

The ghosts are gone. Swallowed. Just like that.

CHAPTER 35

A gas cloud looms near where the ghosts disappeared, and now the birds race into it and change shape, dissolving into cosmic dust. The cloud grows and grows and grows, moving toward us, and what was crow iridescence a moment ago becomes lightning, immense cosmic storms churning within the depths. The cloud towers higher and higher as it comes toward us.

The wind begins to blow again. Only this time, it's blowing at us. For a moment, we're too stunned to act.

"Weapons!" Wanda yells, just as Ebb reaches us, shaking his head at me. *Homer's gone.*

Lined up side by side in empty space, watching the dust storm approach, I feel our smallness. Our weapons have never felt more absurd. And Flit is the most absurd of all, clawing at my chest now and trying to crawl into it, like she did in the hotel. Even Germ's stuffie, as useless as it seems, stays where it's supposed to be. She holds it up in both her hands, getting ready to direct its lasers.

Ebb and I look at each other. He reaches for my hand, and I can almost feel his fingers go through mine. And then he pushes energy forward, and I push Flit away, making her a shield. It's Aria who shoots into the dust cloud first, singing out a high and agonized note as she hurls a rock into the fray.

The rock disappears, and the cloud keeps coming.

We all attack together now—my mom launching arrows in a glorious arc, Aria slinging rocks, Germ shooting lasers out of her stuffie's eyes. Wanda gets ahead of us, ready to take slices out of dust, and Clara hurls wrenches from her pack.

But while our weapons hit the cloud like meteors, it just keeps coming, and blowing toward us.

The dust is past us and all around us now, knocking

us apart. I watch Germ's stuffie fly from her hand. Wanda gets knocked sideways, her pressure suit bursting at a seam, and goes spinning off into space.

"Retreat!" my mom screams. But it's too late. Behind us I hear an explosion, and I turn to see the Astral Accelerator lightning-struck and burning.

Clara, hit by flying debris, goes limp, and Aria grabs her out of the stream of zooming, deadly shards just as Aria's own suit is punctured. They, too, go spinning away.

One by one, the League of Witch Hunters is being knocked in different directions, weightless and lost to the vast emptiness. Ebb races forward into the cloud, hands raised before him, and disappears, and then my mom is knocked away and it's just me and Germ being pelted and pushed, crackling electricity around us.

Germ lurches for my hand, and I lurch for hers. But before we reach each other, she's swept away.

And then I, too, am spinning, blown far from the burning ship. I lift my flashlight and blast Flit downward like jets to right myself.

And come face-to-face with the Nothing King.

No longer a storm, he is the man we saw looking at us in the yard, in a crow-feather cape. Suspended in the air beside him—in a second feathered cloak as deep and empty-looking as the one its maker wears, only this one is winged—is my brother, a lost wild look in his eyes.

Somehow, he's breathing in space. I guess the breathing and the wings both are witch-given gifts. There were supposed to be thirteen witches to fight. But now there is one more.

Wolf watches me, my backpack in his arms. At his collarbone my moonstone glows. His fingers tremble as he twirls it in his hands, his new wings flapping behind him.

Wolf pulls open the backpack and grasps the blanket made of glass; whatever he's going to do with it, it's going to hurt.

I hold up my flashlight—and Flit—to shield myself. But just like before, Flit retreats, clawing against me, trying to hide.

With no choice, I fire up my jets, and flee.

I race farther and farther out to space, the Nothing King and my brother behind me.

Wrestling with my flashlight to get Flit to work, I hurl her at them as a missile, which the Nothing King catches and throws back at me.

I shoot Flit like a laser. The Nothing King deflects it into passing debris from the Accelerator, and the impact makes an explosion so loud that my hearing blinks out on one side. Shards of the explosion come toward me. My flashlight is knocked out of my hand and goes spinning away. Satisfied, in a flutter of feathers the Nothing King and my brother turn away and race back to grab the earth, leaving me behind.

In the distance, I see the remains of our ship, flaming and turning to ash. I try to start my space suit jets, but they've died, severed by the fight.

We won't make it home. Not anymore.

My ship is gone. My friends are gone. I am alone.

And then a piece of metal hits me, and everything goes black.

CHAPTER 36

"Rosie."

There's a voice coming to me, fuzzy as if through a microphone. I don't recognize it, and I think I'm imagining it. My left ear is ringing loudly.

I'm floating on my back, looking up at endless stars. There's a searing pain along my side, and a bearded man beside me who I don't recognize, staring at me through the lens of a space suit. He's holding me by the hand.

I blink at him. He looks familiar and unfamiliar at the same time.

"Rosie," he says again.

I blink. My mouth tastes like dust. It feels like my throat is on fire.

"We met once briefly," the man says, "in a whale at the bottom of the sea."

Things are coming back to me. "We knew you'd all come back. We've been watching the skies for you."

I blink at him. And then I know: he's Wanda's friend who disappeared when we transported to Glimmer 5.

"Raj," I whisper. My voices rakes my throat like gravel. "From Raj and the Boys."

Raj grasps my arm, righting me. "The boys are on our ship," he says. "Where is everyone else? Wanda? Clara? We came to help you."

Now righted, I see a spectacle unfolding before us: in the distance, millions of crows, dragging Earth across the last bit of space to the edge of the black hole, unbothered by the people who came to fight them, too close to the end to catch now, even if our ship weren't gone.

"The League of Witch Hunters," I answer Raj, gazing in horror. "They're all gone. The league is over, destroyed. None of us left but me."

Raj squeezes my arm, a sadness crossing his face.

"No, Rosie," he says. "Not just you."

Gently, he turns me to look in the other direction, at a cluster of ships in the distance. Silver shuttles and stream-lined rockets. It looks like every spacecraft that belongs to Earth is here.

"This," Raj says, and gestures with his gloved hands, "is the League of Witch Hunters now."

I blink, disbelieving. I can't fathom it.

"We don't have weapons, we don't have moonlight. But we thought you might need our help."

"They're here . . . to help me?"

Raj shakes his head. "To join you. Because I told them a story. About two girls who set off to fight the witches of the world, and a third who joined them. Your story moved the world."

"I thought we were alone," I say, and begin to cry.

"What do you need us to do?" he asks.

My body burns with fear and gratitude as I look out at the hundreds of ships. They're waiting for me to tell them what to do, but even with them at my disposal, I don't know what to say. Every time we've been cornered since this whole thing began, I've imagined my way out of things, but I can't picture us out of this. We have no moon-light to fight with. My friends and my family are gone.

"We could have a million ships, but you can't beat a

void," I say, repeating a warning Rufus made. "So I don't
know what to do." Tears leak out of my eyes. For the world
and the whales and my friends and my family and the trees.

Feeling a small tickle at my chest, I look down to see
Flit snug against the front of my space suit. I place my
hands gently over her, relieved and shocked she's with me
even though my flashlight is gone.

"Thank you, Flit," I whisper. "Thanks for staying close."

It feels, strangely, as if I'm talking to *myself*—like this
brave bird squeezed against me reminds me of the parts of
myself that are the most strange and also the most free. I
think about the night I discovered Flit curled inside my
ribs; I remember her wings stretching along my arms. I
think about Rufus trying to light a pile of wood on fire,
and telling me that the hardest thing to do is transform a
thing into something else. I think how I used my stories to
turn straw into gold when I needed it most.

What's on the other side, once you do the hardest
thing you can do, which is change? How much do I trust
that there's light on the other side of an abyss? How much
do I believe that could be true?

And I think, there is only one story left I could possibly imagine.

I have to imagine a story about endings.

◆ ◆ ◆

"There's so much space they could be lost in," I say. "Take your ships, and go rescue the others if they're still alive."

Raj studies me, surprised.

I cup Flit in my hands as she stares up at me, suddenly alert, and ready—awkward, brave, strong, fierce, weird, clumsy Flit.

All this time, I haven't wanted to let her in. Now I invite her.

I open up my palms, and she slips inside my skin, lighting up my arms as she travels to my heart. The boundaries between us fall, no line where I end and she begins. I glow with the strength of her, and she stretches with the strength of me.

I spread my arms, and they are wings, not attached to a cape like Wolf's but a part of me. I stretch my feet, and they are claws.

Raj, in his space suit, watches me in awe. But that is small to me. Because I am not who I was.

I'm not worried about the same things as before; I am not afraid to stand out or to grow up; I'm not afraid to die. I am a bird, and a weapon. As the Brightweaver said, *There's only one thing and we're all it.* So why shouldn't I fly?

Leaving Raj behind me, I take off, as fast as light. Maybe faster. I must look like a comet to the world.

I race toward the black hole and its unstoppable pull, its spaghetti string of eaten stars and its mouth that might eat me too, but I do not slow down.

The crows know I'm coming. I meet them at the edge of the event horizon, and they cluster together in front of the world in a pulsing, breathing storm. I fly into the fray, dodging lightning as it strikes toward me, then snapping my beak around its glow. I eat electricity, and it courses through me.

The storm collapses in surprise. Around me, shapes swirl: clouds, then crows, then meteors. Spinning shards of ice, and mountains of searing dust.

Trying to get hold of me, the Nothing King changes from one thing to another, from creatures into wind, from weapons into weather.

But I change too.

CHAPTER 37

The Nothing King retreats. And I, Rosie Oaks, follow him.

Time and space do not matter to us. We barrel across valleys on unknown planets; we race across light-years.

In the sky he's a comet; I'm a streak of ice trying to smother him. In the rain forest on a distant world, he's an armored green insect and I'm a shining black bat tracking him. In an empty corner of the universe, he's a towering nebula and I'm the wind blowing it apart.

We use planets as stepping stones, we are impossibly small and infinitely large, we are timeless. We grow as small as molecules, as big as planets, and still I don't let him out of my sights. Everything Little One ever became, everything Flit ever tried to be, I slip into as easily as into water. Everything I can imagine, I am.

Do not count out the human imagination, says *The Witch Hunter's Guide.* And to fight the nothingness of the Nothing King, I don't.

He becomes a witch in white, running across the snow, and I become a seal swimming alongside the frozen shore, gnashing its teeth. He grows into a giant, and I hang from a thread of his sleeve, crawl into his robes, and launch spears into his skin. It is when I am sure I've got him that he strikes.

I'm a coyote tracking his snake scent across the desert, rattlesnake blood in my nose, when I see him under a rock, watching me. I am not afraid. I lunge and catch him. And, dangling from my mouth, he strikes.

I fall back. I feel the poison race from my cheek, where his fangs grip me, into my chest.

A fierce wind whips up as he rises and changes, now a man at last, and blows me across the ground. My body skids and scrapes along pebbles and dirt.

I feel something strong and bright leave me, and I look to see Flit lying limply by my side, unconscious. We lie across a dirt trail. I roll toward her, placing my hand on her chest. I feel her heart flailing, stopping, flailing again. Every part of me aches.

I sit up, Flit shining bright but dying in my hands, a pain in my chest where Flit—till a moment ago—soared.

I look around, dazed. I am somewhere that does not exist . . . but as I've learned, that doesn't make it less real.

We're in a fairy-tale forest, like the one in *Hansel and Gretel* . . . or a million other stories. There's a cottage in the distance where all scary things hide, waiting to eat a person up. It's a story and a cottage as old as words. A story to hold all the fear that we carry.

The Nothing King stands a little down the trail, watching me, still cloaked and faceless. And then Wolf comes out the cottage door, his winged cloak flapping. He's watching us, holding his jagged blanket of glass in his arms.

"Come away, o human child," the Nothing King says, taunting me with the words that beckoned me into the museum. His voice is in the air around me, like he's become the molecules. "You've proven a hard one to devour."

I feel the burn of the snakebite, deep in my chest. My pressure suit is leaking air and blood. The Nothing King kneels beside me but doesn't touch me. I feel his coldness around me, like everything that ever meant something disappearing.

He nods to Wolf.

"Wrap her up," he says. "Tear her piece by piece. Show me your devotion to the dark."

Wolf steps up beside us and lifts his blanket, all its pointed edges poised to pierce into my skin. My heart is breaking, and I move to shield myself. But Wolf looks at me, with a slight shake of his head, like he did in my bedroom back on Glimmer 5.

He shifts beside the Nothing King. And then he swivels, and lunges, and—with a wild cry—wraps the blanket around the Nothing King's arms.

And I realize, in that moment, it wasn't a blanket Wolf was making.

It was a plan.

CHAPTER 38

The forest falls away around us, like a movie set that has disappeared.

We're back in space, on the verge of the event horizon where we were before I changed, Earth spinning in the distance. Only, this time Wolf is on the Nothing King's back, his jagged weapon wrapped around the witch's neck. He is flapping his crow-wing cloak and trying to drag the Nothing King backward. He's failing. The Nothing King is fighting him off, trying to shape-shift and pushing him away.

As Wolf is shaken loose, he gets one hand free and reaches for the moonstone necklace at his collarbone. The gesture is so small, I normally wouldn't notice it. But Wolf knows witches. And I—even in this moment—am learning to know Wolf.

He holds the necklace forward as the Nothing King struggles. It's the only moment we have.

I gasp at the pain that claws my chest, and gaze down at my hands, where I still clutch Flit, limp, but breathing. And then, with both hands, I launch her into the air. She flaps her wings, flying her crooked way toward the necklace, and the two collide.

Flit's glow hits the necklace, which sends light flying at the shards of glass around the Nothing King's shoulders. And the blanket—or now, I see, the *net*—comes alight. Each piece of glass, each strand of thread, holds the light and shines.

Struggling in the net of light, the Nothing King screeches but can't wiggle free as Wolf drags him backward and away from me. And though Wolf struggles to keep hold, he's dragging the Nothing King swiftly into the distance, with wings beating harder and harder, fighting for every yard he gains, until they've gotten far *enough* and the black hole's gravity takes hold.

"Let him go!" I scream at Wolf, but he ignores me, still holding on to make sure it gets done. The hole's gravity is pulling them in now, Wolf no longer flapping his wings as they move faster and faster away, sucked deeper toward the dark.

"Wolf!" I scream again, uselessly, but I know that it's too late. There will be no escaping gravity now. Both Wolf and the Nothing King vanish.

A burst of light flares in the center of the black hole. And then the light goes out as my brother, and my bird, and the witch are swallowed into the void.

I stare, frozen, bleeding, disbelieving.

And then I see that something's floating down toward me from above, as gentle as a snowflake. It's a small ball of light as delicate as fluff. It hovers by my chest. In its glow, I can just make out a familiar coiling sphere of light waiting to be filled.

Clutching my stomach, I stare at it for a moment in shock and then feel for the key dangling from my neck. I tear it off its chain, place it gently into the sphere, and hope that that's enough.

In the distance before me, the vastness of the black hole swirls for a few seconds more, and then it collapses into itself. It blinks out, and then it's gone.

There's nothing but silence, and space, and stars, and Earth—peaceful and blue and safe.

And then I see the ships. First just one, and then a cluster of them. Coming to take me home.

CHAPTER 39

When the crows begin to fall slowly from space toward Earth, it looks almost like rain.

I watch through the window of Raj's ship—the remnants of the Nothing King, coming to an end like a meteor shower. Sitting down beside me, someone wraps a blanket around my shoulders, and I see that it's Aria.

The ship that has saved us is shiny and perfect, gleaming, functional, and not shabby or magical in the least. Most important, it hasn't been obliterated like the Astral Accelerator. And even better, it's taking us home.

The others are okay, we know, though other ships collected them. Ebb is with Clara and one of "the boys." Mom and Wanda are together. And Germ is here, sitting on the other side of me, bruised and battered but okay. Though she worries that Eliot Falkor has a headache.

The three of us don't speak about Wolf at first. I can't say the words. Around us, the ship purrs instead of putters as it gets underway.

"Not quite the balmy eighty-five degrees I'm used to on spaceships," I say, grimacing with pain where the ship doctors have stitched me up. I'm still hooked up to an IV that's fighting the poison in my skin—but I also have to smile.

"No Doritos like on Chompy either," Germ adds.

From the ship's window, we can't see anything left of the Accelerator at all. I suppose now it's nothing but shattered parts floating out in space.

"We'll be on the ground in a few hours," Raj says over the intercom.

"And not in the form of exploded toast," Aria adds.

We stare out the window at Earth—moonless, but still there, still whole.

"He loved us all along," I finally whisper.

Germ wraps her arms around me tight. I think about

Wolf, the two of us making a burst of light. But my heart is heavy.

"It's happening," Germ says. "Home. Life. The things we wanted."

I nod. But maybe I just can't grasp it. Or maybe I'm just too tired to try.

The ship hums quietly as we make our way to Earth. Even without its moon, it looks the same from above as it always has: blue, and white, and green, and perfect from far away.

But also, it is not at all the same.

CHAPTER 40

A helicopter brings us from the tip of New Hampshire, where we've all been in the hospital for three days, to Maine. We've been isolated, quarantined, tested for strange alien bacteria and changes in our brain chemistry. We've been debriefed by defense ministers and government people in suits, as we've told the story of Glimmer 5 and the Museum of Imagined Things. And now we're coming home.

The homey lights of Seaport glow up at us from the dark.

There are seven ghosts in the cockpit. The pilot tells us, making conversation, that once he got the sight, they started asking him for rides. He also says we're heroes, and famous. And that our lives will never be the same.

I feel like I am dreaming as we land softly on the grass behind my house on Waterside Road. Someone's turned its lights on to welcome us home, and in some ways, this feels stranger than landing on Glimmer 5. Maybe because I've longed for it so much, and seen it so many times in my mind.

Climbing out onto the lawn, my legs feel like jelly, my knees weak. We cover our heads in the strong wind of the copter as it lifts and flies away, and then the yard is quiet. This is the way we wanted it, to be left alone at first . . . for a few hours, at least.

We're standing only feet away from where (what seems like a million years ago) I burned my stories. I can hear the ocean churning past the cliffs, though it's louder than before.

"It's gonna be weird," Aria says, "to be in a world without witches or a moon."

"And where everyone has the sight," Ebb adds. Fred, having survived near certain death, scurries up Ebb's shoulder. My mom takes my hand.

And without Wolf, goes unspoken.

We stand there in the quiet yard looking at each other, wondering what there is to say.

"I'm not going to stay the night," Wanda announces, surprising us all. "I just wanted to see you all home. There's a car coming for me. I'm headed to New York, to meet with Raj and figure out what's next."

"What do you think you might do?"

Wanda looks upward, shrugs her shoulders, and sighs. "For once, I have no idea." She smiles. "There's talk of organizing the witch hunters from all over the world, to all be together at once. You're invited as keynote speakers, of course." She winks at me, because we all know I'd rather fight another witch than give a speech.

Our smiles rise, and falter, and rise again. It's hard to think about those who aren't here. Rufus and Wolf and all the ghosts.

A few minutes later, a taxi pulls into the drive, as if it's some kind of normal night. But Wanda lingers, reluctant to go, looking up at the blank night sky.

"I haven't given up on the moon yet," she says. "I haven't given up on *her.*"

We all look up, remembering the Moon Goddess and her light.

We all hug Wanda tightly, my mom last of all. And then she's gone. And things around us feel so normal, so peaceful—and impossibly strange. Tomorrow we'll be meeting with reporters, talking about all that's happened. But tonight we can rest.

"My mom is on her way," Germ says.

Mrs. Bartley's driving skills have never been the best, but the way she peels into the driveway a few moments later is one for the ages. Five Bartleys tumble out of the car at once, and Germ—running to the drive—is swallowed in the tangle of them. Soon everyone is crying, even her oldest brother, David, who used to find us annoying.

Only one figure hangs back by the headlights, a little more reserved, waiting to hug her.

"D'quan," Germ says, extracting herself from the knot of her family, and standing before him, suddenly shy. D'quan has always been a guy of few words, but I've never seen Germ at a loss for what to say. For all her talking about him all the time, she's now at a loss for words.

"I wrote you some poems," he says, fishing them out of his backpack. "One compares your freckles to lava."

Germ turns bright red. "Cool." Awkward silence. "I almost fell into a black hole," she says.

"Cool," D'quan replies. And then he slides his hand into hers.

Now we all lump together, hugging, my mom and Mrs. Bartley hugging longest, crying together.

"Thanks for bringing her back," Mrs. Bartley whispers. I cry too, though 2 percent of me wants to laugh because she's wearing her T-shirt that says *I'm Kind of a Big Deal.*

"We're eager to get Germ home," she says to Mom, then looks at me. "But we'll see you in a couple of days."

I nod, a little panicked. Germ and I have been together every single day since departing on our whale last summer.

But before I know it, she's leaving me, squeezing into the car with her brothers and D'quan and pulling away.

After we watch them go, my mom drops her hands to her sides.

"Let's get you girls situated," she says.

Clara and my mom trail into the house to set things up for sleeping. Aria and Ebb linger for a while, and then Aria too yawns, and heads toward the house.

Only Ebb remains.

"I haven't given up on the Moon Goddess either," he says.

Studying his face, I realize I agree. It isn't over with her. I feel like I am only waiting for what reveals itself next.

Despite myself, and wanting to take in this night forever, I'm almost sleeping on my feet.

"I guess I'll see you tomorrow night," he says.

"I'll see you then," I say with a happy twist in my heart.

We pretend to fist-bump, my clenched hand hitting nothing but air. And then Ebb floats away across the lawn and down the cliff trail, just like old times. He looks back every now and then to see me. And then he's gone.

That night, Aria, Clara, and I sleep in sleeping bags on the living room floor, reluctant to be apart. We wait for the moon to rise, we wait for the sparkle of the Beyond—but it doesn't come. And we talk about the future.

Their future, the one I visited on Chompy, no longer exists quite the way it did. But they say that when things settle down, they'll board one of the time whales and try to find their aunt and uncle in 2062.

"And then we'll maybe bring them back," Aria says. "If we can."

"You all could stay here," I say. "When you get back." My mom and I have already said this many times, hoping they'll say yes.

Clara looks at Aria. "I guess it depends what Aria thinks," she says. Which makes me smother a smile in my hand. Clara's never said it matters what Aria thinks before. But I guess anything can change, particularly when your little sister saves you from being pelted to death by space debris.

"We'll see," Aria says, casting me a satisfied look. We are, in many ways, exhausted, and at the same time too excited to sleep.

And that's how we end up being awake to see them.

They flutter down slowly like ash, and I suppose it has taken them all this time to make it from space to Earth: the Nothing King's dead crows, their bodies exhaling light. Aria and Clara and I leap up to the windows to watch, in shock.

Because it's not *really* light they're letting go of but ghosts, thousands upon thousands of ghosts, the ones they devoured in the sky, who glide down like parachutists, many of them landing on our very own lawn. I see Homer among them, and press myself against the window, waving wildly, my heart bursting. He gives a small wave back, but he does not come in. He floats into the woods with his friends. And just at dawn, a real dawn that comes with a real sun and real morning light, everyone's breathing steadies. I am the last one to fall asleep.

CHAPTER 41

It's a different world we've come home to from the one we left. We find this out over days and weeks. On the news, there's talk of peace between some countries that were at war when we left Earth, money being given away, old grievances resolved. People throw parties for the living and dead, and find gifts they never knew they had. Bakers discover that their bread has healing powers; poets watch their words glow as they write them down. With the sight that Dread once stole, people can see the ships of ghosts where they hover on the sea, and form committees to protect time whales and their habitat, knowing that the past keeps going on beneath the waves.

Some things aren't as easy to pin down. Without the Griever, sadness tugs at people but does not drag them under. People understand each other better without Babble's magpies capturing their words. Miss Rage no longer stands on hillsides casting hornets from her hands. Time no longer flies on summer days, weekends seem to last a little longer, and the phrase "They're growing up too fast" fades away because, without the Time Witch, it's no longer true.

There's a buoyancy to people. Most of all, there's a feeling in the world that there is always more than what we see, even when we think we've seen it all.

It's not that things are perfect without witches, not at all. People still stress about their taxes, get annoyed and angry, grow old, cry, pass away. Bad things still happen to good birds (and people), and the world's ghosts wonder what will ever become of them without a Beyond to go to. But there starts to be a feeling that what's broken can be fixed. And though the Nothing King is only locked away and not completely vanquished, remembering his darkness makes us think much more of light.

I think that's why, every night from the yard, Ebb and I watch for the sparkle of the Beyond, the round glow of the moon, hoping against hope to see it. And I think it's why Aunt Jade sends the letter. One day, opening the mailbox, we find it—the last thing we ever expected to see.

It only says two words:

I'm sorry.

And nothing more.

My mom stands with her lips firm as she reads it. She does not write back. And we do not hear from Jade again.

On the lawn each night with Ebb, together but apart, I'm restless. There's nothing left to chase, no witches left to conquer. It seems adventure has grown on me like dragon scales. I used to be a girl who wanted to hide. But now I itch for something new. And then one night, when Germ is sleeping over, I wake to see a ghost standing by my bed.

"Rufus!"

He's standing in the doorway, glowing in death, but there.

"What are you doing here?" I gasp as Germ stirs in her sleeping bag.

"I was just passing through," he says flatly, then smiles his salesman's smile. "What do you think? I came to see you."

"How?" I press as Germ sits up and blinks at us, rubbing her eyes. "You died light-years away."

"Well," Rufus says, tilting his cap a little, "I told her I wanted to have a chat with you, about my latest business venture, so she let me tag along."

I stare at him, bewildered. "You told *who* you wanted to talk to me?" Even in the dark, I can see the amusement glinting in his eyes.

"She wants to talk to you too, out back," he answers cryptically. "Might as well get everybody up." And then he floats out through the bedroom wall. Standing up, I glance out the window, but see no one there except for Ebb, keeping watch as he's always done. Though, at this moment, with his back turned, he's glowing extra bright. I go and wake the others, and we shuffle onto the back lawn, confused and half-asleep.

The first thing we notice is the moon. Behind me, Aria and Clara let out yelps. It's back—full and round and bright and low, its ladder dangling down. The Beyond sparkles as a pink, mysterious haze around the world, and the cloud shepherds move back and forth across the sky.

The night is full of old magic, the kind I saw the first night I could *see*.

And the Moon Goddess is back too. But she's not where she usually is—distant, faint, aloof.

Instead she's standing on my lawn, as silver as the moon itself.

I open my mouth and close it again, too stunned to talk.

The goddess keeps her distance, her face smooth and silver and expressionless, though not unkind. Her eyes are somehow soft and sharp at the same time, as if she sees everything at once, as if she has bigger things to think about than us. As if the whole world, maybe the whole universe, is in her eyes all the time.

Ebb, who saw her first, floats beside me, protective.

"You fell into a black hole," I murmur, summing up everything that's impossible about their presence—the Beyond, the moon, and her. "You can't come back from that."

The goddess seems unfazed by this. "You don't think the world would be so foolish as to let a black hole be the end of things, do you?"

I shake my head, though I thought that was exactly what black holes are.

"They're also beginnings," she says, "though I'm sorry it took me so long to come. It wasn't easy climbing out. Especially with all I had to carry." Beside her she lays down a silver sack, as luminous as she is. "I've brought the moon back as a gift"—she glances at the sky—"among other things. But I myself am moving on. Now that humans have the sight, they'll be coming after me." She looks to my mother knowingly. "And half the point of a Moon Goddess is that she can't be reached. But I wanted to bring you each a gift before I go."

"I've given Rufus unlimited access to moonlight," the goddess goes on, nodding to Rufus where he's come to stand beside us, "and he will deliver to Wanda a new ring." She looks at Aria and Clara next, and her mouth tilts up in a smile. "Did you know you're descended from royalty?"

Germ snorts. Because *of course*. Aria's not a lover of fine cheeses for nothing.

"I've made your family tree for you." She hands a small hand-bound book to Clara. "One day you'll see your parents in the Beyond. But for now, you'll find more cousins here on Earth—in the present and the future—than you'll know what to do with."

"Germ," the goddess continues, reaching into her

silver robes and holding out a second book. "I know how long you've wanted this." Not sure how to act, Germ takes the book with an attempted curtsy-bow-type move that could only be described as awko taco. She reads the title and lets out a small happy squeak, then shows it to the rest of us. *Ten Easy Steps to Reading Your Pet's Mind,* it says. I think of Eliot, safely tucked in Germ's sleeping bag, asleep. He doesn't know what he's in for.

Now the Moon Goddess turns to look at Ebb, and for a moment an expression like affection crosses her smooth and austere face. "You've tried so bravely to protect this witch hunter." She glances at me, then back at Ebb. "And you've defied the limits of what ghosts can do. But I can't bring you back to life. Some things are beyond me. However, I *can* erase the mark you took upon your soul when you drifted into Limbo."

Ebb hovers there, listening nervously, with a look on his face I once thought of as grumpiness, but which I know now is worry and confusion.

"And now you have a choice," she continues. "You can move Beyond and be reunited with your parents, this hour if you wish. Or you can stay a ghost."

The silence around our group is thick. I suck in my breath, aching while I should be happy.

"I've given this choice to all the ghosts who fought beside you. Their business here is done. And so is yours. But only if you want it to be."

Ebb and I exchange a look that makes my heart thud in my chest. I know he's longed to see his parents for longer than I've been alive. But in his eyes, I can't read what he'll choose.

"You don't have to decide now," the goddess continues. "When you've made your choice, tell Rufus. He'll send a messenger to me."

And then she does something that makes even this enormous development—Ebb's possible departure from this world—vanish from my mind. Her eyes glide to my mom.

"For you, witch hunter," she says as she lifts one side of her silver robe.

And out steps Wolf.

My mom lets out a noise between a howl and a shocked, joyful whimper and drops to her knees as Wolf lets her take him in her arms. Soon the both of us are wrapped around him tight.

He is still wild-looking. His hair stands up in all directions, he doesn't say a word, his eyes are restless and mysterious. My brother will always be a puzzle to me; I realize that for the rest of my life, he might be a book I can only half read and understand. And now, he's seen the other side of a black hole, which makes him even more enigmatic than before. We'll always be more different than I used to hope, I guess. But then again, I didn't think to hope he'd save us all. And give his life to save us.

And then come back from the void.

"His cloak protected him until I reached him," she says. "He was wrapped in a void, and nothing can destroy that."

Turning toward the Moon Goddess, I see that she is looking at me with a strange kind of smile. As if she has singled me out last, even though Wolf is my gift too.

"And now, Rosie," she says. "For you I have an invitation."

I tell myself to breathe. I'm not sure it's the kind of invitation I will want.

"To where?" I ask, wary. The last time she invited me somewhere, with her ladder instead of her words, it was to the moon, to embark on a journey to save the world. And I am tired. And tired of being scared.

She lifts a bundle of mist out of her robes and places it in my hands, though it feels like nothing against my palms.

"What is it?" I ask.

"The basket was destroyed, I'm afraid," she replies, "but I'd think that by now you'd recognize the Museum of Imagined Things."

I stare down at the bundle in my hands—there but not there, empty but also full of infinite things. I guess, like the Moon Goddess herself, like even the Nothing King, it couldn't be destroyed.

"You're invited for one last visit, before it gets put back where it belongs," she says. "By morning, it'll be gone."

"But—but," I stammer, and among all the things I want to say, I come up with this: "I've already been there lots of times." I don't mean to sound ungrateful, but that's the way it comes across.

The Moon Goddess only smiles. "Your bird will know the way," she says. I open my mouth to let her know that Flit is dead, but she's already turned and is moving away toward the woods. It's hard to really tell if she walks or drifts or floats, if she's living or a ghost. Maybe she is all the things—it's hard to know for sure. We stand in a group, watching her go.

And that night, when the ladder rolls up toward the moon, it is for the last time.

It does not appear again.

CHAPTER 42

This is how it happens that I enter the Museum of Imagined Things one last time.

The lobby is not the way I left it. At the info desk, there are cloud shepherds of shifting shapes, cataloguing things. More are tidying up the lobby: sweeping up debris, carrying escaped creatures back to where they belong.

By the elevator—to my shock—I see the Brightweaver, waiting for me. She smiles just as if she saw me yesterday and nothing's changed since then.

"There you are," she says. "I wanted to see you while I could."

She wraps me in a hug that warms my soul, and I realize I'm a figment again. And then she pulls back and looks upward. Something is fluttering down toward us.

Flit!

The bird lands on my shoulder and nuzzles against my cheek as I choke back tears.

"She died," I whisper to the Brightweaver in wonder.

"You imagined her, so she lives here," she says, smiling indulgently. "You have about an hour, Rosie, before I take Flit and the rest of the museum back to the clouds. I've promised the shepherds that you'll be the last visitor; it's just too much for them. I hope you make the most of it. You have your bird now to lead you."

She looks down at Flit, who's glowing a bright golden brown, all her adult feathers grown in at last. She hops along ahead of me, into the elevator, and, trusting wherever she leads, I follow. A number lights up without my pressing it, and I wave to the Brightweaver as the doors close.

When I get out again, we're in the Hall of Musicals.

Flit bops her head to the distant tune she likes, and I

laugh. "It figures you would bring me here," I say as I let her lead the way. She tilts her head and looks up at me, and for a moment I feel chills crawl across my neck.

Because the distant music . . . as we get closer, I think I know it. It's "A Spoonful of Sugar," a song from *Mary Poppins*. The movie my mom and dad went to see on their first date.

I feel a prickle of unreasonable hope and cast a warning glance at Flit.

"Don't do this to me, Flit," I say. I've had my hopes up too many times to believe that hope leads to anywhere good. But Flit only chirps and swirls and flies down the hall, ignoring me like she doesn't have a care in the world.

When we reach the red velvet curtains that I can tell by listening lead to *Mary Poppins*, I hover and brace myself for disappointment, a quiver inside my chest as she slips inside. And then I follow.

I recognize the place because I've seen the movie—the park where Mary Poppins takes the kids to the carousel with Bert, the ship-like house where an admiral keeps the time, the cathedral courtyard where an old lady feeds the birds. I follow Flit through these scenes and up the steps of the cathedral, where she flutters in through the open doors.

Inside, the place is hushed and empty. But up above, in an alcove, someone's moving in the shadows. I know enough to see that he's a ghost and not a part of the movie that contains him.

My breath catches in my throat.

I climb the stairs.

At the top, a man is waiting for me. He's dressed in fisherman's clothes, smiling and kind-faced and stubbly-chinned and a little wet. And of course translucent.

"They told me you were coming," he says.

I begin to cry.

My dad floats over to me, and wraps me in a hug.

"Oh, Rosie," he says. And I feel his arms around me tight. We hold on to each other for a long time without words. But then, mind reeling, I remember that the Brightweaver said I only have an hour. I can't hug my dad forever, even if that's what I want to do.

"What are you doing here?" I whisper, pulling back to stare at him, at a face I've only seen in pictures, as I wipe tears off my cheeks.

My dad looks at me sadly and sweetly, as if he can't think what to say first because there is so much.

"Come sit, Rosie. We have so much to catch up on."

And so, after a few more minutes of my hugging him, and struggling to grasp that he's here and real, we sit. And though I can hardly believe I'm doing it, I tell my dad about Germ and Aria, about the Memory Thief and Chompy and Ebb and the League of Witch Hunters, and Glimmer 5 and the Nothing King. And he tells me about his past, how he came to be here in an attic of *Mary Poppins* as a ghost.

"After I drowned, I was heartbroken," he explains, smiling sadly. "I died so far from home, so far from your mom, and I couldn't bring myself to leave the world. Even though I knew I was supposed to go Beyond, even though it tugged at me day and night, I resisted. I'm stubborn, you see. I suspect that might be something you inherited, from what I hear."

I can't tamp down the grin that rises on my face.

"For months, I lingered on a busy beach by the edge of the sea, caught between one world and another, not knowing what to do. There was a movie theater there along the strip, and I'd noticed all these ghosts going in and never coming out. So one night, curious, I trailed another ghost inside and watched him float into the screen and disappear right before my eyes. I felt I had nothing left to lose. I followed."

"It was a doorway," I say, "to the museum."

He nods slowly.

"And that was it," he goes on with resignation. "I'd come into the museum, and I couldn't get back to the world. Those doors go only one way, as you know. I was stuck. And so, eventually, I found my way here to *Mary Poppins*. I think I had the slimmest hope that someday your mom—great witch hunter that she was—would find me here, that she'd discover the museum one day, and trail into the movie we saw on our first date."

He examines his glowing hands thoughtfully. "All these years I've been waiting. Even when I heard we should leave for Limbo, I couldn't bring myself to go, knowing it would mean leaving her—and you—behind." He smiles sadly. "Hope can be an absurd and painful thing."

I look at him and nod, knowing this all too well.

He laughs a bittersweet laugh. "I didn't even know your name until yesterday when the Moon Goddess came, or that you were a twin. But I've loved you since the day your mom told me you were on your way—you and Wolf both. And seeing you is worth all the waiting."

I feel something relax inside me, almost like I've been waiting to relax my whole life.

"What will happen to you now?" I ask.

"Well, I'm due in the Beyond," he says, his mouth crumpling a little, "after you leave. Where I was always supposed to be."

Outside, the clock of the cathedral chimes, and my dad looks deeply sad.

"We only have a little time left, Rosie. There's so much I wish that we could do. But tell me, what can I do right now that would make you happy? I could just sit here and hug you. I could ask you so many questions I have—like who your friends are, and what your favorite food is, and what you love."

I study him, suddenly nervous and shy. I know what I want . . . what I've always wanted. Even if I'm not a little kid anymore.

"Can you tell me a story?" I croak.

He looks surprised, and then smiles. "I'd love to."

And so, for the first and only time until we meet again in the Beyond, my dad holds me in his arms and he tells me a story.

It's a story in which the way is dark, the shadows are long, and the woods are deep. It's a story where things are hard to bear or even understand. Nothing in it is as shiny or as safe as the characters would like—and even when dreams come true, it's not in the way that anyone expected.

But still, it has a happy ending, as any story should, if it's going to be at all realistic. The hero finds her strength, and the people she meets along the way bring joy against the dark, and she discovers that even at the other side of black holes there's light. The story my dad tells me before we say goodbye is—like all the happiest and most hopeful things—true. And that makes it enough, and worth the telling.

EPILOGUE

I suppose my backyard is as good a place to end an adventure as to begin one.

I am standing on the grass, waiting for a shuttle to arrive. My friends—Aria, Clara, Germ, and Ebb—are with me. My mom and my twin brother, too. And the entire Bartley family.

The ship, I see when it lands in the clearing by the cliffs, is not the rickety bucket of bolts that the Astral Accelerator was, but it's not an earth-ship either. It's not so bound to reality as that. It's something in between, a combination of moonlight and metal. It's Rufus's latest triumph.

He calls it the Earthward Ambulator. My mom has painted the logo for him, shining in rainbow colors on both sides of the ship. And this is its first passenger voyage, from Earth back to space. We'll be the first passengers to ride it, and the first people to arrive on Glimmer 5 with the intention of staying for good since Rufus landed there all those years ago.

We are leaving home to build a space-travel destination for all of humankind to enjoy. The plan is for it to have a beach, an ocean of moonlight, and lots of themed hotels. Of course, there will be shuttles taking people and ghosts on tours, and restaurants, and amusement parks. There will be snacks and cars and castles available from the Everything Vending Machine. There will be plenty of things we haven't even pictured yet—maybe a chain of planets, maybe resorts beyond the galaxy.

I don't know what Glimmer 5 will look like when we get there, whether we'll find it all in the disrepair we left it in. Rufus says he's fixed it up with Zia's and Fabian's help. But he tends to oversell things.

And yet, I'm optimistic. I'm excited to begin.

Aria will captain all the tours, and of course, Clara will

take care of all the ships as the fleet begins to grow. Two of their cousins are coming with us as well.

I'll be the one dreaming up rides, and imagining what the planet can be, with moonlight and engineers to make it all come true. Wolf will draw the vision of every building that goes up, and my mom will do the art for all the marketing materials. And Rufus—mostly retired and pleasantly dead—will watch it all unfold.

We are saying goodbye to Earth. Though Rufus says soon his ships will be so advanced that a trip to Earth will be a cinch, I think we'll have to see. Even if that happens, Waterside Road will no longer be home. My school will no longer be my school. Even if I come back to visit, I am still—in a way—leaving home for good.

As we stand loading our suitcases onto the ship, dusk falls, and soon I see Ebb coming up the rise along the cliffs. He doesn't need to pack, but he's coming with us too. Not forever, maybe not even for more than a year or two; he doesn't know when he'll go Beyond. We'll take it day by day. For now, it's only time to say goodbye to those who are staying behind. There are hugs, and crying, and then everyone climbs aboard the ship. I'm the last to go.

The Bartleys retreat to their car, all except for Germ.

They want to give us space. We're about to have a lot of it.

Germ and I stand facing each other.

"I wish I could send half of me with you," she says.

"Me too," I say.

But I also know that wouldn't be enough—for her or me. I know that home on Earth is where Germ needs to be to have what she's always wanted, a normal life. Like most best friends, we're growing in different directions. But I know by now that it doesn't mean we're growing apart.

"Come visit?" I ask. "When that kind of thing is possible?"

She nods, her freckles pale like they always are when she's devastated. Like they were the day I met her crying by the kindergarten door. Tears run down her cheeks.

"You too," she says. "Write me. Especially silly stories with happy endings."

"That's so immature," I tease in a whisper.

We hug each other tightly.

All things change. That's one thing I am learning the longer I live. We all have to transform. But we don't have to end.

As the Earthward Ambulator lifts off, all of us with faces pressed to the windows as we leave, I watch Germ wave and grow tiny below us.

Still, for me she's larger than life. And that's the way she'll always be.

It is not what I pictured, my life once our hunt was over. I didn't picture us living at the edge of the galaxy resurrecting an abandoned hotel. I didn't picture my mom too busy painting logos to sit beside me and read, or Wolf too quiet and wild to whisper secrets with me in the dark.

I didn't picture losing my dad twice, or that in a world without witches, hurt people still hurt other people, like my aunt Jade once hurt my mom.

I didn't picture sitting on Glimmer 5's one hill, watching the stars every night with Ebb sitting beside me. Or holding hands with him, thanks to one of Rufus's latest post-death inventions, which he calls—what else?—the Figment Fabricator.

It can't last.

I'm getting older than Ebb, little by little. I'll be fourteen in a month, and someday not too long from now, the growing gap will feel too strange. When that day comes, Ebb will leave for the Beyond, and the warm embrace of his parents. But for now, he tends to the plants on Glimmer 5 so they grow into a forest, and holds my hand, and makes me laugh, and my heart flutter.

+ + +

I like to think there is a use for black holes. I like to think there's a reason the Nothing King still needs to be there, alive but locked in place.

I do think there are happy endings nestled inside sad ones. I think that's the light that magic promises me. Even now, even though I have the sight, that deeper magic stays beyond what I can see.

And it will always be saying there's more . . . there's more.

There's more.

ACKNOWLEDGMENTS

Thank you to Kristin Gilson for navigating this last part of Rosie's journey with me with such kindness and honesty. Thank you to Liesa Abrams for so many seeds planted and to Rosemary Stimola for friendship and wisdom I treasure more with each passing year. I'm in awe of Bara MacNeill and Jen Strada for their attention to detail, and I owe much gratitude to Khadijah Khatib and Heather Palisi for bringing such beauty to this book cover. I'm also deeply grateful to the team that has taken this trilogy out into the world: Tara Shanahan, Antonella Colon, Nadia Almahdi, and Anna Jarzab. Thank you always to Dannie Festa. And finally, I want to again say thank you to the teachers and booksellers and librarians who build bridges between young people and the stories that save them. I'm so lucky to be in your orbit.

ABOUT THE AUTHOR

Jodi Lynn Anderson is the bestselling author of several critically acclaimed books for young people, including the May Bird trilogy and *My Diary from the Edge of the World*, a *Publishers Weekly* Best Book of 2015. Jodi holds an MFA in Writing and Literature from Bennington College. She lives with her husband, two children, a dog who takes everything too far, and two hermit crabs.

THE
SEA OF
ALWAYS

Thirteen Witches

BOOK 2

THE SEA
OF ALWAYS

JODI LYNN ANDERSON

ALADDIN

NEW YORK   LONDON   TORONTO   SYDNEY   NEW DELHI

ALADDIN

An imprint of Simon & Schuster Children's Publishing Division

1230 Avenue of the Americas, New York, New York 10020

First Aladdin hardcover edition April 2022

Text copyright © 2022 by Jodi Lynn Anderson

Jacket illustration copyright © 2022 by Kirbi Fagan

All rights reserved, including the right of reproduction in whole or in part in any form.

ALADDIN and related logo are registered trademarks of Simon & Schuster, Inc.

For information about special discounts for bulk purchases, please contact Simon & Schuster Special Sales at 1-866-506-1949 or business@simonandschuster.com.

The Simon & Schuster Speakers Bureau can bring authors to your live event. For more information or to book an event contact the Simon & Schuster Speakers Bureau at 1-866-248-3049 or visit our website at www.simonspeakers.com.

Designed by Heather Palisi

The text of this book was set in Adobe Caslon Pro.

Manufactured in the United States of America 0222 FFG

2 4 6 8 10 9 7 5 3 1

CIP data for this book is available from the Library of Congress.

ISBN 9781481480246 (hc)

ISBN 9781481480260 (ebook)

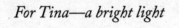

For Tina—a bright light

You are the cloud-builder; you are the grower of wings. You are the one whom Earth entrusts its stories to; you are the singer of songs.

Reader, look behind you. You have left moonlight where you've walked, though you may not remember it.

—*Inscription from a cross-stitched pillow in the Brightweaver's cottage*

THE
SEA OF
ALWAYS

PROLOGUE

*I*n the middle of the night, in a house at the end of
Waterside Road, two women sit by a window looking
out at the sea. They lean toward each other in their
chairs as if closeness will protect them from something they fear.
Outside, the frigid wind blows at the glass. It is dark moon, and
Annabelle Oaks has an uneasy feeling that something is coming.

On her left, Elaine Bartley is wearing a sweatshirt that
says I Could Be Wrong but Probably Not *in faded puffed
letters. She's flipping through the pages of a mystery novel but
barely reading it. Annabelle is elegant in a tiered cotton dress,*

and smudged with paint as she stares at a canvas she is dabbing at with a brush.

They're unlikely companions, and yet the months since their daughters left have brought them together evening after evening, in this ritual of watching and waiting. On a table between them, a piece of paper lies open. It's never far from Annabelle even when she sleeps. It's the note their daughters left behind the night they went away:

I'm going to find him, *it reads. And then, below that, in a postscript scribbled crookedly at the bottom:*

I'm going too.

The first sentence is neat and steady, as if the few words it contains were measured out carefully by its author. The second sentence is sloped and wild, as if one girl were catching up to the other on her way out the door . . . as if it were written at a sprint.

This is the note the women showed the police—who believe the girls have run away to track down lost fathers they will never find. Annabelle, of course, knows better.

A sailor in a yellow rain slicker drifts into the room and then right through Elaine, to get to the kitchen. Elaine sits up taller, shivering.

"That's Soggy that went through you," *Annabelle says.* "Sorry. He's really quite distracted since losing Crafty Agatha."

Mrs. Bartley shivers again, looking around, then turns back to her book. She doesn't have the sight; she can't see the ghosts milling about the room, but she does sense the cold of them. The room, which would look empty to almost anyone, is actually full of spirits. More and more have come every day since Rosie left, ghosts from nearby towns and counties trying to get a glance at the Oaks family home before drifting back to their graves by morning. The death of the Memory Thief has made this house more infamous than it already was.

Annabelle knows that her companion believes her about all of it: the ghosts, the witches, the Moon Goddess, the war. She knows it's easier to believe in impossible things than to believe that someone you love is truly lost; better to think your daughter is off on a dangerous journey she chose than to believe the alternative. But Annabelle knows, also, that Elaine does not know enough of witches to fear them as she should.

Finally Annabelle's visitor stands up. "Heading home," she says, laying a gentle hand on Annabelle's shoulder before turning and shuffling toward the door. Most nights, she's here until she can barely keep her eyes open. And then she returns with circles under her eyes the next evening.

After she goes, Annabelle turns back to her painting, smudging and dotting the canvas with her brushstrokes, rendering a portrait of her grandmother. As with all her other work, there is something foreboding about it. The things Annabelle renders can't help but take a dark turn: flowers wilt in their vases, faces frown, storms whip forests of trees. There is a warning in her grandmother's eyes.

"They're out there swimming, waiting for me," Annabelle says to no one—to the painting, to the ghosts, the walls, the air, the stars.

In her mind she sees her children: Rosie, short, quirky, strong, and brave; and Wolf, a baby boy she only knew for moments before she was robbed of him. She aches with the memory—now returned to her—of the two of them on the day they were born. The tight, trusting grip of Wolf's tiny hand, the sweet smell of the top of his head, the wide wonder in his eyes looking out at the world. Rosie weeping after he was taken away that morning, reaching for him as if she'd lost her own arms.

One child stolen. The other now grown, and off like a thief in the night with her best friend to save him . . . wherever in time he might be.

It is this that draws Annabelle out of her chair to stare at the sea. They're out there swimming, *she thinks, looking out on the cold dark waves of the Atlantic.* And I can't keep them safe.

◆ ◆ ◆

The lonesome house glows like a beacon through the long night. Annabelle hates when the ghosts leave her alone just before daybreak, and as darkness creeps close to dawn, she watches with regret as they drift into the woods. The yard grows quiet and still. And then . . . she hears it. The rustle through the trees, as if the leaves are whispering about something they are afraid of, before falling utterly silent.

And suddenly Annabelle sees why.

A figure stands at the edge of the yard, where the grass meets the horizon of the sea. Annabelle's hands begin to shake.

The witch standing across her yard doesn't move. She is far enough away that her face is only a white oval in the dim light. Annabelle doesn't recognize her except to know what she is.

"Annabelle Oaks," the witch calls across the still air, "your daughter will die."

And it feels like boulders hung around her neck, to hear such a thing.

And then the witch turns and drifts down the trail at the side of the cliff, still moments before the sun can rise. Once she's gone from view, Annabelle sinks to the floor, all the strength leaving her.

She would swim to Rosie if she could.

But no boat, no submarine, could carry her there.

There's only one way to travel through the Sea of Always. And Rosie took that with her.

CHAPTER 1

The problem with living inside the belly of a magical whale for eighty-eight days is the boredom. My best friend, Germ, and I are making the best of it by playing War.

"You got all the aces," Germ says. She is lounging on a La-Z-Boy, eating Doritos. "You always get aces."

"You're exaggerating," I say. But she's right, I do get all the aces.

I look at my hand, the wrinkled cards we've played a thousand times since boarding. My pile is huge and Germ's is dwindling. This happens all the time, and yet . . . and yet . . . somehow, even though it's purely a game of chance, Germ always wins. I'm so close to victory, I can taste it, but I'm pretty sure it will slip away.

I know this is not typically what anyone would expect to find in here, two twelve-year-old girls playing cards and stuffing their faces. To look around, you wouldn't even know we're inside an ageless, time-traveling creature at all. If anything, it looks like Germ's grammie's house, which I visited once when we were little.

Off to the right is our bedroom, with an orange rug and two beds where we sleep. Here in the center there's a TV and two beat-up La-Z-Boys, with bowls full of our favorite snacks on a table in between. There's also a dining table and a shag rug, and a treadmill and mini trampoline for Germ, who can never sit still for long.

Still, there are *some* indicators that we're not in Kansas anymore. For one thing, there's a giant glass "moonroof" above that affords us a view of the blue ocean water above. There are travel brochures littering the room that offer guidance on trips to the Stone Age, the Bronze Age, specific eras like the Han dynasty, the Gupta empire, and so on. There's also a full-color coffee-table book called *Welcome to the Sea of Always* that includes a primer on the magical creatures of the ocean of time, and a terrifying who's who profile on someone called the pirate king and his army of bones. Plus a rundown on the rules of time travel, which includes things like:

No crossing paths with your former or future self unless you want to create a troublesome wormhole.

People of the past can't see you unless they have the sight.

No returning to your starting place until your journey is at an end.

The book and brochures came in a gift basket that was waiting for us when we boarded—the kind you get from nice hotels, full of colorful tissue paper and apples and pears and a pineapple and some chocolate bars, plus spare toothpaste and some welcome papers. Germ and I long ago devoured the chocolate, tossed the fruit, and made tiny spitballs out of the tissue paper to shoot through straws at each other.

Anyway, we basically have everything two twelve-year-old girls could need while traveling through time—

except our moms, and school, and humans besides each other.

Germ's theory is that the whale (whom she's named Chompy . . . since her favorite name, *Chauncey*, didn't fit right) provides everything you need for whatever kind of passenger you are, hence the Doritos and the Pop-Tarts. (The first three days, I ate Pop-Tarts until I barfed.) It also explains why there are photos of her boyfriend, D'quan Daniels, and Olympic women athletes magically pasted on the wall beside her bed, while on my side there are favorite books of mine like *The Secret Garden* and *One Crazy Summer* and *Because of Winn-Dixie*, and some of my favorites from when I was little, like *The Snowy Day*. It explains why Germ's favorite show, *LA Pet Psychic*, is on permanent loop on the TV and why we have several copies of *Pet Psychic* magazine on the coffee table. There are also cinnamon-scented candles (Germ loves cinnamon-scented candles) and matchbooks everywhere to light them.

We have everything we need. But the truth is, time feels endless inside the whale, and I guess that's because it is. I think it's safe to say that in the outside world (the one we left behind), time is passing . . . but within our whale, time stands still. I know this because I have a tiny hourglass necklace given to me by a witch, and not a grain of sand has dropped through it . . . and yet, according to Germ's watch, eighty-eight days have passed. We keep track of *that time* (home time) by marking the wall with a Sharpie (thanks, Chompy!) every time Germ's watch circles noon. So somehow time is moving, and also it's not.

Either way, we're excruciatingly bored—and so we've passed the days by trying at least fifty ways to wear eyeliner, played at least a thousand games of War, painted our toenails every color of the rainbow, had hour-long burping contests, ranked all the boys at our school back home in terms of cuteness. (Germ is devoted to D'quan but says you can't blame a girl for looking. And anyway, D'quan doesn't know the real reason why we disappeared and might think we're dead.)

We've discussed what seventh grade is going to be like if we live to see some of it, and I have promised to let Germ drag me to more parties, and promised to at least try to like her other bestie, Bibi West (who now prefers to be called by her full name, Bibiana, though we can't get used to it and always forget). We've read all the travel guides Chompy has provided. We've read and reread our most important book of all, *The Witch Hunter's Guide to the Universe*, backward and forward a thousand times. Germ has made me a special friendship bracelet to hold my whale whistle to my wrist. And now . . . we're back to War.

"Aw! Isn't Chompy sweet?" Germ squeals, looking over at a small bowl of M&M's that has appeared beside me. Staring at my M&M's, I bite my tongue. Chompy *does* seem to anticipate all our needs. (He's very subtle about it. You look away for a moment, or blink your eyes, or start to daydream, and that's when he changes things on you.) BUT Chompy also used to serve a witch (granted, the witch is dead) whose whistle now belongs to us.

"He'd probably be just as eager to provide witches whatever *they* needed," I say. "Like, we get M&M's. . . . They get cauldrons for cooking children in."

"Shh. You'll hurt his feelings," Germ hisses, glancing at the domed ceiling above us.

Chompy gives a shudder. Which makes me, for a moment, panicked. I'm always nervous that at any moment something on Chompy could go haywire. In the grand scheme of things, we're a very tiny vessel surrounded by seawater that could drown us, after all.

"See?" Germ says with accusing eyes.

"He was avoiding that octopus," I say, pointing out the moonroof at an enormous red creature floating above and past us.

Germ softens again, and she grins. "Every time I think of octopuses, I think about that time in first grade."

I lay my ace down and swipe Germ's jack, flustered. *Here we go.*

It's one of the infamous moments of my childhood. At school we were playing the Farmer in the Dell, where everyone picks partners until someone is a supposedly lonely, solitary piece of cheese. (Don't ask me, I didn't invent the special brand of torture that is the Farmer in the Dell.)

Someone had already picked Germ, so I knew I would be the cheese at the end, which would be horribly embarrassing. And so when the game was whittled down to about three people, I pointed out the window and yelled that purple eight-armed aliens were invading from outer space and we all needed to run for our lives. Somehow, I was so convincing that I got everyone to look out the window at the sky.

"That was the best," Germ says, ignoring the fact that being the girl who pretended we were being attacked by aliens turned out to be way more embarrassing than being the cheese. She lays down an ace, her only one, and we go to war. She wins with a seven to my five, and gains a bunch of cards. The next round is a war too; Germ wins again. My pile dwindles.

I feel a reluctant smile creep onto my face. Germ seems

to think that all sorts of things about me are charming, things I wish I could change—like how I scowl at people I don't know and spend most of our schooltime looking out the window imagining how nice it would be to walk through a door into the clouds, away from everyone but my best friend.

She lays down a nine that brings us to war. While I've been ruminating on my shortcomings, she's managed to get the last two of my aces. Ugh.

The rest of the game follows suit. Germ's hands move quickly as she confiscates my best cards. Soon they're all gone. She looks at me apologetically.

"Sorry, Rosie, I really wanted you to win."

"That's okay," I say. "I wanted you to win too."

She yawns. "I'm gonna turn in."

Germ goes to our room and shimmies into a hot-pink pajama ensemble, provided by Chompy of course, that sets off her pale pinkish freckled cheeks and strawberry-blond hair and fits her ample frame perfectly. I change into an oversize T-shirt and sloppy flannel pants. Germ brushes her teeth and washes her face with this new cream she's been using. I run a brush over my teeth but skip the washing. Germ says "I look gorgeous" to the mirror and crawls into bed—a waterbed she's always dreamt of having. I glance at my own reflection—unbrushed brown hair, teeth too big for my mouth, shoulders too high for my neck. I've been waiting for a growth spurt all my life, and now that I'm having one, it seems like all my body parts are growing at different rates.

Germ kneels by her bed and does her nightly ritual: a Hail Mary and an Our Father. Then a prayer to the Moon Goddess for good measure. It's not all that conventional for a Catholic to believe in a goddess who lives on the moon, but Germ is her own person.

"Moon Goddess," she says to the ceiling, "please look after Ebb, wherever he is . . . even if he's nothing."

I wince; an ache flares in my chest. The last time we saw our ghost friend Ebb was the night the Time Witch came and did something terrible to him. (We'll probably never know what.) He was already dead when I knew him, but he's probably *worse* than dead now.

"And please," Germ adds, "send someone, preferably an adult, to help us kill the witches." She pops an eye open to glance at me for a second, then closes it again. "Rosie's great and all, and I'm sure she'll nail it," she says unconvincingly, "but come on, some help would be nice. Thank you."

Then she lies down. She lies with her eyes closed, but keeps talking.

"What do you think my mom's doing right now?" she says.

I'm quiet for a moment. "Missing you."

Germ sighs and pauses briefly before continuing.

"Do you think people are sleeping over at Bibi's right now? It might be Friday night. Friday nights are party nights when you get to seventh grade."

"I think party nights are more like when you're in high school," I say, though Bibi does have a lot of sleepovers.

Germ nods, her eyes still closed, a slight frown playing on her lips.

"I don't want to miss seventh grade," she says.

"I know, Germ," I say back.

"But I want to be here too."

"I know."

And despite what we are here for, and where we are going and why we are on this whale at all, Germ falls asleep quickly. She sleeps the sleep of the untroubled and the brave.

I stay awake; I am neither untroubled nor brave. My courage has yet to show up.

You'll have to go through them to get to me. That's what the Time Witch said, the night she came to me. Eleven witches left. And to save Wolf, I am to kill them all. Somehow, beyond all laws of reason, I—homework-forgetting, cloud-watching, non-friend-making Rosie Oaks, the girl who hides in the corner at school dances, *the one who has to be the cheese*—am the world's last and only witch hunter.

I would never tell Germ this, but I know—*know* for certain—I can't do it.

Restless, I walk on soft feet to the front of our ship and tread up the three carpeted steps to the soothing space nestled like a large berth above Chompy's mouth and a few feet above the level of the living room, where his brain would probably be if he weren't a magical creature. This is the strangest and most magical section of our vessel. We call it "the Grand View."

There are two velvet curtains parted to either side, framing a dark, open space with two comfy leather seats facing a concave black wall. Just in front of the wall, on the floor, is a circle glowing with silvery light—like the kind you might see in a pool at night. But unlike pool lights, *this* light is magical, and projects a beam upward and all around us in a kind of sphere that holds luminous, three-dimensional images.

They float and fly around me, representing a 360-degree view of the ocean that surrounds us—blue 3D images of underwater volcanoes, dark sea-floor caves, giant fish, and so on. Right now, aside from the odd giant jellyfish or squid, the glowing space is bluish and blank, showing the ocean around us as mostly empty.

In the very center of the room is the *map*, which floats blue and translucent and flat, as if laid out on an invisible table.

The map itself is really two things overlaid: a flat view of the seven continents of the real world laid out along lines of latitude and longitude, and a tightly coiled spiral line stretching and swirling on top of it. In other words, it's a spiral within a grid. The grid, we've figured out, represents the real and concrete space of Earth. The spiral represents time, and spirals inward from the moment we left home (where it's cut off by the map's edges) to a beginning point right in the center, which we can only suppose marks the beginning of history. The spiral circles inward above the map of continents, coiling too many times to count. (I suppose magic makes this possible; it seems there are an almost infinite number of coils. Germ says she doesn't really "get" the map, but I think it's kind of beautiful and symbolic.) And there is always a tiny blue glowing whale marking the location of Chompy somewhere along it.

Swimming the Sea of Always—for a time whale, at least—works like this: if you want to get to South Africa 1890, you follow the spiral around and around past that general location on the map over and over until you get to the coil of spiral that also represents the time you want to reach. Of course, to travel the entire spiral, or to pass every moment in history, would take too long to contemplate, but Chompy takes shortcuts—veering right across from one section of the spiral to another, though what his plan is when he's taking these twists and turns, we don't honestly know.

Floating words to the left of the map spell out where we are in time, to be helpful. Right now, apparently, we're swimming past Yugoslavia, 1990. In the upper right corner of the map, our destination is also spelled out in floating letters: San Francisco, 1855. Beneath that is our days until arrival: six. *Six* days, whale time . . . and Germ still sleeps like a log, while I go hot and cold every time I see that number get lower! Six days until my chance to steal back the precious person the Time Witch stole from me.

On the concave wall at the edge of this space, I have taped two photos: one of my mom and dad before I was born (and before my dad died), provided by Chompy. The other is one I brought aboard myself, an old-timey photo of my brother (the only one I have of him) standing in front of an old building, looking beyond the camera. I think he was looking at the witch who keeps him prisoner, because he looks petrified.

My mom told me a few months ago, when the memory came back to her, that I cried for a month straight after he was taken. She said most newborns cry but that I was inconsolable, and looking back, she believes it was the loss of my twin that broke my heart.

The photo is all I have to go on, because it's the one clue the Time Witch gave me the night she set me her gamble: thirty days to save him. Thirty days that begin once we are off this timeless whale, days that will be tracked by the small hourglass hanging around my neck.

I turn and make my way back downstairs, to our room and my soft bed. I take my Harry Potter *Lumos* flashlight out from under my covers and shine it onto my bedspread, making a tiny, luminous bluebird appear. She is a witch weapon of my own making, and she is our only chance.

I snuggle into my covers and watch Little One waddle around over my feet. I flick her across the room to tidy up my bookshelf. Ever since we boarded, I've been teaching her silly tricks, having her fetch me snacks, or pencils, or anything else I'm too lazy to get myself. Now she looks at me—small, and shivery, and uncertain. "You look like I feel," I say to her.

I turn the flashlight off and roll onto my side and try to drift off. I watch Germ's back as she sleeps.

Sometimes I'm able to forget we are ten thousand leagues under the sea. Other times, I can't forget the ocean and its dark deep water beyond these walls. I listen to Chompy's groans, soft calls, and whale song that echo all around us. Germ often says he's singing us to sleep, but I don't believe it.

I start to drift off.

And then, something changes. I'm shaken awake.

As I blink in the dim light, I realize it's Chompy that's shaking. This time violently.

Germ tumbles out of bed, hair sticking straight up.

The vessel around us is shuddering, changing course. Chompy tilts backward with a sudden jolt, and I slide off my bed too.

We are rising. Fast.

"DESTINATION APPROACHING," comes a loud, detached computer voice from the Grand View.

"What's happening?" Germ gasps.

"I don't know." I untangle from my covers and pull myself toward the front of the ship and up the steps. On the monitor, the ocean is still and empty. The destination still says San Francisco, 1855, six days.

"ARRIVING AT DESTINATION," the voice says.

"We gotta get ready!" I gasp.

I run, slide, stumble back to my bed as we feel Chompy level out. I snatch my flashlight, stuff it into my pocket, and wrap my fingers around my hourglass necklace nervously.

Chompy rocks to a violent stop, and my heart drops to my stomach.

It's about to begin. Our war against the witches. Too soon.

There is a sound like a creaky door as Chompy begins to open his enormous mouth.

"Act normal," I say quickly to Germ, though we've been over this before. "This is gonna be a busy, hot city, full of people from 1855. Some of them may have the sight. If we run into anyone who takes notice of us, never, *never* tell them who we are."

Germ nods, and then points to the hand I hold at my collarbone. My hourglass has leapt into motion. Sand has begun to trickle into the lower half. As it enters the bottom half, the sand transforms into a deep red liquid that floats within the glass, and slowly spells out the number thirty. I swallow. The blood-red thirty spins slowly, so that I can see it from all sides. It's like a tiny version of the holograms of the Grand View, only creepy instead of magical.

Normally fearless, Germ has gone ghostly pale with nerves as she sees it too. We are just at the surface of the sea, and water begins to trickle in at our feet. It is so frigid, it takes my breath.

And then I realize that maybe I'm supposed to give a pep talk. I am the last witch hunter, after all.

"We're ready for them," I say. "We know where we're going, and we know what we're looking for, and we know Little One can do this."

Germ nods, trying to look convinced.

I stand poised, with my weapon ready.

And I find I am, altogether, wrong.

We are not ready for this at all.

CHAPTER 2

We gape, standing frozen in the mouth of the whale. It is breath-shatteringly cold as we stare across a white expanse of tundra covered in snow—distant, jagged cliffs clawing at the dark sky beyond. Ghosts roam the windswept plain before us, moaning. Even the ocean waves around us move strangely: still and calm and flat one moment, then lapping wildly at Chompy's sides the next.

Ever since I burned my childhood stories in frustration (and accidentally got the sight in the process), I've been able to see a ladder dangling from the moon. (One night, I even climbed it to meet the Moon Goddess.) But now, up above, the moon looks like a cold distant marble, smaller and farther away than I've ever seen it . . . and there's no ladder, no sign of the Moon Goddess, at all.

Even the sparkling Beyond—its unknowable depths holding the spirits of those who've died and moved on—has gone hazy, like a gray fog has obscured its pink dazzle. If there are misty, watchful cloud shepherds guiding clouds through the sky, I can't see them.

Still, the marble moon gives off just enough light for us to see several silhouettes standing on the cliffs across the snowy expanse in front of us. The shapes begin to howl. *Wolves.*

Germ and I look at each other.

"Do you think this could be San Francisco?" I ask Germ.

Germ looks doubtful. She's about to respond when we both see it: a different kind of silhouette, moving on the cliffs amongst the wolves—a human one. The figure is holding a flickering lantern, orange and inviting in the dark, but a moment later the flicker disappears. We watch the dark shape hurry along the cliffs and disappear behind a jagged outcropping of rock. Whoever it is, they don't want to be seen.

"A witch?" Germ says.

I don't know, but it seems like if a witch saw us, she'd attack, not rush away.

"Whoever it was," I say, "this feels like some kind of trap."

"Chompy wouldn't do that to us," Germ says. I repress the urge to roll my eyes.

"We should get back inside," I say.

We step backward, deeper into the warmth inside the whale. And I realize I don't know how to command Chompy to close his mouth, to leave, to do anything really. The first time we climbed aboard, he did it on his own.

"Chompy, can you please get us out of here?" I ask.

But nothing. Chompy is perfectly silent, his mouth stretched wide and still. And all I can think is, *This is the whale who knows to provide copies of* Pet Psychic *magazine for Germ, but he won't carry us away from a deserted, frigid tundra we clearly don't belong in?*

"Let me try," Germ says. She closes her eyes and concentrates.

"What are you doing?" I whisper, still eyeing the shore.

Germ pops one eye open and looks at me. "ESP. I feel like Chompy and I have a bond."

But several moments of Germ doing ESP, not surprisingly, make exactly nothing happen. We stand there in limbo, unable to go backward, and knowing forward looks too un-survivable to contemplate.

And then Chompy lets out a giant breath, and we go flying out of his mouth, through the air. We land on the edge of the snowy shore. My *Lumos* flashlight tumbles a few feet away from me.

We sit up, panting, and gape back at Chompy in shock. Before we even know what's happened, he *chomps* his mouth closed and sinks beneath the surface of the water. I pull up my whistle on my wrist and blow it, soundlessly. Nothing happens.

The ocean grows as still as a lake. He's gone.

"I knew it," I gasp. "I knew we couldn't trust that whale."

We are alone, stranded on a barren and frozen island, in clothes meant for lounging about on La-Z-Boys. We won't last an hour in this cold. I am already so frozen, I can't feel my feet.

"What do we do?" Germ says.

"We find whoever was on those cliffs," I say finally, rolling toward my flashlight and snatching it up with fingers already going numb. "It's our only choice."

But, looking toward the cliffs, I don't know how to begin. Everywhere snow is lifted and drifting back and forth in the wind; if there were any tracks on the cliffs, they're probably gone. The few ghosts I could see from Chompy, whom we might ask for advice, have floated away—too far to reach.

And then I remember. My heart flutters with a tiny hope as it always does when I remember what Little One can do. I turn her on. Bright and luminous, she perches in the snow, looking up at me, unbothered by the cold and waiting for my command. It's comforting to see she's okay even while Germ and I are soon to be on the verge of hypothermia.

"Little One," I croak, "find whoever was on the cliffs and lead us to them. Fast."

Little One takes off like a bullet. She returns only seconds later, chirping for us to follow. Germ and I huddle against each other, taking a last look at the place in the water where Chompy disappeared (he might be halfway to the Bronze Age by now, for all I know), steeling ourselves to set off into the brutal frozen wilderness. Above me, I can see out of the corner of my eye, something shimmers, hums, and darts away. It's gone before I can catch a real glimpse of it. Little One chirps once and then goes quiet, waiting.

We wrap our arms around ourselves against the cold, and follow.

· · ·

We stumble through the snow for what feels like hours but must only be minutes. I nearly cry with relief when up ahead a shape comes into view, the same shadowy human figure we saw before, hurrying along—perhaps unaware that we are following. The person is distant, but we can see that they are deeply concealed in thick warm clothes of some sort, and hooded. A few more minutes of walking, and we see what must be their destination up ahead: a small wooden hut nestled halfway up the cliffs at the water's edge, with one light burning bright in a window. The cliff is almost flush to the sea, in the shadow of an enormous white cruise ship marooned in the shallows, anchored and rusting and tilting precariously. I see ghosts drifting along the decks. Seeing it—how abandoned it is—gives me a sense of foreboding. It's another thing that feels wrong.

The figure climbs a treacherous set of stone steps that leads up the cliffs, and disappears into the hut. Little One lets out an excited volley of chirps. Beside me, Germ's teeth are clacking together so violently, I can feel the vibration as our arms touch. We look at each other. We might be walking into a trap, but the idea of getting out of the cold outweighs everything. We push on.

"Remember," I say, teeth chattering as we pick our way carefully up the steps, which are icier and more treacherous the higher we go, "whoever it is, they can't even see us unless they have the sight. That's what the time rules in our *Welcome to the Sea of Always* book said. But if they *can* see us, we tell them we're lost. Maybe . . . a shipwreck. Nothing about witches or hunting or anything else. Nothing about who we are. Right?"

Germ nods.

The wind begins to blow harder as we reach the hut. We try to peer through the windows, but they are so fogged from the warmth—*warmth!*—inside that we can't see through them. Finally, throwing caution to the wind, we pound on the door. No one answers. We look at each other again.

Slowly, with numb fingers, I grasp the door handle, and turn . . . slowly, slowly. My heart pounding, I push it open, and we step across the threshold and into the room, closing the door against the cold behind us. We gulp the warm air while we take in what we see.

We are in a simple room, rugged and rustic. A fire blazes in a fireplace in the corner. There is a simple single bed, a stack of wood, something that smells good cooking in a pot on a stove. There are musical instruments everywhere:

a guitar, a flute, a banjo. And standing on the other side of a small round table, there's someone watching us. The figure is still obscured by the leather parka, face wrapped in a scarf so that only the eyes are visible. Whoever it is can obviously see us . . . so either our time rules are wrong or this person has the sight. I can tell, because they're pointing a slingshot loaded with a jagged rock right at us.

A strong female voice emerges from the muffled scarf. "Tell me who you are, or you'll each lose an eye."

Germ shifts from foot to foot and looks at me.

"Um, I'm Rosie and this is Germ," I sputter. "We're travelers. . . . We need help. . . ." The figure in the parka doesn't budge, and the slingshot is still aimed squarely at my face. "Can you tell us where we are?"

But she doesn't answer us. She only narrows her eyes, which flash to Germ.

"I want to hear from this one," she says, nodding at her. "How did you get here?"

Germ looks at me. My heart in my throat, I wait for her to answer.

"Um, by ship?" she says.

"There hasn't been a ship in this port for over five years," the woman says.

I open my mouth to speak, but she shoots me a look.

She's the kind of person who, when she shoots you a look, you keep quiet.

"Um . . . ," Germ says. "Ummm . . . well, we came on a"—she looks at me—"really *small* ship. Like . . . a canoe. You probably didn't notice."

There is a long heavy silence. I can't be certain, but I think the figure rolls her eyes. Finally she speaks again.

"I know you came by whale. I saw you. Which means you've come from some other time. So you might as well tell me who you are and what you're doing here and how you got your hands on a time whale in the first place."

She says this all to Germ, who's clearly become her soft target. (If there's one thing this stranger is, it's a good judge of character.) At the words "time whale," Germ's eyes widened.

"We'd rather not say," I interject. I shake my head ever so slightly at Germ. "We'd rather know who *you* are."

The woman hesitates. And then she lowers her hood and slides off her leather parka, and reveals that she is not a woman at all but a teenage girl, maybe fifteen or sixteen. She's tall and willowy, black curly hair pulled back in a bun.

"Well, if you could have ended up anywhere," she says, this time definitely with an eye roll, "you've come to the wrong time." She points to the world outside, to the marble of the moon, the hazy fog-covered Beyond, the wild and wrong sea. "I'm Aria," she says. "Welcome to the witch-ruled world."

CHAPTER 3

*A*ria works over the stove, ladling whatever's in the pot out into bowls.

"My sister, Clara, always said we should feed anyone who came across our threshold, no matter how unwelcome. So there you are. Fish stew."

She practically throws the bowls onto the table. Germ and I peer into them, then at each other. We're not hungry, but the warmth of the soup is tempting. Aria moves back to the stove for her own bowl with a kind of confident tread, brushing escaped puffs of hair occasionally from her freckled brown cheeks.

"Um . . . thanks?" Germ says, not sure what kind of manners to use with someone who clearly wants us gone. Aria kind of reminds me of Germ's older brother David, who is generally annoyed by our existence.

"Where . . . when . . . are we?" I ask. "How do you know about time whales and witches? Do you have the sight?"

Aria ignores the last question, maybe because it's too obvious. "It's 2062." Germ and I gasp. Chompy has taken us many years ahead in the future.

"You're on the island called Mari, eighteen hundred miles from the nearest continent, in the middle of the emptiest part of the Pacific Ocean." She sips her stew as she watches us, openly suspicious.

"Does anyone *else* live here?" Germ asks.

Aria shakes her head. "Clara—my sister," she reminds us, "brought me here when I was seven. We were the only ones. I've been here ever since."

"But why *here*? Why so far from other people?" I ask.

Aria looks toward the window, her gaze growing heavy. "Clara said the world had gotten too dangerous. The weather has gone wild; wild animals roam the cities.

And the witches . . . With the moon getting farther and farther away, they've gotten fearless. Its light is too dim to deter them from cursing anyone they like, at any time. People are more and more careless about each other and nature. . . ." She presses her lips together slightly.

"Though, to be honest, I don't know what's happening beyond these shores anymore. And it's not like anyone can escape it, not really. This used to be a tropical island; it's *not* supposed to be frozen solid. The moon isn't supposed to be so far away. All I know is that the witches have covered the world in so many curses, it's propelled the moon away from us, and things are . . . frightening. And it feels as if there's worse to come."

We listen in stunned silence. *In only forty years, the witches do all this?*

Aria is watching us, a slightly new look in her eyes. "But mostly we came because they were targeting and cursing anyone with the sight," she says. "We needed to hide from them, like you." I watch her eyes slide to Germ, and realize it a moment too late.

"Oh, we're not hiding. We're *looking for them*," Germ says matter-of-factly. As these last words leave her lips, her hands pause with the spoon, and her eyes dart to mine. She puts her hand over her face. I open my mouth to interject, but Aria holds a hand up to quiet me. She has gone deathly still. It's as if the air itself has gone tense and tight.

"I want to hear from *her*," Aria says, nodding to Germ, narrowing her eyes intently. "*Why* are you looking for witches?" She asks the question urgently, as if everything depends on the answer.

"Well," Germ says, looking at me uncertainly. And then . . . well . . . months of being cooped up on a whale with no one to talk to but me, and Germ being a natural extrovert, break her open, like a dam bursting. "Rosie's the last witch hunter left on Earth, and I'm, like, her . . . assistant," she gushes. "We've come because the Time Witch stole Rosie's twin brother when he was born. She wanted to end Rosie's family. But she didn't realize he had a twin sister and when she found out, boy was she mad. She kept yelling, 'Tricked! Tricked!' It was awful. And she told us where he is—in the year 1855—and now we're on our way to rescue him. It's like this giant game for the Time Witch; she says we'll have to kill all eleven of the remaining witches to get to him. But our whale, *Chompy*, messed up and brought us here, even though he's a *good* whale, no matter what Rosie thinks. He just sort of *malfunctioned* or something. Maybe if you could help us figure out *how* to be on our way, we could be out of your hair." She looks over at me. I am gaping at her. "Sorry, Rosie," she says. "You know I can't keep a secret. And she seems nice. I think we can trust her."

Germ thinks we can trust *everybody*, I think, scowling. But it's hard to really focus on anything but the startled, tense way Aria is looking at us now. It feels like something sharp and dangerous has landed in the room between us.

She watches us for another split second, and then, abruptly, she walks to the window to look outside. When she turns back to us, she's unreadable but intent. She's got the concentrated look of someone mentally adding up a math problem.

"Your whale, he must have brought you here on purpose," she says.

"Why?" I ask.

"Because . . ." And then she freezes. She's listening to the air. "Listen."

I try, but all I hear is the wind coming in off the sea.

Then I hear it too. A low, distant buzzing, growing louder.

Aria's eyes widen. "The Time Witch knows you're here," she says flatly.

She grabs her slingshot off the table, and throws open the door.

"We'll have to make a run for it. To the caves."

"Caves?" I say sickly, panic seizing my bones.

"A hiding place. Let's go." Within seconds she has pulled on her parka and hood and slung a sack over her shoulder. She throws an oversize parka and a fur over-layer at us from a corner of the room. Each of us takes one, and she flings open the door. The wind whooshes in, chilling our only recently warmed blood, and we bundle ourselves. I am suddenly shaking with fear.

She leads us down the treacherous stairs quickly, taking each jagged step as if it's been memorized through a thousand uses. Germ, who's agile, stays close behind her with ease, while I stumble my way down. We follow, freezing again, fanning out onto the snow at the bottom of the stairs.

"It's at the other end of the beach, there," Aria says, pointing. I see nothing but snow and cliffs in the distance.

We start hurriedly across the snow, but only make it a few steps before Aria stops sharply and looks up at the sky. Something glimmering and opalescent is spreading out there, coming from above the cliffs and moving in our direction. The strangest sound reaches us, like a billion tiny rubber bands being plucked at once. And it's growing louder.

I yank my flashlight from my pocket and bring Little One back to life. She appears on the ground at my feet, ready, alert, agitated. She flits up to my shoulder, chirping a warning.

Aria looks at Little One, then us, and then at a strange bubbling on the ocean's surface where we arrived in the first place. A smooth hump rises out of the water. Shocked, I realize it's Chompy resurfacing.

Aria looks toward the other end of the beach, then at Chompy lying at the ocean's edge, now fully aloft on the water, mouth open. She's gauging which is closer, the cliffs or the whale.

"What can you do with her?" she asks, nodding to Little One.

"Make her . . . really big," I say. "Big enough to eat things." Aria's face falls. She's disappointed. I feel, suddenly, unsure of my weapon—though a moment ago I thought she was magnificent.

"Change of plans," she says. And levels her slingshot at the sky. She shoves me at my back, toward Chompy. "Go!"

We run, all three of us, in the direction of Chompy's waiting mouth. We're sprinting toward him, but it's clear we won't make it in time. Whatever is descending upon us is too fast, too numerous. Like a giant arrow made of a thousand parts, it's diving toward us.

And now I see what the swarm is made of: hummingbirds, multitudes of them. Aria is right. The Time Witch has found us.

We're nearly fifty yards from Chompy when they are suddenly just overhead. I turn Little One toward them and, stumbling in the snow, barely manage to keep my grip as she blasts into the air. She rises fearlessly, streaking into the sky, growing, growing. I watch as she tears one bird, then another and another from the air, ripping out their throats with her claws as she goes. She's the size of a tiger now, airborne, her claws huge. I imagine her bigger, stronger, deadlier. She is soon the size of a horse.

Beside me, Aria fumbles to load her slingshot with a rock. (There's no time to tell her that rocks are no match for a witch.) With Little One as cover, grabbing anything that gets in our path, we run again. But the hummingbirds come on faster. There are twenty or thirty catching up to us, then a hundred, then hundreds of them. And even as Little One grows in size—she's now as big as an elephant—taking more and more hummingbirds out with each bite, they surround her. Over my shoulder, as we run, I see her struggle.

And then, with a terrible screech, she tumbles out of the air. She plummets to the ground, and is engulfed. I stumble too, the flashlight dropping from my hands.

Even Germ falls, fighting off hummingbirds with her fists as she plunges to the ground. They pummel us from all directions. I grasp my flashlight again and try to shine Little One. She only flickers and flares, writhing as the hummingbirds engulf her. I watch helplessly as our *one* weapon against the onslaught vanishes. We're not going to make it. We're beaten already.

Just as I lose sight of the world and the swarm of hummingbirds surrounds me, I see Aria finally lodge her rock in tight to her sling as she's knocked to her knees. As she yanks at her sling, she lets out a sound: a piercing, howling melody she screams into the air, as beautiful and shattering a sound as anything I've ever heard. She shoots her rock upward, and a bright light bursts out behind it, like a bomb shredding the sky.

At first I don't understand that the two are connected, the scream and the flash of blinding, bright light.

Thousands of hummingbirds fall from the sky, blown apart at once. They fall like ashes, every single one of them destroyed. The air goes silent and still, and the sky around us goes suddenly peaceful, dark, empty. We look at each other in shock.

And then, behind us, I hear something else—a deafening and earthshaking *groan*.

I turn in time to see it, the cruise ship in the shallows, tumbling sideways toward the cliff where Aria's hut resides. It falls with a breathtaking, gnashing sound, ghosts screaming from inside as metal collides with jagged rock. Water splashes in all directions as the cliffside crumbles down to the sea, Aria's hut and all.

We watch, stunned.

"No," Aria whispers. "Not again." And then she yanks me to my feet as Germ slowly stands up behind us.

"How?" I sputter, gaping at Aria as she coolly watches the last remnants of her home fall to the ground. Then she looks at me.

"You're not the last witch hunter," she says as she pulls me forward.

And we run toward Chompy's waiting mouth.

CHAPTER 4

The second we are in, the giant wall of Chompy's mouth slams closed behind us. In a moment we are diving and everything is thrown forward.

Collapsed on the rug, panting, holding on to whatever we can grab to steady ourselves, we see that one tiny hummingbird has managed to make it in with us, and is lying injured on the floor. Jerking up, I rouse Little One with the flashlight still clutched in my hand, and she pecks the hummingbird frantically. A tiny spark of light bursts against the carpet as the creature disintegrates.

I fall back, exhausted. We lie there, gaping at each other, as Chompy steadies out. Then Aria leaps to her feet and scrabbles up the steps to the Grand View.

"To the Narrows," she says, and the map flickers to life before her, casting her in a dim blue light. Germ and I look at each other. Can you really just tell Chompy what you want, and he'll do it?

And then we are rocked and tumbled as the whale lurches violently again, tilts, . . . and dives. We listen as the depths of the ocean envelop us. Long moments of silence pass as we wait for something terrible to happen.

"Your whale is fast," Aria says. "We might lose them yet. They can see us from the air, you know, to about a hundred yards deep. But we'll do our best."

"The hummingbirds? I thought you destroyed them all."

"Impossible. There are millions of them. But with any luck, none of the birds that found us made it back to the others."

I stand and hurry up to her side, having finally caught my breath. "How do you know so much about time whales?" I ask. The only thing we've successfully commanded Chompy to do so far is swim to 1855, and even that was already pinpointed on the map when we boarded.

Aria looks at me, then stares around the room as if taking in an old haunt. "I rode one once, a long time ago, when Clara and I came to the island. And Clara knew everything, including how to 'hot-wire' a whale to come get us. She never told me how. But I know that when you're commanding a time whale, you've gotta speak clearly and confidently, like you really mean it."

She descends the stairs and crosses to the bedroom, pulls her leather sack off her shoulders, and plops it down. Following her, I notice that our room has grown to accommodate a third bed, which has appeared across the carpet from mine. Aria begins unpacking her meager things onto it. It's like she's had a go-bag fully loaded even though she's been stranded on an island for years. She lays out her parka, her slingshot, some dried jerky—all practical items except for a small glass snow globe. This she cups in her hands a moment before sliding it gently onto a nightstand that's appeared beside the bed.

"What a day. I'm gonna need some chocolate," she says. Some chocolate appears on her pillow, in a blue velvety box with a magenta ribbon. I notice that Aria's bed is somewhat nicer than ours. It's got a silk comforter and a million pillows. The lamp on her nightstand is vintage, as is the nightstand itself, and a set of speakers appeared beside the lamp in the moment I looked away. Posters of cool-looking bands I've never heard of have appeared on her wall. Suddenly music comes on—something indie.

Aria sinks down onto the bed with a sigh and immediately opens the chocolates, puts one into her mouth, and savors it, then runs her hands along the silk comforter. She re-twines her curly black hair into a bun at the back of her head, as elegant as a ballet dancer.

Germ and I watch in awe. And I think, *This is what a real witch hunter is like.* She takes each of these luxuries as if she expected them, with a bedrock kind of self-assurance. In five minutes she's made herself more at home on our whale than we have in eighty-eight days.

"How did you do that?" I ask.

"Do what?" Aria asks, chomping on chocolate.

"Kill the hummingbirds, save our lives, destroy that entire ship?"

Aria clenches her lips together for a moment at the last words. And I see a flicker of that self-assurance disappear. But then with a flick of her head, she shakes the moment off.

"The ship was a mistake," she says. "My weapon is . . . on the fritz. But I'm a witch hunter, like you. Your whale brought you to me on purpose, to save you. He must have known that wherever you landed in time, the Time Witch's humming-birds would be watching. So he brought you to me. He's gotta be the same whale that delivered us to the island years ago."

"I think he's partial to me," Germ says. "That's why he wanted to save us."

Aria shrugs.

"I don't understand any of this," I say.

Aria looks up at me from under her eyebrows. "The Time Witch set you a game to go and rescue your brother in 1855?"

We nod.

"How long did she give you to complete your task?" she asks, casting her eyes at Germ for a moment.

I hesitate, trying to take it all in. "A month," I finally say. "Thirty days. Not counting our time on the whale, of course."

Aria looks at me solemnly, then looks at the space at the top of my collarbone, and nods, reluctant. "Look how much time you have now."

It takes me a moment to realize it's my hourglass neck-lace she's nodding to. I reach down to look at it and gasp. It looks like a third of the sand is gone now. In the globe of the bottom half, the spinning, blood-red, glowing number is now *twenty*.

"The hummingbirds stole time when they engulfed you," she explains. "They sucked ten days away from you. You've been witch touched already."

I think back to the night the Time Witch came to my room, long after I'd killed the Memory Thief and I thought the witches might have forgotten me. I remember how I opened my eyes and she was there, waiting with her photo of my brother, her dare for me to come find him. She must have laid a hand on me then to curse me. A witch can only curse someone by touching them, as if leaving a scent. But now touched, I am cursed forever, and her birds can steal from me with ease.

"What was your plan . . . once you got to 1855?" Aria presses.

"To have Little One devour the witches one by one," I say, holding up my flashlight.

Aria rolls her eyes. We have known her less than an hour, and already I feel like she's rolled her eyes at us at least twenty times. She's clearly unimpressed with me changing Little One's size.

"That doesn't happen."

"How do you know?"

Aria leans back. "Well, for one, you don't think the Time Witch would be ready for that? She's the *Time Witch*;

she knows everything before it even happens. She'd notice if someone tried to devour all the witches of the world one by one using a magical bluebird." She sighs. "No wonder your whale brought you to me. If I hadn't been there, your whole month would already be gone. Your chance at saving your *brother* would definitely be gone." She looks almost sorry for us, though still kind of annoyed in a teenager way. "You really don't know what you're doing. You were headed for certain death, for sure."

She yawns, and eats another chocolate. Germ and I stand there feeling ridiculous, and Germ gives me a look. It's obvious what we are both thinking. *She's so cool.*

"And now?" I ask.

"And now it's only *mostly* certain," Aria says. She tilts her head. "A witch once killed—anywhere in time—is killed forever; she couldn't go back in time to fix *that*. *But*, like I said, you kill one, and she'll be right there the moment you do, ready to pounce. On the other hand, if you go straight to 1855 San Francisco, all the witches will ambush you at once. I'm sorry, Rosie. It's over before you've even started. You're a mouse and she's a cat; she's just toying with you. It's kind of her thing.

"You're better off going back to the when you came from, going back to your time and living with your losses and finding a way to move on. Hope is a trick, Rosie."

Aria's words sit on me like a pile of stones. Of course the Time Witch would have known where we were headed and what we planned to do. How could I have been so foolish?

"For another thing," Aria says, plunging on, "I live in *your* future. And you saw what it was like."

I think about the future I've just seen, a world covered in ice, with a faraway moon and a Beyond gone dim. As Homer—our local ghost gossip back home—once told us, the witches are always using their curses to tilt the world toward darkness. They want to capture the world in a web of darkness and break the magical thread of connection that runs through all things, sending the moon and its goddess spinning off into space. Only, now I see it's happening faster than I ever dreamt.

"In *your* future," Aria goes on, "I know that only two witches have ever been killed."

"The Trapper . . . ," I say, because I know that my grandmother killed him.

Aria nods. "And the Memory Thief," she finishes for me.

"The Memory Thief's the one Rosie got," Germ says offhandedly, reaching out to touch Aria's silk comforter admiringly.

Aria goes still. It's the first time Germ has said anything that has caused Aria's eyes to go wide instead of roll. For the first time, it's Aria's turn to be surprised.

"Well, I'd like to hear *that* story. But for now, we've got some big choices coming up. And I need a nap before that happens."

"What kind of choices?"

But Aria doesn't answer. She pulls a silk eye mask out of her nightstand and arranges it on her head, perched at the top of her forehead.

"I don't skip naps," she says. Then she reaches to one side of the room, where a red velvet privacy curtain is hanging where it wasn't before. She pulls it as a divider between our space and hers. And all goes quiet.

Our new passenger rises just before dinner that evening, and appears at the table as Chompy fills it up with food. By then I have a million questions for her. Who and where is her family? If she's a witch hunter too, does that mean there are more? If so, does she know how many there are and how to reach them so they can help us? But Aria doesn't meet my eyes as she approaches the table; she's listening to music on a pair of headphones and is generally aloof to both of us. My questions catch in my throat.

Tonight, instead of the usual spaghetti or burgers or other things we love, the table fills with what looks to be *fine* cheeses, steaks, fresh baked bread, cherry turnovers, something Aria says is penne à la vodka, filet mignon, and so on.

"Ah, I've missed whale travel," Aria says. "Even as a kid, I had a taste for the finer things."

Germ and I don't know whether we should be insulted or excited that Chompy prefers to feed us junk food. But Aria, while she eats ravenously, keeps her eyes sliding upward to the Grand View, watching for signs of danger. She keeps one hand poised near her slingshot, ready to jump into action at any moment.

Even though I've always hated fine cheeses, I try to look like I know what I'm doing as I take a big slice of a green moldy-looking one and shovel it onto a cracker. Germ makes a grossed-out face at me, but I ignore her. *A real witch hunter probably does not live on Pop-Tarts,* I think.

I keep lifting my hourglass necklace nervously, making sure again and again that the grains of sand have stopped falling, now that we are back in our timeless vessel.

"So I've gotten us clear of the witch attack," Aria says, dabbing her mouth with a cloth napkin and sliding her headphones onto her lap, "but now, tonight, you're going to have to make a choice. We're almost at the Narrows. They're undersea cliffs with tunnels etched through the middle—enormous underwater gorges. It's the place I thought to take us because Clara told me it's one of the most hidden parts of the sea. The problem is, if we stay high above them, we'll be well within a hundred yards of the surface of the ocean, and there's a good chance the Time Witch's hummingbirds—if they're still in the area searching for us—will see us from the air. But if we go down into the Narrows where they can't see us, there are . . . other dangers. Giant sea creatures—some magical and deadly—volcanoes, the army of bones, dangers we can't even imagine . . ."

She trails off. Germ seems to have a sudden thought. She stands, crosses the room, and grabs the *Welcome to the Sea of Always* book. She flips through the maps and the rules of time travel to the two-page glossy spread that made us both shiver the first time we saw it:

The Pirate King and His Army of Bones. There is a fuzzy picture of a decayed pirate ship sunken underwater but still somehow sailing. It's taken from far off, as if whoever took it was too scared to get close.

"It says," Germ summarizes as she glances over the pages, "that the Narrows have been hunted for a *thousand years* by a pirate king who's put a bounty out on the head of any witch hunter. He's got a crew of hundreds of ghosts. He's pulled countless ships to their doom."

"Yeah, there's that," Aria says.

I feel my stomach flip sickly. Germ and I look at each other.

"Anyway," Aria pushes on. "You'll have to choose."

I swallow, hard. "Can *you* decide?" I ask. Aria is clearly far better at all this than I am, even if she did destroy half her island in the process of saving us. I basically want her to decide everything from now on. And then I add, desperation making me bold, "And then can you help us save my brother? Or at least tell us if there are other witch hunters who could help?"

Aria looks at me silently, and then shakes her head sadly.

"I wouldn't know about other witch hunters." She pauses, thinking. "I *guess* I can help you with the Narrows," she finally says. "I don't think I have much of a choice. But . . . I can't help you save your brother. You saw what happened with my weapon." She pauses, squinting a little as if the thought pains her. "I was thinking you could simply drop me off after we're in the clear, somewhere safe and tucked away but nice and warm for a change. Barbados in the 1960s or something." Germ and I exchange a crushed look.

I scramble for something to say to change her mind, my pulse thrumming. "Maybe you wouldn't *have to* fight," I say. "Maybe you could just . . . stay with us? Help us decide things, navigate things until we get to my brother? We could make it worth your while. We could pay you in um . . . unlimited filet mignon?" I think helplessly. We really have nothing to pay anyone with. "Please. You can't leave us."

"Nah, I'm good," Aria says breezily. "There's really no chance you'll succeed. Sorry."

Then her eyes go to the gift basket. She hesitates, like she is having a little debate with herself. "I mean, I did think for a moment . . . well, you might have something on this whale that I'd really like to have."

"What?" I ask, curious.

Aria stands and lifts the gift basket, then sits again.

"If you want the shower cap, you can have it," Germ says to Aria, "but I have to warn you it's been used."

Aria blinks at her, shakes her head in annoyance, and then pulls an envelope out of the very bottom of the basket. She opens the envelope and tugs out a white piece of paper with an image of a red ribbon printed across the top.

"I'd like to have *this*," she says. It's the first time I've heard her sound nervous. She hands it to me to read. "Clara said there was always one in the welcome gift."

I take it from her, and Germ leans over my shoulder as we read it.

Welcome! This voucher entitles you to one forever stop, any-where and any-when in the past. Next to this sentence is an asterisk, and at the bottom the statement is qualified: *The usual rules of time travel apply. You will not be seen except by those with the sight, you may not cross yourself in time unless you either are a ghost or wish to create a troublesome worm-hole, you may not tamper with the course of human history, and so on.*

We look at her. "What's a forever stop?" Germ asks.

"You get to go to any day you want, and stay there forever."

I stare at the paper. Beside me, Germ widens her eyes at me. "It doesn't feel right, Rosie. What if we need it for something else?" She looks apologetically at Aria. After all, we didn't even know we had it until a minute ago.

"What would you do with it?" I ask, looking at Aria curiously.

Aria's eyes grow sad, but she blinks the look away. "That's up to me," she says with a toss of her head. Germ and I look at each other again. "But I guess if you were willing to let me have it, I could help with planning, logistics. But if there's any witch-fighting, it will have to be up to you and . . . your bird."

I hold the voucher out to her. "It's yours," I say. "If you help us get to 1855 in one piece."

Aria smiles, relieved. "Thanks." She softens a little. "In return, I'll help you as much as I can."

I nod, swallowing.

She studies us thoughtfully. "So, do we take our chances with an army of bones that wants to drag us to our doom, or the hummingbirds above?" We look at each other in silence. "I'm gonna need to think about this," she says. "I like to listen to my gut. And I usually like to do that by looking at fashion magazines."

We spend the next hour mostly quiet, each in our own nervous thoughts. A fireplace has appeared at one end of the room, and hot chocolate warms on the stove. Aria must really love chocolate.

A mug appears for me even though hot chocolate is not really my thing. Chompy must know how much I want to do things like Aria does them. Already, posters of bands

I only vaguely know have appeared on the wall beside my bed. And I find myself rolling my eyes when Germ puts on her shower cap for her bath that night and asks me if she looks like a mushroom. Germ notices the eye roll, and gives me an odd look, like she's a little embarrassed for me. Which is funny considering she spent all last year falling over herself with caring what people in sixth grade thought of her. I guess we've switched places, but I try not to think about it.

Aria lies on her stomach on her bed, listening to music on her headphones and tuning us out, flipping through French *Vogue*s. I sit on the rug with my back to her bed and pull out my *Witch Hunter's Guide to the Universe*, as if reading it for the thousandth time will give me some clue as to what to choose. I scan the faces and names of the witches who are still alive, the terrifying and skillful images of them my mom drew: Miss Rage, Babble, the Griever, Hypocriffa, Mable the Mad, the Greedy Man, Convenia, Dread, Egor, the Time Witch, Chaos.

Colorfully dressed male and female witches fill the pages, some grimacing or making funny faces, while others have such menacing eyes that they are hard to look at. I scan the chapters I know so well, written by my mother long ago: "The Invisible World and Its Beings," "The Oaks and Their Weapons," "Legends," "Secrets of the Earth and Moon," "What Is a Witch?"

I don't realize Aria is looking over my shoulder until she sits up behind me.

"This is impressive," she says, and it occurs to me I should cross out "The Oaks and Their Weapons" and expand it to include Aria and her sister. She points, as I'm flipping past it, to a note I've made about the sight, how it allows people to see the invisible fabric of magic in the world and how it makes them shine like a beacon to witches. "You should add that there are ways to dim yourself so you don't shine so much. Clara taught me how to do it." She bites her bottom lip thoughtfully, laying her hand on the book for a moment. "I can fill in some of the stuff that's missing, if you want."

"Was your mom a witch hunter too?" I ask. It's clear, from things she's said, that Aria's mom is not around anymore.

Aria tightens her lips together, almost imperceptibly. "My parents died. I don't remember them. But my mom taught Clara most of what she knew."

My eyes trail to the snow globe sitting on her nightstand.

"Do you mind if I look at that?" I ask, my curiosity outweighing my shyness.

She studies me for a moment, hesitating. Then she lifts the snow globe carefully, as if it's her most prized possession in the world, and hands it to me.

I gaze at the peaceful, beautiful little scene within. It's an olden-days kind of village, covered in snow, the soft fluffy kind you want to play in and sled in and walk in under the moonlight. I shake the globe and watch the flakes whirl and fall around the tiny houses. For a moment, something strange happens. A light goes on inside one of the cottages, and then goes out again. I stare at it for several seconds, disbelieving.

"You saw it, huh?" Aria says. She takes the globe from me, peering into it. For a moment she is soft and vulnerable, not annoyed or exasperated. "I see it too, sometimes." A sadness plays at the corners of her mouth. "Clara got the globe at some hippie magic shop in Idaho, shortly before we made our journey to the coast. She was twelve, I was seven." She glances at me and then back at the globe. "The shop owner had the sight, knew all about witches. He said some witch hunter had won the globe from the Time Witch in a card game, and had sold it to him when she was down on her luck." She shrugs. "I think he only *said* that to get my sister to pay more. Which she did. I've never even seen evidence that there *are* other witch hunters."

"Same," I say, swallowing, "not any outside my own family."

"This guy said there was a whole league of them . . . ," she says, and then her voice trails off. "The League of Witch Hunters."

I stare at the globe. The light stays off.

"Clara used to watch it," Aria says. "That light. She was always puzzling over it. She was *obsessed* with it, actually. Never went anywhere without her snow globe, was always staring into it when she thought I was sleeping. She said if anything ever happened to her, I should take care of it."

Goose bumps prickle across my arms.

"*Did* something happen to her?" I ask quietly, nervous.

There is a long, tense silence. "She's gone," Aria says finally, shrugging her shoulders as if she doesn't care. The freckles under her eyes squinch inward a little. "And she's the worst." Her expression goes cold for a moment, and she puts the globe back onto her nightstand. "How does your weapon work, by the way?" she asks, changing the subject.

I turn on my flashlight where it lies beside me, and shine Little One, making her retrieve a pen from my bed

and drop it into Aria's hands. "She's powered by my imagination," I say. And then sheepishly, because it sounds so
silly, I say, "I make up stories. I made a story about hope,
and it made her big enough to eat the Memory Thief."
I look around at my books. I used to think I needed to
grow up and realize that made-up stories were not all that
important, but now I suppose the future of my brother—
and possibly even the world—depends on my ability to
wield them.

Aria doesn't balk at this. Instead it's the first time I see
her really smile. "That's cool," she says.

"How does *yours* work?" I ask, nodding to the slingshot
she keeps constantly at her side.

"Music," she says. "I sing." And then her lips compress
into a thin line again, her freckles wrinkling around her
nose. "But my power's broken, ever since Clara . . ." She
trails off. "It . . . goes overboard. As you saw. If I tried to
kill a witch, I'd as likely destroy half the city we were fighting in. It's not safe."

I think of the ship tumbling down, destroying Aria's
hut and the cliffs with it. And I understand why Aria
doesn't want to fight. I wouldn't want to either, if my powers did stuff like destroy my own house.

"Well, it saved *us*," I say.

Aria proffers a smile, but a sad one. "And I hate to be the bearer of more bad news, but I've been listening to my gut for the last hour, and my gut tells me *you've* got to make the choice about the Narrows, Rosie. And it's gonna have to be stat. We're coming up on them now."

We climb the stairs again and gaze at the swirling three-dimensional shapes that circle the room, showing us the ocean surrounding us. There's a breathtaking sight ahead—two towering sets of cliffs, one on either side of a deep tunnel that looks like a scar running right down the middle. It isn't the kind of place you'd ever dream of going into. It's the kind of place where anyone is bound to get trapped.

I take a deep, ragged breath, and I think—suddenly—about the Moon Goddess. How before we left home, I climbed the ladder to the moon to meet her, even though now it seems as if I dreamt it. I wonder if she can see us beneath the sea. I wonder if she is rooting for us right now, if she even cares. What would *she* tell me to do?

The thing about the Moon Goddess is that the moonlight she reflects is filled with a magical kind of hope (that can also burn witches), but she doesn't really tell people the right answers. I wish she would make the sky fall onto the witches; I wish she would send me a sign.

I tug on my hourglass necklace. I feel claustrophobic as I stare at the entrance to the Narrows. But then I think of the Time Witch, her reptile eyes, her merciless grin. The terrors of the Narrows must be awful indeed, but I know that the Time Witch is the most terrifying thing I've ever seen.

"The Narrows, I guess," I finally say uncertainly.

And Aria nods.

"Dive. Take the low route," she says firmly to Chompy. And this time the whale moves slowly, ever so slightly changing direction down, down, down.

The sea around us dims, and grows even quieter. Inside, the lights glow softer. Chompy is trying to go undetected.

"We'll have to hope he can pick the right way forward, and hope to go unnoticed by the things these caves hold," Aria says.

The fear has gone from a distant one to a chill that makes me shiver. The high underwater cliffs rise up on either side as we approach, glowingly depicted in the dark space that surrounds us, and the silence of deep water settles in. The mouth of the Narrows looms closer and closer. And then— our vessel feeling dwarfed by the size of the emptiness—we enter, and descend in the dark.

CHAPTER 5

We watch the images of the Grand View reveal the beasts that drift around us: glowing giant jelly-fish with long tentacles trailing behind them, and blind sharks hunting within the dark crevices of the jagged underwater cliffs of the Narrows. By Germ's count (via Sharpie), we've been traveling for three days in this dark crevice that goes on, and on, and on. The glowing map of the Grand View shows us making a meandering line to the southwest across the spiral of time. We are constantly tense, watching for telltale signs of the pirate king and his army of bones, or the sunken ships of victims they've left behind. Every once in a while, as we dive to avoid an overhang of rock or a particularly large squid, Chompy begins to quake a little.

"Chompy can't go any deeper than this," Aria says. "There are places in the ocean so deep that even a magical whale can't survive them. The weight of the water above becomes too heavy to bear."

I swallow. As if being surrounded by the dangers I already knew about weren't intimidating enough.

Still, after so long of it being only me and Germ, it's nice to have another person around (including one who basically wants nothing to do with us). It's nice to hear another person's breathing in our room at night, especially when it's the breath of a fellow witch hunter (even if she *is* a broken one).

Aria wakes us up each morning with a vigorous shake as if there's no time to waste, despite the fact that we're living in a timeless vacuum. She has the pragmatism of a girl who's lived alone in a frozen hut for seven years, and yet she can tell whether the pastry Chompy serves us is French or Italian. She keeps telling us that too many Doritos will give us worms, but we suspect she is messing with us.

She spends half the time sitting with a purple marker in her hand and combing through *The Witch Hunter's Guide to the Universe*—nodding at some things, shaking her head at others. She corrects anything we've got wrong or incomplete.

She has stapled in a blank page and created a section called "Time Whales and the Sea of Always," which has been conspicuously missing because, until a few months ago, I thought time travel through the sea was a rumor spread by ghosts, and I'd never heard of a time whale. She's formatted the page to be a lot like the ones my mom wrote:

WHAT IS THE SEA OF ALWAYS?

Time on Earth does not disappear as it passes, but rather, it sinks into the sea, becoming an invisible layer of history hidden within the ocean. Just as—above—there is surface reality and then the magical layer underneath, in the sea there is the real ocean and the invisible ocean of time. Still, the time ocean is very real in its own way, and any changes to time inside the sea will impact the course of history above.

WHAT ARE TIME WHALES?

Time whales are magical creatures adapted to swimming the magical sea. For most living things, swimming in the ocean won't mean swimming through time. But time whales have an inner space-time compass that has evolved in them alone, which allows them to navigate time's spiral.

Time whales are naturally hospitable creatures and are magically equipped to provide whatever their riders need. In witch hunters' cases this might mean a living room and favorite foods. In the case of witches, it might mean darkness and emptiness and the smell of despair in the air.

WHAT ARE WHALE WHISTLES?

To aid herself and her fellow witches in their tasks, the Time Witch used her skills to create whale whistles, a whistle for each witch to keep in her robes. She fashioned each one out of silver and space-time, carving a shell on the

surface of each with her fingernail to mark it.
Any time whale called by a whistle must
respond. And while most witches use the
whales to spread curses through the past and
hide from witch hunters, the Time Witch is
fearless and instead prefers toying with those
who would hunt her.

"The Memory Thief lost her whistle," I tell Aria as I watch her write. "My dad was a fisherman. He found it in his nets, and gave it to my mom."

Aria takes this in appreciatively.

Mostly I think we get on her nerves more than anyone else she's ever known. She picks up our clothes—which we tend to leave lying around the room, along with used napkins and dirty plates—as if she might catch something from them. She watches us stuff junk food into our mouths like she is watching a train wreck. When Germ insists that once a week we should have "sloppy joe days" because that's what they'd do at the school cafeteria back home, Aria just blinks at her and then turns and walks back into the bedroom and closes her curtain. At one point on the second day, Germ patted her arm and called her "Big Ar." It did not go over well. She's basically like the coolest big sister we never had.

Germ insists on continuing to make a mess, but I start picking up after myself. I start trying to do my hair in two puffed buns at the back of my head like Aria does (though, mine doesn't look as good because my hair is straight). And when Germ offers me Pop-Tarts one morning, I wrinkle my nose and opt for toasted brioche instead. I know what Germ is thinking: I've always harped on us being ourselves, and now I'm trying to be like Aria. But it's different, because Aria is a real, proper witch hunter, and I *need* to be one. I need to be calm, collected, and sophisticated instead of messy and daydream-y. In school, I was always Germ's sidekick, the unnoticed one. But now I'm supposed to be the leader, and I'm pretty sure getting it right means being a little bit less . . . *me.*

As tired as I am night after night, I don't sleep. I lie awake, shining Little One onto the ceiling above, making her larger, larger, until she is almost too big to fit in the room, before turning her off. I've seen how easily the hummingbirds defeated her, and it makes me anxious. Not to mention what Aria said: *You're a mouse and she's a cat; she's just toying with you. It's kind of her thing.*

We talk in circles about what to do, about how the Time Witch will know of any victory over a witch we have, the moment we have it, and travel back in time to stop me. Aria rightly shoots down every idea we have. I doubt right now that we could take on a pirate king and his army of bones, much less a witch. We are relying solely on luck.

Finished with the whale and whistle section, Aria turns the *Guide* pages back to the spread that shows the Time Witch—her pale white face, familiar reptilian eyes, her necklace of pocket watches. Germ has drawn a mustache on her, to make us feel better. Aria frowns. She adds a couple of lines here and there. In the end, the Time Witch's section reads:

The Time Witch: Most powerful of the witches, besides Chaos. She is catlike, loves to play games and gamble with people.

Curse: Manipulation of time. Like all other witches, the Time Witch must touch someone to curse them.

Skills: Compresses, stretches, grows, and shrinks time. Makes people age too fast or takes away their ability to grow older.

makes happy moments last less time and sad moments last more. She can hear time, and hear when the course of it has been changed by a time traveler. She sometimes steals scraps of time and tucks them up her sleeves.

Familiars: Hummingbirds, distinguishable by their empty blue eyes. They steal, distort, and warp the time surrounding their victims.

Victims: A person cursed by the Time Witch might age rapidly, or age in reverse. They might lose entire years without knowing it. Ghosts, fairly or unfairly, blame the Time Witch for their own angst-filled relationship with time.

I bite my lip, remembering how—the night the Time Witch came to my bedroom to set her challenge—her birds fluttered around me, and the time all around us went still: the clock, Germ's snoring, everything. It was like we were in a long and silent space between two beats of a moment. As soon as she left, time caught up again.

I don't relish thinking how simple it was for her and her hummingbirds to do that.

Aria turns to the last page, to the witch called Chaos. The drawing of him is not really a drawing of a witch at all . . . only a single black feather, like the feather of a crow.

"My sister called him the Nothing King," Aria says, pointing to the word "Chaos." "Has more of a ring to it, don't you think?"

I nod.

Aria takes this as a cue to erase "Chaos" and write "The Nothing King" in its place.

I nod, satisfied. If Aria called him "Mr. Pee Pee Pants," I'd probably still be on board, just because Aria said it. Anyway, Aria's parents passed things on to Clara that my mom, still recovering her memory, couldn't pass on to me.

The Nothing King: The most powerful of all witches.

Specialty: Nothing.

Skills: Nothing.

Curse/familiars: Crows.

Victims: Everyone and everything.

It's kind of a funny entry, as if nobody really knows anything about him.

"Your guide is right that he's the worst of them," Aria says. "The Time Witch is nothing compared to the Nothing King. He's more powerful than all of the rest combined. But he's imprisoned in a black hole at the other end of the universe. He had a big fight with the Moon Goddess in ancient times, and she prevailed." She scratches her chin with the cap of her marker. "If he weren't locked away for all eternity, he'd be a real problem. Anyway." She shrugs. "With the Trapper and the Memory Thief gone, it's only ten more witches you have to get through, not eleven. He doesn't count."

Aria stares off into space for a moment, and a faraway look comes over her face. She's looking over my shoulder toward the Grand View, curious. We can see something blue and bright coming toward our ship.

"Huh."

She stands. We all move toward the Grand View to get a closer look, climbing the stairs.

A glow is emerging in the murky, foggy water up ahead.

The shape is hard to make out at first, the water is so dark, but as we get closer, its luminous glow reaches us so that we can see more fully what we are approaching.

"It looks like a cloud," Germ says.

"Not a cloud. It's too round. More like . . . the moon," I say.

My pulse begins to pound. The orb glowing ahead of us is beautiful. It does look, as impossible as it may seem, like the moon itself. My mind races for an explanation. Has the Moon Goddess sunk the moon to come and help us? The moment the thought crosses my mind, I am sure it's true, and my heart leaps inside my chest.

We do nothing as Chompy swims closer, as mesmerized by the light as we are.

All I can think is, *We're saved. We're saved. We're saved.*

We see the shape moving all around the moon, but not in time.

"What *is* that?" Germ breathes.

And then we lose our footing, because suddenly Chompy is jerking back. He lets out a rumbling, screeching sound underneath and all around us.

At the same moment, we see that the moon is not a moon at all but an enormous, glowing eye looking straight at us. Out of the shadows, swimming toward us so that now both glowing eyes are visible, is a squid as gigantic as any ship I've ever seen. There's a chain around its neck, tying it to one of the soaring cliff walls. And its tentacles, I see too late, are already stretching all around us!

"It's a trap," Aria breathes. "Chompy, rise!"

But it's useless. Chompy butts against something that slams down on top of him, and we fall with the stomach-dropping weight. He tries to slip backward, but that way too is blocked. And this time we see by what.

It's a rusted and glowing submarine with a hole in its side, and ghosts running to and fro along its decks and beyond its round windows. There's an enormous red skull painted at the nose. A net shoots out from the front of the ship, spreading like algae in the water.

"Swim past it!" Aria yells.

Chompy zigzags downward, and we narrowly miss the net as we dive for the depths below. But we see that this, too, is hopeless. We are diving straight into a pit, not a passageway. Inside it waits a pirate ship, completely submerged, sails torn. Hundreds of ghosts poke out of the windows and stand on the decks. They are going wild, like blood thirst has caught them in its grips.

The net settles around us now, and is dragging us down into the pit toward the ship. The light from the squid's eyes above disappears, and but for the glow of the countless ghosts surrounding us, the world around us goes black.

Already, ghosts are jumping off the ship and crawling all over our moonroof like ticks. We can hear the moaning of the dead as they begin floating in through Chompy's sides, appearing around the room.

I leap toward the bedroom to reach my *Lumos* flashlight, but two ghosts appear in front of me with rusted daggers. And as much as I've heard that ghosts can almost never hurt people, these two look very confident that they can.

"Wait for the king," one says.

My eyes dart to the flashlight on my bed. I am about to dive for it, right through them, when a figure appears behind them, and both spirits drift aside.

He is *dim*. So dim that he's nearly invisible. Frail. Withering. I can see at a glance, he is dying. Not the dying people do but something even worse. The pirate king is as *near to becoming nothing* as a ghost can get.

And Germ and I both suck in air at once.

"If you want to live," he says flatly, in a cold, steely voice, "you'll do as I say."

And then, so slightly that only I can see it, he gives me a wink. And I want to scream and wail and faint with joy at once.

The pirate king is Ebb.

CHAPTER 6

'm so breathless, I might as well be a ghost myself. I would leap out to hug Ebb, but I'd fall right through him. Still, I jerk forward before stopping myself. Ebb's eyes are cold, as if he's never seen me in his life. My arms drop to my sides in confusion.

"How . . . ," I breathe. "How . . ." It's all I can get out. Beside me, Aria has her slingshot raised and is ready to smash a song-driven stone into Ebb's face (and also possibly sink our whale in the process).

"Ebb!" Germ says. "You're alive! I mean, not dead. I

mean, you're *dead* but you're not *nothing*! I mean . . ." Germ is wringing her hands, and her face is practically exploding with emotion. Ebb ignores her, and looks at the two ghosts beside him.

"I've heard the loud, light-haired one suffers from delirium," he says.

One of them points a hand toward Germ's hair. "We can remove the hair if it's a problem. Or the head."

Ebb shrugs. "The Time Witch will want them as they are," he replies. The other two nod, hanging on his every word. "Hurry to the ship," he continues. "Take the others. Steer to the surface, find her birds. Tell her we've got them."

"Ebb," I gasp. He shoots me a look, his eyes drilling into mine. I shut my mouth.

The pirates—all at once—drift out through the walls of Chompy and disappear. As soon as they're gone, Ebb's shoulders fall, and he looks at us.

"We gotta move fast," he says. "If we can make it through the gap, we've got a chance."

I don't have time to answer before he peers around and then steps up quickly to the Grand View, searching with darting eyes the holographic image of our surroundings that spin around him. We are not in a pit at all, it appears, but a set of caves that was not even on our maps a moment ago. And then, in the glowing blue shapes of the sea around us, we see a thin, crooked slit on a distant stone wall, with the vaguest hint of a silver glow within it. He points at it. "There it is. It's a tricky bit—a slit through time to another part of the sea altogether, a kink in the spiral. We only have a few minutes to get through it before they return." He looks at me. "Can you steer your whale there?" he asks. "Into that narrow gap?"

I look at Aria, who doesn't answer. Now that I've seen how *she* does it, I'm hoping I can do it too.

"I think so," I say.

Aria shakes her head. She's still aiming her slingshot at Ebb's face.

Ebb swallows. "You're going to have to trust me," he says.

"Trust a pirate who's sworn to have the head of any witch hunter on Earth?" she says. "I'd rather be dead."

His eyes flash at her. "You'll be worse than dead if you don't do what I say. Rosie, tell your whale to dive."

I hesitate. I don't know what's happened to Ebb, why he is so dim and empty-looking, why his voice is so steely and mean. And then I see Fred, his pet spider, crawling up the sleeve of his worn, ripped coat. It feels like seeing an old, close friend.

I look an apology at Aria, who is shaking her head at me.

"Through there, Chompy," I say, the way I've seen Aria do—with confidence, though my voice quakes more than I'd like. Still, just like that, the whale listens. Germ looks at me, and I raise my brows at her, as surprised as she is.

The moments pass as we swim toward the gap. We are diving into an emptiness. Either we are about to disappear into a fathomless nothing of a pit, or we're about to be delivered from danger.

And then, in another moment, we are in and through. Light suddenly cascades down through the water in beams. The darkness falls away behind us. And something unexpected opens out in the view beneath us.

A sunken, ancient stone city.

Ebb turns to us, and his anger collapses into an expression of physical pain. He winces, and as he does, he brightens and then dims—light, dark, light, dark.

"We'll be safe here. Also," he says, looking up at my double buns that I've made to be like Aria's, "what's up with your hair?"

And then he flickers out, and disappears.

He reappears a moment later, dim and drawn-looking.

"Rosie," he breathes. "Germ." He grimaces a smile. He looks at me, taking me in.

We are swimming over the rooftops of the underwater city. Germ says she thinks Chompy likes the view because he's making gentle whale sounds, like someone oohing and aahing at a museum. Sharks weave in and out of streets below us; algae covers what looks to be a temple. It's beautiful.

And then I notice, Aria is still armed and ready to thwap Ebb in the face. "Can someone explain to me how you all know each other?" she demands. "And why I shouldn't get rid of this guy?"

Germ must see this as her moment to convince Aria we're not the silly little kids she thinks we are. She suddenly hearkens back to an etiquette class we had in fifth grade.

"Aria, this is *Ebb*. Ebb, this is *Aria*. *Ebb*, Aria is the second-to-last witch hunter on Earth and enjoys fine chocolates and filet mignon. *Aria*, Ebb is a ghost who has haunted Rosie's house all her life, until the Time Witch got him. Also, he showed Rosie that the invisible fabric of the universe exists. He likes . . . um, *us* . . . and spiders . . . and listening to nature and trying to understand what it's saying." She turns to Ebb and blinks as she runs out of polite introductory things to say. "What are you doing here?" she asks. "Why are you pretending to be the pirate king?"

Ebb's eyes shoot to mine, then flick away.

"I *am* the pirate king," he says.

"But . . . ," Germ begins. There are so many buts. *But the pirate king has haunted the seas for a thousand years, and we only saw Ebb last June. But the pirate king does terrible things to people on behalf of the Time Witch. But the pirate king is evil.*

Germ gives me a look that says, *Awkward.*

"And what is this place?" Aria asks, cutting to the chase. "How do you know we're safe here?"

Ebb's forehead wrinkles in brooding thought, a familiar expression that I've missed for so long.

"I've uncovered so many hiding spots over the years, but this is one of the best. You stumble on these kinds of things, eventually, when you roam the sea for so long. This is the city of Helike, lost to the world above." He looks sad, and won't meet our eyes, as if there's a lot he doesn't want to say. "I don't think anyone knows about it really, even the Time Witch. It's absolutely forgotten by history."

Watching the city drift beneath us, I can easily imagine that no one remembers it. Sharks swim through the streets, and giant clams lie at the foot of elegant staircases. It looks like something out of a fairy tale.

Pulling my gaze from the view, I see that Chompy has already changed things to accommodate Ebb. There's a dusty attic-like space for a bedroom at the other side of the main room, some vintage things like an old catcher's glove and a pogo stick, and a prefab web up in the corner all ready for Fred the spider to move into. Ebb lifts Fred from his sleeve and places him on the web.

I watch him, mystified. How could a boy who's so kind to spiders menace the Sea of Always for a thousand years? But then I keep thinking how the other ghosts treated him: like a leader, and someone they were scared of.

"Fred's gotten dim too. It's all the years away from our grave," Ebb says, swallowing. "We're fading away. I thought it would happen a lot faster, to be honest. I haven't had a time-traveling whale like you, but life under the sea, it slows things down."

His words slice right through me. *Of course. That's* why Ebb is so dim. All these years, he's been away from his grave. He is fading into nothing at all.

"What happened to you after we last saw you, Ebb?" I ask. I feel sick, waiting to hear the answer. I may not want to know what it is.

Ebb flickers out for a split second, then reappears.

There's a long silence as he looks anywhere but at my eyes.

And then, of all the things I never expected to hear, Ebb tells us how he came to rule and terrorize the ocean of time.

CHAPTER 7

"Everything was so peaceful the night she took me," Ebb says. "It was dark moon, so of course I knew it was a riskier night with the moonlight gone, but it'd been so long since you'd destroyed the Memory Thief that I wasn't worrying about it. The witches hadn't come for you: no revenge, no attacks, nothing. I was starting to feel like you and your mom were safe.

"I remember you were up in your window that night, reading a book while your mom was cooking dinner. It was the picture of what I'd always wanted for you—a happy home, your mother's love. I was out on the grass by the cliffs, guarding the yard and your house, as usual. I guess I had gotten too comfortable with things."

He thinks and swallows. I can see fear pass through his dim frame and over his face, a kind of terror.

"One minute I was alone, and the next minute I just . . . wasn't. She was . . ." He pauses, then continues, "Standing there, a few feet away.

"It was her eyes I saw first, those empty blue eyes, gleaming in the dark across the lawn. I tried to move, but I wasn't fast enough. It was like she moved at the speed of light. You wouldn't believe how fast. And then her arms were wrapping around me. There was only time to think, *I'm gone.*" He shakes his head. "The only other thing I thought about was *you.* I thought, *She's after Rosie next.*"

He looks down at the floor.

"Anyway, the next thing I know, I'm in a cellar. I didn't know where or *when* I was, but there were other ghosts jailed with me: a ghost of a baker from Portugal in the 1600s, a ghost named Lin Mei who was a dancer, a professional thief from the 1970s named Steve. They told me everything: what year we were in—1018; and what place—some abandoned castle in what is now Spain. Basically, the

Time Witch keeps a few ghosts around to gamble with. I was one of those ghosts."

"Gamble with?" I ask.

"Sort of like poker chips. If she's gambling with someone, she'll bet them five ghosts, that kind of thing."

"But why would someone want ghosts?" Germ presses.

Ebb has made it clear many times that ghosts, unable to touch and move things except for in rare circumstances, are generally useless.

"Turns out some people with the sight like having ghosts around," he answers. "To sing to them, or be gentle alarm clocks, or be night-lights, or to keep the people company. And the Time Witch sometimes *gives* things to ghosts, half-magic, half-real things they can use to make them less useless. Like brooms for cleaning, stuff like that. She gave my crew their daggers."

"But why don't the ghosts just escape from her jail?" I ask.

"Lead walls," he says, his eyebrows lowering. "ANY-WAY," he goes on, "I passed year after year in that cellar, waiting to be gambled away, hopeless. And you know me. I like to *listen*. I noticed the water whispering that there were tunnels under the lead cellar. The mold grew in a certain direction like it was trying to point the way out. It was like all the life in that cellar wanted to help me escape. Only, I didn't have the will.

"She caught me one day, when she came to collect another ghost she'd lost in a game of cribbage. She caught me whispering to Fred and listening. And I suppose it made her think she could use my services. She wanted me to try to teach spiders in the castle to be her spies.

"Well, she started having me come to different rooms upstairs to talk to the spiders and so on. And that's when I got more of the lay of the land—the layout of the castle, the fields all around and the ocean beyond. I spent a lot of time up there, and after a while she barely noticed me. By that time I think she'd long forgotten where she'd collected me, or why. I'm a ghost, *harmless and powerless*, you know?

"And every night, it was back to the cellar. The ghosts came and went, and passed the time with gossip, like they always do. I listened to that, too." He glances at his feet. "That's how, one night, I learned you were still alive. They were talking about a witch hunter, about the game the Time Witch had set for her." He looks up and meets my eyes. "They said the Time Witch had dared the witch hunter to rescue her twin brother. I knew it had to be you." He kneads his hands together. "They said you were doomed."

A long silence.

"Around that time, I started to develop my plan. Every night, the Time Witch would head out to spread her curses while I organized things at the castle—getting the insects to spy, getting the other ghosts to behave, getting more and more of her trust. When I told her I could whisper the creatures of the sea into attacking ships and whales, she was intrigued." He stares at his fingernails and looks up at Germ. "Basically, I told her I could organize the Sea of Always the way I'd organized her castle, have it all at her command. You'd be surprised how much of the sea—how much *nature*—is really beyond her control, so she was tempted by the offer.

"She gave me a ship. Really, what she wanted more than anything else was more weapons against any witch hunters who might come after her." He glances at me again. "Even the ones she invited herself.

"I gathered a menagerie of loyal sea creatures, and a crew of thousands of ghosts . . . the bad ones. You know, ghosts who'd done horrible things in life and never moved on."

I nod. I know all too well how some ghosts move on to what is Beyond, and some don't.

"I built my undersea army. Ghosts can't usually fight, as you know, but we had our witch-given daggers. *And* we had our nets, which the Time Witch also provided—

half-real and half-magic, like I said. And then . . .”

“And then . . . ?” Germ asks. We are both on the edge of our seats, wanting him to tell us that it’s all a big misunderstanding, that he didn’t do those unspeakable things we read about in our *Welcome to the Sea of Always* book. Then again, for Ebb a *thousand* years have passed. Enough lifetimes to change someone into a person—or a ghost—you don’t even know anymore.

“Then what?” Germ finally demands. “Ebb, did you do all those horrible things the book says you did? Maraud the sea for riches, pull countless ships to their doom? Did you do all that to survive the Time Witch?”

Ebb looks at her a moment, his eyebrows low, and pauses for what seems like forever.

“If there’s one thing I’ve learned over a thousand years,” he says, “it’s that ghosts like to gossip.” And then he turns his eyes on me. “But you can’t believe all the ghost gossip you hear.” For a moment, his eyes have a twinkle. “I’ve encouraged my crew to, um, embellish our adventures a bit.”

I see Germ visibly breathe a sigh of relief. I am pretty sure I do the same.

“Well, what about the squid?” Germ demands. “You’ve got him chained in the Narrows!”

Ebb shrugs. “You mean Inky? Oh, Inky’s all right. He’s

better at unlocking that collar than any ghost could ever be. He's very dramatic, a top-rated performer. I'm glad I took a chance on him."

He smiles at Germ and Aria, but doesn't look at me again. I get the feeling more and more that he's avoiding my eyes . . . that he'd avoid me altogether if he could. And I don't understand why.

"I've kept plenty of secrets from my crew. One of them is Helike, and another one is that I'm not out to kill witch hunters after all. They'll be enraged when they find I'm not on their side."

Aria, still looking distrustful, says, "I'm not so sure *ours* is the side you want to be on."

Ebb blinks at her. "What do you mean?"

Aria looks steadily at him. "Rosie's hopes of saving her brother are pretty much crushed. The Time Witch knows Rosie's every move the moment she makes it. It's a trap in every direction. Basically, your friends are beaten before they've started."

For a moment, an expression crosses Ebb's face that shows the old Ebb—moody, protective, determined— making an appearance at last. He pushes his flickering brown hair out of his flickering ghostly brown eyes.

"I can fix that," he says simply.

CHAPTER 8

We stare at Ebb. A tangle of nerves zings in the pit of my stomach.

"What do you mean, you can fix it?" Aria asks suspiciously.

Ebb puts his hands into his pockets. "I mean, all those years I was watching and listening to the moss on the walls, and the water under the floor, I watched and listened to the *Time Witch*, too. And I learned." He looks back and forth between Aria and Germ, and only occasionally at me. "I learned that witches wash their faces with dirt. I learned that some of them snore. I learned that even though they roam the Sea of Always in their whales, they hate water. I learned that the Time Witch likes to hide stolen scraps of space and time in random places; I know a ghost who says he found a forest from the 1700s that she hid in a sock once. And I learned something else, too."

By now he's looking a tiny bit full of himself. "This one night when I was up in her room, she opened this rusty square metal box she had beside her bed, like a jewelry box but really plain, and took something out of it. It was as if she wanted to look at it for only a second, to check on it. Then she stuffed it back into the box. It was the only time I ever saw her do that in two hundred years. But I'll never forget it."

"What was it?" Germ asks.

He smiles, and looks rather pleased with himself. "Her heart."

We all blink at him, speechless. "Her *heart*?" I breathe.

"Clara," Aria offers slowly, her eyes on Ebb, "once told me she'd heard that witches and their hearts aren't attached. That witches carry their hearts around, like accessories."

Ebb nods. "It's true. I'd heard the rumors, but I'd never given them much thought until that night. A witch's heart doesn't pump her blood, but she still needs it to live." He looks up at me. "In other words, if you destroyed a witch's heart, she'd die."

Aria gets up to go check the Grand View and then returns, as wary as always even in this hidden place.

"But this doesn't fix anything," I say to Ebb. "Even if we managed to steal a heart and destroy it, the Time Witch would know the second we did it, and she'd go back in time and destroy *us*."

"Well," Ebb says, "I was thinking that, but then I was thinking about fire ants."

"Fire ants?" Germ and I echo simultaneously.

"Well, there's this kind of ant that attacks its victims in a sneaky way. Basically, a whole bunch of ants crawl up a creature's legs, unnoticed, until they're all over its body. Then one of the ants sends the signal, and they all bite at once. It's like, they spend all their effort setting up the attack. Once they actually bite, it's too late, the animal is overwhelmed."

Germ looks conflicted. "Smart little guys," she says. "Also, poor animal. I don't know who to root for." Aria gives her a look like, *You can't be serious*. But Germ is the kind of person who can't help but root for both sides in any battle. (One time, she cried when I told her the basic plot of *Snoopy, Come Home*.) For now, she's been rubbing one of the walls as Ebb has been talking, so she doesn't notice Aria's look. "I'm giving Chompy a cheek massage," she says.

Finally we turn back to Ebb. "Okay, so what do fire ants have to do with killing witches?" Aria asks.

Ebb clears his throat, his full-of-himself expression melting under Aria's skeptical gaze. "Right. So yes . . . the Time Witch is one step ahead of you and always will be because she knows anything that happens at any time. So killing the witches one by one won't work, and neither would killing them all at once—even if you got the chance. You'd be no match for all those witches at the same time.

"But, well, I've had about a thousand years to think about this. And I was thinking, if the Time Witch is so careless with her heart, the others probably are too. I mean, witches are pure evil. They're not exactly *in touch* with their hearts, you know? I bet they all keep them somewhere nearby but neglected."

We don't answer because we don't know how. Ebb has taken on a brightness that was not there a few seconds before. For a moment he's almost as luminous as his old self, more *here* than gone.

"If we were to *sneak* somehow like fire ants do, to steal their hearts one by one—hearts they never check on anyway—the Time Witch would never know. Nobody would notice that their hearts were gone, not for a while."

And then he dims slightly. "I wouldn't be able to help"—he nods upward—"out there. I'd have to stay on board. Another day out of the sea with time passing, and I'd probably fade away completely. It would be up to you three."

There is a long silence as we take this in. Germ is the first to break it.

"And then what would we do with the hearts, once we have them?" she asks.

He shrugs, as if this is the simplest part. "We have Little One eat them. All at once."

"But then there's still the Time Witch," I press.

Here he falters, flickering a little with doubt. "We'd have to count on the element of surprise with her. I can't think of any other way. We go to 1855 as our final stop. She'll have all the witches there waiting to attack. What they won't know is that we're already holding their lives in our hands. We have Little One devour the hearts the minute we face them, and take advantage of the Time Witch's surprise to have Little One attack her before she can react."

We are silent.

It's actually kind of a good plan.

"How would we find them? All the witches?" I ask.

Ebb opens his mouth to reply. "I don't kn—"

"Whale song," Germ interjects. "Chompy can ask around." I look to Aria, trying to gauge whether this is a crazy idea or not, and surprisingly, she looks intrigued as Germ starts to think out loud. "The whales are probably friends, you know? *I'd* be friends with the others if I were a time whale. Just because the witches command them doesn't mean they don't like to chat with each other."

"They could tell Chompy *where* in time they last dropped off their witches," Aria offers. She's tense, but I can see her grudging appreciation of Ebb's and Germ's ideas. She's softening toward Ebb, for sure. "We'd have to make our landings on or around dark moon nights, when they're getting bold enough to be out and about. Obviously, the Time Witch would be keeping your brother in San Francisco on a dark moon night, so that one's a given. Then it's just a matter of stealing hearts from the nine most fearsome souls on earth before we get to her."

"Even if she's caught off guard, the Time Witch could have us cursed in a second flat," I offer. "She's the Time Witch."

Everyone nods grimly.

"I still think it's the best option we've got," Ebb says. His eyes dart again to my hair, in the buns. I'm beginning to feel self-conscious about them, and about him noticing how much I'm trying to be like Aria. I casually roll them out.

"There's one major drawback to the plan," Aria says. "If even one of the witches catches us stealing, notices what we're up to, it's over. We have to pull off all nine thefts perfectly, from nine terrible beings. And *then*, like you said, we still need to defeat the Time Witch. All before Rosie's remaining time runs out."

"The witches won't wander far from shore and the safety of being able to call the whales they command," Ebb offers. "They're lazy and scared of the moonlight and don't like to be out in the open for long. We could find them."

We sit in silence for a long while, all weighing the choice we face. Aria is the first one to speak. And her voice is softer, kinder as she looks at Ebb.

"Well," she says, "up till now this mission has felt completely impossible. Now it only feels *mostly* impossible." She tilts her head, smiling slightly, the kind of smile that might belong to a girl who has not given up on battling witches as much as she says. "I guess I could help, with a plan like that. Even though I can't help to fight."

Germ, too, is clearly warming up to the plan. Then again, Germ is always the brave one.

They all look at me, like I'm the person everything hinges on. I do not like being the person everything hinges on. I like to be the one watching from the wall.

"Ebb, the first place we're going is home," I say. Ebb is fading, and he needs to get back to the place where he died, to recharge.

"You can't," Germ says sadly. "The time rules."

She retrieves our *Welcome to the Sea of Always* book, opening to the rules page.

We scan the list, past the rule about tampering with the course of human history (I suppose witches don't listen to that one, and maybe since they're half-magical, it doesn't count) and the one that forbids any living person to cross themselves in time. Then Germ points to the rule she's remembering:

No extra stops beyond one's central mission, EXCEPT when using a forever voucher.

"See?" she says. "The only way to make an extra stop is by using the voucher. And you promised the voucher to . . ." Germ looks at Aria, who shakes her head.

"I can't give it up. I'm sorry, I really can't."

Ebb seems to catch on vaguely to what we're talking about. He looks at the hourglass around my neck. "I've waited a thousand years. I can wait twenty more days, more or less."

But I can't help thinking about something that makes my stomach churn. If I hadn't promised Aria the voucher, we could have taken Ebb back to the time before he died. Not only could he have recharged, but he could have seen his parents again, before they died too. He could have spent a day forever with them.

Again, everyone is silent. They are waiting for me to make a choice.

I stand, and walk up to the Grand View to look at the old-timey photo of my brother, his wide eyes like mine, his fear at whatever or whoever lies beyond the camera.

The sea is peaceful and safe around us, and time on the whale stands still. We could swim the ocean for a long time trying to look for other solutions, safer ones, hoping to escape the Time Witch's notice. I am not like Germ and Aria. I could burrow into a hole with my stories and the people I love, and never mind not venturing out or saving the world at all, if only I could know that Wolf was okay. Then I would happily let someone else fight the witches.

"I need to think," I say. "It's gambling it all in one shot. It's risky."

"I get it," Ebb says. "But I'd say decide soon. My crew will be looking for us. The Time Witch will be looking for us. And there's something else." Ebb flickers. "Something more I learned about the Time Witch, watching her over the years. She's planning something. I don't know what, but whatever it is, it's more than just covering the world in darkness. There's something deeper she's trying to do."

"Deeper than covering the world in darkness?" Aria looks dubious.

"I know it sounds weird. It's nothing I can put my finger on exactly. Only . . . something's up. Something we don't understand."

We all take this in uncertainly, because it's hard to get upset about something possibly worse than fighting to save the world from a web of evil that, in Aria's time, has sent the moon spinning away.

"Well, if we kill them all," Germ says, looking on the bright side, "we'll never have to find out."

CHAPTER 9

Several days pass as we go over and over the possibilities, safe and static on our whale as he circles the hidden backwaters of the city of Helike.

Aria and Ebb carefully lay out what our plan would look like if we *were* to go through with it: the amount of time we'd have to steal the heart of each witch (about fifty-three hours per witch, on average, which doesn't seem like much when we don't know how far inland we might find them), and how we'd go about doing it unnoticed by witch spies.

Aria explains what she learned from her sister about

the sight. To dim the sight so that witch spies and witches don't see you, you basically close your eyes and imagine turning down the volume of your *inner self*, as if you were using the volume on a remote control.

"To be clear," she says one evening, "dimming yourself *won't* make you *invisible*, especially not to a witch. It'll just make it so you don't shine out to her and her familiars like Rudolph the Red-Nosed Reindeer. We will need to be sneaky."

As I listen, I fiddle around with Little One, whipping her around and making her dart faster, grow bigger, dive, bite, grab things around the room. I know she's going to have to be the key to all our thefts, but I'm not exactly sure how. With the Memory Thief, I made Little One enormous. But there's nothing sneaky about a luminous bird the size of a house. Not to mention that after what happened with the hummingbirds, I'm afraid she's not as strong as I hoped.

Ebb and Germ and Aria go on talking, but quietly enough that I can't hear. They giggle about something together. In the three days since he boarded our whale, Ebb has ignored me almost completely—leaving conversations when I join them, not looking me in the eye. There are things I forgot about him, like how he blushes brightly like a lamp when he's embarrassed, and how curious he is about everything. Now, feeling hurt, I watch the three of them chatting so easily. Whatever makes him avoid me, it's not impacting his friendship with Germ or his getting to know Aria.

I know I should ask him. But I'm pretty sure I can guess the reason why he doesn't seem to like me anymore: I'm the girl who let him get caught by the Time Witch. I'm the one he was trying to protect, and instead it got him a thousand years wandering the world alone, and nearly got him obliterated.

Eventually Germ comes and perches on my bed, crossing her arms around her knees and looking at me.

"How's it going with Little One?" she asks.

"I'm trying to figure out how we'd use her to get the hearts in a sneaky way. But it's hard because . . . I don't know what to expect, you know?"

Germ nods. She looks me over. I'm wearing pj's that are almost an exact imitation of Aria's white silky ones.

"You don't have to be like Aria to be a good witch hunter, you know," Germ ventures, like she's walking on eggshells. "I mean, Aria's great, but so are you."

Dubious, I glance over at Aria as she chats with Ebb. Not only does she know everything about witch hunting, but she's also better than I am at being friends with the ghost who's looked out for me my whole life.

"I wish I was as good at making friends as you guys are," I say. Even back home, I've been trying to be more outgoing with Germ's huge and growing array of friends. But it's not as easy for me as it is for her.

Germ is thoughtful. "I'm no witch hunter like you and Aria, so what do I know . . . but maybe you don't need to be friends with *a lot* of people, just the right people." She pauses. "As for Ebb," she says, looking over at him, "whatever his problem is, he'll come around."

I want to think Germ's right. But I also wonder if I will never be quite the right fit anywhere. And I wonder how someone who's not the right fit anywhere can save the world.

Germ is sitting and watching as I make Little One swipe a dust mote out of the air, when we both look up to find Ebb watching me.

"What are you looking at?" I ask flatly. I try to sound cool, calm, aloof, like Aria.

"I was . . . remembering something," he says. "About how when you are concentrating, the tip of your nose sort of . . . crinkles up."

"Oh." It's a weird thing to say to someone you are

basically ignoring, and I don't know how to respond to it.

Ebb drifts away, and the moment passes, leaving my head full of the mystery of it.

Germ and I are sitting in the main room playing Spit, and Aria is up at the Grand View studying some Portuguese men-of-war floating by, when it happens. I'm trying to smack-talk Germ about my card-playing skills even though I know I'm bound to lose, when Aria makes a strangled, surprised kind of noise, "OH."

She looks back at us, suddenly tense.

"What is it?" I ask.

"You'd better come look," she says, her voice like gravel.

We all head up to the Grand View as Aria watches us gravely. Then she turns and points to tiny glowing shapes floating here and there around us.

"There," she says. "And there. And there."

I can't quite make them out at first. Whatever they are, they look like small faraway fish—only they *drift through the water* rather than swim. More and more come into view as they come closer to Chompy. There must be hundreds of them.

"What are they?"

"Bottles," Aria says after a moment.

And I see now, upon closer inspection, she's right—the shapes are floating, green glass bottles. All with something curled up inside them.

"They're *messages* in bottles," Aria says. "And I'll bet you anything they all carry the same message."

"Why?" Germ looks up at her. "Why do you think that?"

She taps the air where one of the bottles appears, and we get a zoomed-in closer look. "See? They're all addressed to Rosie, in the same hand."

Sure enough, the closer she zooms (I didn't even know zooming was possible), the easier I can make out the words: *Rosie Oaks, c/o the Time Whale She Rides On.* I recognize the writing from the back of Wolf's photo. It belongs to the Time Witch.

"She must have sent out hundreds of thousands of them, floating through this part of the ocean, hoping one would reach you," Aria says. "Chompy, can you swallow one?" she asks. "And bring it on board?"

A few moments pass as we get closer and closer to one of the floating bottles. There is a slight intake of water, trickling in through the entrance at Chompy's mouth. And then the water gets siphoned back out again through the clever little drains along the edges of the rug, and all that's left behind is one old-looking green glass bottle with a piece of paper clearly rolled up inside.

I snatch it up, but then Germ takes it out of my hands, gently. It's like she's anticipated that whatever's inside is going to hurt me.

Germ fiddles with the cork for a moment, which is so wedged into the top of the bottle that it's almost impossible to pry out, but finally she gets it free.

She unrolls the paper carefully but quickly, and—as she holds it flat—her eyes skim its surface.

Germ goes pale. She looks at me.

She doesn't seem to be able to read it out loud, because she hands it to me silently, looking pained. And I read it instead.

Greetings and salutations, witch hunter!

Dropping a line to ask you how Helike is this time of year. I'll bet it's lovely! I'd come to see you there, but the truth is, it would make our game end rather too quickly, don't you think? I had really hoped you'd be more of a challenge than this, my dear. I thought I'd explained to you how terribly bored I am. I'll give

you one more chance to entertain me.
Incidentally, your brother is well.
He can't send his regards because he
doesn't know that you exist. Just today
I explained to him that in twenty days,
I'll have to take all his years away until
he is . . . no more. You can imagine how
distressed he was by this news, given
that he is not aware there's a soul on
Earth who wants to save him. But I
feel it only fair to apprise him of the
inevitable. Particularly because your
attempts to defy me have been so paltry
thus far.
It's a shame. Had you never attempted
to come after him, had you ignored my
game, I suppose I would have forgotten
about him altogether and let him at least
live out his life. But things take some
unexpected turns sometimes after all. I
wish it happened more often.

All good wishes,
The Time Witch

The horror creeps over me in inches. When it reaches my knees, I feel them turn to jelly.

"She's going to take all his years away!" Germ tells Aria and Ebb. "Until they're gone. Until . . . he's gone." Ebb meets my eyes, and he looks so stricken that for once it's like he knows me again, and cares. Perched on the coffee table, Little One trembles and begins to chirp frantically. She sounds as desperately wounded and terrified as I feel.

Aria takes the letter, reads it swiftly, then crumples it up and tosses it to the ground. "Don't you believe that, Rosie. She's enraged. You've slipped her traps so far—the hummingbirds, the pirates," she says. "You've worried her, that's why she sent this letter—to intimidate you. Don't let her make you think anything else."

My eyes are drawn to my photo of Wolf again, taped on the wall. How lost he must be, how alone. He doesn't even know about me! He should be home having a normal life. He should be going to school and playing in the yard. And the world should be *good* for him. In the world my brother deserves, witches don't exist. And now, by setting out to save him, I've put him in more danger than ever.

But this doesn't make me angry at myself.

It makes me angry at the witches.

I feel the fear turn into something hard and steely inside me. I see it in Little One too, as she glints and gleams like blue, glowing steel. I forget about the future. I forget about the dark web being woven through the world. I only want to tear every witch limb from limb until my brother is safe.

I look to Ebb. "I'm in," I say. "For the plan. When do we start?"

For a moment no one speaks. Germ closes her eyes. She's doing ESP, but whatever she's trying to communicate to our whale, it's not working.

"Chompy?" Aria finally says, taking control. "We need to find a witch. Any witch."

We hear a howl of whale song. And then singing. Beautiful, haunting singing.

"What's he doing?" Ebb asks out loud.

"He's calling out to the other time whales. Asking where they are."

The haunting sound is all around us for several minutes. And then silence. The timeless ocean, so far from the tumult and change of the world above, stays quiet.

"They're not answering," I whisper.

"Maybe they're too far away," Germ says.

And then there's a faint sound, so faint that it seems

almost imaginary. Somewhere far across the ocean, some-one is answering back.

Chompy is perfectly still for a few moments, as if lis-tening. And then there is a tilt and a swish of the room as he rises and sets himself in motion.

I find, now that I've made my choice, I can't wait to start.

The witches have stolen so much from the world: memories, love and connection, my only brother.

I grip my hand around my *Lumos* flashlight, and watch the monitor scroll and toggle and swirl across a vast map of the sea. I don't care where I have to go, as long as I find them.

Now we start stealing from them.

The dark moon is back, and Annabelle Oaks is busy. For the third day in a row, her nightly companion has stayed home. Elaine's other children are missing her, she says. "They're teen-agers," she pointed out three nights ago, the bags under her eyes darker than ever, "but they're here, and they need their mother too."

With Germ's mother gone, the ghosts demand all of Anna-belle's attention. They tell her their troubles, and she listens, consoles them about lost friends, and friends who have moved

Beyond. She advises them on how to make their graves more inviting. She reads to them and changes the TV to their favorite late-night shows. She paints their portraits.

She cares about these ghosts. But whenever they allow her a moment to herself, she paces, frets, walks the stairs up and down, up and down, all through the long November nights. She can't eat and her body has become willowy, too thin. It's been a month since she saw the strange witch in her yard. Will she come back, now that the moon is dim? Annabelle fears such a return, but she also longs for it.

What does the witch know of Rosie, and how? Why did she come? To warn her, or taunt her? Did she come to curse her? Did she come to help? Annabelle goes to the window for the thousandth time of the night, to watch the sea. It's almost dawn, and she is on the verge of giving up for the night. Once the sun rises, there's no chance the witch will appear.

And then the wind begins to blow, and the hair on the back of Annabelle's neck stands up. A family of squirrels scurries up the side of the house and into the attic for shelter. The trees shiver. The ghosts dart out through the walls in a rush and zip across the yard to the woods. Annabelle's heart leaps as if it has touched an electric wire.

One moment the witch is not there, and the next moment, she is.

This time, she's closer—halfway across the yard—and illuminated by the dim light of the windows shining onto the lawn. She has a dark mole at the side of her mouth, and purple eyelids that match her dress. This time, iridescent white cats, all wearing sparkling purple collars, saunter around the grass that surrounds her, brushing lazily against her ankles.

Annabelle realizes, with a shiver, that she knows this witch, or stories of her. She was almost killed once, the story goes, trapped inland by a hunter and almost burned to death by the moon. According to the tales, a hundred years old at least, some mysterious circumstance led to her escape.

Convenia is her name.

When she sees that Annabelle has spotted her, the witch turns toward the footpath that leads down to the ocean along the side of the cliffs. She walks it for a way, then looks back, waiting. She does this twice.

She wants to be followed.

Annabelle takes a shuddering breath, steeling herself. She turns to her bed and kneels beside it, and digs from underneath it a bundle of disused arrows, a dusty bow—her weapon, useless for years. But because she can't imagine walking into danger without these things, she takes them on her way out.

When a witch has news of your daughter, even if she's

luring you to your death, you have no choice but to go.

On the beach at the bottom of the path, Convenia is waiting for her. Annabelle steps softly onto the sand. She cradles her arrows in her arms but doesn't try to use them. She waits to be cursed, drowned, killed . . . but she also waits with hope.

Convenia reaches underneath the collar of her dress, untucking an obscured silver whistle, and blows on it.

And then, something moves in the water near the shore.

The round, foaming eddy of a surfacing, speckled whale.

The whale opens its mouth. Convenia watches Annabelle, an invitation in her eyes.

It might be doom. But it also might be Annabelle's only chance to reach what's more precious to her than life.

She walks into the mouth of the whale, and the witch follows her in.

In another moment, they vanish beneath the waves.

CHAPTER 10

April 5, 1692. 7 p.m. Salem, Massachusetts.

That's the date and time and place that have appeared on Chompy's floating screen overnight. We are standing in the dimness of the Grand View, our faces bathed in blue light.

"Isn't it weird that it's Salem?" Germ muses as we watch the tiny hologram Chompy make its way across the spiral. Beneath our feet, the real Chompy's belly is growling; wherever we are, there aren't much krill. "That's the time of the Salem witch trials. But I thought the Salem witches weren't real. Do you think our teachers were wrong about that?"

"I guess so," I say. But really, I don't know. We learned about the Salem witch trials in fifth grade, but to be honest, I spent a lot of that year staring out the window, imagining the squirrels outside wanted me to be their forest queen.

I remember the basics that Mr. Dubois told us back then, but only vaguely: that the Salem witches weren't r*eal* witches, just *people* who acted a little bit weird or different. And that people sometimes got scared of *weird* or *different*, so they imprisoned them, or worse. (I remember thinking I'd have been in trouble if I'd lived in the 1690s, since I can act pretty weird and different myself sometimes.)

But maybe Mr. Dubois was wrong. After all, I'm pretty sure he didn't think ghosts and magic and moon goddesses were real either. So in general he was kind of off the mark.

"Maybe they're all there, already caught," Germ says hopefully, "and we can swoop in and take *all* their hearts while they're in jail."

The map shows Chompy moving us through a place where New York and 1981 intersect, moving further and further back in time. As we curve past New Jersey, Germ says, to no one in particular, "My grammie says the 1980s never really ended in Jersey." Aria re-tucks her bun and nibbles on something she calls truffle cheese, giving Germ her patented *What are you talking about* look.

I glance over at Ebb, who lingers near his dusty bedroom space, dim and brooding. He doesn't like that we're going to steal from witches without him; I think he's worried for us, though he'd never say it . . . at least not to me.

But then I notice, looking behind him, that Chompy has provided two photos on his nightstand: one grainy black-and-white one of his dead parents—kind-looking people with love in their eyes, his mom blond and light-eyed and his dad dark-haired and bearded with deeply tan skin. And then, weirdly, a picture of me—as a silhouette in my window back home, waving. And then Ebb notices me noticing. He startles, and frowns, and shakes his head slightly. A moment later, the picture vanishes as if he wished Chompy would take it away.

At that same moment, the familiar whooshing of Chompy's tail slows; the bubbling hum of him moving swiftly through the water goes quiet. We've arrived.

"Dim yourself," Aria says to me as we hurry to our room to grab our things. Behind us, Chompy's mouth cracks open, the front wall rising. "Get ready." We grab three knapsacks we've packed with food, sleeping bags, and

water. In my mind, I turn the volume down on my sight—
something I've been practicing for days. I wrap my hands
around my hourglass, and watch the sand start to trickle.

Here we go.

Cold ocean water floods in and laps at our feet as we take
in the view of a serene, rocky beach. A grassy green field
lies beyond it, and the smell of wood fires wafts through
the air. As Chompy's map indicated, it's evening, the sun
just sinking toward the horizon.

"We'll be fine," Aria says, but I can tell she's as nervous
as we are. One by one, we step into knee-deep water and
trudge ashore.

Watching the sky for hummingbirds, Aria heads
straight for the edge of the woods to a path that leads into
the forest. She crouches, staring at a spot on the ground,
and motions us closer to look at it too. At first I think it's
only a shadowy blotch, a trick of the light. But then I see
it's not a shadow at all. The closer I look, the more clearly
I see the vaguest outline of a shoe.

"Whoa," Germ says. "Creepy."

I would have never noticed it on my own, but now that
Aria has drawn my attention to the footprint, I see them
evenly spaced up ahead along the path, like the barest hint

of shadows. I reach out to touch the one in front of me, and my fingers feel immediately cold.

"Witches leave footprints wherever they walk," Aria explains. "You can even see them in daytime, once you're really paying attention. It's the absence of light that makes them stand out. A regular shadow can be beautiful, but a witch footprint looks . . . empty. Like you're staring into nothing."

"I've never even noticed them," I say, frustrated with my lack of hunting abilities.

I expect Aria to give me one of her superior looks, but she softens a little. "Well, obviously you need the *sight* to see them, but even after you get it, they're very subtle." She pats my shoulder kindly. "Anyway, Clara always said that if you noticed all the invisible things in the world—ALL the fabric at once—you'd go mad. You've got to adapt a little at a time."

"Well, I sure could have used it when I was trying to find the Memory Thief," I say.

"Butter late than never," Germ says. It's a random thing we like to say whenever we add butter to our pancakes after sleepovers; for some reason it cracks us up. Aria glances at Germ with an unimpressed look, then turns back to the path.

"Why would she land so far up the shore from town?" Aria wonders aloud, glancing around for any signs of human life. "I suppose she wanted to curse people living in the outskirts along the way."

We keep the trail of footprints as our eerie marker as we forge into the woods, the witch's path running a few hundred yards from the ocean, but parallel to it. We have no idea what witch we're following or if she or he knows we're coming. As the sky darkens, Little One lights our way. I check my hourglass often to look at the sand trickling down, watching the glowing red number twenty fade as the evening wears on. After a while, we sit on a fallen log to eat and rest. But we don't linger long.

By full nightfall we can hear the distant sound of children playing and smell chimney smoke in the air. The magical world is coming alive for the night, and we soon pass a ghost in a beautiful suede beaded robe sitting on a log, making something intricate out of wood. He looks at us for a moment and then gets back to what he's doing, unconcerned. Ghosts, of course, can see everything, sight or not.

Eventually we pass a farmhouse with warmly lit windows. A man stands in the front yard, picking a cabbage for his dinner. Beside him, a shaggy dog sniffs the air and glares at us, barking. The man follows the dog's gaze, his eyes brushing right past us as we stand frozen in place. Then he returns to his work. Unlike the ghosts, he doesn't see us—not even a bit. If he's cursed, I can't see any evidence of it.

We eat a late dinner of beef jerky and beans, resting our legs but not for long. Other than a ghostly couple who drift through our campfire at one point (they nod to us but are too deep in conversation with each other to slow down), we are alone. It's the night before dark moon, so only a waning crescent of moonlight rises above, with only the tiniest hint of a ladder dangling from its side.

I feel a moment's sadness that the Moon Goddess seems more unreachable than ever, though around the moon the beauty of the Beyond has begun to sparkle. Cloud shepherds move through the air far above, and Aria lets out a longing sigh.

"It's nice to see the sky the way it's supposed to be," she says softly. "By the time I was born, it was already dim."

By morning, we realize that we'll need to sleep if we are going to sustain ourselves. We find a tucked-away glade well off the witch's path and close our eyes for a few hours

before resuming midday. The deeper we get into civiliza-
tion, the more clear it becomes that, to everyone we pass,
we are invisible. Kids traipsing through the forest ignore
us; women carrying bundles of wood walk right past us.
Only animals and ghosts know of our presence, squirrels
scurrying out of our way, dogs perking their ears toward
us. We eat under the canopy of an oak tree.

"This must be what it's like to be a spirit floating
around," I say to Germ. "We're here, but we're not. We're
real, but we don't belong."

I think about it as we walk, Aria keeping careful track of
the witch's path as we go: the people we see along our way
are doing things they haven't actually done for hundreds of
years, living lives that ended long before I was born.

And yet all these lost moments are still happening,
thanks to the Sea of Always. It makes me think, with a
pang, about my dad. He died, but also, in the past, I guess
he's not dead at all. Somewhere he's alive and doing the
same things he used to do, on and on forever. If only I
could find him in time, I could see the little things no
one can really tell you: what his face looks like when he
laughs, what his voice sounds like, how he smells. Those
are the kinds of things you want to know about a dad
you've never met.

"Rosie!" Aria whispers.

Daydreaming. I turn my inner volume down the best I can and look around me. It's dusk again, and I see that while my mind's been somewhere else, we've arrived at the edge of Salem. Plain but pretty brick buildings line up in criss-crossing rows ahead of us, and doorways flicker with lantern light. We see draft horses tied to posts, dimmed stores, one clergyman hurrying toward what looks like a courthouse. But that's not why Aria has grabbed my attention.

There's a creature waddling across the road in front of us. It's a chameleon, green and bright . . . and totally out of place in Massachusetts. The evening is just dark enough for us to see its ghostly glow. My heart thuds faster; there's no mistaking the iridescent sparkle of a witch's familiar. The creature ignores us completely, which means that, at least, the dimming is working.

I try to remember which witch chameleons belong to. I should know, since I've read *The Witch Hunter's Guide* about a million times. But in my nervousness, the witch's name and face elude me. Even Aria appears to be drawing a blank.

The creature scurries to the edge of the road and into the grass. It's joined by two more at the top of a rise, and then they disappear across the field.

"There should be more people in town. Where is everyone?" Germ says nervously.

"I don't know," Aria says, "but those chameleons were on a mission."

We stare in the direction the chameleons went. The witch's footprints lead the opposite way, through town and out the other side. But it feels like, to find the witch, we should follow her pets. At least, that's what worked with the Memory Thief. I look at my hourglass anxiously. The number twenty has faded completely, and the number nineteen is now in its place. A little over twenty-four hours have passed since we landed. We don't have time for mistakes.

"Let's follow those chameleons to see where they're headed," I say. "Only for a few minutes."

We are luckier than we expect. We find the missing people, *and the witch*, all gathered at the edge of a river not five minutes later.

The witch has been captured, and is about to be drowned.

Completely unnoticed, we slip up to the back of a gaggle of people gathered at the water's edge. A severe man wearing a sour, wrinkled expression and a white curled wig, some kind of magistrate maybe (I do remember the word "magistrate" from Mr. Dubois), stands at the front of the crowd. There are torches planted in the dirt on either side of him to illuminate the scene. I gasp as I see a chameleon climb out of his sleeve and slither down his leg and away, glowing with whatever it's stolen from him. *He's been cursed already,* I realize.

The crowd jostles a little, and finally I see that the person at the center of all the attention is not the man in the wig, but a small, wild-haired woman to his left. She's standing at the river's edge, flanked by two men holding her arms, and glaring back at the crowd defiantly.

The man in the wig gestures at her, and speaks loudly. I recognize the look on his face as he does. It's the look my mother used to wear under her curse, like he is here, but also far away.

"Gentlefolk, we are here tonight to carry out the sentence passed upon this avowed witch, based upon the testimony of our good citizens in this year of our Lord 1692. We hereby attest that this witch has cursed our crops and caused them to fail, challenged the magistrates in a most blasphemous manner, and struck terror into the hearts of the God-fearing citizens of this town."

The crowd begins to murmur as I study the woman, whose defiant expression is dissolving into fear. She doesn't match any of the drawings in my book; she's pale, and small, wild-haired, and twitchy. She doesn't look so different from *me*, and she certainly doesn't look scary. Then again, my mother was drawing from rumors and stories. Maybe she missed this witch, or didn't get her right.

In the murmurs around me, I can tell that all are in agreement that the woman before them is evil. But amongst the noise and motion, I do notice an old man standing at the outside of the crowd, silent and set apart— looking disgusted with his neighbors. For a moment, I could swear there's something special about him, something particularly alert and awake.

As the judge continues, I see more chameleons— slithering around under the skirts of women around me, between people's feet, out from under robes and coats. Aria and I look at each other nervously. For one thing, we don't want the creatures to notice us. For another, it's clear that it's not just the magistrate but most of the people around us who've been witch-touched and cursed. We're surrounded by them.

"Gentlefolk," the judge says again. "I have listened with care to your accusations. And we have come here to mete out the punishment that is required."

I watch the woman's face shudder at these words. And suddenly it comes back to me who chameleons belong to.

Hypocriffa. She's the sixth witch in the *Guide.* I remember her clearly now: a woman with sewn-up ears and a finger poised before her lips. And suddenly I know what's happening.

History was wrong about witches, but not in the way I thought. There *were* witches in Salem, but they weren't the ones who got drowned. *And this woman is no witch.*

"Martha Parker," the judge goes on, "you hereby stand convicted of witchcraft. You shall now face trial by water. If you drown, you will die the death of the innocent. If you float, we will know for certain that you're a witch."

The woman, Martha, slumps and lets out a moan.

"I never understood the logic there," Germ whispers.

"They're lying! They're *all* lying!" I whisper, panicked. Aria reaches out an arm to settle me. "*They're* the ones doing something terrible, not her! Only, they don't know it. They're all cursed."

The injustice of it panics me. They can't drown this woman. They can't!

Germ, who never needs to be convinced to take me at my word, immediately starts to jostle forward, ready to fight, ready to save Martha Parker. She's ready to make a one-girl charge at the crowd, despite being both invisible and weaponless. I draw Little One out of my pocket. Aria grabs our sleeves and pulls us both still.

"Absolutely not!" she hisses. "If we change this woman's fate, the Time Witch will hear the change *immediately*. She'll come back in time and trap us *immediately*. And all will be lost. Everything. Not to mention, we're not supposed to tamper with the human past."

Germ gets red. She looks to Aria, uncertain.

"I want to help too," Aria whispers. "But the best way to help people . . . *all* people," she continues, "is to destroy *all* the witches. All at once. Like we've planned. This woman is lost to us. We have to find the witch who's laid this curse, the one who sent the chameleons in the first place. She's not here, and"—she nods at the hourglass at my neck, where the number nineteen has already started to fade from the top down—"we're losing valuable time. We've got to go."

In a moment, Aria has us moving away. She's tugging us along by our sleeves, while we resist less and less. I know she's right, but I can't help looking over my shoulder at the crowd behind us, horrified.

And because I'm looking back, I notice one curious thing as we hurry away. I see the old man, the one who *seemed* so alert and awake, moving away from the crowd quietly. He makes his way to the trees at the edge of the water, as if he doesn't want to be noticed—though I can't understand why. All I can see is that, even though he looks old and frail and not like any kind of magical person at all, he leaves a silver glow, faint and subtle like moonlight, along the ground behind him as he walks. It disappears quickly, and it's so dark, I think I must have imagined it. But it gives me a strange kind of hope for the woman by the river, for no reason I can explain.

The last I see of the crowd or anyone else is the man walking into the woods at the water's edge. And then he slips out of my sight.

CHAPTER 11

ack in town, we reconnect to the witch's trail and follow it down the main avenue into the forest at the other edge of Salem, weaving onto the outskirts of the town and beyond, moving inland and away from the sea. This forest is deeper, thicker, full of the calls of owls and the sounds of unseen animals scrabbling through the trees. The night of dark moon has arrived, and Little One lights our way in the moonless dark. Our legs ache.

Here the footprints—even now they can be distinguished by their absolute foot-shaped emptiness—come closer together, as if the witch were tiring, taking smaller steps. As we walk, my heart stays with the woman we've left behind and the cruelty of the people around her. I feel terrible leaving her.

A few more hours pass before our trail turns through a fence into a small yard, surrounded by trees and full of thick and impossible brambles. We slow, holding our breath as we trail the footprints to one small, narrow opening in the thorns. After squeezing in and through them, careful not to rustle them for fear of being noticed, we emerge to find a tiny clearing and a brick cottage with untamed roses growing all around it.

A few chameleons squeeze under the gap at the threshold of the front door. I reach for my flashlight and clutch it tightly in my pocket. Looking at each other, eyes wide, we tiptoe slowly up to the windows and peer inside. And gasp.

The inside of the house is old and decrepit, with walls half-eaten away by termites, soot-covered broken furniture, a bed so crooked that the yellowed mattress has been moved to the floor. And all of it—every wall, every floorboard, every piece of furniture—is covered with chameleons. Chameleons crawling on the empty iron stove, slithering through the rotting hay strewn across the floor.

The witch sits in the middle, on a crooked wooden bench, her profile to us.

She is smiling to herself, plump and beautiful and contented as she sits on her bench in a bright turquoise dress. But her ears are sewn shut. And there is a steely set to her smile, as if the moment she were to stop smiling, she would start screaming in rage. I know, from my mom's description of her and from her even for a moment, that she is not a *listener* like Ebb, trying to hear and understand the whispers of the world. Hypocriffa, I remember, is the opposite of that. She steals whatever it is that lets us put ourselves in other people's shoes, the recognition of one soul from another. And in the absence of that, she leaves an empty opening for distrust.

The chameleons crawl onto her lap like a cozy blanket and around her feet like slippers, and something curious happens as they do. As they move over and around her, their breaths rise up—visible, like dandelion puffs floating in the air, only made of the same dark emptiness as the footprints we've been following.

The breath fluff is like a cotton candy of nothingness— not the beautiful color of crows or still black nights with stars, but something instead that seems to swallow light and devour it.

"What's happening?" I whisper. I don't think there's much chance of a witch whose ears are sewn shut hearing us, especially when we're on the other side of a wall. But I keep my voice very low just in case.

"It's like," Aria speculates uncertainly, "whatever they're stealing, they're breathing out the emptiness of witches—something its opposite. Like how people breathe in oxygen and breathe out carbon dioxide." But she looks as confused as I feel. When *Aria* looks confused, it makes me nervous.

The witch waves her hands above the creatures, collecting the darkness in her fingers. She plays with it a bit—fluffing and smushing and expanding it. And then she tucks it, handful by handful, into a rough-hewn basket with a lid, like a sewing basket. She then pulls a long, thin wooden contraption out of her sleeve, unfolds it, and rests it on the ground—a spinning wheel. From her bench, she leans over the wheel and begins to spin the tufts into long, dark yarn, pumping the spinner into motion with her foot, letting each long thread of tufty fluff through her fingers slowly as she pulls it out of the basket.

"I always heard witches described as crafty, but I didn't know they meant, like, *crafts*," Germ whispers. Aria blinks at her. "I feel bad for the chameleons, though," she adds. "She took their breath."

"Germ." I level my gaze at her. "They are *literally* pure evil." Aria doesn't understand—like I do—that Germ's love for everything and everyone is her greatest weakness. A witch who steals people's sympathy for each other is pretty much Germ's opposite in every way.

"How are we going to steal her heart if she's surrounded by, like, nine hundred guards?" I whisper. "We don't even know where the heart is." I'm looking around the room, but it's so disheveled that it's hard to tell where the furniture is, much less a heart.

And then, I finally see something that reminds me of Ebb's description. Aria nudges me and points to it at the exact same time. It's a small but heavy-looking metal box, rusted and covered in soot like it's been through a few fires. It sits beside the yellowed mattress, as if it's important enough to keep close but not quite important enough to take good care of. Just as Ebb said, it's clearly a neglected appendage. We're betting the world on it being, also, a *necessary* appendage. It lies only a few feet across the littered floor, and yet it may as well be miles away, the room is so packed with familiars.

I look at Aria. "Any chance you can do something?" I ask.

She shakes her head, and for a moment her eyes flare

with something—anger or sorrow or both. "In the old days, I could have sung something, put the chameleons to sleep, laid a song over them like a blanket. Now . . ." She shakes her head again. "Anyway, none of us can do *anything* till she sleeps."

The witch goes on spinning, and we stay crouched by the window, waiting. I toggle back and forth between obsessively watching the sand slide through my hourglass and trying to think of what to do.

Finally, somewhere close to dawn, the witch leans back in her chair, drowsy. She stands, walks to the doorway, and leaves the ball of yarn she's made on the threshold outside the door, as we duck back farther behind a bush, watching.

Then she walks to her yellowed mattress and lies down on it, and goes still immediately. Germ may sleep the sleep of the untroubled, but this witch sleeps the deathlike sleep of someone who has no conscience at all.

I turn my flashlight on. Little One sits there amongst the twigs and dried leaves at my feet, waiting for my command. But what *is* my command? How do I retrieve a heart from a box surrounded by hundreds of reptiles who will wake the witch on sight of me?

Aria and Germ stare at me. "Okay, Rosie," Aria says.

"Okay what?"

"You gotta . . . do whatever it is you do."

"There's no way those chameleons won't see Little One," I say. In the Memory Thief's cave, I had to *fight*, but I didn't have to go *unnoticed*. This is a whole different thing.

"Can you please *try* your weapon?" I ask Aria sheepishly.

Aria gives me a flat look. "You know I'd knock the whole house down and half of Salem. Not much of a secret."

I think quietly, trying to ignore that we are losing time. I have flashbacks to Little One being pulled out of the sky by the horde of hummingbirds at Aria's island, so helpless. Self-doubt turns my throat dry.

Germ looks at me, flushed. "Maybe you could shrink her into a *tiny* bird, so they don't notice her."

"But she'd still have to carry the heart past them," I say.

They both stare at me. "No pressure, Rosie, take your time," Aria says sarcastically, while her eyes bulge out at me in urgency. We sit there and sit there and sit there, staring at each other. I wish I were alone to think. People watching me, even Aria and Germ in this case, are my kryptonite.

And then, because I can't take any more of the staring, I close my eyes. I try to forget there's a witch on the other side of the wall that could destroy my chance of ever saving Wolf. I try to imagine I'm alone . . . alone and safe to dream. I tighten my hands around my *Lumos* flashlight. I try to remember where Little One came from and why: a story to devour all the cruelty of witch darkness. I wanted to fight back against something too big for me to win against.

"Don't let your sight glow too brightly," Germ whispers. But if I'm glowing like a beacon that witches can see, for now I can't help it. I can't dim myself and imagine at the same time.

I think how a witch like Hypocriffa—who steals people's sympathy—tells only one story, a story that's big and simple and loud: *distrust, fear, judge.* That's the story people were telling, at the water's edge, condemning that woman they thought was a witch.

And then I think of the woman's innocence, and it wrenches at my guts how I couldn't help her. I think about how a truthful story is not loud or simple at all, how a real story lays small and slight things along a path you have to be curious enough to look for. It reminds me of a cricket: a cricket is so tiny, but its little song can keep a person up all night. The true things of the world seem kind of like that.

Once, I think, *a cricket hopped near the ear of a dragon, to sing about what was quiet and real. The dragon thought the cricket was no match for him. He swatted, and roared, and breathed fire to quench the creature's tiny song. But the cricket— being so small—hid in crevices, ducked behind rocks, and kept singing. It drove the dragon so wild, singing day and night, that in trying to set it on fire in a rage, the dragon set himself on fire instead. And the loud, blustering giant burned into ash.*

It makes me feel a little better, telling myself this story. Even if it doesn't—

"Rosie," Germ whispers, touching my arm. "Um. I think you broke Little One."

I open my eyes. And lose my breath.

Standing on the ground in front of me, Little One is not Little One anymore. Or at least, not the Little One I know. I only recognize her by her glow, and the bond between us that's tied around my heart, but she is no longer a bluebird at all.

She's a cricket.

I look at her in shock. "She doesn't *have* to be a bluebird?" I whisper, even more surprised than Germ and Aria, whose mouths are hanging open. "She can be *other* things?"

"She's *your* weapon," Aria says in wonder. "And you are truly weird. I love it."

I'm trying to think of what it really means, that Little

One can shape-shift. Could I turn her into other animals? What are the rules?

"But, Rosie," Germ says, squinting in the pained way she does when she gives me bad news, "what can a cricket do? This does *not* solve our problem."

But Aria seems to get it before both of us, because her eyes are twinkling.

"Well, what do chameleons eat?" she asks.

And I see it, that without even completely thinking about it, I've made Little One the juiciest, most delicious cricket a reptile could ever see. And then I realize why.

"She's not going to go in and sneak in past them," I say. "She's going to *lure them out*."

I stare at this new version of Little One, grasping how much I don't know about my witch weapon and what she's capable of, even after all this time. And then I slowly lift my flashlight and shine it at the bottom of the cottage's front door, my heart in my throat.

"Be careful," I say to her, but she ignores me, like some fearless part of my soul. The cricket version of Little One hops under the crack under the door. And we watch through the window as, suddenly, she has the attention of every chameleon in the room.

It only takes a few moments. The chameleons all look

in her direction, and their tongues begin to dart quickly out of their mouths, tantalized. Little One is quicker, and hops back out under the door again. We watch in relief as the chameleons follow, squiggling out through the small crack after her. Every single chameleon in the room jockeys to be the next to clamber outside after its prey.

Breathless, I shine Little One toward the woods, worried for her. We watch in awe as the multitude of chameleons follows, numerous and as squiggly as worms, down the path and around a curve. The moment they are out of sight, Germ stands abruptly.

"I'm going in," she says.

"Germ," I hiss. But Germ slips up to the door before Aria or I can stop her. She is bolder than she is reasonable. And while Germ generally has no "inside voice," she is also incredibly graceful, and she moves through the room like a cat burglar. We watch her through the window as the witch sleeps, as still as a corpse.

Germ crosses the room to the metal box, gently lifts the lid, and stares at what's inside with a shuddering, disgusted look on her face. She puts the thing into a small cloth sack (provided by Chompy, I suppose) she pulls from her knapsack, and goes to put the lid back on, but she is moving so quickly, with such nervousness, that she knocks the box over. The lid makes a clatter even we can hear from outside. Germ is stock-still, staring at the witch.

Hypocriffa doesn't budge.

Then I feel a tug at my sleeve. Aria draws my attention to the woods. My stomach churns.

The chameleons have given up. They've cleared the bend in the path and are headed back toward the cottage. I see in the distance the tiny glow of Little One behind them, hopping wildly and trying to get their attention again. Without success.

I tap on the window gently, so that Germ looks over as she's just tightening the sack closed. I wave for her to hurry out, but she thinks I'm giving her the thumbs-up. Her mouth widens in a huge, goofy grin, and she gives me the thumbs-up back. Watching the chameleons close in across the grass, an iridescent army moving like water, I begin to gesture frantically.

Finally Germ seems to get what I'm communicating. Her eyes widen in panic, looking toward the door.

She rushes toward the window on tiptoes and slides it open as quietly as she can. Then, like a contortionist, she slips in and out and through, scooping her body sideways.

As she slides out with a hiss and shuts the window with a creak, the witch startles. She sits up, gazing around the

floor with sharp turquoise eyes. The chameleons are filtering back into the room under her gaze, curling and uncurl-
ing their tails, wiggling as they walk. We duck, the sack
clutched close to Germ's heaving ribs as she tries to catch
her breath. Can the witch sense us out here in the dark?

We wait for the witch to come to the window, for an
explosion of chameleons to burst out through the door.
But nothing. I slowly lift my head up, and peer back inside.
Hypocriffa has gone back to sleep.

Germ slides the sack into my hands.

My palms drop under its weight. Whatever's in it, it's
heavy, wet, and like Jell-O. I stuff it into my coat pocket,
along with my flashlight—and the cricket version of Little
One disappears.

I begin to stand, but Aria grabs my wrist and yanks me
back down. Crouching again, I follow her eyes.

A figure is approaching, a person of some sort, and the
closer they get, the more troubled I feel. Who would be
coming, in the middle of the night, to find a witch? It's
only when he rounds the bend that we see for certain, the
answer is: another witch.

This time, I know exactly who this one is. Dread. He
looks very much like my mother's drawing in the *Guide*—
tall and gaunt, with bottomless eyes glinting in the dark.

A hyena follows behind him, luminescent, nipping at his heels—though he takes no notice. I remember that, in the *Guide*, I always thought he was with a wolf, but either the book got it wrong or I did. The hyena somehow looks much worse.

Dread walks up to Hypocriffa's door and takes the ball of yarn from where she's placed it on the threshold. He tucks it into his sleeve and, without even pausing, turns and walks back into the woods.

We wait for several minutes, hoping that he's really gone. And then we emerge from the bushes.

"Why would he be here?" I whisper to Aria. "What would he want with a ball of that yarn?"

"I don't know," Aria says, looking as troubled and bewildered as I am. "But I don't think we'll be getting his heart tonight." I look in the direction Dread has gone. I fear the day we'll have to steal from him, but for now, I think Aria's right. We're exhausted, and we need to get a handle on exactly what it is we've stolen.

"We're *hours* behind schedule," Aria adds. "It'll take less time than coming, but still probably all day and most of the night to get back to Chompy."

Once we're sure Dread is gone, we sneak on soft feet into the woods, and walk silently until we are a safe distance away from the cottage. It's not until we are making our way seaward, that I really start to breathe again.

Like thieves in the night, we hurry on our long journey back toward the ocean's edge, carrying our strange quarry with us.

CHAPTER 12

E bb, Aria, Germ, and I are gathered on the shag rug in a circle, looking at the little sickly jiggling sack in my hands. By my hourglass, we've given up two and a half days for this first heart—the blood-red number eighteen is faded almost down to the middle. But we did *steal a heart*. And that's something.

We've already asked Chompy to look for the next whale. He's been calling for an hour into the great blue yonder, but so far, no answers.

"Should we look at it?" I ask, worried what a witch

heart is capable of. Could it bite us, cling to us like a leech? Can it sense we have stolen it? Tell the witches where we are?

"Duh," says Germ, never one to err on the side of caution. "Of course."

My hands shaking a little, I begin to loosen the drawstring on the sack.

Germ grabs the empty Dorito bowl from the table, and I upend the sack so that the heart slides into it, and lands on some crushed orange crumbs.

We stare into the bowl.

The heart is not the kind of heart any real creature would actually have; it is not heart-shaped at all. It's a gleaming red apple.

Wincing, I poke at it, and my finger sinks into its surface, like sinking into Jell-O. Like the witches, it's like it's half-real but half-unreal, there and not there.

Germ reaches out to touch it too. Her touch rolls the apple onto its side, and we all groan. There's a rotten hole on one side, brown and decayed and smelly.

I quickly drape the sack over it, scoop it in, and pull the drawstring tight, and then drop the sack beside me, disgusted. I won't be looking at witch hearts any more than I need to, I decide.

"That seems like the perfect heart for Hypocriffa," Aria says. "Good on the surface, rotten and cruel underneath. Like that judge. Like all those cursed people accusing that woman." We already have *The Witch Hunter's Guide* lying open on the floor beside us. Next to the picture of Hypocriffa my mother drew are some words she jotted down in messy handwriting as if following a train of thought: *For those she's cursed, it's easy to make harming others feel right. It's easy to make other people out to be monsters.*

But Hypocriffa's heart raises more questions than it answers. Do all witch hearts look like this . . . not like hearts at all? Is each one different, reflecting the essence of whom they belong to? There is so much about the invisible layers of the world I have yet to learn.

Still, none of those answers matters as long as I can destroy them. And it looks easy enough. Little One has devoured an entire witch—heart, guts, and all. One small rotten apple heart won't be a problem. I only wish I could have her do it right now.

"So chameleon breath was being spun into yarn?" Ebb asks. He still won't meet my eyes, though he looked like he was about to faint with relief when we reached Chompy a few minutes ago.

We've filled him in on most of what happened since

we left him, but we're also still figuring it out ourselves—
the dark, empty tufts of breath Hypocriffa was spinning
at her wheel, and the strange appearance of the second
witch, Dread. Ebb flickers as we talk. I think worry for us
has drained him a bit.

"I don't know," I say. "But there's something about
that yarn that's important. Otherwise why would another
witch come to collect it?"

My imagination goes wild wondering what the answer
is. Are they knitting a rope ladder to the moon? Or a lit-
eral web? What does it have to do with the dark void left
by witch footprints? Still, the others don't seem as fixated
on the yarn as I am. Germ always says I let my imagination run away with me.

"The awful Salem judge said this ridiculous thing
about how witches float," Germ tells Ebb, interrupting my
thoughts.

"Well, they've got it mixed around," Aria offers matter-
of-factly. "Witches can't swim. Even though they're always
traveling the Sea of Always. Clara told me that; she thought
it was ironic."

This gets our attention. We all blink at her for a moment.
"We could drown *them*!" Germ suddenly exclaims. "Let's
drown them all instead of stealing their hearts."

Ebb and I exchange a smirk; we know Germ couldn't drown a fly. But then Ebb remembers he's avoiding me and drops the smirk.

"If you could ever catch one to drown," Aria says bitterly. "Much less nine of them . . . plus the Time Witch."

Germ's shoulders slump.

Aria ignores her disappointment. "But if stealing each heart is as hard as stealing that one was, we don't stand a chance." She looks at me. "We have to be faster, Rosie. I mean," she corrects, seeming to remember she is only helping to get her voucher, "*you* need to be faster."

I swallow. "Next time will be easier," I say. "Next time I'll know what to do. I'll know I can change Little One."

We all look at each other, uncertain.

"What do *I* know?" Germ murmurs, to no one in particular, with disappointment and maybe a tiny bit of longing. "I'm only the assistant."

It's a little bit of a to-do, deciding where to keep the dark heart of one of the most sinister creatures in the universe. Aria suggests we each take turns sleeping with it, and Germ is certain Chompy will think of something and give us the perfect place for it like he always does. But no padded safe or lockable pirate chest is forthcoming, so I end up putting the heart into my backpack, in the main compartment. (Since I always keep at least one favorite book in the front pocket for good luck. Right now it's *The Snowy Day*, which I've borrowed from my shelf because it always reminds me the world is beautiful.) My rationale is that at least my backpack has a zipper, and surely a witch heart cannot unzip something and escape, considering it has no opposable thumbs.

That night in bed, while Germ and Ebb and Aria are goofing off playing gin rummy in the living room (our card game repertoire is expanding by the day, thanks to Aria), and Ebb is filling the extra time by showing them how to empty people's pockets without them knowing (something he learned from his years of imprisonment with the ghost thief named Steve), I fiddle around with my flashlight, trying to see what else I can turn Little One into. But it's slow going. She occasionally flickers into a cricket again, and once, I get her to be a mosquito, but that's about it. Apparently, I can't transform Little One if my whole heart isn't in it. And that's not easy when I'd rather be playing gin rummy and learning how to pick pockets and not be feeling left out.

I watch them even though I pretend not to. It's clear that Ebb and Germ have picked up their friendship right where they left off; they laugh and joke with each other, discussing over cards the pros and cons of talking to nature. (Sometimes, according to Ebb, trees tell you things you don't want to hear by, say, pointing a branch toward an oncoming storm.) But it's like they're talking about two different things. Ebb wants to learn and understand everything. He's deeply curious about how nature works and how it whispers to us in ways most people don't notice. Germ, on the other hand, just wants to be able to ask Chompy if she can give him a hug.

"Like the other day, I told him via ESP to eat some krill, and he definitely did," she says unconvincingly. Ebb smiles at her affectionately, glowing a little brighter.

Meanwhile, Ebb and Aria are also clearly hitting it off.

On a whim, I decide to channel my inner Aria to see if that changes things. I lower my eyelids in an aloof *I don't care* kind of way and try to walk up to the game of gin rummy with a casual elegance.

Ebb looks up at me, staring for a moment.

"Are you okay?" he says flatly.

"What do you mean?" I ask in what seems to me a cool, aloof voice.

"You're doing something weird with your eyebrows," he says, then turns back to the game.

I slink off and up to the Grand View, restless, worried, and hemmed in all at the same time. I watch the years and miles roll past as Chompy circles the time spiral, waiting for the next call.

I turn my mind to Salem again, my thoughts revolving around the innocent woman by the water. Was she really drowned? I feel so responsible for her. And then it occurs to me: If Chompy can provide anything I need, could he provide me something I need that's also from the past?

"Chompy, do you have any newspapers from Salem, the week of April 5, 1692?" I ask. I'm not sure if, back then, newspapers even existed.

I look up at the monitor, and when I look down again, there's a small newspaper rack attached to the wall at the side of the Grand View. I pull out the one newspaper hanging from the top bar, a browning paper crowded with small black type in heavy square paragraphs.

I flip through the pages gently until I find what I'm looking for.

Woman, Martha Parker, escapes trial by drowning.

My pulse spikes.

I read on, about how Martha Parker was condemned as a witch. About the evening she was scheduled to be drowned. When I get to the next paragraph, I feel a wondering grin stretch across my face: *It's believed she was aided by a man belonging to the seditious and nefarious Witch Freedom Society of Salem. A bounty has been placed on the heads of all individuals involved.*

My heart lifts. The man I saw. It was he who saved her, I am sure of it. But how and why did he leave that misty light behind him?

My thoughts are interrupted by a sudden, haunting sound. It's a low distant hum—beautiful, mournful, a call from somewhere far away.

In another moment, Aria pops up beside me to look at the Grand View. We watch as tiny Chompy's circling comes to a halt and he heads left, cutting across the spiral quickly and surely. By the swish of the water around us, we can tell he is picking up speed.

"It's the next whale," Aria says, "calling out to him. We're on our way."

CHAPTER 13

We are headed to 1952, to a town called Onno on the coast of Nigeria.

As we get close to shore, my heart beating a fast rhythm, an enormous shape swims just in front of us, blocking everything else. It brushes right up against us, and Chompy goes wobbling, knocking us all off our feet.

We watch the Grand View monitor in shock as the shape that's hit us makes itself clear. We see the large black eye of a whale, and then its body as it swims away. We shake, wafted in the current of its tail, and Chompy lets out a cry.

"He's annoyed," Germ says, touching her temples and trying to sound like she is reading Chompy's mind. "I think these two are in a tiff about something. That's what I'm picking up on."

"What would whales even argue about?" Aria scoffs.

"I wonder which witch it belongs to," I say.

At that moment, as Germ's about to hazard an uninformed ESP guess, there's an enormous *whoosh*. Chompy jerks upward in something of a leap, opens his mouth without warning, and just sort of . . . spits us into the open air. I let out a yelp as we fly through the sky, and then land on hard ground, tumbling and groaning.

I sit up, my hip and shoulder aching from the landing.

Out on the water, Ebb stands in Chompy's open mouth, glowing in the darkness and looking as if he's embarrassed by Chompy's bad behavior, and holding up one hand to wave. "Good lu—" he calls out, but he's cut off as Chompy slams his mouth closed and dives.

"Told you he's annoyed," Germ says.

"I don't trust that whale," I say.

After sitting stunned for a moment, we stand and brush ourselves off, dimming ourselves and looking around. I pull out Little One and send her ahead several yards so she can illuminate what's around us.

We're on a slim slice of beach; it's a warm night, and again the tiniest sliver of moon hangs in the sky, with its unreachable hint of a ladder. By its position, Aria reckons it's about three a.m. At the edge of the sand is a field that leads up into rolling green hills that disappear into the black night. It's peaceful, beautiful, inviting, but as our eyes adjust, we also start to see *it*, the trail of shadowy footprints mostly obscured by tall grass, easy to miss or mistake for dips in the ground. A witch has come this way, and the sand in my hourglass is, of course, already falling.

"We've gotta move quickly," I say, "and make up for lost time."

We walk in a tight row into the field before us, looking around for the shadows that mark our trail. There are wild animals in Nigeria, Germ informs us, bigger than anything Maine has to offer. She saw it on *Wild Discovery: Animal Whisperer*. We don't want to meet them, particularly when, even with Little One's light, we can only see a few yards around us. While we've prepared ourselves for witches, we're not prepared for a stampede of elephants.

We walk . . . and walk . . . and walk . . . for hours and

into dawn. Unlike in Salem, there's no sign of a town or people nearby.

Seeing me reach for my hourglass again, Aria stays my hand. "It won't make this go faster," she says.

And it's a good thing I stop obsessing, because a few moments later we come upon a gathering of enormous, living silhouettes in the dark. After a heart-stopping moment of terror, the glow of Little One reveals it is a family of giraffes, staring at us with curiosity from behind the trees.

"Oh!" Germ gasps, jerking to a stop. "I love them soooo much."

For once I have to agree with her. It's magical to come across giraffes in the wild, maybe as magical as witches and ghosts. In another moment, though, I have to nudge her to keep walking. I suppose if we stop and linger at every place we find interesting in this past world, we'll never make it anywhere.

Shortly before dawn, we pass a group of ghosts standing and chatting by a river—all women. But the rest of the morning is uneventful. We rest around lunchtime—lying down for a brief nap under the shade of a tree—and move on as soon as we're rested and fed. We push on for the rest of the afternoon and into evening, snacking but not stopping, trekking long past sunset and into the night. Little One lights our way as another night, this one moonless, descends, our feet weary and our legs aching.

It's getting late, and we're thinking about stopping to rest for a bit, when we come to the rise of a green hill and find, on the other side, a town. From above, it looks like a small gathering of shadows only barely visible in the dark. There are maybe fifty or so modest houses nestled in the valley before us.

The whole place appears to be asleep. But one figure moves from house to house, a white glowing shape wandering the village's edges. If he glanced up the hill now, he'd see us. But he's too focused on what he is doing to look.

The witch is already at work.

We stand frozen in place and watch, afraid to move. Even from here, he is terrifyingly skeletal and all too familiar: *the Griever.*

Words about him from the *Guide* leap out in my memory: blind, mournful, acute hearing. Steals joy.

He has a pale white, ancient face, like the grim reaper I've seen in stories—gaunt, hollow cheeks; wide, empty eye sockets. He wears a flowing white robe. Flapping gently around him at shoulder height are his familiars: a clutch of iridescent bats. We see all this as he cranes his neck, tilting his chin this way and that in the direction of the houses, as if sensing his next victim with his ears alone.

"He's listening for the sound of people breathing," Aria says ever so lightly, so that barely even I can hear her. But even that whisper, from fifty yards up the hill, seems to reach the Griever's ears. He jerks his head in our direction and stands still for a moment. We hold our breath, and wait.

Finally he turns back to the house he is next to. He scampers through its dark window with the speed of a spider. Whoever the person is sleeping inside, I fear for them. I look at Germ and Aria, and we nod to each other, then walk softly toward town through the tall grass, watching for any sign of the Griever emerging from the house.

When we see his head appear at the window, we freeze, and watch as he scampers out. He peers back inside for a moment, watches, and bites his fingers as his bats enter the room. There is a dazed smile on his face. And then he turns and moves on, the bats following. He comes to the next house, listens for a moment, and scampers inside.

We move slowly down the hill, pausing whenever we see the witch emerge from indoors. We watch as another and another house is invaded. The bats flutter in and out of the windows, sparkling with what they have stolen. Meanwhile, we make our way closer and closer to the first house, and when we reach it, we peer inside.

Little One casts her glow on a man asleep in bed. A few bats are still here, moving over his body busily. A gray cat sits in a corner, staring at them and us, alarmed.

In his sleep the man stirs, and the bats flutter away and out the window. The sleeper sits up in bed as if shaking off a bad dream. He's maybe fifty years old, but he moves as if he's a *hundred* and fifty—slowly, as if it pains him. He stands and turns on a small bedside lamp, then walks to a table across the room where a photo sits, of a woman with bright eyes and long black hair. Staring at the photo, it's as if the man's soul has gone small inside.

The three of us look at each other, but don't dare to whisper a word. It's easy to guess that this woman is no longer alive. And the Griever, I realize, has made it so this man will never recover from losing her. By the look on the man's face, I can see that the unseen things that offer hope of what's *beyond*, and all the *maybes*, are far beyond his reach even in dreams. He gives off the feeling that deep inside, he is mired in a swamp. I've felt that swamp before, when I thought my mom would never love me. Maybe everyone has felt it. There is sadness . . . and then there is forgetting that happiness can even exist. The Griever's specialty, I see with utter certainty from looking at this cursed man, is the second of these.

"I've felt like that too," Aria whispers, looking at his face with pity. And I wonder what she means, and when. Who and what could have made someone as perfect as Aria feel like that?

The man crawls back into bed and holds the place where his wife must have slept. There is a painting of a waterfall on the wall beside his bed, and I stare at it, because for a moment in the dimness, the water looks like it's moving—though of course it can't be. And then a movement far off, seen out of the corner of my eye, makes me look up. I nudge the others. In being mesmerized by the scene before us, we've lost track of the Griever. He's skulking away from the village and up into the hills.

We reluctantly retreat from the window of the man so lost in his loss, and follow.

The witch is drifting farther and farther inland. We follow far enough behind to be out of earshot—at least, that's what we hope. And still the Griever keeps going, deeper and farther across the fields.

I look at my hourglass again. A red seventeen now spins inside the glass.

Where could he be headed? I want to whisper. But I don't dare risk the noise.

Finally, a little before midnight by my reckoning, the Griever begins to behave strangely, looking around like he is making sure he's not being followed, and then he slips into the dark gap between two large boulders. We follow, as stealthily as we can, though it feels like we could become trapped in such a place. We squeeze through the gap, and find ourselves in a kind of swamp, thick and hidden beyond the boulders and surrounded by impenetrable marsh.

It's a gloomy place, in the shadow of rocky overhangs where the bats now settle in. They hang themselves upside down, clinging to the undersides of the arching boulders, rustling like the skin of a dog when it shakes itself off. The Griever waves a hand at them. And—as with the chameleons—they exhale dark tufts of emptiness, as if changing light to emptiness inside their lungs.

The Griever gathers armfuls of these breaths, then waddles mournfully to a rock where he sits and pulls a spinning wheel, exactly like the first one we saw, out of his sleeve. As Hypocriffa did, he spins yarn out of the fibers, muttering to himself words we don't quite hear. Then, leaning back, exhausted, he hangs the finished ball of yarn from a branch at the swamp's edge, as if leaving it for someone to retrieve.

He lies down in the muck and goes, suddenly, to sleep. At least, I *think* it's sleep. His skeletal face remains blank, his empty eye sockets wide, white, and open. Tears stream out of them, but he remains still. And beside him, we see the container that surely must hold his heart, a faded trinket box that looks as if it could be made out of bone.

All around, the bats flutter and move restlessly, wide awake, as they probably will be till morning.

Germ looks at me meaningfully, points at the sky, and then makes a sleeping motion with her head tilted into her hands. She is suggesting we wait till the sun rises and the bats sleep, but I shake my head. That means waiting several hours we can't afford to lose. And by then, the Griever will be waking up.

I lift my flashlight, turn it on, ruminating. Little One, in bluebird form, looks up at me expectantly.

I think back to the story I told to Germ the day we met, about a bat that swallowed mosquitoes and burped out stars. The story came to me because, at the time, we had bats in our attic. My mom didn't even notice the noise, but I'd hear them leaving at night and returning just around dawn, when the sun was beginning to rise.

I close my eyes and think about those mornings: the calming of the bats at first light, the reassurance of the sun rising like a fresh start. A new day, I think, is the opposite of the Griever. It brings the unexpected, the possible things, the maybes. I can still picture it, the sun like an orange yolk on an early morning, bringing brightness after a long weary night.

I open my eyes, my flashlight pointed toward the ground. I imagine the sun rising despite the hour—a strange and impossible idea—but when I move the beam forward, a warm, round glow appears.

Germ lets out an audible, amazed sigh. Suddenly Little One resembles a ball that's caught fire. I look over at Germ, and we stare at each other in wonder. Little One has changed into a tiny *sun*, floating close above the ground, burning and glowing and golden bright. For a moment I can only gape at Little One—dazed by the beauty of her glow.

"You can make suns?" Aria breathes. She holds out her hands to the warmth of it as it burns brightly in the air.

"I didn't *think* that I could make suns," I say. I thought other animals was shocking enough.

I shift the direction of my flashlight's lens along the ground and into the air, a few feet away past the trees, where, if I were a bat, I might think a sun could be rising far in the distance. It's a trick of space and perspective, but miraculously, all along the rocky overhangs the bats' restless motion immediately begins to still—it happens instantly. Hundreds of bat eyes start to flutter shut. And finally, thinking its dawn, the bats settle down to sleep.

I blink at the light that's lulled them. *I have made a tiny sun in the middle of the night*, I think, again and again. If Little One can be a cricket and then a sun . . . what *can't* she be?

This time, getting the heart is easy. Aria takes it upon herself to tiptoe right in on silent feet, open the box lying in the mud beside the Griever, and slip whatever's inside into the sack in her hands.

Once she's back at my side, she slides her prize into my backpack. In minutes we are on our way, rising back into the hills and heading for the shore. As soon as I can take a moment, I look at my hourglass, still a bright and barely faded seventeen, and wild bubbles of happiness rise inside my chest. We will make it back long before our fifty-three-hour goal has passed. We are making up lost time!

We pass the town again on our way back toward the sea, this time poised before waking as the real dawn arrives.

As we crest the hill from which we first saw it, I turn to take another look. And catch my breath.

The Griever's footprints, stretched from house to house, crisscross the village below, outside every window and marking every road and pathway through town. It steals my joy for a moment.

I can see, looking from up high, how the footprints cover the town like a net. So many broken hearts, so much stolen light, and I know the witches have left behind towns like this everywhere, all over the world and all *over time*.

I remember what Homer the ghost said to me once, that chaos is to witches as water is to fish. How much of the planet have the witches entwined in this emptiness? How much goodness have they stolen? And what will become of the world if I can't defeat them?

I take one more look at the valley below, reminding myself that this is what's at stake if I let the world down. And we hurry on.

Chompy and Ebb are waiting to welcome us back when I blow my whistle, and soon we are diving to safety. Ebb and I almost try to hug each other, which is confusing, though Ebb's ghostiness stops us anyway. We've run down a little more than four full days on my hourglass. But we also have two witch hearts to our name, and I suspect Little One has powers beyond what I've ever dreamt.

We all lean over the kitchen table, dumping the heart into the snack bowl again.

This one is a flower—a red poppy wilting and going brown around the edges. Again, as real as the flower looks, when I poke it, the surface gives under my fingers like jelly.

"Every time I think things can't get weirder . . . ," Germ sighs. But she's smiling. We can't help staring at each other and breaking into grins, in fact. Because I know we're all thinking the same thing.

I'm good at this. That's the surprising thing. For the first time since we began, I actually think we have a chance. More than a chance.

I'm thinking we might just pull off this whole thing after all.

CHAPTER 14

It's terrifying and exhilarating and also completely weird, but we are a witch hunting crew, roaming the world, looking for hearts to steal.

Germ and I are in seventh grade. Right now, our friends are going to dances that Germ says are *awko taco* and learning to sew pillows in Life Skills class. Not *one* kid we know would even for a second believe that there's an invisible fabric surrounding them that includes witches trying to rule the earth . . . much less that I, Rosie Oaks, could be fighting those witches. I know that if we ever make it back to tell them, they won't believe us anyway. Mostly we just want our moms. We'd settle for any adult, really, who could help us. And yet here we are.

In the middle of a lightning storm in Russia in 1820, near a mine being plundered for ore, we find the Greedy Man—green-faced and asleep—nestled in a hollow of dirt underneath a forest of beech trees. He's surrounded by thousands of beetles—glowing with the generosity they've stolen from the owners of the mining company nearby—and sleeping in the space left behind by all the roots the insects have devoured.

Little One steals the witch's emerald-shaped heart by becoming a handful of caterpillars, burrowing into the leather pouch in which he keeps it, and slithering it out for Germ to reach down and grab. The whole thing—from tracking the Greedy Man through the rain, to getting his heart, to making it home to Chompy—only takes twelve hours, and we don't even break a sweat. A small clutch of hummingbirds passes us as we retreat, but our dimming works and they don't see us.

We find Miss Rage in the Sahyadri hills of India, from which—at night—she likes to shout at the top of her lungs (though no one living, besides people like us, can hear her) as she sends her sparkling hornets down into the valleys below to steal forgiveness and sow hatred in its place. I make Little One a starling that sends her hornets scattering simply by coming to roost in a tree above and giving them a hungry look.

That morning, hurrying back to our whale, a monsoon lets up long enough for us to see a rainbow arcing overhead. Afterward, it rains so hard again that we have to stop under a tree for shelter, knowing we are losing time. But with Miss Rage's heart in a sack in my hands, I feel buoyant with our success.

We find Babble living in Canada, near a small town where two groups are fighting over a statue in the town square, their words twisting like curveballs on the way to each other's ears. Babble's magpies, we deduce, have stolen their understanding of each other. The people are speaking the same language, but they don't really hear each other.

I make Little One a fox to scatter the magpies from where Babble sleeps in an abandoned school bus, and Little One captures Babble's heart, a tangled knot of thread, in her teeth. I can still hear the townspeople yelling from half a mile away.

At each stop, my hourglass reflects my time to save Wolf trickling away. But we are, shockingly, on schedule. We are even getting ahead of it.

I don't sleep much. Here and there, we see the Time Witch's hummingbirds patrolling the shores, and there's always a chance they've seen us without letting on. Constantly there's the chance that the witches have found out, and that the next heart or the next stop is a trap. The more we steal, the more likely it is that they've noticed us stealing, that *someone* has noticed a heart missing.

It's like scaling the side of a cliff without any ropes. The closer we get to the top, the farther we are from the safety of the ground. I am so scared of falling, I lie awake at night in the glow filtering down from the Grand View, watching Germ and Aria sleep. I watch Ebb float through the cabin while he thinks I, too, am sleeping. He flickers in and out, letting his worry (for me? for us? for himself?) show when he thinks he's alone. I feel like saving him—saving *everyone*—is up to me. And still, I long for my mom, for a dad who is somewhere alive in the past, for someone to take care of me . . . and Wolf . . . and the world.

Meanwhile, at each stop, we watch the witches spinning, spinning yarn out of darkness, making a substance so empty-looking, it haunts me. We know it is Dread they are spinning it for, and it doesn't add up with anything we've learned about them. They're up to something beyond what our *Guide* can tell us or what our mothers and sisters knew. Whatever it is, the thing that unsettles me most is the *not knowing*. I wonder what the Time Witch is doing, where she is and where she thinks *we* are, if she even suspects we could be unraveling things beneath her feet.

There is one more thing that confuses me. There's the movement of the waterfall painting in Nigeria. In Russia, passing by a shop window, I saw motion inside a dollhouse, and I heard voices from a mouse hole in India. I wonder if maybe my imagination is unraveling my brain, if my imagination is truly running away with me at last.

I pass the long days on Chompy waiting for the next stop. I read my well-loved and well-worn books for comfort—the ones that appeared on my bed when we moved in. I study *The Witch Hunter's Guide* until I know it not just by heart but *in my cells*. (One thing I do not do is look at the hearts we've stolen once they're put away. I can't stand to do that; they are too gross, too frightening.)

I play with Little One, who's more daring and more wildly imagined all the time, a bird that once grew and shrank now able to transform into anything I can dream of.

"It's what *you* are," Germ says one night before bed, when I'm sitting on the edge of my bed flicking Little One into a shark, a worm, a butter knife, still troubled that it's not enough. "That's what makes what she can do possible. Your weird brain was supposed to be weird all along, Rosie. I always told you that." But it's hard for me to really believe it. When something has always been with you and made you feel different, it's hard to think of it as very spectacular at all.

And so the days go on, leaving me hopeful, and fearful, and worried, and exhausted.

And then we learn something new. It's about Aria.

We are in Iceland, 1683, tracking the witch named Egor. We realize it's him we're chasing when we see his peacocks strutting, unseen by the people around them, through the middle of downtown Reykjavík.

Unseen also, we've wandered into the heart of the city in the late afternoon, and there is a crowd gathered in the square, including a few nosy ghosts dressed like Vikings. A man at a podium is talking to the gatherers, the peacocks lurking behind him. We've arrived midspeech, but apparently he is mostly talking about himself. We guess this from the way he keeps puffing out his chest, pointing to himself, and smoothing his hair.

Whatever he's saying, we can tell it's boring. Beside me, Germ starts to drool because she's falling half-asleep, and Aria is looking at her fingernails. The man at the podium preens and swaggers and sucks in his stomach, and the crowd seems to love him. They clap and cheer every time he pumps his fists.

"I bet if we swam through the Sea of Always long enough," Aria comments dryly, "we'd run into ridiculous people beloved by crowds throughout time."

I nod, fearing, from the reaction of this crowd, that she might be right. It's with relief that we find the rest of the trail we are looking for—dark shadowed footprints across the white snow along the curb—and follow it toward the outskirts of the city.

We see it looming before us as we follow Egor's trail out of town. At first, it looks like a mountain amongst all the other mountains. But as we get closer, we see that it's oddly shaped, and after a while of walking, we see that it is actually *witch*-shaped. It's a mountain, but the snow-drifts that cover it have been carved, or blown, or piled into a sculpture: jagged chin, ski-slope nose, long robes, wide-open eyes. I'm familiar with this figure from my *Guide*. It's the shape of Egor himself.

"He must have created this as soon as he arrived," Aria says. "This guy's a legend in his own mind."

Does Egor go all over the world fashioning likenesses of himself out of any material he can? I wonder. It seems kind of pathetic.

As we get closer, the mountain arches above us, foreboding. At the base is a small hole that leads inside a snowy crevasse. And here is where we find Egor the witch, staring at us.

He's lying on his side facing us, his bed a sheet of ice. Around him is a circle of mirrors, also made of ice, that glint in the dim light of the snow cave like knives.

A moment of sheer terror passes before we realize he's not really staring at us at all, but at one of the mirrors beyond our shoulders to the left of the entrance. We stand stock-still for several minutes under Egor's gaze, but he doesn't move, or blink. In actuality, he does not look like the monolith he's carved to guard his cave at all. He is a small, gnarled man, withered and sad-faced.

By the bed is a tiny silver box, crusted with ice, where he must keep his heart. And next to it is the usual ball of yarn, dark emptiness spun into thread. Peacocks strut around him, ignoring us—they are too busy preening their feathers to notice us. We don't even have to hide from them; they're so preoccupied, they make terrible guards. They glimmer with what they've stolen: their victims' true worth.

"Is he asleep?" Germ finally whispers.

I shrug.

Aria, impatient, takes action. She uses her slingshot—not as a witch weapon but as its regular old self—to shoot a rock at the snow beside him so that if he flinches, we can make a fast escape. An icicle breaks and falls down right in front of him. A few iridescent peacocks flutter, but Egor doesn't flinch. "He's asleep," she says, and smirks. "He can't even keep his eyes off himself when he's unconscious."

Still, the ice box holding his heart is there in the mirror too, right where he's looking. He may not notice us, but he might notice anything interfering with his view of himself.

"What can you imagine, Rosie," Aria asks, "for a witch who's looking at exactly what you want to steal?"

Weirdly, I already have an idea. I turn on my flashlight, and Little One glows bright blue against the white snow. Then I close my eyes and imagine what Egor probably wants most.

I feel Germ shudder beside me and grab my arm. Aria lets out a small, strangled gasp. I open my eyes to see what I've created. By their fear, I know it has worked.

I've transformed Little One into Egor *himself,* standing there staring at us. But I've also made a few adjustments. *This* Egor holds a small Earth in the palm of his hand, as if it's nothing compared to the size of him. He looks full, whole, powerful—not hungry and empty inside. He looks like the real Egor probably wishes himself to be.

Now I shine Little One Egor onto the surface of the mirror that *real* Egor is staring at.

The witch shudders for a moment, as if surprised—and I worry I've made a huge mistake. And then his shoulders relax, and his mouth twitches into a smile. He softens. For a moment, believing himself to be bigger and more important than anything and anyone else in existence, he rests. And his eyes flutter shut.

As he does, I let Little One slowly, ever so slowly, float over to the ice-sheet bed. He bends over, removes the heart gently from its box. And then he drifts over to us and lays the heart at my feet before turning back into my brave, curious Little One, tilting her head to watch me. The peacocks, still too busy preening to notice us, never see us leave.

There's a ledge that looks out at the mountain range around us. We noticed on the way in that it looks down on a village nearby, and we sit on this ledge for a moment to catch our breath before our trek back to Chompy.

We stare out at the valley, just going dim, Egor's footprints crisscrossing the town below.

It's been like this again and again in every witch-cursed place—the trail left behind as the witches take what is hard in the world and make it harder, turning losses into voids, mistakes into battles, words into weapons. And the more I see it, the more I see that in every single case, their curses do this by separating one human being from another. And by separating every person from the trees and animals and the earth around them. As if all living things weren't a family. As if, in Egor's case, feeling more important than everything around you were really all that great.

It is while I'm thinking this that I see the woman wandering through the village below.

She is waddling down the main street of the small town, handing something out. She is poor—I can tell by the threadbare clothes that wrap her up against the cold— but she is giving out homemade bread to the people on the street. In the footsteps she leaves in the snow, a faint silver light glows and rises.

"What is that?" Aria asks, squinting at the woman.

I don't really know. The woman clearly isn't someone with the sight, and yet her footprints have that glow. But I finally share what I saw with the old man in Salem. I tell Germ and Aria about the man who saved the innocent *non*-witch Martha Parker. How he left light behind him, and how I read later that he'd saved her.

We stare at the woman as she disappears around a corner of a house, the silver light in her footsteps fading.

"Maybe it's not only witch hunting that pushes back against witch darkness," Aria says.

We sit in silence, thinking. We don't know what to make of it. We watch the peaceful village, children playing, sitting together talking and laughing around fires.

"*We* used to do that," Aria says thoughtfully, "in my childhood town. Before we left to hide. Sit around a bonfire together with our neighbors. It was like warming up the winter." She sighs, her cool teenage exterior gone. Germ and I are both silent. Waiting for Aria to share things about herself is like trying not to startle a butterfly.

"When we got to our island, Clara stopped making fires outside. She stopped doing anything fun or happy like that. She spent all her time staring into that snow globe. All because of what that store clerk had said, that a hunter had owned it. She wanted to believe there were other hunters in the world so badly, she felt like everything depended on it. I think"—Aria's voice catches here—"she was probably thinking of leaving for a long time, to look for them."

Aria hesitates, and doesn't meet our eyes.

"I started sleeping in front of the door. I was so scared she'd leave without me." She swallows. "But it didn't do any good. One night she . . . vanished anyway. I guess she probably crawled through a window to avoid me. It was like she couldn't wait to go. She didn't even say goodbye, or leave me any advice on how to survive without her. I don't know how she made it off the island. She was just . . . gone."

Beside me, Germ lets out a small sniff. I don't have to look at her to know she is crying. I am as still as it is possible to be, afraid Aria will stop talking.

"I guess she didn't want me to slow her down or be a burden she had to worry about." Aria shakes her head. "My snow globe is all I have left of her, really. I figure if she ever found those rumored witch hunters, they're all dead or worse. Either that or she didn't *care* enough to come back. I don't know which scares me more. All I know is that I'm so mad at her, and my voice—the *magic* in it—

hasn't worked right since I woke up that morning after she left, and it probably never will."

She looks over at me. "I know you keep trying to do things like I would do them, Rosie." At this, I blush, because I hadn't thought Aria noticed me trying to be exactly like her, and it's embarrassing. "But I'm just mad and hurt. That's all. It's not a strength, trust me."

Germ reaches for Aria's arm and links hers under Aria's elbow. Aria wipes at her own eyes, and then Germ's.

"I'm not crying, *you're* crying," Aria says, and smiles weakly.

We sit silently, my hourglass forgotten. And I take it in sadly, how Aria's grief and anger has broken her voice. I wish I could fix it for her, like I wish I could fix the things in myself I think aren't quite right, like I wish I could fix the world for Wolf.

"That's why I need the voucher," she finally says. "I want to go back to a day long before Clara left, when I wasn't so angry, and when I still trusted her not to leave me behind. I want to stay there forever. Even if I know it's not the truth."

I don't know how vouchers work. I don't know if *this* Aria would trade places with her old self, or if she'd just be an unseen presence, an unseen time traveler, lingering in happier times merely to be near them. But I do understand why Aria wants to go back.

She looks up through her tears, down at the peaceful village. The woman has appeared again. Her arms are empty of all the bread she was giving away, and she's waddling her way home through the snow. We've just left behind a witch who thinks only of himself, but the world is so full of people like this woman: generous, selfless, kind.

And then Aria does the thing—I guess—that helps her like stories help me. She hums, and as she does, the notes move like colors into the air in front of her mouth— the way warm breath puffs out on a cold day. She reaches out and touches the colors, poking them. They glow in the dusk.

Aria strings a few puffs of color together with her hands—a trick I have never imagined, much less seen. She raises her slingshot, tugs back the rubber band, and lets it flick gently against the colored puffs, which float down the slope and away from us, and finally over the woman walking through the village, like a lantern to light her way home. For a moment, Aria's powers aren't broken at all. But as quickly as her song illuminates the woman's path, the thread of colors floats right past her and into a snowbank, disintegrating, and causing a tiny cascade of snow to tumble to the ground. The woman's path goes dark again.

"See? Even when I try to do the most delicate things . . . ," Aria says sadly.

Germ tries to change the subject. "I'd love to hang out with those people for a night," she says, looking in the direction Aria's voice has gone.

"I'd love to hang out with *any* people," Aria says. "I mean, but I'm happy I have you guys."

Germ and I try not to react. But we exchange a look, both surprised by the compliment.

"You know what I miss?" Germ says. "The carnizaar."

I smile slightly. Germ's mom used to take us. It was a school fundraiser that was half carnival, half bazaar, with handmade crafts to buy. It used to be the highlight of our summer when we were kids. "Do you think my mom will take my brothers without me?"

"I can't imagine your family's doing anything but worrying about you, Germ," I say.

From our perch, we watch the rounded valley beneath us. The more I see of the world through time, the more Earth seems to me like a living creature—nurturing us, growing us, rooting for us, an intelligent animal growing other animals on its back, rumbling and churning and creating.

I try to imagine, for a glimmer of a moment, what it could be like if everyone could see the magic that ties them to the world, the moon, the clouds, the trees, each other—the beautiful magic that the black night reveals. Gravity was always there, invisible, and then we found it. Couldn't it be the same with magic, too?

My imagination falls short when I try to picture what that could look like. And maybe that makes me less of a witch hunter than I need to be.

But, in any case, the world I see from the ledge tonight is the opposite of witches like Egor. And it is worth fighting for, whether there is anyone out there to help us or not.

CHAPTER 15

It's evening, though day or night never matters much on Chompy. By Germ's count, it's our 105th day at sea. We haven't heard a whale call in more than a week.

There are bags under Germ's eyes, and Aria's jaw is permanently clenched. Ebb floats and flickers along the corners of the rooms, steering clear of me as usual, looking gloomy. I can see it on everyone's faces and in the way their shoulders slump. We are tired—more tired than any of us has ever been. The days and nights hunting hearts have worn us down.

Then again, we have six hearts . . . and eight and a half days left in my hourglass to capture the last three. The exhaustion of our crew is so intense, you can practically touch it, but we are also happy. We are, in fact, in very good shape.

Still, as miraculous as Little One's transformations have been, I feel like somehow I am falling short with her, like whatever I've turned her into is still no match for the Time Witch and what faces us in San Francisco. Occasionally I catch her giving me a look that seems almost bemused, as if my own imaginary bird thinks I can do better.

Germ—who's been playing solitaire for hours—stands up. "I need a break," she says.

"All we do on this whale is take breaks," Aria says. "It's a timeless whale."

Germ shakes her head. "I don't mean sitting around being bored. I mean a *real break*. Something different, something fun." She drops her shoulders listlessly. And then she seems to have a thought. "We need a party."

Reflexively I let out a groan.

Germ and I went to a few parties in fifth grade. (In sixth grade I was mostly occupied with ghosts and my mother's curse.) Back then, Germ always had fun at the parties, and I always felt like I'd rather be pulling my fingernails out one by one. One boy, who'd learned in Life Skills class that it was good to make small talk, asked me awkwardly which season was my favorite, and I literally ran into a closet. It was humiliating. But now Germ's eyes are widening in a growing excitement that makes me very wary.

"We need to have a seventh-grade dance," she says with finality, clenching both her hands together in fists.

"A *what?*" Aria says. Something tells me Aria's seventh grade was very different from ours, considering the darkness of the future. Ebb, who's been brooding in his room, lifts his head.

"A seventh-grade dance," Germ says. "It's great. There's soda, and music, and everyone's nervous, and you have to ask someone to dance, and it is a total disaster if they say no." Standing behind Germ, I shake my head at Aria in warning. Ebb all but disappears, floating through a curtain and out of the room.

"That does sound . . . great?" Aria says flatly, casting me a side-eye.

But Germ has latched on to the idea so fast, she's

unstoppable, a seventh-grade-dance juggernaut. "Chompy knows everything we want to hear—it's basically like he was born to DJ. And we should have a theme. Maybe oldies. Like, stuff from the year 2000."

To my surprise, Aria is beginning to look slightly interested. Germ has her at the music stuff. When Aria sees me still shaking my head, she shrugs. "Well, it's not like we're not in a timeless vortex," she says.

In the end, I am overruled by Chompy. I don't know if it's because he's grown partial to Germ or if he *was* actually born to DJ, but before we can even discuss the possibility further, the seventh-grade dance appears. Sparkling garlands materialize along the ceiling, and the Grand View monitor comes to life with a light show that sends colored spirals around the room. An upbeat song comes on. There are cakes and games and amazing party costumes hanging from racks that have appeared along the walls. There's a bathtub full of jelly beans, a trampoline, a Velcro wall and Velcro suits on hangers along a rail.

I decide, begrudgingly, that if this is going to happen, I at least need to dress more presentably. I disappear into the bedroom and try, of course, to do my hair like Aria, and put on some deep fuchsia lipstick and pull on a denim dress. I can't decide if I look nice or if I just look like someone sadly trying to look like a teenager and failing.

When it comes to fun, Germ is all business. She sets her chin and drags Aria into the middle of the living room floor before the last garland appears.

"Oh, we're doing this now?" Aria says, casting me a helpless look. Germ starts to twirl her like a tetherball, then grabs my hand and pulls me into the circle. And despite myself, I am soon doing some involuntary dancing.

I have to admit, it does feel a little bit good. Like letting gunky air out of an exhaust pipe. Eventually Ebb appears, drifting along the edges of the room skittishly, watching for the slightest motion from Germ to include him, so he can hurry out through one of the walls.

But, it turns out, a seventh-grade dance is fun. Maybe that's because only my best and most trusted friends are at this one, and in real life it would be different. But it does lift my spirits. Germ is right. A little dancing, it seems, goes a surprisingly long way.

For the rest of the evening Aria, Germ, and I find out new funny things about each other, like that Aria's favorite show is actually *The Wiggles*, and how Germ has never admitted—even to me—that she wants to be a pilot in the Alaskan wilderness someday.

Aria shows Germ how to do a French manicure, and Germ shows Aria how to stuff as many marshmallows as possible into your mouth while still being able to say the words "fuzzy bunny." Germ gives Aria the full lowdown on D'quan Daniels' perfect eyelashes, and Aria tries her best to look riveted. In other words, for a few hours, we act like we are twelve (and in Aria's case, fifteen). Only *Ebb* acts older, steering clear of us like a grumpy old man, probably because of *me*—and also, I guess, because he is, technically, a thousand years old.

But as Aria and Germ curl up in sleeping bags so that Germ can show Aria *Notting Hill*, a romance movie she has made me watch a million times even though her mom says we're not allowed because it's PG-13 and inappropriate, my thoughts of the witches and their mysterious yarn creep back in. So I slide out of my sleeping bag and climb to the Grand View and sit down. I open the *Guide* and look over the three witches we have left besides the Time Witch: Dread, Mable the Mad, and Convenia. Up beside the monitor, my mom and dad look down at me from the photo taped to the wall. I shine Little One on the floor and watch her pecking around—she looks frazzled, uncertain, weary, like the rest of us.

Then I feel a presence over my shoulder, and look up to see Ebb, hovering there.

"It's weird. Convenia," he says, pointing to the page I have open, the witch with the tired eyes and the cats surrounding her. "She's one of the weaker ones. She should have been one of the easiest to find. But now she's one of the last."

We study the drawing. She seems fairly insignificant, as witches go.

"You look awful," he says.

I glance up at him. "You're the one fading into oblivion," I say.

Ebb flickers with a smile. "What's troubling you?" he asks.

I stare down at the book. What's *not* troubling me? Still three witches to go, plus the Time Witch. Wolf still out there alone and afraid, in so much danger, not knowing I'm trying to save him or even that I love him. And then there's the strange spinning of the yarn. I know I am missing something important, but I don't know what.

"It's just . . ." I falter. "I've figured out all these ways I can use Little One, but she's still only Little One and I'm still only . . . *me.*"

"What's wrong with *you?*" he asks with the hint of an encouraging smile. I shrug.

"I'm . . . messy," I say. "Like, messy in every way."

"Well," Ebb says after thinking a few moments. "What makes you strange and messy makes you strong. It's your weird and wild parts that are going to save us."

"That's what Germ said," I reply, "but it's hard to believe it. And anyway, I couldn't save *you*." I glance at my feet, a lump welling up in my throat.

Ebb looks away awkwardly. "What do you mean?"

I swallow. "I understand why you're not my friend anymore. I let you get caught by the Time Witch." Tears well in my eyes. "But I'm really sorry, Ebb. More sorry than I can ever say."

Ebb goes very dim. He looks, from what I can tell, surprised. And then he clears his throat.

"I didn't know you thought that," he says. He's quiet for a long time. "You know, I was in the Time Witch's basement for a few hundred years after she got me. I assumed she'd cursed you, destroyed you. During that time, I didn't even try to think about how to escape. I lost my will to try." He clears his throat. "And then I found out you were okay. That's when things changed for me. I decided to win the Time Witch's trust. I worked, I spread rumors, I lied, I stole. I spent a thousand years building up my crew and my reputation."

"You did what you did to survive," I say, thinking he's asking for reassurance. "I understand."

He blushes, and his glow brightens for a moment before dimming again.

"Rosie, I became the pirate king so that when the time came—when you finally came into the past and the Time Witch had you in her sights—I could be in the right time and the right place to help you."

I listen, my face flaming up. I can barely speak because of my confusion.

"But . . . you don't even like me anymore," I sputter. "You're not even my friend."

He looks away, and now it's his turn to look embarrassed. "That's not why I don't talk to you anymore." He seems to be searching for words that are hard to find. "It's just—after a thousand years, I'm not growing. I'm the same age. But you're already so different after only a year. I mean, you look different and do your hair different and dress different sometimes. You're leading a quest against the witches. You're . . . different than I remember. You've always been like my little sister." He frowns. "But soon you'll be older than me. You'll grow up and you'll live a whole life I'm not even old enough to understand. Like, I'll never go to a dance like you and Germ, you know? You'll do all that a ton."

"I hope not," I say. He flickers, smirking. "Germ's older, but you're still friends with *her*."

He shrugs. "It's not the same. Ever since you were born, my afterlife has been about *watching over you*. But now you're a ship that's gonna sail right past me. You're gonna outgrow me. And I feel like I have to start letting go."

This makes me feel embarrassed but also relieved inside. And I think maybe, in some small way, I understand what it's like to be scared of someone you care about. I've missed twelve years of Wolf's life, and it scares me. What will he think of me, if I *am* able to rescue him? Will he even like me?

I don't know whether Chompy does it on purpose or not, but a slow song comes on.

"Would you want to have a dance with *me*?" I say.

Ebb looks startled. I don't like him the way Germ likes D'quan; that would be weird. But I do feel warm inside that Ebb really loves me after all . . . enough to spend a thousand years trying to help me. Germ is still my favorite person on earth, with Aria running a close second. But Ebb is mixed in there somewhere too, in some weird space I can't define.

I stand and we try to touch our hands together. Of course, they don't really touch, but we do the best we can.

We walk to the living room and move around the room in an awkward but fun, slow way. We laugh at each other. We are like two people almost the same age.

Slow dancing is all the things Germ has promised: embarrassing and kind of nice. The fact that Ebb is a ghost, and a fading, flimsy one at that, doesn't make any of that less. I don't know where to put my eyes, so I look up at Fred in the corner, who's weaving the words:

> *I think that I shall never see*
> *A poem lovely as a tree.*

I wonder if maybe it is worth being weird and awkward and not fitting in most places if I'm the person Ebb wants to have his first dance with, and the person Germ sees as her best friend, and the person who can make tiny suns that put monsters to sleep, and do things that make my friends believe in me. Maybe Germ's right that you don't have to have a big group of friends as long as you have the *right* group of friends.

In the bedroom, Aria has fallen asleep. Germ is writing "fart" on her forehead. We are misfits. But also we are normal in our own weird, witch hunting, time-traveling way. Being misfits is, maybe, what everyone in the world has in common most of all.

And despite being hyped up on orange soda and Oreos, on this night, I sleep the sleep of the untroubled, and the loved.

CHAPTER 16

Germ and I are in our beds a few nights later, settling in to sleep, when I hear Aria's voice from the Grand View.

"You guys, come look at this."

We slide out of bed and walk up the front stairs to see.

The dates on our monitor keep disappearing, scrambling, speeding up, slowing down.

"It just started. I don't know what it's doing."

Suddenly we are rocked backward as Chompy takes an abrupt turn up. Stumbling back over my feet, I look at

Aria, who looks at me, eyes wide and afraid. It feels like Chompy is headed for the surface, but why?

"Where are you taking us, Chompy?" Germ asks, having fallen back against a wall, closing one eye so she can concentrate. But Chompy, instead of answering her in ESP, keeps swimming (no surprise there).

And then the numbers stop altogether. They blink and then go out.

It's too late for questions. Chompy slams to a halt.

I hear the familiar sounds that come whenever we emerge from water: the silence as Chompy's tail stops propelling us, the lapping of waves. Chompy's enormous mouth is beginning to open, and the dimness of evening is streaming in. Water pours in over our feet.

Wherever we're going, we've arrived.

The hot air that envelops us is steamy and moist. Ahead of us, we see a valley in dim dusk light, scattered with giant ferns at least a hundred feet high, stretching to the base of a steeply rising range of mountains, brown and rocky and towering above and casting evening shadows across the beach.

Chompy waits for us to disembark. We look at each other.

"Do we have a choice?" I ask, but I already know the

answer. There's a witch here; there must be. We have to swallow our fear, and follow.

We gather our things and slowly climb out, stepping into the warm seawater and wading onto land. I feel sweat collecting along my temples and running down the sides of my face. It must be almost a hundred degrees.

In the distance, the tip of a volcano peeks up far beyond the cliffs, rumbling and coughing. Every time it sputters, the ground beneath our feet rattles. The air smells thickly of decaying plants and rich, fragrant dirt. And the sounds of life are almost deafening—birds squawking, insects buzzing, and the growls of things we can't see and maybe *don't want* to see.

"That must be the problem with the monitor," Aria says. "I think we are back before humans kept track of time. Maybe before humans, period."

There's no question, this is not a place we could survive in for long. The volcano spews as if it will erupt any minute. We need to get out of here faster than even my hourglass demands.

"But why would a witch come here?" I ask. "If there's no one here to curse?"

I look at Aria, who shrugs. We are looking for the dark trail that will tell us where he or she has gone, when Aria holds an arm out in front of us and stills us. She nods up to the rocky mountain face ahead.

We don't have to look for the witch's trail after all.

We see him already.

His long gray robes dangle as he climbs the mountain ahead of us, scrabbling from ledge to ledge like a mountain goat. Unsure if he might see us if he looked down below him, we fling ourselves behind the nearest fern, and watch through the gaps in the greenery as he climbs. He keeps looking at the deepening dark sky as if he's hiding a secret from it. I recognize him, of course. *Dread.* The memory of the yarn and his connection to it disturbs me.

"Doesn't matter what he's here for," Aria says, as if reading my mind. "We only need his heart."

We follow at a distance, keeping to the sides of the jagged mountain. At first we climb easily, but soon we are scrabbling with our hands and fingernails, the ledges getting narrower and harder to find purchase on as we get higher and higher.

Germ, of course, climbs with her usual natural ability. She moves as if she could climb the mountain backward. Aria and I, on the other hand, are fairly certain this is the moment we will meet our deaths. About halfway up, Aria pushes her face against the cool rock and shakes her head.

I am feeling like my arms and legs have turned to jelly and that we'll never make it, when things begin to level off a bit. Soon we're on the top of a plateau, in a woodsy scrub.

We crest the rise and see the valley on the other side, waterfalls pounding down distant mountains, barely visible in the very last of the day's light. Far ahead, we see the bobbing head of the witch, still on the move. As we follow, staying far behind but always keeping him in our sights, night falls.

We walk for about an hour. As the night deepens, the magical things come out to glimmer: the Beyond sparkling and pink and far away, the strange and misty shapes of cloud shepherds crossing the sky. It reassures me that even here before "time," these things are present. But it's a fully dark moon night, and even the slim sliver we sometimes have to light our path is gone.

In the darkness, it becomes harder and scarier to traverse past bushes, over rocks, but at least Dread's trail glimmers up ahead in the dark. And then, at last, we come to a rocky outcropping where there is a kind of fissure through the rocks, and a clearing in the middle where he's come to a stop. We hide, tucking ourselves into the folds of the rocks from where we can watch the clearing without being seen. Dread has built a small fire and he's sitting near it, doing something with his hands. A rough-hewn sewing basket sits on the ground beside him, and I know without seeing what it contains: the yarn he's collected from all the witches. When I see what he's doing with it, I feel my stomach tighten with a warning.

He's knitting something. Silver knitting needles flash and glint in the firelight. Whatever creation he's making, it lies half-done across his lap like a kind of blanket.

Germ, Aria, and I look at each other, not exactly surprised that this is how the yarn is being used, and yet deeply worried. Dread knits and watches the path and waits. I feel a bottomless terror, watching him. It's as if he breathes fear into the atmosphere. It raises the hairs on my arms, makes the back of my neck tingle.

Something throbs lopsidedly in his pocket, and I nudge Aria. It might be his heart. Either that or he's got a bullfrog in there—breathing, moving, squirming.

But I can't steal a heart from this witch, I think. I can't even imagine going close to him.

And then what he is waiting for arrives.

Or rather, her hummingbirds arrive first.

"You're late," Dread says, as mildly as if a coworker has come late to a meeting.

From the edge of the darkness, the Time Witch drifts into view.

She walks up to the side of the fire, hummingbirds fluttering around her hands and shoulders. Aria clutches my arm, and we push back into the rocky crevice around us as if we could melt into it. We dim ourselves further, if that's possible. My heart begins to pound so loudly, I fear it can be heard from miles away.

The Time Witch settles on the other side of the fire.

"I was busy," she replies. Her reptilian eyes glint in the light of the flames.

"With your games, no doubt," Dread shoots back. "Gambling something. What is it this time? A piece of space-time from your sleeve? One of your little knick-knacks?"

"My games keep me from losing my mind, you know. Eternity is long and flat."

"Your games will ruin us someday. You take unnecessary risks. I hear you are taking them with witch hunters now."

"That's a bit dramatic, don't you think?" the Time Witch replies. "Besides"—she shrugs—"gambling against humans is like playing a game against a slug, or a puppy."

Dread is silent for a long time.

She sighs. "Have I ever lost? And besides, is that any way to speak to someone who's brought you good news across time?"

"Well?" He sits back. "And what is this good news? Why have you asked me to meet?"

"I've just been to the very edge of the future," the Time Witch says. "And conditions are ideal. We've spread enough curses around the earth to sever people almost completely from moonlight. The Beyond has grown dim for them; the moon—even when it shines—is distant. It's all perfectly prepared. It will be comfortable and easy for him, when he comes. A soft, warm welcome for a traveler who's journeyed far."

Germ and Aria and I glance at each other in confusion, wondering who she means, but for the moment, Dread looks as confused as we do.

"You've been making something for me," she says. She puts out her hands eagerly.

Dread holds it out to her. As he dangles it in the air, it looks like a half-finished blanket.

"It's beautiful," she says, deeply moved. Maybe there are some things new under the sun after all, for the Time Witch. This appears to be one of them.

"Will you finally tell me what it is we are making?" Dread asks.

"Isn't it obvious, by looking at it?" She holds up the dark fabric in her hands. It's missing a big piece, but still, its emptiness as she holds it up is staggering. "You really haven't guessed?"

"A shawl," Dread says blandly, annoyed. "An afghan. A table runner."

The Time Witch smiles then. I know that smile; there's only hatred in it. "A hole."

Dread is now surprised. He stares at her, waiting.

"Turns out the best way to reach a black hole . . . is with another one."

Dread stares at her another long moment, and then he, too, grins.

Aria understands what this means a minute before I do. She wraps her hand around my wrist and digs her fingernails into my skin. Just as the meaning is on the tip of my brain, Dread says it.

"We're making a black hole, to bring the Nothing King back?"

The Time Witch sifts the fabric through her hands, running her fingers along it as if admiring its softness. "It's really like burrowing a tunnel, from one place to another across the universe," she says. "Once it's finished, the Nothing King can step through it. And then he has only to grab hold of the world and drag it back in. Do you know what's inside a black hole?"

Dread shakes his head.

"Chaos. Obliteration. All of this"—she gestures upward—"the world and all the magic that surrounds it will be gone."

"And us?" Dread asks.

"We will finally have the disorder we crave. I can finally enjoy myself for once." Her teeth glint in the fire-light. "I've been so very bored. Did I mention that?"

Dread looks both excited and terrified.

I remember Aria's words. *The Time Witch is nothing compared to the Nothing King. He's worse than all of them combined.*

The Time Witch shakes her shoulders, as if impatient. "Don't let me interrupt your other chores, here at the beginning of all things," she says. "You've come, after all, for an important job."

Dread nods once. He stands up, stretches his legs, as if getting ready for a day at work. He tugs at his gray robes, and something stalks out from underneath them. A hyena, glowing, hungry-eyed, starving, in fact.

"The first thief," he says with a hint of pride. "The first humans will be born soon, and the first familiars will be ready to steal from them. My pets will take their *sight*."

The Time Witch smiles at the hyena. "Who's a good boy?" she says, leaning forward to pet the creature, who looks as if he might eat her face if she's not careful. The Time Witch is unafraid. "Stealing such a gift from humans before they've barely begun. They won't see the Beyond, or the dead, or the goddess on the moon." She pats the hyena one more time, then stands, looking at Dread. "You will miss a few. They'll become psychics and have TV shows, and some will hunt witches."

"I know," he says.

"But in the end, it won't matter," she adds.

Dread tilts his head thoughtfully. "So the witch hunter you are toying with? She dies?"

The Time Witch shrugs, back to boredom. "Of course she dies. They *all* die—the twin brother, the loud friend, the girl with the broken voice, the boy ghost. They die in San Francisco, 1855."

Aria, Germ, and I look at each other. My stomach has fallen to my feet, and my mouth has gone hot and dry. And then Dread lowers his hands and opens his robes entirely. More hyenas emerge, one after another after another. They come slinking out—a slow, luminous parade—and spread in all directions along the top of the ridge.

In the end, hundreds of hyenas materialize from under Dread's robes, and lope off into the trees in the glowing darkness. They descend into the valley below to wait for the first humans, as Dread said. We watch in despair as they fan out over the surface of the roiling, young Earth, the seeds of disconnection and fear planted right at the very beginning of things.

People were supposed to see the magic all along, I realize with a deep, aching sadness—the light lying under the dark, the same living fabric shared by babies and mountains and birds.

"We should destroy them both right now!" Germ hisses. "Turn Little One into a beast that devours them both."

I reach into my pocket for my flashlight, but Aria stays my hand. "You can't fight both of them at once. We've got to stick to the plan. For Wolf's sake."

My hands shake as I try to weigh what she's saying against my overwhelming urge to destroy the witches before me.

Wolf. All this has been for Wolf. I can't abandon him.

And so, with the witches and their horrifying blanket in my sights, I hide. And watch the seeds of dread fan out over the earth. The Time Witch watches Dread's iridescent familiars disappear beyond the trees, and then she turns and floats out of sight, carrying an almost-finished black hole in her arms.

There is only one small victory.

At the exact moment Dread brushes past the fissure where we hide, Aria does the quickest, most *un-seeable* seeable thing I've ever witnessed.

If I weren't looking straight at her, I wouldn't even notice it happening. She reaches out with one arm in a smooth, seamless motion, and slips Dread's heart right out of his pocket. She is shaking as she pulls her arm to her chest. We *all* are. But Ebb's pickpocketing lessons have paid off.

We wait for several moments, and then she opens her palm to show us.

Dread's heart is a sleeping dove, a beautiful thing. But in her hands it shifts and jiggles like jelly, like all the rest, and I know that it is rotten to the core. It is almost too heartbreaking to look at.

Still. He may be the witch at the heart of all the fear in the world. But his heart is in my backpack now.

CHAPTER 17

We have arrived at our last stop, though we don't know it. I wake to a beeping.

Bleary, I slide out of bed and walk to the monitor to see what it means.

I've slept fitfully, dreaming of the campfire at the beginning of the world and two witches discussing the end of it, the black hole in the hands of the Time Witch. My first thought—aside from wondering about the beeping—is, *We lose, we die, I don't save Wolf.*

As the sleep-fog of my brain clears, I slowly make

sense of the beeping and what I'm seeing on the monitor. We are closing in on London.

Chompy must have heard the whale call sometime while we slumbered.

"It can't be true," Aria says, shuffling up beside me, rubbing her eyes and continuing a conversation that ended when we fell asleep the night before.

We spent much of last night—once we'd returned to Chompy and shared with Ebb everything we'd seen and heard—debating what we should do, whether we should give up on our plan entirely, or whether we should forge ahead. We decided, before passing out from exhaustion deep in the night, to at least get the last two hearts before facing the Time Witch, and then decide.

And now, suddenly, here we are. We're here to find either Convenia or Mable the Mad. There's no way to know which yet.

We still have plenty of time to get them both if we do everything right. But it's what comes after that we dread most: San Francisco, 1855. Where, supposedly, we die.

Germ, just out of bed too, is staring out the moonroof, her face drawn and pale.

"Why would she say it if it weren't true?" she asks heavily. "Why would she lie to another witch?"

Aria visibly struggles to answer this. "She was only talking about one possible future, one where we fail," she presses. "There have got to be *lots* of possible futures. The time-traveling whales make that possible. The future she's seen can't be the one where we've collected so many hearts."

Germ and I are silent, unconvinced. I want to believe her. But I can't help thinking of what she said when she first boarded Chompy what seems like forever ago. The Time Witch knows our moves the moment we make them. She's a cat and we're the mice.

Ebb is standing at the monitor, watching the years and places tick by.

"You know, Rosie, the London where we're headed to is in 2001. Your dad was alive then, right? He probably used London as one of his ports." He looks back at me. "What if we run into him?"

I know Ebb is trying to think of one thing, anything, to bring brightness to our dark moods. But I also know that running into my dad would be like coming across a pearl lost in the ocean. It's not going to happen. And then, seeing how unimpressed I am, Ebb points out something else. "Also, it's the home of Harry Potter," he says, giving me a look that's meant to be encouraging.

I smile at him sadly. Ebb does know me, in some ways,

better than I know myself. I've longed to see Leadenhall Market and King's Cross Station and all the places that my favorite stories have changed for me from something real into something *more*. And I do feel a tiny sizzle of curiosity, in the pit of my stomach, despite the sense of doom that's descended on us all like a thunderstorm. When we finally whir to a stop in the port of London, I am even a little bit excited.

"I recognize that whale," Ebb says, staring at the Grand View's image of the killer whale we've come upon swimming near the wharf. "I saw it from my ship once, a couple hundred years ago. It belongs to Mable the Mad."

"Mable the Mad it is, then," Aria says, her face going still with determination. I know she is thinking the same thing I am. That all of this could be pointless, and maybe we've already lost. But we have to try.

Chompy's mouth begins to open.

"*Notting Hill* was filmed here," Germ says, apropos of nothing.

And despite the heaviness we all feel, and despite the witch and the whale, and despite the newfound realization that there are even worse things than a web of curses over the world, for the moment I'm just a girl who loves Harry Potter, standing on a whale, getting to see London at last.

We find ourselves stepping out of Chompy's mouth onto a fog-enshrouded wharf in the middle of the night. The smell of rotten fish hits us like a wall, and we see the London Eye, a great twinkling Ferris wheel, in the distance, closed and still for the night but still alight. Big Ben chimes somewhere we can't see, along with all the other far-off sounds of any modern city that goes all night. But here, at the wharf, all is deserted and dark.

"There," Aria says, pointing to a dark trail that leads up the docks past a row of buildings, taking a sharp right behind a wall. We follow it, winding around corners past a string of town houses, a small coffee and antiques shop called A Gathering of Lost Things, a pub with a lion on the front. Soon it all starts to blur together as we make our way into the snaking streets of London. It seems we cross half the city in our slow pursuit of Mable the Mad, and a few landmarks I've read about stand out: the London Zoo, the Millennium Bridge, all mostly deserted in the dark. Ghosts congregate on the steps of churches and old stone buildings. Finally, near dawn, the trail leads us to a small, crooked apartment building with a narrow staircase.

We can see that the witch has already been and gone. We find people in the hallways muttering to themselves, sitting and weeping with their doors open, speaking to nothing and no one. Mable's dark footsteps mark the floors leading to each door. Her curse, among all the witches' curses, is particularly cruel. She doesn't disconnect people from each other; she disconnects them from themselves. They don't know what's real and what's not. As we walk past one apartment, I see the tail end of one of her rabbits hopping out a third-story window and disappearing into the night.

At the very top of the stairs, the footprints turn back on each other. We've come to another home with its door open, where a little boy is peeping out from behind a chair. There are no footprints in here, no sign of the witch, but it catches my attention because the boy is looking straight at me. *He can see me.* He smiles. He must have hidden from her.

I peer around the room. The TV is on, and cartoons are playing quietly in the background.

"Where are your parents?" I ask him.

"At work," he says.

He's here all alone, I realize, hiding from a terrible thing. I know I have to leave and keep following the footprints, but something draws me to the boy. Back when my mom was under the Memory Thief's curse, I was all alone too.

"Are you real?" he asks. I swallow, then nod. "I see

things no one else can see," he says. "Sometimes I wish I didn't."

"I know what you mean," I say.

Being different, I know all too well, can make you feel alone. And feeling alone can make you feel dusty inside.

"I saw a witch." He shivers, fear crossing his face. He seems to reflect on this. "Some things are so scary, they make you want to crumple up," he says.

I feel an ache rising in my throat. "I'm trying to fix some of that," I whisper.

"We've gotta catch up to her." Aria, who's been standing behind me keeping a lookout, tugs my sleeve. "Let's go."

I turn to follow Aria out, but on second thought I turn back. I pull my *Snowy Day* book—the one I packed for good luck what seems like forever ago—out of my backpack's front pocket, and slip it into the boy's hands. I can't really explain why I do it, except that when I was little, the book kept reminding me that there is always wonder in the world.

"There are beautiful things too," I say. "And you are not alone."

I look up, and Aria is shaking her head at me, an angry expression on her face.

"It's only a book," I whisper. "It won't make any difference. Nobody will notice."

The boy takes the book, and opens to the first page. I don't know if he will read it or if it will mean to him what my books have meant to me. But it's the best I can do. Aria is pulling me forward, and we move on.

We find Mable the Mad three blocks away, where she's sleeping in an empty Tube tunnel that has long since fallen into disuse. To lure her rabbits away from her, I turn Little One into a carrot dangling at the end of a string. It works like a dream. We retrieve her heart tucked in her sleeve—a piece of rope frayed at the edges—and soon we are snaking our way out of the abandoned tunnel into the dim light that comes before the sun rises.

Stores are still closed, but a few people have begun milling about as London comes awake. Up ahead, the antiques store we passed on our way in, A Gathering of Lost Things, has opened its doors. I suppose because they sell coffee and want to catch the morning commuters.

I'm rounding the corner to pass it when something brings me up short. It's a man I glimpse who's just walked in. Through the glass of the storefront, I watch his profile as he crosses the room. He looks like he could be a sailor, head nestled into a weather-beaten coat, hair windblown and messy, not the usual kind of man you'd see in an antiques store. There's something deeply familiar about him.

"I need to do something alone for a second," I say to Aria and Germ. "Is that okay? I'll catch up with you at Chompy."

"You sure?" Germ asks. I nod. They both look reluctant, but also, Germ can read all my faces. She knows when I need to do something on my own, and she knows when I'm determined. "Okay, we'll see you there," she says. She takes Aria's elbow and they walk away.

After they've turned the corner, I walk closer and peer in through the shop window, my heart pounding everywhere it shouldn't—in my knees, my feet, my head. The man is standing at a counter at the back of the shop, holding out his hand for the antiques dealer to assess what he holds.

Now my heart skitters so fast, I think it will burn itself out.

It looks, from here, like what he holds might be a silver whistle. A whistle like my dad found, long ago.

I hurry inside.

Considering it's not even quite light out, the store is empty but for the man and the shopkeeper. There are cracked vases, old coins, mismatched ceramic tea sets.

There are all sorts of old clocks ticking away the hours, each set to a different time. I make my way through the dusty aisles, past shelves full of lamps and jewelry boxes, toward the back of the shop. But when I get close, I see that the man is not holding a whistle at all.

He's got a handful of silver spoons, and he's trying to get the best price for them. And then I see his face. And suddenly I want to evaporate, or spill onto the floor and right through the cracks. He is not my dad. Of course he's not my dad.

I guess, since what Ebb said, I've been watching for him even though I didn't know it. I've been wishing, hoping against hope.

I turn back to leave. But as I do, I notice that something has changed. At first I can't put my finger on what. And then I realize that it's *silence*. The clocks have all stopped ticking. I look over at the counter where the clerk stands. She is completely still, her eyes frozen on one spot. The man with the spoons stands as petrified as a statue. Hummingbirds flutter around him.

And then I feel a pair of eyes on me. I turn to see a darkly dressed figure watching me from the end of the aisle, pocket watches dangling from around her neck. I yank out my flashlight and turn it on.

The Time Witch moves quickly and easily. She waves a hand, and Little One freezes in midair—stopped in time. She comes walking toward me. She smiles.

"You left a trace," she says. And she waves her hand once more, levitating my *Snowy Day* book out of her robe. She cocks her head. "I heard the change when you gave it to the boy. Like threads of time gone wobbly."

She sends her hummingbirds all around Little One, who is easily and quickly pulled onto the ground, flickering in distress. As I dive forward to help her, the birds surround me. They peck at me little by little. I try to bat them away, but there are too many. At first I don't know what the feeling is. My feet ache. My legs feel as if they're being stretched. And then I realize, I'm growing, getting older.

I am losing time.

We don't die here, I think, frantic. *We die in San Francisco.* But it's only a desperate thought.

I'm starting to feel my bones creak when there is a sudden, screeching sound. Something hits the window, and around me windows shatter in a deafening crash. Antiques come flying from the shelves; the clocks all burst into pieces. A shard of glass hits the Time Witch right in the chest. She stumbles backward against a shelf, and it falls over on her. Behind me, a wall crumbles and falls.

And still the screeching continues. I'd know the sound anywhere. It's Aria's broken voice.

In another second, Aria and Germ are standing over me in the rubble, Aria with her slingshot aloft, and I grab Germ's offered hand. And then we're off, careening out of the shop and toward the wharfs where Chompy's open mouth is waiting.

It flashes across my mind that if we were trying to avoid tampering with history, that's all over now. I don't see until we are rounding the corner that it's not just the antiques shop that's been destroyed by Aria's scream but the whole block. The fronts of buildings have practically disintegrated, and people stand amidst the debris, looking around in shock. Their eyes glide right over us.

"I'm sorry!" Aria yells, as if she weren't saving my life.

And then I'm hit by another wave of hummingbirds— we all are.

Spun by the force of them, I tumble onto my back.

The Time Witch is closing the distance before me— moving down the block. She's lifting her arms—to freeze us? to throw more curses?—when Aria lifts her slingshot and lets out another scream as she lets fly a rock. We are all blown back by the sound of it, including the Time Witch, who is blasted to the ground. For a moment, all is still.

And then we hear a piercing creak. In the distance, we see the London Eye shake, and with a heart-stopping moan of metal and glass, it begins to topple.

Even the Time Witch, still on the ground, watches in disbelief as the Ferris wheel crashes down with thud after deafening thud. It's just long enough for me to lift up my flashlight again. I try to think how Little One can save us from time itself standing still. But I'm helpless, frantic, lost.

"There was a place that saved us," I whisper, in tears, trying to picture that place in my mind, a place away from everything that scares me. "We got out."

Little One, flailing, disappears. She snuffs out. She's gone.

But where she vanished, a door appears—open, empty, and uncertain. I know it on sight. It's the door I used to imagine as a kid that took me out of my classroom and into the clouds.

Aria screams and shoots her slingshot again, hard enough to knock the closest hummingbirds back to give us cover. We run, all three of us, through the door, dragging each other along.

And then everything disappears in a blinding flash of light. And the doorway swallows us whole.

CHAPTER 18

I wake with a start, shielding my face.

After a moment I lower my hands, blinking into bright light. I hear birds and some kind of rushing water nearby, maybe a river.

Slowly I sit up, looking around and trying to make sense of where I am—a bright, airy bedroom with yellow walls. There are two other beds in the room, where Aria and Germ are deeply asleep under piled mounds of white comforters. Silently I slide out of bed onto shaky legs. I don't know where we are, but it doesn't look like a place the Time Witch would keep someone prisoner. Still, I don't know for sure.

Near the foot of the bed is an easy chair, with a cross-stitched pillow propped cheerfully on its seat. It's one of those old-fashioned sorts of cross-stitches that certain kinds of grandmas make, with a threaded picture of a little pink-and-blue house. But the cross-stitched words are curious:

> *You are the cloud-builder; you are the grower*
> *of wings. You are the one whom Earth*
> *entrusts its stories to; you are the singer of*
> *songs.*
> *Reader, look behind you. You have left*
> *moonlight where you've walked, though you*
> *may not remember it.*

I squint at the pillow, trying to understand it. Then I feel another moment of panic. I clutch at my hourglass necklace and lift it to see.

"No, no, no," I whisper. *NO.*

There's almost no sand left. The floating red number is a faded one, mostly gone. There can't be more than two or three hours' worth of sand inside.

It can't be. I keep shaking my head as if I can make it

untrue. My time to save Wolf, all the time we had left . . . it has almost completely vanished.

I am so devastated, I forget to be quiet in case we are somewhere dangerous. I walk out into the hallway, shutting the door behind me. I startle as I see someone staring at me from across the hall, then realize I'm looking at a mirror.

It's an understandable mistake. My reflection is me, but not a *me* I know. I touch my face. It takes me a moment to realize why. I'm older! I can see it in the way the size of my head has caught up to my ears, how my chin is more pronounced. I'm taller, though not what anyone would call tall. My legs have grown thin and long like the legs of a deer.

"She's taken a year from you," I hear a voice say. "You're thirteen now."

I step gingerly down the hall, following the sound into a round room surrounded by tall, wide windows, their sills teeming and spilling with plants. On one far edge of the room a woman sits with her back to me, guiding a needle through a cross-stitch on her lap and tapping her foot to music I can't hear. More plants sit tucked on shelves, in corners, perched on top of books and tables. It's messy and wild and disorganized.

I am a swirl of feelings: agony about the time in my hourglass, shock about suddenly finding myself thirteen, confusion about the Time Witch and where we left her and where we are. But all I can do is clear my throat.

The woman turns. She's wearing a brown caftan, her long brown hair falling around her shoulders. She is curvy and dewy-faced. She holds up what she's stitching so I can see it—a kitten dangling from a tree branch, with the words "Hang in There!" stitched underneath in yellow.

She puts the project aside and nods to a comfy chair in a corner. "Why don't you have a seat? You look out of sorts. Would you like some tea?"

"Um." It's all I can manage to get out.

"I'll take that as a yes." She leaves the room for a moment.

The chair she's directed me to has another cross-stitched pillow on top:

Come away, O human child!
To the waters and the wild
With a faery, hand in hand,
For the world's more full of weeping
than you can understand.

There are others around the room, a mixture of silly sayings like *Me? Sarcastic? Never!* and more profound things like *Anything you lose comes round in another form.* I blink at them as I sit, waiting.

The woman returns with a mug of tea. She hands it to me and I take a sip. It tastes like lemons and cinnamon. It's soothing.

"It's the little things," she says, smiling.

"Where am I?" I ask.

The woman shrugs and looks out the window as if gauging the answer to my question.

"I suppose we're over Ohio about now," she says.

"Ohio?"

"Well." She nods toward the window. "Maybe closer to Indiana. Have a look."

I stand slowly and walk to the window. We are surrounded by thick, rolling hills of mist; it seems to stretch for miles around. Far to the east I see the shifting shape of a cloud shepherd blowing at the edges of this mist, his cheeks puffed out and his mouth pursed.

And then I look down over the edge of the windowsill. That, it turns out, is a mistake: my stomach drops to my feet. Through a pothole-shaped gap in the mist, I see we are miles above the earth. Suddenly I feel the terror of falling. I cling to the wall next to me, wanting something to hold on to.

"Are we . . . ?"

"On a cloud?" The woman nods. "Isn't that where you wanted to be?"

"Clouds don't hold houses up," I sputter. "They're vapor."

She nods, agreeing with me. "Nevertheless, here we are." The woman begins to tidy up her sewing materials, putting them into a basket. The thread she was using seems to shimmer and move in her hands.

"Who are you? Am I dreaming? Am I dead? Are you an angel?"

She points to a small sign over the doorway.

BRIGHTWEAVER: MENDER OF SPIRITS, SOULS, AND HEARTS. FREE ALTERATIONS! ALL ORGANIC!

"I've been called different things by different people over the years. Fairy, angel, muse . . . I can't be fussed either way. I'm here to help; that's all you need to worry about." She smiles. "It was a close one. But you found me just in time. It's nice, I so rarely have visitors. Most of what I do is mail order."

"How did I . . . come here?"

"By imagining your way to me, I suppose. It seems to be your strength, witch hunter."

"But the Time Witch. We've lost." It's all landing on

me at once. The realization that our plan has failed, that my time left is practically nonexistent. "She found me in London, after I interfered with time and gave someone a book. The witches are going to swallow the whole universe into a black hole." I breathe. "We heard them talking about it."

The Brightweaver looks startled for a moment. But she doesn't question me. "I see," she says, nodding. "Well, I can tell you're weary." She lifts the corners of her mouth in an encouraging smile, though I can see I've rattled her. "A tour will help. And we haven't got much time together." She sniffs the air. "It smells like rain. We'd better wake the others."

The Brightweaver gives Germ and Aria a quick meal. ("You look older," Germ says, squinting at me in confusion as we sit at a round, wooden kitchen table. And then, her shoulders slumping forward, she says, "We've lost, haven't we?") Then the Brightweaver explains to them where we are. She leads us all out the front door, and we find ourselves stepping onto a trail that winds across the misty hills of the cloud beneath us, into a peaceful glade growing out of a valley in the mist. The trees, too, are made of vapor. In the air around us, cloud shepherds blow and herd the fluffy shapes of it. Our feet sink slightly beneath us, like we're walking on marshmallows.

But if walking across a forest of clouds is strange and spectacular, it pales in comparison to what we see amongst the trees. A towering, cloudy castle rising up as far as the eye can see.

"What is that?" Aria breathes.

The Brightweaver tilts her head casually. "The museum." She leads us down the path. "The cloud shepherds maintain it. It's taken them infinite time to compile it. It contains records of all languages ever invented. All the human languages of course, but also dog, bear, jellyfish, crabgrass, the carnivorous and non-carnivorous plants, local colloquialisms of mosses—you name it. Also," the Brightweaver goes on—proudly, "all the maps ever made or imagined, including ones of imaginary worlds, maps of the minds of each person alive. Sheet music for every note ever sung. Every picture ever drawn, painted, or imagined. Every dream ever dreamt. Every word that ever left a person's mouth. Who knows what else is in there. I've never been to the top of it, though I've climbed and climbed. I don't know if there *is* a top, to be honest."

We walk past a ghost sitting on a bench outside the

castle, reading a book that the cover says is a translation of *Eastern Volcanic Rock* into Spanish.

"How . . . ?" Aria asks. "How is that possible?"

"Simple chemistry, I guess," she says. "All those words and ideas and dreams are lighter than air, so it all floats up. And gets stuck up here, snags on the vapor of the clouds."

"How can dreams leave a trace?" I say. This does not sound like chemistry to me. "They're not real." I think of some of the dreams I've had. The one where Jennifer Aniston came to my house for French toast. The one where I was driving Germ to get her parachute license and eating a shoe.

The Brightweaver eyes me sharply. "Everything leaves a trace." She clears her throat. "But none of that's your concern today. Your concern," she says, looking at us, "is moonlight, of course."

She leads us into a glade, close and thick and mysterious. The trees are splashed in colors, in so many shades that I've never even dreamt could exist. Shimmery paintings with edges that aren't quite solid dangle from the branches of trees. The very air looks like it's painted, the sky above the trees covered in polka dots, stripes, bright blotches like waves.

"The art that people dream up tends to get snagged

in the trees particularly," the Brightweaver says, moving along. "The cloud shepherds will collect it all for the museum."

Germ is gaping down through another gap in the clouds as we pass it. "Wow, is that Des Moines down there?" She backs up, and bumps into a tree of mist, which dissipates at her touch. "Sorry," she says, blushing.

"Oh, it's fine," the Brightweaver says. "There's only one thing and we're all it." Then she smiles and walks on. Germ and Aria and I look at each other. It's not a comforting feeling, to see the mist that holds us thirty thousand feet above the earth dissolving so easily.

"A witch hunter's heart has to be strong. And full. And bright," the Brightweaver says as she walks. "There's no room to be wishy-washy, especially for you three."

"Rosie and Aria are the witch hunters," Germ offers, but the Brightweaver only plunges on.

"And there's only one way I've got to mend a hunter's heart . . ."

The Brightweaver turns at a fork in the path. We come to a small stream. Up ahead we see a cave; haunting music drifts toward us from within.

But the music is not acting like music should. It's attached to something visible and bright, a long, fragile, blue thread, as if it has been turned into a color and a shape floating on the air toward us. The thread of music ruffles my hair gently, touches my cheek as if to console me. It draws a pair of wings behind Aria's back and ties them to her. Another thread—alongside the sound of a violin—curls into a ball at the ground outside the cave in exquisite indigos and teals and burgundies, as if to cry.

"A lot of the music ends up in the caves because of the good acoustics," the Brightweaver says. "It'll be gathered up too."

"My music used to do stuff like this, when it worked," Aria says, touching one of the wings now attached to her, a soft smile on her face. The wings loosen, and disappear.

"Yes," the Brightweaver says as she steps onto a bridge built purely out of the round, yellow sound of drums, crossing the stream in front of us. "Music sneaks like vapor under doors, shines lights, leads to places you never expected. And here, you can see it. Up here in the clouds, I suppose you get to see what you've always known was real all along." She sighs, as if she's surveying a really nice garden. "I love that about this place. And I love that about humans and their hearts. All the magical things they create, it really adds something."

What she's saying reminds me of the things I've made

with Little One: the rising sun, the hopping cricket, the doorway to a safe place. I think about the one cloud shepherd I've ever met, and something he told me about imagination. *"Imagining is a little like the opposite of witches, don't you think?"* he said. *"To stretch and grow beauty from nothing at all?"*

"I wanted you to see all of this before I do my mending," the Brightweaver says. "To show you there are more ways of fighting witches than you can dream of—in the trail left by your mom's arrows, in the songs you sing and the words you speak. Every person's got such gifts. Anyone can fight witches, because everyone leaves traces," she says simply. "If only they could see all this, I think they'd believe in that more."

I think of the woman we saw from the mountain in Iceland, handing out bread, something so simple and small. I think of the man in the crowd in Salem who helped Martha Parker escape. Was this what they were leaving behind? Can people leave moonlight behind them the same way witches leave darkness?

"You three are not alone," the Brightweaver says as I try to take this in. "As much as it may feel like you are. Ah." She turns, leaning over a rough-hewn mist fence, looking at something beyond it. "Here's my favorite."

We are looking out at a valley, enormous, gently sloped. Cloud shepherds—there must be a hundred of them—are crisscrossing the valley, gathering something up in their vaporous arms.

The thing they gather is sparkling and pink, a lot like the color of the Beyond at dusk. And as they gather it, it hugs around them softly. Some of the cloud shepherds giggle as they work. The sparkling pink mist dances around them, sweeps under their feet, and lifts them up like balloons as they gather it—delicately. It's hard to watch them without feeling calm and comforted. And no matter how much they gather, more keeps appearing.

"What is it?" Aria asks.

The Brightweaver shrugs. "Love."

She smiles, then turns to look at us. "Okay, if I'm gonna fix you all, I'd better get started." She looks down at the cloud beneath our feet, which has taken on a gray color while we've watched the shepherds gather.

"Rain's gonna start any minute now," she says. "We'll have to be quick."

"What happens when it rains?" I ask.

"You'll fall to earth," she says with a shrug.

I look down at the world so far below us, my stomach swimming like I'm at the top of a roller coaster.

"You'll be fine as long as you stick the landing," the Brightweaver says.

And before we can ask how one does that, she hurries on.

My fear and worry about how and what the Brightweaver is going to do to us is growing, as we come to a pond glowing silver and bright.

"Is that . . . ?" Aria asks.

"Moonlight? Yep. I gather it in buckets on bright nights, when it's really coming down from above, and keep it in the lake to use later. I dye my threads with it. It's the hope it carries that I'm after."

"*Rosie's* been to the moon," Germ offers proudly.

The Brightweaver's eyes widen; she's impressed. "What was it like?"

I don't know what to say.

"Like a dream. I guess. Kind of like being here."

"I feel *bad* for the Moon Goddess," the Brightweaver says. "It's gotta be a big responsibility, creating hope for the world and all that, but she's not the best communicator. You'd think if you were going to fill the universe with magic, you'd also tell everyone about your existence, you know? It feels like sending a sealed envelope but you forgot to put the letter in."

"Dread stole the sight," I say. "At the dawn of human-kind. Without it, people *can't see* magic."

The Brightweaver nods. It's clear she already knows this. "Yes, but still. Surely she could have come up with something better."

I feel the weight of her words, and the weight of my own distance from the Moon Goddess. The Brightweaver is only saying what I've felt all along. "It's kind of like she doesn't care that much," I say.

"Oh, I doubt that, very much." She lifts a basket of threads from the ground and dips it into the pond, shaking it around a bit. "You'll be surprised how the hope she gives can help people help themselves." Then she starts sorting some tools out of a basket that look rather ominous, needles both sharp and shiny. "But yes, some communication every once in a while would be nice. I like to think I help to mend the gap a bit, when I mend a heart. Though I know I'm only two small hands working against a tide." Her face grows sad, worried. "I try to stitch as much hope as I can into the hearts in my care."

She sizes me up.

"Anyway, stick out your chest."

"Um . . ." I look at the tools in her hand. "I don't . . ."

"I'll go," Germ says, puffing her chest. I stare at her in

awe. But then I've always been in awe of Germ's ability to charge into anything with courage.

The Brightweaver gets very businesslike. She points to Germ. It's as if a light has been turned on in Germ's chest, like when you are baking cookies and you turn on the light in the oven. (Germ and I always leave the light on when we bake because we can't tear our eyes away from what we're about to eat.) But instead of seeing the things you'd expect to see inside a person's body—a heart, bones, blood—a luminous, tiny lion rises inside Germ's rib cage, as filmy and bright as the music making bridges and wings. Its ears are only a little torn, its paws matted around the claws.

"I thought my heart was just a lumpy blob of cells," Germ says, eyeing her chest, her chin pressing against her collarbone.

"That's your *other* heart. The material and less important one," the Brightweaver says, seeing the wonder on our faces. "Now, I just need my needle and thread." She pulls her little basket to her side, and guides the threads she's dyed through one of her needles. "If you will face me, Gemma Bartley, and poke your chest out a bit more so I can get at it. It won't hurt. You are mostly good, actually."

Germ does as she's asked. And the Brightweaver begins to stitch. She doesn't touch Germ; she merely moves the needle and thread through the air in front of her, leaving thin threads of light behind that reach inside Germ and wrap around the lion—mending a torn paw here, a scratched ear there.

"Every person," the Brightweaver says, "who hopes to hunt witches has to hunt them in their own way. There's no such thing as destiny." She looks Germ firmly in the eye. "You're no sidekick."

Germ blinks at her, confused. But before Germ can say more, the Brightweaver turns to Aria.

"You."

Aria, nervous, swivels toward her, and her chest lights up. Inside, the shape of a bright red cartoon heart appears, torn down the middle.

The Brightweaver frowns. "You, my dear . . . Oh, I'm so sorry. Yours is just . . . completely broken. What *happened* to you?"

Aria looks away, on the verge of an eye roll.

"Her sister left her," Germ says. "She's gone, like, forever. And Aria doesn't know where."

The Brightweaver nods, still all business but with the tiniest hint of a pitying frown, and begins to stitch the rip in the middle of Aria's heart, pulling it tenuously together with silver thread. "I'm sorry, my love. I hope you don't mind me saying it, but you never know when you might be underestimating people, even the ones who disappear. Maybe you don't want to hear that." She sighs. "Anyway, I'll try to sew you up the best I can. But you're going to have to forgive her, you know. It's never good to let hurt turn to anger. That destroys things, as you might have noticed."

She finishes quickly, clearly in a hurry as she keeps looking up and turning her head, listening to the thunder that has begun to rumble nearby. Finally she turns and stares right at the center of my rib cage. I look down at my own chest in wonder. What floats inside—when the light illuminates me—looks like a tiny, haunted mansion with all the shutters closed.

"Ugh, look at you," the Brightweaver exclaims. "All dusty old rooms and hidden closets and dark basements. It's like you feel like you have something to hide." She pats my arm before she begins to stitch, her threads pulling open windows, dusting cobwebs from the eaves of my heart-shaped house. "Who *cares* about those who'd make you feel that nothing about you is right? Who cares about any of that when you have *friends?*"

I feel myself blushing. She looks at Aria and Germ, who look worried for me, then back at me. "Don't worry, I've seen much worse. Some have hearts that turn to mold, or mud, or porcupines, or ice, or sharp teeth. I can handle this, believe me."

She looks me sharply in the eye, then Aria and Germ. "But I hope you realize, mending you with moonlight isn't snapping my fingers and having things be fixed. It's only helping you toward being who you are. And I certainly can't patch a black hole, or kill a witch, or save the world. You'll have to do the rest yourselves, you three. I'm sorry, I don't envy you, and I don't know if it's possible. But being *certain* that things are possible doesn't really enter into it. We all must do our part anyway.

"Now." She leans back as the light in my chest goes out. "I do mail-in orders," she says. "So if any of this doesn't work, send it back. You'll simply have to have your bird make a doorway to me, or do what other people do, I suppose . . . wish on a star or pray or hold a lucky penny and hope, or whatever. But you will need to have patience. I have this one order from a man in Versailles whose heart is a puffer fish with clogged gills; he wished on a star three months ago, and I have yet to get his heart back to him. I'm way behind."

Underneath us, thunder rumbles.

"Better get ready," the Brightweaver say. "It's going to pour."

We look at each other nervously. Panic rises in my chest. Not least of all because I don't want to hurtle from the clouds toward earth. But also because . . . I don't want to face what's waiting for us down there, whatever that is. I want to wait a little longer, to put off the end of everything and probably the end of us.

"But we're not ready to go back," I say, raising my voice above the thunder. "The witches said they know the future and they win. We haven't found Convenia, the last witch we need, and we won't even have time now. I don't think we even have time to find Wolf. And I didn't get to ask you, since you know so much about magic and the unseen layers of it, about these things that I've been seeing all over the world. A painting of a waterfall in which the water actually flows, things moving in Aria's snow globe, voices from a mouse hole . . ."

The Brightweaver, her hand moving to replace her needles in her basket, pauses. For a moment, I've intrigued her enough to stop her in her tracks.

After a second, though, she only offers—haltingly—a thought. She has to speak loudly as the storm whips up beneath us. "All I can tell you is that the rules of space and time are bendable. There's a phrase," she goes on. "'A tempest in a teacup.' People think they're being funny when they say that. But rumor has it, a tempest really could fit into a teacup."

"What's a tempest?" Germ bellows. The thunder is almost deafening now.

"What I mean is . . ." The Brightweaver shouts something to us, but we can't hear her.

"What?" I yell. She says it louder, but we can't hear her reply.

Thunder roars. The cloud opens.

And, along with a torrent of rain, we drop from the sky.

CHAPTER 19

A speckled whale swims underwater, its enormous tail sending jellyfish swirling in its wake. In the open air above, there is a storm.

From within the belly of the whale, Annabelle can hear the muffled sound of torrential rain on the water above, though all around them things remain peaceful and still. They are closing in on their destination. Annabelle knows this because the whale is slowing down, its tail swishing slower and quieter, the numbers on the screen creeping closer to 1855. Up ahead, watching the numbers tick by, Convenia has not spoken since they left the coast of Maine. She's watching for something, waiting; Annabelle does not know for what. Annabelle still doesn't know whether she's a prisoner or an ally, a captive or someone the witch wants to help.

And then, in the silence, Convenia turns to her. It's only fitting, given all that has led them both here, that her first words to Annabelle are the beginning of a story:

"As you may know," Convenia says, "I am a witch who steals forbearance. I take that in people which is steady and thoughtful and leave something much lazier in its place: carelessness, rashness, thoughtlessness. It's been fun, I can't deny that. The fights when two people share this curse at the same time are quite something to behold, like sparkling fireworks. But I have this scar."

Convenia lifts her sleeve and produces a small tin box from it, shoddily made. She opens the box to show Annabelle what's inside—an object shaped like a small, leather-bound book, open to show that its pages are blank. Convenia's heart. It's scarred across the middle with a bright pink tear.

"Did a witch hunter do that?" Annabelle asks, staring at the scar. After so long not speaking, her voice comes out creaky and afraid. Convenia stares at her with cold marble eyes, then shakes her head.

"I was caught out in the woods on a full moon night, after

a witch hunter gave chase. I suppose it was in the 1300s or so. I was in a wide-open meadow in medieval Armenia when the clouds passed and the moon emerged. It burned me; the pain was excruciating. I almost didn't make it back to my whale, and by the end I had to crawl, the moonlight had injured me so." She shivers. "When you're a witch, the thought of dying— there is nothing worse. You see, it's not as if what you love goes on without you, because you love nothing."

Annabelle considers her words. She wouldn't want to die, but if she knew Rosie and Wolf were okay, it wouldn't be the worst thing imaginable.

"A human was waiting for me at the end of the trail," Convenia goes on. "She was a girl, no more than nine. I don't know who she was, but she was no witch hunter. Still, she had the sight.

"She knew I was a monster the moment she saw me. She knew enough to be afraid of me. And with one shift of her foot onto my sleeve, she could have held me there, in the moonlight to burn. But that's not what she chose to do."

"What did she choose?" Annabelle asks quietly, after a stretched silence.

The witch looks up at her. "She had mercy on me." Convenia frowns. "The girl believed in it, as foolish as that is. She knew I could have cursed her in return. But she let me go anyway.

And that puzzled me. And because it puzzled me, it scarred me, right here." She nods again to her book-shaped heart, traces the pink mark with her finger. "And now I'm not whole. I'm not all of any one thing; I have this seed of something else, of wretched mercy. And because of that, I can't let your daughter die. I can't let the witches do what they plan."

Annabelle does not know whether or not to believe this. The witch is a liar, after all. All witches are. But she still asks, "What do they plan?"

"We have to find your daughter," Convenia says, not quite answering. "And save her."

"My weapon is broken," Annabelle answers. Liar or not, this witch has brought Annabelle all this way, thinking she has a power that she does not have.

Convenia nods. "That may change, once you have a chance to use it in the service of your children."

Annabelle holds her arrows in her hands, sifting through them thoughtfully. In twelve years she has not even shot one successfully. Not since Wolf was stolen.

"Wouldn't you rather have one broken chance than no chance at all?" Convenia asks. "When they are walking into a trap?"

Annabelle looks up at her sharply. "Rosie knows all about the Time Witch, everything I could teach her and tell her. She has enough imagination to anticipate a trap."

"It is not the trap she thinks," Convenia says.

A silence stretches between them. And then they see the dark shadows up ahead. Ten of them, still beneath the water's rainy surface, waiting. Enormous, dark shapes just under the surface of the sea.

Whales.

"They're here," Convenia says, a tremor in her voice betraying her first sign of fear. "They're all here."

I wake. I am in my familiar bed, inside the familiar walls of Chompy the whale.

I roll over and look at my things—my books, my backpack full of hearts lying by the bed. Have I dreamt it all? The Brightweaver, the library in the clouds, the stitching of my heart?

Ebb is hovering in a corner of the room, watching me. He looks relieved that I've opened my eyes. But in another moment, that's replaced by consternation.

"You're older again," he says.

"The Time Witch stole a year," I reply, my voice sounding heavy and groggy. It takes a moment to realize that I am now about the same age as Ebb.

"Any advice," I ask, trying to lighten the worry on his face, "for being thirteen?" I think about things he said while we danced. How I know, compared to Ebb, I won't be thirteen for long. How I am a ship sailing past him.

"Uh, don't die," he says with a smirk. "It's not as fun as it looks."

I glance over and see that Germ is sleeping, and Aria's curtain is closed, so she must be too.

"How did we get back in here? Have we been here long?"

Ebb shakes his head, his eyebrows scrunched in confusion. "We were waiting for you, me and Chompy, at the wharf. But when we heard the commotion and saw the London Eye topple, Chompy dove. I was screaming at him to go back up for you, when you suddenly appeared in your beds, all three of you. I couldn't believe it. I thought for sure you'd been lost forever."

I slide to sit up in the bed. Ebb moves as if to reach for my hand, but then—either because he's a ghost and can't *hold* a hand or because I'm older again, or both—he leans back. "You were talking in your sleep about haunted mansions. I couldn't wake you. What happened to you? How did you just appear here?"

I shake my head too, because even *I* can't explain it. But then Germ's voice chimes in from her bed.

"We went to the sky because Rosie made a door to

her happy place," she murmurs, slowly sitting up. "There was, like, an infinite museum. And this lady who was an angel or a fairy or something. And basically we learned that nature talks, like you always say, and it's all translated in books. I'm going to try to learn Iguana when I get home."

"*That's* what you got out of that whole thing?" I say, swiveling. "That you can learn Iguana?"

Germ shrugs as if to say, *Why wouldn't it be?*

We tell Ebb the rest, and Aria eventually shuffles out from behind her curtain in silk pajamas and fuzzy fuchsia slippers to fill in the bits we miss—the Brightweaver, the hole through which we could see Ohio, the power of unseen things, the mending of our hearts.

Ebb listens to it all as if, at this point, nothing would surprise him, as if he is very tired of magic in general. But also, very relieved we are okay.

I do feel a little different in my chest. It's like this tiny voice that's always been inside me, asking if a quirky, messy person like me is the *right* kind of person to be heroic and brave, that voice has gone quieter.

"Well," Ebb says, "we're already stopped. We've been swimming all night."

"Swimming where?"

He gives me a look but doesn't answer. My heart flutters at the warning and worry in his eyes.

And then I rise to take a few steps toward the Grand View and see the monitor. And fall silent.

"Ebb, we're in 1855."

Ebb flickers. And a fear grips me tight in my stomach. *We are here. We are here, we are here, we are here.*

In the swirling images, I see an enormous shadow in the water. It's another whale. Looking around, I see even more. We hear the whales calling softly to each other.

"Their whales are here." Which means . . .

"The witches are here," Aria says, her face drawn and shocked.

"But . . . the Time Witch found us in London. What if she knows?" I say. "If she knows we stole a heart from Mable the Mad, she knows we're stealing them from all of them."

"Even if she does, that doesn't change the main thing," Ebb says. "You still have the hearts."

He's right. I look at my backpack, slouched at the foot of my bed. I heft it into my hand, feeling the jiggly weight of the hearts inside.

"We won't have time to steal Convenia's," I say. "We only have a couple of hours, at most." I look around to see if all the witches' whales are accounted for, but in the shadows, with the movement of the whales, I can't be sure. I hold up my hourglass; the very faded red one is spinning in the bottom half. "It'll take all that just to find Wolf, and that's if we're lucky. When and if we fight the Time Witch, I guess we'll have to fight Convenia, too."

This seems beside the point now. There is ice in my lungs. But I know we have no choice.

Aria agrees.

"They'll probably be waiting to attack us as soon as we surface," she says.

"Well." Germ stomps her feet a little, like a bull spoiling for a fight. "We'll attack first. You've gotta have Little One ready to eat the hearts. Have your backpack ready."

Aria paces nervously, clearly feeling uncertain as she grips her slingshot, as if she could will it into working better. We look at each other; my breath rattles in my chest. We could stay here, safe and timeless, forever. That has never been more tempting than it is at this moment. How do you bet everything on something that is far from certain, even likely to fail?

"Are you sure you all want to do this?" I ask them. "Our plan?" I could go alone. I *should* go alone. But Germ and Aria don't even grace this with a response.

"I could come with you guys too," Ebb says. "Maybe I'd last long enough to help."

"Most likely," Aria replies, "you'd flicker out and disappear forever. Who knows how much time onshore would finish you."

Ebb nods. Clearly he knows she's right, but he hates it.

Chompy is swishing his tail, facing the shore, but he is waiting. All we have to do is rise, and we'll be in my brother's time and place. So close to where he lives and breathes . . . scared, alone, and never in a million years expecting me.

I can't help but imagine what we must look like from the outside, from an unseen eye—maybe the Moon Goddess's—looking into the sea: a whale, enormous but small in a vast ocean, surrounded by other whales and facing a shore where all the witches on the planet wait for us.

I think how once there were two babies born in a hospital in Maine. The first a loud baby, crying, a boy. The second a girl, and one who liked to keep to herself. I didn't always know it, but all this time, all my *life* really, I've been waiting to be here. To see my brother again. And to destroy the ones who took him, the ones who want to take everything.

It could go one way or the other. Only minutes from

now. We could lose. We *do* lose, according to the Time Witch.

Listening, I notice that the rain has stopped.

I nod. I clutch my flashlight to my chest, and turn it on. Little One hovers above me. Aria holds tight to her slingshot because it's the only thing she's got. Germ looks like she wishes she had a weapon, but she also looks determined to do whatever small things she can. I hoist my backpack full of hearts onto my back, comforted and terrified by the weight of it and what it holds: the key to our victory or loss, tucked into a JanSport Classic.

"Okay, Chompy. Take us up," I say.

We rise.

CHAPTER 20

The witches are not waiting for us on the shore. They don't attack us as Chompy rises out of the water to let us out. They don't even attack us when I see my brother for the first time.

It happens like this.

It's a cold wet evening, we find, as we breach the ocean's surface in 1855. Chompy opens his mouth, and fog pours in around our feet along with the ice-cold seawater. With our weapons poised, we wait for an attack, peering around into the mist that surrounds us, nearly blinded by it. It's the perfect moment for them to set upon us. But nothing comes.

We slide out of Chompy's mouth into the shallows, hearts pounding, sure that at any moment we'll see a flash of a hummingbird's wing, the glimmer of a hyena's eye, a witch's hand reaching to touch and curse us in the dimness of the early dark moon night. But nothing. We walk, waterlogged, onto the beach, soaked up to our knees and shivering. It isn't easy when everything's engulfed in fog, but we can just make out the dark shapes of hills and gullies in the distance. And one thing is clear. We are alone, for now.

I tug my hourglass and watch the sand trickle again. It's so little time, and already I feel like I am vibrating with stress. We have to move fast. I feel the kind of shiver that goes through you when you are near the end of a race. It's when you are closest that you feel the most like you can't go on, that the possibility of losing is too terrifying.

"I thought California was warm," Germ says, wrapping her arms around herself, shivering.

"The coldest winter I ever spent was a summer in San Francisco," Aria offers.

"You've been here before?" Germ asks, blinking at her.

Aria sighs. "It's Twain."

Germ shrugs. She's always been too restless to read, but I make a mental note of the quote.

The fog blows off for a few moments, revealing empty rolling land and a wide dusty road ahead of us. We see buildings far in the distance, their flickering lights (gas, I'm guessing; I don't think there's electricity *back now*) dim in the fog. The city of San Francisco. But there's no witch trail. No dark footprints leading us in the right direction. Nothing.

"They might've gathered up their tracks. Since they expect us here," Aria says.

"Well, what do we do if there are no tracks?" I ask, my stomach starting to burn with panic. Not that I expect Aria to have all the answers. I thought—I was *sure*—the witches would be wherever we turned up, ready to pounce on us. But I don't even see a single hummingbird patrolling the shore. It's extremely unextreme.

"We find Wolf anyway," Aria says, staying collected—though her eyes betray doubt. "That's what we do."

We're all acutely aware that we have only about two hours before the Time Witch snatches all the remaining years of my brother's life away from him. I try not to think of what that means. I turn to Germ, who's looking out at the water, staring very intently at Chompy.

She notices me watching her. "I'm telling him that when we get back, we might have witches on our tail," she says. "I'm telling him we're going to need all the help we can get." Her eyes dart to mine, embarrassed. "And I'm telling him I love him. I hate to be the one who says it first."

Aria and I look at each other. I turn Little One toward the ground to light our way.

We walk.

The harbor echoes with the sounds of bells and city voices carried by the fog. The mist comes and goes as we trudge on, sometimes obscuring what's in front of us and sometimes drifting to reveal ships beyond the shore, an observatory on a scrubby hill, busy boulevards up ahead, dirt roads leading out of town, orderly rows of buildings and houses. Ghosts drift around us as we pass through a gorge gouged out between two hills, for a few minutes losing sight of the sea.

"The gold boom," Aria says, low, as we enter the outskirts of the city. "I bet none of this was here a few years ago. We learned about it in school the year before Clara and I fled. Even then, all our history books were disappearing—stolen by people who were already cursed, to mess with things."

A noise startles us, and I cling tight to the straps of my backpack and hold my flashlight like a dagger. But it's only a slamming door. We hear an old-time piano playing somewhere. We pass buildings busy with people who are out and about for the evening. They all look past and through us. A street marked CLAY appears to be the main road, lined with stores: a shoe shop, a grocer, a hat shop, a drugstore, hotels, a dentist, all their lights flickering to welcome evening customers.

"Can you imagine going to the dentist in 1855?" Germ says, trying to buck up our sagging spirits, our agitation at the trickling time. "I'd rather let my teeth fall out."

We wander the city as quickly as we can, all the way to the other end. But nothing. No sign of witches, of Wolf, of anything.

This is not what I expected at all. And I realize, with feelings like ice spilling down my spine, *this is how they beat us.* We just go on wandering around and around San Francisco until our time is up. I see the same realization and fear mirrored back to me by Aria and Germ, the looks in their eyes, how Germ has started to wring her hands. Horrified, I check my hourglass with shaking fingers. The one has almost vanished—only the base of it remains, a tiny red line spinning in air. The sand is almost gone.

"This is how it ends?" I whisper, my throat aching. "This is how we lose him forever?"

We are standing there looking at each other, our eyes welling up all at the same time, when something grabs our attention.

Someone is whistling. And the thing that gets us is that the song could not possibly be from 1855. It sounds distinctly like someone is whistling "Don't Stop Believin'."

We turn to see a man standing in a doorway, watching us. For a moment, his tune wavers, and when he starts again, the song sounds more like "Jingle Bells." He's dressed in a vest and trousers, with a handlebar mustache and a long wooden cane in one hand. He looks nervous.

Finally he goes silent. He begins to walk toward us but doesn't look at us. As he reaches us, he crouches as if to tie his shoe and whispers, "You with the League of Witch Hunters?"

I blink at him. I don't have the heart to tell him we *are* the league of witch hunters. Witch *hunter*, if you don't count broken slingshots.

"I've seen her. The Time Witch," he says.

My mouth drops open, trying to form words. But he doesn't wait for us to speak before he continues, still kneeling in the road, making a double knot. "I know where she hides. Wherever the rest of your group is, you'll need all of them to get through her."

"The r-rest . . . ," I stammer quietly, glancing around the street to make sure we are not being watched, "are coming?"

I don't want to put a foot wrong and have this strange man give up on us altogether. For the moment, his hope is our only hope.

The man gives a slight nod. He stands, and turns, and makes his way back across the road. He pauses once and throws a look at us over his shoulder and leans on his cane for a minute before continuing down an alley that runs alongside the hotel.

"Should we follow?" I ask Aria and Germ. I lift my hourglass and look at the time, feeling sick. Half an hour left, more or less. "It could be a trap."

"I don't know if we have a choice," Aria says.

We cross the street and trail down the alley. Things get quieter and quieter as we walk several paces behind the mustached man. I pull my backpack off my shoulders and hold it tight to my chest, ready to whip the hearts out at any moment for Little One to eat.

The man does not acknowledge our presence again; if he hadn't spoken with us, I'd assume he didn't even know we were there. And then, so subtly that we almost miss it, he nods and lifts his cane, pointing it down a dark street.

Apparently this is where his courage gives way. Before we can get our bearings or understand where he's pointing, he's already gone, turning down an alleyway and vanishing from sight.

We are standing in front of a row of gas-lit brick buildings that look abandoned and very tucked away.

"He didn't tell us where," Aria says, pulling at her fingers in frustration. "Which building?"

Mere minutes left, and we're as confused as we were before the man *helped* us at all. But a moment later, I find myself staring at a doorway across from us. The hairs are standing up at the back of my neck. The wide double doors of the entrance look familiar to me, as if I've been here in a dream. And then I realize why.

"This is the place where Wolf had his photo taken," I breathe. "The one the Time Witch gave me. He was standing right here."

There's no mistaking it, I've memorized it so deeply: my brother's terrified expression, the intricate pattern of the paneling in the flicker of gaslight, the crack in the wood at the top of the right-hand door. He is *close.*

I walk up to the building and touch the bricks, run my

hands along them. I get on tiptoes to look in through a high, small window. Dim.

And then I see a hummingbird flutter down a hallway inside, glowing in the dimness.

"She's in there," I say. Which means Wolf must be too.

I try the door, absolutely certain it will be locked. But it swings open, quietly and easily.

"Rosie, it's too easy," Aria whispers, holding on to my sleeve. I know she's right. We are so close to running out of time, but also, this could still be a trap. But again, what choice do we have? Mentally I try to dim myself down to zero. My fingers tremble on the door.

We enter and find ourselves in a deep and obscure corner of a long hallway. We duck back into the alcove of the doorway a second before a smattering of hummingbirds flutters past, and hold our breath until they're gone, concentrating on staying dim.

As we step into the hall again, I see we have to choose a hallway to the left or to the right. I choose left, and we come to another intersection, where I choose right. Then left, then right again. The hallways are all the same—all musty and dim and empty. We are at another corner, and I'm beginning to lose my grip on staying calm, when a glowing ghost in a bowler hat floats by, wringing his hands and failing to notice us. He looks nervous. As we watch him get farther down the hall, casting a soft glow as he goes, I think maybe we should follow him. If he's scared, it might have something to do with the Time Witch. Maybe he's a prisoner like Ebb was. Maybe that's why he's so afraid.

I nod to the others, and we follow on soundless feet, staying dim with all our strength.

After a couple of minutes of winding up and down corridors, the ghost visibly stiffens. I see him shiver and shrink as he passes an archway at the end of the hall. It's as if whatever is beyond that archway is dangerous to him.

Once he's rounded the corner, we approach the opening. Aria clutches my wrist, ready to run. Pressing myself into the shadows of the wall to its right, I peer around the corner. It is hard to believe what I see.

I am looking across an inner courtyard that lies at the heart of the building, dim and dark and lit by gas lanterns, open to the moonless sky. In the far corner is a silhouette I'd know anywhere, a familiar black sleeve. The Time Witch is sitting in a wooden chair, turned away from us. She's got a blanket full of nothing on her lap—is knitting the last ragged, undone edges of it. To her left, an hourglass that matches mine—only much bigger—sits on a wooden stand beside her chair. The sand at the top is just about gone.

As clever as she is, it doesn't seem as though she knows we're here. A female ghost in old-fashioned riding clothes is equally ignorant of our presence, standing in the corner of the courtyard, waiting on the witch patiently and looking petrified.

"Shall I bring the boy?" the ghost finally asks. "It's almost time to take his years."

I swallow.

The witch keeps her face turned down to her knitting, slipping knots of emptiness over her needles as if deeply relaxed. It scares me that she isn't even keeping watch for us. Why isn't she nervous? Why isn't she trying to find us and fight us? Where are all the other witches?

"He has about ten minutes left. No need to rush," she replies. "I play fair."

Aria tugs my sleeve again. She gives me a look, and I know what she's thinking: we've got to find Wolf NOW. She's got to be keeping him close by.

Luckily, at that moment, the Time Witch turns even more fully away from us, picking something like lint off the top of her shoe. We slip away from the archway and hurry down the corridor ahead of us. With each footstep I wait for the Time Witch to burst into the hall behind us, to appear in front of us with her birds. But nothing comes. We round another corner, beginning to breathe again, and it's at that moment I hear something that makes my skin tingle.

The sound is familiar, but I can't place it at first. All I know is that it reminds me of *home*, in some way I can't describe. I follow the sound, winding left, then right, deeper into the building.

I end up at a nondescript wooden door, slowing to hear the sound still issuing from behind it. At the height of my knees there's a small metal slot—like the kind you might find in jail, where they slide meals to prisoners.

Chills cascade in waves down my skin. This is a place where someone is being kept.

Breathless, I kneel. Beside me, Germ and Aria kneel too.

The room contains a single shape of a person, standing and facing a wall. He is small, fragile and thin. A boy. I can't see his face, only the back of his head.

I start to feel dizzy, as if I'm floating above myself. Beside me, Germ sucks in her breath.

I take in several things at once. The sadness of the boy's posture, even from the back. The grimness of the room. The strange knickknacks along the ledges of the walls:

pebbles, old corks, pieces of broken glass. This prisoner has collected anything and everything he could get his hands on—no matter how useless or broken or small. Most of all, I notice what he's doing.

He is *painting*.

That is the sound of home I heard.

He has fashioned a brush and paint out of old frayed rope, a cup of water, and gathered ash heaped in a broken wooden bowl. I try to fight back the tears that flood my eyes. He is painting, like our mom.

Beside him sits a small tray with a candle that has almost run out, cobbled together out of old pieces of wax. He steps to the side to dip his brush in water, and when he does, he moves out of the way of the candlelight, and I gasp. The candle illuminates the walls of the room . . . and shows what a boy trapped for many years, with nothing to do, has accomplished.

Every inch of the cell is covered in paintings. Floor to ceiling, hundreds of pictures are sketched all over the walls. The lowest ones are rudimentary, as if he did them when he was very young. The higher ones are intricate, beautiful, haunting: a house on a hill, groups of people holding hands, someone yelling into the air, a ladder dangling from the moon seen through the bars of a window, a gathering of witches like crows. I know two things at once, from this room: Wolf has the sight. And he contains more darkness and light than I could ever imagine.

His drawings are half hope, half nightmare: tornados, beasts, rainbows, earthquakes, tidal waves, floods, angels, spinning beautiful planets. I can see in Germ's eyes what she's thinking. *What do you expect from a boy raised by witches?*

And then I see one painting in particular that makes my hands shake: two babies lying side by side, their little hands clasped tightly together. The second baby is dimmer than the first, and shaded. But it is me. I know it's me, because the babies are like two halves of each other, mirror images. Just like I always knew there was some piece of me missing, Wolf has clearly always known too.

I am almost too shocked to move.

I do not have to fight the witches.

I can free him, right now.

I feel a strange tickling at the back of my neck and along my back, but I ignore it.

"Rosie, I don't like this," Aria whispers. "Something is very, very wrong about this."

But I ignore *her*, too. I can't think of anything but the boy in the cell.

All my life, because of my mom's curse, I thought I

knew what loneliness was. But I always had Germ. And hope. And now I see what being alone really is, and that my brother knows it so much better than me. And, of all the things I've seen the witches bring, all over the world, I think it might be feeling alone that's the worst.

And then Wolf steps back to the wall with his freshly dipped brush, and paints a few words.

My last day alive. And I'm not scared.

His hand trembles. He's lying. He is very scared.

The boy with no name was here.

He lays his brush down, and looks at the moon out the window. I wonder if it has sent him dreams and beauty that way, despite the walls around him. It's clear he thinks this is the last time he'll see it.

He sits gently on his bed, and folds his hands to wait.

And then a small bluebird appears at his feet.

He looks down at her in surprise.

I am pointing Little One through the slot, and she's looking up at him quizzically. He watches as she nuzzles up to his threadbare, torn left shoe.

I don't dare to call out to him, even in a soft voice. Instead I send Little One fluttering through the air, this time leaving words behind her like a miniature blue skywriter. *Only the witches would have you think there is more darkness in the world than there is light,* I write. *Only the witches would have you think love could ever really leave you.*

The boy shifts and pivots his head, eyes shooting to the window first. And then he looks around behind him, at the slot . . . at me.

There is the tiniest dawning of wonder on his face, mixed with the shock, as he meets my eyes. He looks just like me: dark hair, big brown eyes.

After a second, wonder is replaced by fear. His eyes dart up and down the door; he cocks his head to listen for the Time Witch. I hold my finger to my lips, heart pounding.

He slides off the bed and tiptoes to the vent, crouches down to look at me.

"Are you okay?" I ask. Which seems a silly thing to ask, in hindsight.

He blinks at me for a moment, and then shakes his head. He points to his mouth. *Is he saying he doesn't speak?* He was the loud baby, the one who got taken. And now he doesn't make a sound.

Still, I reach my hand through the slot and grab on to his. I whisper what I've dreamt of saying since the moment we set out on the whale, what seems like a lifetime ago, to save him.

"I'm your sister. I've crossed the Sea of Always to rescue you. And now I'm taking you home."

I release Wolf's hand. Little One, already inside the room, begins to grow at my command.

I turn her into a saw slicing her way silently through the door between us. My fingers tremble on my flashlight as she cuts a square quickly through the wood, and I hold it gently as it falls. The noise is barely a whisper, and the Time Witch doesn't appear.

Through the newly opened gap, Wolf studies me—and my hand nestling into his again—uncertainly.

I should be troubled by what Aria said because I know she's right. It does feel *too easy*, after all this time. But inside, I'm floating. *I am holding my brother's hand.* I tug him gently, and finally he crouches and slides through the hole into the hall, where I can finally wrap my arms around him. In my arms, he stands as stiff as wood.

"I'm sorry it took me so long," I say.

With Germ pulling my arm to get us moving, and all of us looking around like the sky is about to fall, we hurry out of the building, me holding my bag of hearts in one arm like a hostage. With the other, I am pulling Wolf behind me. His fingers feel, to me, like gold.

CHAPTER 21

We are hurrying along the road out of town, far on the outskirts where the city and houses give way to scrubby wilderness, walking as fast as we can. The sand has completely run out in my hourglass, but it doesn't matter—I have what I came for. The stars shine in the moonless sky above us. Fog blows across the land, occasionally obscuring what little we can see in the dark.

His hand is still in mine, but Wolf hasn't said a word.

Germ and Aria and I keep looking over our shoulders, knowing that any minute the witches will be after us. The

Time Witch, no doubt, has come for Wolf's years by now and found him gone. And yet here we are, untouched. I still don't understand it.

We are following the line of the sea, looking for the first sign of Chompy to show above the waves, straining our eyes for a glimpse of him.

"What about saving the world?" Germ says, keeping her voice low in the dark. "We won't stop the witches from unleashing the black hole if we don't fight them."

I don't know what to say. I never even considered that we'd get my brother without destroying the witches; I have eight hearts in my backpack, and the Time Witch still has hers. Still, all I can think of is getting Wolf to safety. Once we make it to Chompy, we can think about everything else.

Aria and I have our weapons up, and I'm growing warier as we close the distance between the city and our landing spot. The tide is out; the water has receded, making the sea farther to reach. All around us, patches of fog play hide-and-seek with the world.

We pass into the same narrow gorge between the two hills we came through earlier, which means we're getting closer to our goal. Still, its rocky walls are high, and I don't like losing sight of the sea even for a few minutes.

And then, beside me, Wolf stiffens, and begins to tremble like a leaf.

He stops walking altogether. Holding on to him, I'm jerked to a stop too.

"Wolf, we have to keep moving," I say. "We have to get you to our whale."

Wolf looks at me, his eyes wide and haunted. Something is wrong, and only he knows what. And then . . . we all see.

As the fog drifts past us, we get our first glimpses of them, shadowy blotches in the mist. They are in a circle that surrounds us, like a murder of crows.

It's strange, but as much as terror washes over me, relief washes over me too.

The moment has arrived, at last. There are no surprises. The witches are going to attack us, as we knew they would—just a little later than we planned.

The Time Witch is the only one I can make out at first, hummingbirds swirling around above her. But we are as ready as we'll ever be.

I shine Little One onto the ground and instantly grow her, her mouth enormous, hovering at my shoulder, ready to swallow in one bite the hearts of all the witches before me but one. I step forward and hoist my backpack into my hands. I open it and reach inside.

But what my hand touches is not hearts. I look down.

It's worms—a squirming, writhing tangle of worms, wriggling where our stolen treasures should be.

The hearts are gone.

CHAPTER 22

All is motionless except the fog; the last wisps of it drift inland and rise away from us into the dark hills. The clear night air reveals the rest of the witches now encircling us: Hypocriffa, the Griever, Egor, Miss Rage, Babble, Mable the Mad, the Greedy Man, Dread . . . all those we've robbed. Convenia, still, is nowhere in sight.

My mind races. How and when did they take the hearts back? My thoughts shoot to the abandoned building where we found Wolf, the tickle at my back as I knelt by Wolf's door. And suddenly I know it: the Time Witch replaced the hearts, in the moments I looked at my brother for the first time. She was toying with us, as she has from the beginning.

But before I even finish this thought, Wolf is no longer in my grasp. He's in the arms of the Time Witch instead, wrapped in her cloak. He lets out a strangled sound, like an animal. The Time Witch nestles him into one arm and holds up something silver in her other hand, dangling it back and forth and smiling at me. I reach on reflex to my wrist, and find that my bracelet and the whale whistle attached to it are gone. My heart drops to my feet.

Little One is poised above the bag of missing hearts, flapping frantically near my shoulder. The Time Witch goes on smiling, stroking Wolf's hair.

"That long walk into Salem, those nights standing in doorways in the rain, that trek through Iceland? All that time you thought you were the three of you alone, saving the world. But my dear, I knew, I waited, I watched. My birds may be thoughtless creatures, but they know how to be subtle." She looks almost gentle, the way she caresses Wolf's hair as she talks. "I could have destroyed you at any moment. I'm the *Time Witch*. As I told Dread that night by the fire—when you were spying on us from behind the rocks—playing a game against a human is like playing with puppies. It's easy. I was hoping it wouldn't be. I was hoping you would entertain me. It has been . . . disappointing."

And then she pats her sleeve, and I see a corner of the black hole blanket dangling out from where she's tucked it. Her smile deepens. "At least once the Nothing King comes, I won't need such games to feel fulfilled."

I am still in shock, still grappling with the hearts being gone, the crumbling of our plan before my eyes. All of my doubts have come true: I've made a huge mistake.

Of course she dies. They all die. That's what the Time Witch said. Who was I—Rosie Oaks—to think I could change the future?

My mind goes blank, like blacking out at a spelling bee when a crowd is watching. I look to Germ, but her eyes are closed. She pops one eye open and looks at me, trembling.

"I'm asking Chompy to help," she whispers urgently.

But Chompy couldn't rescue us even if he *could* hear Germ's ESP. We can't get out of the gorge without getting past the witches. We can't reach the water.

In another moment, on some signal I don't see, the witches move—so fast, they're a blur. They zip close around us and dart away, one after the other, as fast as light. I jerk up my flashlight but not fast enough. I feel hands flutter against me; beside me, Aria and Germ stumble left and right. We are being touched, and marked. They encircle us again, once they've finished. The whole thing has taken less than a second.

"Rosie," Aria gasps, holding her slingshot close to her doubtfully. "We need you to be extra Rosie right now and dream something up."

I blink at her. I'm trying to think of how to be something *more* than Rosie right now. Clearly I need to be *more*, but I can't imagine how. What would a *really powerful* witch hunter do? What would Aria do if her weapon could work? How would my mom fight? How fearless would Germ be? I even think of Bibi West back home. How would *she* battle us out of this if she were a hunter too?

I shine Little One onto the ground before me. I imagine her as a bomb—the most destructive thing I can think of. But as soon as she changes shape and barrels out toward the witches, the Time Witch waves a hand, and Little One's fuse burns backward . . . and then snuffs out.

I bounce the flashlight's beam along the ground, regrouping, making Little One a silver arrow a moment before I fling her at the Time Witch. She waves another hand, and the arrow slows, then turns, flying back at the three of us. Aria lets out a scream, and we all duck. It barely misses us.

I am frantic now. I make a flame, a missile, a sword, grunting as I try to send each shape pummeling toward the Time Witch, but she fends them off by barely lifting her fingers.

And then she raises her arms, as if to surrender. And out of her sleeves, the hummingbirds come. Hundreds of them pour out into the air, rising from the witch's arms like storm clouds. The other witches, on her cue, do the same.

All around us, familiars flutter and flap out of sleeves, crawl and lope from within the folds of robes. They spread into the air and across the ground toward and all around us: chameleons slithering across the dirt, magpies and hornets and bats fluttering into the air. They pin us in from all directions, coming to steal everything from us: our courage, our hope, our years. Little One flares and flickers and becomes merely her small bluebird self, chirping in terror. My imagination feels frozen shut. I simply can't get it to work.

I look to Germ for ideas, but Germ has finally abandoned her ESP, and I can see the deepening certainty in her eyes. We can't fight this. We can't even come close.

Above, the hummingbirds and bats rise high enough to block out the stars. Below them, thousands of tiny beetle feet tap across the dry ground, but it's the hyenas that reach us first, leaping out of the night toward us.

Screaming, Germ falls back under the weight of one, defenseless, but Aria holds her slingshot aloft and aims at them as they struggle. She tries to sing, but her voice cracks as it comes out. Her shot goes crooked and crazy, missing Germ and the hyena completely and slamming into a boulder that breaks apart.

"Save her!" I say to Little One. I make her a lion, the strongest, most powerful Little One I can think of, who lunges at the hyena's throat and fells it. She lunges at another that's leaping for Aria's face. She takes down three more hyenas before the bats are on us.

First it's one by one, but soon it's a torrent. I think as fast as I can, changing Little One again and again: she's a bear knocking bats from the sky, a badger devouring chameleons, a silver shield blocking the onslaught of hornets, a whip slicing at peacocks. She is brilliant, bright, changing as she fights. She is everything I try to make her.

But she is facing impossible odds.

At my side, a swarm of hornets reaches Aria, who lifts her slingshot just as they knock her over, her weapon flying out of her hands. She lunges for it. I turn Little One into a gust of wind that blows the hornets across the air. But I can see the rage they've left, all over Aria's face.

Another hyena bites me from behind, and I whip Little One toward it in the shape of a panther. The hyena goes limp as it's devoured, but I feel an aching space inside where the hyena bit me.

I'm spinning so fast, I can't even *see*, as I lash out wherever I can. I feel creatures biting me, pecking me, scratching me—and deep things inside fall away with the bites. I see it happening to Germ and Aria, too. They look confused, hopeless, enraged—all the things we can't let ourselves become. The witches are overrunning us, easily.

Aria is still trying to load her slingshot. She manages to nock a rock and howl a broken note as she unleashes it, but her shot goes crookedly careening into the dirt.

"The water! To the water!" Germ yells. But there are too many fighting against us. I'm knocked onto my back by a bloodthirsty peacock, and before I can move to get up, I'm covered by shiny brown bats. I try to make Little One a door like before, but above me, she is pulled out of the sky by hornets.

"Rosie," Aria yells, nocking another rock and letting out a scream-howl. This one clears an opening in the space between us just enough for us to see each other through the storm of creatures. "She *knew* we were at the fire that night! She was lying, *because we were listening*! This isn't where we lose. This isn't where we die!" But a growing hopelessness is taking over her face. "Rosie," she cries, "this is where we win!"

I turn my neck to see her better, but she's being devoured by curses, and despair comes over me in waves. I turn my face to the sky, the iridescent creatures swarming over me.

"This is where we win," I say in the direction of the stars, as if because Aria said it, it can be true. I see, at the edges of my vision, witches tightening a circle close around us. But instead of trying to fight, I concentrate. I remember how I used to coach myself, back before my mom remembered me. *You are the Rosie who keeps quiet*, I think as I swipe a beetle out of my mouth and clutch Little One to my chest, tears of fear squeezing out of my eyes. *You are the Rosie who makes doors in clouds. You are the Rosie who's messy, but you are the Rosie who made Little One. You are the girl who Aria and Germ and Ebb believe in.*

Peacock feathers are falling all around me as the birds nibble at my shoulders, and a witch, Dread, has come to stand over me curiously, staring down at me with his depthless gray eyes, almost pitying. I ignore him. "You are the girl who got picked last in the Farmer in the Dell, but you are the girl who got everyone to look at the sky."

I point my *Lumos* flashlight upward from my chest, grasping on to these last words in my mind. While the witches close in, they are all looking down at us. And that is why I try it.

I direct the beam up to the sky. And because it's the only thing I can think of, even though it's bizarre and even embarrassing, I send Little One shooting up toward the stars.

When she comes back down, she's not alone. Or rather, she is not just *one thing*. She shoots up into the air like a bottle rocket by herself, but when she comes down, she comes down like meteors.

The witches look up all at once to see an unexpected sight: glowing figures descending from the heavens like a swarm of octopuses.

"Are those . . . ," Dread begins to ask as I look over at Germ, who—under the weight of the familiars swarming her—is looking back at me with a dawning half-horrified, half-excited realization.

"Yes." I gasp for air as even the familiars fall away from me to gape up at the sky at thousands upon thousands of purple eight-armed aliens.

The first problem for the witches is that what they're seeing is too absurd to be real. So when the aliens begin shooting from their ray guns, the witches are too slow to move.

Fiery balls of light careen down onto the fray like rain, wiping out a swarm of bats, knocking out hordes of rabbits. Flocks of peacocks go flying into the rock walls of the gully. Throwing their arms over their heads, the witches dart for shelter, but Egor is hit and is suddenly engulfed in flames. He streaks down the gully, his robes flying behind him, until he disintegrates. Miss Rage tumbles to the ground, batting at the folds of her robe, her legs alight. The Time Witch stares at her in shock a moment before she lifts a hand to fix it, the fire reversing its course under the wiggle of her fingers, turned back in time to nothing.

The distraction leaves barely enough time for me to leap to my feet. I close the distance to Wolf at a sprint and rip him out of her arms, sending her stumbling.

But I see only too late that with impossible speed she has snatched something from me in return. My flashlight.

I hear the sickening crunch as she breaks it in two. And then, as she again lifts a hand, the aliens come to a stop in midair, and then fly backward up into the sky. Like dying fireworks, they fade into the nothingness they were before I invented them. The last glowing purple embers of them disappear into the sky.

The Time Witch grinds her foot into my flashlight, crumbling it into pieces, obliterating it.

All goes quiet.

And the time torture begins.

CHAPTER 23

I fall back, utterly defenseless, as hummingbirds engulf every inch of me. There's a sharp ache all over my body—I am being stretched like gum. But it's what's happening to my friends that scares me most.

As the birds swirl around my face, batter my eyes, my cheeks, my arms, I catch glimpses. Germ's face is getting plumper, her hair longer, her legs shorter. She's getting smaller and smaller. She looks like the Germ I knew when she was eight. Then more like Germ at five—the Germ I met in kindergarten. And then she's a baby, sitting in the sand and surrounded by hummingbirds, all reddish-blond curls, her freckles gone. She lets out a wail, tears running down her baby cheeks.

Aria's time is going forward *and* backward. She shifts into a little girl with two black braids batting the birds away, then an old woman freckled all over and curling over herself in fear, then a teenager but older than she is now.

"Rosie, what—" she cries in a creaky voice, her eyes boring into mine. And then her hair starts to turn gray; her smooth brown skin wrinkles.

Wolf's hand, which I'm clinging to despite the hummingbirds careening into us, is getting smaller. I look down at my own fingers holding his. My skin is growing creased and dry and pale. My arms are tired, wiry, and thin. My muscles ache so much, I can barely stand. The hummingbirds are taking years so fast, I am already too old to fight back.

I sink down to the ground, holding Wolf, who is now the size of a toddler, squirming in my arms. Despite all the creatures flinging themselves against me, I'm determined not to let go.

But I'm too tired, too frail. I don't have many years left to take; my time is almost gone. Aria is small again now, maybe eight or nine. Germ is crying and pounding her tiny fists on the ground.

I look at little girl Aria, who looks at me, her bottom lip quivering.

Biting down, Aria pulls her broken slingshot up high and nocks a pebble in, aiming it at the nearest witch, Dread. She lets out a half-scream, half-song cry, the deepest and most pained cry of hurt I can imagine. As she does, she shoots the rock straight at him.

There is an enormous creak, as if the sky is being torn. Several witches are knocked backward by the force. Dread, the one the rock actually *hits*, is lifted like a rag and thrown across the air. He hits the side of the gorge, and melts into iridescent gray vapor as he flies apart; gray drops of him spatter everywhere. His remains fall like rain.

The baby Germ has stopped crying. She points her hands at the rain, and laughs.

Aria and I look at each other in shock, but it's only a fraction of a moment before there is a deeper, louder sound—a kind of creaking rumble.

And then the gorge begins to shake, and its walls give way, fault lines snaking through the rock a second before it crumbles. The walls topple all around us, forcing us into the middle of the gorge as the entrances at either end collapse.

The remaining witches rise up willy-nilly from where they fell. The Time Witch takes in the view around her, and her shoulders seem to relax. Now we are outnumbered, *and* trapped. The passageway is now a pen surrounded by high walls of jagged fallen stone. Our only escape is lost— our path to the sea, gone.

I gape at my friends. Aria is a little kid. I'm at least ninety years old. Germ is a baby. Even if we were at our best, we couldn't get over that rubble. And now . . .

The hummingbirds swarm to finish us off. Young Aria scoops Germ into her arms, trying to protect her from them. I thrust Wolf's hand at her.

"Take them both! I'm too old to run!"

Aria balks for a moment, not wanting to leave me. Then she snatches Wolf's hand from mine and makes for the rubble. I watch her scramble up the mountain of broken rock, small but determined. With no strength left, I turn my back on the birds showering over me, but I keep my eyes on Aria, *willing* her and Germ and Wolf to make it up the fallen rocks for a clear run at the ocean.

And then, in horror, I see that a figure has appeared at the top of the hill above them, coming from the other side of it. She is all in purple, and she's late. But she's come just in time to cut off the escape of the people I love.

Convenia. The last witch. Behind her, a woman—silhouetted in the dusk—rises to stand, a bow arched in her hands.

My heart shudders. She draws back and shoots, an arc like a rainbow across the sky.

My eyes follow the arrow's trajectory as it flies over my head, over the thousands of hummingbirds coming to take my last breath, and straight into the heart of the witch who cast them.

The Time Witch clutches her chest, and falls into the ground. It happens so fast, you can barely see it. One moment she is there, and the next, she is swallowed into nothing. As if she never existed at all.

And beyond the ashes of hummingbirds falling from the sky, I see my mother running toward me.

CHAPTER 24

There is no celebrating, no hugging.

Instead my mom lifts me and throws me onto her back with a moan while Convenia whips baby Wolf and baby Germ into her arms so that young Aria can run free.

Already I can feel my age leaving me, the years rolling off me, my strength returning as bits of obliterated humming-bird rain down on me from the sky. But the remaining witches, screeching, terrified, enraged, are flinging every-thing they've got at us as we make our tripping, falling way up the rubble mountain—my mom and Convenia fighting them off the best they can.

Convenia's cats tangle with the creatures behind us, leaping into the air to snatch bats out of the sky. In the fray, one of Babble's magpies manages to peck the whale whistle from around Convenia's neck and make off with it. My mom shoots arrows behind her, but with me clinging to her back, they fly astray. Miss Rage dodges one and then another. Six witches still pursue us.

We crest the mountain and half tumble, half run down the other side. The ocean comes into view, blue and waiting and not so far away.

But it's what's missing from the ocean that stops us in our tracks.

Chompy. Chompy is nowhere to be seen. Just as I always feared, he's deserted us . . . at the moment when we need him most. And I have no whistle to call him back.

We keep running to the water's edge, and turn. Our backs to the ocean, up to our shins in the water, we face the witches coming for us. It's pandemonium as our ages twirl rapidly back to what they were. Aria, Germ, and Wolf cry out as they stretch and grow. My body burns as I get younger, stronger, taller.

We stand united but still vastly outnumbered, and now

I have no Little One to fight with. My mom shoots arrow after arrow, knocking familiars out of the sky. But she can't manage to get another witch.

"We've got to swim!" Germ says.

We all gape at her. The ocean behind us is endless. There is nowhere to go. We'd be swimming to our deaths.

"It's the only thing left to do. Chompy's coming for us. I know it! He must be rallying the whales!"

We know it isn't true. But we back into the frigid water and begin to paddle out into the sea. We have no choice.

To our shock, Convenia stays on the shore, protecting our retreat, casting her curses this way and that, her cats leaping at birds, lizards, rabbits, but she is being swamped. Finally a cloud of bats descends on her at once. From within the whirlwind, we hear her scream, and then go silent.

Breathing hard, I paddle alongside my mom, who's taken Wolf in one arm. Beside us, Germ and Aria are stroking wildly, out of breath. We are paddling into an empty frigid vista, with nothing to keep us afloat.

The witches, on the other hand, have options. They gather at the edge of the water for a moment, doing something we can't make out, and then we see their familiars all coming together—forming a fluttering writhing boat to hold them, its hull made of chameleons and scrabbling beetles, its sail made of birds and hornets. We watch in horror, helpless, as the witches climb aboard this writhing vessel and sail swiftly toward us, faster than we can swim. We paddle farther and farther, but not fast enough.

When the water begins to churn around them, we think it's only the power of wingbeats from the sail, stirring up the wind. But the foam keeps rising beneath them. The waves bubble and froth, churning foam.

"What's happening?" Aria yells.

I couldn't say. It's a familiar sight, but I can't think why.

And then I realize it's the kind of splash Chompy makes when he rises. Only, it is everywhere, all around us.

The whales all breach the surface of the sea at once. Eleven of them rise from the ocean, swamping the creature boat in waves, sending familiars scattering into the water, where the whales devour them like krill. The whales snatch scores of them in their powerful jaws before plummeting back underwater. And as they do, what's left of the boat capsizes, and all of its inhabitants—six stunned witches—tumble into the sea.

The surface of the water whips and swirls as they disappear under the waves, creating a swirling whirlpool beneath us that we fear will suck us in. But then we feel a smooth surface rising up underneath us. Chompy lifts us above the water, fighting against the current to swim us away from it.

A few more giant ocean bubbles burble and pop. And then, the whirlpool disintegrates. The sea goes quiet.

We're all silent for several moments, disbelieving, trying to catch our breath, as the waves roll in and out and swoosh against the shore.

The witches have drowned in the same sea that carried them through time.

Gasping, we slide off Chompy's back and paddle with the last of our strength for the shore, where we throw ourselves onto the sand and stare out at the water, in shock.

"What just happened?" Aria breathes as we all watch the ocean, which is still and calm.

"Chompy loves me," Germ says. "He wanted to help."

I blink at her, trying to take it in. Does Chompy really love Germ like Germ loves Chompy? I blink at her, panting, feeling foolish. I always thought Germ's loving everything and everyone no matter what was her weakness. Instead it rallied the whales . . . and I guess, possibly, saved the world. I guess Germ's witch hunting weapon is love.

The sun is rising. And we watch it, in awe.

"The tide's coming in," Aria says. But none of us bothers to move.

My mother is holding on to Wolf with both hands as the waves lap at our legs. I lean against her arm, and the three of us hold each other tight. There are so many questions I want to ask. But Wolf beats me to it with one of his own.

He is staring at the woman who won't let go of him. And then he looks at me, questioning.

I can tell he wants to ask who this woman is who's holding on to him for dear life. But whether he has no voice, or simply can't bring himself to use it yet, I don't know.

"That's our mom," I say with a smile. "She's a witch hunter like us."

I say it without thinking it through. But it feels like a sudden release, like a breath of comfort, like *rest*.

For so long I thought I was the only witch hunter, and then—even after Aria came, I thought I had to do it mostly alone. But I was wrong.

And not just because my mom has arrived and gotten back her power. But because Germ called the whales with her love and they saved us, and Aria, even with her broken songs, kept us from harm. And Wolf has the sight . . . and who knows what gifts to go with it? And people, just by doing little things, leave moonlight where they walk.

We are so different in the ways that we fight—and we are so small in the face of the dark—but we are, none of us, alone.

And then Chompy rises, resurfacing. He opens his mouth to allow us in, waiting.

Wolf cringes back, afraid.

Already Germ is standing and retracing our steps, throwing each and every whale whistle she can find, left behind from the witches, angrily into the sea.

The whales will never answer to us or anyone else again, unless it's by choice.

It will take Wolf time to learn he is safe. It will take time for me, too. I know I will need to reassure him about so many things.

"It's okay, Wolf. I think he wants to take us home," I say. "Are you ready?"

Off the coast of San Francisco, on an evening in 1855, it is high tide.

The waves lap at what's been left behind. Familiars that haven't flown and crawled and loped away to return their stolen quarry to the world have disintegrated on the beach, and their ashes have been slowly swept away by the waves. Shells tumble in the lapping water, as do shreds of colored cloaks, and a broken tin box that once belonged to a witch who had a seed of mercy planted in her heart. A pink glow is fading around it, as if its contents might not have disintegrated like the rest. As if what it held might have moved on to somewhere pink and sparkling instead.

A limp black blanket, recently completed, easy to mistake for a cloak or a rag, lies upon the shore, its edges fluttering as the waves lap farther and farther up the beach to claim it. Finally it is washed into the sea. Pulled out into the deep, it flutters open in the water, spreads like a flower or a blob of ink.

The blanket, as empty as emptiness can be, is pulled into the currents. It's so full of darkness, it almost turns the corner into light. Its depths are endless.

And out of this blanket something seemingly small and insignificant flutters down toward the ocean floor, something from another side of the universe.

A crow feather, but not the usual beautiful color of a crow. This feather is the color of a void.

It spins and churns as it descends.

And as it falls, it grows.

CHAPTER 25

We are swimming across the Sea of Always and—though we are hundreds of years and three thousand miles from home—we do not have far to go.

We are on the shag rug in the main room, where we're gathered in a circle, sitting together in silence. I think the people around me are all trying to imagine what a world without witches means. But all I can think of is Little One.

My mom has Wolf wrapped in a blanket and in her arms, as if she can make up for all the time she did not get to baby him, by never letting him go. He hasn't spoken since we left the shore.

He's a quiet boy after all, silent in fact, and a mystery. It'll take a long time to get to know him. We're the family who's loved him for years, but we're also strangers—people he never expected to exist. And it will take months, maybe years, to prove to him how much we'd give to make him safe.

But also, it's like I always thought between us. He has my eyes and my smallness. We both scratch our nose in the same way. I suspect he feels it too, that we know each other in our bones.

And I know that soon, we'll tell him his history. But for now, we take our time.

In the corner, Ebb is the faintest wisp of a flicker of a ghost, but he's also still here. As soon as we've dropped Aria off, we will head back home to Seaport, and back to the safety of his grave. He'll recharge—we hope—to the bright and glowing ghost he was before the Time Witch stole him. We just have to make it that far, and I know that we will.

The question is, what kind of world are we returning to? What will it be like to rise to a place where everything witches have stolen has been returned? Some things are beyond even my imagining.

"Where are we headed?" I ask Aria finally. She's been at the front of the ship giving Chompy his orders. "Where and when is your never-ending day with your sister going to take place?"

Aria smiles sadly, and shakes her head.

"It's not," she says.

"What do you mean?" Germ asks as we all look at her sharply.

"I don't want to go back in time and pretend Clara isn't going to leave," Aria says. "And I don't want to stay in one place forever, even if it's a happy one. It wouldn't be enough after all I've seen of the world, and witches, and you guys. . . ." She frowns, uncomfortable with being so mushy. "I don't need to hold on to Clara forever, pretending she's not the person who leaves me. I need to let her go. Really, I need to let being *mad* at her go. I want to stop holding on so tight to the *wrong* of it. Even if I still don't know how."

"Maybe it's like, forgiving someone is a gift you give yourself," Germ says quietly. Germ, as smushy-hearted as she is, finds forgiving as easy as breathing. The rest of us have to work at it.

Aria nods at her, and looks at Ebb. "I asked Chompy to head to May 4, 1934. The day before you died, Ebb. I'm giving you the voucher."

Ebb's glow flares up so suddenly and brightly, I worry he might go out altogether.

"I know," Aria goes on, "there are two people there you really want to see."

We arrive at the backyard of the only house on Waterside Road in 1934—*my* house, long before it was destroyed by the Memory Thief—on a clear, fully moonlit night. I'm so excited to see the full moon in its glory, I could hug it if I could reach that far.

We climb, one by one, out of Chompy's mouth, step ankle-deep into the water, and walk up onto the beach. Familiar ghosts wander around on the sand, barely noticing us, ghosts that I've been seeing on and around this property ever since I got the sight.

We step onto dry land near the cave where Ebb was caught by the tide the day he died. And where he showed me my mother's weapon, back when I vowed I would only ever hunt one witch.

The moment we are on solid ground, all our hopes come true. Ebb begins to charge up like a light bulb. He glows bright and luminous and fully ghostly again, as easy as that. He is home.

He looks up, as if to smile at the Moon Goddess. We

all do. The moon sits in the sky with its ladder dangling as if nothing has happened at all.

I have the sense, which has been with me ever since I got the sight, that everywhere the world is speaking—crickets telling each other "I'm here," owls grumbling as the darkness wakes them from their long day's slumber.

The Beyond sparkles above it all, serene, mysterious, full of the unknowable—not the silver glow of moonlight and hope, but the pink sparkle of something even better. Gazing up at it, we suddenly hear voices, laughter. Up on the hill we see a boy doing something with his dad. He does not see us, of course. This version of Ebb—the living one—doesn't have the sight.

I hear his dad call out to him. *Robert.*

Ebb stares up at the cliff, his eyes wide, his glowing face flickering and flushed. His parents are there—not waiting for him, but there for him to haunt for one never-ending, happy day of his living childhood. To watch over. To be close.

He looks at me. I put my hand toward his, though we can't touch. I look back at Chompy's wide-open mouth, waiting for us even without the whistle to call him.

Above, the sky is darkening, the stars seeming to blink out one by one—though there are only a few small clouds in the sky. I register it, but only vaguely. It's strange but unimportant. I'm too sad about letting Ebb go. I feel like a part of me is tearing away.

I watch our hands, mine a little smaller than his, so close to each other but unable to touch. I wish I could have known Ebb when he was alive. I wish, for just once, we could hug.

I know the moment can't last forever, so finally I let my hand fall. It's then that we feel the breeze kick up. We all look out at the water, at a dark patch—now definite, circular, and widening—growing in the sky above the sea. It reminds me of an ink blot spreading, creating a shadow on the water below.

"What *is* that?" Aria says. But none of us can answer. It's a moment when things go from predictable to strange . . . a sudden pivot into fear.

In the distance, we see ghosts pointing at the vast expanse overhead. Above, clouds and cloud shepherds are being whipped across the sky as if by a hurricane-force wind, then sucked upward toward the widening dark. Beneath us, the ground begins to shake.

We gape for a moment in shock as the emptiness in the sky spreads. Even the living Ebb on the hill and his dad stare above in wonder. Behind them, someone is shouting to them urgently to come inside. This is something *every-one* can see, living and dead. Down the beach, the ghosts begin to scream.

"A hole?" Germ says, her voice wooden in fear. "Is that a black hole?"

At the moment she says it, I feel it's the truth.

The Time Witch, her blanket. She left it behind. There's no time to reason it out or try to understand.

"Let's go," my mom says flatly, jumping into action. She grabs my hand and Wolf's and pulls us toward the water where Chompy waits; she nods to Germ and Aria to follow. I look back at Ebb, a question on my face that I can't put into words.

We trail along behind my mom, stumbling toward Chompy on instinct, knowing we need to hide . . . that the whole *world* needs to. I look back again with relief to find Ebb hurrying along behind me, the last of the group. He's following, but he keeps looking back at the boy on the hill in the arms of his dad—gaping at the sky.

We climb into Chompy's mouth, stumbling over ourselves; even Chompy is shaking and eager to move. Glowing and wincing, Ebb leaps on board behind us, whooshing between the whale's jaws as they close. There's a vicious rocking as Chompy turns course, and we all fall

all over the room—which goes topsy-turvy as he tilts and dives toward deeper water, hurtling into the sea and down, down, down as fast as he can go. Getting her footing by grabbing a wall, Aria runs into our bedroom and emerges with her snow globe. She cradles it in her hands, keeping it safe just in time, because Chompy now turns so steeply downward that we all roll along the floor, and then become plastered to the wall.

The numbers on the monitor spin. We can hear water gurgle and churn beyond Chompy's walls as he dives deeper and deeper, as fast as a bullet. Around us, lights begin to flicker.

"He's not supposed to go so deep," Ebb says. "He'll break."

"I know, I know," I gasp. But what are we supposed to do? Where can anyone hide from a black hole? Even the Sea of Always and all it contains will be swallowed up.

We go deeper, and deeper, and then suddenly Chompy stops. The whale shudders. And the lights on board flicker and go out.

"We can't go any farther down," Ebb says. "That's it."

We sit, touching each other's hands in the dark. All we can do is wait.

Around us, we hear the heavy sound of far-off crashes,

thuds. Is it cliffs crashing into the sea? Mountains crumbling, cities toppling? The whole world ending at once? My mind flies to the things and people we love up there. The living Ebb and his parents, Germ's mom, Bibi West, D'quan Daniels, the ghosts in my house, the store clerk in town, all the people everywhere, animals, bugs, stop signs, people, buses, trees, cities. Our beautiful living breathing Earth.

Chompy lets out a long slow whale call—crying out for the other whales, calling to anything that might be out there. But the sea is silent.

We blink at each other without seeing each other in the dark. We are quiet for a long time, waiting for whatever is coming. There is nothing else to do.

And then I notice the tiniest hint of a light, coming from Aria's lap.

"It's my snow globe," Aria says after a moment. The tiny light has come on in the little house. She caresses the globe gently with her hands.

"It looks so safe in there," Germ says wistfully, as if longing to curl up inside it. "I wish we could hide in *there*."

We stare at it for a long time.

"A tempest in a teacup," Aria whispers. She looks up at me. Something is connecting in her eyes. They have a sudden twinkle of recognition in them, but I don't know what it means.

"The Time Witch," she says. "Her trinkets. Her gambles. Voices from a mouse hole. A forest in a sock." She takes a deep breath and lets it out. "Clara." She rubs her hand along the glass. "The Brightweaver said time and space are entwined and bendable. What if they are bent . . . in here?"

She cups the snow globe lovingly. "Clara would know. But it's the end of the world, and I won't see her again. Oh, Clara," she whispers. "I love you."

And then she begins to sing. A song that sounds like what losing someone is. She sings *sadness*, the kind of sadness you feel when you forgive and finally let go.

A thread of light trails out of Aria's mouth, like we saw in Iceland. Colorful, like the rainbow mist that flies behind my mom's arrows and the luminous light that makes—*made*—my precious Little One glow. It is purple and pink and beautiful, and it moves like a ribbon slowly through the air, wrapping itself around Aria's hands and the snow globe inside them.

And then it does something strange.

It threads right through the glass into the snow globe, and reaches the tiny door of the house with the light on.

Inside Chompy, you could hear a pin drop.

The tiny thread of Aria's song wraps around the tiny knob of the door and pulls it open. And then . . . five very tiny figures come swimming out, unmistakably human, each the size of a pinky nail. That's when Aria's hands jerk in surprise, and she drops the globe.

In the dark, we hear it shatter.

The tiniest light from the globe is lost. And the despair around us is complete.

And then, in the blackness, we hear murmuring in the middle of the room.

"Ugh, I think I cut myself," a gruff voice says.

"Oh, get a Band-Aid, you'll be fine," says another, annoyed.

"Still clumsy," another voice says, and this one makes Aria gasp.

Only Germ thinks to find where the scented candles have fallen, and light a match.

In the glow, five new people sit facing us: a woman with pink freckled cheeks and a peg leg; a man with a white beard and glasses; two black-haired boys who look almost the same age; and a teenage girl who looks a lot like Aria, with one puff of a bun above her head, wearing a hot-pink hoodie. I know it's Clara, without even having to ask.

"What did we miss?" she asks, smiling at Aria, before her sister falls on her with a scream.

As soon as Aria stops squeezing her neck, it rushes out of Clara, how one night while Aria slept, Clara found her way into the snow globe—where she suspected other witch hunters might have been trapped by the Time Witch. How she found them . . . but then found herself trapped too. How she's been hoping Aria would save them all ever since.

The two sisters sit back, wiping away ecstatic tears. Clara says she has a lot to be sorry for, but clearly sees by our faces that now is not the time to go over it.

"Okay, but seriously." She looks around the room as she turns solemn and nervous, as Germ lights the only candle that hasn't shattered. "You all look *bad*. What did we miss? Where are we? How *are* things?"

We all look at each other in the flickering light.

"Well," Germ blurts out, "it's nice to finally meet you. I'm Germ. I like my iguana, Eliot Falkor; shows about pet psychics; and my boyfriend, D'quan, who might think I'm dead and also might be doomed. Also"—she clears her throat, glancing around the room at the rest of us—"the Nothing King has unleashed chaos, and the world is about to be swallowed by a black hole." She takes a breath. "We're mostly sure the earth is pretty much destroyed. We might be all that's left of it because we're at the deepest part of the Sea of Always. But it can't be long before the black hole devours us, too." She leans back, out of breath. "So . . . things are . . . not great."

The newcomers look at each other in silence.

"Well," the woman with the peg leg says after a moment, standing and brushing glass off her legs and sighing. "Sounds like we're in a bit of a pickle. I guess we'd better get going."

"Going where?" I ask, looking around. We're trapped in a whale at the bottom of the sea on a doomed planet.

"You don't spend endless years stuck inside a witch's snow globe without learning a thing or two about space and time," the woman says.

She scans the room, noticing the magazine crumbled by our La-Z-Boy.

"Oh, this'll do nicely," she says, staring at the photo on the cover. It's *Pet Psychic* magazine, *The Outer Space Issue*. There's a picture of the swirling Milky Way on the front with an inset of a thoughtful-looking Labradoodle in the upper right-hand corner. The headline reads: CAN YOUR PET CONTROL DISTANT PLANETS WITH ITS MIND?

She traces a circle around the Milky Way photo with

her finger. One moment the picture is just a picture. The next, the Milky Way sparkles with motion and light, like the waterfall painting I saw.

The woman slips a fingernail under the circle she's traced, and tugs. It opens, like a door, and there are stars swirling beyond its small opening.

"Prepare yourself. Things are about to get a little weird."

We—my mother, my brother, Aria, Germ, Ebb, and I—stare at her like she has to be joking. Things are *about to* get weird?

Little One is gone. The moon and its goddess are probably gone too. The cloud shepherds have been sucked into a void of nothingness. And we are being summoned into a piece of paper by what I can only assume is the League of Witch Hunters in the flesh. Looking around at them, they are kind of a lopsided lot—disheveled, not necessarily warrior-like.

Immediately I like this about them. If I'm honest, it feels just about right.

The doorway on the magazine keeps growing, growing, growing until it is big enough to at least stick a hand into.

I reach for my flashlight but remember it's gone too. How climbing into such a place will help us save the world from a black hole and the Nothing King, I don't know. But by now, I guess anything is possible.

Our group climbs into the hole, one by one, feet first. Despite the fact that the doorway is about the size of a fist, once each person gets a few toes in, they manage to get the rest of themselves in too, and then shimmy down inside. I'm reluctant to let Wolf and my mom out of my sight, and I tug on Wolf's shirt as he goes to step in. But my mom shakes her head to reassure me she's got him. Finally I am a kid, and my mom is leading the way. I let him go.

It looks like it must be painful.

Germ, because she's always so brave, goes before me. She shrinks to the size of the hole bit by bit as she enters it. And then the woman with the peg leg, bringing up the rear, nods to encourage me to follow.

What I am stepping into is anybody's guess.

But I am with my friends—my weird, broken, strange, wild, lopsided friends. Perfectly imperfect. Not a *lot of friends*, but the right ones.

I take the hand Germ reaches back to me, and follow her toward whatever waits.

ACKNOWLEDGMENTS

Thank you to Kristin Gilson and Liesa Abrams for shepherding this story and lighting the way. Thank you to my agent, Rosemary Stimola, for all of the sharing, wisdom, and support. I'm so grateful to Kirbi Fagan and Heather Palisi for the beautiful cover, Bara MacNeill for her awe-inspiring attention to detail, and Chelsea Morgan for their guidance.

I could not have written through a pandemic year if it were not for Tina Mueller and her family: our bond has been the great gift of a challenging time. Thank you to Robyn for always being my trusted reader, friend, and style consultant. Thank you to Mark for being my incredible partner and love. And thank you finally to my mom, who read to me and with me, who kept all my books on her shelf and sent them to her friends, and who always let me be my dreamy and woods-wandering self. I miss her more than words can say.

ABOUT THE AUTHOR

Jodi Lynn Anderson is the bestselling author of several critically acclaimed books for young people, including the May Bird trilogy and *My Diary from the Edge of the World*, a *Publishers Weekly* Best Book of 2015. Jodi holds an MFA in Writing and Literature from Bennington College. She lives with her husband, two children, a dog who takes everything too far, and two hermit crabs.

THE
MEMORY
THIEF

Thirteen Witches

BOOK 1

THE MEMORY THIEF

JODI LYNN ANDERSON

ALADDIN

NEW YORK   LONDON   TORONTO   SYDNEY   NEW DELHI

ALADDIN

An imprint of Simon & Schuster Children's Publishing Division

1230 Avenue of the Americas, New York, New York 10020

First Aladdin hardcover edition March 2021

Text copyright © 2021 by Jodi Lynn Anderson

Jacket illustration copyright © 2021 by Kirbi Fagan

All rights reserved, including the right of reproduction in whole or in part in any form.

ALADDIN and related logo are registered trademarks of Simon & Schuster, Inc.

For information about special discounts for bulk purchases, please contact Simon & Schuster Special Sales at 1-866-506-1949 or business@simonandschuster.com.

The Simon & Schuster Speakers Bureau can bring authors to your live event. For more information or to book an event contact the Simon & Schuster Speakers Bureau at 1-866-248-3049 or visit our website at www.simonspeakers.com.

Jacket designed by Heather Palisi and Jessica Handelman

Interior designed by Heather Palisi

The text of this book was set in Adobe Caslon Pro.

Manufactured in the United States of America 0621 FFG

4 6 8 10 9 7 5 3

Library of Congress Cataloging-in-Publication Data

Names: Anderson, Jodi Lynn, author.

Title: The memory thief / by Jodi Lynn Anderson.

Description: First Aladdin hardcover edition. | New York : Aladdin, 2021. |

Series: Thirteen witches | Summary: When sixth-grader Rosie begins to see magic, she learns that her mother's dwindling memory is tied to an age-old battle between the light of the moon and the darkness of witches.

Identifiers: LCCN 2020003256 (print) | LCCN 2020003257 (ebook) |

ISBN 9781481480215 (hardcover) | ISBN 9781481480239 (ebook)

Subjects: CYAC: Witches—Fiction. | Magic—Fiction. |

Mothers and daughters—Fiction. | Memory—Fiction. |

Good and evil—Fiction.

Classification: LCC PZ7.A53675 Mem 2021 (print) | LCC PZ7.A53675 (ebook) |

DDC [Fic]—dc23

LC record available at https://lccn.loc.gov/2020003256

LC ebook record available at https://lccn.loc.gov/2020003257

For Harry, who has rescued me too many times to count

PROLOGUE

In a stone courtyard at the edge of the woods, a ghost with glowing red eyes floats back and forth past the windows of Saint Ignatius Hospital, waiting for a baby to be born.

In the decades that he's been haunting this place, the ghost has seen it all: visitors and patients coming and going, the hopeless cases, the lucky people with small complaints. He's kept his glowing eyes on the hospital doors in peacetime and during terrible stretches of war. He's seen more babies born than he could ever count.

So when cries drift out through the far west window of the maternity ward, and then relieved laughter, and another set of cries, the ghost knows exactly what it means: a particularly rare event, a miracle magnified. The other ghosts in the courtyard go about their business as usual, unnoticing, but the ghost with the glowing red eyes floats to the window for a glimpse.

Only, then something else happens that the ghost does not expect. Something that, in all the years he's haunted the stone courtyards of Saint Ignatius, he's never seen.

The night, all at once, becomes still. A silence falls over the woods; the dark sky—already moonless—dims. An owl calls to the stars and then goes quiet. A cat consults with a mosquito, eats it, and then scampers off in fear. Leaves whisper to each other a little lower than before. Sensing an approaching darkness, knowing the signs of the presence of a witch, all the ghosts of Saint Ignatius flee—zipping off through walls and into woods, vanishing in the night. All except one . . . who hides . . . and watches.

Slowly two women emerge from the edge of the trees.

The first looks sad and mournful, with a forgettable face, and hands that reach through the air as if grasping for something that isn't there. Strange, translucent moths flutter behind her, and a faint cloud of dust, as if she's just stepped out of a closet full of antiques. The other is far more frightening—with empty powder-blue eyes, the pupils like pinpricks, smudged all around in dark purple circles. She smiles with a hungry mouth full of sharp teeth. From around her neck dangle pocket watches, too many to count.

While the sad, grasping witch flicks a wrist and drifts in through the slowly opening doors, now obscured in a kind of misty haze, the blue-eyed witch waits. The night waits. The animals wait. The air waits. Nurses, doctors, patients coming and going—none of them notice two witches in their midst. The living remain blind to them, as they always are.

Finally, silently—the sad witch emerges through the doors, this time with something bulging under her cloak.

"Is it done?" the second witch asks, and the meek, empty-looking one nods.

"I've laid my curse. The Oaks woman's memories are mine now," she says, moths fluttering out of her sleeves as she speaks. "She won't remember anything—not us, not our secrets, not the *sight*, not even herself."

The second witch considers for a moment, her mouth crooked in bitterness. She glances at the ghostly moths fluttering through the air, then turns her eyes to the lump under her companion's robes.

"And this?" she asks.

"No one will remember *him*, either." The sad witch waves a hand, and the folds of her cloak part to reveal a baby, hovering in the air just in front of her stomach. She smiles down at him. There is something terribly needy and desperate about the smile.

"Strange. The Oakses are always girls," the blue-eyed witch reflects.

The grasping witch clearly longs for the baby. She appears to be the kind of witch who longs for everything. "Can I keep him?" she asks.

The blue-eyed witch fingers the pocket watches around her neck and looks down at the baby with disgust. Then she waves a hand, and the baby floats across the space between them. He begins to cry as the blue-eyed witch glares at him.

"I want no more of this family. The last of them comes with me."

"What will you do with him?" the grasping witch asks.

The other witch smirks, her eyes as blank and endless as a reptile's, and then she gazes in the direction of the sea, though it is too far off to be seen. "It's a fine night for sinking to the bottom of the sea," she says before waving the child toward her, into the folds of her own cloak, which close around him like curtains.

The two witches look at each other meaningfully, their dark hearts beating a thorny, unsteady rhythm. And then, as quickly as they appeared, the witches drift into the forest from which they came.

And—but for the trees and stones and spiders and crickets and cats—nobody sees. Nobody but one curious haunt with glowing red eyes and a rash around his neck.

Ghosts have endless time to fill with talk: stories and rumors and legends to pass the long nights. But because the ghosts have fled, there will be no whispers of this moment later—no rumors of what's occurred—drifting amongst the spirits of the seventh ward.

No one will whisper that when two witches came to Saint Ignatius Hospital to settle an old score and take the memories *and* the firstborn child of a woman named Annabelle Oaks, Annabelle Oaks saw them coming . . . and had just a flash of a moment to hide an infant away. There will be no one to reveal the fatal mistake of a sad and grasping witch confusing one baby for another (a quiet baby, as it turns out; a baby who knew how to keep to herself) . . . of one innocent baby doomed and another saved. Only one ghost knows of these things, and—for reasons of his own—he will not talk.

For now, the crickets in the grass listen in silence for a few moments longer, but then they go back to their chirping. The forest resumes its usual noises. A moment is swallowed into the past.

And a restless, angry spirit keeps his secrets. For a time.

PART 1

CHAPTER 1
ROSIE

It's on the night I burn my stories that the danger begins. Or maybe that a *life* begins that's different from the one I knew before.

It starts with me and Germ, the way most things do. I am in the backyard reading Germ a story I wrote.

The story is about a woman asleep in a pile of white feathers. No matter how her daughter tries to wake her, the woman is so deeply asleep, she won't stir. She sleeps for years and years and years.

Then one day the daughter finds a beautiful black iridescent feather buried deep amongst all the white ones. She plucks the black feather, and there is a shudder as all the feathers begin to move. And the girl sees that the pile was never a pile at all but instead that her mother has been sleeping on the back of a giant feathered beast who has been holding her captive and enchanted.

The girl's mother stirs as the beast does. She tumbles off the back of the beast, and together they escape to a remote village at the edge of the earth. Safely hidden, they live happily ever after.

Germ listens in silence and stares out at the ocean as it crashes against the rocks far below my yard. She wraps her coat tighter around herself to ward off the early fall chill. She's got a new look today—thick black eyeliner. It looks weird, and Germ is clearly aware of this, because she keeps swiping at it with her thumb to wipe it away. She's trying to look older but not doing a very good job. I don't know why she tries, because her eyes are pretty as they are.

When I finish and look up at Germ, she frowns out at the water, her brows lowering uncertainly. I can predict something like 1,021 of Germ's moods, and I can tell she's reluctant to say what she's thinking.

"What?" I ask. "You don't like it?"

"I do," she says slowly, stretching and then settling herself again, restless. (Germ never looks natural sitting still.) Her cheeks go a little pinker. "It's just . . ." She looks at me. She scratches the scar on her hand where—at my request—we both cut ourselves when we decided to be blood sisters when we were eight. Her freckles stand out the way they do when she's feeling awkward.

"Don't you think we're getting too old for those kinds of stories?"

I swallow. "What kinds of stories?"

"Well . . . ," Germ says thoughtfully, "the mom waking up." Germ looks sheepish. "The happy ending. Fairy tales."

I look down at the paper, my heart in my throat, because it's so unexpected. Germ has always loved my stories. Stories are how we *met*. And what's the point of writing a story if there isn't a happy ending?

"It's just . . ." Germ flushes, which again makes her freckles stand out. "We're in sixth grade now. Maybe it's time to think about real life more. Like, leave some of the kid stuff behind us."

If anyone else said this to me, I would ignore them, but Germ is my best friend. And she has a point.

Suddenly I find myself studying the two of us—Germ

in her eyeliner and the plaid coat she saved all of last year's Christmas money for; me in my overly large overalls, my too-small T-shirt, my beloved Harry Potter *Lumos* flashlight hanging around my neck like a bad fashion accessory. I've been doing this more and more lately, noticing the ways Germ seems to be getting older while I seem to stay the same.

"Well, I'll revise it," I say lightly, closing my notebook. Germ lets her eyes trail off diplomatically, and shrugs, then smiles.

"It's really clever, though," she says. "I could never come up with that stuff."

I knock her knee with mine companionably. This is the way Germ and I rescue each other—we remind each other what we're good at. Germ, for instance, is the fastest runner in Seaport and can burp extremely loud. I'm very short and quiet, and I'm stubborn and good at making things up.

Now Germ leaps up like a tiger, all athletic energy. "Gotta get home. Mom's making tacos." I feel a twinge of envy for Germ's loud, busy house and for the tacos. "See you at school."

Reaching the driveway, she hops onto her bike and peddles away at top speed. I watch, sad to see her go, and thinking and thinking about what she said, and the possibility of a choice to make.

Inside, the house is dim, and dust scuttles through the light from the windows as I disturb the still air. I walk into the kitchen and tuck my story away into a crevice between the fridge and the counter, frowning. Then I make dinner for me and my mom: two peanut butter and banana sandwiches, some steamed peas because you have to eat vegetables, Twinkies for dessert. I use a chair to climb up to the top shelf over the counter and dig out some chocolate sauce to drizzle onto the Twinkies, scarf my meal down—dessert first—and then put everything else on a tray and carry it up two flights of stairs.

In the slanted attic room at the end of the third-floor hall, my mom sits at her computer, typing notes from a thick reference booklet, her long black hair tucked behind her ears. Her desk is littered with sticky note reminders: *Work. Eat. Take your vitamins.* On her hand she has scribbled in pen simply the word "Rosie."

"Dinner," I say, laying the tray down on the side of her desk. She types for a few more minutes before noticing I'm there. For her job, she does something mind-crushingly boring called data entry. It's mostly typing things from books onto a computer and sending them to her boss, who lives in New York. There is a sticky note on the corner of her computer where she's written down the hours she's supposed to be typing and the contact information of her boss; she never stops early or late.

Against one wall, a small TV stays on while she works, always on the news. Right now there's a story about endangered polar bears that I know will break my heart, so I turn the TV off; Mom doesn't seem to notice. She does that strange thing where she looks at me as if adjusting to the *idea* of me.

Then she turns her eyes to the window in dreamy silence. "He's out there swimming, waiting for me," she says.

I follow her eyes to the ocean. It's the same old thing.

"Who, Mom?" But I don't wait for an answer because there never *is* one. I used to think, when I was little, she was talking about my dad, a fisherman, drowned at sea before I was born. That was before I realized that people who were gone did not swim back.

I fluff up the bed where she sleeps to make it look cozy. She sleeps in the attic because this is the best room for looking at the ocean, but her real room is downstairs. So I've decorated this one for her, lining the shelf with photos of my dad that I found under her bed, one of my mom and dad together, one of me at school, a certificate of archery (from her closet) from a summer camp I guess she used to go to.

I don't have my mom's artistic skills, but I've also painted lots of things on the walls for her. There's something I've labeled *Big Things about Rosie*, which I've illustrated with colored markers. It stretches across years, and it's where I write the things I think are big and important: the date when I lost my first tooth, the date of a trip we took to Adventure Land with my class, the time I won the story contest at the local library, the day I won the spelling bee. I've decorated it with flowers and exclamation points so that it will get her attention. I've also painted a growth chart keeping track of my height (which goes up only very slowly—I'm the shortest person in my class). I've also drawn a family tree on the wall, though it's all just blanks except for me and my mom and dad. I don't know about the rest of my family. I guess we don't really have one.

Still, as strange as it may sound, none of it means anything to her—not *Big Things about Rosie*, not the family tree. It's as if none of it's there. Then again, most of the time it's as if I'm not here either.

"Tell me about the day I was born," I used to say to her, before I knew better.

I knew the *when* and *where* of my birth, but I wanted to know what it had *felt* like to see me for the first time. I wanted to hear my mom say that my arrival was like being handed a pot of gold and a deed to the most beautiful island in Hawaii (which is what Germ's mom says about her).

But eventually I gave up. Because she would only ever look at me for a long time and then say something like, "Honestly, how could I remember something like that?" Flat, exasperated, as if I'd asked her who had won the 1976 World Series.

My mom doesn't give hugs. She's never excited to see me after school or sad to see me leave for the bus. She doesn't ask me where I've been, help me shop, tell me when to go to bed. I've never in my life heard her laugh. She has a degree in art history, but she doesn't ever talk about her professors or what she learned. She never says how she fell in love with my dad or if she loved him at all.

Sometimes when she's talking to me, it's as if my name is on the tip of her tongue for a while before she can retrieve it. Before meetings with my teachers or my pediatrician, she asks me how I'm doing in school and how I'm feeling, as if to catch up before a test. It's all she can do to keep track of the *facts* of me.

I've known for a long time that my mom doesn't look at me the way most moms look at their kids—like a piece of light they don't want to look away from. She barely looks at me at all.

Still, I love her more than anyone else on earth, and I guess it's because she's the only mom I have. My paintings on her wall are one of my many ways of trying to love her into loving me back. And I guess my stories are my way of pretending I can change things: a pretend spell and a pretend beast and a pretend escape to somewhere safe together. And I guess Germ is right that they're never going to work.

And the thing that bothers me is, I've been thinking that too.

I head out into the hall. I flick my *Lumos* flashlight on because one of the chandelier bulbs has burned out, and go down the creaky old stairs to the basement. I throw a load of laundry in, then run up the stairs two at a time because the basement gives me the willies.

On my way through the kitchen, I pick up my story from where it's wedged by the counter.

I have a plan.

And, though I don't mean it to, it's my plan that makes it all begin.

CHAPTER 2

My bedroom is something special, decorated for me by a mom I feel like I've never met. Long ago—before I was born—she painted it in bright beautiful colors, creating rainbows and guardian angels on the ceiling. There's a window around which she painted the words "Look at how a single candle can both defy and define the darkness," which—I found out later—is a quote from Anne Frank's diary. I love the person who painted that on my wall. I dream of that person, but I certainly don't know her.

I've added lots of my own touches over the years. For one, I've filled the room with all the books I've stolen from my mom's room: fiction, histories, biographies, art books, piled on shelves, tucked willy-nilly wherever they aren't supposed to fit, perched on my nightstand. (Other things I've stolen from her include a silver whistle engraved with a shell, a pair of silk slippers, and a matchbox from a restaurant she must have gone to once.) There is a second bed in the room, and a second set of blankets and pillows that my mom has stored in the closet, as if she's always expecting company. I've made the bed a fort for all my old stuffed animals. There's a loud, ticking old clock on the wall.

I've put lots of my own sticky notes on the wall around my bed. *Sleep tight. Don't let the bedbugs bite.* And *Sweet dreams, sweetie.* On the mirror: *You look taller today, sweetie.* And *Those crooked front teeth make you look distinctive, sweetie.* I try to encourage myself with things a normal mom or dad would say, because if I let myself feel sad about not having a normal mom or dad, I'd fall into a black hole and never climb out.

Now I sit on my bed and pull onto my lap the story I was reading to Germ.

I open my closet and take out the pile of others; there

must be a hundred or more. My heart gives a lurch. These stories have always felt like they fill in a half of me that's missing. (I don't know whether it's missing because of my mom, or my dad, or something else, just that it is.) They've always been my way of spinning my feelings into something comforting, like spinning grass into gold. I also retrieve, from my dresser, my lucky pen and my blank notebooks.

I shuffle them all together. Then I carry them down to the metal garbage can that stands outside the kitchen, off the patio, and dump them in. I know how to handle fires just like I know how to fix the refrigerator and reset the furnace and order everything I need on the computer with a credit card—after years of having to do things Mom doesn't.

I get the garden hose unraveled and ready, to be safe. Then I take a match and drop it into the can, and watch the papers begin to burn. All those words I've spent so much time unfolding from my brain—tales of injured dogs that find their way home, elves who give the breath-less new sets of lungs, stories about rescues against all odds and lights in the darkness—flame up into ash before my eyes and float away on the ocean breeze.

The firelight flicker illuminates the trees and burns like a beacon in the dark yard. I imagine it must look, from the water, like a miniature lighthouse, the lonely peninsula of Seaport tacked to the eastern edge of Maine like a lonely outpost. Above, the sky lies, cloudy and heavy, over the crescent moon.

I think again about how stories are how Germ and I *met*. On the first day of kindergarten, Germ laid herself at the foot of our classroom door, screaming for her mom. All the other kids steered clear of her—I guess because of the banshee-like wailing. I knew what it was like to miss someone, even though for me it was someone right nearby. So I sat beside the wild-eyed, wild-haired stranger and awkwardly patted her back and told her a story I made up on the spot about a bat who ate ugly old mosquitoes and burped out stars instead. By the end of the story, Germ had stopped crying and I'd won a friend for life.

Now I snap back to attention as the fire sputters out. I close the lid and go inside to get ready for bed.

I ache over what I've done. But Germ is right: my stories are fairy tales I don't really believe in anymore—that anyone can just save the day. I'm too old, I've realized, to hope for things like this.

And despite the ache, I swell a little with pride. Because I think I've figured out the three main things about life:

1. If the person you love most in the world does not love you back, you can't keep hoping they will.
2. If you are not loved (and if nobody cares about polar bears on the news), there is no magic in the world to speak of.
3. If there's no magic in the world to speak of, there's no point to writing stories.

I am done imagining things differently than they are. I feel a distinct tingle behind my eyes and ears and in my heart—as if I have really changed—and I wonder if the tingle is a growing-up thing, and I hope it is.

Outside, the crescent moon glimmers for a moment through the clouds, then is swallowed up by them.

I get into bed and drift off to sleep.

I have changed my life forever. I just don't know it yet.

I wake sometime deep in the night to the sound of someone talking. For a few moments I'm half in and half out of a dream, trying to make sense of what I'm hearing. Then my eyes flutter open and fear sets in.

There is a man whispering outside my door—his voice low and rumbly like sand being shaken in a glass jar.

"The nerve of her. I hate her. Hate her. It's my place. MY PLACE!"

I lie still. The moon peeks out behind a cloud for a moment through the window, then disappears. I stay as stiff as a board, but my heart thuds at my ribs like hooves.

The voice moves off, as if whoever owns it is heading down the hall toward the stairs, though I hear no footsteps. And then, silence.

I wait and wait. Several minutes go by. I start to think maybe I've been dreaming, but my skin crawls. I wish I could get into bed with my mom, tell her I heard something strange. But those wishes have never worked out. I am the protector of this house; no one else is going to do it.

After several long minutes I force myself to silently slide out from under my covers, grabbing my *Lumos* flashlight from my nightstand as I go. I tiptoe to the door, pull it open silently, and peer out into the hall.

There's no one there, but—with a jolt—I hear the voice, still there, though moving away from me and down the stairs.

I step out onto the threshold and peer in both directions as all goes silent again. I tiptoe down the hall and then descend the stairs, my heart thudding.

At the landing I step into the parlor and come to a stop. Because there, hovering in front of the door that leads to the basement, someone is watching me.

He is shimmery and glowing bright blue, frowning at me, his eyebrows low. He floats at least a foot off the ground.

He stares at me for a long moment, as if in surprise. Then he turns and floats through the door into the basement, and is gone.

I stand gaping for just a moment longer before I turn and run up the stairs, hurtling up to the attic. I slam the door shut behind me, then stand with my back to the door, trying to catch my breath.

Then I walk over to my mom's bed, and after hesitating a moment, I shake her awake.

She blinks at me, groggy.

"Mom, there's a ghost downstairs," I whisper.

Mom squints at me, trying to wake up.

"I'm sleeping," she says, annoyed. And then she covers her head with the pillow.

"Mom," I whisper again, shaking her arm, my voice cracking. "Mom, I need your help."

My mom reaches out from under the covers and gently bats me away. "Leave me alone," she says, her voice cold and far away.

After a moment, I hear her breath get steady and even. I step away from the bed and sit down on the floor with my back to the door, watching her sleep, trying to steady my own breathing.

There've been so many times when I've had to do things on my own: comforting myself after nightmares, nursing myself through colds and the flu. One time a raccoon invaded our house, and I had to trap it in a towel and throw it out the front door. Still, it makes me almost breathless, the hurt. I feel starkly alone.

I listen in the dark, but all the noises of the house have gone silent.

I give myself a talking-to:

There's no such thing as ghosts, sweetie, I tell myself. *You've always had an overactive imagination. This is exactly the kind of thing you've decided you don't believe anymore, as of this very night.*

And then, when that doesn't quite work:

If you can just make it to morning, you'll be fine. Ghosts only come at night. I think.

I wish Germ were here. Together we would know what to do. Together it's like we make one fully formed human. I just have to make it to the bus and Germ in the morning, and everything will be okay.

I sit staring out the window all night, until the sky begins to lighten above the horizon. And when the day grows hazy outside, I watch my mom get up from bed and pull on her robe and walk to the door, like a person in a trance. She doesn't see me till she nearly trips over me.

She blinks at me a moment. And then she merely waits for me to get out of her way.

I follow her into the hall and peer downstairs.

The parlor below, the hallway, the kitchen, all seem quiet and normal.

I come to the bottom of the stairs and look at the closed basement door awhile. All normal at first glance.

And then I see the clock hanging in the parlor. I'm going to be late for the bus.

CHAPTER 3

azed, I rush into an oversize sweater and a pair of stretchy pants and two socks that don't match and put my flashlight around my neck. I make a jelly sandwich and hurry back up to the attic to check on Mom, who's already in front of her computer working.

I set the alarm on her computer to remind her to eat. "There's spaghetti in the fridge," I say. "And drink some milk. It's good for you."

I kiss her—a gesture she pulls away from. And then I race outside to the safe harbor of the bus just as it pulls up.

When I see Germ, I let out a breath I didn't know I was holding. Seeing her familiar freckles, her impatient gestures for me to sit down, makes me feel like I'm *safe,* even if she is wearing that goofy eyeliner again, and now lip gloss too.

I plop down next to her as the bus lurches into motion. I'm on the verge of telling her everything that happened last night, when she turns to me.

"I think Eliot Falkor has a stomach virus," she says. "He's not acting like himself. I think he may have a fever. I tried to take his temperature by sticking a thermometer under his armpit, but his armpit isn't really an armpit, you know?"

I do know. Eliot Falkor is Germ's iguana. He doesn't completely have armpits.

Germ continues, talking faster than I can think, with her usual lack of decibel control. "Maybe he picked something up when I took him to the park yesterday. I thought he'd start barfing. I mean, I don't think iguanas barf, but he was *green.* I mean, not the normal green but a *pukey green.* But I read this thing once in *Reptile Enthusiast . . .*"

I glance back at the other kids as they board the bus. Should I interrupt and say something? What if someone overhears?

"Did you watch the news last night, the thing about polar bears?" Germ is obsessed with the news. She lies awake worrying about it, or sometimes stomps around in anger about something she saw. It does seem, even to me, that things on the news are always getting worse.

She talks about polar bears as we pass the immense Seaport Civil War cemetery and Founders Square, which make up the center of our small town. "Sometimes I feel like the world is ending," Germ goes on, and then enumerates why. By the time we get to school, she hasn't paused for breath.

And so, before I know it, we're at school and my secret is still bursting to get out. But in the light of the day, my fears are also beginning to fade a little. The more I look around at kids doing the things they do every day, and the bored face of the bus driver, and the cars converging on the school parking lot like always, the more it feels like last night was a strange dream, and impossible. I guess it feels like ghosts couldn't possibly exist in a world where some kid just threw fish filet all over the front of the bus.

And then, as a last aside as we're walking through the double doors into school, Germ says—a little awkwardly— that she's doing a talent for the Fall Fling with Bibi West on Sunday night, and I nearly fall over my own feet.

Of all the things Germ and I are known for in our

class, the biggest is that once, in second grade, I bit Bibi West because she called Germ "Germ Fartley" instead of her real name, Gemma Bartley. Germ is famous for then promptly adopting the nickname and introducing herself that way from then on. The cruelty of the nickname, though, was not an isolated incident.

Bibi is this complicated combination of cruel and charming. She likes to make up funny dances and do them behind teachers' backs (charming). She gives the people she likes little presents constantly—scented erasers, squishy soft pencil cases, special candy from her trips to Portugal to visit her grandparents (also charming). Once, in third grade, she even handed out lemons to a select few third graders, setting in motion a trend of lemon-giving that lasted several months and worked its way down to the kindergartners. She is the kind of person who can make you want lemons for no reason at all.

On the other hand, she loves to talk about people behind their backs (cruel). And she has a way of finding out people's secrets and using the resulting information like money in the bank.

But recently Bibi—and seemingly everyone else in the sixth grade—has decided she wants to be friends with Germ.

Germ holds funerals for her lunches every day. She likes to run laps around the playground at recess to see if she can beat her previous time. She is blond and freckled and fleshy and restless, proud of her large, round, powerful body when some people seem to think she shouldn't be.

But it feels like she came back from summer vacation with a new kind of air around her, or at least everybody *else* came back different. Because now the loud self-confidence that used to put kids off is something people admire. Kids who used to tease her have started seeking her out. Even the name "Germ" sounds suddenly cool in people's mouths.

The new air has definitely not extended to me. I'm so small and quiet that sometimes people forget I'm there (although, I do have a bit of a kicking-biting streak). I'm ridiculously clumsy and unathletic and always get picked last for teams. I cut my own hair, so my head is kind of a disaster, and that doesn't even come close to my clothes, which are a combination of Mom's old oversize things and the results of a yearly shopping trip I talk my mom into, where she stares into space while I fail at figuring out the rules of coordinating. I barely talk to people I don't know. Even when I make the effort (which is rare), my tongue just freezes in my mouth. Long story short, I tend to fade next to Germ. Although, Germ says that if I'd just share the contents of my brain with the rest of the world, they'd see it's like the ruby slippers from *The Wizard of Oz* in there.

I'd rather keep to myself. But now kids gather around Germ in corners to talk, or laugh, or just linger. I walk into rooms and find Germ sitting with people I don't know, chatting, and it makes my heart pound a lopsided jealous rhythm, because I've never seen Germ look so happy or flattered (and also nervous, tucking her hair every few seconds). And even though I'm really, really scared of the ghost I think I saw (*did* I see it?) last night, the Bibi thing is my worst fears realized.

We make our way to our lockers. I still can't get a word in because Germ is telling me all the details of the Fall Fling excitedly: how Bibi asked her; how the talent they're doing is so secret, she can't even tell me.

And then my chance to speak up comes because Germ pauses to catch her breath. And instead of my telling her about the ghost, something else entirely comes out.

"But, it's *Bibi*," I say. Germ gives me a sideways, wary look as I falter on. "Remember when she used to chase Muffintop the stray cat around the parking lot, trying to step on his tail? Remember when she used to call Matt Schnibble 'Freckly Little Schnibbles' and make him cry?"

Germ gets quiet. "She's not like that anymore," she says, uncertain and a little annoyed at the same time. Her freckles stand out on her cheeks as they flush. "She was going through a hard time then. She was really insecure. She's not that bad."

I don't reply. Something about the way she defends Bibi, like they've had deep talks, makes me shut up like a clam. For the moment, my thoughts of the ghost have flown to the back of my head. I don't blame Bibi for wanting to be friends with Germ. Germ is bottled lightning; Germ is the most likable person I know. But my feelings are swirling a million miles a minute and . . .

"Bibi will be good, but I'm gonna be terrible," Germ says. "They're gonna spitball me."

I think this is probably true, so I try to be helpful.

"Just make sure you don't wear eyeliner," I blurt out. It's like the words just escape my mouth before I've really thought about them.

Germ is silent for a moment, blinking at me. "I *like* eyeliner."

"I know. It's just, it's not very, um, *you*," I muddle out, biting my tongue.

"I can like new things," Germ says quietly.

I nod silently.

We get to our lockers. I unpack the lunch I made, and scribble a quick note to myself on my lunch bag before putting it into my locker. (I write poems to myself on my lunch bag every day in my mom's handwriting so that people will think my mom is really loving and no one will think I'm being neglected. Probably 89 percent of the energy I spend at school is on making it look like everything is normal at home so no one will ever have a reason to take me away.)

D'quan Daniels, who Germ used to crush on in fourth grade, passes us and waves at Germ, who picks at her hair before waving back. He looks at me as if he might wave to me, too, but then quickly breaks eye contact. Some of the boys are scared of me because last year I kicked a kid in the shins when he tried to tackle me in keep-away.

Germ, blushing with a combination of self-consciousness and pride, watches him walk away. It's a look she wears more and more, and I don't like it. Germ has never cared what people think, but these days she seems to care a lot.

Still, as her eyes catch mine, she suddenly zeroes in on me. She cocks her head, looking at me and placing a hand on her hip, her annoyance with me gone.

"Are you okay?" she asks. "You look kind of off."

"I'm fine," I say nervously, now unsure how to tell her about last night, or even if I want to. "I didn't get much sleep."

Germ folds her arms, unconvinced.

"What's going on with you?" she asks sharply. "Tell me." Now that she's focused on me, she reads me like a book.

I look around the crowded hall. Everyone is busy talking, laughing. My throat tickles with nerves. I suddenly feel ridiculous.

But I lean forward and tell her anyway.

"I think I saw a ghost last night," I say, low, feeling my face flush.

I wait for Germ to laugh, or be annoyed, or both, as she looks at me for a long moment. Sometimes I worry that she is losing that strange, wild, fighting-spirit piece of herself that makes us fit together so perfectly.

But now she lets out a breath decisively.

"I'll ask my mom if I can sleep over," she says.

CHAPTER 4

We go over it all several times on the bus ride home: the sound of muttering in the hall, the glowing man hovering by the door of the basement. Germ makes me slow down over this or that detail now and then, but she never laughs. She looks uncertain but not amused.

"Nobody's gonna believe you," she says, ruminating. "And your mom won't be any help, no offense." She gives me an apologetic smile. "I guess the first thing we have to do is see if he's there again tonight."

"And then what?" I wonder aloud.

Germ stares out the window, thinking. "On *Los Angeles Pet Psychic* they got rid of a bad spirit by burning something called a smudge stick all around the house. It had, like, oregano in it or something."

I blink at her. *Los Angeles Pet Psychic* is one of her favorite shows. She's always waiting for them to do a segment on an iguana, but it has never panned out. Still, I doubt how much burning oregano could help if I do end up seeing a ghost again.

Walking into the house, I see that half the groceries I ordered online earlier this week are scattered on the counter: eight of the same Swanson frozen dinners, four boxes of Pop-Tarts, four frozen pizzas, a box of spaghetti, eight cans of soup. There's a whole bag full of candy—Twizzlers and caramels and all sorts of treats I order too because my mom doesn't care.

Some of the bags have been unpacked, but it looks like Mom got halfway through and then forgot and moved on to something else. Even after all these years being friends with Germ, I flush with embarrassment. But Germ briskly crosses the kitchen and starts putting things away as if it's the most normal thing in the world, and I help her, gratefully.

After we finish, we find Mom upstairs in her attic room, staring out the window at the sea, as she does for hours every evening. The pull to the ocean and this window view of it is so strong, she starts muttering nervously to herself whenever she has to leave the house, and we always have to hurry home.

"Hey, Mrs. Oaks," Germ says, behind me in the doorway.

"He's out there swimming," Mom says automatically, her eyes on the sea.

"Yeah," Germ says, turning a kind smile to me. "His legs must be tired." Germ reaches out and gives my arm a squeeze. I know she feels bad for me, but she also tries to be funny about it. I think she understands that you only have the mom you have.

"Germ's sleeping over," I say. "And I have some progress reports I need you to sign." My progress reports always have some variation of the same note at the bottom: *Rosie is very bright but doesn't speak very often. Rosie daydreams too much.* I know my mom will sign them without reading them.

Mom gives a vague smile to both of us. "That's nice," she says, and then looks away from us in silence.

Outside, the sun is low and distant in the cloudy sky. Dusk will be here quickly, and Gram and I have both agreed that night is the best time, probably the only time, to see a ghost. Germ has to get home at the crack of dawn tomorrow for soccer practice.

"I guess we should get online and find out everything we can about warding off spirits," I say. Germ nods.

"If we even see any spirits," she adds, to manage expectations.

So we spend the next hours digging up information on charms and ghost repellents (ghosts don't like silver, apparently) and exorcisms. Since exorcisms need a priest, and we don't know any priests, we get a bunch of silver spoons from the kitchen and hang them from strings on doorknobs and wall hooks, making do with what we have.

In my room, Germ goes to my closet to get the spare pajamas she keeps on hand, and notices that my stories are missing from where they're usually piled up on the floor. She turns to me quizzically.

"I burned them," I say nonchalantly. "I'm finished with stories." Her eyes widen significantly, but she doesn't say anything. Tact is not really her strong suit, but sometimes even Germ knows when to keep her thoughts to herself.

"Now what?" she says.

"Now we station ourselves at the basement door. And wait, I guess."

"You know you get low blood sugar," Germ says. "You're gonna need some snacks."

In the living room, in a fort we have built from pillows, Germ and I sit and stare at the basement door while eating Little Debbie cakes and Twizzlers, and wait, our legs up the wall beside each other. We are having a burping contest, which is hopeless on my end, given Germ's innate gift for burping. As the sun gets lower on the horizon, I grow more and more nervous, chomping the Twizzlers so hard that my teeth clack together, and even Germ has to tell me to slow down or I'll go into a sugar coma.

Mom drifts through at one point and nearly trips over us. She stares down at us in surprise.

"What are you doing here?" she asks. And I wonder if she means here on the floor or in her life in general.

"We're trying to see a ghost," I say.

Mom nods as if I've said we're doing our taxes, and circles past us to get a snack from the kitchen. Germ shrugs at me.

After a couple of hours we start to get bored. Eventually my mom goes to bed—I listen to her familiar shuffling tread in the hallways above, as if she doesn't know quite where she's going until she ends up there. We lie with our feet up the side of the parlor couch.

"Do you think D'quan or Andrew Silva is cuter?" asks Germ. Germ is increasingly boy crazy. To me, boys seem as uninteresting as they always have.

We wait. And wait and wait. In fact, we wait for half the night, long past midnight, and no ghost appears. No creaking, no booing, nothing. We watch part of a PG-13 movie that Germ's not allowed to watch. We wait because we want to see something, but also, we're afraid to go to sleep. Eventually we do sleep, though, me lying in one direction in the fort and Germ the other.

I only stir when I hear the whispering. For a moment, I can't move. I slide my eyes to the clock. It's two a.m.

"Hate her," the voice rasps. It's coming from the direction of the basement.

My body goes hot and cold. My heart thrums, my stomach drops like a roller coaster, a heaviness and coldness comes over me.

I nudge Germ with just the slightest movement, and feel her stir awake.

Slowly we sit up, facing each other.

"Do you hear that?" I mouth silently to Germ. She looks at me, head cocked, then shakes her head.

"My house," the voice says. It gets louder. I wait for Germ to acknowledge it, but she only gazes at me with wide, confused eyes.

We move slowly to the entrance to our fort, and crawl halfway out. I stare at the basement door.

There's no doubt; the voice is coming from behind it. And there is a glow. And as the voice gets closer, as if its owner is climbing the stairs, the glow gets brighter.

I can feel my hands begin to tremble.

"Rosie, what is it?" Germ whispers. "Are you okay?"

"You can't hear it? Really?" I whisper, low.

She shakes her head again. But instead of looking like she doubts me, she appears to listen harder. I'm panicked. I *need* Germ to hear it. I need to know I'm not crazy, at least.

"Never tell, never tell," the voice says, growing ever closer.

Germ looks to be straining her ears with all her might, though the voice is as loud and clear as day. I reach for her hand, terrified, and squeeze it tight.

"Serves them right."

At that moment, Germ's eyes widen.

"I hear it," she mouths. But she's straining, even though the voice is loud by now.

I point to the door, to the glow coming from under the crack.

Germ stares hard at it. She squeezes my fingers harder. And then the glow flares, as if in anger. And we both jump, and Germ grasps my sleeve.

"I see it," she whispers.

We both cower in the blankets, facing the door, clutching the spoons we've hung around our necks.

"The yellow-haired one is never quiet," the voice says suddenly, suspiciously. Its owner has reached the top of the stairs, just on the other side of the door. He knows we're here.

And then Germ, for some reason, startles and looks over my shoulder, not toward the basement door but over the top of the fort, and slowly she stands.

"Um, Rosie?" she says, not whispering anymore. "What does a ghost look like, exactly?" She sounds sick, panicked.

"Like, um, dead and see-through-ish," I whisper back, eyes glued to the basement door, thinking, *Everyone knows what a ghost looks like.*

"Um. Rosie?"

"Yeah."

"I think there's more than one."

I notice now, what she's talking about, and I feel sick with fright. The glow isn't only coming from in front of us, but all around us.

I swivel, slowly.

A woman stands in the parlor staring at us, a ball of yarn in her hands. A man is just behind her wearing a yellow rain slicker, sopping wet and pale, starfishes stuck to his arms. There is another woman by the couch, very old, all in white. And closest—just inches from us—is a boy with floppy brown hair and a dour expression, like he's just tasted something rotten. He's a dreadful sight: maybe thirteen or fourteen, wide brown eyes, a furrowed forehead, pale, his dark hair plastered wetly down around his ears, bluish skin. He glows with a bluish light that casts a dim glow onto the wall behind him.

We're surrounded.

CHAPTER 5

The boy raises one finger and points at me, frowning. My heart pounds in my fingers, my feet, my ears.

"You," he says, "can see us?" His voice is as clear as a bell, like a real living boy talking to us, but there's nothing living about him—he's pale and limp, a shadow of a person who looks half-drowned.

I swallow, and nod.

He stares at me for a long moment, and then he seems to crumple into himself, hanging his head and shaking it. "No," he says. "No, no, no."

Germ and I gape at him, exchanging a look of confusion and fear. I don't know what to say, or if I should say anything, or if we should run. I eye the silver spoons we've dangled all over the room. Whatever they are supposed to do, they are not doing it.

The boy looks Germ up and down, uncertainly. Her face is pale white, her freckles drained. "You see me too?"

She hesitates for a moment, then nods furiously.

The boy lets out a long, slow sigh, his eyes full of sadness. "Well, I guess you've really done it now," he finally says. Germ and I exchange another confused look.

Then a voice behind us makes us leap. *"Done it now!"*

I swirl around to see the man I saw last night, who is now standing on the landing on this side of the basement door. He grins at me, then lets out a loud, mad peal of laughter. "Danger now. So much danger now." He laughs again. I flinch at each barking sound, but try to steady myself. His eyes glow like coals as he glares at me, full of hatred.

The dead boy floats up beside me and glowers at the man.

"Don't worry about *the Murderer*," he says. "He's harmless." But then he pauses, and appears to rethink his words, because he adds, "I mean, everybody does call him 'the Murderer,' and he *does* want to murder you, and he's pretty territorial. But it's not your fault."

The boy reaches an arm toward me. I leap back and let out a small scream, but not before his arm has sliced right through me—with no effect, just the faintest feeling of a cool breeze running through my stomach. "See? He can't touch you. None of us can." He frowns, and glances at the man—the Murderer—again. "Still, don't go into the basement at night. Some ghosts do sometimes figure out . . . alternatives."

Germ and I are both too scared to respond. There are too many questions swirling in my head, and my heart is beating too hard for me to speak.

The other ghosts hover around us, staring at us intently. I try to steady my breath enough to settle on one question, the one that burns the most. "What are you doing here?" I manage to whisper. It sounds more like a croak.

The boy looks at me a long moment. "We're *always* here. We've been here your whole life. I'm Ebb," the boy says. He looks around the room, his mournful eyes wide, as if deciding something. "Well," he finally says, resigned, "I guess you'd both better come with me."

He begins moving toward the stairs, and casts a dark, strained look back at us. "If you could keep up, I'd appreciate it."

Germ and I eye each other, bewildered.

Ebb pauses at the landing, then floats halfway through the banister toward us. "Night won't last forever," he says, "and we disappear at dawn."

Germ looks to me, her eyes questioning if we should follow. I shake my head uncertainly.

"You couldn't have always been here," I make myself brave enough to say. "This is impossible."

Ebb sighs, hovering impatiently.

"I was afraid of it happening when I watched you burn your stories."

I give a small start. The thought of being watched the other night prickles my skin all over, makes me sick to my stomach.

"I guess you've given up on writing them," Ebb continues. "It happens all the time; people give up on fanciful things as they get older. But for people like you, from a family like yours . . . If you push magic away in one place, it will find you in another. I think probably when you burned your stories"—he pauses, trying to think of how to explain—"you closed a door and opened a window. And that window is *the sight*."

"The sight?" I whisper.

Ebb shakes his head, as if we are wasting time. "It's

how you can see me now, all of a sudden. You must have triggered your sight."

I'm still trying to grasp what he's saying, when Germ says nervously, "What about me? What triggered *my* sight?"

But Ebb only floats up the stairs, pausing in the upper hallway at the top, staring darkly down at us. He floats back and forth, as if pacing.

"It's very important that you come," he insists. "There are things I need to show you."

I nod to Germ. As dour as the dead boy looks, I don't think he wants to hurt us. We move toward the stairs, though slowly.

When we reach him at the top, he pivots and continues down the hall.

He leads us down the hallway and stops in front of the antique dresser tucked into a nook by a small, octagonal window looking out onto the yard. With pretty turquoise handles and lovingly carved inlays, the dresser has always seemed—like so many things—as if it belonged to someone I don't know, instead of to my mom. Now Ebb looks down at the floor just in front of it, nervous, uncertain. He glances up at me.

Upstairs in the attic, I hear my mom's bed creak. No

footsteps, but it sounds like she's stirring. We all wait silently. Finally, all settles again.

Ebb stares down at the floor, then at us, as if we're supposed to know what to do.

"Um," Germ says.

Ebb, exasperated, sighs and rolls his eyes. I'm beginning to notice he sighs a lot.

"You'll need to move the dresser. I can't exactly do it myself." He pushes his arm into a wall and pulls it out again as if to demonstrate.

Haltingly, Germ and I sidle up beside each other, then gently lean into the dresser from the right side so that it slides to the left.

I turn my gaze again to the floor. There's a gap between two of the boards, only noticeable if you are looking straight at it. I kneel slowly and tuck a fingernail into one of the tiny crevices and pull. To my amazement, the board comes up easily. My heart, already thrumming, begins to skip and flutter.

There's a small, dark space here. I grasp my flashlight from around my neck and shine it in. Spiders scatter in the beam of light, and dust whorls fly up around me; the hole smells like old wood and paper, and my light strobes across a shape, rectangular and dusty.

I reach in to pull it out.

It's a book, square and worn, leather bound. On the cover someone has etched an illustration of the earth, with figures in the space surrounding it: men and women, each one with a malicious, angry face. These figures seem to be casting threads from their hands that weave around the world. In the upper right-hand corner is the moon, and a tiny figure standing on its surface with her back turned, tears flying into the air around her head.

It's a strange and disturbing etching. And at the top, in familiar handwriting, are the words "The Witch Hunter's Guide to the Universe."

"My mother etched this," I say.

Ebb nods. "She hid this here, before you were born. She wanted to keep it close without you ever seeing it. Then she"—he looks at me apologetically—"forgot."

"Forgot?" Germ asks.

He hesitates. "Forgot everything," he says, his eyes flashing down at mine for a moment, before flashing away. "At least everything that matters. Once they took it all away from her."

I feel a creeping, sick feeling. Like I have known something bone-deep all my life but no one has ever named it until now: that there is something really wrong with my mom. Something beyond what a doctor could say.

"*They?*" I ask.

Ebb looks down at me for a long time, hesitant. "There are worse things in the world than ghosts in the basement, Rosie," he says. "You'll need to know about them now if you want to live."

CHAPTER 6

In second grade, I stopped talking for a whole month. It just seemed like every day I said less and less until it was whittled down to zero. Germ said it was my quiet way of yelling for help.

At home, my mom didn't mind or notice, and when my teachers asked her about it, she said vaguely that the doctor was helping, and when my doctor asked about it, she said the teachers were helping, but neither thing was true.

Germ minded a lot. She tried to coax me into talking by waving my favorite candy in my face but telling me

I had to ask for it. I didn't budge. So she started talking through all the silences. She talked more so I could talk less. It felt like she was carrying all the words for me that I couldn't say.

And then, in the middle of some facts she was telling me about her bike one day, she stopped and took a deep breath and said, "Rosie, tomorrow, things are going to change. You are gonna say good morning to me, and then ask me some things, and that'll be the end of it. It's time to rejoin the world."

It was an overwhelming feeling, to know that the next day I would have to talk again and try to act like a normal person in the world, again. I wanted it and I didn't want it at the same time.

Holding the book with my mother's writing on it, I have a similar feeling. A feeling of moving toward something I'm not sure I can face.

I sit on the floor. My hands shake as I grasp *The Witch Hunter's Guide to the Universe,* and open it. And then flip through its pages.

It's not a very thick book, but the pages are dense—full of drawings and tight, cramped notes.

And witches. It is a book full of them. Over the next twenty-six pages are profiles of thirteen witches—some harmless-looking, some clearly malicious. For each witch there are descriptions on the right-hand page, written in all sorts of different handwriting, some very faded, as if different people have undertaken to write the notes over the years. But for each witch there's a drawing on the left-hand page created by my mother.

The witches are beautifully drawn, shaded with charcoal. Some wear wild clothes, grimacing or sticking out their tongues; others have quiet faces with murderers' eyes. There's a picture of a greenish-tinted witch clutching a bag of gold tightly to his chest. There's a tall man in a suit with his hand on the back of a wolf, a woman with a necklace of watches, and a bearded man holding a handful of spiders (though his picture has a big *X* through it). They have names like the Greedy Man, Hypocriffa, the Griever, Babble, Miss Rage, Chaos, Convenia, Mable the Mad, the Trapper. In my mom's skillful hands, they look as real as someone you might see on the street, only monstrous—with evil in their eyes, and mouths that smile with malice.

I keep flipping until I reach a drawing that makes my hands freeze. It's a woman staring out at me in desperation, dark black circles around her green eyes. She's covered in webs, and moths and caterpillars—perched on her shoulders, clinging to her sleeves, and entangled in her hair. Her face, as scary as it is, is *nondescript somehow*, the kind of face you might see a hundred times and still never manage to recognize. My mom has spent a lot of time, probably the most time, on this one. It's the most complete.

But it's the description that has frozen my hands. My mom has underlined the words again and again in several spots.

The Memory Thief: Weakest of the thirteen witches.

Curse: The removal and hoarding of memories. Forgetful herself, this witch covets the memories of others.

Skills: Keen sense of navigation, direction, and smell. Sees ultraviolet, sees in the dark. Sensitive to the slightest movement.

Familiars: Her moths are her weapons and her spies. They spread out all over the world at night and steal from her victims. They can be distinguished by the shifting, sparkling

*patterns on their wings, which are actually
the shifting dust of the memories they have
stolen.*

*Victims: A person cursed by the Memory
Thief may appear normal, go about their
normal lives, but they've lost memories
of the past, of the people they are close to,
even how to love others. At times, entire
towns have lost their histories to this
terrible witch.*

I feel sick as I read these words. I stare at the moths in
the drawing, tracing them with my fingers.

I move through the rest of the pages faster, skimming through the varied handwriting, squinting at some
pages yellowed with age or stains. There are labeled sections:

"The Invisible World and Its Beings"
"The Oaks and Their Weapons"
"Legends"
"Secrets of the Earth and Moon"
"What Is a Witch?"

At the last section, which is written in my mom's unmistakable handwriting, I pause again and read:

There are moments in life when we hear about something so terrible, it feels as if we've been punched in the stomach. That feeling—that sense of despair—is a witch's greatest thrill; it is like the air she breathes.

Witches are made of the darkest shades of a hidden and invisible fabric that permeates the world. Like ghosts, most people can't see them. However, they contain just a hint of the physical world too, and so they are sturdier and far more powerful than other magical beings. While they can't walk through walls like ghosts can (they're too solid), they can open doors and windows with a flick of the wrist, make small items float in the air. They control great multitudes of familiars—half-magical, half-real creatures just like them—who do their bidding.

Witches are not solid enough to kill, but they are excellent thieves. They're known to steal and hoard anything they can get their hands on: jewelry right off of human necks, favorite mementos, socks, even the odd pet. They steal for the sake of taking what is ours and what we care about: to keep it for themselves, but most importantly to make us feel the loss of it. Most of all, witches steal the good things inside us. What's inside us is the thing they want most. That's where their curses come in.

To lay a curse, a witch must touch her victim, as if laying a scent. Her familiars do the rest: gathering the good things she means to pillage—memories, time, wisdom, and so on. Each witch treasures a different prize.

By stealing what is good in us, the witches leave voids behind. And humans full of voids lose all the things that matter: hope, connection, love. They lose even the vaguest whispers in their hearts that there is magic and beauty in the universe. By cursing as many victims as they can and stealing all the good, the witches hope to capture the world in a web of despair so thick that it reflects only the ugliness of their misshapen hearts. In such a world, their power will be boundless.

But witches do have their limits. They can float but not fly (though sometimes winged familiars can help). They cannot be two places at once, or disappear from one place and reappear in another. And most of all, because moonlight has hope in it, witches cannot tolerate it. It burns them. This means they choose only to travel the world and lay their curses at the dark moon, when the moon reflects no light at all.

What's more, witches are not all-knowing or all-seeing, and they rely on their familiars as messengers and spies to find the things they seek.

This is how they've always found witch hunters. It is how they will find me.

I turn the page, but the rest of the book is blank. This is where the guide ends, with my mother talking about how she will be found.

I lay the book down, still open, and reach my arms around myself. I look up at Ebb.

"Is this all real?" I whisper. "Are these witches"—I nod to the book—"real?"

Ebb nods. "As real as I am. The women in your family have kept track in this book. They've kept everything they could learn about witches in one place."

The three of us sit in silence for a long time, as I try to make sense of what he's saying. I stare down at the last page again. *This is how they will find me.*

I touch the words, trying to touch my mom's old self that wrote them.

"They found her?" I ask.

He nods solemnly.

"Yes." He clears his throat. "Witches don't take kindly to those who hunt them." He avoids my eyes.

I take this in for a few moments, a strange, sea-urchin feeling prickling in my chest. I gather my breath. "*Hunt* them?" I finally ask.

Ebb nods, and his expression is unreadable.

"You come from a long line of witch hunters, Rosie," he says. "And your mom is the last known witch hunter alive."

CHAPTER 7

"My mom's not a witch hunter. She's a data entry specialist," I say.

My stomach churns hotly. Beyond the octagonal window, the thick sliver of moon darts out from behind a cloud for a moment and then dims.

"This isn't true. None of this is true," I say. "There are no witches. I've given up believing things like this." There has to be an explanation for all of it: dreaming, hallucinating, a bad sloppy joe at school. I wait for Ebb to evaporate the way dreams do when you realize you're in one.

But Ebb only looks back and forth between me and Germ, as if he's deciding something against his better judgment.

"I can show you something more. I think it would convince you about witches and everything else," he says. "*But* you'd have to promise me that you'd both do as I say. Even the witch's familiars—as mindless as they are—might notice Rosie now that . . ."

"Now that what?" Germ asks for me as I hesitate.

"The sight changes you. It's an extra sense, and witches and their familiars can pick up on it like a light in the dark."

Germ swivels her head, studying me as if looking for the change.

Glancing out the window at the height of the moon, Ebb floats backward.

"It's about time for them to arrive," he says. He turns toward the stairs to the attic, then suddenly pivots back to us.

"You can't disturb what's happening. You can't meddle in any way. Promise me that you won't. You couldn't stop it if you tried, anyhow."

"We promise. But stop what?" I ask. And I hear my voice teetering.

He turns reluctantly to the stairs. "Your mom's curse. Are you coming?"

Ebb nods to us, then floats up the stairs and through the door of my mom's attic room. I follow with Germ at my heels, take the knob, hold my breath, and open the door slowly.

My mom is sleeping peacefully. The moon peeps out again from behind the clouds, then disappears behind the overcast sky. Nothing strange, nothing out of place.

Ebb ushers us into the closet, then drifts in behind us and nods to Germ to close the door. It's slatted, so we can see out, though it's harder to see in. I used to hide in here when I was little, watching my mom, trying to figure her out.

"We're safe here," Ebb whispers. "They're mindless creatures, like I said. Your sight's the only reason we even have to hide at all. And they won't look for us or notice us if we stay quiet and hidden."

"'They' who?" Germ asks. But Ebb is intently watching through the slats now, staring in the direction of the attic window, and he doesn't answer.

We follow his gaze and wait. For several minutes, nothing happens and nothing comes. And then Ebb raises an arm slowly, extending a finger to point at something beyond the window.

In the distance, a strange shape is making its way toward us over the ocean, like a ribbon threaded through the air. Whatever it is, it's made of the same diaphanous glowing stuff as Ebb, and moving fast. Before long, it's close enough that I can see it's not *one* shape but a cluster of smaller ones—hundreds of tiny, glowing silhouettes fluttering and flapping in the breeze.

"What are those?" Germ whispers.

"Moths," I breathe, a feeling like rocks in my stomach, remembering the page from *The Witch Hunter's Guide to the Universe*, the picture my mother drew.

"The moths and what they carry are deeply precious to the Memory Thief," Ebb says, "like a collection of jewels she hoards away. There are billions of them, I imagine. Far too many for her to ever even notice. But it doesn't matter; her greed for what they steal is limitless. They come here like clockwork every night to collect. Ever since the night your mom was cursed."

The shapes get closer and closer. The moonlight glints off their wings, which undulate with color. The first few arrive at the attic window like in an air ballet—graceful, delicate.

"They're gonna hit the window," Germ says, but as these

words leave her lips, the shapes gather along the bottom of the windowsill. The window creaks open as if they are lifting it, and the first of the moths flutter into the room.

They're unlike any moths I've ever seen. Some are purple in the moonlight; some glow yellow and white. The patterns of sparkling, iridescent dust on their tiny wings move and change.

The creatures land gently on my mother's bed. They crawl and flutter over her shape under her blankets. As they do, they seem to brighten and change color, as if they are taking something from my mother that charges their wings like batteries.

I feel my skin go cold. And it sinks in that this is not a dream, because in dreams things do not really hurt. But it hurts to watch this, because I know exactly what's happening, as clear as day. They're stealing everything that should make my mom love me. All the memories that add up to someone's love. I feel the loss of it, watching them. All the things that have been taken.

Beside me, I see recognition crossing Germ's face. First comes the look of shock, then sadness. Then a familiar kind of anger.

I see what she's going to do a moment before she does it.

She can't help it. Germ has always been my protector like I've always been hers.

Her fists are tight. Her face is clenched. She coils back.

"No!" I hiss, reaching for her—but it's too late. She springs toward the closet door, knocking me forward, and we both tumble into the room.

Germ lunges toward my mom's bed and slaps at the moths. Ebb zips forward as if to stop her, but falls right through her.

The moths scatter, and circle around our heads, once, twice, three times, as if sizing us up. Then they race toward the window—out, and up and away.

Germ freezes. My mom tosses in her sleep and lets out a small moan, but does not wake.

Ebb zips closer to the window and looks out, then back at me. "They must have picked up on Rosie's sight," he says. "That's why they left so fast. A girl with the sight, in the house of a witch hunter." He shoots a glare at Germ.

Germ looks wild-eyed and ashamed all at once. "I'm sorry. I just . . ."

But Ebb turns away from her and watches the sky, his face tight and fearful. Minutes pass; we wait—for what, I don't know. Time moves slowly, but nothing happens. The sliver of moon pokes out of the clouds again and illuminates the room.

Ebb's shoulders seem to relax a bit. He turns and looks at us. "I should never have shown you," he says.

The way he says it lets me breathe a little easier. Like whatever he's afraid of is not coming.

But then there is the smallest shift in the breeze. Clouds cross over the moon and linger there, and we are engulfed in darkness.

A moment later—somewhere outside and over the ocean, far away but unmistakable—a distant shriek carries across the air.

Ebb turns back to the window, tilting his head, listening. "Maybe it has nothing to do with us," he whispers. "Maybe . . ."

The wind begins to blow.

The ghost in the yellow rain slicker bursts through the wall in a panic. Noticing us, he whispers, "Hide," and then zips through the opposite wall and out of sight.

Fog is rolling in thickly off the sea. On the air, I hear what sounds like the softest of whispers—so soft, I think I'm imagining it. "Tricked?" the whisper says, far away but also, somehow, close, and as ancient-feeling as dust.

"Back in the closet," Ebb whispers, and Germ lurches for the slatted doors as I step back.

"My mom," I whisper, moving to grab her arms.

Ebb floats in front of me and hisses, "There's nothing left for the Memory Thief to take from your mom but you. You've got to hide."

I feel Germ grab the back of my shirt and pull me backward.

Into the closet we stumble, Germ closing the door behind us with her free hand. Ebb zips through the door and settles beside us.

Just as we settle, I hear it. The sound of the window sliding open again.

Beside me, Ebb is dim and trembling. The thought crosses my mind that he should have nothing to fear since he's dead, but all thoughts flee at the sound of rustling outside the window, a sound like thick silky fabric rustling. Germ gently grasps the inner edges of the door as if to secure it with her bare hands.

I press my face close to the slats and peer through them.

With the moon gone, it's almost black, but I can just see the outlines of a figure in a dark dress moving about the room, looking all around it as if for something it has lost. I can't see the figure's face, but I can hear her sniffing the air. She flits through the dark carefully, softly—stopping to study and sniff this and that. She reminds me of some animal, and after a moment I realize it's an insect, a moth—fluttering and feeling her way along. She moves to the foot of the bed, where my mom still sleeps.

I take a breath, and for a moment the figure pauses, swiveling slightly toward me, listening. Ebb shakes his head at me, and I hold my breath.

Eventually the woman turns back to my mother.

She speaks, in the same dusty voice of the whisper from the air.

"Annabelle Oaks, how long has it been? Ten years, eleven? It's good to see you after all this time. You do look much changed, much less lively. But . . . have you been hiding something from me? Something my moths have seen?"

Her voice is full of controlled rage and something else: longing, loneliness. She studies my mom asleep in the bed, clearly thinking.

And then she turns and begins to sniff around the room again.

"I do smell a child," she whispers. "Or is it something burning? I can't tell."

She listens, sniffs, and my heart is nearly bursting out of my chest.

"It's not possible. We took . . . ," she says, and is silent for a few moments. "Unless . . ."

And then she makes her way over to the wall to the side of the closet, putting her hands on it.

"Did you cheat me? Is there a child here?" she asks. "A *hidden* child? A girl child?"

Germ reaches for my fingers and squeezes them tight. I don't know if it's to comfort herself or me or both. The woman moves away from the wall, and I silently let out a breath.

And then suddenly a face appears up against the slats. The woman has crept up to the doors and now she's peering in.

Green, sad, empty eyes meet mine. A pale gaunt face. A slim snake of a smile spreads across the woman's lips. Germ grips the doors tight, hopelessly, while I stay glued to the slats, unable to move, paralyzed.

"Come out, come out. I won't hurt you," the woman says, her eyes going from me to Germ and back. A cloud of moths rises from behind her and toward the slats of the door, landing and crawling on them. The slats start to creak, coming loose from their grooves.

Despite myself, I let out a small moan. There's nothing to keep her from us. As more and more moths gather, the slats begin to pull away. Germ lets go of the doors and grips my arm.

But at that moment, there is another change in the room. At the back of my mind I register it: the clouds shift. Moonlight, sudden and bright, floods in on us. The witch—inches from me—startles, and turns. She shrieks, then floats to the window. Pausing for just a moment, crouched on the sill, she turns back to look at us.

"Watch for me at the dark moon, child," she calls over her shoulder. "At the dark moon, I'll end you."

And then, moths gathering around her, she falls out of the window, and is gone.

CHAPTER 8

We wait for several minutes, but nothing happens. The house lies still around us; the moonlight remains bright through the windows. And then the man from downstairs, the one in the rain slicker, floats into the room, muttering to himself. "Scare of my after-life," he says. "Never been that close."

I feel sick, and Germ looks mortified. Ebb turns to glare at her.

"Half an hour of *seeing*, and look what you two have

done," he says, pulling at his hair in agitation. "This is the worst thing that could have possibly happened."

"I'm sorry," Germ whispers.

There is a long silence as Ebb glowers at Germ, then me. "I should have never shown you," he says, shaking his head. "I'm so stupid."

Germ can't stand anyone putting themselves down, so she reaches out for Ebb's hand, and her fingers slip right through his. "Don't say that," she whispers. "Never say that."

I can only think back to the witch, her eyes on mine, the things she said. *Tricked. A hidden child. A girl child. End you.*

Ebb waves off Germ's attempt at kindness, angry and cold-eyed. "All I know is, if the clouds hadn't moved, if the moon hadn't come out, you'd be . . ."

"The moon?"

"She didn't want to get burned," he says curtly. And then I remember what *The Witch Hunter's Guide* said about this, why witches fear the moonlight.

Then he changes tack again, filled with too many thoughts at once. "She means what she says. When the moon is at its darkest phase, she'll come back for you. She'll punish us ghosts for knowing about you. We're all in terrible danger now."

"When does the moon go dark?" Germ asks.

Ebb stares out at the sky, counting to himself on trembling fingers, his eyebrows low over his eyes. "Dark moon is Wednesday night. Four days," he says.

"Four *days*?" Germ puffs, shocked.

I'm trying to make sense of it. Less than an hour ago I didn't even know witches existed, and now one is coming for me? In four days?

But Ebb is too distracted to respond. He's pacing, in a ghostly way, floating back and forth across the room, dim and drained-looking.

"You should run, leave here tonight." Then he seems to reconsider. "No, it won't be enough. You won't survive on your own. Now that you have the sight, you're a bright target; she'll find you. I know witch curses can't kill, but when she says she'll end you, she means it. You'll need help to get away."

Germ looks at me, guilt written all over her face. Lost for words, I shake my head at her and give her a well-meaning wince. I know she was only trying to fight for me and my mom.

Ebb looks down at his floating feet, thinking. "We need to talk to someone who knows more than I do," he finally says decisively, moving toward the hallway. "I have an idea. Come on. I'll take you. It's not that far away."

"Far away as in we're going out*side*?" Germ says. "Ummm, no. There's, like, a witch out there."

"Trust me, these walls mean nothing to a witch—locks, doors, windows—none of it. If she wants to come for you, she will."

I don't want to follow either, but without a moment's delay, Ebb floats through the wall and disappears. Through the window, I see him floating out into the yard and looking impatient.

I take a deep breath, let it out, and then we walk into the hall and down the stairs.

There is only one ghost in the parlor when we get there. I stop short, chills spilling down my back.

"Fool child," the one Ebb called the Murderer says to me. Germ and I stop in our tracks. He floats slowly closer, his eyes—red like coals—boring into me. They're the eyes of someone who would happily squeeze my life away with his bare hands if he could. I see now there is a red rash around his neck, as if made by a rope. "After what was lost to hide you."

I swallow the lump in my throat. "What do you . . . ?"

But the Murderer doesn't let me finish. "Nevertell, nevertell, nevertell," he whispers. "Never, never, never." His smile drops off his face and he glares at me. And then he floats across the hall, through the basement door, and is gone.

Stepping out onto the front lawn, I shiver. Germ has pulled on her coat, but I've forgotten mine and I instantly regret it. Still, Ebb is already halfway across the yard, and it's all we can do to keep up. My attention is so glued to his back, trying not to lose him, that I don't notice what surrounds us until Germ jerks to a sudden stop beside me, grabbing my arm.

"Rosie," she says. I look back at her impatiently. She's staring out across the lawn toward the sea, and after a moment I follow her gaze, and gasp.

Everything is different.

Far above us, where there was only sky before, is a distant and beautiful pink haze circling the outermost edges of the atmosphere between us and the stars, like the rings around Saturn. Beneath it, distant figures—made of white mist—move amongst the clouds like bees moving from flower to flower. I can't quite make them out—they seem to change shape as they move—one moment becoming part of a cloud, another moment appearing to push clouds along ahead of them. Out on the ocean far beneath the sky, transparent ships float far away, projections of luminous light on the dark water.

It all takes my breath away. It's strange, and frightening, but most of all, it's beautiful.

Beside me, Germ's standing with her mouth hanging open.

"Um, can you please hurry?" We turn to see that Ebb has doubled back, and he looks more miserable than ever, if that's possible. A few ghosts float in and out of the woods behind him, barely noticing us, including an elderly lady in the moonlit yard moving back and forth as if hanging something on a clothesline.

Ebb follows my gaze out to the ocean and the sky. "Oh. Now that you have your *sight*, you'll start to see everything. The world as it really is, all the terrible and wonderful things just under the surface. It's all part of the invisible fabric—that's what witches and ghosts and all the magical, unseen things are made of. And it's all much more visible at night—it glows in the dark, but only to people with the sight." I immediately think of glow sticks and glow-in-the-dark stickers, how they only show up in darkness. "Your eyes will take a while to adjust."

"The invisible fabric I read about in the guide, it's basically magic?" I ask, nodding to the strange and marvelous sights around us.

Ebb looks up, unimpressed, the same way I would look at an airplane or a car driving by.

"Yeah. Like me, all this has always been there. You just haven't noticed."

Then, as simple as that, he turns back toward the cliffs and we follow him—down the rambling dirt path that leads along the grassy clifftops toward the woods. I've walked this path before, but never at night. And I have no idea of how far we're going, or where. Luckily, the moon lights our way.

After a few minutes of silence, Ebb seems to take pity on us, because he hangs back a little. "Of course, ghosts are the flimsiest of all, the least powerful, the fabric spread *thin*, I guess." He clears his throat. "Witches, like you read, are made of much sturdier stuff—as are their familiars. They are part magic, part real, like the book says, though still invisible to most humans."

As we walk, we catch sight of the occasional ghost drifting along the path or through the nearby trees. Most turn to look at us, and then, seeming to dislike being seen in return, hurry away.

"I didn't know our woods were so haunted," I say.

"Oh, this is nothing. Every place in the world is haunted. Living people completely miss the whole thing.

Makes them feel quite alone, the things they don't see."
And then he adds, pensively, "I was surprised too—when I
died and saw it all. You get used to it."

Ebb floats on down the path, and we follow, getting
farther and farther away from home. Once or twice I see
him do something puzzling—reach down to his shirt
pocket, open it, and whisper to it. Is it possible for a person
to be dead and also delusional?

"I thought ghosts were supposed to be scary," Germ
whispers to me as we walk. "But this one just seems kind
of . . . moody. And I still don't know why I have the
sight."

I speak up, so Ebb can hear. "You said *people like me,
from families like mine* have a strong connection to the
unseen things. Is Germ from a family of witch hunters
too?" Germ's mom seems even *less* likely to be a witch
hunter than mine. She bakes cookies. She wears sweat-
shirts that say *I Could Be Wrong but Probably Not*. She
watches home decorating shows.

Ebb looks over at Germ, perplexed, and shakes his
head.

"I have no idea why Germ can see it all too. I never
heard anything about her or her family having the sight."

I'm starting to lose my bearings, and Germ and I have to step around or over bushes and brambles that Ebb floats right through—so we are soon out of breath, our arms and legs scratched up. Then we crest a small hill, and what's on the other side comes into view. Germ stumbles in fright as I let out a small cry.

There must be fifty ghosts gathered in the hollow below us, so many luminous spirits in one place that the whole field is aglow—some dressed as sailors in rain slickers, some in handspun clothes, others in finery. They're scattered among a hodgepodge maze of crooked, crumbling headstones, and they're all looking at us—but it's clear from the very first moment: they're not happy to see us.

Hovering in front of us, Ebb gestures for us not to move.

SEAPORT HISTORIC CEMETERY, a sign says, just within my view at the edge of the field. ESTABLISHED 1782. DEDICATED TO THE PEACEFUL REPOSE OF OUR TOWN'S SOULS.

A ghost floats up the hill toward us. He's mean-looking—one arm lopped off below the shoulder and bound with a rag, the other covered in tattoos of giant squids, mermaids, dragons, and anchors. His face is horribly scarred, copper-colored skin gone bluish and bright, one eye sagging.

I realize suddenly, Ebb is not our friend. He's led us here, away from witches, to a cemetery full of angry ghosts instead. He is a vengeful ghost leading us to our deaths.

The man floats closer, and I notice that worms can be ghosts too when I see a translucent one squiggling out of his ear. He leans down to look into my eyes with his one good one. Then he looks at Ebb, straightening up.

"There's word a witch is about in these parts tonight," he says to Ebb. "I hope you don't bring trouble here."

Ebb shifts nervously, floating back and then forward an inch.

"This is Rosie Oaks," he says. "Annabelle Oaks's daughter. Rosie, this is Homer."

The man stares at me another long minute, this time in surprise. His face softens, and his anger is replaced by recognition. And then concern.

"And I'm afraid we do bring trouble," Ebb adds nervously. "We've got a problem." He gives me a sort of encouraging look. Maybe he's not leading us to our deaths after all.

"The Memory Thief has found out about her?" Homer

says heavily, as if a weight of worry has just landed on his shoulders.

Ebb nods. He recounts the events of the night quickly, looking down at his feet sheepishly. When he gets to the part about Germ charging the moths, Germ flushes bright red and starts looking down at her feet too.

Homer stands for a long time, taking it in. Then he turns to me.

"Your life has changed forever, Rosie Oaks. You've gotten the sight, and I'm afraid you can't go back now to unseeing. And now you have found out that the world is both better and worse than you thought." He looks around at the other ghosts, up at the sky, still moving with its strange cloudlike figures and pink light. "I'm sorry about it. But now we have to figure out how to keep you alive." He mutters something under his breath at the moon. And then he sighs. "Come with me," he says.

CHAPTER 9

We stumble our way across the cemetery. The ground is sunken over graves in places and makes a sickening squish beneath us. I trip into a headstone, which elicits a cry from one of the ghosts.

"Respect my grave!" he yells across the hollow.

"We're sorry!" Germ mumbles, her face flushing.

The ghosts don't part for us, even though we keep saying, "Excuse me, excuse me."

"Forgive their manners," Homer says nervously, scanning the woods as if expecting danger at any moment.

"Most of them haven't been noticed by a living person since they died. Just walk right through them."

After hesitating for a moment, I step through a ghost blocking my way. Then another. Then another. Germ does the same. It gives me an icky, unsettling feeling, and Germ looks slightly nauseated.

"I know they're a gloomy lot," Homer says with an apologetic look. "You would be too, though, I guess, if all you wanted was to move *Beyond,* to the *up there*"—he casts his eyes to the pink hazy ring of the sky—"but you were stuck here."

"Why can't they just go up there?" I ask. "Just float up to the sky?"

"We can't fly, for one thing." Homer looks at me, his urgent expression softening into a smile. "And anyway, we are *tied*: earth-tied, home-tied. We have our haunts—our graves, the place where we lived, the place where we died, perhaps a place or two that has special significance to us. But trying to leave those places *thins* us, drains us."

I look up at the pink hazy sky.

"Why would you want to go up there anyway?" I ask. It does look beautiful, but also mysterious, strange, unknowable.

Homer comes to a stop for a moment, considering.

"Why *there*, my dear, is moving on. It's where we're all meant to go. Eventually. And until then, we wait. Some ghosts get to move on right away." He nods to the sky again. "And others don't. A lot of us just can't let the past go, and some of us—I think—have unfinished business of some sort. Something we need to wrap up, or fix, before we depart this earth. That's my theory anyway. Nobody ever tells us."

"What's *your* unfinished business?" Germ asks.

Homer shrugs. "Me? Could be to avenge myself against the squid who drowned me," he says pensively, "but I just don't know. I wish I did. It's dreadful to be *stuck*." He casts another glance around at the woods, then moves on.

At the far end of the hollow is an enormous crypt, and we make our way in that direction as Homer chatters on—clearly on edge, but also kind. He has a gentle, thoughtful air about him as he talks. Already, I like him much more than I like Ebb, who toggles from melancholy, to friendly, to angry and annoyed so fast that I can't make him out. Right now he's kicking at stones sullenly, his foot passing through them.

"Still," Homer continues, "once you die and become a ghost, you start believing the impossible . . . because you yourself are impossible. And that's comforting in its way."

He points to a tattoo on his biceps, the one of the giant squid. "Got this long before I died. Kind of ironic, considering what killed me, but still glad I have it. Reminds me to always stay present. I found out about meditating after I died. Helps a lot. Ghosts aren't usually good at *being present*, considering we are actually shadows of the past." He looks around, bemused.

"I cope with it all by staying nosy. I know way too much about every living and dead person within five miles of Seaport, plus local history, all the sports teams within fifty miles, and of course, you and your mom." He points to his head. "I'm a stickler for gossip, is what it boils down to. That's why Ebb's brought you to me. I know all about your mom. Then again, *everybody* knows *something* about your mom. And now we all know what kind of danger you're in."

We've come to a stop at the edge of the crypt, which has the words "Homer Honeycutt, captain of the *Mary Sue*. Sunken on the rocks of Cape Horn and devoured by a squid, 1886."

"Well, this is home, such as it is."

Homer gestures for us to sit on a low stone ledge of the crypt. We perch awkwardly, Germ swinging her legs like she does when she's sitting on bleachers at a football game.

"Respect our graves!" a ghost yells at us from behind, making us jump, and Germ's legs go still.

"So," Homer says, folding his hands, an ominous worry settling over his luminous features, "the Memory Thief has found you. And now if you're to escape her, you need to know some things. Things that have been hidden from you, just as you yourself have been hidden."

Homer is about to go on when a ghost lets out a moan, and Homer shoots him a look and shakes his head.

"So far in your life, you've learned only the history of the seen and the living. Now, if you are to survive, you need the history of the living *and* the dead, the seen *and* the unseen."

Beside me, Germ shivers—possibly with fear, possibly with excitement. I cross my arms over my chest. If there's one thing I know how to do, it's to be quiet and listen.

Homer lowers his head, as if thinking about where to begin. To our surprise, he starts with the moon.

"At the beginning of time," Homer begins, eyeing us sharply, with urgency, "there were the thirteen witches and there was the Moon Goddess, all made of magic. The Moon Goddess, hidden and mysterious—who herself created our moon and many others—gathers up light and sends it down at night as a dim glow onto earth's darkness, bringing strange powers with it: hope, dreams, imagination . . . mysterious things we don't fully know or understand. The witches, on the other hand, are made of all the ugliness you can imagine. You simply can't have a thing without having its opposite, and the Moon Goddess is so powerful, it took thirteen witches to balance out her worth.

"The goddess and the witches have been at war, always. But they fight each other in different ways. The Moon Goddess is subtle, and I guess unfathomable. She stays far away, and doesn't meddle directly in earthly things. The witches, on the other hand, are not subtle at all. Their desire is to sow chaos, unhappiness, and discord among humans. War, despair, loss, grief, anguish . . . their fingerprints are on all of it. And they love it; chaos is to a witch what water is to a fish."

Homer pauses. "Now, all living creatures die, the world churns. Darkness and light, you see, are part of nature, and neither can ever fully leave us. But the witches are always trying to tip the scales in their favor."

His brow furrows as he goes on. "In the last hundred years or so, it seems they've been succeeding. They've sown more discord upon the earth than ever before."

Ebb, who has been hovering at the edge of the crypt, looks at me sorrowfully. Homer falls into silence, wincing as if what he's about to tell me will be the hardest part of all. And then, instead, the corner of his mouth lifts into a kind smile.

"But there's hope, merely because there are people who've fought back. And this brings us to your family." He looks at me for a long time, and my arms begin to swim with chills.

"The women in your family have all had the gift of sight. People call it ESP, or being psychic, or whatever else. Mostly living people are"—he shrugs in a defeated kind of way—"oblivious to the unseen things all around them. A few are more aware, but they use their abilities for small things: telling fortunes, finding missing socks, stuff like that."

Germ nods sagely beside me and interjects, "Reading pets' minds."

Homer blinks at her for a second, then looks at me. "*Your* family has used it differently," Homer continues. "You are the last in a long line of women who used their seeing abilities—abilities they could have used to find socks, or read fortunes, or read pets' minds, I suppose—to seek out witches and how to hunt them."

"Like, with swords and stuff?" Germ asks.

Homer shakes his head. "Witches can't be wounded by any mortal method. Lunging at a witch with a sword is like fighting air. But the women in your family, they *have* invented their *own* weapons, capable of hurting witches—and killing them—though to our knowledge that only happened *once*, in Sweden in 1612, when your way-back-quintuple-great-grandmother killed a witch called the Trapper."

He shakes his head again as if trying to shake the image out of his mind.

"Since then, no one has managed it." He pauses. "Because, well . . . the witches can no longer be found."

"Can't be found?" I echo.

Homer tilts his head to look at us solemnly.

"Witches, as powerful as they are, are cowardly creatures. After that first killing, they disappeared somewhere beyond this world—nobody knows where, or how. They only return once a month at the dark moon, when the moonlight can't find or burn them, to lay their curses, before fading back to wherever they hide. The few witch hunters on earth haven't even had a fighting chance of killing witches because they haven't been able to track them down. One by one, *they've* been found instead, and cursed."

Homer looks out over the horizon at the sea. A shadow creeps across the crypt as a cloud crosses over the moon.

"But the Memory Thief . . . ," I say.

"It's rumored that the Memory Thief is an exception—that somehow, while the others hide far away, she was left behind to lurk on earth for some reason we don't know."

"Still, there's one strong, brave, *exceptional* person who we've come to suspect *did* find the witches, who discovered the great secret of how to reach them where they hide, and destroy them. Not just the Memory Thief, but all of them." He turns to look at me. "The problem is, of course, that she's forgotten."

I have a prickly feeling. A sea-urchin-in-my-chest feeling.

"That person, Rosie, was your mother."

CHAPTER 10

An old ache, a buried hurt, rises up beside my confusion.

My mom is not strong or brave. She doesn't even like to walk down the driveway to get the mail. She doesn't even make toast. She doesn't even know how to love me. And yet she has figured out the key to fighting the greatest forces of darkness in the universe?

I feel all the things I've missed piling on me at once. Birthdays she could have cared about, nights when we could have read together, hugs and inside jokes. I think of the mom who painted my room, the one who painted, *Look at how a single candle can both defy and define the darkness.* Was she once really all the things Homer says she was? I want to believe it and I'm scared to believe it.

Germ lays a hand on my arm. Homer sighs, looking at me with pity, which angers me. I'm angry and sad and hopeful at once.

A breeze blows cold across us.

"All of this brings us to you," Homer says. "And how you yourself are an impossible thing."

I hesitate. "Impossible how?"

"Well"—he pauses, looking around the cemetery and up at the sky, as if gauging the time he has to answer—"the stories of you both are woven mostly of rumors and gossip. We ghosts have quite a network—ghosts meeting up in fields, at cemeteries, out on the sea, passing along information. I can only tell you what I know. But I'll have to do it quickly.

"I know that your mother left home at sixteen to travel the world searching for witches, and preserved everything she learned in *The Witch Hunter's Guide to the Universe.* And that *her* mother—your grandmother—had passed along the book to her just before being cursed by Mable the Mad and wandering off into the woods, never to be seen again." He eyes me for my reaction as I listen breath-lessly. *My grandmother, cursed, lost.*

"I know that somewhere in your mother's travels, while crossing the sea by freighter on one of her journeys, she met your father. I know that she showed up here in Sea-port after he died, with just a suitcase and a growing belly and a key to the house on Waterside Road."

My skin prickles at the mention of my father, but Homer pushes on quickly, before I can ask more.

"It didn't take the ghosts who haunt your house long to figure out who she was—we ghosts have known about the Oakses for years. And it didn't take long for us to see she was hiding, and to guess whom she was *hiding from.*" For a moment pity overtakes him, deepening the lines on his face. "The ghosts at your house, including Ebb, watched her stash *The Witch Hunter's Guide* under the floor and wait for your arrival. She was hiding your history from you, I suppose. She was already, before you were born, hiding your sight. She was turning her back on all of it."

"But why?" I finally interrupt.

Homer looks at me sadly. "As I think Ebb has told you, those with the sight stand out in the world like a beacon, easy for witches to find. Most of them pose no threat to witches. And a witch hunter can learn to sort of . . . *dim* themselves, a mental trick that's hard to master. But the daughter of a witch hunter, a defenseless child . . . well, I suspect that, despite all her courage, she couldn't face the possibility of losing you."

I swallow the lump in my throat.

"And she might have had a chance to live a normal life with you. Only . . ."

"Only?"

Homer wrings his hands together and lowers his voice, looking around the cemetery again as if keeping an eye out for the Memory Thief herself.

"Only, somewhere in her travels—we believe—she'd discovered the enormous secret of finding and reaching the witches. The rumors circulated quite a bit at the time. And those rumors, I believe, made it to the witches' ears." He leans back, as if he doesn't want to say what he has to say next. "And even though the famous Annabelle Oaks had given up hunting witches, a witch came for her anyway. And for you. And that's the impossible thing."

"What?" I ask, confused.

"Why, isn't it obvious?" he says. "You're still here."

Homer drops his voice lower still. He leans toward us, and speaks so quietly, we have to lean forward to hear him.

"The night you were born, your mother was cursed. That much is obvious. When she went to the hospital to have you, she was the same powerful woman we had always heard about. But when she came out, her memories were gone; she was just a shell of a person.

"As the newborn daughter of the woman who had so threatened the witches and their secrets, the Memory Thief should have hated you, even feared you. And you were but a helpless baby; it would have been so easy for her to curse you, too, or to bid her familiars to steal you. But for some reason that we can't begin to guess, you weren't taken. Your mother's *memories* were—but not you." He smiles gently.

"Your mother somehow saved you, Rosie. We don't know how. In my heart, un-beating as it is, I believe that means something—a powerful secret. There's no other way to explain it. But no one can imagine what it might be."

"The Memory Thief," I offer, "she said something about being tricked."

Homer contemplates this, then shakes his head. "I don't know. I've spoken to every ghost who haunts that hospital, and none of them can tell me anything useful. They all fled when they sensed a witch in the vicinity that night, and never looked back. It's a dead end, no pun intended."

He gazes at me, then leans back, swipes a worm gently out of his ear and drops it onto the ground. He looks at us. He thinks for a long time.

"All I know is that the Memory Thief is coming for you *now*. And to *stay* safe, you'll have to go far from here. Give up everything you know. Go into hiding."

"For how long?" Germ asks for me.

He blinks at me a moment, taken aback. "Why, forever."

He does not seem to notice that he has shocked us. He looks down at his hands as if counting on his fingers, working out logistics under his breath. "There are people who could hide you, take you in, all over the world—in Japan, in Zimbabwe . . . a few brave people with the sight, scattered remnants of witch hunting families who'd take the risk for one of their own. All that matters is that you're safe and away from here come the dark moon."

"What about Germ? Is she in danger too?"

He looks at Germ, then shakes his head. "She's got the sight for some reason I can't guess. I suppose it *could* be a coincidence. But she's not a witch hunter. As long as she stays uninvolved, they'll ignore her. It's you the witch wants. And she'll be angry. A witch can't kill, directly. But her familiars are something to be reckoned with, and there are many ways a witch's curse can cause you to end up dead—to wander off a cliff, say, or jump from the deck of a ship."

I'm afraid—so afraid that my heart feels like it has fallen into my feet—but an entirely different idea now catches hold of me. And I know, now that it's caught, it won't un-catch. I don't say it at first.

"My mom would never come with me," I say instead. "She won't leave sight of the sea." I think of how agitated she gets when we're away from the shore for just a couple of hours.

And then I find the courage to ask what I most want to know. It causes that same prickling, heavy, sea-urchin-in-the-chest feeling that I've felt all night. And now I realize what it is. The painful, lopsided, unfamiliar feeling that has been rising in me for hours is a scary, risky, prickly kind of hope.

"Um, Homer, you talk about all these curses that witches cast by touching someone. Can a curse be broken?"

Homer blinks at me and leans back, his brow furrowing in concern.

"Rosie . . ."

He hesitates for a long time before he finally speaks again.

"I don't know everything about witches, but I do know that the only way to kill a curse is to kill the witch who wields it. And only one person, by some fluke we can't begin to guess at, has ever killed a witch. Even an adult twice your size would not be able to do it. Even a trained soldier. Even your mom couldn't."

"But if I could get my hands on a witch weapon like the kind you were talking about—"

"It's not so easy to do that, I'm afraid. The witch hunters have secrets just like the witches do—and the biggest one is their weapons. We don't know how they made them, or where any of them are. I doubt even the guide will give you much help there."

"But . . . ," I say, and can't find the words. I think of how Germ's mom says the day Germ was born was like getting the deed to a Hawaiian island. If I broke the curse, would my mom feel that way about me? Would she look at me like Mrs. Bartley looks at Germ? The thought makes me dizzy.

An itchy, watched feeling makes me turn to Ebb. He's staring at me intently with a strange look on his face—sorry and guilty and uncertain all at once. But before I can try to make sense of the look, Homer speaks again. "Rosie, once, your mother loved you with all her heart, and that counts for something, even if she's forgotten it now. And her only wish was that you be safe. She would have never wanted you to be a witch hunter."

"I don't want to hunt *witches*. I just want to hunt *one* witch. I could just stay and kill the one witch."

"You can't stay. It's out of the question."

Beside me, I feel Germ studying me. She clearly wants me to run, like everyone else, but she also knows me better than anyone else. People assume that because I'm small and quiet, I'm also easy to go along with things. I am not. Germ shakes her head.

"Rosie won't go," she says.

Homer stares at us a moment, then scans the woods around the cemetery, nervous.

"We ghosts couldn't help you, you know—we ghosts— if you got in trouble." He looks at Ebb, who's been listening quietly in the background. "We're only shadows, remnants—our uselessness is our greatest burden. Even if we could fight, which we can't, the fate of a ghost who crosses a witch is worse than death. If you stay, if—and *when*—she comes for you, we can't save you. You'd be completely on your own."

I sit very still. My stomach hurts. It feels like I've swallowed a bag full of rocks. But Germ has always said I've had a piece of iron lodged in my back that won't budge once I decide something.

I can't leave my mom. Especially when I know there's a tiny, tiny sliver of a chance I could . . . fix her.

Homer sighs, relenting, but exasperated.

"If you want to kill the Memory Thief, Rosie, you'd have to do two things: find a witch weapon or how to make one, and find out how your mom saved you the night you were born—why and how you were never taken. But let's be clear: I'm against it."

He sounds bitterly worried and disappointed as he continues, "Remember, at the dark moon, she'll be back for you. There's no getting around it."

I knead my hands together, too filled with worry to reply. And seeing this, Homer seems to take pity on me. He slumps a little, and smiles at me.

"Take heart, Rosie," he says. "Only the witches would have you think there is more darkness in the world than there is light. Only they would have you believe that love could ever really leave you."

He ruminates for a moment, then stiffens. "The moon is low. You'd better go so Ebb can get you home before he disappears at dawn, like we all do. I've kept you too long."

I stand on unsteady legs and glance at Ebb, who still has the guilty, uncertain look on his face.

"I'd shake your hand," Homer says, "but you'll just have to settle for me saying it's an honor to meet one of the famous Oaks women at long last. And I hope our paths cross again."

Germ tugs my sleeve. Ebb is already making his way across the cemetery, impatient now, and we turn to follow him.

Looking over my shoulder, I see Homer waving as we hurry away, until he is hidden beyond the trees.

CHAPTER 11

"I like him," Germ says wistfully. "He's moody but he's kind of cute."

We're rambling back along the uneven cliff-side trail toward home, and I realize, after puzzling over it for a minute, that Germ is talking about Ebb—who leads the way, his head hanging low. This makes it official that Germ thinks every boy on earth is cute, even dead ones. And also that Germ can face anything in the world, even the news of a magical unseen layer underneath all existence, and still stride through life like usual.

"Though, I guess he'll be thirteen forever," Germ muses. "Then again, we'll catch up to him in a couple of years," she says brightly. "Then again," she says flatly, "we'll get older than him really fast."

Up ahead, Ebb is gloomy, lost in thought. And then he pivots suddenly toward us.

"You should run, Rosie, like Homer says. I don't think you understand what you're up against. You only just learned about all this stuff and you have no idea how terrifying it can get. Even if you had a weapon . . . ," he says, and gets lost in a thought for a moment, then refocuses, shaking his head. "I can't help you when she comes. We ghosts are useless, like Homer said. We can't affect *anything*, really. And if we tangle with witches—" He stops himself.

"What?"

Ebb doesn't answer. He looks down at the ground, thinking. All the while, he seems to be patting something in his pocket, checking on it occasionally.

"Maybe we can get someone *living* to help us," Germ says. "Like someone . . . adult."

I nod in agreement. "And I can show my mom the book she hid. Maybe things could come back to her if she sees what she wrote with her own hands."

Ebb looks unconvinced. "Trust me, none of it will

work. Nobody will believe you. And your mom won't understand. That piece of her is gone."

"Ebb," Germ ventures, as if she's going to say something profound. "You can be kind of a downer," she blurts out instead. "I'm just being honest."

Ebb brightens and fades momentarily. I suppose it's the ghost version of a blush. Then he goes blank, like he's given up. He pulls whatever it is out of his pocket, cupping it gently in his hand—and I finally see what it is. A spider. Or at least, a ghost of one. Germ and I exchange a look.

"Is that your . . . little friend?" Germ asks softly, casting me a look.

Ebb glances back at us. "We died on the same day," he says curtly. He replaces the spider in his pocket and floats on in silence.

"And it talks?" Germ asks, never one to pick up on subtle social cues, like when people don't want to discuss something.

"*All* of nature talks in its own way," he says, but won't elaborate further. Germ looks at me like she's not so sure that Ebb isn't crazy.

As we linger for a moment, I look to the horizon for any sign of the memory moths returning or a witch approaching (though, I'm not sure exactly how witches approach places—on brooms?), despite Homer's reassurances about witches steering clear of moonlight. Dread sits heavy in the pit of my stomach.

But then, something else in the sky takes my breath—not a witch, but something even more stunning and strange.

I don't know how I could have missed seeing it. It lies low over a cliff that juts out into the ocean: the bright crescent moon and something—a *ladder*, as impossible as that is—dangles down from its edge, just grazing the clifftops.

Ebb and Germ both follow my gaze.

"What is that?" I ask, nodding toward it.

Ebb is quiet for a moment. "It's an invitation, to any brave enough to accept," he finally says.

"Invitation to what?"

He shoots a look at me as if I've asked a really obvious question. "To the moon."

I think back to what Homer was saying about the Moon Goddess. It's hard, in a way, to believe she really exists. But the ladder makes it suddenly real. I think for a moment about astronauts, landing on the moon and not knowing there's an invisible Moon Goddess hovering around them.

My heart leaps.

"Why don't we just climb the ladder? We could ask her what we should do about the Memory Thief. She could help us!"

I feel sudden hope flooding over me, but Ebb is shaking his head.

"It's probably been centuries since anyone's climbed up there," he says. "You can only climb it if the Moon Goddess allows it. Otherwise, when you get about halfway up, the ladder disappears and . . ." He whistles and makes a plunging motion with his hand. "Nobody ever really tries it."

My spirits drop. "That's terrible. I thought she was supposed to be good."

Ebb flickers as he thinks how to explain. "The Moon Goddess *is* a force of good, but she keeps her own plans, and she's very exacting, and I suppose only the pure-hearted and brave can make it all the way to her. Otherwise the witches would probably climb up." His shoulders droop with gloom. "Anyway, she wants people to help themselves; she can't fight their battles for them. At least, that's what all the legends say."

I look up at the moon, anger prickling. What's the

point of being a good and wise Moon Goddess if you don't *help*? But Germ's mind is on another tack.

"Ghosts have legends?" she asks.

"Sure," Ebb says. "Like that beyond that pink haze is a paradise for all the souls who've moved on. And like the sea contains all the time that's ever existed and you can travel through it in the mouth of a magical whale."

"Is that true?" I ask.

Ebb considers for a moment, then shakes his head slowly. "It's just wishful thinking."

"Wishful why?"

Ebb shrugs.

"Ghosts and time. It's the thing that torments us. Too much of it now that we are dead, too little of it when we weren't." He smiles ruefully. "The Time Witch has a lot to answer for with us."

I remember skimming past the Time Witch in *The Witch Hunter's Guide*, a woman with clocks dangling from her neck. But the Memory Thief is the only witch I can think about.

We stand gazing at the setting moon—which glows, aloof and distant, above the mirror of the sea for a few more moments before it sinks out of sight. I think of my mom and dad, meeting somewhere out at sea so long ago—somewhere in the time when the ghosts lost track of her, before she showed up in Seaport with me in her tummy. And then a spark ignites inside me.

I turn to Ebb, try to grab his arm, but my fingers, of course, slip through him instead.

"My mom likes to say, 'He's out there swimming, waiting for me.' I used to think she was talking about my dad. Do you think he could be a ghost, out there somewhere, swimming? Do you think she's talking about him?"

Ebb looks at me for a moment. He glances sadly up to the glowing haze above.

"I'm sorry, Rosie. I've heard nothing about your dad except what Homer said, that your mom met him on a freighter while crossing the ocean back when she was chasing witches." He squints as if trying to remember. "And that he drowned before you were born. Not because of witch mischief or anything like that, I don't think. Just because . . . bad things happen."

Unanswerable questions rise up one after the other about my dad—*What was he like? Did he have the sight too? Did he love my mom from the moment he met her?* I feel an empty place inside ache. Ebb waits for me to say something, but I'm silent, so he continues.

"The ghosts who stay behind are a rarity, Rosie. Most times people are just *gone*, Beyond. Your dad—if he were out there somewhere, I think we would have heard about it by now."

I stare down at my feet, crestfallen. But why would my mom always talk about someone waiting for her in the sea, if it's not him? I tuck and fold the hope inside me to think about later in secret. Maybe that feeling of always missing another half—maybe that's my heart knowing my dad is somewhere out there, trying to find me and help me.

There's a deep kindness in Ebb's voice when he speaks again.

"I know it's not the same as having a mom and dad who are really there for you, but you were never alone, Rosie, even though you felt like you were. The times you've woken up from nightmares and your mom wouldn't comfort you. The times you've fallen and she didn't get you a Band-Aid. Your first steps that she ignored. I've been here through all of it; all of us ghosts in your house have. You just couldn't see it."

I stare at him quietly, feeling my face flush. Even though he's trying to be nice, I don't like the idea of ghosts lingering around for my whole life without me knowing it—not at all. I've always been a secretive kind of person—especially about my feelings. I like to keep myself a secret from pretty much everyone but Germ. And now I wonder, how many of my secrets does Ebb know?

The night is just beginning to fade when we see the warm lights of my house up ahead, glowing through the dark wet dimness. Several ghosts are floating across the lawn as if leaving after a long night's haunt.

A small creature, all fangs and claws, is running across the grass toward us, and he lunges at my leg, though he passes right through it. He growls and snarls up at me before lurching away.

"What was that?" I ask, shuddering. *An evil creature?* I wonder. *A witch's familiar?*

"Just the ghost of a rabid possum," Ebb says. "He's a mean old thing, tries to bite everybody. We all wish he'd move on, honestly."

We are just venturing onto the grass when I almost walk right into a flesh-and-blood, breathing man.

I stumble back, shocked. It takes a few moments of staring and getting my bearings to realize it's only Gerald, the guy who sometimes fixes things around the property, whom I pay with my mom's checkbook.

Germ and I stand frozen in our tracks, Ebb hovering between us. We stare at Gerald and Gerald stares back. And then he smiles.

"You two are up early," he says. Neither Germ nor I can find words to reply, because we are waiting for him to notice Ebb.

"Um," I say, "we were . . . bird-watching."

Gerald cocks his head at me. "Birds?"

"You have to get up early to see the red-breasted, uh, warble . . . um . . . jay," Germ puts in.

Gerald stares at us for a moment, then nods. At the same time, a translucent old woman—the washerwoman I saw last night—barrels through him with an arm full of filmy sheets, and Germ almost loses it, snorting into her hand.

"Bless you," I say.

"Well, no rest for the weary," Gerald says, after giving us another strange look. He then walks across the lawn to his truck to get his supplies, as the last of the ghosts but Ebb trickle into the woods beyond him. We let out the breaths we've been holding.

"Well," Germ says, eyeing Gerald but turning to me. She has circles under her eyes. "I better get home. My mom wanted me there by seven. And maybe she *will* believe me, about everything. Maybe she can help."

I look at her, feeling guilty suddenly—all the night's seemingly impossible events catching up to me.

"Germ" I say, "I don't know how you can *see*. But the witches . . . all of this is my problem. I don't want you to be in danger too."

"It's *our* problem," Germ says. "I feel like I caught the sight from you somehow, and I'm happy I did." She frowns. "But, Rosie, I want you to be safe. I think you should really think about running like Ebb and Homer say."

"I'll think about it," I say slowly, looking to Ebb, who watches us silently. It hurts a little, because I can't imagine ever leaving Germ, and I wonder how she can encourage me to leave.

She gives me a quick wave and gets on one of the rusty old bikes that we share, by the shed. As soon as she's gone, things feel emptier and scarier.

"Well, I'll be back tonight," Ebb says.

I turn to him. "From now on, maybe you could give me some privacy," I say. "I really appreciate all your help, but would you mind just . . . staying outside the house from now on? I mean, you're a boy, for one thing. It's sort of . . ."

Ebb's mouth drops closed, then straightens into a thin,

embarrassed line. His glow dims a little. He nods. Then he turns and drifts across the grass without another word. A moment later, as the sun rises above the lip of the sea, he vanishes completely.

Inside, I climb the stairs and look in on my mom, who's asleep.

She is peaceful in her bed, despite the wild night that's passed.

When she wakes, I'll show her the book and see if she can remember. But in my heart of hearts, I think that she'll wake and look at me with foggy eyes and try her hardest to remember things, and fail, like she always does. She'll go about her day as if I'm not here. She'll sit and look out at the sea.

For now I crawl into bed and hope for a couple of hours' sleep. I tap out on my fingers the four days till the dark moon. I have so much to find out before then. What secret saved me the night I was born? Is it the same secret my mom found out about fighting witches? What weapon can I use to defend myself?

I pull *The Witch Hunter's Guide* into bed with me and flip slowly through the pages until I reach the section called "The Oakses and Their Weapons."

As Homer warned, it's a disappointment. There is only

one simple paragraph about weapons, at the very beginning of the section. It reads: *A weapon is as much a part of a witch hunter as her fingernails or her teeth. It is tied right to her heart, and that's where she keeps it close. The secret of it is passed on from mother to daughter, a gift of magic and material combined: an embroidered dress for a shield, a sword made of song, a net knit from poetry.*

It doesn't make sense. How does anyone knit a net of poetry, or embroider a shield? It sounds simple and impossible at the same time. And one thing is for sure, my mother never passed on the secret to me.

Beyond this, there are old photos pasted onto the pages, from as far back as the days of blurry old black-and-whites of ladies in long dresses with bustles. My family—all the women. People I have never heard of, but whom I long for. A woman with a severe gray bun, *Dorothy Oaks, cursed with madness*—my grandmother? A woman with scraggly brown hair, holding a fine leather-bound dagger, *Mary Lee Oaks, struck with babble and confusion.* A woman in a beautiful dress stitched all over with pictures, *Eugenia Oaks, cursed to forget.* And my heart sinks seeing them, as I read the curses by their names.

Women who knew more than me, who never had their sight hidden from them, who grew up learning to fight, and were told the secrets of their family tree. They *all* met terrible ends. They were blotted out. Every single one.

Who am I—a girl who didn't know even about the invisible fabric until this night—to think I can do what they couldn't?

I look out the window, thinking about the Memory Thief. How she blotted my mom out—taking all the love out of her, and with it, all the fight. She is going to blot me out too, in four days, if I can't figure out how to kill her first.

Maybe I should run.

But then I think again about my mom. I wonder if maybe the love Homer says she felt for me could be hidden inside her like a muscle memory, like the way a person plays the piano without thinking about it. Like if once she got a little of it, it would all come back to her.

And then it lands on me—the sudden, breathless, horribly hurtful hope. To have someone look at me like I'm a light their eyes are drawn to. To have a real mom, which would mean a real family, which would mean I, myself, am a real, lovable daughter.

If that's not worth risking your life for, I don't know what is.

PART 2

CHAPTER 12

I wake in the late morning with Homer Honeycutt's words in my head: *Find a witch weapon or how to make one, and find out how your mom saved you the night you were born.*

I know the first place I need to start, but it doesn't fill me with much hope. I need to start with *her*.

Bleary-eyed from so little sleep, I tuck the *Guide* under my arm and head downstairs to make myself my first-ever cup of coffee. It's bitter and I don't like the taste, but it wakes me up. *You're gonna stunt your growth, sweetie,* I think.

I make my mom a cup and bring it to her in the attic, where she already sits, rocking and staring out the window.

She looks up at me and narrows her eyes. I glance around at all the things I've put up to help her remember me. I kneel beside her with the book. I slide *The Witch Hunter's Guide to the Universe* onto her lap.

Her eyes go from her coffee cup to the book, then to me. There is something there. A glimmer of a spark of memory.

"Mom, do you remember this book? It's a book you helped to write," I say, "full of secrets you helped to learn."

She blinks at me, then stares back down at the cover. I slowly open it for her, and flip through one page and then the next, my heart beating in my throat with hope. When I arrive at the page of the Memory Thief, her eyelids flutter. She turns her gaze to the window.

I look hard at her. "Mom," I say, low, because my voice falters. "What happened the night I was born? How did you protect me? What secrets did you know?"

She turns her eyes back to me. And that's when I see it, or I think I do. Somewhere deep inside her eyes, something trying to get out, to reach me. Maybe I'm imagining it, but I don't think so; it's like the smallest pinprick of light still inside her. And then it fades.

"What are you asking me?" she says. "What is this? Why are you bothering me?"

I squeeze her hand tight. *What did you expect?* I think.

"I'm not giving up," I say. "I'm going to find you—the old you. I'm going to rescue you from the monster in the fairy tale. I'm going to bring you back."

She blinks at the book. She shakes her head a few times as if clearing it of a dream. "That would be nice, Rosie," she says, and then she looks away as if I've already left the room.

I close the book and pull it onto my lap, fingering the edges, knowing that any help my mom could offer is not worth hoping for. I know she'll sit all day staring at the sea, forgetting me, the book, everything, like a ghost herself. I'm on my own.

I call Germ and leave her a message, just checking in. And then I set my mind to the first thing I need to do. Booby traps.

There's an old movie Germ left here once called *Home Alone*, about a boy who has to protect his house from thieves, and I rewatch it to see how he lays traps for the bad guys, taking notes in one of my school binders. Homer said no human weapon can hurt a witch—I haven't forgotten that. But even *he* said he didn't know everything about witches.

Based on what I learn, I get a shovel and a twenty-pound dumbbell I find in the attic. I turn broomsticks into spears; a jar of pennies, some soda cans, and some string into a homemade alarm system; and a box of nails into a gruesome paddleboard bat. There's an axe that hangs on the wall down in the basement, but I decide to steer clear of the basement altogether. I just don't have the courage to go down there now, even in daytime.

I break glasses in paper bags and place the bags by my window to use as bombs. Then I take a long tour through the fuse box and watch an online video about how to get wires to spark.

Once I'm finished with the traps, I turn to my mom's bedroom, not the one in the attic but the room that is *supposed* to be hers. Despite her general indifference to most things, it makes me nervous to sneak in without her knowing. So I try to do it as quietly and quickly as possible.

Coming in here has always felt like walking into a museum of the person my mom once was. There are old photos on the wall of her standing on a boat or in front of the Egyptian pyramids, holding a bow and arrow aloft proudly at summer camp with a blue ribbon on her chest, riding a horse, gazing at my dad with a joyful smile—a wild, brave, happy person. There is her diploma for art history. A soft purple bedspread lies over her queen bed; all sorts of stained-glass baubles hang in the window to turn sunlight into rainbows. There are paintings she once made of flowers and statues and people, things she painted while traveling the world. (Though, now I realize, with a deep chill, she was traveling the world *hunting witches*.) All her subjects have personalities: a rose looks self-confident; a building looks tired; a statue of a man in robes, glimpsed through a painted window, looks curious and kind.

There are empty spots on her shelves where her books used to be, empty spaces left where I've stolen her knickknacks—retreating to my room with treasures in my arms, trying to steal bits of my mom, I guess.

Mostly she has either not noticed what I've taken, or not cared, but a few books she has stolen back: *Where the Wild Things Are, Hansel and Gretel, Rapunzel.* I go to them now, flip through the pages—which are full of witches and monsters, faeries and magic. Does she keep taking these books back because the secret to finding and killing witches is hidden on their pages? A witch getting pushed into an oven, a monster being tamed when you stare into its eyes?

But if there are clues in these books about how to fight a witch, I can't find one. I doubt I could push a witch into an oven or tame one with my eyes.

As quietly as I can, I search the rest of the room. It's disheveled and disorganized. I find Mom's wedding ring in a ceramic mug next to a chewed piece of gum; I find Mom's bank card in a pile of receipts, and an engraved pendant with her birth date on the floor. I look through folders, boxes, plastic bags.

And then I find, amongst a pile of blank postcards from places she must have visited once, my birth certificate.

It reads:

State of Maine Certificate of Birth
Place of Birth: Saint Ignatius Hospital
Date of Birth: September 1, 2010
Name of Child: Oaks, Rose Kristen
Sex: Female
Weight: 6 lbs, 8 oz
Hair: Brown
Eyes: Brown

I've seen the sign for Saint Ignatius Hospital many times. It's just at the edge of town, in a patch of woods at the start of a long empty road through the trees, the sign rotting away so that now it only says SAINT IGNAT SPITA. I don't even know if the hospital is still open, but I do know it's been displaced by a new, shiny hospital downtown. The new one I know really well because every time Germ breaks a bone doing something daring, we go there.

I gaze at my birth certificate for a while, at the date, wishing I could read more into this simple piece of paper than a few meaningless facts. And then—just as I'm tucking it back amongst the postcards—I notice there *is* something. Because on the back of the certificate, in a loose scrawl that is still my mom's, only messier than usual—are these words:

> Swimming.
> Swimming.
> Swimming.
> Waiting.
> Where is he????
> Where they hide from me.

As I stare at the words, my body prickles with chills.

Questions rise one after the other. Who is "he"? Does "where they hide" mean the witches?

Swimming, and the night I was born, and how I was saved, and where the witches hide—the great secret my mom supposedly discovered. They're linked somehow; they have to be. But how?

Just as I move to put the birth certificate away, I hear my mom stirring in the attic, then creaking down the stairs. I hurry out right as she comes to the landing. She looks at me for a moment, as if suspicious, and then brushes past me into the room.

By the time I fix dinner, the day is dimming to dusk. My heart begins to thrum a little faster, to know the night is coming, and all the strange things it brings with it. I can barely eat, I'm so nervous. I try Germ again on the phone, but she doesn't answer.

After I eat, I turn to *The Witch Hunter's Guide* again. I fight off sleep as I flip through the chapters, glancing at the legends. (There are plenty about the Moon Goddess and her ladder, and just as Ebb said, one about a whale who can swim through time, and some about ancient ghosts who tried to mount a rebellion against the witch Hypocriffa and lost.) There's a long description of the moon and gravity that I decide to come back to later.

Under "The Invisible World and Its Beings," there's
a disclaimer that there are plenty of magical beings left
to be discovered, followed by a list with drawings and
descriptions of the ones that are known. The Moon Goddess. Ghosts. Witches. Witch familiars. Cloud shepherds.
Curious, I zero in on this last one.

*Made of mist like the clouds they guide, the
cloud shepherds watch the happenings of the
world from above. They are rain keepers,
snow spillers, wind blowers. They are restless
observers. They climb high over towns, wrap
themselves around forests, whip over the
waves. They've seen dinosaurs thrive, Atlantis
sink, and Pompeii fall under ashes. And all
the while, they watch the world, and listen,
and see all. With a bird's-eye view and a vast
memory, they know almost everything about
human affairs and have memories of each
person on earth.*

*They will sometimes share their
knowledge if only you can reach them, but
they are extremely elusive—only touching
earth in fog: grazing mountaintops, lying*

over the water, and they will dissipate
and disappear when approached. Like the
Moon Goddess, they do not interfere.

I sit back. What I would give to find a cloud shepherd
and talk to it. But I suppose the likelihood of catching a
cloud is about as high as the likelihood of pinning down
the edge of a rainbow.

My eyelids are heavy, and none of this is helping me to
uncover the secrets of killing a witch. I lay the book down,
then walk up to my room and watch out the window as the
sun sets. As it does, the magical world comes into focus.

Up in the sky, the cloud shepherds—now that I know
what they are—move about, changing shapes as they go.
The phantom ships materialize on the horizon, and the
moon rises at the lip of the sea, its ladder dangling.

A light fog drifts up from the ocean and across the
lawn. And then the ghosts begin to arrive. They emerge
from the wispy edges of the fog—there must be twenty or
more, and I catch my breath as I watch them.

Five peel off toward the house: the knitting woman I
saw last night in the parlor, and the washerwoman from this
morning (the two appear to be friends). The starfish-covered
sailor in the yellow rain slicker, the lady in white. And—I

shiver—the Murderer. As if he feels my eyes on him, he looks up at where I stand, and I go still with fright. For a moment our eyes meet, and his bore into mine with hatred.

Then the group drifts below and out of sight, no doubt floating into the rooms below.

After watching for another minute, I'm just about to turn away from the view when I see Ebb. He's standing at the edge of the trees across the lawn, apparently obeying my request not to come into the house, which makes me feel a pang of regret. (I'd much rather have Ebb here than the Murderer.) He doesn't notice me, though. For some reason he appears to be whispering to a cluster of fireflies.

I don't realize I'm being watched until I hear a strange dripping sound. Someone is standing behind me.

"It's the tragic ones who linger the longest, ain't it, little one?"

My arms swim with gooseflesh at the raspy voice. I turn to see—not the Murderer but the starfish-covered sailor standing in the hallway, dripping luminous water that doesn't wet the floor.

I don't think I'll ever get used to ghosts.

"Tragic?" I manage to say.

The man shrugs. "Nothing cheerful about how the boy died. There's a reason he's called Ebb," the man says. "Used to be Robert when he was alive. Loves animals, that boy. Even bugs, always drawn to them."

I wait for him to say more.

"He's looked after you since you were a baby, as much as a ghost could, which I suppose isn't much. Kept you company even though you couldn't know you *had* company."

I stare out at Ebb, trying to reconcile the boy he's describing with the ghost I've met—angry at me one minute, melancholy the next, sometimes kind and sometimes not.

"Don't mind his moods," the man in the slicker says, as if he's read my thoughts. "You'd be moody too if you were tied to earth while your parents had moved Beyond."

I turn. I want to ask about Ebb's parents, and what happened to them, but before I can summon the words, the man floats through the wall and is gone.

I swivel back to the window and watch Ebb move from tree to tree, whispering to tiny insect ghosts. He must sense me watching him, because he turns and looks toward the window, then lifts his hand in a half wave. I half wave back, blushing with shame for being so mean to him. And then I turn away.

I look around my room, feeling defeated. The first day is already gone, and I'm no closer to finding anything that could help me fight a witch, except for the cryptic note on the back of my birth certificate. I will go to the hospital tomorrow, I decide, though I have no idea what I'll look for. Hopefully Germ can come with me.

I nervously fiddle with my mom's knickknacks on my shelf—the matchbox, the shell-engraved whistle, an old wrinkled Playbill, and then my fingers move to a few of my worn, faded books: *The Wind in the Willows*; *Aesop's Fables*; *M.C. Higgins, the Great*; *Anne Frank: The Diary of a Young Girl*; all the Harry Potter books; and on and on.

My books have sheltered me from the moments that are hard, and whisked me away when I needed to escape. They're like wool that keeps you warm in the cold and cool in the heat. On days when I find it especially hard not to crumple up because I wish I had a different mom or a different life, I escape to them.

Now I read my favorite, well-worn chapter in the whole Harry Potter series, where Ron, Harry, and Hermione make an escape on the back of a dragon they once feared. It's my favorite because I like how by saving themselves, they save the beast, too. I love most of all the moment when they rise up, and fly.

And like always, even in the face of witches and curses, it works. It calms me. It saves me the way it always does.

And I sleep deeply afterward.

And the witch doesn't come.

CHAPTER 13

The phone rings downstairs, waking me with a jolt Sunday morning. Before I'm even out of bed, I'm thinking about time: three days till dark moon. *Three days, three days*, I think with each step down the stairs.

I hurry to the kitchen and pick up our ancient phone from the cradle. (We have an old answering machine, too—all left over from some unknown owner of the house years ago.)

It's Germ. She's out of breath, and her words spill out all in a rush.

"So sorry I didn't call yesterday. After soccer, when I got home, I tried to convince my mom that ghosts exist and told her that we talked to a bunch of them last night. But now she thinks I'm having seizures. She looked it up on WebMD, and it says when you have seizures, you hallucinate. So now she's not letting me out of the house. Like, except tonight for the Fall Fling. She said I couldn't call you because we just 'egg each other on.' She thinks I'm calling Bibi right now."

"You're allowed to call Bibi?" I blurt out, more hurt-sounding than I want to be, feeling betrayed by Germ's mom.

Germ pauses for a second. "Because of the Fall Fling. We have to organize for tonight. Do you think . . ." She hesitates. "Do you think you still might be able to come?"

"What?" I ask. My promise to go to the Fall Fling has completely slipped my mind until just this moment.

Germ pauses. "I know, I know, it's really crazy to ask, with everything going on. It's just . . . I can't back out because of Bibi, and . . . it's going to be a disaster and I'm going to be humiliated. But I know it's not a big deal compared to . . . everything. I know."

I've never heard Germ sound so agitated. She took on ghosts last night with relative calm. Now her voice quivers with fear. I feel a tinge of disappointment that Germ even cares about any of this stuff right now.

And then I think, *If I'm not there to comfort Germ if she does get humiliated, which is fairly likely, who will be?*

"I'll be there," I say, keeping the disappointment out of my voice. "Of course."

I can practically hear her sigh of relief at the other end. "Thanks, Rosie." She pauses. "I did do a bunch of internet research on witches and stuff like that yesterday. But sorting out make-believe stuff from real witches is, like, impossible. There are all these books that say witches don't float. And I read a bunch about the Salem witch trials, which just sounds like people back then were afraid of women who did what they wanted. I'm gonna keep looking."

Behind her, I can hear the news, which she always has on, and then the doorbell.

"Uh-oh, that's Bibi at the door. My cover's blown— gotta go."

She hangs up before saying good-bye.

I sit there for a moment, engulfed in jealousy I don't like and that I wish I didn't have.

Get it together, sweetie, I tell myself.

And then I look at the clock. It's already eleven o'clock.

+ + +

By afternoon, I'm on my bike riding alone to the hospital, in the rain, in an oversize raincoat I borrowed from Mom since I don't have one. I wear my *Lumos* flashlight under my coat for good luck.

I pull off the ramp where I've always seen the decrepit sign that reads SAINT IGNAT SPITA, and wind down a woodsy road. It's deserted, and I wish again that Germ were with me, because she always makes me feel at least 75 percent braver—but I steel myself and keep pedaling. Whenever Germ is afraid, she says she thinks of gummy bears with ketchup on them, and it's so disgusting that it helps. But it doesn't work for me.

In the dim rainy light, I marvel at the loneliness and emptiness of this place. It must have felt to my mom, when she came here to have me, like she was going to the ends of the earth to hide.

I pedal on and on, and it looks like nothing is back here until the moment that, up ahead as I round a bend, the hospital looms up from the woods.

I brake, and catch my breath.

No wonder Homer said this was a dead end.

The building stands in the middle of a clearing carved out from the surrounding woods, its walls jagged and crumbled like old teeth. It looks like it's been in a fire—black smudge marks snake across its white stone. It's covered in ivy and moss, and its doors are blocked with yellow tape, though most of the tape lies sagging along the concrete landing. The building is surrounded by an overgrown field that must have been a lovely lawn once. A few of its windows are boarded with plywood. On one of them there's an eviction notice. In the wetness, mushrooms have sprouted everywhere.

This is the place where I was saved, by a secret. I wish a place could share its memories the same way people do. I wonder what *The Witch Hunter's Guide*, with all its talk of magic, would say about that.

I take a deep breath and walk into the tall grass. The front doors, behind the tape, stand propped open. I step up to the threshold and lean forward to peer inside.

An empty hall with waterlogged papers all over the ground, a few overturned silver trays. I step gingerly inside, wind down the hallway and then through a series of rooms where old bedding lies in drifts against the walls. Broken glass crumbles under my feet. It's clear right away that I'll find *nothing* here—no records, no sign of the lives that used to be lived here. And Homer says none of the ghosts know the answers.

At the back corner of the building, I find the long suite of rooms that once made up the maternity ward. I walk past one room after another, peering in. The rooms are painted white but have gone a dingy gray. After toeing through some trays and cups on the floor of one of the rooms, I find my way through a door and out into a small courtyard.

I wander along the stone pavers, then turn to look back at the empty building behind me. An old broken clock hangs over the entrance. My heart sinks. Whatever saved me that night, whatever secret spared me that might help me again when a witch comes for me, there's nothing here to find.

It's dusk by the time I get home, and ghosts are floating up Waterside Road as I pedal up the drive. The light from the attic window where my mom sits glows like a beacon. There's a circle of ghosts playing cards by the pathway to the front door. There are two ghost children playing tag in the yard. They all nod a wary acknowledgment to me as I move past.

In the parlor I find the knitting lady and the washer-woman already sitting on the couch passing the time, talking about how a ghost they know lost his life to killer bees, and how that compares to dying of typhoid.

Walking into the kitchen to make dinner, I tune them out as they move from one topic to another, and I only vaguely overhear snippets.

"You know, Crafty Agatha, I hear she sucks the meat off children's bones," the washerwoman says.

"No, she doesn't," the knitting lady—Crafty Agatha, I suppose—says. "But I do hear she cooks people in pots. I hear she hides in a big hollow tree with a cauldron hanging from one of the limbs."

I'm beginning to realize what a gossipy, superstitious lot they are—just as Ebb said. When they're not talking about the weather, or each other, they're talking wild theories about witches, the Moon Goddess, and what lies past the pink haze of the *Beyond*. In any case, they sound like they are going on half wild rumor and half fact, and it's impossible to tell which is which.

"She hides inside a volcano in Hawaii," a voice says from the other side of the room. I turn to see that the drowned sailor in the rain slicker is passing through the room, and now he hovers by the couch. "She was left behind by the others because she lost something the rest of them have, some way of getting to their hiding place, so now she's stuck hiding here on earth. I've heard it from several reliable sources." He gives me a sheepish look. "Sorry, little one. I know it's probably unpleasant to hear."

"What do you know about it, Soggy?" Crafty Agatha says.

"Are you talking about the Memory Thief?" I interject nervously, and they all turn to look at me. "The one who was left behind and can't go where the rest of them go?" The two women on the couch look at each other meaningfully. I'm curious. I wish they could tell me where the Memory Thief hides. Then if I ever figured out how to fight her, I could find her before she found me first. Still, I can't tell what parts are idle gossip and what parts are real.

"Never you mind, little one," Crafty Agatha says. "I'm sure all will be well." They exchange another look that says they really don't think all will be well.

Subtle, I think.

Just then, another ghost drifts in and whispers to them, looking at me.

"She was?" Crafty Agatha says, looking over at me with one eyebrow arched.

I sigh. Now, I guess, I'm the subject of the gossip.

"What?" I finally ask.

"Some spirits saw you riding home from Saint Ignatius Hospital just after sunset."

I nod. Annoyed. I don't like everybody knowing what I'm doing all the time.

"Well, it's just, it's a good thing you weren't there at night," Crafty Agatha says. "Hate to see you caught out by the Murderer so far from home. That could just about frighten you to death, I imagine."

My skin prickles.

"The Murderer?"

The washerwoman and Crafty Agatha nod.

"What would he be doing there?"

"Oh." Crafty Agatha waves her ball of yarn in the air. "Well, he's always either there or here. He comes and goes between the two all night long." I blink at them, waiting for more of an explanation, which they finally seem to realize they should give.

"We don't really know why," the washerwoman says. "Only that he does the same thing every night."

My stomach sinks. *Never tell*, the Murderer always says, like he's keeping a secret. Homer said none of the ghosts know anything about what happened at the hospital that night. But what if there were one ghost, I suddenly realize, who's decided to never tell? Could what happened the night I was born, and the Murderer's secret, be linked?

I look toward the basement door, and steel myself to approach it.

"Leave him be, child," Soggy urges me, floating up beside me. "Ghosts have ways of hurting you, no matter what Ebb says. If they're angry enough. Haven't you ever heard of falling chandeliers? Plates flying across a room? If a ghost is angry enough, he can kill. And trust me. That one is angry enough."

I swallow before I take the last steps toward the door.

I open it, and peer down the stairs, then walk down them, one by one.

I look around, dreading the sight of the Murderer, the coal-red eyes, the rash around the neck.

But the basement is empty.

He's not here.

CHAPTER 14

My mom drives us to school that night. I only have to remind her once or twice why we're going, while she nods like Germ is some vague acquaintance I've barely mentioned before. The rest of the time, we're silent. And the farther we get from the house and the sea, the more she fidgets and rubs her hands against the wheel.

As we turn onto Main Street, I pause at the sight of several ghosts hurrying to cross the road, dressed in suits as if for work. In the school parking lot, a ghost mother and child drift across the pavement, the mother dragging the child as if he's late for school. Mom drives right through them, though they don't seem to mind or veer off their path in any way.

I take a deep breath as we climb out of the car, then cross the lot and step through the double doors of my school. Only when I'm standing in the hallway, surrounded by crowds both living and dead, does it really sink in what kind of a night it's going to be.

Seaport Middle School is 102 years old, and it has the ghosts to prove it. A handful of dead children float up the hall, yelling so loudly, I can barely hear anything else. A translucent teacher in a long dress shushes me as if I'm the one being loud. A ghost custodian is lying on the hallway floor.

The crowd of living parents and kids meandering through the hall and buying their tickets and fundraiser candy is oblivious to all of it. They walk right through the ghosts, discussing dinner and grades as luminous shades of the past surround them.

I try to paste a look of indifference onto my face, as if there's nothing unusual to see. It's especially hard when the dead custodian lying on the ground turns his head and smiles at me, and his head nearly comes off. How strange it is that the world goes on as usual—with announcements and basketball tryouts and algebra—when the past circles all around us. I walk faster, my mom shuffling along behind me.

I catch a glimpse of Germ as we make our way to the bleachers. She looks out at me as she climbs the stairs to backstage, then glances at a ghost boy who's being particularly loud, and rolls her eyes, exasperated. She's pale and putting on a brave front. In fact, she looks panicked.

"I'll sit over here," my mom says, gesturing to some folding chairs in the far corner of the room. She likes to be away from people—the noise upsets her, and she doesn't know how to make small talk because she has nothing to say. I hurry over to Germ.

"I feel like I'm gonna barf," she says. "Do you think I caught something from Eliot Falkor?"

"I think you're nervous," I offer.

"You're right," Germ says, nodding, her eyes wide and dazed with fear. She blinks at me for a moment, then shakes her head and shoulders, as if trying to shake off the nausea. "What did you find out?" she asks.

I tell her about the birth certificate, and the abandoned hospital, and what the ghosts said about the Murderer. Her eyes widen.

"I wonder what he knows," she says. And then a voice calls her from backstage, and she whips around to listen, then turns back to me.

"I gotta go get dressed."

With that, she hurries up the stairs and disappears through the doors.

I sit beside my mom, looking around. There's a dead referee down on the court, blowing his whistle. And after a few more minutes of waiting, the curtain goes up.

I start a little in surprise when I see that the first two performers are Germ and Bibi, standing there beside each other on the stage, looking very small while they wait for the crowd to go quiet.

The opening act is always reserved for the showstopper. (Usually it's this girl named Lewnyi who's the best at piano of anyone in school.) The other thing is that Germ is wearing a skirt—A SKIRT. The eyeliner is back too, and now there's lipstick.

And then, the act begins.

It turns out, the act is whistling.

They are whistling a medley of show tunes. It all begins slow, with "Singin' in the Rain," followed by "There's No Business Like Show Business." But then they get into more complicated territory: the soaring chorus of "Memory" from *Cats*, the highs and lows of "Send in the Clowns."

I sit there staring, listening, shocked. I didn't even know Germ knew how to whistle. But there she is, her high-pitched trill weaving melodies in and out of Bibi's low harmony, and though they start out nervously and miss a few notes, they are soon careening ahead with a galloping rendition of "Ease on Down the Road"—watching each other carefully as they do it, so that they're perfectly in time. They are so in tune with each other that it begins to sound seamless, like one unit whistling instead of two people.

The whole audience is completely silent. Even the dead referee stops blowing his whistle. Nobody throws spitballs, or laughs quietly into their hands.

And I realize something—I guess at the same time that the rest of the school does. Germ and Bibi are really, *really* good.

When they finish, Germ and Bibi beam at each other and fall into a huge hug, and the crowd erupts into cheers.

And then it happens. Though Bibi's performance was solid, it's clear that Germ's whistling was the breakout piece of the act. And that really hits home when the kids start chanting. It's unintelligible at first, but then I recognize the sound.

They're chanting Germ's name.

CHAPTER 15

When she sees me through the crowd that gathers after the show, Germ smiles and leaps toward me for a hug.

"That was . . . wow," I say. "That was amazing!"

There are all sorts of feelings swirling around in me, but I try to make happiness for Germ be the only one. It isn't that I wish people would chant for me like that one day—I wouldn't like that; it would only embarrass me. But it's hard not to wish they wouldn't chant for Germ, either.

Bibi is right beside her, and for a moment, we exchange a glance—neither of us smiles at the other.

"And you look . . . really nice," I say to Germ.

I do mean it. But also, in her skirt and with her hair done so perfectly, Germ looks like an animal *tamed* somehow. My favorite Germ is the Germ running ahead of all the boys on the playground, hair flapping in the wind behind her as if she weren't going to stop even if she ran off the edge of the earth. It's hard to think of her doing that in a skirt.

The crowd starts to thin, and Germ turns to Bibi as Bibi whispers something to her. They both laugh. And then Bibi steps off into the crowd somewhere. Germ turns to me, her face becoming uncertain.

"Bibi wants me to come to her house and celebrate with some cake her mom made. But . . . ," she says. She looks unsure.

"I thought you weren't allowed out."

"Well, my mom made an exception because of the show; she'd be coming too, to meet Bibi's mom." She looks hesitant, and flushes.

"Bibi is the worst," I say. It just slips out. I think I suddenly understand the term "green with envy." I feel like the color of barf inside.

Germ frowns at me. "I know you and Bibi aren't on great terms . . ." She trails off. "But she said you could come with us."

"I've got to go home and figure out how to save myself from a *witch*," I say flatly.

Germ bites her lip, and her cheeks flush red. She looks like she's going to cry.

"I'll convince my mom she should let me come over to your place instead. Or maybe I could ride home with her and then sneak out. I don't think she's going to—"

"No, that's okay." I sound harsher than I mean to. And then more just comes burbling out. "Go do what everyone else wants you to do. You're getting really good at that."

Germ is stunned for a moment. She opens her mouth to say something, but I never get to hear it. A wave of kids sweeps around us—a loud, chattering group we always said we didn't want to be a part of, and they start to tug at Germ. Bibi clasps a hand around her elbow, pulling her away, as Germ looks over her shoulder at me.

I don't know what to do. I just stand there and watch her disappear out the gym doors. My best friend looks at me once, with an unreadable face—an edge of anger and hurt—but she doesn't fight the current.

For the first time, a shocking thought has popped into

my head and is clinging there, tighter the more I try to push it away. *What if I'm not always Germ's best friend? What if I'm not even her best friend* right now? I've never even considered the possibility—it's like thinking, *What if this arm I've been using all my life to draw and write and brush my teeth with turns out not to be my arm?* And it makes me think of that feeling of having a big missing piece inside. And how if I miss Germ too, I'll be missing, like, three quarters of myself. I'll be, like, one quarter of a person.

I touch the scar on my palm. I worry the line where we once cut and promised each other to be blood sisters forever. But we're not really sisters. We're not stuck together like that—like family. Germ is not really my other half; she's someone who can drift away.

It's a feeling like a hole opening inside, the feeling of a stomach drop as you fall.

Even with what's happened the last few days, it might be the scariest thing I've ever felt.

All the way down the winding cliffside road, looking out at the sea and the sliver of moon above it, I'm thinking I was horrible to Germ and regretting it bitterly. But I'm also angry. I don't understand how anyone could be so excited about what everybody thought of their talent skit, when there are witches in the world.

Maybe it's better this way, I think. Better if Germ stays away so she doesn't get hurt. After all, it's me the Memory Thief is after. But jealousy still grips my heart, and as hard as I try, I can't imagine facing the scariest thing I've ever faced without the person I lean on the most.

As we pull into the driveway, I'm pulled out of my daze by a dazzling sight.

The trees. They're blinking.

Every tree lining our driveway, every tree in the woods surrounding our yard, appears to be alive with light. It takes me a moment to realize why: they are all covered in insects, including what looks to be thousands of fireflies.

"Mom," I whisper, "look."

My mom doesn't respond as we climb out of the car, though she, too, is staring at the trees.

In the air there's a hum, a buzzing from all directions—there are grasshoppers and dragonflies, spinning and flying through the air or gathered on trees, on bushes. Spiderwebs sparkle in the gleam of our headlights. And of course, there, kneeling in the center of the yard, whispering to a handful of regular moths (not the scary kind), is Ebb.

He turns to look at me, almost smiles. Then he gets up and floats in the other direction across the grass.

My heart pinches with regret, and confusion. I look at my mom, who has turned off the car and is still staring at the trees. For a moment I hope she can see the beauty, the way she used to see beauty in everything.

"We should call an exterminator," she says, and turns to head for the door.

Inside, Crafty Agatha knits away silently in her chair. I light a fire in the fireplace because Mom is shivering, but soon she shuffles off to bed without saying good night. I can hear her getting changed and ready for bed upstairs, and the ticking of the grandfather clock on the wall, but otherwise the house is quiet.

Then there is the smallest noise downstairs, a mutter.

I look toward the basement door, and Crafty Agatha speaks.

"He's here," she says. My stomach flops over sickly.

I stare at the door. I don't want to go down. But what choice do I have? I glance up the stairs and wish my mom could come with me. Then I cross the room, wincing at each sound of the floor creaking. I crack open the door, and pull the string to turn on the one dim lightbulb that hangs in the staircase.

Heart pounding, I take the first step down into the dimness. I'm a big giant pounding terrified heart with legs.

I can't see him at first. It's only when I've reached the basement floor and peered in all directions that I spot him in the corner, in the shadows beyond the glow of the light, his red eyes glowing like embers in the dark, his fingers rubbing against each other as if he's holding himself back from lunging for my throat.

"My basement," he says. "My space. My house, my house, my house."

I take two steps backward, but then shakily stand my ground.

"I need to ask you something," I say.

He stares at me, his lips moving as he mutters to himself, but I can't tell what he's saying.

"About the hospital. And the night I was born." Except for his twitching hands, he doesn't move, only watches me. "Were you there when the Memory Thief came that night?"

He stands for a moment longer as if frozen, and then a smile spreads on his face.

It sinks into my heart like a heavy stone. *He knows.* He knows something.

"Please tell me," I whisper. "How was I saved? What

was my mom's secret about the witches? Was it something that helped protect me?"

He chuckles softly to himself.

"Why do you hate us?" I whisper.

He stares at me a long time. "My house, not yours," he says flatly. "I hate anyone who lives in my house."

I stand there at a loss, searching my brain for a way to get him to talk—a way to pull out the secrets that are so close, I can almost taste them.

"But don't you hate witches, too?" I try. "Don't all ghosts hate the witches?"

He shrugs. "Witches are no business of mine. Only my house. MY house."

I look down at my fingers, thinking and thinking. And then it comes to me.

"What if I promised, once this is all over, that I'd figure out a way to get my mom to move out of this house?" To be honest, I'm not sure I can make this happen, but if I can fight the Memory Thief and break my mom's curse, it seems like moving would be the least of my worries.

The Murderer is silent a moment, as if considering, but then he shakes his head. "Don't think so. No. Don't think so at all. Don't believe a promise like that."

I look at him for a long time, and my eyes trail to the mark around his neck. A question pops into my mind.

"What did you do, that was so bad that they hung you? Why do they call you 'the Murderer'?"

In less than a second, the Murderer is moving. He zips toward me, and stops just within an inch of me, and across the room, the axe falls off the wall. His face is in my face, his red eyes boring into mine.

"GET OUT," he hisses.

I back away slowly, to the bottom of the stairs, then run up, taking them two at a time. I slam the door behind me, though I know doors don't help. And I try to catch my breath.

The Murderer is a dead end too.

CHAPTER 16

On Monday, two days till the dark moon, I skip school for the first time in my life. I convince my mom to cover for me. Turns out, it doesn't take much.

"I'll dial," I say, standing by her computer as she punches data from an enormous book of numbers onto her keyboard. "And then you just read this," I say. "Okay?"

Mom barely glances from the screen as she nods. "Okay," she says.

I lay a sheet of paper down in front of her that explains I won't be in today because I have a cold. And then I dial the phone. And though she sounds like a robot as she reads my script to the person who answers, she is polite and unmistakably, at least, my mother.

"Thanks," I say as she hangs up. I give her a kiss on the cheek, and she flinches.

I curl onto the couch with *The Witch Hunter's Guide*, and that is where I spend my morning, looking for anything I've missed.

I read "Secrets of the Earth and Moon," which gets increasingly stranger as I read.

> *There is a magical thread of connection through all things. Most people sense this even if they don't say it. Water, trees, grass, animals, insects, and people are tied together by it, each with gifts to share: water quenches the thirst of the trees, the trees shelter the animals, the animals are masters of motion and flight and song, and the people build worlds beyond what animals can dream. Even the moon has gifts to share—reflecting magical light for people to dream and hope by, its gravity steadying the earth on its axis.*
>
> *But the witches have begun to break this*

thread, their curses turning people to their
darker natures, causing them to forget, to take,
to grab at the world around them. They want
people to forget their connection to all the other
pieces of the world, and to magic itself.

If the witches succeed—and break the
thread that binds us—they can send the
moon and its goddess spinning off into
space. Without the moon, nights will
become unspeakably dark. The earth will
lose the rhythm of its tides. The weather
will grow wild. Witches will be undeterred
by moonlight. Untold chaos will reign on
earth. And people will forget, once and for
all, that they are connected to anything but
themselves. And we will all be lost.

I sit back, my heart sinking, feeling a deep sense of
dread. I think of how much Germ worries about what she
sees on the news. Are the witches and the world so ines-
capably tied? Is the world really in so much danger?

I flip back to the section on witches and find the Time
Witch—whom Ebb spoke of with such bitterness.

Revisiting Mom's drawing makes my skin prickle and

my hair stand on end. It shows a woman with a hungry mouth and sharp teeth staring out at the reader, dark black circles around her empty blue eyes, the pupils as tiny as pinpricks. She wears an old-fashioned black lace dress and a necklace of pocket watches, but it's her eyes that scare me most. They're deep, limitless, empty—like the eyes of a fish. The first time I looked through these pictures, it was the Memory Thief who struck fear into my heart—but now I feel relief that it isn't the Time Witch who wants me dead. There's a hunger to her and a malice and a deep empty coldness that makes the Memory Thief look meek in comparison.

I read the description of her.

The Time Witch: Most powerful of the witches, besides Chaos. She is catlike, loves to play games and gamble with people.

Curse: Manipulation of time.

Skills: Compresses, stretches, grows, and shrinks time. Makes weapons out of time. Makes people age too fast or takes away their

*ability to grow older. Makes happy moments
last less time and sad moments last more.*

*Familiars: Hummingbirds, distinguishable by
their empty blue eyes. They steal, distort, and
warp the time surrounding their victims.*

*Victims: A person cursed by the Time Witch
might age rapidly, or age in reverse. They
might lose entire years without knowing
it. Ghosts, fairly or unfairly, blame the
Time Witch for their own angst-filled
relationship with time.*

The shrill sound of the phone startles me, and chills race up my spine. I sit still, not answering, and wait for our ancient answering machine to pick up.

Germ's voice rings out after the beep. She must have finagled access to someone's phone at school.

"Rosie, it's me. If you're there, pick up?" I stay where I am, frozen. For some reason, I can't bring myself to pick up. I suppose it's a mixture of hurt and protectiveness. The more danger I find in the world of witches, the more I want Germ to stay away. And the more I think of Bibi, the more I want to hide from Germ.

"Why aren't you here today? I hope you're okay. I have stuff to tell you. I'll call you when I get home."

After she's hung up, I turn back to the book, and read the last few lines of the "Secrets of the Earth and Moon" section.

> If the grass and the animals and the trees
> have gifts, people have their own part to play
> too . . . their own gift.
>
> Imagination is a piece of the hidden
> fabric that only humans can wield.
> Imagining is to humans like flight is to
> birds. It is faint and invisible and hard to
> see at times, this gift—just a shimmer in
> the human heart. And it's the reason why
> witches have always hated and feared us. It
> is our deepest power.
>
> The hearts of witches are fearsome,
> and have been unstoppable for as long
> as time. But do not count out the human
> imagination. It's a whispering, quiet
> thing, easy to drown, easy to kill.

But it has a power that can destroy the
most terrible darkness.

I trace the words with my finger. I don't understand it, or what it could mean about how to fight.

But when I close the book, I'm convinced. The world needs witch hunters. It needs people like my mom—or who she used to be—who are brave enough to do what she did. I'm just not one of them.

I'm in my room at around three, staring at the walls and lost for what to do next, when I hear gravel crunching in the driveway and see Germ riding her bike up to the house. She must have raced over from her house as soon as the bus dropped her off.

I step back from the window, and listen to the sound of her feet as she clomps up the stairs and knocks. She waits, then knocks again. Upstairs my mom stirs, but she never answers the door if she can help it.

Germ walks around to the side of the house and taps on the parlor windows.

"Rosie," she calls up to my window, but I don't answer. "Rosie, are you here?"

I tighten my hands around the cover on my bed. I want to hurry downstairs and open the door, but I stop myself. I'm a swirl of confusing feelings—anger at her, guilt about being angry, wanting her to stay safe and away.

After a while, Germ yells again. "Okay, I'm going!" she yells. "But I left some stuff by the front door."

I hear her feet crunching across the gravel a few moments later, and step back to the window just in time to see her pedaling down the driveway and disappearing onto the trail that runs between her house and mine through the woods.

Once she's gone, I walk down the stairs, open the front door, and find a pile of papers held down by a rock. On top is a note in Germ's big, messy, greedy-for-the-page writing:

> Found some interesting stuff at school and printed it out. I figured sometimes the internet might know more than ghosts do. Hope this helps.

I take the pile inside and sit down on the sofa, sifting through what turns out to be mostly printed newspaper articles, all about—for some reason I can't guess at first—a man named Hezekiah Thomas. He lived in Seaport in the

1920s and was hanged following a strange and sad saga. I become more and more riveted as I read.

The saga begins with a woman named Helen Bixby, who moved to town when Hezekiah was twenty. He fell so in love with her that he learned carpentry and built her a house with his own hands as an engagement gift. Only, Helen Bixby turned him down and married someone else—and then lived happily with her husband just down the road, Hezekiah's only neighbors.

The tragic part comes next. One night, Helen— her husband away for work in the city—showed up at Hezekiah's house in a blizzard. She was having a baby and it was coming very early, and she needed help getting to the hospital. Hezekiah, seeing her outside and consumed with bitterness, ignored her cries at his window, the sound of her fists pounding at his door. He watched her wander away in the snow. Helen Bixby, I read on breathlessly, never made it to the hospital; she died in the snowstorm.

And then I come to the part that really makes me pause.

The articles indicate that no one would have been any the wiser about the terrible thing Hezekiah had *not* done if he hadn't—drunk on whiskey one night—confessed all of this to his brother, who turned him in. And he was hanged for his crime, though many said it wasn't a crime at all. One of the headlines of the articles reads: WHAT MAKES A MURDERER?

My arm hairs begin to prickle at the words.

I shuffle now, fast, through the articles until I come to one with a clear photograph, one that I can make out more easily.

There is the photo of Hezekiah Thomas. His eyes are fiery and full of anger. His skinny frame is coiled as if he'd like to lunge at the photographer. He is standing beside a beautiful white house, built by his own hands. *My* house.

I know him, of course. His face is only too familiar to me. He lives in my basement.

He haunts the hospital because he should have brought her there that night, I think. *He can't let the past go.*

I feel a small—just a tiny—prick of sadness for the Murderer. Clearly his guilt and rage have made him a monster.

The phone rings again; again it's Germ, and I don't answer. She calls a few more times, then gives up completely. As the afternoon fades into evening, the house is quiet again.

Watching the sun sink slowly in the sky, I feel a weight in my stomach—about the Murderer, about the witches, about my mom. All of this knowledge, and I'm no closer to really knowing anything that can help.

Is Ebb right in telling me I should go, leave, run away and never come back?

I walk to my closet and pull my orange backpack out. I start to think about what to take if I do leave—I lay aside a couple of books, some warm clothes, a bag of Twizzlers I keep in my drawer. I put it all in the backpack, just in case.

Downstairs I make dinner for my mom and me. The wind is blowing, but clouds only briefly cross the moon before they float onward. The sound of the wind whistles against the windows.

"Some say the wind is the goddess, trying to blow the world's troubles away," Crafty Agatha says abruptly, startling me. I hadn't realized dusk had arrived. "Sometimes it feels like she will never stop."

I follow her eyes to the window. I don't see—at first— the lonely, forlorn figure floating along the edge of the cliffs, surrounded by fireflies. But then my eyes and attention focus, and I realize I'm looking at Ebb. I bite my lip for a moment, then—suddenly decisive—pull my coat on, slip my trusty flashlight around my neck, and hurry outside.

I catch up with Ebb by the cliffside. The ghost of the rabid possum is out tonight, and he nips at my heels viciously as I walk, before he finally hobbles away. The wind is wild, whipping at the bugs and the grass and the trees, but Ebb doesn't seem to notice. Still, he's a lonesome sight.

When I reach him, he's talking to a grasshopper on a leaf.

"What are all these bugs doing here?" I ask flatly. I'm not the best at starting conversations. A *hello* would probably have been better.

He looks at me for a moment, and I worry, since I've been so rude to him, that he's going to ignore me. But he finally says, "They came to get a glimpse of you. Insects spread news pretty fast." He shrugs. "They came to see the girl they think is going to fight witches and save the world."

I shake my head. "One witch," I say. "And why do they care?"

Ebb takes this in, then looks down at the grasshopper again. "Animals, insects . . . they see the invisible world much easier than people do. Like, you know how dogs seem to be barking at nothing sometimes?" I nod. "It's not nothing. Anyway, animals hate witch darkness as much as anyone else does."

I watch him. "How do you talk to them?"

"It's mostly listening, really. When you're dead," Ebb says, "you can't make a sound that the living will hear. You learn to listen instead."

Ebb pulls his ghost spider out of his pocket, and gently pets the creature on the head with his pinkie I try not to stare.

"I don't understand," I say. "Like . . . what would a tree even *talk about*?"

Ebb shrugs. "Oh, I dunno, bird nests, the weather, wind, earthworms tickling their roots, what the soil tastes like on any given day, when their bark feels dry. Stone is the hardest to understand—very slow to say anything, pretty aloof, concerned with ancient news—volcanoes, floods long ago. Mosses are kind of interesting." He tilts his head thoughtfully. "Constant gossip about when it's going to rain. Nature's always talking, if you know how to hear it."

I think of what *The Witch Hunter's Guide* says about nature and magic, how it's all connected.

I look around, and my eyes settle on a small cedar tree at the edge of the property where the land plummets down to the sea. "And what's that tree saying right now?" I ask him, fighting back a smile, the first I have smiled in days.

"It just keeps pointing its branches to the water. All the trees in the yard do. Like they're trying to tell us something. But I can't figure out what."

Words rise into my mind. *He's out there swimming, waiting for me*, I think. But I shake the thought away.

"Have you had any luck," Ebb asks, "finding more clues?"

I tell him about the hospital, and the Murderer, and everything I've read in my book, and how none of it has led anywhere. The more I talk, the more my frustration and worry tumbles out.

"I still don't even know how a witch weapon works," I say. "I still have no idea how to find one. I'm completely defenseless, which means I'm no closer to finding out how to kill a witch."

The wind is blowing so hard, my hair keeps flying into my mouth as I talk. Ebb looks at me shivering, then up at the sky.

"Let's go somewhere away from the wind," he says finally. "I want to show you something."

Ebb leads me down the path that crisscrosses down from my high yard to the beach, winding through rocks and steep crags.

"Where are we going?" I say, looking up at the cliffs all

around us, feeling nervous the farther we get from home on such a wild night. Far above, the cloud shepherds are busy herding shapes of mist. Ebb's answer doesn't exactly reassure me.

"Better just see it when we get there. It'll sound too creepy otherwise."

Still, I follow, scrabbling clumsily down the steep rocky trail as Ebb floats easily ahead of me. We emerge onto the beach, at the edge of a cave Germ and I used to explore when we were younger.

He leads me to the lip of the rocky hollow, and we hurry inside out of the wind.

"Don't worry. High tide won't be for a while," he says. "If there's one thing I know now, it's the tides."

I turn my flashlight on and look around. It's a dismal place—dark and empty, musty, mildewed and forlorn. Ebb turns to me, looking almost embarrassed.

"Where are we?" I ask. But with a sick thud in my chest, my eyes light on something that gives me the answer before he can.

On the wall of the cave, just visible in the beam of my light, are words etched in stone: *Here on this day May the 5th, Robert Alby and his parents were taken by the tide.*

Ebb clears his throat. I realize, in a sudden flash, how a Robert might come to be known as an Ebb. How *ebb* is what happens when the tide goes out.

"This is where I died," Ebb says, looking everywhere but at me.

CHAPTER 17

"I used to use this place as my hideout, back when I was living. I called it 'pirate's cove.' I loved to come down here and look for fish and shells and sea critters. That was eighty-seven years ago. . . ." His voice trails off for a moment.

"The afternoon I died, I'd caught this spider in a match-box and named him Fred." He nods to his shoulder, where Fred is now perched as if listening raptly to us.

"It was such a hot lazy day. I didn't mean to fall asleep.

I just lay down on that ledge over there to rest my eyes for a few minutes, enjoy the coolness of the cave."

Ebb pauses a long time.

"I woke to cold water lapping all around me, the waves crashing in too fast and hard for me to escape. I screamed for my parents. I guess they were out in the yard above, because somehow they heard me. They tried to rescue me. But none of us made it out. Not even Fred." He reaches for his shoulder, and strokes the spider gently.

"My parents, they moved Beyond right away. One minute we were all waking up as ghosts, looking at each other, trying to understand what had happened. The next moment"—he looks up and out of the cave—"they were surrounded by pink sparkling dust, and then they were gone. I was left behind, stuck here on earth. That's how it is."

I feel such sorrow for Ebb. To spend eternity tied to this lonely hole by the sea and a house that used to be his. I want to say something consoling or kind. But as usual, the words don't come when I need them. Being quiet is a hard habit to break. When even your mom doesn't want to hear about you, you learn that your feelings have nowhere to go but in.

"I used to fantasize that I could learn from your mom—

to hunt the Time Witch. That maybe if I could hunt her, I could make her give my time with my parents back. But I've learned over the years—we ghosts hide from witches; we don't fight them." He hangs his head.

"Why do you think you didn't go with them?" I ask.

Ebb shakes his head. "I know it's different for every ghost. The Beyond, and what ties us here, is such a mystery. But I think . . . I caused something terrible to happen, and I need to cause something good to happen to make up for it—I've believed that for years." He dims and glows, like a ghost blush, as he looks at me. "I always thought if I could protect you, like I didn't protect my parents, maybe that would be it. But if anything, I helped get you in trouble in the first place. And also I just want you to be safe." He blushes again.

As he speaks, something catches my eyes in the dim moonlight that filters into the cave. Ghostly spiderwebs. Hundreds of them, sparkling in the moonlight like fine, delicate strands of silver. The webs are glowing—luminous webs made by a luminous, ghostly creature. They are beautiful and strange, delicate and miraculous.

But the strangest thing of all is that they've been— impossibly—spun into *words*.

*"Burp," went the bat. And out came
a galaxy, the inhabitants of which never
learned that the bat that burped them out
had ever existed.
"I'm Higgle Piggle, the Elf in the shoe,
and I'm going to give your breath back to you."*

"Hey," I say as a strange recognition slowly dawns on me. "Those are words from my stories."

Now Ebb practically turns supernova bright, a massive blush.

"I taught him," he admits, gently cupping Fred from his shoulder and depositing him at the center of one of the webs.

"Taught him my stories?"

Ebb glances away, embarrassed. "Yours, and lines from the books you read too. He likes the words. *I* like them too. They . . . help me."

"What do you mean?"

Ebb thinks for a long time, looking sheepish, before continuing.

He sighs. "All I know is, my afterlife was pretty glum until you showed up in the house. Even as a baby, you were quiet, but full of something *bright*. Then you got older and started writing your stories, and I read them over your shoulder. And . . . well . . ." He looks at me, at a loss as to how to explain. "There's so much to be afraid of," he goes on. "Even the world's sweetest, most innocent things are not safe from witch darkness. But your stories always made me feel like it was possible that everything could be okay somehow."

Now it's my turn to blush. I don't know what to say. I think of all the times the books in my room have helped *me* when I felt sad or lost, and to think that my stories could do that for Ebb feels strange, and good. I feel deeply embarrassed and warm inside. I reach out toward one of the webs, and just barely touch it. There is something so beautiful and delicate about it, fragile but strong somehow.

"I'm sorry for kicking you out of the house," I finally say. It's a big step for me.

Ebb nods. "It's okay. I understand."

"I guess we both just want our parents back," I say.

Ebb nods. "I want to be in the Beyond with mine, and you want to be here on earth with your mom."

"Tomorrow is only one more day till the dark moon," I say, turning glum.

Ebb looks at me for a long time. "I suppose you're not going to run," he says, sounding resigned.

I think of my packed backpack, then shake my head. I know in my heart I couldn't bring myself to leave, to give up.

Something seems to move across Ebb's face, some kind of choice being finally made. "Then . . . I have something else to show you," he says.

He moves toward the back of the cave, and gestures for me to follow.

"I'm sorry I didn't tell you before," he says. "But I wanted you to run instead of giving you false hope." He pauses and looks at me. "If you're staying, you're going to need it."

He leads me back deeper into the cave, to a little nook completely protected from the water, where only something smaller than a boy could fit. Then he turns to me very solemnly.

"I'm not the only person who used this cave as a hiding place. Someone else did too, many years after I died."

He nods me forward, and I look inside. I can't tell what's in there, so I pull it out. It is heavy in my hands.

"I don't know how it works," Ebb says in a warning tone.

I unwrap whatever it is from the bundle of cloth. And gasp.

It's a quiver full of arrows, and a bow, but it's also unlike any bow and arrows I've ever seen—like a weapon, but also something *more*. Each arrow is painted with tiny, exquisite scenes: forests and flowers and sunsets and dreamy landscapes. The bow, too, is covered in brightly colored depictions of rainbows and fields and mountains. The paint is faded, but I would recognize my mom's art anywhere.

And though I have no experience in these kinds of things, I realize what Ebb has been holding back.

And I know a witch hunting weapon when I see one.

CHAPTER 18

If my house is isolated, Germ's is almost impossible to find. It's not on GPS or any maps because it's not really supposed to exist. Her dad, when he was around, parked their mobile home there because the land was unclaimed and it didn't cost anything, and they just . . . stayed. It's like the house that isn't, tucked behind an old junkyard.

Tuesday afternoon, one day till dark moon, that's where I go, breaking my promise to myself about leaving Germ out of things.

I do this for two reasons: One, I can only stand not talking to Germ for so long; forty-eight hours is about the maximum. Two, if anyone can teach me how to shoot a bow and arrow, it's Germ, who never met a physical activity she wasn't great at. I once saw her do a front handspring in gym class, her heavy frame flipping deftly end-to-end, simply after watching someone else do it *one time*. She can ski backward. *I need her* for this. And, I reason to myself, it doesn't involve her fighting a witch, only her helping me figure out how to do it myself.

Above, the sky is so overcast, the clouds look like a wet soggy web. Worried that we could be in for a dark, moonless night, I bundle the bow and arrows into my backpack (they poke out the top, but I wrap them in an old towel) and climb onto my bike.

I steer into the woods—down the well-worn path between Germ's house and mine. As I ride, I keep thinking about last night and everything Ebb told me. I keep coming back to something he said about his death—that he feels like he was responsible for something terrible, and now he needs to do something good to rectify it.

It's not just the sadness of the story that clings to me. It's that it feels like it *means* something important, but I can't quite figure it out. The meaning is out of my reach, something that keeps slipping my mind.

A few dragonflies follow behind me as I go deeper into the woods. As I pull up at Germ's, I leap off my bike and lean it against the usual tree, and on second thought, tuck the bow and arrows behind the bike in case Mrs. Bartley is home from work early. (Usually she works till long after dinnertime.) Germ's brothers do sports after school and are rarely home before seven.

Germ thinks her trailer is shabby, but I've always loved it because it's overflowing with her and her mom and her loud and unruly brothers. Today the sight of it makes me nervous as I climb the stairs. Usually when I need to apologize but can't find the words, Germ says, "Let's pretend we already did this part," and all is immediately forgotten. But this—Bibi West and how Germ is changing and I'm not—is bigger than any fight. It's not something that can just go away. And that's something new.

I knock, and wait. After a minute the door opens and Germ appears. She looks unsure whether she's happy to see me. A hint of a smile flashes across her face, but then it moves aside for anger, and also, maybe, uncertainty.

The gulf between us feels wide. I wonder, with a feeling like an astronaut floating in space, if it might even be unfixable. I swallow the lump in my throat.

"I have something to show you," I say.

We are standing over the bow and arrows, which I've laid on Germ's bed.

She stares at them for a long time.

"Why're they painted?" she asks.

I shrug. "I don't know. *The Witch Hunter's Guide* . . . the women who hunted witches in my family, their weapons . . . they all involved beautiful things, music and embroidery and stuff. I guess it's connected to that somehow."

Germ takes it all in, looking hesitant. "Well"—she nods to the bow and arrows—"*does* it work?"

She looks at me. I look at her.

"You haven't *tried* it yet?"

"You know that if you don't help me, I'll end up hitting the nearest person within a mile and killing them."

Germ thinks on this, and nods. "That's true," she says. "But, Rosie, dark moon is tomorrow." She heaves a sigh. "You've got almost no time to learn."

"I don't have a choice," I say.

We go out into the yard, which is really just scraggly woods all around the trailer. Germ selects a big old dead oak tree as the target. Dusk is falling quickly. I hold out the bow and arrows to her to try first, but she shakes her head.

"You're the one who's good at this stuff," I say.

"But you're the one who needs to know how to hunt witches," she says.

"*Witch*, not *witches*. *One* witch."

Still, I guess she's right that it has to be me. At the same time, if all that's standing between me and a witch is my athletic abilities, well . . . I try to push the thought out of my mind.

Germ helps me get my stance right, back leg facing forward, front leg bent slightly to ground me, arms strong.

I'm pretty sure we both expect this to be the first of about a thousand tries to hit the tree.

But things do *not* go as we expect.

The arrow veers far wide of the tree—that much isn't surprising. It sails in the direction of Germ's brother's junky old car, which he saved all his money last summer to buy. It's going for the windshield or the hood or the front right tire, depending on how fast it spirals downward.

But as it's flying, something miraculous happens. A shimmer—a puff of something—appears, filmy and delicate but unmistakable, like the trail of exhaust you might see from an airplane. Only this is in a wave of colors and small, diaphanous shapes so exquisitely beautiful, so full of light, so warm and clear and sparkling that just looking at it makes something feel better inside you. The shapes are the shapes my mom has painted on the arrows; the colors are my mom's colors come to life—as real and unreal, at the same time, as ghosts. They shimmer in the air for a moment, then disappear.

I turn to Germ just in time to see the same look of awe on her face a moment before the arrow hits its mark, landing with a *thwack* in the car's front tire after all. There is a loud hiss as the tire loses air.

Germ says two things.

"Well, that was something."

And then,

"David's going to kill me."

We practice for two hours, until my arms feel like they're going to fall off and I can't feel the pads of my fingers. When I want to give up, Germ makes me practice some more while she runs little circles around the yard and picks up the spent arrows. We take a break for dinner, and then we start again.

For a while, the beautiful shimmering trail of color flies out behind the arrow each time, but it gets dimmer and dimmer. Soon, it stops appearing altogether, which worries me.

"Maybe witch weapons have to rest," Germ says.

By seven p.m., after about three hundred shots, I've hit the tree a total of four times. Still, three of those are in the last twenty tries, so I'm getting better. At this rate, if I practice all day again tomorrow, I should have a 20 percent chance of actually hitting the witch when she comes for me tomorrow night. As long as she stands as still as an oak tree, I guess. It's not great odds, I have to admit.

Finally, spent, we lounge on the metal landing outside Germ's front door, which all the Bartleys jokingly call "the veranda," and drink Gatorade. We are quieter with each other than usual. Sometimes when we lie out here, we pretend to talk with our feet, so not talking with our feet is another sign that something is off. I know we are both worried about our friendship, underneath all the other things we are worried about. And what I really want to say is that I just wish things could always be the way they have been for us. But I don't say that.

Instead I tell Ebb's sad story to Germ. I tell her about my failed conversation with the Murderer, and how I even thought of running away before Ebb took me to his cave last night.

"Do you think the arrows can really hurt the Memory Thief?" I ask, thinking out loud. "I mean, they just make a kinda weak puff of colorful stuff. Even if it's a magic puff."

"Puff the magic puff," Germ says listlessly. She's lying on the one decrepit, strappy outdoor chair, with her legs dangling over the arm. "Maybe it could, though. Maybe you just have to hit her one time. What if you get her with just one arrow, Rosie, and all your troubles are over?" I think about this, but it's too hard to imagine.

"I wish we knew where she was hiding," she goes on after a moment. "It's weird to sit and wait for you to be attacked."

Something nags at me.

"There's this giant piece missing," I say. "I still don't know what happened the night I was born. There's some big part of the whole picture that I can't see, and it's important. I know it is. The thing about someone out there swimming, waiting for her, and how it's tied to that night."

Germ nods slowly, thoughtfully. "And I guess that's the one thing the Murderer won't tell." She runs a hand through her thick blond hair. "He's not really the kind of person to do a good deed."

I loll a lazy, tired foot in agreement. And unbidden, my mind drifts back to Ebb—to the things he said about his parents, to his own wish to do a good deed to cancel out a bad one.

And I sit straight up.

"Unfinished business," I say.

Germ looks at me in surprise, confused. "What?"

"It's something Homer said about moving Beyond. And then Ebb was saying he feels like if he can just save someone—just one person—he can cancel out his guilt for what happened to his parents."

Germ squints at me, not quite following.

"What if it's the same for the Murderer?" I say in a rush. "What if, if he helps me by telling me his secret, he makes up for the person he didn't help? And what if that could let him move Beyond? Every ghost wants to move Beyond, more than anything else, don't they?"

Germ, catching on now, smiles.

"I've gotta talk to him," I say, standing up and moving quickly toward my bike, feet crunching in the dry leaves.

Behind me, Germ hurries to her bike too.

"You can't come," I say.

"It's just talking to a ghost," she says. "It's not mortal combat or anything."

And because Germ can be as stubborn as I can, I don't argue.

We pedal into the woods and ride for home, and the Murderer.

CHAPTER 19

When we get to my house, Ebb is just arriving for the night, floating across the lawn with Soggy and Crafty Agatha. Seeing us, he brightens and floats over.

Behind him, bugs are everywhere—swarming the trees, the grass, all over the tree trunks. There is such a huge number of them that I can hear the sounds of millions of tiny mouths devouring the leaves, the pitter-patter of thousands of minuscule feet, possibly even the sound of bug poop falling.

"What's with the bugs?" Germ asks as Ebb approaches us.

"They think I'm gonna fight witches and save the world," I say.

"Oh," Germ says flatly.

"We're looking for the Murderer," Germ explains to Ebb as he reaches us. "Is he here?

Ebb glances over his shoulder, and then looks back at us and shakes his head.

"He's not with us tonight. He went the other way."

I nod. "To the hospital?" I say. "We'll go find him there."

Ebb looks uncertain, then looks up at the sky. "I don't know if it's the best night to go looking for the Murderer or anyone else. So cloudy tonight, the moon is blocked. It worries me. What if . . ."

But I'm already climbing back onto my bike, because it's too important to wait. And before Ebb can finish, Germ and I are careening down the driveway and barreling onto Waterside Road.

"Be careful!" Ebb calls to us helplessly from the driveway, and I cast one look at him over my shoulder and nod before we vanish behind the trees.

Within half an hour we're on the lonely, woodsy road to Saint Ignatius. I've clipped my Harry Potter *Lumos* flashlight into a place I made on my handlebars to act as a headlight. Patches of fog roll by us as we ride north. Crickets and tree frogs sing from the trees.

Finally the broken-toothed silhouette of the hospital looms up ahead. Even Germ slows down at the sight, her feet going still on her pedals.

In the dark, with the magic fabric visible, the place is transformed.

The yard around the hospital is full to the brim with soldiers—young men in green uniforms, some in much older-looking blue ones, some missing arms or legs, some with bandages around their heads—too many to count. There are also nurses in old-fashioned dresses, doctors in old-fashioned attire, one doctor with a beard all the way to his waist. Scattered among them are a few other patients—women and men in civilian clothes, but not many.

The night is growing dark, but the gathering of ghosts casts a glow big enough to light the whole hospital. They all turn to look at us as we inch slowly toward them.

I scan the crowd for the Murderer, but my heart sinks—he's not in the outer yard.

I climb off my bike and slowly walk into the crowd of spirits, trying to look unafraid. Germ follows my lead. The crowd mostly parts for us. Some ghosts we walk through and others move aside. I hold my breath as we make our way in through the decrepit double doors.

The hospital is just as crowded inside. Germ and I thread our way down the halls, looking at every face to see if it's the right one, but no luck.

It's not until we get to the courtyard at the back of the building that we find him. He's alone, floating back and forth outside the windows of the maternity ward, muttering to himself.

Of course, I think. *Of course he wants to be near the mothers and babies.*

For a moment, we watch him through the window, scared to approach.

But then the Murderer turns, and his eyes slide to ours through the glass. He stops floating, and I go completely still with fear. His eyes flame up like coals as they lock on mine.

"I think I'm going to have to do the talking," I say to Germ.

Germ looks over at me and says flatly, almost in despair, "Well, then this will go well."

I lower my hands to grip the door, and step out into the courtyard. Germ follows.

The Murderer grins as we approach. His teeth glinting, he reminds me of a cat showing its jaws to a mouse before eating it.

I take a few steps closer, nonetheless. Behind me, Germ's breath is quick and nervous.

"Terrible night to be out," he says, looking up at the cloudy sky and smiling. "What brings you?"

I take a deep breath and blurt it out. "Helen Bixby," I say.

At the name, the smile slides off the Murderer's face. If he hated me before, his expression now holds something worse. Pure unadulterated rage.

I force my voice to leave my throat, to keep going.

"I think you have unfinished business, Mr. Thomas. And I'm hoping I can help you finish it."

He blinks at me, confusion for a moment dimming the coals of his eyes. I've caught his attention.

"I know you didn't help when you should have, and because of that, a woman and her baby died. I know that's why they hanged you."

He frowns now, rubbing his hands together agitatedly. Behind me, something falls. A bust from the hospital roof.

Germ jumps closer beside me, but for some reason I don't budge. I am too close to everything to be turned away. My heart pounds in my chest. I have to convince him. Convincing him is everything.

"I think once, a long time ago," I say, "you didn't help someone, and it cost everything. And I think that now . . . you have a chance to help me, by telling me a secret. And maybe it will set you free."

I look up at the sky. Even on a dark, cloudy night, the pink haze of the Beyond swims above, dim but there. The Murderer, I notice, looks up too. And if it's not just my imagination, there is longing in that look.

"I need to know what saved me that night. What secret my mom had, to protect me from the Memory Thief. How those things are linked to the sea."

He looks down at me, and his frown is now a sad, lost kind of thing. But then he begins to quake with anger, and another stone bust falls from the hospital roof. This time Germ and I both have to dodge to avoid it.

"You can't save Helen Bixby and her baby anymore," I push on. "But I think you can save me and my mom."

"You don't know that that will move me Beyond," he says. "Nobody knows that. The Beyond does not make promises, or spill its reasons."

I hesitate. I know he's right. And yet, it also feels like

JODI LYNN ANDERSON

this has to be the moment his afterlife has been waiting for. I just don't know how to convince him.

He looks around. "You and your mother took my house. It's MY house."

"I didn't know it was yours," I whisper apologetically.

His angry quaking slows, but his eyes remain hateful.

I cast about for anything else to say. "This has to be what you've been waiting for. Two lives lost, two lives saved. It evens out. It all makes sense."

He blinks at me for a moment, and strangely everything seems to change. He looks at me, then Germ, then back at me. Suddenly, inexplicably, he laughs.

"Two," he says, then laughs again. "Two lives."

Something about the way he says it makes me feel knocked off balance. He's laughing at what I don't know, and it scares me.

"You were a quiet baby," he says after a moment, turning serious.

I wait.

"It's what saved your life that night," he goes on. "Not any great secret. Not any discovered power."

I blink, wary now, worried. "What do you mean?"

The Murderer shakes his head. He looks up at the sky again, straightens up again. Now he looks solemn.

"They came for her that night," he says begrudgingly. "And they came for the last of the Oakses."

I stare hard at him, chills rising on my arms. The weather is changing, but I barely register it. It's getting colder, the fog thicker.

"*They* who?" I ask. "The Memory Thief? Who else?"

The Murderer goes a little dim, maybe the tiniest bit of fear crossing his face.

"*Two* witches," he says. His eyes widen at me. "*The Memory Thief. The Time Witch.*"

Confused, I'm trying to think what to ask next. But the Murderer goes on, unprompted.

"And they took *him*," he says. "That is the only secret, nothing else. No great power or discovery or secret protection."

Looking at him, I think he must have spoken wrong, but the hair on the back of my neck begins to prickle. Germ, on instinct, reaches for my hand and grasps it.

"Him *who*?" I ask, barely above a whisper. The woods all around us seem to have gone silent. The crickets and tree frogs that were roaring at our arrival are quiet. The moon has disappeared.

"*Three* lives, not two," he says. "And they took *one* to the bottom of the sea."

"I don't understand," I say, shaking my head. I can feel the blood draining from my cheeks. I feel like I'm slipping down a slope with nothing to grab to stop my fall, because of something that has always been *not there*. A missing piece of me. A second half. It all flares up like something my heart knows but doesn't know the contours of.

Beside me, Germ has gone so pale, her freckles float on her skin like in a bowl of milk.

The Murderer just stands there, ruminating, looking up at the sky, distracted. "They took him," he repeats. "Dropped him in the ocean, I guess."

"Him who?" I press. "Dropped *who*?"

He turns to look at me, as if just now remembering I'm there. "Your mother only had time to hide one of you. *He* was crying; you weren't. They never knew there were *two*." His shoulders sag as if in release, or surrender, or both. And then he says the only thing that really matters. "Twins."

Now the sound in the trees is growing louder. Leaves flutter. Insects begin to chirp, hum, and cry. The woods are agitated about something.

But I can only focus on what the Murderer has said. From the moment I hear the words, I know it's true, and a howl rises in my heart.

And then the Murderer cocks his head, as if listening intently to something. Whatever he hears, it makes him turn his face sharply to the woods, and then the sky, and then to me.

"She's coming," he says.

"Everybody, leave here.

"Leave now.

"Run."

CHAPTER 20

Above, a flock of birds takes sudden flight, and flees across the horizon. In the trees, squirrels scurry and leap from branch to branch, all headed in the same direction—*away*. We stand watching them, frozen.

"Um, that can't be good," Germ says.

But I can't think about what I see around me. All I can think about is the word "twins."

"Rosie," Germ says, looking up at the sky, "we have to go. We have to get home. Your bow and arrows . . ."

Germ yanks on my arm, and after a moment I fall into step behind her. But as we launch into motion, I turn my head back to look once at the Murderer. Something strange is happening to him. He is holding out his hands, staring at them. A pink, sparkling dust has appeared around him. He looks at me and lets out a laugh.

This is the last glimpse I have of him—surrounded by sparkling dust and rising slowly from the ground as Germ and I turn away and race across the hospital lawn.

I don't have time to wonder about his fate. I only run.

We're on our bikes within seconds, standing on our pedals and thrusting up the hill. It's so dark, we can't see more than ten feet ahead of us, and that's only thanks to my flashlight.

Heart pounding, iron taste in my mouth, I look up at the sky. If there's a witch out there, it's too dark to see her. I scan the darkness of the trees. I look for the sliver of the moon to show from behind the clouds.

"It's too early," I say to Germ as we pedal. "It's not time. She can't be coming."

Germ casts me a doubtful look as we chug our exhausted legs up the incline. "I think maybe she's going to take a chance," she says.

We take a shortcut past the edge of town, soaring downhill. Germ is like lightning on her bike, but she keeps slowing to wait for me. It occurs to me for the millionth time that she's much more of a fighter than I am.

"Strange weather," someone calls out to us as we pedal past the convenience store. "Be careful, guys."

And they're right. Up ahead, lit from below by the lights of town, clouds are gathering very fast beyond the trees, in the direction of my house. I don't like those clouds. And then, as we round the bend onto the beginning of Waterside Road, something happens that makes my heart falter. A luminous moth flutters past my face, just barely missing me. I watch it flap past—its iridescent, pattern-shifting wings are unmistakable. Germ and I exchange a panicked look.

A few minutes later, another slaps against my handlebars and tumbles off into the air.

The closer we get to home, the more memory moths fly out of the dark at us. We're riding so fast, they only graze us as we whip past them.

We cut left, into the woods, onto one of our shortcuts. Branches slap at our faces, snag and tear our clothes, but we don't slow down. I follow Germ's eyes up to the sky, and gasp. A blanket of magical moths is headed in the same direction as we are. There are thousands now. Some drift down through the canopy of the woods like snowflakes at the beginning of a blizzard.

My legs feel like they're on fire, my lungs about to burst. The woods have started to look familiar now. This tree, that boulder—we're close to home. But then we burst out into the open clearing of my yard. I skid to a halt in the grass and tumble off my bike in shock.

I feel rough hands pulling me up, Germ yanking me to my feet as I gape.

My house is no longer my house. It is covered, every inch, in fluttering, squirming, shimmering moths. Moths blot out the sky and cover the lawn.

In the woods, panicked grasshoppers and fireflies, spiders and crickets and dragonflies, swarm out from the trees and circle the roof.

A flash of light zips back and forth across the lawn, and I see it's Ebb.

From somewhere inside, there's the sound of glass shattering—and a moment later a cloud of moths bursts out through one of the windows. Roof shingles fly across the yard. The front door, as we watch, comes flying off its hinges as a swarm of moths explodes out from behind. The ghosts of the house have scattered onto the lawn, confused and terrified. Crafty Agatha is swirling in circles, uncertain where to go. The washerwoman ambles past us into the woods. So much for my booby traps.

And then I hear a bloodcurdling scream from inside the house.

As I run toward the sound of my mom in terror, she appears in the doorway, hair in a million directions, clutching her heart.

"Mom!" I scream, and run toward her.

And then I see . . . out above the ocean, perhaps a mile away, a shape is coming toward us. It glows purple against the dark.

"Inside!" I yell, unable to think of anything else. But as we turn toward the house, a cyclone of moths, spinning wildly in circles, barrels into the side of the house, and— with a sound like ripping and then a deafening crash—the whole front wall of my house comes crashing down.

We turn to look at the sky. The shape is now close enough to make out, closing in on us fast. The clouds are gathering low behind it.

It's a chariot, streaking across the sky toward us, but it's made of moths, thousands of them all flying together in unison. And holding on to the reins is a figure all in black. She has one hand in the air, and moths gather around her hands like a flame.

The Memory Thief.

"*She's* the *weakest* witch?!" Germ yells. The sound of moth wings is deafening now. My mom cowers by the front door of the house.

I swallow, and turn my attention to the rubble falling around me, my hands shaking. I have to find my bow. Right now.

I pick up bits of rock and splintered wood and throw them aside. *You can find it, sweetie*, I think. *Just focus, focus, focus.* As I do, bugs swirl through the air like a tornado.

Each time I glance over my shoulder, the chariot looms closer and larger, and I feel so scared I think I might vomit. The bow is nowhere to be found.

But just as I'm about to fall back in despair, I spot it: the corner of the top of one of the arrows. I lunge at it and free the bundle from the debris piled on top of it.

Around us, the clouds are moving faster, and for a moment I catch a glimpse of a strange shape in the mist across the grass, before I turn away.

My eyes on the sky, I try to fit the arrow onto the string, but I can't get my fingers still enough to do it. Suddenly Germ is beside me. She grabs both of my hands, hard and steady, and looks at my face.

"You can do this," she says.

But Germ is a terrible liar. I can see by her eyes that she's not sure at all.

Still, I manage to steady my hand enough to fit the arrow.

The witch is descending toward us.

I want to shoot, but I know I need to wait until she's close enough. As close as the oak tree in Germ's yard.

She comes. And comes. And comes.

She is so close now, I can see her sad, longing eyes. She grins at me.

And then, when the distance is right, I let the arrow fly.

At first, it looks to be far off the mark; it arcs up as if it's going to go clean over her head. But then, on its way down, I see it. It is going to hit. It sails downward, picking up speed, and I can't believe it, but it's headed right at her, trailing colored beams of shapes behind it.

Germ grabs my arm. The shot hits its mark.

And then sails right through her and out the other side. Without even slowing her down.

The wind whips as the chariot reaches the ground, and the Memory Thief leaps out—cast in the glow of ghosts circling the yard. She floats toward me with her arms outstretched, her feet zipping across the ground.

"Come with me, little one," she says. "Come forget with me."

I stumble backward, but not before she reaches my shoulder with her hand—just the tip of her finger. I feel her touch, and with it, a deep frozen chill.

The witch slows in the air for a moment. Then the moths around her swarm directly at me, barreling through the bugs surrounding me.

They land on my shoulders, my face, my ears.

Forget, they seem to whisper through my skin—*forget*. I sink down onto the grass, not because I can't stand, but because I don't remember why I should. Beside me, Germ is yelling something, but I don't know what.

Memories float in my head: drinking Gatorade with Germ on the veranda, Bibi West looking at me at the Fall Fling. Each vision rises up and begins to sparkle like dust, then disappears.

And then the moths are knocked back. The wind is whipping. Patches of fog blow toward the trees. It's unmistakable: shapes loom in and out of the fog, though I can't make them out.

The Memory Thief takes several stumbling steps backward. And just as the clouds part far above to reveal the last sliver of moon in the sky, it dawns on me: *The cloud shepherds are helping.*

A stream of dim white moonlight falls down onto the lawn. The Memory Thief lets out a cry, stumbling backward and shielding her face. With a howl of rage she reaches out for the figure nearest her—Crafty Agatha. A cluster of moths swarms Agatha as she screams. A moment later, the moths fly apart—and Agatha is gone.

Across the grass, Ebb lets out a cry.

The Memory Thief leaps onto her chariot, which lifts up and into the sky, and shoots into the air like a star. In another moment, she's beyond our sight.

I lie on the grass, paralyzed for the moment. My head turned to the side, I gaze at the clouds lingering just at the edge of the field—the strange, misty faces looming out of them, looking at me, almost beckoning me. I can hear Germ and Ebb talking to me, but it's like they are far away. I can only focus on the cloud shapes as they float toward the edge of the trees.

I sit up slowly, and look back toward the house at my mom, then up ahead, at the strange patch of foggy cloud. This may be the only chance I will ever get.

I find the strength to stand. And then, I run. I chase the cloud shepherds into the woods.

CHAPTER 21

The thinnest sliver of moon shines down through the trees. I've been walking for a long while, though I've lost track of time. I only know I've wound my way far from the sound of the ocean and deeper into the woods.

A few memory moths flutter along behind me. Every time one flutters close, my shoulder—where the Memory Thief touched me—aches, and so does my mind. But soon I've left them behind. I think I may be cursed, but only just barely, if that's possible.

The patch of cloud that floats ahead of me acts strangely. Whenever I speed up, it does too, and whenever I slow down, it too slows. It *wants* to be followed, but at a distance, it seems. So one after the other, the cloud and I snake our way through the trees.

I'm tired and my feet hurt and my heart feels heavy. And though I'm determined to keep up with the cloud, with every step, I'm thinking about only one thing: *I had a brother.*

Small mysteries click together, now making sense— my feeling of missing a second half, my mom's long days of staring out the window at the sea. *He's out there, swimming. Waiting for me.*

The Murderer said that's where they took him and dropped him in.

And there is one thing I know now, most of all: it was never some powerful secret that saved me at the hospital that night, not any key to undoing witches. It was a mistake. *I* should have been taken, not him.

This is the thought that makes my feet as heavy as lead. I have to force myself to keep going or I'd curl into a ball and never get up.

Soon I can hear the ocean again, louder and louder, and I know I must be getting close to the shore. It's mistier here. The wet air tickles my face, and I squint to see the cloud ahead as it blends with its surroundings.

And then I take a step and nearly fall over as my stomach drops out from under me. I am standing on the edge of a cliff overhanging the sea.

I jerk back and steady myself. The cloud has disappeared ahead of me into the fog. I can't follow any farther.

My hope faltering, I call out, "Hello?"

Nothing but stillness. I begin to panic.

"Please come back!"

Nothing.

I sink down to sit at the cliff's edge.

Don't give up, sweetie, I think.

But the truth is, I give up.

I stare down at the ground between my knees for a few minutes, thinking I'd rather be a blade of grass, an ant, a speck of dirt—anything but a girl who can't save her mom, a twin with a missing half. I've tried my best and accomplished nothing. I've only found more trouble than I started with.

And then I feel a tickle of moist air on my cheek, and look up.

The cloud is hovering inches away from me.

I see a face loom out of it, made of mist—a round face that disintegrates and rearranges into a long and thin face, then into a bushy-browed face, and then it has no eyebrows at all. But every face appears to be a kind one. It smiles at me gently again and again as it changes.

And then a sound weaves through the mist, as if several threads of voices are joining together at once.

"Chin up," it whispers.

The face keeps changing—one minute old, the next minute young.

"Are you a cloud shepherd?" I ask.

"We are we." The voices gather and whisper.

Now the bushy eyebrows are back, over a bulbous nose, and another gentle smile.

"Cloud shepherds don't save people," I say. "But you saved me. Why?"

"We've watched you. We watch everyone. And we took pity. We know you are weary, young witch hunter."

I shake my head. "I'm not a witch hunter. But can I ask you some things?"

"We will answer what we can."

"Did my mom discover a great secret to finding and fighting the witches, or not? Is there any chance my brother is alive? Why didn't my weapon work?" The questions come out in a rush. I can't help it.

The cloud frowns. There is a long silence.

"We're afraid we don't know your brother's fate."

My heart sinks.

"But we can tell you a story. It begins with a lost item. Found by a man. Given to a woman."

I wait breathlessly.

The cloud dissipates, and the face disappears completely. A moment later, a shape rises up before me—a girl, about twelve years old—all made of mist. I know instantly that it's my mom.

Figures appear all around the girl, and by the way they circle and float, I can see they are ghosts. I smile. It's my mom seeing ghosts, and talking to them.

The girl grows. She's now a young woman, climbing aboard a ship. Setting off to search for witches, I guess. A few miniature clouds float in and out of the scene, high above her, with kind eyes watching her.

The clouds rearrange themselves again and again, to show my mother climbing a mountain, walking the edges of a snowy field, walking into villages, talking to people (though I can't hear the words), sleeping in a doorway in the rain—no doubt searching for witches and their secrets. The moments rise up and then drift out of sight. My heart swells with pride in the person my mom used to be.

And then a beautiful ship rises up out of the mist, and

my mom—a grown woman—stands at one of the rails. Across the deck, a figure watches her. A fisherman with a kind, familiar face. My heart flutters because I know this face by heart, even from photos. This is the moment she meets my dad. I reach my hand out and let it drop as it moves through nothing but mist.

The picture vanishes. The face of the cloud shepherd smiles at me again.

Another scene rises up, just briefly. It's my dad, pulling in his nets near a shore.

"Once," the cloud shepherd says, "each of the thirteen witches was given a special whistle—forged for them by the Time Witch to help them travel into the past. The Memory Thief, forgetful as she is, lost hers one night. And your father found it in his nets."

In the scene, my dad stares at something strange and small caught in the ropes of his fishing net. Then the scene vanishes, and another appears.

Now my dad is leading my mom down to a beach under a misty full moon. He opens his hand to her, and shows her what he's found, and my breath catches in my throat. Even in the mist I recognize it. It's the whistle I stole long ago from my mom's room, with the shell engraved on it. The one that sits on my shelf back home.

"How did he know about magic, if he didn't have the sight?" I ask.

"Love gave him the sight," the cloud shepherd whispers. "Love can sometimes make us see what our loved ones do. And so, he gifted her with the magical item he had found. And it changed everything."

I watch as, in the scene, my mom holds the whistle to her lips, and blows. And something rises out of the water. An enormous shape emerges from the waves.

My legs go weak. I take a deep breath.

This is the secret my mom found, I realize, my heart knocking around inside me. *She was never talking about my dad waiting for her, swimming in the sea. She was talking about something else entirely.*

There are three things that I know at once are true:

The sea really does contain the past.

The witches are hidden in it.

And now I know how my mother planned to reach them.

I don't know I'm crying until the face of the cloud reappears, and reaches out a hand of mist to touch my cheek, and smiles sadly at me.

"My dad drowned at sea," I say. "He's never coming back, is he? I thought before, it might be him in the sea, but no. He's gone Beyond."

The face is blinking at me, watching me with concern and kindness. It nods.

"Does he still watch over me, even though he's gone?" I ask.

"That mystery is the beating heart of the world," the cloud whispers. "Even *we* don't know."

I pull my knees up to my chest and wrap my arms around my knees, feeling small.

"Why did my mom's weapon fail?" I ask.

"Simply because each hunter has to use her own weapon, not someone else's. A weapon has to be just yours, and its power is limited only by the boundaries of your own heart."

I take this in. It's something I should have figured out, from reading *The Witch Hunter's Guide*.

"And what's *my* weapon?" I ask.

The cloud seems to shrug.

"Just take your *gift* and combine it with a weapon close to your heart. That's all."

"I'm not really *gifted* at anything," I say. "Just making things up."

The cloud smiles at this, as if I've said something incredibly silly. "Here's what we've seen people make up: Skyscrapers. Countries. Cures. Ships that fly to the moon.

It took a dream to make the first house. The first language. Made-up things make the world." An arm of mist reaches out as if to pat my head, and though I can't feel it, the gesture feels nice inside. "Imagining is a little like the opposite of witches, don't you think? To stretch and grow beauty from nothing at all?"

I am silent for a moment, at a loss.

"I don't think I can figure it out, or do any of this, on my own," I whisper.

"You are not alone," the cloud whispers. "Don't you realize that now? The past and the ghosts and the trees and the bugs and the animals and the moon and the hum of things—that you are connected to all of it?"

The face scrunches up a little bit and shifts this way and that, looking around, then smiles at me. "It's going to rain."

And then, without warning, the face disappears, and the rain falls down around and onto me from above.

And I sit staring out at the sea, legs dangling, like I'm staring off the edge of the world.

CHAPTER 22

I'm trudging home through the darkness just before dawn, shivering cold, finding my way by following the shore, when it reaches me—the sound of quiet voices singing something beautiful and sad, but not in any language I've ever heard. The closer I get, the more certain I am—it's coming from home.

Around me the woods are quiet as if listening too. And when I make my way out of the trees and into the clearing of my yard, I find what seems to be every ghost within a five-mile radius, including every ghost from the historic cemetery, joined together in the song.

I see Germ across the yard. When she sees me, she runs across the grass and tackles me in a tight hug. She is covered in dirt and bruises, and her hair puffs out like a tangled mane. I'm sure I don't look so great myself.

"Is my mom okay?" I ask.

"We're all okay," she says. "Your mom's asleep in a pile of clothes and blankets I made in the kitchen. She doesn't have any idea what happened, really. She thinks it was a tornado." She nods back over her shoulder to where Ebb and Homer are sitting together on a log across the yard. "Ebb went to get Homer, but he and the others were already on their way."

She looks at me, waiting to hear what happened in the woods. When I hesitate, she presses.

"Did you catch the cloud shepherd?"

I nod.

"Did it tell you anything important?"

I look at her for a long moment. And then I shake my head. This may be the first lie I've ever told Germ, even with a nod or a shake. But I'm thinking of the whistle, and the shape that rose from the waves. And I decide, I will keep my mom's great secret a secret for now. The witch I'm after is here on earth, hiding somewhere in the now. And that's my only concern.

I look around me at the spectacle of hundreds of ghosts gathered on my lawn. "What are they singing?" I ask. I see that Homer and Ebb are now floating toward us.

"It's a song for Crafty Agatha," Germ says, turning solemn as she follows my eyes. "I guess it turns out that when a ghost is killed by a witch, it's forever. No going Beyond. She's just"—Germ looks down sadly—"been turned into nothing."

Floating up beside her, Homer shakes his head. "We're singing to the moon, in a language even the earth can understand, to mourn her. We're mourning that witches exist at all."

I think of Crafty Agatha, who never bothered or hurt anybody. And my heart fills with rage at all that the witches have done. What could the world be like without them? What if their ugliness and greed were *not* just an inevitable thing? I guess that question is what sent my mom wandering across the earth looking for ways to destroy them in the first place. For once, I can imagine what compelled her so strongly to go.

"Does the singing help?" I ask.

Homer tilts his head thoughtfully. "I don't know why

it helps to just share how we feel, and to sing something beautiful at the darkness, but it does." He clears his throat and wipes a small tear from the corner of his eye.

"How are *you* feeling, my dear? I hear you were touched by the witch?"

"Just barely." I think about the strange sense of memories being lost, yet still leaving their mark on my heart. I think of my mom and how it must feel for her, to have it go so much deeper. "I feel a little . . . empty in places?" I admit.

"You must have the smallest graze of a curse, but manageable," he says. "The moths may pilfer a memory or two here and there if they can get close to you. But you got very lucky, considering." He looks at me a long time, sympathetic.

"Ebb told me what you learned from the Murderer," he says sadly.

I swallow. "Do you think my brother could still be alive?" I ask.

Homer hangs his head gently. Clearly he does not want to give the answer he believes.

"I'm hoping you've put the Memory Thief on the defensive for now. I'm hoping she'll lie low for a while, lick her wounds. She's not used to being defied, and it must terrify her—even if your weapon didn't hurt her. Now that we know the risks she's willing to take, she could return at any time when the moon is obscured. And now that we are dealing with, well . . ." He takes a deep breath.

"To anger the Memory Thief is a terrible thing. But to trick and tangle with the Time Witch . . ." His voice trails off. "The Memory Thief is a force to be reckoned with, but the Time Witch is something else entirely. Some say she's the worst witch of any of them, besides Chaos. If she hasn't heard about you yet, she soon will, and she will be angry. She will play with you like a cat plays with a mouse. She's twisted. Unpredictable." He clears his throat. "It would be madness not to go into hiding now. Obviously"—he nods to the shambles of my house—"you have no choice. I know a ghost in Arizona, in Coronado Cave. She can take you in at first, and help you figure out your next move."

Beside me, Ebb is very quiet. I keep shooting him looks, but he only stares down at his feet.

"We can stay at my house so you can get some rest before you go," Germ offers. "My mom won't mind. We can tell her it was a tornado that hit your house. Would that be okay?" She looks to Homer.

"Well," Homer says, "I think the Memory Thief will be too rattled to return right away, even on a dark moon. I'd give yourself a day, maybe two, to get ready. And then I'd leave as soon as you're able."

"And your mom can stay with us as long as she needs," Germ says.

"Sun's coming up soon," Ebb says sadly, looking at me.

"Oh yes," Homer agrees, looking out at the horizon for the first pink rays of the sun as they snake, just barely, their fingers above the line of the sea.

And a moment later, something strange begins to happen all around us. Tiny, glowing spirits of bugs that were killed in the fray, crushed by falling walls and pummeled against trees—fireflies and dragonflies and crickets and ants—begin to float up from the ground, all tiny luminous ghosts rising and surrounded by sparkling pink dust.

"What's happening?" I ask Ebb, leaning close to him.

"Their spirits are going Beyond," he whispers back.

And now I know for certain, this is what was happening to the Murderer, too. He was moving on.

I lean back and watch in awe as they lift off—hundreds of them, rising into the sky. It is a beautiful, triumphant, and sad thing. I don't want them to go, but I also know they are going to a place where they belong. It's comforting because it makes me feel like the broken things of the world have a place after all, and that they get put back together again somewhere else.

Ghosts begin to trail away to their graves as the morning arrives. Ebb and Homer wave before departing.

Germ and I watch the last of the ghosts of bugs rise into the dawn—a beautiful glowing ballet of tiny spirits.

And I don't believe that any witch darkness could blot out the beauty of them rising.

CHAPTER 23

If Germ Bartley is a force of nature, her mother is a gentle breeze.

Mrs. Bartley is shorter than Germ and rail thin, and is always looking for someone to split a piece of toast with her because she can't eat the whole thing (which Germ finds agonizingly funny). She has impeccable manners, but when it comes to defending Germ, she's so fierce that all the teachers at school are scared of her. She's also no fool—but because she can't imagine Germ ever lying to her, she believes just about everything Germ says. One time Germ and I ate all the ice cream out of the freezer, and Germ told her we must have been sleepwalking, and Mrs. Bartley read a bunch of books on sleepwalking and made Germ do a hypnosis program to break the habit.

So when Germ tells her, after the three of us drag into the driveway of the trailer Wednesday morning, scraped and bruised and disheveled, "Rosie's house was destroyed by a small tornado," she believes us immediately. And when she calls the police, she tells them the same.

A thin layer of ice forms on the puddles in the yard, and icicles dangle from the eaves of the trailer. The trees beyond the junkyard are all covered in a layer of frost that sparkles in the sun.

We are interviewed and poked and prodded by three police officers, an insurance agent, and two medics. If they are concerned by the way my mom barely remembers what happened, they attribute it to the shock.

Of course, after inspecting my house and yard for themselves, they believe it was a tornado too. How else could all that destruction be explained? At one point I do float the idea that something else did it, just to test one more time if there's any hope for help from any adults at all.

"Do you have any police tactics for handling, um, supernatural forces?" I ask. But the policewoman just blinks at me a moment and then has paramedics come to double-check my pupils to see if I'm concussed.

Germ's brothers hover around us, bringing us juice and applesauce and peanut butter toast because that's what they know how to make. It's a nice break from how they usually just torment Germ by licking all the sweets in the house to claim them for themselves. Eventually Mrs. Bartley shoos them outside because it's too crowded. Germ and my mom and I take turns taking showers. Washing the grime off, I want to cry, to think I'm washing away the particles of *my house* and how I may never see it again.

"You and your mom stay as long as you need to," Mrs. Bartley says to me once we've settled in, squeezing my arm. "We love the company." I try to ignore that she's shouting it over the din of Germ and her brothers bickering.

We sleep half the day, exhausted. My mom is established on the couch that night, though she spends most of the dusk outside, staring through the trees in the direction of the sea. Does she remember my brother with the same muscle memory I hope she remembers me with? Or is it the other thing, the rising shape in the waves that the cloud shepherd showed me, that she is thinking of? Is it both?

I have brought my orange backpack, and Germ keeps slipping things into it that she thinks I might need if I run.

"Your mom can stay with us as long as she needs," Germ says as she tucks a pack of tissues into the front pocket, a compass she nicked from one of her brothers into the flap at the front, money for a train ticket she's taken from the savings she keeps rolled into her pillow. "We'll look after her. My mom'll make sure the insurance company handles things. *I'll* make sure nobody sends your mom away. Don't worry about that, Rosie."

I make my bed up on the floor of Germ's room, occasionally glancing out the window at the moonless night. What if Homer's wrong and the Memory Thief does come back tonight, not "licking her wounds" after all? How long would it take for her to find me here?

Germ puts a sleeping bag beside me. When we have sleepovers, neither of us sleeps on the bed. Out of habit, Germ switches on the news.

We listen to the sounds of everyone else going to bed, including my mom. And then we lie in silence in our sleeping bags, staring at the ceiling while the news drones on in the background.

"I think the witch took some memories of us. I don't know—there's just some hollow places in my head."

Germ smiles. "There's always been hollow places in your head," she teases.

"Remember when we used to build little frog hotels out of logs?" I say, after a long silence. Germ nods.

"I still remember that," I say.

For a long time again, we don't say anything. I'm thinking about what the cloud shepherd said about my weapon needing to be my gift. But my mind keeps wandering.

"Do you think, if I leave, Bibi will be your best friend?"

As I say it, I realize what I'm hoping for. I'm hoping Germ will say, *Of course not! I could never have a best friend besides you!* But Germ only sighs. "You're both my friends," she finally says.

"Well," I offer slowly, uncertainly, "it's just maybe you feel like she gets you better now than me anyway . . . now that we're older," I say. This is as close as I've come to telling Germ my true feelings about things, and my heart pounds.

Germ, exasperated, sits up, cross-legged, her face flushed as she looks at me. "It's true, there are pieces of me Bibi *gets* that you don't. And there are a LOT of pieces of me that you get that *she* doesn't." She glances at the TV, and then at the ceiling, then at me, at a loss. "I'm changing. I can't help it. I know you've never really wanted to grow up, or change, or make new friends. I sometimes think maybe it's because you never got to really be a kid, with your mom and everything. Or maybe it's that since you never had her cheering you on, you're afraid to take chances, you know? I think I understand. I do.

"But I just . . . Rosie, I think maybe you can't stop time." She pauses, and corrects herself. "Well, maybe there's some witch who can. But *you* can't. We're growing up; we can't stop it."

As little as she likes to talk about deep things, when she does, Germ is almost always right. She goes on, interpreting my silence the way she usually does—as permission to keep talking. She takes a breath as if to say the thing that's hardest.

"It's just sometimes . . ." She hesitates. "I feel like I have to pick between *you* and growing up. And between you and everyone else. It's not really about Bibi. It's about me and you. I can't promise we'll ever build frog hotels again or things like that. We may not always be like we *have* been."

She looks at me, and tears glisten in her eyes. She feels bad for me, because she's never really been this honest with me about what she thinks. And it doesn't feel good to hear it.

Outside, the wind is blowing and we both look out,

fearful what the night could bring. I pick at the hem of my shirt, lips sealed tight.

Maybe she's right about all of it. I feel my own pride prickle. I could give up almost anything on earth not to have things change with me and Germ ever. And Germ doesn't really understand and I could never really explain it to her. She has her mom and her brothers—they're all stuck with each other. I don't have anybody like that. If Germ's not stuck with me, nobody is.

She looks down at her hands. "It's hard for me, too, you know. Changing. It's like . . . good to have new friends and care and participate—it feels so good sometimes. And then other times, I care too much. I get caught up and worried that maybe I don't deserve all the attention. I worry about what people think in a way I didn't used to. I lose the brave pieces of myself sometimes, and I don't like it. You never seem to lose yourself like that. I'm not as brave as you that way. You don't care what anyone thinks.

"But I want a normal life," Germ sighs. "Like, to go out with people and go to the movies and kiss D'quan maybe."

I make a face. "He eats dirt sandwiches."

Germ looks annoyed. "Rosie, that was second grade," she says flatly. And then we look at each other, and for just a moment, laugh.

She looks at me solemnly once we've quieted down.

"Rosie, I'm here. Whatever comes for you, I'm here—just tell me how I can help, and I will do it. But with the future, like the *future* future, I think we just . . . don't know who we'll turn into. I may just turn into an average girl who likes going to the movies. And if things go well—you'll be off hunting witches."

"I only want to hunt one witch," I whisper.

Germ shakes her head, thinking something she won't say at first. She looks up at the news, and is quiet for a long time.

"It sounds pretty terrible and hard and scary being a witch hunter. But sometimes I see things on the news I wish so badly I could fix. I wish I could fix everything for everybody." She pauses. "I'm not an Oaks. I don't know why I got the sight—if it's a fluke, an accident. But I guess, even though I'm scared for you, I wish I were powerful like you. Maybe I'd be brave enough to give it all up—all my hope for a regular life, to have a chance to make the world better. I don't know—I think in the end I'm too wrapped up in everything else. But not you, Rosie. You may not know it yet, but you're the bravest person I know. You just seem to forget it all the time. Now that you know about the witches, you won't be able to sit back and do nothing. Not ever again. You're too stubborn."

I think about the times when Germ and I have rescued each other. The time Germ got her mom to show up and cheer when I won the library essay prize, because my mom wouldn't get out of bed. The time after Germ's dad's one visit, when we were eight, when I made her laugh through her tears after he'd gone—with stories of his brain being possessed by gremlins. Without Germ to rescue me, how can I do anything at all, much less be a witch hunter? How can I even be a whole me?

I look at her. "There's some things I haven't told you."

Germ sits upright a little. I tell her about seeing my mom and dad—what the cloud shepherd showed me in the mist, how my dad had the sight because he loved my mom. I still don't tell her about the whistle or what it brought. But I tell her the rest.

"The cloud shepherd told me I have to make my *own* weapon. That's why my mom's didn't work. He said I have to make it out of what I'm good at. Take my gift and a weapon that's close to my heart and combine them. I just don't know what that means, really." My thoughts trail to the other secrets, the ones I'm not yet ready to tell.

"I wonder if my mom had time to name my brother before the witches took him," I say.

Germ is silent.

"I'd name him Wolf, and make him match his name, so he could fight them. I'd give him sharp teeth to bite them with and fast legs to run away and a sense of smell to find his way home even if he's worlds away." I look up at Germ, self-conscious. I realize I've lapsed into my old habit of trying to change what I can't by making things up.

"Stories," Germ says simply, looking at me.

"What?"

"They're your gift. I think you need to a write a story you think can overcome witches."

I take this in. I try to picture myself storytelling a witch to death, but it seems about as likely as whistling a ghoul into a marshmallow.

"It's sort of what you already do anyway, Rosie. You try to change the bad things by imagining them differently."

"And what do you think my weapon would be?" I ask. "Even if you're right?"

Germ shrugs. "Mom's got a chain saw in the shed."

CHAPTER 24

When I sit down that night to write, long after everyone—even Germ—is asleep, I come up blank. I chew my pencil and stare at my paper and think about Doritos and where the Memory Thief might be and everything but an idea. What kind of story could hurt a witch? It has to be simple, but capture everything that matters about the witches, everything I feel. It has to tell the truth but also be made up, because those are the kinds of stories I like best. For some reason, I think about birds—how small and delicate they are, and also how they fly, what a special gift they have that no other creature has. Weirdly, it's easier to write about witches if I write about birds instead.

I set my pencil to the paper, and start.

Once there was a beautiful world full of
all sorts of birds: cardinals and parrots
and peacocks and birds you have never
heard of in all colors. It was a world where
sometimes baby birds got taken by snakes
in the dead of night, and nice birds were
caught by cats, and good birds got sick
and fell from the sky, and sometimes mean
vultures won in the end, and sometimes
mom birds forgot to love their baby birds.
　　Meanwhile, though there were some
very terrible birds and terrible things,
there were also birds who made nests out
of beautiful shells, and birds who fought
badgers and rattlers and raccoons for
their babies and friends at any cost, and
birds who sang even when they were
in cages. And anyway, just about all
the birds—even the most unloved and

underestimated birds—could fly. Every bird
could tell you what worms smelled like and
which constellations pointed where. Every bird
could hear a grasshopper from two backyards
away. Every bird contained multitudes.

The point is, the bird world was full
of so many bad things. But it was full of
beautiful things too.

And there was one particular bluebird,
very small, who could not really chirp
around birds she didn't know, and who
sometimes was clumsy enough to fly right
into tree trunks, and her feathers were
scraggly, and her mother bird never
brought home worms for her, so she was a
little starved inside. But this tiny bluebird
decided she was going to gobble up all
the darkness of the world, grab it with her
little beak and devour it. Nobody had ever
thought of that before, so nobody had ever
tried it. (And there were plenty of birds
who thought it was impossible.)

And it was hard, and uncertain—but
the tiny bluebird tried anyway, and she

succeeded. By eating up all the darkness,
she made the bird world better.
   And no more bad things happened to
good birds anymore.

I look at the story and feel that familiar feeling of something both made-up and real. I wonder why that feels so good and always has. Maybe it's just like the cloud shepherd said—that a story makes a space in the world that wasn't there before, and that feels like the opposite of witches somehow.

I don't know if it's the story I'm supposed to write, and I don't know how it will work—if it will shoot colors out behind it like my mom's arrows, or do something else. I don't know how to make my story into a dagger or a sword. But for now, even just writing it gives me hope.

I tiptoe past Germ, then out into the den, where my mom sleeps on the couch. It's no small feat to walk through a trailer full of six sleeping people without waking anyone, but I've always been good at being quiet. After bundling into a coat, hat, and mittens, I walk out into the deep moonless night.

I shiver from the cold as I make my way to the shed. I

wish for my flashlight, but it's still attached to my bike—which I left abandoned back home. So I find my way by feeling through the dark with my hands. I find the chain saw in a corner next to the lawn mower. I can't even lift it, and I don't like the thought of trying to use it. I think it has something to do with the bright red WARNING sticker on it showing a person accidentally cutting off their own arm. Still, I hoist it up into my skinny arms and carry it outside. I pull some tape out of my pocket that I brought with me, and tape my story to the side of the chain saw. And then I wait. And I wait. I shiver and wait for the next twenty minutes to see if something magical happens—some puff of color and light.

When nothing happens, I try other things I find in the shed: an abandoned fencing sword, an old slingshot David made of wood, a screwdriver. (I'm getting desperate.) Nothing—when I throw it, shoot it, swing it—gives off any magical color or glow of any sort. I don't try to turn on the chain saw, but something tells me it's not really my style of weapon anyway.

I think about *The Witch Hunter's Guide* and what it says about weapons: *A weapon is as much a part of a witch hunter as her fingernails or her teeth. It is tied right to her heart, and that's where she keeps it close.*

I think how the cloud shepherd, too, said it needed to be a weapon close to my heart.

But there's nothing close to my heart in this shed. These aren't even my things. All my things are at home.

And that's where I think I need to go.

I ride Germ's bike since I don't have mine. I'm so tired, I swerve on the path now and then. I pedal the long curvy trail through the woods to my house, finding my way by memory alone, since there is no light. I'm scared that the Memory Thief may be lurking about, but I'm also scared not to figure things out as fast as I can.

When I get to the end of the driveway, I lay the bike down and stare at what remains of my house. Somehow, there is one lamp on in the parlor, though one parlor wall is missing. It casts a shadowy light in the dark night.

The house is half caved in—all the windows smashed, half the roof gone. Furniture, blankets, and clothes lie tangled across the yard. As I walk closer, I find small and familiar things—a broken cookie jar, one of my mom's shoes.

I climb the collapsing front steps carefully. There's broken glass under every footstep. Walking gingerly inside, I jump at the sight of Soggy, sitting in the one upright chair in the parlor (where Agatha used to sit), looking back at me blankly. Down the hall, I can hear another ghost crying.

There's no rhyme or reason to what's been broken or not. A glass vase sits on the kitchen table, but every chair has been knocked across the room. The coatrack is standing, but the corner cabinet's been smashed to pieces. Feathers from pillows lie everywhere.

I make my way across the parlor to the stairs. I test them one by one, trying to be quick but careful.

Getting to my room, I swallow the lump in my throat. Papers from textbooks and school binders are strewn across the floor. I step in quickly and retrieve the one thing I want most from here—the engraved silver whistle—and slip it into my pocket for safekeeping.

My mom's room is even worse off than mine. All her paintings, all her knickknacks and reminders of the old her: destroyed. And then I see the pile of books on her floor, the ones she kept taking back from me, tumbled on top of each other: *Where the Wild Things Are*, *Rapunzel*, *Hansel and Gretel*. I pick up *Where the Wild Things Are* and flip through it, thinking how just a few days ago I looked for answers to fighting witches in its pages.

And then it comes to me: why my mom wouldn't let these books go.

They're all about lost children.

It settles around me; my skin swims with chills.

And I realize . . . maybe my mom has returned to these stories again and again for the same reason why I turn to the books in my room: to fill in the places that are missing, to push back against the darkness that has taken those things. To remind herself—*because* she has no memory— that monsters can be destroyed, and heroes can win, even if it's only pretend. Maybe stories make us stronger because they make a bridge to things we've lost. Maybe stories make powerful things out of broken ones.

"You're not supposed to be here," says a voice behind me.

I turn.

Hovering in the doorway, looking very dim, and grumpier than ever, Ebb frowns at me for a moment. Then a smile lights up his face.

We sit near the edge of the cliffs looking out at the ocean, me in my coat and wrapped in a blanket, and Ebb undisturbed by the cold. The haze of the Beyond is extra-bright pink in the pitch-dark sky, putting on a rare show. I think how Ebb will be tied to my house forever, even if it crumbles to nothing—until he moves on to the pink haze above us.

"So we just need to find a weapon that's close to your heart," Ebb says. "Surely there's something lying around here you can use."

"Believe me, there are no weapons close to my heart," I say flatly, leaning back on my mittened hands, frustrated. "I'm not really a weapon-y kind of person? I *have* bitten a few people."

We're quiet for a long time, and I feel a little shy around Ebb suddenly. Even though he's a dead boy and an older one, it's a little awkward to sit alone with a boy at night. Maybe not for him, but definitely for me.

"Are you going to leave if you can't figure it out?"

"I guess I have no choice," I say.

"Especially with the Time Witch involved," Ebb adds, his face hardening.

"To think of leaving my mom and Germ . . ." I trail off because I can't put it into words, what this feels like. "My mom's already forgotten me. What if Germ forgets me too?"

Ebb is silent, just listening.

"I wish she and I could make a pact, like we did when we were little. To always be each other's favorite person in the world, best friends. But you can't promise stuff like that."

Ebb looks at me openly.

"I doubt you'll ever really lose Germ. Maybe you just don't have to hold on so tight."

He looks full of something he wants to say.

"I'm sorry I brought all this on you. I'm sorry I showed you the witch book, and the memory moths that night. Things would be so much easier for you if I hadn't."

I consider this, then shake my head. "The hidden world is full of all this terrible stuff. But it's also full of incredible things, and bigger than what I knew before. It feels like something I always longed for, to know there was *more* than just what I see around me. As scared as I am, I wouldn't go back to not knowing."

Ebb goes dim, then bright, then dim.

"You were right about my dad," I finally say. "He's not out there. He's just gone."

Ebb leans back, thinking. "With all the magic in the world, some things still can't come back. But maybe it's okay. Because of what lies up there that we can't know."

I take this in.

"I only wish it wasn't up to me to fight," I say. "I just wish someone else could, somebody bigger and stronger and braver than me. But there's nobody else."

Ebb is still and silent for a long while. Then he reaches into his pocket, pulls his hand out again, and lays it over my palm. As he pulls his fingers away again, I see that he's placed something in my hand.

Fred the ghost spider.

I twitch my fingers. I can't feel the spider, but still he sits there—a little glowing speck on my palm. I suppose he manages to perch on me the way ghosts manage to sit on chairs and move across floors—some kind of friction between the real and the unreal, perhaps. But it's such a delicate balance that when I move my hand too fast, he floats through it.

"He can't fix anything for you. But maybe he can give you courage," Ebb says. "When you feel alone. Having him with me always helps *me*, at least. He told me he wouldn't mind."

I slowly hold up my hand, and watch the spider scurry across my palm, then down into my coat pocket.

"But what about you?" I ask.

"The witches aren't after *me*," he says. "You need him more."

I sit quietly for a moment. And I wonder if inside my coat the spider can hear the *beat, beat, beat* of my heart as I realize that Ebb has become my friend—that I've made another friend besides Germ—just when I'm about to leave. Maybe it's hard not to grow and change. Even for me.

"Thank you, Ebb. After this is all over, if I ever get to see you again, I'll give him back."

But Ebb is looking at me strangely.

"A weapon close to your heart," Ebb says. "And you're not a weapon-y kind of person. Maybe your weapon is not necessarily weapon-y either. Maybe it isn't exactly a weapon at all."

We look at each other, and Ebb waits for me to catch on. "What's your favorite tool for fighting the dark?" he asks me. And suddenly I see where he's going.

I stand up, and Ebb follows. I know where I left my bike when we arrived at the attack, but I don't know if it will still be there.

But then, I see it's where I left it—lying on the grass at the edge of the driveway. And attached to the handlebars is my *Lumos* flashlight.

I detach it and hold it in my hands, then look at him. "Do you think it could work?"

Ebb shrugs. "It can't hurt to try."

The night is quiet around us. I wrap my story around my flashlight, secure it with the rubber bands I find in a still-intact kitchen drawer, and we wait. It's not exactly embroidering a dress, or painting arrows, or weaving a net—but I'm only eleven, and rubber bands are the best I've got.

I turn it on, but nothing really happens—just a normal beam of light.

"Maybe we need to let the magic settle in," Ebb suggests.

So we wait for something magical to happen.

Ebb just floats around the yard because ghosts don't sleep. But I start to doze, and dream of the Memory Thief and the Time Witch, huddled over a fire, holding my baby brother between them and laughing.

I wake to a sound of growling nearby, a shape moving toward me across the lawn, jaws open wide.

I let out a cry, jerk back, and—in the dark—grab my flashlight and turn it on, swinging the beam toward the sound. I only realize it's the rabid possum a moment before it happens:

As the beam of my light hits the ghostly little creature, something changes. A shape, small and impossibly fast, shoots right from my flashlight toward the possum like a lightning bolt. It lands on the back of the possum, who lets out a snarl, then explodes in tiny sparks, and disappears.

The next moment the shape from the flashlight is coming back toward me—sailing through the air gracefully, made of bright blue light. I realize in wonder that it's a tiny, luminous bluebird—small and quiet as it perches beside me on the grass. It looks up at me and lets out one tiny chirp.

Ebb has zipped close to me, and now hovers a few feet away.

I turn to gape at him, and he gapes back at me.

He looks at the flashlight, then at the little bluebird perched at my side.

And smiles.

CHAPTER 25

"Well, go on. Use it again," Germ says.

It's the following night and the three of us are together now: Germ, Ebb, and me. We sit in my abandoned living room shivering, staring at my *Lumos* flashlight, which I've placed in the middle of us. The moon is a new, tiny sliver above.

I slept most of the day, exhausted while Germ went to school. And now, with everyone back at the trailer asleep, Germ and I have snuck over here together, bundled against the cold.

I study the flashlight, biting my lip. "I'm scared I'm going to hurt someone with it," I say.

"It probably only hurts bad guys," Germ says.

"*You* try it," I say to her. "You're good with aim and stuff."

Germ shrugs, picks up the flashlight, points it at a wall, and turns it on. But it's only a beam. She hands it back to me. As soon as I take hold of it, the bright, breathtaking bluebird appears—and then wreaks havoc. She circles the room, tearing down the chandelier above the overturned dining room table, knocks over the one vase that was still standing, and nearly eats Fred the spider as he sits on my knee. Just in time, I cover Fred with my free hand, and turn the flashlight off again before she can reach him.

"I don't think she just destroys bad guys," I say.

"Um, yeah," Germ says.

Under Ebb's worried gaze, I shepherd Fred into my pocket.

"This time," Germ suggests, looking thoughtful, "maybe see if you can control it more. Like, be calm, know what you want to point it at. Try to think of it as an extension of you. Like your arm or something. That's what we learned in nunchucks class." Germ has taken every athletic class known to mankind.

I warily hold the flashlight again, taking a deep breath before I turn it on, then direct it at a safe, empty corner of the room.

The little bluebird appears again. This time, though, she is slow and gentle, pecking around the floor at imaginary seeds. She seems to suddenly notice us, looks over, cocks her head inquisitively. I tense up as she hops toward me, nervous she'll hurt me. But she only hops up onto my hand.

My fingers twitch a little. She feels like part air and part feathers. Like a half-imaginary, half-material thing. She appears to like me. To want to *please me*, actually.

"We should name her," Germ says. "How about 'Chauncy'?"

"Chauncy" is Germ's name for everything that needs a name, because she thinks it's funny.

"I knew a boy named 'Chauncy,'" Ebb says wistfully. Germ snorts into her hand.

The bird sits on my finger, nuzzling up to me, chirping very softly—as if she didn't harbor a powerful, destructive side. She doesn't have much of a voice, but her liquid dark eyes hold cleverness, I decide. And courage, despite her size.

"Little One," I say decisively. "She looks like a Little One."

We walk out onto the lawn, so that we won't break anything else in the house. (Not that it matters with the house already so broken—we just don't want things to land on our heads.)

"Get her to do some stuff," Germ says.

I direct my flashlight—and Little One along with it—at a piece of paper on the grass. She pecks at it, and it bursts into small flames. I direct her up into the air, and watch her fly, quick and sure, darting in and out around trees, diving and soaring. I point her at a chair that's been tossed out of my house, and she flies right at it, takes one little peck at its leg, and the leg breaks in half.

"She's, like, a barreling bluebird of destruction," Germ says, impressed. "Do you think she'll be enough . . . if the Memory Thief comes for you?"

"I don't know," I say.

I think we're all wondering, not *if* but *when*. I hate the thought of always hiding, always waiting for the Memory Thief to appear.

"I wish we could find her first instead," I say. She *is* the only witch, it seems from what I've learned, that might be reachable somewhere in the world.

As I ruminate on this, something happens to Little

One. Fluttering up toward a tree branch, she begins to fade, and suddenly blinks out.

I shake the flashlight, but nothing happens.

And then I realize. "Batteries."

As Germ and I search the kitchen for more, I think about something the cloud shepherd said.

"A witch weapon is limited only by the boundaries of your own heart," I say to Fred in my pocket, sardonically. Your own heart, and battery life, I guess.

It takes the wind out of my sails. My weapon is a dinky little plastic flashlight that cost three dollars, and it's useless without batteries. Little One may be able to crunch on chairs and paper and moths, but a witch is a much bigger thing. What if Little One's not strong enough? She seems pretty ferocious, but she's also tiny. As much as I hate to admit it, it's still hard to think she could be any match for a witch.

I turn the flashlight beam on again once the new batteries are in. Little One appears perched on a chair, looking at me inquisitively. I walk outside again, to where Ebb is waiting, looking thoughtful.

As she flutters up toward a tree, something draws Little One's attention toward the woods. Suddenly she's executing a thrilling dive through the air—barreling across the distance faster than I've ever seen anything move. I see, just before she reaches her target, what she's going for: it's a memory moth, floating out of the edge of the woods, probably looking for me. Whatever the reason, Little One swoops down on it like a dive-bomber. Though it's almost as big as she is, she snatches it out of the air and eats it in one gulp, chomping with bright-eyed satisfaction, tilting her head this way and that as if to savor the flavor.

We wait breathlessly for a distant screech, the sound of the Memory Thief losing one of her precious creatures. But there is nothing, no sound, no anything. Maybe Homer's right, that the witch is somewhere licking her wounds. I look at Ebb and Germ, and after a few minutes of waiting, we all exchange a giddy smile.

Then Little One tilts her head, staring toward the woods again. She chirps and chirps and chirps at me.

And then she again barrels into the woods.

I see just a flash of her—soaring toward a treetop—and there's a bright flicker as she catches another memory moth in her mouth, then gently lets it go. She circles back to me, chirping, restless.

"I think she's telling you something," Ebb says.

I look at Little One, uncertain. "What?"

"Maybe you don't have to wait for the Memory Thief to come for you," Germ offers suddenly. "The moths are all sent by *her*, right, from wherever she hides?"

I nod, slow to catch on. And then it hits me.

"Little One can follow the moths," I say, breathless.

"I'll come with you," Ebb says, "as far as I possibly can."

I try to process what he's saying. It hits me hard. I feel scared, maybe even more scared than I did the night I first got the sight. Because I know what this means.

It means it's time to find the Memory Thief, and fight.

It's not easy to pack everything you need to survive a journey to find a witch, especially in a trailer full of sleeping people without waking anyone up. But my mom sleeps soundly as Germ and I move about the main room, stuffing my backpack full of granola bars, water bottles, Gatorade, nuts and peanut butter, Slim Jims, bread, and peanut M&M's.

I roll up my sleeping bag and connect it to the pack with Germ's brother's belt. I'm wearing layers: a sweater, tights, coat, hat, and scarf. I've already taken all the money out of my mom's wallet, and left a piece of paper with the letters *IOU* in its place, because I saw it in a movie once. I slip Fred the spider into my pocket, ever so slowly. He's already, in the short time we've been home, built a web in the corner of the room with the beginnings of a word.

In the bathroom, I splash warm water on my face to wake myself up. In the steam on the window, I write, *You can do this, sweetie.*

Germ lays a note for her mom on the kitchen counter, lingers for a moment staring at it, and then stands at the door, silhouetted by the porch light, waiting. It doesn't register, for the moment, why she'd do such a thing. I am too lost in thoughts of leaving, my throat aching.

I stand over my mom on the couch for a moment, looking down at her sleeping form. I crouch beside her, and think: *Either I'll succeed and see her again and the curse will be broken, or I'll never see her again at all.* Ever so gently, I touch her shoulder and give her a soft kiss on the cheek.

"I'm going to fight the Memory Thief. I'm not sure if I'll be back," I whisper. "But if I do come back, I hope you remember me then."

I step toward the door. Then I gasp. *Extra batteries. I almost forgot.*

Germ directs me to a pack in one of the kitchen drawers, and I stuff them into my bag. Then I follow her out into the yard. Ebb has promised to meet us halfway between our houses.

It's not until we are a few minutes down the trail (walking, this time—too loaded down to bike) that I realize Germ is also carrying a backpack. I halt abruptly.

"You're coming?" I say.

Germ looks slightly sheepish.

"I thought I could take you just as far as I can."

I stand there hesitating, unsure whether I should let her come or not.

"I left a note for my mom. I told her I'd be gone for a few days and I'd explain when I got back and to try not to worry. If at the end of three days, we haven't found anything, I'll turn back."

"That's six days. And worry? She's going to lose her marbles."

Germ doesn't say anything for a minute because she knows I'm right. "I brought tons of beef jerky. *Tons.*"

I still don't know. The thought of having Germ with me as I set off into the woods is about the most comforting thing I can imagine in the world right now. But I want her to stay.

"Rosie," Germ says. "I know I can't fight a witch. I know it's not my destiny like you. My destiny is to be, like, a normal person. But I still want to help. I'll come as far as I can. And then I promise, I'll let you go."

I don't know how many days or miles it will take to get to the witch. It may be that it's a distance too great to travel and that I'll have to turn back anyway. But I soften as I think, *At least I will have Germ for part of the way.*

"Okay," I relent. "But when it's the right time, you've got to let me go."

Germ nods. "I will. I promise."

Ebb is waiting for us in a patch of moonlight at a familiar boulder where I asked him to meet me. There's a light dusting of frost on the ground, and trees that make everything sparkle.

"You packed light," Germ jokes, because of course he is just floating there like he always is.

"Are you sure you want to do this?" I ask Ebb.

He nods.

"I haven't ventured more than a mile or so from home since I died," he says, "but there's a first time for everything," he says. He looks scared.

We stand for a moment, staring at each other. And then I pull my flashlight from around my neck. I point it at the horizon to the north, and Little One appears, sitting on a path of dry leaves ahead of us, tilting her head at me quizzically. I breathe deeply.

"Follow the moths," I tell her. "Just don't eat them. We don't want to draw attention to ourselves."

Little One is zipping over the trees—a flash of luminous bright blue against the dark. And then she is gone. We stand there in silence and wait. Minutes pass. We look at each other, nervous, the forest hushed.

And then there's a *woo-wup-woo-wup-woo* far off in the trees. And Little One shoots up above the treetops in the distance like a tiny firework, chasing a tiny, luminous moth. She stops midair, and then hovers. She's waiting for us to follow.

We trudge into the woods.

I glance over at Ebb, who appears pained.

"You okay?" I ask him. And he looks over at me and nods.

"Does it hurt?" Germ asks.

Ebb considers this like he isn't sure. "I feel like my soul is at the end of a yo-yo string that's stretched too far. Yeah, it hurts."

"Do you want to turn back?" I ask.

He shakes his head. "It's bearable," he says. He takes the lead before I can argue.

When we catch up with Little One, I point my flashlight forward again like a kind of command, and she takes off. She covers lots of distance, but never goes so far that we can't hear her *woo-wup-woo-wup-woo,* and see her little figure when it rises, victorious, from the trees. Each time she finds a new moth, she circles like a beacon—her bright blue shining iridescent in the dark sky.

"The moths may end up stretching all the way to Japan," Germ says.

And with that cheerful thought, we walk into the night and whatever it may hold.

CHAPTER 26

The sounds of Seaport—the occasional hum of far-off cars, the ever-present sound of the sea—fall away behind us as we walk deeper into the woods. Soon all we can hear is the rustling of leaves and the occasional but reliable *woo-wup-woo* of Little One as she finds another memory moth. Up above, the stars look as if someone has thrown a handful of bright seeds across the sky.

Occasionally we cross a road cutting its way across the forest, or pass a remote house nestled in the trees, but mostly we are on our own.

At dawn, we come to a stop, as the memory moths and Ebb and Little One—all the invisible world—disappears.

"I'll wake at my grave at dusk," Ebb says. "And get here as soon as I can." A moment later he fades and then is gone. Germ and I sleep in a patch of sun for most of the day, our sleeping bags huddled together, trying to keep warm.

At dusk we rise. Fred has crawled out of my pocket and made a web in the tree above us, with a half-finished picture of a flower. I gently reach up to where he sits and drop him back into my pocket. We eat, and wait for Little One to come to life in the beam of my flashlight and for Ebb to return.

It doesn't take long. By the time the growing sliver of moon is rising above the trees, we see his luminous form coming toward us in the dimness. He's not winded, of course, but looks more pained than yesterday. The separation from home is clearly wearing on him more tonight. We don't say much to each other as we pack up and begin again.

As we make our way along the miles in the night, and stop to eat now and then, we quickly realize that what I thought was a month's worth of jerky and peanut M&M's is not going to last that long at all. The more I think about it, the whole thing—setting off to find a witch who could be anywhere in the world—seems like a crazy idea. I think reality is sinking in for Germ, too. I'm starting to get blisters, and even Germ has been limping a little. Turns out Keds are not the best hiking shoes.

"My mom's gonna be so mad," she says glumly. "I'm sure she's called the police by now. What if they send bloodhounds after us?"

"I think that was only in the 1950s, they did that," I say, but I'm not sure.

The one bright side is that as we walk, the number of memory moths appears to be growing. Instead of flying so far ahead that she's almost beyond hearing distance, Little One is now finding the luminous moths more and more frequently and closer together as the night stretches on. It's as if they are gathering, all moving in the same direction toward some common destination. Then again, that could be wishful thinking.

But by three a.m. by Germ's watch, there are so many of them that we can follow the moths ourselves without Little One's help. They look like clusters of stars on the trees, crawling along the ground. Ebb takes to floating on ahead of us, to see if he can find out anything interesting in the near distance.

He zips back a few times, but then he doesn't come back at all.

And then the sky begins to get light. We realize we are not going to see Ebb again this night, and keep exchanging worried glances.

Finally, legs aching, feet sore, exhausted from walking more than we've ever walked in our lives—we nervously go to sleep and hope he'll come back at nightfall.

We wake well past dark. Ebb is there waiting for us, perched on a rock and staring into the distance ahead. He turns as I rustle awake, and his face is hard to read. Something has happened.

"What is it?" I ask, sitting up and rubbing my eyes, the cold outside of my sleeping bag a rude awakening. Beside me, Germ stirs too.

Ebb looks at me a long time, and then says, "I found something last night, just before I vanished."

"What?"

"Better if I just show you, I think."

We follow Ebb through the woods. At his urging, I

leave my flashlight off, so we only have the moon and the stars and moths and Ebb as light. Finally he leads us into a thick scrub of bushes and thorns. On and on we go, picking our way slowly through the dense, forbidding undergrowth, through ravines and crags filled with thorns. I wonder if maybe he's forgotten we can't float through obstacles like he can. My hands, even through my mittens, are pricked, my clothes torn.

But then, pushing prickers and scrubby bushes aside, I see that he's come to a stop—and that he's staring at something ahead of him that's hard to make sense of. It looks like a big glowing, fluttering mouth looming up from the dark ground, its lips squirming with glowing light, purple, yellow, deep pinks, blues.

A few steps closer, and I see that it's not a mouth at all—but an opening into a rocky outcropping, every inch covered in moths. It's a cave.

Moths are crawling in and out of it. It's covered in a kind of strange material, and I realize it is the gray, silky fabric of a cocoon. The silk is so thick that, if it weren't for the illumination of the memory moths, it would blend in and just appear to be more rock.

Nobody has to tell me that the Memory Thief has been here.

"But how . . . so close?" I wonder out loud. Not three nights' walk away from my house, and we're at the entrance to her hiding place? It's too much of a coincidence.

Ebb already has this figured out, however.

"She must have these entryways all over the world," he says. "Hidden where no one ever finds them. This must be how she comes and goes. I'll bet there are thousands of them, maybe tens of thousands. I bet they all lead to one place."

We stare at the cave for a long time. A slight, cool breeze emanates from inside—it smells old, a stony, musty breath of the earth.

"She's in there somewhere," I whisper.

We stand there several minutes before it really sinks in that this is a place I have to enter. And one I have to enter without Germ. Who knows how much farther and longer the journey will be once I'm inside?

I turn to look at her, and by the pained, confused expression on her face, I can see she's thinking the same thing. She opens her mouth to say something, but I say it for her.

"You can't come with me," I say.

Germ looks torn, like she thinks this is the truth but also doesn't want it to be.

"This is something I have to do. Nobody else," I say. "This is my fight, not yours."

Germ nods, but there are tears squeezing out of her eyes.

"Will you be okay to get home on your own?" I ask.

"Oh sure," she says, "definitely." But she's bluffing. I can see that a solitary, three-day hike in the woods is not exactly an easy thing to contemplate.

"Will you start back now?" I ask. She nods.

"If you need me . . . ," she says. "If you need anything at all, send Little One for me."

I nod. And then I reach my arms around her neck, hugging her hard. She squeezes me back fiercely. I don't want to let go, but finally I do.

We all stand there, waiting for someone to make a move first. And then I realize that that someone has to be me.

I take one last glance at the beautiful, full-of-life, out-side world, and the sky full of stars. I look at Ebb, and he nods at me sadly. I wave good-bye to Germ, and I guess to everyone and everything else, too. And then I step across the threshold, pushing my way through the thick silk of the entrance. It gives and comes apart around me as I enter, and I brush it off me with a shiver.

Ebb puts his hand over his heart, gives a gentle smile to Germ, and then he follows me.

I turn on my flashlight and shine it down into the dark. Little One flutters ahead, though she flutters lower and slower than before, pausing here and there to perch and look around her. Even *she* looks scared and uncertain.

Together, we enter the cave and leave the world behind—only one of us with a beating heart that pounds as we move forward—enter the cave and leave the world behind.

CHAPTER 27

We are in a narrow tunnel of rock stretching back into the dark, on a slight tilt downward.

Ebb at first trails along behind me, but soon he passes through me and takes the lead. He begins disappearing around curves up ahead to scout things out. Moths line the way, fluttering along the walls, but with Little One close by, they stay away from me. With each step, the air gets cooler.

I haven't been walking long when Ebb comes drifting back to me, looking at me strangely.

"What is it?"

"Well, the tunnel sort of ends up ahead."

"Ends?" I ask. This can't be the end.

"*Sort of* ends," Ebb says, but with a nervous look, full of dread.

"What do you mean, '*sort of* ends'?"

He simply turns, and I follow.

I see what he means a few moments later, when we reach a dead end with only a small hole in the rock wall ahead of us. It's just big enough for a person to fit through but not by much. It's covered in the same silky cocoon material as the cave mouth. As I shine my flashlight deeper in to take a look, my heart quickens.

"It's not a path anymore," I whisper to Ebb. "It's a slide."

"I tried floating down a bit, but I didn't get to the end. It just seems to keep going and going down. So I floated back up."

"But . . . ," I say, staring down into the darkness into which the slide plummets, "if I slide down, there's no way to get back up. Not for *me*."

This, I realize, is why Ebb looks so filled with dread. He nods solemnly.

My heart is beating so hard, it feels like it could stop as

I force myself to move the silky covering of the slide aside, and climb up—crouched—into the hole.

My fingers clutch the rock wall on either side of me to hold me still. The slide is so steep that already it's hard to keep myself from sailing down into the darkness.

"Will you go first?" I ask breathlessly. "And meet me at the bottom?"

Ebb nods.

I peer down into the silky, slippery tunnel. I remember a lake Germ's mom used to take us to as kids, and how it felt for us to jump in—those first days in late spring when the water was still so cold. How Germ would take the leap right off the bat but I would linger, scared of that first moment of being airborne, when I couldn't turn back.

"You'll be with me down there?" I ask Ebb.

"Yes," Ebb says. "I will."

"Okay," I say. I try to slow my breath, but it's coming fast. "Go ahead."

Ebb nods, floats down into the darkness, then disappears. Soon even his glow is gone.

I hold my breath, and think about my mom.

And then I let go, and slide.

◆ ◆ ◆

At first I think I'm imagining it. Far below me in the dark as I slide, a haunting, scratchy music echoes. An old-timey voice croons,

> *"We just discovered each other*
> *Tonight when the lights were low.*
> *One dance led up to another*
> *And now I can't let you go."*

I've been sliding down and down and down for what seems like forever, my stomach lodged in my throat, my legs numb with the feeling of cresting the peak of a roller coaster. As the time has ticked by, I've steadied myself a little so I'm not slipping around so much. I've pointed my feet, with my hands at my sides to stabilize me. The slide twists and turns, it spirals, it dips so steeply at times, I almost lose contact. It feels like I'm sliding right down under the ocean, right down to the center of the earth. I try to remember if the core of the earth is hot or cold, but I can't. I shouldn't have daydreamed through geology. How far and long have I gone? Hours? Miles?

But now, the music. And—if my eyes aren't playing

tricks on me—a glimmer of something far below me. A flickering of light.

And then seconds later, with a shock, I'm truly airborne and out of the darkness, falling through nothing but empty air.

I land, and bounce, and land and bounce again.

After a few moments, I'm still enough to see what, exactly, I've landed on, but I can't quite make sense of it. I'm on the top of a huge pile of . . . old mattresses.

I stare up at the stone ceiling high above, and the hole out of which I've fallen, in a daze. With a sinking heart, I know I'll never reach that hole again. Then I look down and see that Ebb is hovering near the ground below, staring up at me, a mixture of relief and fear on his face.

"You okay?" he asks.

I nod.

I roll onto my side, and off the mattresses, tumbling down little by little till I reach the ground. The music is still playing.

> "So tell me I may always dance
> The 'Anniversary Waltz' with you.
> Tell me this is real romance,
> An anniversary dream come true."

We're in an enormous craggy underground space. There are cobwebs in the upper curves of the ceiling and memory moths fluttering around, but there are also signs that there is someone in these underground caverns besides us. The space is lit by torch-lined walls, and I see that everywhere inside the cavern there are piles and piles of *things*: books, old bicycles, video game cartridges, old clocks with broken faces. And far off along one of the craggy walls, an old record player is spinning its scratchy tune.

I crouch next to the nearest pile of books and sift through it. They're books written in languages I don't know, books of Greek mythology, coloring books, old romance novels.

"There's a path—but much bigger than the tunnel, more like a series of caverns. It just keeps spiraling down," Ebb says, his glow still very dim, his face almost sick.

"It looks like," I say, peering around, "she's really . . . nostalgic." Ebb is quiet.

"What's with the music?" I ask him.

Ebb stares hard at me, then looks over at the record player. I don't think I've ever seen him quite so worried, if that's possible.

"This was my parents' song," he says. "It was the song they played at their wedding. They used to play it for me, on their anniversary, and dance with each other."

He looks at me.

"I don't know if it's a coincidence. But maybe she knows we're here. Maybe she's toying with us."

A shiver runs through me. I wish I could reach for Ebb's hand, but the distance between the dead and the living is too big for that.

"Well," he says, glancing over his shoulder, dim and drained-looking. "We should be quiet, so that if she doesn't know we're here, she won't find out." He doesn't look so hopeful about that, though. "Shall we?"

I follow him toward the opening of the next cavern, and we move ahead.

The more we walk, the more honeycombed and vast the caverns become. Smaller tunnels branch off from our main path in all directions, and everywhere there are things stacked in corners and pathways: old paintings, and ancient carved wooden figures piled up next to used tires, stop signs, model trains, all covered in cobwebs.

"She's a pack rat," I breathe in wonder.

Yellowing photos stand propped against walls. Ancient marble statues, beautiful illustrated books, woven silks, entire sections of elaborate tile walls. In one enormous cavern we come upon a weather-beaten merry-go-round, paint chipping off the ornate carved horses. In another, a rusted tugboat looms up above us, leaning against the enormous stone walls. It's like a museum, or a big dusty closet, and beautiful in a way. Mementos of life on earth, hidden away inside of it. It doesn't feel like a dark and terrible lair; it feels more like a melancholy person's attic.

"Why would she want all these things if she hates people so much?" I wonder out loud.

Ebb shakes his head. "The same reason she wants their memories, I guess. She just wants to steal, and to desperately hold on to everything, I think."

I consider the times I've seen the Memory Thief. Her empty eyes. Her grasping hands. And I realize, Ebb is right. She's clinging to all this stuff, and I suppose to memories that don't belong to her too. Like she's trying to fill a hole that is too big to fill. Maybe all the witches are trying to fill something that's empty inside them; maybe they are all an absence of something beautiful.

Ahead, Ebb floats on, rounding a curve and disappearing from sight.

The minutes pass, and I don't see him again, and I start to worry. "Ebb?" I call, in a loud whisper. But no one replies.

And then I catch sight of him. He's come to a standstill and is looking down on something. Only when I'm standing beside him do I see what it is.

It's a canyon—enormous, seemingly bottomless—opening out in front of us. And it's full of moths. Bright, beautiful moths, pulsing with yellows, oranges, and golds. Millions of them, maybe billions of them. A multitude.

A gossamer bridge made of silk is suspended over the canyon. And out above the abyss, at the middle of the bridge and towering several stories into the sky, is an enormous cocoon.

My body swims with chills. I know, without even having to question it, that *that's* where I'll find the Memory Thief.

We stand silently, staring. I glance again down at the canyon below, full of moths and therefore full of lost history, lost love, repeated mistakes.

"So many memories," I say after a moment's shocked silence, anger pulsing from my head to my feet. "These *belonged* to people. They were never supposed to be hers. All because she's too empty to have her own."

The more I stare at all the countless memories taken, the more enraged I get. The more I hate this witch and all the other witches too.

There's something I've noticed over the years. When I'm angry, I'm especially clumsy. I bump into walls. I crash into things. It's like my negative thoughts drive me to run into the closest thing I can find.

And now is no exception. As I turn abruptly away from the canyon, in a cloud of rage, I twist off kilter on one foot and lose my balance, and then stomp against the ground to right myself. I don't mean to kick anything out of place. But there's a tiny pebble right where my shoe lands, and it goes flying out into the void below us. It clatters along a rocky outcropping as it falls downward. For a split second, Ebb and I go still, and wait.

And then the entire abyss of moths erupts with the sound of millions of wings as the hoarde of creatures— all at once—lifts into the air, flapping all around us. They swirl and spin for several seconds and then settle back down as quickly as they took flight. Still, the sound has been deafening.

Inside the cocoon, a light flickers on.

We gape at it, and the long narrow bridge that leads to it. I feel like I'm going to be sick.

"I think she knows we're here," Ebb says.

CHAPTER 28

We've been standing for a couple of minutes while I wait for the courage to set foot on the bridge— as if courage were some kind of package that just arrives at your door and then you have it, and then you're okay.

But I suppose courage is not just going to show up inside me all of a sudden. I guess it probably didn't work like that for my mom, either, when she crossed the world looking for witches. I guess it's more like jumping into the lake behind Germ: you just make the move. You take the step. I'm going to have to put one foot in front of the other and step onto the bridge, courage or no.

I lay my backpack down and pull out some new batteries, and replace the ones in my *Lumos* flashlight just in case. My hands are trembling as I slip the flashlight back around my neck.

Ebb stares at me, dim and mournful. I long to shake his hand, or give him a hug, but both things are impossible.

"I wish I believed I could do this," I say.

"I think you could take on a witch and then some," Ebb replies.

"Why do you think that?" I ask, wishing he could convince me, but knowing he can't.

He stands for a moment, thinking. "Because you give me hope. And that's not a little thing."

I swallow, embarrassed.

"If I don't come back, I hope you get Beyond soon."

He nods. "I know you'll be back. I'd never count you out, Rosie Oaks."

"Thanks, Ebb."

"I'll watch from here for as long as I can."

I nod. "Okay."

I take a deep breath.

I turn to the bridge.

I take the step.

My stomach dips with weightlessness as I move my feet along the narrow path perched above the canyon. I want to look back at Ebb, but I'm afraid I'll lose my balance. I'm also afraid to look down.

It's just like the path to Germ's house, sweetie, I think. *It's just as narrow as that.* But then I think of how many times I've tripped on the path to Germ's house or knocked my bike into a tree, and I try to think of something else.

I keep my eyes on the cocoon in front of me, scared that any moment the Memory Thief might come hurtling out at me, or set her moths on me. But, though the light continues to flicker in the one window, all stays still and quiet.

There's a kind of landing at the end of the bridge, spun tightly of cocoon silk. At first I think it might not hold me, but testing one foot on it, I see it's incredibly strong. I climb onto it, and look back at the canyon with relief. Far on the other side, so far away that he looks small now, Ebb lifts his hand in a wave. I wave back.

I pull my flashlight from around my neck and turn it on.

There are three silken stairs that lead to a hole in the cocoon that serves as the entrance.

I climb the stairs slowly, take one last look back across the canyon at Ebb, and enter.

✦ ✦ ✦

Inside, the cocoon doesn't look like a cocoon at all, but like the interior of an old house frozen in time. There's a curving staircase with a carved railing that climbs to the floors above. There's a parlor and a dining room table, lit only by the flickering flames of a corner fireplace, black-and-white photos of random people from different eras on its mantel. There's a record player in the corner playing some old jazz number with no words. Everything—the photos, the mantel, the record player, the dining room table and chairs—is covered in cobwebs.

As I stand there taking it in, the song comes to an end and the record begins to crackle and squeak, ready to be turned over. And then I hear something else.

The sound is faint at first, but unmistakable the longer I stand there in silence. It's a *creak, creak, creak, creak* coming from the floor above me.

I clutch my flashlight and point it at the ceiling, where Little One appears, fluttering in the rafters. She flies down near me and perches on one of the cobwebbed dining room chairs, pecking at her feet where the cobwebs stick to her, perturbed. Even she looks afraid, shaking the sticky cobwebs off her beak.

I point her toward the stairs, and she flies to the bottom one, flutters above it.

Together, we make our way up.

Somewhere above, the creaking stops.

At the top I find a hallway that stretches down past a long series of rooms.

I make my way past each of them, peering inside—each full of old, homey things: toys and dressers and beds and calico curtains, web-covered, dusty. The windows—which are really just holes with no glass—are enclosed by silken strands so that it all feels shut in and claustrophobic.

I make my way to the very end of the hall and the last room. After looking side to side to make sure it's empty, I cross to the one small opening that looks down to the canyon below. This is where we saw the flickering, but now the room is only shadowy and dark. Ebb must have left, because I can't see him where I left him at the edge of the bridge.

And then I hear it.

Creak, creak, creak. Right behind me.

I turn and see what I missed—tucked just to the side of the open door and obscured by it.

A rocking chair. And a woman sitting in it.

She's covered in cobwebs too, and is so still, she looks

almost petrified. Her face is neither young nor old, beautiful nor haggard. She is all in purple, and she looks—not terrifying like she did the last time I saw her, when she was reaching out to curse me, but—lost. On her lap is a blanket covering some shape I can't make out. There's pain on her face, and her fingers are grasping, grasping at the air as if plucking at invisible mosquitoes.

"You've come to take something from me," the Memory Thief says.

Little One, who's been fluttering about the room, alights on my shoulder and perches there making a *click, click, click* sound with her beak—either for fear or warning.

I try to take courage from the fact that she's with me, but she's agitated like me.

"I only want what belongs to my mother," I say.

The Memory Thief frowns softly, and looks down at her lap. She pulls the blanket aside. As she does, chills swim up and down my arms, because there in her gnarled hands is a metal cage. And in the cage are hundreds of tiny purple and blue and yellow and pink and orange moths. I know in my bones what they are.

My mother's memories.

"I've been looking them over for the first time," the Memory Thief says, "all these memories. I steal so many—

millions, billions—even the interesting people are hard to get around to. Though I *should* have looked, I suppose. I would have known about *you* even before you had the sight." She sighs, low and deep. "These ones are lovely. There is so much love, so much courage. Your birthdays, your milestones—they're here too." She waves to the air, indicating the world at large. "I may not ever get to see even a fraction of the memories I've collected, but every single one is precious to me. I'm afraid I can't give these ones back to you."

She looks so fragile, sad and wounded. Not the vicious witch I've been so afraid of meeting.

"You've come a long way with your little friend." The Memory Thief nods to Little One. "But you've been very foolish. It's not for children to defeat witches, no matter what the storybooks say. And it's not for sweet little birdies, either." The Memory Thief stands, frowning at me. "I know how it is. You want to hold so tight to the things you love, never let them go. But only *I* can truly hold on to the past, Rosie. Not you."

I start to feel a prick of panic. Because I'm realizing quickly, she's not afraid that I've found her, and not afraid of Little One. As frail as the Memory Thief appears, she does not seem frightened at all.

Unintentionally, her eyes dart toward the ground. It's the only warning I get. I look down and let out a cry.

Moths have crawled into the room, thousands of them. They cover the floor and, though I haven't noticed them, are all over my legs.

I stumble backward with a cry. I grasp my flashlight and shine it down at my legs.

Little One dives, but is instantly swarmed by moths. They're on her so fast and thick that her wings flap only once before she tumbles onto the ground. She flaps madly, tries to lift off again, but they're clinging to her back, her beak, her tail.

And then I feel a cold hand grip my arm, and I turn as my flashlight is pulled out of my grasp. The Memory Thief darts backward, my flashlight in her hands. And just like that, she reaches the one small window, extends her arm, and drops my flashlight out.

I watch in horror as Little One, in her struggle with the moths, flickers a few times and then disappears completely. A cacophony rises from below, thousands of moths rising from the canyon into the air.

I turn my eyes to the cage of my mother's memories, lying on its side near the rocking chair. I lunge for it, but the Memory Thief is there in a moment, blocking my way, shaking her head. She latches one gnarled hand on to my arm, and her grip is like steel—nothing like the touch of the frail woman she appears to be.

"It looks like you've come all this way, dear, to be disappointed. Witches can't be killed. You must have been told that, and still you've come. You were right when you burned your stories that night. Oh yes, I know about that. There is no magic in the world to speak of. Not the kind you hoped for, at least."

She holds her free hand out above the floor, and the moths begin to rise. They start to land on me, though I try to knock them away. But I'm covered, drowning in dusty shimmering wings.

It happens so fast. The witch's fingers send a feeling like ice through my arm as she curses me. My memories begin to leave me, not in a trickle but in a wave. I observe them as they go:

My mom, sitting at the window, saying, "He's out there swimming, waiting for me."

My mom as a girl in a cloud shepherd's misty hands.

My mom and my dad in the photo in the attic, looking at each other with so much love.

Watching D'quan Daniels eat a dirt sandwich in the second grade.

Telling a story to Germ on the phone to help her sleep.

Germ and me racing in the yard.

Germ on the first day of kindergarten, huddled at the foot of the door.

Germ wearing eyeliner for the first time.

Ebb and me sitting on the cliff and watching the sea.

Homer Honeycutt saying, "Only the witches would have you think there is more darkness in the world than there is light."

So many memories, all beginning to blur and fade away. I feel tears running down my cheeks as I watch these visions turn to iridescent dust and fall through the air, gathered on the wings of the moths that flutter all around me.

And then I can't remember why I'm crying.

And then I feel myself lifted by the moths, carried through the halls of the cocoon as if on a moving, fluttering bed.

And then I forget to notice anything at all.

CHAPTER 29

I wake in the dark, in a round cave with no door. There is just the tiniest flicker of dim light coming from a small hole in the stone ceiling far above me.

I sit up slowly, trying to remember. Why am I here? Have I been here before? Can I walk? Can I stand? I remember vaguely the faces of a blond freckled girl and a dead boy and a woman who sits by an attic window watching the sea, but not what they mean to me or why they are in my head.

I only remember that I'm trapped and that there's no escape and that I'm small. And I remember the witch. Memories of the witch are still in my head.

I don't know how long I've slept. It could be hours or days. My stomach feels empty, but I don't remember if it's ever felt this empty before.

I stare at the wall in front of me, lit just barely by flickering light from the hole above. Then I fall back asleep.

For who knows how long, I wake and fall back asleep. My dreams are vague and shapeless and they seem to stretch on for years.

I wonder if you can disappear just by wanting to—just by sheer lack of wanting to *be*.

I roll onto my back, and close my eyes again, but just as my eyelids flutter shut, I catch a glimmer of something, and open them again.

In the faint glow from the hole at the top of the cave, I see them. In the crags and corners of the cave, in the little nooks here and there.

I think I'm imagining them at first, because they are words floating in the air on nothing, and that makes no sense.

But as my eyes adjust again to the flicker-light, I see that the words are not floating on nothing. They are woven into the thin crisscrossing silk of webs—just barely visible in the gossamer threads:

I am responsible for my rose.

The moment you doubt whether you can fly, you cease forever to be able to do it.

Hoping is such hard work.

Look at how a single candle can both defy and define the darkness.

I stand slowly, on shaky legs. The words are so familiar, even though I don't remember them. I think they are from stories.

They're woven all around me, hundreds of them. And then I see their creator—a tiny, ghostly spider working steadily in a corner of the room. He is putting the finishing touches on another one.

Nevertheless, as they climbed higher and higher, London unfurling below them like a

*gray-and-green map, Harry's overwhelming
feeling was of gratitude for an escape that had
seemed impossible.*

I don't understand it, but one moment there's such a
hollow place inside me, and the next moment the words
are filling that place up. Something inside that was empty
and lost a moment before feels *un-lost*. It's like the words
remember something for me that I can't, and give something to me I can't find by myself. The words build something out of nothing. They put something beautiful and
strong inside my chest, and the beautiful and strong thing
starts to overflow into imagining.

I imagine rescues against all odds and lights in the
darkness. I imagine help is coming even if everything is
broken and all hope is lost.

I imagine that stone walls can't hold me. I imagine that
I am the one who makes the rules, and that I am bigger
and stronger than I think, unbound and unstoppable. I
imagine that with nothing to lose, there is also nothing to
hold me back. I call help to me, believing I can.

And then I hear a tiny . . . the tiniest . . . of sounds.

A small shape comes fluttering through the hole of the

cave. A luminous bluebird whose name, it suddenly occurs to me, is "Little One." And though she's too small for it, she's carrying a flashlight in her mouth.

"Little One," I whisper to her as she lands on my finger. She drops the flashlight into my hand. "I don't remember what to do."

Little One flutters out of my hand and around the webs above, waiting.

I read some of the words again.

> *Harry's overwhelming feeling was of*
> *gratitude for an escape that had seemed*
> *impossible.*

I take courage.

"Little One," I say, pointing my flashlight at the floor so that she perches there, looking at me expectantly. "We can fly," I say, with only the overflowing hope that the words can be true.

Little One chirps as if excited, as if she's been waiting all along for this.

And then, she does something I don't expect. She begins to grow.

She grows and grows and grows, so big and bright and blue that the cave starts to feel small. It's getting tighter and tighter inside the cave, and I hurry over to slip the spinning spider into my pocket.

And then there is a deafening crash and rocks begin to crumble around us. Little One has outgrown the cave, and burst its walls.

In another moment, we are standing in open air— the canyon walls towering impossibly high above and all around us.

Little One looks down at me with enormous glittering black eyes as big as I am, and then she lowers one wing. I climb onto her back.

And we fly, fueled only by wishing and words.

I'm clinging tight and we're barreling up, up, and up. I don't remember where we need to go, but Little One does. And then, up above us, and getting closer fast, is an enormous cocoon.

A dark figure comes crashing out of the entrance and onto the landing, throwing her arms into the air as she sees us. We do not slow down.

She runs out onto the bridge across the abyss, letting out a horrible screech. Thousands of moths rise from all around us. But we are too fast, too big, too enraged.

Just as the figure reaches the middle of the bridge, we dive. I only know what Little One will do a moment before she does it.

She soars at the witch, opens her beak, and devours her.

With a scream cut short, and a cage of moths busting open as it flies out of her hands, the witch disappears into the bird's gaping beak.

And is gone.

I watch the moths fly out of the cage, and flutter upward. They are not the only ones.

If the moths of the canyon were loud a moment ago, they are chaos now. They flap so loudly, hitting the walls, that it feels as if my ears will break. It's a hurricane of them, so many, I can barely see anything else. The walls of the cavern begin to give off a low moan.

Walls begin to crumble all around us.

And moths begin to land on me, but I'm not afraid. Because these moths are familiar to me—or at least, their whispers are. And as they crawl and whisper over me, I begin to remember.

Little One is searching, searching for something, along the walls and tunnels that are coming apart.

And then I see a small luminous figure hovering and staring up at us. Little One swoops a wing at him, and brushes him onto her back beside me. And again, we fly up, up, up.

As the cavern bursts open, we soar into the open air.

The moths—millions of them—go with us. They flee in all directions, filling the dark sky. I watch them in disbelief.

"What are they doing?" I ask.

And the ghost boy (his name is Ebb, I remember; things are coming back fast) says, "I think they're going home."

I look upward again.

Have we set them all free? Could something that wonderful really be possible?

Flying through the air toward home, we soon see a small figure below us, a blond and freckled girl walking home through an enormous forest. She has a long way to go.

Little One dips. She takes Germ gently into one claw, and lifts her up, and soars.

CHAPTER 30

We land in my backyard, on the beach at the bottom of the cliffs. It's almost dawn.

Little One bends a wing so that Germ, Ebb, and I can slide onto the grass, and then she straightens up again.

"Thank you, Little One," I say, and turn off the flashlight, and she disappears. I know that no matter what, I'll be able to call her back when I need her.

Germ and I hug each other. Ebb swirls around in a circle, extra bright.

"Tell me everything," Germ says.

So we tell her all that happened after we left her: the tunnels of the cave, and the hoarded old things, the canyon full of moths, the cocoon, and the witch. And then, when I get to the dark room and my lost memories, I pull Fred out of my pocket and slip him onto Ebb's hand, and tell them both the rest. How Fred's words filled my empty places. How they made me imagine things I thought were impossible.

All the way home, moths have been returning memories to me. It feels almost like the memories never left. I suppose the same thing is happening to people all over the world—as the escaped moths spread out across the sky and around the globe. At least, that's what I hope. I hope that lots of people are still there to receive the memories that were taken from them.

Ebb looks down at Fred in his hand, petting him gently on his head, then slips him onto his shoulder. The sun is rising, and they have to go.

"I knew you could do it, Rosie," Ebb says. And then he begins to flicker.

In another moment, he's gone.

Germ and I watch just the slightest hint of the sky lightening as the clouds of distant moths streak out toward the horizon.

The enormity of what I've done begins to sink in.

What forgotten things are going to be remembered? Will it ever, in the smallest way, change the world? All because of a story and one tiny little imaginary bird?

Germ, who's been grinning from ear to ear, finally grows serious.

"Well, I've really got to get home. I've been living on M&M's for the past twelve hours. And my mom . . ." She looks sorrowful and deeply guilty. "I may be grounded for, like, life. But when I'm allowed, I'll call you."

"What will you tell her?"

"I'll tell her I was sleepwalking," she says, and winks. And then she gets serious again. "No, I'll tell her the truth. And she won't believe me. And she'll probably put me in therapy or something. But at least *I'll* know it's the truth. And I'll keep trying to convince her, somehow.

"Rosie . . ." She hesitates. "I was thinking about it all the time I was walking home, and I'm pretty sure I've fig- ured it out. I think the reason I got the sight is because I love you, just like how it happened with your mom and dad, how loving her so much helped him to see what *she* saw. I think maybe loving a friend can help someone see what they see too."

She hugs me again; then we pull back and look at each other. There is still that uncertainty between us, that little bit of distance. But we are too happy to be bothered by it now. And I think maybe she is right about the sight, and how she got it.

"I'll walk you up to the driveway," I say.

We are just stepping onto the steep trail up to the yard when I hear it.

I put a hand on Germ's arm.

She turns to me with a quizzical look.

"What?" she asks, but I hold a finger in front of my mouth, and listen hard.

It's an unfamiliar sound, coming from the direction of the cliffs. I know what the sound is, but it makes no sense. It's hard to distinguish above the wind off the sea. But I have a prickling, itching feeling.

"It sounds like someone calling my name," I say.

Germ tilts her head and then nods. "I hear it too."

It's definitely coming from up on top of the cliffs now. Someone is calling, calling me.

We make our way up the path as fast as we can. Just as we crest the ridge, I see her walking along the cliff's edge, her long dark hair blowing in the breeze. She's staring in the opposite direction, searching for something.

"Rosie!" she's calling. "Rosie!" Out of breath, as if her life depended on finding me. She's so disheveled and upset, it looks as if she's run all the way here.

"I'm here!" I call to my mom, and she whips around to see me.

She clutches her hands to her chest. Her eyes fill with tears.

"Rosie?" she yells, her shoulders sinking in relief—the way you feel when you find something you've lost that you care about more than anything else in the world. She smiles so big, the way you might smile if someone gave you an island in Hawaii, I guess.

"Where have you been?" she calls to me.

And then she opens her arms, and I rush into them.

PART 3

CHAPTER 31

ere's a thing or two I've learned about memories. They are like seeds; love can grow from them. They look different depending on the day when they are remembered. They are slippery, malleable things, apt to be altered. They can be clutched too tightly. Their absence can cause fractures that run deep between people, towns, whole countries. They are meant, sometimes, to be let go. And yet, the night the Memory Thief was destroyed and the memory moths set free, the world became a little better for it.

Everywhere, strange, subtle things have happened—
stories I see on the news: Grandparents who've forgotten
names and faces suddenly smiling at their grandchildren.
Amnesiacs showing up in their families' backyards. Towns
publicly reflecting on histories long forgotten. Even if
people don't see the invisible moths in the sky, dropping
dust on them like snow, maybe they feel it.

Even the reporters look happy as they relate these
stories.

Like memory, time is both a measurable thing and an
immeasurable one. It's true that at the end of our curling
and lonely road in Maine, the months pass. It's also true
that, under the surface of the sea, time stays in one place,
or rather a million places at once. And I think about it all
the time. I think about *them*. The witches.

Are they coming for me? Are they scared of me? Do
they know who or where I am? Do they know what I did?
The days pass, and there are no answers, and I settle into
a fragile kind of safety. The longer it lasts, the less likely
it seems they will ever arrive. Maybe the idea that a witch
hunting weapon has succeeded again, after all these years,

is enough to keep them away forever. Homer did call them cowardly creatures. I count on it now.

It takes my mom time to remember everything, and some of the years are still foggy. The days before I was born are vivid to her—her time hunting witches, meeting my dad, hiding her books, that terrible night at the hospital— but the years since then are hazy. What's not hazy is how much she loves me.

I am getting to see who she really is, and coming to know the person who once filled my room with wonder and colors and powerful words. That person has exploded into my world, and I see why the witches feared her.

She is curious. She listens much harder than she speaks and plows through books and newspaper articles, soaking up things like a sponge.

She is angry in a way that makes me feel strong.

"Nobody's doing anything about the polar bears?" she demands, the edge of a fight in her voice. "We'll see about that, Rosie," she adds, as if she thinks anything can be fixed if you just have the right strategy. She has that "We'll see about that" tone in her voice about a lot of things—a mix- ture of rage and purpose. Her voice is colorful and lively at these moments—like gravel and roses. (At other times, when she's just talking with me about nothing at all, it lilts like a feather in a breeze.)

She is efficient—not one for moping over what she's lost. One of the first things she does is tackle my room: organizing my books, replacing all the notes I've put on the walls with notes of her own:

You are a magnificent creature.
You are a miracle.
You are funny, you are smart, you are brave.

She is tireless, and when she's not tending to me, or reading, or working, she's creating. Painting everything she can see—the sea, the trees, *me*. Only, she doesn't just paint what's *there*—she captures something elusive: the hopefulness of a tree, the mystery of the ocean and what is lost in it, the sadness in my eyes when I think about my brother. She says that—like poetry and stories—art is a way of looking for something true. "A great man once said, 'An artist is here to disturb the peace.' That means an artist makes people think twice about what they don't think about hard enough."

She is hard to look away from—with cleverness and interest in her eyes.

But she is also, oftentimes, lost. She spends many days in and out of a fog, fearful and weak. "Life can sometimes break something inside you," she says, "and sometimes you can't fix it." By "life," she means what happened to my brother.

We almost never talk about Wolf (which is what we've decided to name him, since he never had a name). Those times when he comes up, a heavy helplessness settles over her. It's like the memory is too painful to fully hold in her mind. She starts to drift away, and I have to pull her back with talk of other things. I think, more than anything, it's that she doesn't know what to do to make it better. The few times she's tried her arrows, they've done nothing at all. Her witch hunting days, her longing for the thing that waited in the water for her, are over—that much is easy to see. Some things can't be fixed. And to be honest, I'm often relieved. I just want her safe.

It turns out insurance is a boring but useful thing. While we are squeezed in with the overcrowded but always cheerful Bartleys, our house is slowly rebuilt. When it's finally finished, we move back in, and the ghosts trickle back. Mom can see them now, and she and Soggy catch up on old, new, and mutual friends. He cries on her shoulder about Crafty Agatha. She has a knack for comforting ghosts. She tries to make the afterlife brighter for him and the others with jokes and compliments and music on the record player, and soon our house is full of all the neighborhood spirits (they're ghosts, so of course word travels fast)—dancing in the parlor, laughing in the kitchen, swirling up and down the stairs.

Germ likes to join us sometimes, but not as much as she used to. Sometimes she's at Bibi's house, or sometimes at D'quan's. Sometimes I am too. I'm not trying to hold on to her when I go with her. I'm just trying to see if maybe people change, even me. I'm trying to take down my walls. And the more I do, the easier it becomes. I'm even beginning to think—though I don't like to admit it to myself—that Bibi seems actually kind of okay as a person. Maybe she's even nice, I don't know.

Things with Germ and me may never be exactly what they used to be, and sometimes I worry about that. But I also try to trust that the changes are good, too. After all, I can't get back what's already gone.

Still, I know something gnaws at Germ—I can see it, just like time gnaws at *me*. She likes to flip through the newspapers and clip out the upbeat stories, then tape them to the wall in her room. With bad news, she bites her lip. She thinks and thinks, like she is figuring something out.

It's a problem, this knowing we have more power than we thought we did. Even for a non-witch-hunting, boy-crazy, longing-to-be-normal person like Germ.

Mom and I like to sit on the grass in the afternoons watching the late spring flowers bloom, basking in the sun, and taking in the breeze from the ocean. And at times like those I know we're thinking of Wolf, and how it doesn't seem right to be here without him.

Sometimes we laugh and talk, and sometimes we're quiet thinking about Wolf, and I find myself staring at the ocean. I'm happy, but I'm troubled all the time. To never really know what happened to him—it keeps me up at night, and makes my stomach ache. He might be out there, and he might not. He might be forever gone, but then, he might not.

We talk about the witches and all the things my mom has learned. There are no surprises, but there's one thing she is very careful not to mention—the thing the cloud shepherd showed me that night, that clearly she doesn't want me to know.

She only hints at it once, as we walk across the grass on our way inside one afternoon. "If you ever plan to leave me, Rosie, please don't tell me. I don't think I could stand it if you do, and I know I could never let you go." I listen for a moment in confusion. I think I understand, but I'm not sure. And I don't bring it up again.

The days go on this way: small victories, slow recoveries, sometimes giddy happiness, and sometimes deep regret and worry about what we've lost. But I'm restless. And every night, I watch the moon rise, and wonder. And every night Ebb floats around the yard keeping watch, especially on dark moons. We never know when one of the other witches might come for us, or if—as we hope—they've forgotten us altogether and moved on to things bigger than a small girl and her imaginary bluebird.

And then one dark night, when Germ is sleeping over in her sleeping bag on the floor, and the rest of the house is asleep, I wake to the sound of something in my room, or rather, the sound of nothing. It's completely silent. Germ's usual snoring has stopped.

And then I realize, with a sick feeling, what else is different. The old clock in the corner of the room has stopped. I climb out of bed and look at Germ's watch on her wrist; it's stopped too.

A moment later I see the shadow, sitting in the corner, hummingbirds whirring in the air around her.

Her powder-blue eyes stare at me in the dark.

She smiles at me with razor-sharp teeth, and eyes as empty as the eyes of a fish.

I shrink back into the corner of the room. I look at my flashlight across the room on my nightstand, but I don't dare move.

"Shhh," the Time Witch whispers. "Don't wake your mother. She's so harmless, I'd rather let her be for now." She gazes at me a long moment. "Did you think I didn't know? That I wouldn't know where to find you? Did you think I'd forgotten that you've killed my friend?"

I'm silent. I am petrified and frozen.

She seems to rethink her words. "We witches . . . we don't exactly have friends. Still, it angers me. Who are you to kill a witch?" Her teeth glint in the darkness as she smiles at me again. "No, Rosie Oaks, I haven't forgotten you. I've watched you. I've learned. I know what power you have, and what powers you don't.

"Oh, that reminds me. I brought something for you." She lays a tiny paper square on the table next to her chair, and beside it, a tiny hourglass. She looks at my flashlight in the corner. "You're welcome to bring your toy, too. It's nothing either way to me. Consider this my gift, to make up for your friend, the ghost. Turns out he's not very good at keeping watch after all."

It's as if a rock has thudded into my chest. I look toward the window for Ebb outside it. I already know I'm not going to see him.

"What did you do to him?" I whisper suddenly, in a panic. My stomach flops over sickly.

The Time Witch smiles.

"He did try to fight . . . poor, helpless thing. Seems to have a bit of a vendetta against me."

Seems, I think frantically, not "seemed." Not past tense. He might still be okay. It's a tiny detail and an uncertain one. But I cling to it.

"Perhaps you've heard that I'm quite fond of games. Things get boring when the world is at your mercy." She grins. "Well, I've got a game for you. The game is, if you want him, come and get him."

"Come for Ebb?" I whisper, but she only smiles as if at some private joke.

"Of course, you'll have to go through *them* to get to *me*. I think you may have heard that there are twelve of us left. Well, *eleven* now."

She shifts in her chair, looking out at the dark, a hummingbird darting behind her and hovering above her shoulder. The clouds are still covering the half-moon, but the breeze is blowing them. "Well, I'd better be going," the witch says, though she makes no move to leave.

"Maybe I'll see you again sometime. It would be . . . interesting. I long to be interested in something. There's nothing new under the sun these days, it seems to me. But maybe you could prove me wrong."

And then she lazily waves a hand, and the humming-bird at her shoulder darts toward me, circling me. I blink, batting it away, and when I open my eyes, the clock has jumped forward a minute or two and ticked back to life. The witch is gone.

Germ starts snoring again.

And I'm left standing in the corner of the room, watching the spot she occupied a moment before. After a second's hesitation, I make my way to the table by the chair. I pick up the tiny square of paper she left, and squint at it in the dark, then turn on my flashlight to study it further.

It's a wrinkled photo of someone I don't know, who must have lived a couple hundred years ago or more. A boy my age in an old-timey hat. The photo has got that brown tint of very old images, the kind from the Wild West and Victorian parlors, and it's marked on the bottom: *San Francisco, 1855.* The boy is small like me, brown-haired like me. He looks vulnerable, and scared, like whatever he is looking at beyond the camera scares him to death.

And my legs go weak as I realize who he is. And who the witch wants me to come for.

My brother. Alive. Or at least, he was alive when this picture was taken.

I turn it over, and on the back, in a scrawled hand, it says, *You have one month.*

I look outside at the dark grass, the dark sky.

And then I pull on my robe and slip silently out of the room. I know what I need to do.

I tiptoe out into the backyard, and walk all the way down the ocean-side trail to where the half-moon rises above the rocky outcrop of the far cliffs. There I find the bottom of the ladder dangling, an arm's length out over the sea, as if waiting just for me. At least, I have to hope that's true. If it's not . . .

I look up toward the moon and take a deep, ragged breath. I make my mind go blank to forget my fear. I reach for the ladder, grab tight, and—with a small, breathless jump—I begin to climb.

Don't disappear, I think with every breath. *Please don't disappear.*

Several minutes have passed before I even think to look down, and when I do, I grip the rungs of the ladder in terror. I see my house already tiny below. I decide not to look down again, and I keep pushing onward, getting more and more out of breath, my arms sore.

But there is also something dreamlike about the climb. I'm already much farther up than I should be. It's impossible to climb the distance before me, and yet with each rung I get noticeably farther from the land below. Up this high, the air should be cold and thin, but I feel warm and my lungs are full. My legs shake with exertion and fear, but the ladder does not disappear.

After a while, I can see the entire coast of Maine, then the shape of North America, far beneath me. There's no sign of cloud shepherds except very far in the distance and already below me.

I keep going up, up, up into the dark night just beneath the stars.

The moon looms bigger and brighter above me with every step, its light welcoming me. Soon I'm close enough to touch it. And then—impossibly, unbelievably—I'm there. I step down onto the moon's surface, all aglow.

Before me, the Moon Goddess is sitting on a chair—a throne, of sorts, but a modest one. She has long curly silver hair and silver skin and eyes that seem to stare right into me.

"You came," she says. Her voice is a whisper, yet so powerful and confident, I think I could hear it from a million miles away. I have a feeling that whatever I answer the Moon Goddess, it will be something she already knows.

"I know what was waiting for my mom in the water," I say.

"Yes," she whispers, "you do."

"And I think now, it's still waiting. But for me." The Moon Goddess watches me silently. "I don't want to go. I want to be safe and hidden and small. But my brother is out there somewhere, and I think so is Ebb. And the witches are out there somewhere too. And all the terrible things are out there somewhere. And I might be the only one who can help with any of it."

"Yes."

"And there are eleven of them. And all I have are a flashlight and some stories."

"A story can have more sway over the world than an evil man," she says simply, as if I should already know it. "It can touch more lives, change more hearts, build more courage than a dark force. The witches tell a story of emptiness and malice and mistrust and hate. You could tell the opposite story."

She pauses, and I don't speak. "You've suffered, Rosie. Would you like me to erase what you know?" she asks kindly, gently. "Would you like to forget the hidden fabric . . . me . . . your power . . . your brother? I could make you and your mother forget. Sometimes it's easier to forget what we are responsible for and what we are supposed to do. Remembering means choosing," she says.

I think about the magic and the witches and all the scary and beautiful things. How things were easier before I knew, but also harder. And I think that to wait for others to fight is not enough.

I shake my head.

I know that despite everything I want that's different, and all the weeks I've pretended that I haven't, I've already made my choice about whether I'm really a witch hunter or not.

CHAPTER 32

That night, while Germ sleeps on the floor, I climb down from the moon and tiptoe into my room, and pull a small engraved whistle from inside my pillowcase where I've been hiding it, and slip it and the small hourglass into my pocket. I tuck *The Witch Hunter's Guide* into my backpack, knowing too well the terrors it contains: the Greedy Man, Hypocriffa, the Griever, Babble, Miss Rage, Chaos, Convenia, Mable the Mad, and more: witches with murder in their eyes and weapons to curse me.

Downstairs, after filling my backpack with a few sweaters and some food and my *Lumos* flashlight, I stare out the window at the night. The trees sway in the breeze.

I try to take heart.

There's being comfortable, and then there's being brave.

I write a note for my mom—saying that I'm doing it the way she wanted, that I'm not telling her before I go.

I open her door and look at her sleeping. "Please forgive me," I whisper. Passing my door again, I peer in at Germ snoring for a moment, then keep walking, trying to step around the creaks.

Down at the beach, I almost lose my nerve. I listen to the familiar sounds of the waves on the beach and the other sounds of home, and wonder when or if I'll ever hear them again. I hold my whistle to my lips, but before I blow, a noise behind me startles me.

Standing on the sand by the bottom of the cliffs, silhouetted by the moon, is Germ. She has her sleeping bag hastily rolled under one arm and wild just-woken-up hair. She's waiting for an explanation, but it's also as if—at least partly—she already knows. She knows I'm leaving.

"It's true, the legends," I say quietly. "The whale, the sea, time. All of it." I hold up the photo of my brother.

Germ blinks at it, trying to shake off sleep. She looks at the whistle in my hands, and her eyes ask a question.

There are so many answers: Wolf, and Ebb (I hope), and the Time Witch. But they all boil down to one.

"I'm going after them," I say to her, simply.

Germ is silent for a moment, and her eyes focus.

"Me too," she says.

I shake my head, but Germ flicks her wild hair back in annoyance, and tightens her arms around her sleeping bag.

"It's my world too, Rosie," she says, "even if I'm not an Oaks. And I want to fix it."

I think of Germ obsessing over the news, the broken things in the world, and the knowledge that has gnawed at both of us: the chance we can't forget we have. I know I'm not the only one who's been trying to choose between doing nothing and doing *something*. I can't think Germ choosing *this* is also her choosing *me*. Still, my heart flutters with warmth.

"There are ten of them plus the Time Witch," I say. "And I mean to get through all of them."

"Let's get through all of them," Germ says, her mouth closing tight. Her freckles glow brighter with her anger.

I can't help it. I break into a smile.

We look at each other for a few moments nervously, and then I turn to the water and blow the whistle as hard as I can. And though the sound seems to drown in the wind, an answer comes at once. A stream of spouted water blows high into the air, making us stumble back on our feet.

And then comes the rise of a shape—like a hill suddenly emerging from the sea. Getting closer and closer, an enormous tail flaps against the waves—powerful and strong. We wade out to our knees, scared and excited, holding hands as the shape rises before us.

The whale stares at us with ancient eyes. It opens its enormous mouth.

I gasp. Inside his mouth is a small cozy room with a rug and chairs and two beds and a few warm blankets. It's not the kind of thing you'd expect inside any kind of mouth, anywhere.

"I thought I'd seen it all," Germ breathes.

"I think we're just getting started," I say.

We cast one last look at the bluff where my house stands. The trees and grass blow in the breeze—as if the trees are talking even to those of us who don't know how to listen, and the whole yard is waving good-bye.

We step inside. And the whale closes its mouth as it dives into the sea . . . and into the past.

And the witch hunt begins.

ACKNOWLEDGMENTS

Thank you to my editor, Liesa Abrams, and my agent, Rosemary Stimola, for their talent, time, and most of all, their deeply precious presence in my life. Thank you to Dannie Festa for making me feel like I have the best team in the world. Thank you to Ani Kazarian and Alison Turner for our time writing in the woods; Mara Anastas for infinite patience; Tammy Coron for showing me a better way to do things; Sarah McCabe for a fresh perspective; Chelsea Morgan, Bara MacNeill, Alison Velea, and Jen Strada for letting nothing slip through the cracks; and Heather Palisi, Jessica Handelman, and Kirbi Fagan for a beautiful cover. I want to acknowledge my husband, Mark, for carrying me through draft after draft of this story with his feedback, time, support, and love; and Monica, Lauren, Haviva, Lily, and Rebecca for allowing me to devote time to my work by caring for my babies. Much gratitude to Natalie and David for sharing their cabin in the woods!

I want to thank my mom for giving me a love of reading and my dad for always being my rock during storms.

ACKNOWLEDGMENTS

And finally, I am deeply indebted to the teachers and librarians and booksellers who make writing books possible for me and who nurture young people as passionate readers. They are some of the most powerful witch hunters in this world.

ABOUT THE AUTHOR

Jodi Lynn Anderson is the bestselling author of several critically acclaimed books for young people, including *Midnight at the Electric* and the middle-grade fantasy *My Diary from the Edge of the World*, a *Publishers Weekly* Best Book of 2015. Jodi holds an MFA in Writing and Literature from Bennington College. She lives in Asheville, North Carolina, with her husband and two children.